AMERICAN
Pulp

AMERICAN
Pulp

**Edited by Ed Gorman,
Bill Pronzini, and
Martin H. Greenberg**

Carroll & Graf Publishers, Inc.
New York

First Carroll & Graf edition 1997

Carroll & Graf Publishers, Inc.
19 West 21st St., Suite 601
New York, NY 10010

Library of Congress Cataloging-in-Publication Data
American pulp / edited by Ed Gorman, Bill Pronzini, and Martin
H. Greenberg.—1st Carroll & Graf ed.
        p.   cm.
     ISBN 0-7867-0461-6
     1. Detective and mystery stories, American.   2. Crime—
Fiction.
3. American fiction—20th century.   I. Gorman, Edward.
II. Pronzini, Bill.   III. Greenberg, Martin Harry.
PS648.D4A48   1997
813'.087208—dc21   97-17245
                                                       CIP

Manufactured in the United States of America

"Easy Money" by Evan Hunter. Copyright © 1960, renewed 1988 by Evan Hunter. First published in *Ellery Queen's Mystery Magazine*, September 1960. Reprinted by permission of the author and his agents, Gelfman Schneider Literary Agents, Inc.

"The Pickpocket" by Mickey Spillane. Copyright © 1954 by Flying Eagle Publications, Inc. First published in *Manhunt*, December 1954. Reprinted by permission of the author.

"In a Small Motel" by John D. MacDonald. Copyright © 1955 by the Non-Pareil Publishing Corporation. First published in *Justice*, July 1955. Reprinted by permission of the agent for the author's Estate, Diskant & Associates.

"Sudden, Sudden Death" by Talmage Powell. Copyright © 1957 by Davis Publications. First published in *Alfred Hitchcock's Mystery Magazine*, November 1957. Reprinted by permission of the author.

"An Empty Threat" by Donald E. Westlake. Copyright © 1960, 1988 by Donald E. Westlake. First published in *Manhunt*, February 1960. Reprinted by permission of the author.

"Package Deal" by Lawrence Block. Copyright © 1961 by Lawrence Block. First published in *Ed McBain's Mystery Book #3*, 1961. Reprinted by permission of the author.

"All the Lonely People" by Marcia Muller. Copyright © 1989 by Marcia Muller. First published in *Sisters in Crime 1*. Reprinted by permission of the author.

CONTENTS

■ ■ ■

INTRODUCTION
■ ■ ■

Following the success of Quentin Tarentino's film "Pulp Fiction," used book dealers were hit with hundreds, perhaps thousands of requests for pulp magazines.

Many of the people requesting them had no clear idea of what pulp magazines even were. All they knew was that they wanted some. Presumably, they thought the magazines would be much like Mr. Tarentino's raucous and bawdy picture. Some were disappointed to learn that film and magazines bore no resemblance at all.

While the first all-fiction magazine printed on woodpulp paper was *Argosy* in 1896, the pulps, as we think of them, flourished between 1920 and 1950. They measured seven by ten inches, usually contained 128 pages, and were frequently filled with advertising for everything from dentures to trusses to bust enhancers. They made no pretensions to being anything other than what they were: purveyors of entertainment for the so-called "common man and woman."

Pulp magazines tell the tale: *Black Mask, Dime Detective, Magic Carpet Tales, Thrilling Mystery, Weird Tales, Big Chief Western, Snappy Stories, Ranch Romances, Crime Busters, Ace G-Man, The Whisperer, Sweetheart Stories, Captain Satan, G-B and his Battle Aces, Pirate Stories, Gangland Stories,* and *Zeppelin Stories.*

Starting in 1950, television and inexpensive paperbacks made pulps obsolete. But before one gets too choked up about the demise of the pulps, one must consider a sobering reality: most pulp fiction was cliché-filled and godawful.

To be sure, the pulps did produce giants: such names as Dashiell Hammett, Raymond Chandler, Cornell Woolrich, Erle Stanley Gardner, Horace McCoy, Robert Bloch, Frederic Brown, John Jakes, and John D. MacDonald all flourished in the pulps. And wrote some great stories. But looked at objectively today, a good deal of pulp fare was laughable and forgettable.

This was not true, however, when the pulps gave way to the digest-sized magazines of the 1950s and 1960s. *Ellery Queen's Mystery Magazine, Alfred Hitchcock's Mystery Magazine, Manhunt, Accused, Hunted, Pursuit, The Saint, Detective Magazine, Mike Shayne Mystery Magazine, Mystery Book, Mantrap, Verdict, Tightrope,* all consistently produced excellent crime fiction.

This is why, as you look through this book, you'll notice so many stories from the fifties and sixties. For us, this was the true golden age. *Manhunt* alone, at its peak, published two or three minor masterpieces per issue, month in and month out.

The digests were companions of the paperback original. The new breed of writer was generally superior to the old pulpsters. To be sure, they were still writing pulp fiction, but a more fetching and insightful variant of it. Writers such as John D. MacDonald, Charles Williams, Chester Himes, Vin Packer, and Peter Rabe turned out stories and novels that were artful in every respect. Unlike most plot-driven pulp stories, these were realistic tales of character, mood and theme. And these same elements were reflected in shorter works they wrote for the magazines.

We realize that our contention here — that the digests of the fifties and sixties constitute the real "golden age" of the hardboiled crime story — is somewhat heretical; finish this collection, you'll be inclined to take our beliefs seriously.

The best of pulp fiction past and pulp fiction present. You'll have a wealth of good reading ahead.

Ed Gorman, Bill Pronzini, and Martin H. Greenberg

Evan Hunter

EASY MONEY

From *Ellery Queen Mystery Magazine*, September 1960

Evan Hunter is also Ed McBain. In fact, during the heyday of the crime magazines back in the 1950s, Hunter was also a number of other people as well. Hunter has written a number of mainstream bestsellers, not the least of which is The Blackboard Jungle. *McBain has written, most notably, the 87th Precinct novels, still the cutting-edge of police procedurals. Overlooked in all this is the hardboiled crime stories both Hunter and McBain have written. Look up a McBain (non-87th) called* Guns, *a novel that stands shoulder-to-shoulder with the best work of Elmore Leonard and George V. Higgins. Here's a shorter example of his pure crime story.*

E. G.

JEFFREY TALBOT KNOCKED ON THE DOOR AND WAITED. HE stared at the metal numerals stuck to the wood, noticing that one of the screws was missing in the numeral 2. Inside, he heard a faint rustling.

He knocked again.

"Just a minute," the voice came, muffled, low.

He straightened his tie, putting the heavy valise on the floor near the door. Briefly, he went over the pitch in his mind. He looked at the name written on the slip of paper he held in his hand: O'Connor.

He smiled and put the slip of paper back into his jacket pocket. Why didn't she hurry? Or he? Or whoever was rustling around inside?

Patience, Mr. Matthews had said. A little patience goes a long way. Just remember that these people want what you have to offer. It's your job to give it to them. Be patient. But make the sale.

The door opened a crack, and Jeff edged his toe slightly forward, ready to jam into the opening should the door begin to close. Just the way Mr. Matthews had showed him.

"Yes?"

The woman was small and old—at least, she looked old. He sensed immediately that she wasn't really as shrunken as she appeared. If only she would pull back her shoulders and stand erect; if only there wasn't that tired, pained expression in her eyes; if only her mouth would . . .

"Yes?" she asked again, her blue eyes widening slightly.

Now the pitch. Once the door is open the rest is easy, Mr. Matthews said. Just get the door open, that's the big thing.

"How do you do, Mrs. O'Connor?" he said, touching his hand to the brim of his hat.

The woman looked slightly puzzled. A thin network of frowns, spidery, lacelike, etched its way across her forehead.

"I'm from the Home Bible Company," he announced, a pleasant smile on his face.

"Oh?" the woman said.

He sensed her confusion, sensed it sweeping into the hallway, almost overpowering him. There was the smell of panic, and he remembered the smell and tried to put it out of his mind. Why on earth didn't she stand up straight?

"May I come in?" he asked.

"Well, I . . ." she hesitated.

He smiled tenderly, his eyes pleading with hers, the way Mr. Matthews had showed him. Mr. Matthews was smart, all right.

"Well," she said, clutching her housedress at the neck, her thin hand working nervously at the collar, "I suppose it would be all right." She opened the door wider and then added hastily, "I really can't afford . . ."

Jeff stepped through the door into a living-room. The shades were drawn and the room was dim.

"What a pleasant room," he said.

Mrs. O'Connor walked rapidly to a battered green couch, its upholstery worn and faded. She fluffed a cushion and said, "It's really a mess. I haven't felt too much like cleaning since . . ."

"Nonsense," Jeff lied. "It's spic and span."

He was beginning to feel it. He was doing all right. His first approach, and he was doing all right. Now was the time to move in.

He sat down on the couch while Mrs. O'Connor went to the

windows and lifted the shades. The couch was hard. He could feel the springs when he sat down.

He glanced briefly around the room. A radio set stood in the corner. It was an old-fashioned set, with a cabinet that had sliding doors. Both doors were closed, as if the radio hadn't been played for a long while. On top of the radio a photograph in a leather frame smiled across at Jeff.

The man in the photograph had white hair and a broad grin. His jaw was solid, like a square slab of marble. His eyes held a gay twinkle under the shaggy white brows.

"Now," Jeff began, turning away from the picture.

"I do hope you're not going to sell me anything," Mrs. O'Connor said, and Jeff noticed the faint Irish brogue for the first time, like a charming splash of green on her tongue. He wished again that she would straighten her shoulders, perhaps smile out of her tired blue eyes. "I haven't any money to spare."

Jeff opened the suitcase and took out the Bible. He held it on the palm of his hand, the way Matthews told him to, the gold letters facing Mrs. O'Connor.

The Holy Bible.

He paused a moment for effect. The Bible was black, bound in handsome leather, the gold lettering done in Old English stamped deep into the cover.

"It's very nice," Mrs. O'Connor said, "but I don't think I need . . ."

Jeff flipped open the cover quickly and showed Mrs. O'Connor the flyleaf.

There, in attractive script, carefully hand-lettered on the heavy paper was the name: *John O'Connor.*

Mrs. O'Connor's mouth rounded into a little "O," but no sound escaped her lips. Her hand went to her throat, and he watched it flutter there in panic. She gasped, then passed her hand over her eyes, as if clearing away a dreadful vision.

"It's beautiful, isn't it?" he said in awed tones.

Mrs. O'Connor shook her head meaninglessly, and then she nodded.

"Your husband ordered it," Jeff said. That was what Mr. Matthews said would always clinch it.

"My husband," she whispered. There was no expression in her

voice. A mist had risen to her eyes, moistening the blue, lending an artificial sparkle where there was none.

"Yes," Jeff also whispered. "Before he died."

It was almost as if he'd told her for the first time that her husband was dead. She jerked back involuntarily, the thin hands completely out of control now, the tears springing to her eyes.

"John," she said, her voice breaking, the sobs overwhelming her.

"There, there," Jeff said. He rose and put his arm around her quaking shoulders. "There, now. There." He felt rather foolish— felt, too, that he was watching a stranger go through the routine, almost as though he were watching Mr. Matthews when he'd gone through the same act with the Italian woman.

"There," he consoled.

She drew away from him. "I'm . . . sorry. It's difficult to . . . get used to."

The Bible. Never let them forget the Bible.

"He wanted this," Jeff said, placing the Bible on the couch. "He ordered it. Before he died."

He watched her eyes again, waiting for the tears. But there were none this time. Instead, she touched the Bible with reverent fingers, almost caressing it.

"Thank you," she said. "Thank you so much for bringing it."

He cleared his throat uncomfortably.

"Only ten dollars," he said.

She didn't understand. He hadn't said it correctly. He hadn't said it the way Mr. Matthews taught him, the way Mr. Matthews had said it to the Italian woman.

"John saved," she said, misunderstanding. "He probably saved."

In a quiet voice Jeff said, "It isn't paid for yet, Mrs. O'Connor."

He felt momentary panic, and then guilt. He struggled against the feelings and deliberately put them down. This was easy money. The Bible was worth ten dollars any day of the week. And he got five out of every ten. Easy money.

Mrs. O'Connor touched the Bible once more, lovingly. "Ten dollars," she crooned.

"There's no obligation, of course," he said, reaching for the book. "That is, if you don't want it, we couldn't possibly . . ."

"Oh, I'll take it," she protested. "He ordered it. It was what he wanted."

"Well, yes, but if . . ."

"No, no, I'll pay for it." She paused. "Only, well, you see I haven't that much just now."

"You can pay it in four weekly payments, if you like. Two fifty each time."

"Yes," she said, as though he had just offered her salvation. "Oh, yes!"

He busied himself with his order pad, writing her name and address. He checked a box marked "Installment."

"That'll be two fifty," he said.

She walked into the next room, and he heard the protesting squeak of a drawer, the faint click of a purse being opened. He heard the jingle of coins. Then silence.

He waited.

Another drawer squeaked open, and he heard the rustle of clothing, then a tin can being pried open. The drawer shuffled shut, and Mrs. O'Connor returned.

"Here," she said, and she reached for the Bible.

He took the money in his left hand and casually covered the book with his right.

Then he slipped the money into his pocket and picked up the book. She stared at him, the fear working its way into her eyes again. He saw what was mirrored there, and turned away.

"I'll be back next week," he said pleasantly. He gave her the receipt. "I'd like to leave the book, but you understand, Mrs. O'Connor. So many people have . . . well, no scruples. We're forced to take precautions, you know."

"Yes," she said, disappointment in her voice and in her eyes.

"I'll see you next week," Jeff said, putting the Bible back in the suitcase.

She held the door open for him, and as he started down the stairs he heard it close like a whimper behind him.

■   ■   ■

The following Monday, after a week of selling, he sat in the big leather chair in the reception room, waiting to see Mr. Matthews. The receptionist was working on a crossword puzzle, her legs crossed, one shoe swinging back and forth, back and forth.

It's a job, Jeff thought. It's a better job than any I've ever had. It pays well. It's a job.

And then, abruptly, he thought, "But I'd quit if I were half a man."

His own thought startled him, and he glanced up nervously, almost expecting the receptionist to be watching him. She was still busy with the puzzle, her pencil stuck thoughtfully between her lips.

"How much longer?" he asked, twisting in the chair.

"Keep your shirt on," she said. Her voice had a twang in it. He didn't like her voice. She glanced up at the clock.

"Jeepers," she said, "time for lunch." She got up quickly, perching a little hat atop her head. "Be a dear and take any calls, will you?" she said over her shoulder.

I should have said no, he thought after she was gone. That's her job, not mine. My job is selling Bibles. Easy money. The easy way out.

Well, so what? he asked himself. If I don't take these suckers, somebody else will. So it's the easy way, the coward's way.

The word burned in his mind.

Coward.

It was funny the way a man could forget. Or did he really forget? Somewhere, deep in the folds of memory, the picture would always persist, dimly sometimes, but it was always there, always quick to flare up.

A sudden cold sweat broke out over his upper lip. He fumbled for his handkerchief and wiped the sweat away. But he couldn't wipe away the picture in his mind. He looked at the reception desk, at the clock ticking on the far wall, at Mr. Matthews' closed door.

The picture was still there . . .

■ ■ ■

"Jeff!" MacC. was yelling, "Jeff, you can't stay here. They're raking the beach."

A sprinkle of slugs playfully kicked up sand three feet before their eyes.

"Leave me alone!" Jeff shouted.

The machine gun began probing in earnest, the sand rising in angry spurts around them. MacC. dropped his gun in the sand and stood up, his tall form towering over the protection of the dune. He rolled Jeff over, struggling for a firmer grip. Jeff stared up into his face, watched the sweat there, the strain.

And then, magically, he watched in fascination as the dust spouted on MacC.'s blouse. Just little spurts of dust—ping, ping, ping, right across his chest. And right behind the dust the red blossomed, spreading from the little holes like flowers opening in the morning.

MacC.'s mouth opened. He looked at Jeff with accusing eyes that suddenly rolled and went lifeless.

The machine gun kept chattering ceaselessly just beyond the dune . . .

■ ■ ■

"Well, Jeff!" It was Matthews' voice. "Sorry to keep you waiting. Come in, come in."

Jeff mopped his face with the handkerchief, gripped Matthews' hand and pumped it vigorously.

In the office Jeff sat next to Matthews' desk.

"Eighteen sales in one week," Matthews said. "Good work, my boy!"

"Thanks," Jeff said. He was thinking again of the fear in Mrs. O'Connor's eyes. He shrugged the thought away and tried to concentrate on what Matthews was saying.

"And this is only the beginning, Jeff, only the beginning. You'll be lighting your cigarettes with dollar bills soon."

He chuckled, the fat on his jowls wiggling.

Suddenly he became very businesslike. "You understand, of course, that it's to your advantage to get all the money the first time."

"It's not easy," Jeff said. Again he heard Mrs. O'Connor rummaging through her dresser, looking for two dollars and fifty cents.

"Of course not," Matthews agreed smoothly. He was puffing a cigar, the band still on it. The gold of the cigar band rested against the gold of the signet ring on his finger. A ring on a cigar, a ring on a fat finger.

"You should play up the leaving a little more," Matthews suggested. "Make them feel that if they don't give you the whole ten right then and there, it's all off. Get me?"

"I'd lose the sale that way," Jeff argued.

"Possibly. But a lot of these people are holding out on you.

They've got the sawbuck, but they just don't want to part with it."

Did Mrs. O'Connor have the sawbuck?

"Well, I'll try," Jeff mumbled uncomfortably.

"I know you will," Matthews said, a grin flashing across his fleshy features.

■ ■ ■

The next day Jeff got five new customers. And then he went to collect the second installment from Mrs. O'Connor.

He stood in the narrow hallway, the same feeling of oppression bearing down on him. Across the hall, behind a closed door marked 2F, angry voices shouted at each other. Jeff knocked again, and the door next to Mrs. O'Connor's opened.

"She ain't in," the boy said. He had rumpled blond hair and a nose spattered with freckles.

Jeff smiled and asked, "Do you know when she'll be back?"

"Nope."

"Did she leave any messages?"

"Nope."

Jeff stroked his chin thoughtfully. "Have you got any idea where she went?"

"Sure."

"Well, where?"

The smell of boiling cabbage drifted up the stairwell.

"To work," the boy said, and he started to close the door.

Jeff's foot darted out and jammed itself in the crack.

"Where does she work, sonny?" he asked.

"Next door. She helps the landlady. Mrs. Canning."

"Thanks," Jeff said.

"That's all right," the boy answered.

Jeff started down the stairs, the cabbage smell growing stronger when he reached the ground floor. He walked into the street hastily and looked to either side of the tenement. A small grocery store, its windows packed with fat, round salamis and colorful beer ads, was on the left, and another tenement on the right. He walked to the latter and climbed the steps, past a woman sitting on the stoop rocking a baby carriage.

He glanced at the doorbells and rang the one marked "Superintendent."

"You looking for Mrs. Canning?" the woman with the carriage asked.

"Indirectly," Jeff said. "I'm really looking for Mrs. O'Connor."

"Mary O'Connor?" the woman asked.

"Yes," Jeff said, almost astonished that Mrs. 'O'Connor had a first name, even though he had written it on the receipt.

"You'll find her on the third floor."

"Thanks."

The baby in the carriage began to cry as he walked into the dark interior and started up the stairs. The building was pretty much like the one he'd just left: the stairway was narrow, the banister wobbly, the walls full of cracks, and here and there huge chunks of plaster had fallen down leaving large gray holes in the ceiling. Assorted smells of crowded living reached out to embrace him as he winced slightly and climbed the badly lit stairs.

On the third floor he found Mary O'Connor.

She was on her hands and knees. Her hair was stuck to her forehead. She dipped her brush into the bucket and sloshed water onto the floor.

Wearily, she bent over her work. Jeff watched her, embarrassed, and then he cleared his throat.

Mary O'Connor looked up, and puzzlement crossed her face. Then her eyes grew large, and Jeff thought she was going to cry. Instead, she smiled eagerly, scrambled to her feet, and began drying her hands on her apron.

"Hello," she said, "I've been waiting for you."

"Hello," Jeff said. "I had quite a time finding you."

"I took a job," she said. "I . . ." She seemed to debate telling him more than she had to. "I took a job."

"That's nice," Jeff said.

" 'Tisn't much," she explained, "but it helps. John, he didn't leave much. I mean, not that it was his fault."

"Of course not," Jeff agreed. He reached into his pocket for his receipt pad.

"Five dollars a day, Mrs. Canning gives me," Mary O'Connor said.

Jeff's fingers fumbled with the pad. Five dollars a day!

She reached into the pocket of her apron and pulled out two crumpled dollar bills and two quarters.

"Here it is," she said, "just the way you said."

Jeff took the money, still thinking of her salary. Quickly he made the entry on his pad and handed her a receipt.

"Thank you," he mumbled.

Mrs. O'Connor smiled weakly. "You'll be sure to be back next week?"

"Yes. Of course."

"And then there'll be just one more week until I get the Bible."

"Yes."

She smiled in satisfaction, got down on her knees again, and dipped the brush into the water.

Jeff left her that way—on her hands and knees over a wet floor. He walked down the three flights of stairs, not looking back. He couldn't chase a persistent thought out of his head.

Mrs. O'Connor scrubbed floors for a full day to get five dollars. To earn the same amount all he had to do was sell her a Bible that her husband never ordered.

■　■　■

That week his new sales went up to twenty-three.

Once—just once—he thought of quitting. And then he thought of the money again. It was too easy. He'd been a shoe clerk for a time, holding sweaty feet in his hands, flattering customers, cursing them when they were gone. And once he worked in an office, and the boss would come out every ten minutes, look over his desk, clear his throat, and go back into the office again. And then the restaurant job, washing dishes, and the stock clerk job, and driving the truck, and the countless other jobs since the Army.

No, it was too much. He was tired of sweating, tired of being afraid. He was going to take it easy now. He was going to light his cigarettes with dollar bills . . .

Matthews was in rare form that Wednesday.

"How do you like the job?" he asked.

"Fine," Jeff said in a low voice.

"One hundred and fifteen dollars in a single week! That's mighty nice money, boy, mighty nice money."

"Is it?" Jeff asked.

"I'll say it is," Matthews assured him. "And this is only the beginning, boy, only the beginning. Wait'll I tell you the latest wrinkle."

Jeff sat in the leather chair beside Matthews' desk.

"Yes, my boy, a new wrinkle. The obituaries in the morning papers are fine, and we'll still use them, of course. People are dying every day, you know." He chuckled noisily.

Jeff knew someone who had died—on a slug-spattered beach. Matthews puffed on his cigar, warming up to his news.

"I guarantee a hundred sales a week, Jeff. With this new wrinkle there'll be no more duds. These people will think you're doing them a favor, a big favor."

Suddenly Jeff didn't want to hear Matthews' new scheme. He wanted to be left alone. He didn't want any more pep talks. He'd heard a pep talk once, a pep talk punctuated with machine-gun bursts. He'd quit then, and he was quitting now, but he didn't want to be told about it.

He was nothing but a con man—a swindler and cheat playing on sympathy and respect for the dead.

"The casualty lists," Matthews announced proudly. "More and more are being released every day. The War Department is really just catching up with itself."

Casualty lists. Somewhere in the back of Jeff's mind staccato chattering began. Casualty lists.

"Killed in action," Matthews said. "As soon as the names are released we snatch them up—and bingo!"

Ping, ping, ping, right across his chest. Little spurts of dust.

"Your son ordered this, ma'am, asking us to collect for it over here." Matthews grinned and winked at Jeff.

Jeff gripped the sides of his chair, his knuckles white.

"What?" Matthews continued in mock surprise. "Your son was killed in action? Oh, I'm terribly sorry, I had no idea. Then we spring the Bible with the kid's name in it and . . ."

Matthews stopped suddenly.

"What's the matter, boy?"

Jeff reached out and grabbed Matthews by the lapels of his coat.

"You filthy pig," he snarled. "You dirty filthy pig. Casualty lists!"

With sudden fury he threw his fist into Matthews' jaw, staggering him backward, smashing him into the desk, knocking his box of expensive cigars to the floor.

"Just a minute, boy," Matthews squealed, his hands out in front of him. "Just a minute now, Jeff."

Jeff's eyes blazed. His hands ripped at the lapels again, and he lifted Matthews and threw him against the wall.

"I quit, you stinking scum! I quit, do you hear? I'm through, finished! I've stopped doing your filthy work, do you understand?"

Jeff was shouting now. He threw open the black suitcase and began searching among the books, finally coming on what he wanted. He stood up then and faced Matthews who was crouching in the far corner of the room.

"Expect the police," he said simply. Then he left.

■　　■　　■

He felt a little happier as he gave the boy the envelope with the five dollars, and the Bible. The note said, "A mistake has been made, Mrs. O'Connor. This Bible was already paid for. A long time ago."

Perhaps he was still a coward. A more courageous man would have gone up to face Mary O'Connor personally. But when he saw the boy disappear into the building, he felt a lot happier.

Happier than he'd felt in a long time.

Mickey Spillane

THE PICKPOCKET

From *Manhunt,* December 1954

Mickey Spillane's novels, particularly I, the Jury *and the others which star the toughest of all fictional private eyes, Mike Hammer, are well known to all mystery readers (who either love or hate them with considerable passion in either case). His output of short fiction, however, is relatively small and much less familiar. Most of it was produced between 1953 and 1960 and published in* Manhunt *and such men's magazines as* Cavalier *and* Male. *Significantly, none of his short stories or novelettes features Mike Hammer or any other private detective; yet most have the elements of harsh and violent reality that made the Hammer novels huge bestsellers. "The Pickpocket" is one of the few exceptions—an atypical Spillane tale in every way, including its non-Hammerlike protagonist, and one which demonstrates the range of his talent.*

B. P.

WILLIE CAME INTO THE BAR SMILING. HE COULDN'T UNDERstand why he did it, but he did it anyway. Ever since the day he had married Sally and had stopped in for a bottle of beer to bring home for his wedding supper, he had come in smiling. Sally, he thought, three years with Sally, and now there was little Bill and a brother or maybe a sister on the way.

The bartender waved, and Willie said, "Hello, Barney." A beer came up and he pushed a quarter out, looking at himself in the big mirror behind the wall. He wasn't very big, and he was far from good-looking. Just an ordinary guy, a little on the small side. He was respectable now. A real law-abiding citizen. Meeting Sally had done that.

He remembered the day three winters ago when he'd tried to lift a wallet from a guy's pocket. Hunger and cold had made his hand shake and the guy had collared him. He was almost glad to be run into the station house where it was warm. But the guy must have known that, too, and refused to press any charges. So he got kicked out in the cold again. That was where Sally had found him.

He remembered the taxi, and Sally and the driver half-carrying him into her tiny apartment. The smell of the hot soup did more to revive him than anything else. She didn't ask any questions, but he told her nevertheless. He was a pickpocket. A skinny little mug who had lived by his hands ever since he was a kid. She'd told him, right away, that it didn't matter.

He had eaten her food and slept on her couch for a week before he got smart. Then he did something he had never done before in his life. He got a job. It wasn't much at first, just sweeping up in a loft where they made radio parts. Slowly he found out he had hands that could do better things than push a broom. The boss found it out, too, when he discovered Willie assembling sections in half the time that it took a skilled mechanic to do it. They gave the broom to someone else.

Only then did he ask Sally to marry him. She gave up her job at the department store and they settled down to a regular married life. The funny part was that he liked it.

The cops never gave up, though. As regularly as clockwork they came around. A real friendly visit, understand? But they came around. The first of the month Detective Coggins would walk in right after supper, talk a while, looking at him with those cynical, cold blue eyes, then leave. That part worried Willie—not for himself, but for little Bill. It wouldn't be long now before he'd be in school, and the other kids . . . they'd take it out on him. Your old man was a crook . . . a pickpocket . . . yeah, then why do the coppers come around all the time? Willie drained his beer quickly. Sally was waiting supper for him.

He had almost reached the door when he heard the shots. The black sedan shot past as he stepped outside and for one awful instant he saw a face. Black eyebrows . . . the sneer . . . the scar on the cheek. The face of a guy he had known three years ago. And the guy had seen him, too. In his mind, Willie ran. He ran faster than he had ever run in his life—but his legs didn't run. They carried him homeward as the self-respecting should walk: but his mind ran.

Three years wasn't so long after all.

As soon as he came in Sally knew something was wrong. She said, "What happened?" Willie couldn't answer. "Your job . . ." she said hesitantly. Willie shook his head.

It was the hurt look that made his lips move. "Somebody got

shot up the street," he told her. "I don't know who it was, but I know who did it."

"Did anyone else . . ."

"No, just me. I think I was the only one."

He could tell Sally was almost afraid to ask the next question. Finally, she said: "Did they see you?"

"Yes. He knows me."

"Oh, Willie!" Her voice was muffled with despair. They stood in silence, not knowing what to say, not daring to say anything. But both had the same thoughts. Run. Get out of town. Somebody was dead and it wouldn't hurt to kill a couple more to cover the first.

Sally said: ". . . The cops. Should we . . ."

"I don't dare. They wouldn't believe me. My word wouldn't be any good anyway."

It came then, the sharp rap on the door. Willie leaped to his feet and ran, reaching for the key in the lock. He was a second too late. The door was tried and pushed open. The guy that came in was big. He filled the door from jamb to jamb with the bulk of his body. He grabbed Willie by the shirt and held him tight in his huge hands.

"Hello, shrimp," he said.

Willie punched him. It was as hard as he could hit, but it didn't do a bit of good. The guy snarled: "Cut it out before I break your skinny neck!" Behind him he closed the door softly. Sally stood with the back of her hand to her mouth, tense, motionless.

With a rough shove the big guy sent Willie staggering into the table, his thick lips curling into a tight sneer. "Didn't expect somebody so soon, did you, Willie? Too bad you're not smart. Marty doesn't waste any time. Not with dopes that see too much. You know, Marty's a lucky guy. The only one that spots the shooting turns out to be a punk he can put the finger on right away. Anybody else would be down at headquarters picking out his picture right now."

His hand went inside his coat and came out with a .45 automatic. "I always said Marty was lucky."

The big guy didn't level the gun. He just swung it until it covered Willie's stomach. Sally drew in her breath to scream quickly, just once, before she died.

But before the scream came Willie gave a little laugh and said:
"You won't shoot me with that gun, Buster."

Time stood still. Willie laughed again. "I slipped out the magazine when you grabbed me." The big guy cursed. His finger curled under the butt and felt the empty space there. Willie was very calm now. "And I don't think you've got a shell in the chamber, either."

The big guy took one step, reaching for Willie, a vicious curse on his lips; then the sugar bowl left Sally's hand and took him on the forehead. He went down.

Willie didn't hesitate this time. He picked up the phone and called the station house. He asked for Detective Coggins. In three minutes the cop with the cold blue eyes was there, listening to Willie's story. The big guy went out with cuffs on. Willie said: "Coggins . . ."

"Yes?"

"When the trial comes up . . . you can count on me to testify. They won't scare me off."

The detective smiled, and for the first time the ice left those cold blue eyes. "I know you will, Willie." He paused. "And Willie . . . about those visits of mine . . . I'd like to come up and see you. I think we could be good friends. But I'd like to have you ask me first."

A grin covered Willie's face. "Sure! Come up . . . anytime at all! Let's say next Saturday night. Bring the missus!"

The detective waved and left. As he closed the door Willie could imagine the chant of young voices. They were saying:

"Yeah . . . and you better not get funny with Bill because his pop is friends with that cop. Sure, they're all the time playing cards and . . ."

Willie laughed. "Sometimes," he said, "I'm almost glad that I had some experience. Finally came in handy!"

John D. MacDonald

IN A SMALL MOTEL

From *Justice*, July 1955

John D. MacDonald could, and did, do it all. He wrote pure pulp; he wrote glossy slick; and he wrote some powerful mainstream—stories and novels alike. While his Travis McGee novels got him on the bestseller lists, his paperback originals from the 1950s are probably his best work. He had an apt and unforgiving social eye, much inspired by one of his favorite writers, John O'Hara. The everyday detail, the homely detail if you will, fascinated him. And it brought his plots and people alive. What follows is a good example.

E. G.

THE COUPLE FROM OHIO WANTED TWO ROLLAWAY BEDS FOR their two tired, whining kids, and so Ginny Mallory had hurried to her storeroom and wheeled one down the walk to the end unit of Belle View Courts. The man made no move to help her wrestle the bed over the low sill of the door. He stood, a dead cigar clamped in his teeth, watching her struggle with it.

Ginny hurried back to the storeroom and got the other one and just as she came to the door of the end unit, another car pulled up by the office and began honking. The tourist woman was fussing with one of the children.

The rollaway wedged itself stubbornly in the door. As she pried at it, the man said, "Set the other one up over there, girl."

For a moment she thought she would howl like a kicked dog. She stood quite still for a moment, then pulled again. The bed came free and she shoved it into the room.

"I'd appreciate it if you and your wife would unfold this one and put it where you want it. I've got another customer out there."

She turned quickly and as she went down the walk toward the office she heard him holler something about ice. Let him holler.

Thick October heat lay heavily over south Georgia. Though she walked briskly, she felt as if all the heat of the long summer just past had turned the marrow of her bones to soft stubborn lead. She managed a smile as she went out to the big car with Massachusetts plates. A tall, white-faced man stood by the door of the car. He was alone.

"Do you have a single?" he asked, his voice flat and toneless.

"Yes, sir. Do you want to look at it?"

"No thanks. I'll take it. Which one is it?"

"Number three. Down there. The third from the end."

"Can I put my car in back?"

"It will be perfectly safe right in front of your door, sir."

"Can I put it in back?" he snapped.

"Yes, I suppose so. But it—"

"Where do I register?"

"Right in the office." She went in and went behind the counter. He followed her in. She laid the card in front of him. He signed J. L. Brown, gave his residence as Boston, wrote in his license number and the make of the big car, gave her the money and she gave him the key. As he went out the door she asked him if he would want ice. He ignored her. She wished they would all be as little trouble. And she wished more would come so that she could cut the lights on the big red-and-blue neon sign, leaving only the sign that said: *No vacancy.*

She stood behind the counter for a moment, resting a lot of her slim weight on her elbows, the heels of her hands cupped over her eyes. She had finished cleaning the rooms and making all the beds at noon. She had showered, changed to a crisp blue denim sun suit, and had a quick light lunch. Now, at six, the sun suit was sadly wilted. Her long blonde hair, piled high on her head, was damp with perspiration. She smoothed the corners of her eyes with her fingertips. She knew the lines of strain that the long summer had put there. Her eyes felt as if they had sunk back into her head, and they burned like coals.

Out on the highway directly in front of the Belle View Courts the big diesel rigs thundered by. The sun was far enough down to give the world an orange look. There was a hint in the shadows of the blue dusk that would bring the mosquitoes out of the lowlands. And this, she thought, is the slack season. And I can barely keep up with it. And barely keep ahead of the mortgage. *You were so damn proud of this hideous white elephant, Scott. And it was so much easier when you were around.* I don't know why. It just was.

She took her hands from her eyes as the screen door slapped. The man from Ohio said, "How about that ice, girl? We going to get it?"

"Right away. If you wait a minute, I can give it to you."

But he went back out the door, saying, "Bring it over to the room."

She went back into the small room where she slept and ate. She opened the refrigerator and dumped ice cubes into a glass pitcher. She hurried to the end room with it, knocked, walked briskly in and set the pitcher on the tray on the bureau. As she turned toward the door the man said, "Here, girl." He pushed a dime and a nickel into her hand.

Ginny looked quite fixedly at his chin, at the dark stubble, and said, "Thank you, sir."

When she got back to the office she put the fifteen cents in the pottery pig on her window sill. Next came a honeymoon couple, too intrigued with each other to need much service. She settled them in eighteen, and there were only three units left to rent. She wondered if she would try to eat now, or wait in the hope that the three empties would fill up quickly.

She looked with practised eye at the highway traffic. Most of the business was beginning to come from Florida-bound cars. It would continue that way until Christmas, and then the north-bound ones would start to build up, and by April the court would be full of the ones headed home, bright with new tans.

She went outside and leaned against the front of the office, her hands shoved deep into the wide front pockets of the sun suit. She felt sticky and weary. The sun was entirely gone and the world was blue. Peepers were beginning to chant over in the patch of swamp beyond the gas station. Cars had turned on their lights. The big rigs were aglow like Christmas trees.

Across the way, the floodlights made the gas station a white glare. She saw Manuel pumping gas into a battered station wagon. Johnny Benton came out and stood in the glare of lights, looking across the highway. When she waved, he saw her and came strolling across. His weight crunched the gravel of her parking area, and her neon made a red highlight on his shoulder and on the side of his tanned face.

He came up to her, offered a cigarette. She took it and he lit both cigarettes with a kitchen match he popped with his thumbnail. "How's it going, Ginny?"

"Three empties left."

"Not bad for this time of day. Things are picking up a little. We had a good day too."

For a time there was no traffic and the night was still. The station wagon had gone. Manuel was back inside the station. Ginny could hear the Cuban station on the small radio across the way, bongo drums and dry rustle of gourds.

"You beat, kid?" Johnny asked, his voice deep and slow.

"I'll live, I guess."

"You start filling up every night, you get some help, you hear?"

"Sure, Johnny. I'll have to."

"You can get a part-time girl for maybe twenty a week. No need making yourself sick, you know. How much weight you lost this summer?"

"Not much."

Johnny flipped his cigarette away, slapped at a mosquito on his big bare brown arm. He leaned against the wall beside her. "Funny thing," he said.

"What's funny, Johnny?"

"When Scotty brought you up here from Jax and built this layout, we all sort of figured you for something different."

"How, Johnny?"

"Well, you just didn't look like the kind of woman to take to this kind of work, that's all. We figured on you giving Scotty a bad time soon as the novelty sort of wore off. I guess we figured wrong."

"Maybe you didn't."

He laughed again, softly in the night. "You're too bull-headed stubborn to quit now. I don't know as old Scotty would have made this place pay out, but I got a hunch you're going to."

"Scott would have made out," said Ginny.

Johnny was frowning. Ginny could tell by his expression that he was thinking of the senseless traffic accident that had taken Scott's life seven months ago.

Johnny rapped his knuckles on the bar. "You use a cold beer? We got some over there."

"Later on, maybe. When are you closing, Johnny?"

"Around eleven, I guess. Manuel's taking off about eight to go see that gal of his. Look, Ginny. Manuel and I were talking it over the other day. We made the deal with Scotty on that room of yours we share. Scotty set it too low. It isn't right we pay you so little. Manuel and I, we figure the fair thing to do is bump it about fifteen a month."

"I don't want any charity, Johnny."

"Charity, hell! I'm talking about fair."

"Let me think about it, Johnny."

"No need thinking. You're on summer rates now. When the season is on you get twelve a night for that room. Know what that is? Three hundred and sixty bucks a month."

"And look how you've helped. All the little jobs I can't do, Johnny. And think of what it would have cost me to have men come out from town. Last week you fixed the electric pump. And Manuel painting all those ceilings for nothing. Let's not talk about it, Johnny. Please."

"Okay, okay," he said softly. He looked through the office window. "More business, Ginny." She saw his shoulders stiffen. "It's that guy from Jax. Ferris." He moved toward the door. "Whistle when you can use that beer."

She stood in the doorway, heard Johnny Benton and Don Ferris say "Hi" to each other with exaggerated casualness. Don came to the doorway, held her arms tightly, kissed her on the cheek. "Hello, darling," he said.

"Hello, Don. Surprise visit?"

■   ■   ■

Don made a wry face. He was a brisk, thin-faced man with dark hair, quick, shrewd, humorous eyes. "I should have phoned for a reservation, dear. Can I stay over?"

"Of course."

"I really have something important to talk about."

"Don't you always?"

"Now be good." He turned and looked quickly across the street toward the gas station. "Does he pester you?"

"Johnny is a good friend, Don."

"He was a good friend of Scotty's. I suppose he has some primitive idea of protecting you. Actually, I suppose I feel better having him close by. I'd refuse to permit you to stay out here alone."

"Permit, Don?"

He looked at her quickly, grinned. "A manner of speaking. You have to forgive any—proprietary manner. Remember, I did propose three times before you married Scotty Mallory."

"Excuse me, Don. Customers."

They came in two cars, two elderly couples traveling together. They took sixteen and seventeen and seemed pleased with the accommodations. That left fifteen the only one empty, and Don wanted that. With a tired sense of freedom she came back from getting them settled and worked the switch that turned off the big lights and left the *No vacancy* sign gleaming. She looked across the way and smiled to herself as she saw Johnny hold up his arm and make a circle of thumb and first finger. She got the key to fifteen and handed it to Don.

"Would you like ice, sir?" she asked him.

"Enough to make a pair of drinks for us, Ginny."

"I want to clean up, Don. And I haven't eaten yet."

"Let me take you into town. Benton will watch the place."

"He does enough. I don't like to ask him to do that. I've got enough here for both of us."

"No. I'll go into town and bring something back. Please let me."

She thought for a moment. "All right, Don. And thanks."

Ginny went in and closed the door to her room. She took a quick shower, changed to a yellow cotton dress with a wide belt. It was a dress that Scott had liked. So proud of me, she thought. So pathetically delighted with me. She brushed her hair and let it hang long to her shoulders the way Scott had liked it. She made up her lips carefully in the small mirror.

Just as she finished she heard somebody rapping on the counter. She went out and saw that it was the man from Ohio again. He gave her a slightly startled look. "Uh—you got any aspirin. My wife's got a headache."

"Just a moment, please."

She went and got a tin of aspirin. "Two is plenty," he said. "They work good on her. Do—do you manage this place?"

"I own it."

She saw the faint dull flush and knew that he was remembering the fifteen cents he had given her.

He coughed. "It's a—nice layout. We'll stop again sometime."

"Please do," she said, and smiled mechanically.

She saw Don swing his convertible in and park in front of fifteen. He got out with a big paper bag in his arms. He came into the office, gave her a quick bright look of approval.

"Take it right in, Don. On the table."

"Some very special steak sandwiches, darling. Salad. French fries. Let's put the hot stuff in the oven and have a drink first."

She set the small table. He made drinks. He was quick in all his movements, sometimes almost catlike. She liked the crisp whiteness of his sports shirt, the good fabric of his slacks. Once upon a time she had very nearly said yes to him. But Scott had come along. She knew that Don sensed how tired she was. He made a special effort, she knew, to be amusing while they ate. The stiff drink had relaxed her. All the customers seemed bedded down for the night. The peepers were in full chorus. She heard the clattering roar as Manuel drove off to visit his girl.

After they had cleaned up, Don said, "Would we get eaten alive if we sit outside?"

"It might not be too bad."

They went out and sat in the metal chairs on the grass near the florid beach umbrella. Their cigarettes glowed red in the dark. High speed traffic made ripping sounds in the night, stirring warmth against their faces.

"I want you to think over what I'm going to say, Ginny. I want you to consider it very seriously."

"What is it, Don?"

"I know the amount of your mortgage. You can't keep secrets from a lawyer, you know. And I talked to Ed Redling about this place. He's one of the shrewdest real estate people I know. He thinks he can unload it for you, and get you out from under with about fifteen thousand free and clear."

After a time she said tonelessly, "I had six thousand saved and Scott had twenty-one thousand from his uncle. So we put twenty-seven thousand in it, plus a fantastic amount of work, Don."

"Then admit that it was a poor gamble. Take your loss and get out."

"Scott believed in it."

"And because he believed in it—because he was wrong, a girl like you has to do coolie labor, wear herself out, get old before her time, to make something work that was a bad gamble from the beginning. Isn't that being a little sentimental? Scotty had to buy the best in all departments. It gave you too big an investment."

"I can make it pay off."

"All right. You can make it pay off. What is going to happen? Just when your mortgage payments start to shrink to the point where you can make more than a bare living for yourself, somebody will come in and put a fancier outfit within a quarter mile of you. And then you won't even get the fifteen thousand out of it. Ginny, you've got to trust me. I'm thinking only of your good. I guess it's no secret that I want you to marry me. I want you to get off this highway and come back to Jax where you belong. This isn't the sort of thing you should be doing."

She laughed flatly. "Johnny says I'm bull-headed stubborn."

"Let me tell Ed to go ahead with it, dear."

She sat in the metal chair. The night air was getting cooler. For the first time in many days she was completely relaxed, comfortable. It was a strong temptation to let Don go ahead with it. And so much easier to be Don's wife than—Scott's widow. Don would get them a nice little beach house. Long lazy days in the sun. Just a few rooms to take care of. And sleep, sleep, sleep. Thousands of hours of it. It would be so blessedly simple. And he was nice. Quick and funny and nice. It would be cheating him, in a way.

"Suppose I don't love you, Don. Suppose I don't feel that way toward you. More like a friend, I guess. A good friend."

"I'll take my chances. All that will come later. Believe me."

"Do you think so?" she asked in a half whisper.

He leaned forward, took her hand harshly, his fingers pressing deep. "No one can say you haven't done wonderfully here, Ginny. You've done more than anyone had any right to expect."

"Perhaps."

He released her hand, settled back. "I want to be one hundred percent honest with you, my darling. Right at this point I'm onto something big. I've put everything into it. I'm in it with Redling. If we can hang on for another three or four months, we won't even have to think about money for the rest of our lives. And to be brutal about it, that dowry of fifteen thousand will help a hell of a lot. We could borrow, but that would mean letting a third party in on it. And that would cut the profit."

"So you want me for my money, eh?" she said.

In the darkness she saw him twirl an imaginary mustache. "Exactly, my fair young maiden. At heart I'm a confidence man."

"Fool!"

"Seriously, darling, don't be annoyed with me, but I can't help feeling there's something a bit morbid about—working yourself to death to run this thing as a sort of monument to Scott Mallory. And I'm sure he'd be one of the first to tell you that."

"He had such a big dream, Don. This was going to be the first of a whole chain. And then we were going to get into the restaurant business too. And you don't know how hard he worked before—before the accident."

"Really, Ginny! You believed that big fat dream?"

"Don't sneer, please, Don. Everybody needs some kind of a dream, I guess."

"I'm sorry. I came out here to—make sure that next time I come, I can take you back with me."

She brushed at the thin high whine near her ear. "I can't decide—boom, all of a sudden."

"Think about it. But don't think too long."

An airliner went over, running lights green and red against the dark sky. She could see into the gas station, through the wide sheet of glass that turned it into a bright white box. Johnny was racking cans on one of his display shelves. He completed the pyramid and backed up to see how it looked. She watched him turn and walk outside, hook up the hose and begin to wash down the concrete apron in front of the station. A mosquito pierced her ankle with its thin sting. She heard footsteps on the gravel and turned to see Mr. Brown from Boston standing there, tall and angular against the light from the office.

"Yes?" she said.

He loomed over her. "What are you telling this man about me?" he asked, quite coldly.

* * *

For a moment the question dazed her, it was so meaningless. "I don't know what you mean."

"I had my lights out and I've been watching you out here,

talking and talking." He moved his head a little and the flood-lights of the gas station across the way caught the lenses of his glasses. The man sounded righteously indignant.

Ginny stood up, a small shivery feeling at the nape of her neck.

Mr. Brown said, "I suppose you told him I put my car in back."

Don had stood up. "Relax, my friend. Neither of us has the slightest interest in you."

"That's so easy to say," Mr. Brown said. "I heard the plane, too. And the cars slow down when they go by. You must all think I'm a fool, or blind. Why are you all waiting?"

Ginny held her hands clasped tightly. Across the way the small radio was tuned to brassy jazz. A distant truck moved toward them, the sound beginning to smother the music.

Don said, "I don't think you're well. Why don't you go back in your room and let Mrs. Mallory phone a doctor for you?"

Brown took a slow backward step. "Would it be—a doctor?" he asked softly. He turned his head toward Ginny and once again his glasses caught the light. "I suggest you do not use the phone, Mrs. Mallory." The truck roared by, the motor sound changing to a minor key as it rushed south down the dark road. Mr. Brown turned and walked away, his stride long and slow. They watched him go into his darkened room, and they could not hear the door close.

Ginny giggled, and it was a strained thin sound. Don said, "A crazy, darling. Pure and simple. Persecution complex. I don't know what else. A paranoiac, maybe."

"He seemed all right when he registered. He just wanted to put his car in back instead of in front. I didn't think anything about that."

"I don't like this. He might be dangerous."

"What can we do?"

"I can phone to town, to the police."

"Maybe he'll go to sleep now. And leave in the morning."

"And hurt somebody on the highway, further down the road? We have some responsibility, I think."

"He said not to phone."

"How would he know. Come on." He walked beside her. "Don't walk so fast, darling. He's probably watching out the window."

"It's—creepy."

"He just needs help."

They walked slowly to the office, and Ginny went in first. Don followed her and she heard the click of the lock after he shut the door. He went briskly behind the counter, took the phone from under it, listened for a moment, hung up. "Somebody's using it," he said.

She stood, waiting, and she felt that it was grotesquely melodramatic. The man was just a bit odd. She heard a small clicking against the glass panel of the locked door. She turned and saw Mr. Brown standing outside the office door. He held his elbow a bit away from his side. He tapped again on the glass, metal clicking against glass. A small round metal eye against the glass. He motioned to her with his free hand. For a moment she did not comprehend.

Don said, and his voice trembled a bit, "I think you better let him in." She turned and stared at Don and he was looking beyond her, at the door, and he ran his tongue quickly along his underlip. She moved to the door and she had the odd feeling that she was floating, her feet not touching the tiles. The world looked bright and faraway, as though she were looking at it through a long tube. She unlocked the door and the round metal eye looked up a little; looked, it seemed, at her throat. She put her hand there instinctively. The screen door was slanted against his shoulder. Across the way Johnny was hosing down the concrete near the pumps.

"I want you and your friend to come and help me, Mrs. Mallory," Brown said.

"We'll be glad to help you," Don said quickly.

Brown moved back a little, "What is your name?" he asked Don.

"Ferris."

"Mr. Ferris, please walk beside Mrs. Mallory. Walk down to my room and go in and turn on the light as you go in. Don't walk fast."

The concrete walk that led down the length of the court was roofed. Metal chairs were aligned against the wall on the right. They walked side by side. Don whispered, so that she could barely hear it, "Do exactly what he says."

She turned on the lights and they stood inside the room, their backs to the screen door.

"Mrs. Mallory, please stand right there. Mr. Ferris, please close the blinds on the windows."

As Don worked the cords on the blinds, Ginny heard Brown come in and close the door. She knew that he stood close behind her. She thought she could feel his breath stir her hair. The sudden blow against the back of her head shocked her. It drove her head forward, hurting her neck. She stumbled a few steps and her knee struck the edge of the bed and she fell awkwardly, catching her weight on her hands. She realized that he had hit the back of her head with the heel of his hand. She turned quickly. Brown looked at her calmly. She had not looked at him closely when he had registered, receiving only the impression of paleness and height and dark clothes.

He had a thin face, receding dark hair, prominent frontal bones in his forehead. His glasses had thin gold rims, and his face and eyes had an oddly colorless look—the face of a severe, dedicated and trustworthy clerk. His dark suit was poorly cut, and he wore a gold wedding band.

"Mr. Ferris, please place the large black suitcase on the bed and open it. It is not locked."

Ginny saw the metal eye follow Don as he moved. It was a thick-looking revolver with a very short barrel. It had a sullen, dangerous look. Mr. Brown's fingers, wrapped around it, looked long and white and frail.

Don put the suitcase on the bed and opened it. Ginny glanced into it. Apparently the money had been packed with great care, but in moving it about the top layers of wrapped bills had slipped from their orderly stacks. It all had the cold impartial look of money stacked in a teller's cage.

"Sit beside Mrs. Mallory, please," Brown said.

Don sat so close beside her that their thighs touched. Ginny felt a small tremor of his body. "It isn't Brown, of course," Don said. "I saw the pictures."

"Very old pictures." Brown leaned his back against the frame of the closed door and closed his eyes for a second or two, then opened them very wide. "I am sorry to ask you to do this." His smile was quick, thin, almost shy. "All my life I have handled money. Now, for some reason, I find it impossible to count this. I begin, and each time I seem to become confused."

"How did you manage it?" Don asked, and Ginny sensed his

attempt to be casual. Her head had begun to ache as a result of the unexpected blow.

"It was not difficult, Mr. Ferris. A matter, actually, of merely walking out with it at precisely the right time. Mrs. Mallory, I suggest you get that paper and pencil from the desk. Call the totals off to her, Mr. Ferris. The numbers on the wrappings are correct."

Ginny wrote down the neat numbers as Don called them out in a flat precise voice. It took a long time. She had to make two long columns. At Brown's request she added them, announced the meaningless total. Three hundred and seventy-two thousand, five hundred. Brown had Ferris recheck her addition.

"There was more at first," Brown said. "One bundle I checked and I cannot seem to remember where."

"What will you do now?" Don asked.

Brown looked at him, expressionlessly. "I should like to sleep, of course. I rather imagine I am expected to make some sort of attempt at escape. But they've watched me for years. They've forgotten that I know precisely what it feels like to be watched. I haven't slept in a long time."

"You're sick," Ginny said.

He looked at her and he seemed to be puzzled. "Perhaps."

"Where were you planning to go?" Don asked.

"I had never completely decided that."

"They'll catch you," Don said.

"An error of fact. They already have. They caught me—a long time ago. Now they're letting me travel, trying to make me think I'm still—free. I suppose it is a form of torture. I've seen *them* in the restaurants and on the highway. When I turned in here I knew this was where they had planned I would stop. But I was too tired to leave. I can tell by your eyes that you know all about it. Both of you."

There was silence in the room. Ginny saw Brown's arm tremble. He steadied the gun hand by holding his wrist with the other hand.

■　■　■

For a few moments Ginny was able to look at the world through the eyes of the sick Mr. Brown. Everyone knew. Everyone watched him. Everyone watched him with cold amusement, superior scorn.

"But it isn't the way you think it is—" she started.

"It's no use, Ginny," Don said. His voice was odd. She turned and looked at him in surprise. There was an odd look on his face. He said, "You're right, Mr. Brown. We all know about it. We were ready for you when you got here."

"Of course," Brown said quietly.

Don leaned forward. "But we could—change sides."

Ginny saw Brown become rigid. He seemed to cease to breathe for a time. "Why?" he demanded.

Don reached over and placed his hand flat atop the stacked money. "Answer enough?"

"How do I know it isn't a trick?" Brown asked. "You could pretend to help me get away without their knowing. Maybe you would be merely—continuing the sport."

Don said scornfully, "Don't you know us better than that? It's against the rules for us to take any of the money. Once we take the money it means we've turned against them."

Brown frowned at him. "Is that one of the rules?"

"Didn't you know that?"

"How much would you have to take?" Brown asked.

Ginny watched Don take a bundle of the currency out of the suitcase. His hand was very steady. She noticed that he picked stacks of the older bills. Stacks of twenties and fifties and hundreds. He took out ten stacks and set them aside.

"This much," he said.

"It's a lot," Brown said.

"But think of the risk we're taking."

Brown thought a moment, nodded. "That's true. What is your plan?"

"Do you know how we've followed you?"

"That has bothered me. I've changed routes dozens of times when there was no car in sight. But you people have always known."

"A device was installed on your car. It gives off an electrical impulse. And we've followed the car by radar."

Ginny watched Brown, saw him puzzle it out, accept it. "That explains a great deal," he said, nodding.

"I'll disconnect the device," Don said, "and install it on my car. Mrs. Mallory and I will drive north in my car and they will think you have doubled back on your tracks. You head south. If you're clever, they'll never find you again."

"And how will you avoid punishment?" Brown demanded warily.

"While we're traveling north, I'll disconnect it and throw it out at the side of the road. I'll report that we were following you and lost you. They'll think you discovered the device and threw it out yourself on your way north."

Brown shifted uneasily. He looked at Ginny and then at Don Ferris. "We'll go to my car and you will show me the device."

Don shook his head. "I'm sorry. I can't do that."

"Another rule?" Brown asked dubiously.

"Of course," Don said. "I'll have to do that alone."

The gun hand sagged slowly. Brown pulled it back up with a visible effort. "I'll let you out," he said. "I'll stay here with Mrs. Mallory. Go change it from my car to yours and come back when you've done it." He reached behind him and unlocked the door. He glanced out, pushed the screen open to back out. Don stood up and took a step toward the door.

Ginny heard a thud, a grunt of effort, a scrape of shoe leather on concrete. The screen slammed. Don stood poised for a moment. Johnny Benton pulled the door open awkwardly and came in, walking Brown ahead of him. Brown's arm was twisted up into the small of his back, and his lips were flattened back against his teeth with pain. Johnny looked very big, very brown, very welcome. Brown's glasses hung from one ear. As Johnny shoved him roughly forward the glasses fell to the floor and Brown's foot came down on them, crunching the lenses. Holding the man with almost contemptuous ease, Johnny examined the revolver in his other hand. He slid it into his hip pocket.

"What goes with this character?" Johnny demanded. "I never heard crazier talk in my life."

"It's been in the papers and on the rādio for four days," Don said. He stepped beyond Johnny and pulled the door shut. Johnny had seen the money on the bed. He stared at it and licked his lips and stared some more.

"Heavenly hosts," he said softly.

"Let go of my arm," Brown said.

"Sure. You go sit right there and be good," Johnny said. "Are you okay, Ginny?"

"I'm all right." She felt better. Johnny was like a breath of fresh air in the room.

Don stood with his hands in his pockets. He was frowning at the money.

Brown sat on a straight chair by the windows. Without the glasses his eyes looked mild and dazed. He said, "You'll be interested to know that Mr. Ferris and this woman have accepted money. They were going to help me get away. I understand that is against the rules."

"Shut up," Don Ferris said thinly. He walked over to the bed, picked up some of the stacks of money, dropped them back into the suitcase. He took out his cigarettes. Ginny accepted one. He didn't offer one to Johnny. Johnny pulled a single cigarette out of his pants' pocket.

"Is he nuts?" Johnny asked.

"Completely," Don said. "It was one of those crazy things. So damn casual about taking it, he walked right out past the guards. He'd worked there thirty years."

"Twenty-eight," Brown said.

Don ignored him. "He's got delusions. He thinks he's being watched all the time. He thinks we're part of the big gang watching him. According to the radio, they think he holed up somewhere. They don't know he got this far. He was lucky. What luck! A crazy man's luck." He turned and looked sharply at Johnny. "Three hundred and seventy-two thousand, five hundred dollars."

Ginny felt an odd prickling on the backs of her hands. She rubbed them together. Don and Johnny were staring at each other. She could read nothing in Johnny's face.

"Tax free," Johnny said softly.

The two men looked at each other for a long time. Then, as though on some signal they both turned and looked at Ginny. She looked into Don's eyes, and then Johnny's, and she had the feeling she had never met either of them before. It seemed quiet in the room. With the blinds closed the smoke from the cigarettes hung in the air.

"Why are you acting so funny?" Ginny demanded, and her own voice sounded strange to her.

Neither of the men answered her. Johnny stepped over to the bed. Don was watching him carefully. Johnny took the paper with

Ginny's total on it, glanced at it casually, took it over to where the glasses had been smashed against the asphalt tile floor, near the edge of the throw rug. He picked up the gold frames and shook them lightly. Some more fragments of the glass dropped out. He sat on his heels, the pants tight on his blocky thighs. He kept his head tilted to the side to keep the cigarette smoke out of his eyes as he cautiously brushed the fragments of glass onto the paper. When the floor was clean he put the paper down with the frames on top of it and carefully folded it into a small bundle. He squatted there, staring up at Don.

After a long silence Johnny said, "A good eye doctor can take a little bitty hunk of lense and figure out the exact prescription. I read that once in a story."

Don moved back and sat suddenly on the bed, on the far side of the suitcase from Ginny. He sat down as though his legs had gone weak. Ginny looked at him. He avoided looking at her. He put the separate stack of money back in the suitcase. Ginny looked at Brown. His pointed chin was against his chest. His white hands rested on his knees, fingers slightly curled. He looked as though he might be asleep.

"What are you thinking about?" Ginny asked, her voice a bit too loud. They did not answer her, and she knew she did not need an answer.

Don sat on the edge of the bed and counted on his fingers. "His name on the register. The car. Possible serial numbers of the new stuff." He looked at Johnny, who had stood up and who was carefully placing the bundle of broken glass in his pants' pocket.

Johnny turned as though looking out the door. But the blinds on the door were closed, inches from his eyes. Ginny could see the serrated metal grip of the revolver, see the shape of it through the stretched cloth of his hip pocket.

Johnny said softly, "Sure. One at a time. The register is on cards. They aren't numbered in any serial sequence. No trick there." He half turned and gave Don an odd smile and panto-mimed tearing up a piece of paper.

"You can't tear up a car," Don said softly.

"A truck went through that abutment on the bridge near Grover three months ago. It's still wide open. Deep there, and a pretty good current, and you don't have to go through any kind of town to get there. I got work gloves in the station, just in case."

Ginny put her fist so tightly against her mouth that her lips hurt. "No," she said. "No. I won't let that happen."

Don reached suddenly across the closed suitcase and took her wrist in his hand, holding it tightly. His fingers were icy. "Use your head," he said softly. "Insurance covers their loss. And that man is no loss. They get like that, and you can't cure them. Just the three of us. And nobody ever says a word. Ever. One hundred and twenty-five thousand apiece, roughly."

"Not apiece," Johnny said, tucking his thumbs in his belt, planting himself flatfootedly. "Not if I do the dirty work for you, Ferris. I'll take one eighty-five. That's nearly half. How you handle the rest of it with her is your business."

"A third apiece, Benton."

"And for that, what do you do?"

Ginny felt as though her throat had closed completely. Don dropped his cigarette on the floor, stepped on it, turning his shoe. He sat with his elbows on his knees, hands hanging limp from the wrists, head lowered. He looked slowly at Brown. Ginny saw the muscles of Don's jaw bulge, saw an ovoid pulsation at his temple.

Don said in a half whisper, "You take care of the car. I'll—do that." And he made a partial gesture of his head toward Brown.

"Without marks," Johnny said, just as softly.

"I'll go with you," Don said. "I'll stun him and let the water do it."

Ginny saw Johnny nod in agreement. Johnny went over to the bed, standing half between them. He rapped lightly on the edge of the black suitcase with his brown knuckles. "A cruiser," he said softly. "And some of those little lovelies who carry hatboxes. And a sports car. All wrapped up in there."

"Not all at once," Don said sharply.

Johnny turned his head slowly and looked at him. "I'm not that stupid, Ferris."

Ginny suddenly saw what she had to do. She jumped up as fast as she could and ran for the door, remembering that it was unlocked. Johnny's hard arm locked around her middle after she had gone three steps. Her feet slipped on the tiles. He pulled her around roughly, clamped a heavy hand over her mouth. She could smell gasoline on his hand. It nauseated her. She wondered if she would faint. Johnny's voice came from far away. "This is your problem, isn't it?" he asked Don.

Don came over to them. He took Ginny's wrists. He looked pleadingly into her eyes. "Please, darling. There's no risk at all. There'll never be another chance like this one. If we don't do it, local cops will take him. And how much money do you think will be left by the time they turn it over? Say you'll go along with us. You don't have to do a thing, and you get a full third. Will you do it?"

She shook her head from side to side. Beyond him she could see Brown in that same position. His head had tilted a bit to one side. She knew he slept.

"It's no good without her," Johnny said. "It stinks."

Don knuckled his chin. He shrugged. "Hold her, then. Let me think."

"Put her in the same car?" Johnny asked quietly.

■ ■ ■

She saw Don look over her shoulders into Johnny's eyes. He bit his lip and she realized, with complete terror, that he was actually able to consider it as a possible course of action, even as Johnny had been able to suggest it. Terror was like a veil in front of her eyes, distorting Don's face, filming it. It was misty and only the shrewd eyes were clear. At last Don shook his head. "Too risky, Benton. Too many questions. We've got to make her partly responsible, so she can't talk about it."

"Suggestions?"

"Let me think. Damn it, let me think!"

"It's so perfect, Ferris," Johnny said regretfully. "Perfect, all except for Ginny and her big mouth. Stash all that money and use it a little at a time. I know where it would be safe to get rid of the new stuff."

"Can't you shut up!" Don yelled.

"Keep yelling and you blow the whole thing."

"I'm sorry."

"I'm getting an idea. We got to move fast. Knock him out while I'm thinking, Ferris."

Don looked at Johnny sharply. "What's the idea?"

"Do like I tell you. Then we'll bring the car around."

"Walk him out. That's safer."

"Do like I tell you, Ferris. This will work out all right."

She saw Don turn and look at the sleeping man. She saw Don go into the small bathroom and come out at once, wrapping a hand towel around his fist. He licked his lips uneasily as he went up to the sleeping man. He hesitated.

"Go ahead," Johnny ordered.

Don had his back to them. Ginny felt Johnny brush aside her hair with his chin and kiss the side of her neck. Both his hands were busy holding her. The callousness of it made her shudder. She tried to bite the palm of his hand but her teeth could get no purchase on the calloused skin. She saw Don step forward and grasp the hair of the sleeping man, tilt the head back sharply and strike at the jaw with his padded fist. It was a vicious blow and she knew that the scene was implanted so deeply in her mind that she would never forget it.

Brown did not fall. He looked shocked and dazed. He raised his hands slowly. Don Ferris drew the padded fist back again.

Johnny spun her away from him and said in a conversational voice that sounded loud in the room. "Okay, Mr. Ferris."

Don turned slowly, releasing Brown's thin dark hair. He took a step toward Johnny. Ginny, sidling toward the door, saw Johnny pull the stubby revolver out of his pocket, saw Don stop suddenly, midway in his second step.

She saw Don's eyes turn toward her. His voice was thin. "Ginny! He's decided to take all of it! Ginny!"

Johnny backed quickly so he could watch both Don and Ginny. He gave her a slow grin and he kept the revolver pointed at Don. "Kid, go phone the police in town. Talk to Tom Heron if you can."

The towel dropped from Don's fist to the floor. He straightened up. "Wait a second, Ginny. Okay, Johnny. I see your point. It would have been too risky. Look. He's too far gone to even remember what the total was. So let's do this. Grab a few bundles. Not too much. Twenty, thirty thousand. Nobody will possibly know the difference. He's too crazy to make sense. Use your head, Johnny. And what harm would that do, Ginny? What harm? Come on!"

He reached his hands out, palms upward, half pleading.

"Come back as soon as you phone, Ginny," Johnny said softly.

She left. She half ran down the concrete to the office. The line wasn't in use. Tom Heron was at the station. "This is Mrs. Scott Mallory at Belle View Courts on Seventeen. Johnny Benton is holding a man here for you. He's the one who—took all that money in Boston."

She heard a distant startled, metallic gasp, heard Heron say, "Right out. Ten minutes." Fifteen miles, she thought, and maybe they would make it in ten minutes.

She walked reluctantly back to the room. Events, moving so quickly, seemed to have taken her beyond the ability for logical thought. The door to the room was still open. She looked through the screen. The suitcase was on the floor now. Mr. Brown lay on the bed. He was holding a wet towel against his jaw, and his open eyes stared mildly up at the ceiling. Don stood on one foot, the other foot on the chair where Brown had sat. Johnny was lighting a cigarette. The gun was not in sight. As she went in he held the match flame and gave her a cigarette. She leaned close to take the light, looking at the flame, then glancing up at his eyes.

Don looked at her as she turned away from Johnny. Don looked familiar again, his eyes quick and humorous. "Well, it was a thought," he said.

Ginny could not look into his eyes. She turned her back to both of them.

"What's the matter, darling?" Don asked. His voice was easy.

She hunched her shoulders as though she were very cold. She could not answer him. The long slow minutes went by. Cars came from the south at high speed, slowed and turned in, slewing on the gravel. She was glad there were no sirens.

Don said quickly to Johnny, "Don't think you've got anything, Benton. Anything you can use."

"I don't," Johnny said in his deep voice. "Hell, you're a lawyer, aren't you?"

■　■　■

They had gone. The sedans and the money and Mr. Brown. And Don Ferris had gone, leaving number fifteen empty again.

She stood in the night, arms folded tightly, and she saw the floodlights of the gas station wink out. The night was much darker than before. By the time her eyes had adjusted, Johnny was coming slowly across the highway. He came up to her, tall and slow. He stood by her.

"It wasn't a good thing to do, Ginny," he said slowly. "I guess you know why."

"I guess I do."

"Ginny, once when I was a little kid and I was sick, the thermometer got dropped and it busted, and they put the mercury in a little dish. Damnedest stuff. Hold it in your hand and give it half a chance and it would run right out between your fingers. Pretty stuff, but tricky."

"Johnny, I don't want to—"

"You've got to listen to it. He's like that. Coming up here all the time. Nothing you can really put your finger on. Then I see him looking at all that money. Looking at it in a special way. I could tell the way he was thinking. So I had to give him a little chance. Like tilting the dish and watching that mercury run. You see, I was afraid he was going to take you away from here. I wanted to give you a real good look at what I figured Ferris was, all along."

"I—can't ever forget the way he—"

"I know. Funny thing. I found out I'm no saint either."

"How do you mean that?"

"For just a minute there. I don't know. Gun in my hand and all that dough. Just had a sudden crazy feeling about grabbing it and running."

"You wouldn't have," she said firmly.

"Glad you think so, kid." His voice sounded amused.

She turned toward him.

"Johnny?"

"Yes?"

"You didn't want him to take me away from here."

She sensed the way he suddenly became awkward with shyness. "Yes, but I can't say anything yet. Not so soon. It isn't right to speak up so soon. Scotty and I, we—well, you know what I mean."

"I know what you mean, Johnny."

She went into the office for a moment and turned on the big sign: *Belle View Courts. Vacancy.* She went back out and stood beside him in the soft Georgia night, and they waited together for a night traveler, for tired headlights coming down the long straight road.

Talmage Powell

SUDDEN, SUDDEN DEATH

From *Alfred Hitchcock's Mystery Magazine,* 1957

Talmage Powell made his first professional sale in 1943—a mystery novelette that was cover-featured in a pulp magazine. It was followed with some 500 mystery/detective, Western, science-fiction, and men's magazine stories. Of his twenty novels, most of which are criminous, five paperback originals published between 1959 and 1964 feature Tampa private investigator Ed Rivers—a more realistic creation than the bulk of softcover private eyes who appeared and disappeared in the '50s and '60s. "Sudden, Sudden Death," the tense story of a man's relentless hunt for the deliberate hit-and-run murderer of his wife, originally appeared in Alfred Hitchcock's Mystery Magazine *in 1957; Powell later revised and expanded it into his maiden novel,* The Smasher *(1959).*

B. P.

THE HOTEL ROOM WAS LONELY, AND THE REPORT, ARDUOUS. AT the paper-littered kneehole desk, I paused to light a cigarette. As I leaned back in my chair, I caught a glimpse of myself in the bureau mirror. Mr. Everyman. Five feet eleven. Weight one-seventy. A lock of black hair fallen over a ridged forehead. The eyes squinted, the stubbled face just a little gray with fatigue.

I signed the report: *Steve Griffin.*

I stood up, stretched, and discovered that it was dark outside and that I was hungry. I slid the papers into the briefcase resting against the end of the desk and decided to freshen up with a shower.

I didn't get to take the shower.

The phone rang.

"Mr. Griffin?"

"Yes."

"Long distance calling. Just a moment and I'll put your party on. . . . All right . . . go ahead, please."

The connection seemed bad. Her voice sounded distant, faint.

"Maureen!" I said. "This is a surprise! Wait a second. Let me tell the operator the connection is—"

Maureen cleared her throat, a hundred miles away. "The connection's all right," she said in a stronger voice.

I gripped the phone.

"Anything wrong? Penny. Is Penny all right?"

"She's watching some kid TV show. Oh, she's okay. But—but she doesn't know yet."

"Know what? What do you mean?"

"Steve, you've got to come home. Right away." Her voice moved up-scale. There was a moment of silence; then she said quietly, simply, "A man's trying to kill me, Steve. He made the second attempt today. The first time might have been an accident. But not twice. No, not twice!"

I sat down heavily. I heard the distant voice pleading for me to hurry home. The first time had been two days ago, she said. The same car. She'd been out at a suburban plant nursery to get some shrubs for Dudley to set. The car had swung into the intersection, tires screaming. She'd jumped aside, just barely missed being hit. Today, it had happened when she stepped from the curbing at the supermarket, carrying a bag of groceries.

The same car. Heavy. Green. Like ours.

"My God, Maureen! Why?"

"Why?" she said. And she began crying. It wasn't like her. Maureen never cried. She couldn't be crying because somebody had tried to kill her. "I'll tell you when you get home, Steve."

I frowned. "Stick close. I'm on my way. Call the police."

"Yes, Steve—when you get here."

■　■　■

A hundred miles of blackness, with rain beginning to come down. I was driving a coupe that belonged to the sales department. It was light and didn't hold the road too well.

I wasn't hungry any longer. The phone call kept rehearsing itself in my mind. Somebody was trying to kill her, but she wanted to have me there in the flesh when she told me why and when she reported it to the police.

It was unreal, as unreal as our very first meeting had been. That had happened in Germany, in the closing days of the war. Maureen was with a USO troupe and when the German plane came over—one of those lonely, mad-with-frustration vultures that the Luftwaffe had left—Maureen and I landed in the same ditch. It was a muddy ditch. But I slammed her down and threw myself across her. Guns burped and a siren snarled. She was far from relaxed, but she wasn't trembling, either.

It was over in seconds. The plane went away and activity returned to the ground.

"Blood," Maureen said, looking at my back, and went green. Then she bounced out of the ditch and came back with two guys who had a stretcher between them. They lifted me out of the ditch and she ran alongside as we jogged toward the ambulance. She looked small and breathless and the breeze feathered her short, curly blonde hair.

She stood bowed and penitent as they slid me in the ambulance.

"I'll come to the hospital to see you, soldier."

"Swell," I said, speaking through my teeth because the numbness was going away.

It wasn't a serious wound, but a back muscle had been laid open and it was slow to heal. She came to see me three times while she was in the area. I kept my promise to look her up when I got Stateside. We went around together for a while. Neither of us had close relatives. We were lonely. The things we'd seen overseas had changed us. We needed something. We decided we needed each other. One night we went to a party, and when it was over, neither of us wanted to go home. We drove the rest of the night, in a state that could be described as just a little hilarious, and got married early that morning.

It was not the perfect marriage, but we had worked at making it work. We were not, in the usual sense, in love. But we had a lot in common; we had companionship, understanding; we were willing to accept each other's minor imperfections without hurt or irritation simply because neither was judging the other with the yardstick of a romantic ideal.

Our daughter, Penny—five years old, blonde curly hair, teeth white and even in her small face—cemented the marriage.

If it sounds dull, I have given the wrong impression. We visited and partied among a sizable group of friends. Maureen was intelligent, and quick to laugh. Her minor failing was her hatred of details, which was reflected in her housekeeping. Her one major failing, if one had a desire to judge her, was her need for constant appreciation. She was neither catty nor flirtatious, but when she entered a room, she had to know that others knew she was there.

The actress in her? Perhaps. But I was inclined to think the trait stemmed from a deep-seated sense of insecurity.

The first lights of the city flashed by the couple. Traffic grew heavier. I threaded my way cross-town, cutting in and out of traffic with a cab driver's dexterity. I swung into the residential section where we lived—Meade Park—and my fingers were gripping the wheel so hard they ached.

It was midnight and the rain was even heavier than it had been. Houses here and there—new and white and snug behind their lawns—showed lights.

I turned the corner onto Tarrant Boulevard. Our house was halfway down the block. The living-room lights were on and our car was parked under the carport. I pulled up behind the green sedan and sank back in my seat, content for a moment to look at the car and the lights of the house.

I got out of the coupe, turned up the collar of my trench coat and ran across the lawn to our front door.

I opened and closed the door, expecting to see Maureen arise from a chair, but the living room was empty.

"Maureen?"

The silence of the house began to live. The house began to ache with emptiness, as I gave the downstairs a quick search.

I took the stairs two at a time, my heart beating hard. I reached the door to our bedroom and a glance showed me it was empty. Then I rushed to the door of Penny's room. I was too weak to open it. I had to stand a moment, hearing my own loud breathing, before I was able to turn the knob and switch on the lights.

Penny was in bed sleeping. She had one arm flung over her giant panda doll. She stirred, and then sighed into deep sleep.

I went back downstairs, wiping my face and hands. By the time I reached the living room, the handkerchief was sodden.

The main thing was not to go to pieces, to think what to do. I lighted a cigarette and forced myself to be calm. As I dropped the paper match in the ashtray, I saw the butt. I picked it up. It was still moist, soft. It hadn't been snubbed out long. It wasn't Maureen's; there was no lipstick on it. It must be a man's.

I kept from doing it aloud, but my mind was screaming her name, and I found myself at the front door, wet darkness in my face, looking for some sign of her. She might have gone out. But not far on a night like this, without the car, with Penny alone upstairs. The neighboring houses were dark.

I closed the front door. I had the average man's reluctance to call the police. Then I remembered the dim, distant sound of her voice over the phone.

In the small alcove off the hallway, I picked up the phone, dialed, and a quiet, bored voice cut short the ringing at the far end. "Police station, precinct five."

"I want to report a missing person."

"I'll connect you with the bureau."

A pause. I wiped my lips with the back of my hand. Another click.

"Missing persons. DeCoster speaking."

"This is Steven Griffin, 642 Tarrant Boulevard. My wife has disappeared."

DeCoster sighed, as if this were an oft-repeated routine. "Her name?"

"Maureen. She . . ."

"What makes you think she's missing? Sure she hasn't stepped out or been called by a friend or is late coming in from a movie?"

"Listen," I said. "Two hours ago I was a hundred miles downstate. She phoned me. She said someone was trying to kill her and begged me to come home. When I arrived, the lights were on in the house, the car was there—but there's no sign of her. If you've got questions—"

"I'll ask 'em there," DeCoster said.

Eight minutes later, a police cruiser splashed to a stop before the house. I was in the open front door watching for it. DeCoster and a young cop in uniform came through the rain, introduced themselves, and we stood in the living room.

DeCoster was a tall, thin, sallow man. His face was long. He had loose pouches beneath his eyes, but the eyes were gray with sharp lights in them.

"Give it to me," he said, pushing his hat from his forehead.

I gave it to him.

"Got a picture of her?"

I picked up a picture of Maureen from a corner table. DeCoster took it, and I watched him decide that she was, in a unique way, a very attractive woman.

"Pixie," he said, "mischievous. Slanted eyes. Nice teeth. She won't be hard to recognize." He handed the picture to the uniformed cop and told him to take it from the frame, after I'd said that it would be okay.

"Sit down," DeCoster said to me, "and we'll talk."

"Talk! Why don't you do something?" I'd told him of the cigarette stub in my first résumé. Now I mentioned it again. "Whoever was smoking the cigarette couldn't have taken her out of here long before I arrived. Every minute you waste . . ."

He touched my shoulder. "I understand your feelings. But you're jumping to conclusions. Even if you're right, he won't be in the open, a sitting duck waiting with her for us." He nodded at the young cop in uniform. "Get it on the air."

The cop went out with Maureen's picture. DeCoster gave me his undivided attention, as if I were the only customer he'd had in the past five years.

"Tell me about her."

"What do you want to know?"

"Anything you can think of. Her habits, friends, likes and dislikes, activities. Her enemies."

"She didn't have any—not that kind."

He smiled and waited; and I went cold all over. The message was in his eyes: Oh, yes, she did; she had at least one of that kind.

I found relief in talking of her. As long as she could be spoken of in the present tense there was something to cling to. DeCoster was a good listener, attention never wavering.

I tried to show him what she was like, her strange mixture of maturity and perpetual adolescence. Just when you were convinced that her outlook would be forever youthful and unsullied, she would reveal a bit of bitter knowledge about life that should only have belonged to an ancient and rather pessimistic philosopher. At the very moment it seemed she would shy from a puppy's bark, she would show a flash of grit and determination that would have put a mastiff to flight.

With a nod, a word, a facial expression, DeCoster kept me talking. He learned that she'd been an actress who'd achieved only minor success. Her eyes still became nostalgic if talk turned to things theatrical, but she'd spoken little about her acting days since the birth of Penny.

DeCoster learned that I was a minor partner in a plastics firm headed by Willis Burke, who had become my friend during the war. The company had done well. Of a proud old family, Will had used an inheritance to put up most of the money when we started. He was the executive, the organizer, the desk man. I ran things in the field.

"Then you're away from home a great deal?"

"Most of the time . . ." I stopped speaking. We sat looking at each other. Carefully, I put my hands on the arms of the chair. "Do all cops have dirty minds?"

"Now, you just remember this." DeCoster's face seemed longer, thinner. "There are only three possible explanations for someone being after her, Griffin. First, the man might be a nut. Second, he might have mistaken her for someone else."

"And third?"

"Third—in your absences she's been up to something that made somebody want to kill her." He said it gently. But I hated him.

The door chimes sounded. I was out of my chair, reaching the door ahead of DeCoster. Willis Burke was outside. He was a tall man, but gave the appearance of stockiness. He carried himself with that unconscious assurance that comes from never having to worry about money. At thirty-five, his face was still that of the college senior who is president of the student body. A square face with a cleft chin. Heavy, but even brows. Brown hair that formed a widow's peak on the high, clear forehead.

He was bareheaded, with rain speckles on his hair and dark suit. He'd been drinking, just enough to give him a glow.

He waggled a finger under my nose. "Saw the company car in the driveway. Suppose you'll want a bonus for finishing . . ."

"Come in, Will. Something's happened."

He came in and I closed the door. Will looked from DeCoster to me, sensing that my words carried more than casual implication.

"You in trouble, Steve?" Will asked. "Need help? We'll give it the old college try, kid."

"Will, Maureen has disappeared."

He was sober now, staring at me. Then his face went slack. "When?"

"Tonight."

I went on, speaking as rapidly as possible, not wanting to hear the words I was saying. DeCoster listened and said nothing.

Will licked his lips. "Lemme get this. She called. Life threatened twice. Gone when you got here. Look—this is real, isn't it? I'm not passed out and dreaming?"

"You're sober enough," DeCoster said.

"I was afraid of that." Will had brief contact with the shakes. He sat down. Then he got up again. "No wonder she's been looking as if sleep and she had become strangers."

"When did you see her last, Mr. Burke?"

"Yesterday. In the evening. Carla, my wife, and I invited her to dinner. We'd noticed how peaked Maureen was looking. Decided she needed an evening. But it didn't work out."

"No?"

"Carla and I had words. We often do. I forget what the ado last night started over—oh, yes, Carla had forgotten to make reservations at the Penguin Club. I should have called her during the day and reminded her, she said, I knew what busy days she had, how much she had to think of.

"Usually Maureen is amused at minor tiffs. But last night her temper snapped and she walked out on us. Today she called me to apologize. Wasn't herself, she said. Bad migraine headache."

"You didn't see her today?"

"Nope. I asked her over the phone if I could give her an assist. She said she just needed a quiet day or so of rest. She was going to lie down and do nothing more than her grocery shopping at the supermarket late in the afternoon. I let her ring off then. Frankly, my fur was a bit ruffled because of last evening. Carla put an LP record on after Maureen left. I was a thoughtless fool for hurting Maureen's feelings, said Carla, furthermore I was a thorough cad for washing dirty linen in public. I spent the night at the club. Worked awhile this morning; then went out to cure my hangover, a treatment I have not yet completed."

"Did Mrs. Burke see Mrs. Griffin today?"

"I don't know. You can ask her."

"I'll do that," DeCoster said. "I take it that the two families have a stronger link than merely the business relationship."

"We're friends," Will said. "Sometimes I come here when I

want a quiet dinner." Will's glance moved about the living room. "Cozy. Relaxing. Not like my place."

"How often do you come when Mr. Griffin isn't home?" DeCoster said mildly.

The cleft deepened in Will's chin. "Public servant, would you like a punch in the nose?"

"You're not as sober as we thought," DeCoster said. "Or you're very foolish. Now answer my question!"

Will measured the cop. Then he decided to talk instead of punch. "I don't court scandal in the first place," he said. He glanced at me. "Secondly, Steve happens to be my friend."

I was glad he'd said that and I was glad he'd said it in that way. DeCoster's poisonous insinuation about Maureen was gnawing at my mind, despite my efforts to ignore it.

The phone rang. I went into the hall to answer it. The call was for DeCoster.

He listened mostly, speaking only a few monosyllables, glancing at me from under his brows. From the dining room came the tinkle of a bottle neck on glass, as Will dosed his hangover.

DeCoster dropped the phone in its cradle. His face was gray. As if speaking to himself he said, "The quick slash of a scalpel is more merciful than the sawing of a dull knife."

I grabbed his arm. "What do you mean?"

"A woman answering your wife's description was just brought into the morgue."

A strange thing happened to the house. Its walls seemed to expand suddenly with terrific speed and I was alone in a dark place where a cold wind blew.

Then DeCoster's face swam back in focus. He was gripping my bicep. "It may be a mistake. It might not be her. You'll have to go down and say for sure."

It was Maureen, I told myself. They had her picture. She was easy to recognize. DeCoster had said so himself.

I stood at the foot of the stairs, one hand on the wall and one on the newel post. I looked up toward a hallway where a dim night light burned. Where silence held and a child lay sleeping.

I felt DeCoster's hand on my shoulder. "I'll have a policewoman come over. Sergeant Elda Darrity. She's young, and kind, and really goes for kids. If your little girl wakes, Sergeant Darrity'll know what to do."

Will was standing in the hallway. He'd overheard enough to understand. His face looked as if it had been oiled. "Steve, I'll go with you. I'll have Carla come over to stay with Penny."

"I'd like for you to go with me," I said. "But don't upset Carla." I preferred to have the policewoman in the house, if Penny should wake up. Carla prattled. Carla might try to tell a little girl about this big thing.

■   ■   ■

The policewoman was a pleasant and capable-looking brunette. She was husky, but there was kindness in her face.

With Will and DeCoster flanking me, I went out into the night. The three of us got into the back seat of a squad car. A young cop in uniform was driving.

The cruiser was warm and dry. The rain was insistent, streaming across the windows, whispering on the roof. The windshield wipers had to work hard to keep the windshield clear.

I remembered how humbly and tenderly she had watched them put me into the ambulance. "I'll visit you in the hospital, soldier. . . ."

The morgue was a brownstone building. The steps leading up to the double glass doors were worn, scooped out.

The lighting inside was white and harsh after the ride in darkness. DeCoster spoke to a man in a low voice.

"This way, please, Mr. Griffin."

We went down a corridor, into a room where the temperature was kept at a low point. A white-smocked young man moved across the tile floor on rubber-soled shoes. He pulled back a sheet that was draped over a form on a slab, and I made the identification for the one-thousandth time. I had endured the making of it nine hundred and ninety-nine times during the ride over.

The man in the white smock drew the white cloth back over the face of death. I turned away. My flesh felt cold, but sweat was creeping down my cheeks. I tried to recall her laugh, but the dark corridors of my mind held only my final look at her, broken and bloody and stripped of all dignity. Clothing wet and torn. Hair wet about her small, triangular face.

Tomorrow Penny would awaken and ask for her mother.

I was moving and there were two or three people around me, moving with me. I fumbled a cigarette between my lips and someone held a lighter flame to its tip.

Rain in my face again. Then the swirl of blurred lights outside the moving squad car. Will and DeCoster were still with me.

We stopped in front of the house. The three of us got out and went inside. The policewoman said Penny was still asleep; everything was all right.

.   .   .

Everything was all wrong. Everything was out of kilter. Everything was warped, rotten, and unfair. She was needed here. Penny needed her; I did; the house did.

Somewhere in the city, a man was feeling his muscles and nerves relax. Perhaps he was smiling to himself, or having a drink, or grim with a new worry as his mind went over and over the whole thing, seeking flaws, the smallest mistake.

Nobody could possibly need such a man.

DeCoster asked me if I would be okay. I nodded, and Will told DeCoster that he would stick around.

DeCoster turned to me. "Words are meaningless at a time like this; so I won't try to use them. Relax if you can, Griffin, and rest. We'll need all the help we can get. You'll be talking to several people in the morning."

I nodded. DeCoster and the policewoman went out. I sat down on the living-room couch and put my face in my palms. I heard Will in the dining room getting whisky. He came back with the bottle in his hand. "A short one for medicinal purposes, Steve?"

I shook my head. I watched him pour a small drink. He looked tired, almost ill. He didn't toss off the drink. He sat with his elbows on his knees, the glass held in both hands. He was staring at the carpet.

Then he lifted his head. "Steve, I didn't exactly level with DeCoster."

"What do you mean?"

"I've been here when you were away. Now that this terrible thing has happened, I must tell you. I have to make you understand. Steve, she was like a sister to me."

His voice faded away.

I sat perfectly still. "Go on, Will."

He made a vague gesture with his hand. "I know this is risking one thing I've treasured a long time, Steve—our friendship. But I won't take that other risk—having you learn from someone else.

It was all completely innocent, but it might look different if you hear about it in a roundabout way."

He stopped speaking again. He seemed to need help in finding words. I let him sweat; I didn't say anything.

"She wasn't the one-hundred-percent poised young matron you wanted her to be, Steve. God knows she tried! For your sake— and Penny's.

"She had qualities she felt she should get the better of. They weren't really bad. Impulsive generosity. A lonely need for applause, approbation. A too-youthful streak in her that needed constant urging to be adult.

"She admired your character, Steve, your strength and realistic outlook. She was a different person when you were near."

"You were going to tell me," I said, "about you and her. Instead you brand me as a fool who didn't know his own wife."

I didn't realize that I was almost shouting, until I stopped speaking and silence provided a contrast.

Will tossed off his drink quickly. "I've told you," he said, "and I've told you why. We were not alone often. Neither of us entertained any thought of an affair. We would talk and have dinner, maybe go for a ride and make jokes that only children would laugh at."

"Like you were still in college," I said.

He dropped his eyes; a line of white showed about his lips. "Maybe you're right, Steve. I guess we did try to turn the clock back and pretend there was no present reality."

"Then you would go back to Carla."

He stared at the carpet and said nothing.

"Does Carla know?"

"I haven't told her. I don't think she'd understand. Steve, do you want me to get out?"

"No," I said. "I think you've told me the truth. I think you lied to DeCoster because in your way of looking at things you felt you were protecting my honor." I stood up. "So I'm not asking you to leave, Will. But do you think you'd better get back to Carla?"

"She'll be all right. I'll stay here. There might be something I can do. And thanks, Steve."

I went up the silent, hateful stairway toward the master bedroom.

I took off my shoes and lay across the bed, conscious of the empty twin bed beside me. I didn't turn a light on.

The darkness was close and I heard the insistent beat of the rain against the window panes. I might have spent more time with her. I might have come to know her better. I knew now that I had hardly known her at all. I'd been too busy making money, because I'd thought that was the most important thing I could do for her. I hadn't meant to cheat her. . . .

       ■   ■   ■

The girl came to the house early the next morning. Will was asleep in the guest room and Penny hadn't awakened yet. I was in the kitchen making coffee and thinking about one of the toughest problems I'd ever faced—how to tell Penny—when the door chimes sounded.

She was a tall, attractive girl. Her face was well-defined, with high cheekbones and a warm, full-lipped mouth. She had large, dark brown eyes and glossy brown hair which almost touched her shoulders. The details added up to a total that bespoke quiet friendliness.

"You must be Steven," she said, the voice one more warm detail. "I'm Vicky Clayton."

She saw the blankness in my face. "Maureen never mentioned me?" Beneath her quietness, she was nervous. It showed in the way she gripped the newspaper in her left hand.

"She might have, Miss Clayton. My mind isn't working too well this morning."

"Of course." The touch of her hand on my wrist was an unconscious, impulsive gesture. "I'm sorry, Steven," she said simply. "Maureen and I were friends once."

We were still standing in the doorway. I stepped aside and she entered.

"Would you like some coffee?" I asked.

She didn't protest or explain that it was an awkward time for her to be here. She said, "Thank you."

She sat down at the dining table and I brought coffee in. Her newspaper was on the table, and I saw the item. I picked up the paper. A woman had been run over by an automobile. She was a wife and mother; she had once been an actress. Police were searching for the death-dealing car.

I dropped the paper on the table and forced myself to drink some coffee.

"Have you lived here long, Miss Clayton?"

"I don't. I came here only a few days ago to visit relatives. I phoned Maureen. We were planning a lunch and old-times talk."

"You knew her in show business?"

"I was a terrible actress," Vicky smiled.

There was a racket of racing footsteps; a child in rumpled pajamas came into the dining room. Penny stopped short, seeing the stranger. Then she ran forward and bounced into my lap. She flung an arm about my neck and pressed her face against my chest. "Daddy, Daddy! You're home!" She scrambled down and before I could stop her ran toward the kitchen. "Mommy, Daddy's home!"

Vicky Clayton paled and glanced away.

"Mommy . . ."

Penny saw that the kitchen was empty. She came back to me. I picked her up, swung her high. "Is Mommy still asleep?" she asked.

"Penny," I said. Then I couldn't say anything else.

Vicky rose. "Hi, Penny. I'm Vicky. Your mother had to go away on a trip. And you know I forgot to ask her what you like for breakfast. But you can tell me. And we'll have a nice breakfast."

Vicky proved a godsend; the way she handled Penny was remarkable. The phone began ringing and people began dropping by the house. The place became a slow-motion confusion of hushed tones. Will came downstairs, sober and rather severe. He was back on beam and started taking charge with a pleasant but firm demeanor.

Carla arrived, a plump, healthy magpie who wasn't chattering today. She held my hands in hers and wept softly.

Will rescued me by putting her to work answering the phone.

I snatched the chance to go into the kitchen. Vicky and Penny had finished breakfast.

I glanced through the window. They were in the back yard, constructing a village in Penny's sandbox.

The police arrived. A different pair of them this time, both in plainclothes. The one who did the talking showed credentials that identified him as Liam Reynolds, lieutenant, homicide. We needed privacy. I took him upstairs.

He was a young guy and handsome. He didn't look like a cop. He looked like a dancer.

In the bedroom, I motioned him to a chair. I sat on the vanity bench.

He apologized for bothering me at such an inopportune moment. "But," he added, "I know you want to see him got. And got good. I want him, Griffin, and I'm going to get him. I hope he tries to play his string to the end. He doesn't deserve to live to reach headquarters. A jury might let him off with ten years."

Reynolds stopped speaking: then he relaxed. "Sorry. I've got a wife myself. Same size, same coloring." He stood up, walked to the window. "I talk too much. But I don't like things that crawl out from under rocks and prey on women."

He turned from the view of the lawn below. "Let's start with her phone call to you last night. Was that the first indication she was in any trouble?"

I nodded. Reynolds was a surprising man. Looking at him, I somehow began to feel better. Maybe it was his directness, the way he faced reality. Suddenly, the daze I was in cleared. I saw the new day outside. I saw the bed that had supported Maureen's body in sleep. I could say it now: She was dead.

"The reason," Reynolds was saying, "that's what you're afraid of, isn't it, Griffin?"

"Yes," I said.

"We'll find the reason." Compassion came to his face. "Maybe the reason was none of her doing after all. Maybe it was only in the twisted mind of the man who killed her."

He returned to the subject of the phone call. I repeated the call word for word.

"She knew the reason," he said.

"But she didn't tell me—and the reason proved to be more urgent than she thought."

"Money?"

"I don't see how. We have enough for comfortable living. Not so much nor so little to be a danger."

"Bad habits?"

"No real vices. Nothing to cause anyone to . . . Nothing big enough to constitute the reason."

"Affair?" The word was clinical, impersonal.

"She possessed a basic honesty, a great deal of kindness. I realize for the first time how lonely she must have been at times, how vulnerable I left her marriage—but if she had responded to another personality with passion, she would have told me and divorced me. I'm sure of it.

"I think you'll have to look for the reason in some tangent to her ordinary daily living, Lieutenant."

"I'll keep what you say in mind," he said. "Now with your permission I'd like to take a look through her things. So far we haven't much to go on. A few routine facts. Cause of death, brain injury. It might have happened when the car knocked her down. She was found on Timmons Street, a dismal, dirty deserted stretch of waterfront warehouses. She certainly didn't go there alone, afoot. He came here, forced her to go with him, and when they passed down Timmons maybe she fought her way out of the car. She was crazy with panic. She tried to run. He used the car as a weapon."

My mouth was dry. "He wanted to use the car. He'd tried twice before with it. Like a fixation."

"Yeah," Reynolds said. He crossed the room. "Did she have a place where she kept letters, mementoes, bills to be paid?"

"She wasn't methodical. Try the dressing-table drawer. Upper left."

It was a catchall drawer. I stood beside Reynolds as he scanned a few old letters from her friends, the small scrapbook she'd started once with some old playbills and a tiny newspaper notice or two. He removed bills, receipts, notes on scraps of paper reminding her to do things. Then he handed me her checkbook. "In order?"

I flipped the stubs. Then I went through them again. A frown creased my forehead. "No," I said, "it isn't in order. There are too many small ones written out to cash lately. The total's out of all proportion to what she usually spends."

"We'll find out if she endorsed them." He thrust the checkbook in his pocket as a reminder to call the bank. His attention returned to the drawer. It was almost empty when he brought out a sheaf of typewritten, clipped-together paper.

"Looks like a play manuscript," he said.

"I didn't know she was writing a play."

"She wasn't. Here's the author's name and address in the upper left corner of the title page. Randy Price. Know him?"

"I don't recall the name."

"Let's go have a look at him."

We went downstairs. Will Burke was finishing a phone conversation. He came down the hallway toward us. He was collected, efficient, competent, a young chairman of the board. He would remain that way until the Joe College in him kicked up its heels and told the executive to go to the devil. Then Will would shed his gravity, dignity, and cares and have himself a party for two or three days.

I introduced him to Reynolds and left the two of them talking. I avoided the living room, where a few well-meaning people lingered. I went out the side door.

The sun was warm and the sky was a washed-clean blue. Everything smelled fresh and green after the rain. I had to work at it to keep myself from thinking how much she enjoyed this kind of day.

At the rear corner of the house I stopped and watched Vicky Clayton and Penny a moment. The Clayton girl sat on the edge of the sandbox, her print dress drawn over her knees and tucked behind her legs. She was leaning forward, constructing something in the sand. Penny hunkered nearby, absorbed in what Vicky Clayton was doing.

I walked forward and my shadow fell over them. Vicky stood up, the morning breeze toying with her hair. I took her aside, telling Penny we would be right back.

"I'm grateful," I said. "You've brightened her morning immeasurably."

"And mine, too. She's wonderful, Steven. I certainly hope I didn't do wrong. I chatted with her about her mother. I think she's reconciled to her mother's being absent for several days. When she's stopped missing her mother so much, she can be told the truth gradually, without shock."

"I'm even deeper in your debt than I thought, Miss Clayton."

"Oh, I love children. I teach, you know."

"No, I didn't."

"Of course—Maureen never mentioned me."

"I just wanted to tell you," I said, "that I'm going out with the detective. I'll take Penny off your hands and leave her with the woman who baby-sits for us."

"Must you? I haven't a thing to do. But I forgot—I'm a stranger. You might not *want* me to stay with Penny."

I didn't hesitate. I looked past Vicky. "Penny, on your best behavior with Miss Clayton."

"Yes, Daddy," Penny said.

■　■　■

Randy Price's address was on Shady Oak Lane. This was not far from Meade Park, but it was like being in the country. Shady Oak's history began during the between-wars boom, when a development company went broke out there. Streets had been laid out, a number of lots sold, a few low-priced cottages built. Then the crash. After that the city grew in other directions. And in Shady Oak, there were stretches of broken sidewalks. And gaunt, tarnished streetlights, with their glass knocked out, stood like skeleton sentinels, guarding nothing.

Reynolds and I passed two or three of the small frame houses that looked as if they hadn't been repaired or painted since the day of erection. Junky cars sat in the yards and behind one house a cow was grazing.

Price's address was different in two respects. No cow watched our approach and the car beside the weathered cottage was a fairly new model.

The sun was warm and humming insects added laziness to the day as Reynolds and I walked across the porch. He knocked on the front door.

There was no immediate answer. Reynolds knocked again. Then a voice said, as if coming through a yawn, "Okay, okay. Be with you in a second."

Price, finally, came to the door and looked at us through the screen. He was young, dark, and handsome. He would have looked like a teenage boy, had it not been for the Vandyke and neatly clipped mustache.

"Hi," he said with a grin that showed the flash of large, even teeth, "sorry—but I'm not buying anything today."

Reynolds gave me a glance.

"I'm Steven Griffin," I said. "You're Randy Price?"

His face lighted with pleasure. "Say now—Maureen's husband? Holy cow, why didn't you let me know you were coming out? I'd have cleaned up the joint!"

He held the screen door back for us and we entered. The small living room was furnished with a couple of chairs, desk, daybed, straw carpet. Stacks of old books and magazines were at precarious rest on everything except the desk chair and daybed. Randy Price cleared chairs by the simple expedient of picking up the books and magazines and stacking them in a corner. While he was busy with this task, I had a chance to look him over. He was slender, his elbows and shoulders bony. But his muscles were flat, rippling, strong.

Finished with his task, he dusted his hands on the thighs of his trousers and offered his right hand. "Say, Steve, this is a real pleasure. Maureen said she was going to have me meet you when you got back to town. Sorry she couldn't come out. Busy, huh?"

I watched his face and listened to his boyish monologue, trying to come to some conclusion about him.

"Look, you guys sit down. Make yourselves right at home. I might be able to rustle up a beer."

He rushed out of the front room. We heard him banging around in the kitchen.

I glanced at Reynolds.

"Play it dumb," he said. "He doesn't know about Mrs. Griffin."

Randy returned with three moisture-beaded cans of beer and an opener. He set the beer on the desk beside a portable typewriter. He opened the beers and handed them around. Reynolds and I sat down and took a sip out of the cans. Randy half sat on the edge of the desk, smiling at us.

"Do you share Maureen's interest in the theater, Steve?"

"I'm afraid I don't know much about things theatrical."

"You've missed the most exciting thing in life," he said. "Of course, I'm a long way from the theater yet. But I'm learning life and people, which are the sources of great theater. I'm reading, studying, and working." An inner light shifted and began to burn in his eyes. He paced a few steps back and forth, talking of the meaning of the theater.

I could easily understand how this boy might instantly seal a friendship with Maureen. He was intense, eager, enveloped in a dream that had once touched her briefly. He was Youth with a classic, chiseled face. A woman with Maureen's impulsive generosity and kindness would have wanted to help him the moment she glimpsed his dream.

He calmed down enough to retake his position against the desk

and sip his beer. "I'll never be able to repay your wife, Steve. She
has an uncanny natural sense of theater, of what will play and
what will not. I'm writing plays, plays, plays. A trunkful of them.
When I get several that please me, I'm going to New York. I
know," he said with such frankness and simplicity that I almost
believed him, "that I'll be famous. I have it—that extra ounce of
awareness of life and people. The world will some day recognize
what Maureen and a few others recognize today."

He stopped speaking, a shy smile appearing, and the smile
made what he'd said appear less, far less, egotistical than it might
have sounded. I had never before seen such superb, simple self-
confidence.

"Say," Randy said into the little silence his words had brought,
"you guys need more beer?"

Reynolds and I both declined.

"Couple weeks ago when I met Maureen," Randy said, "I had
no idea what a lucky break it was. She still knows a few people.
She's going to get some of my better stuff in the hands of a good
agent."

"We have one of your plays in the car," Reynolds said. "Perhaps Mrs. Griffin intended to show it to the agent."

"Well, she has three of them," Randy said. A frown came to
his face. His glance moved between Reynolds and me. He began
to feel that something was wrong. His feeling seeped into the air
of the cottage. "Say, isn't this a purely social call?"

Reynolds stood up, slid his small leather case from his pocket,
and opened it. Randy stared at the policeman's badge.

"What's wrong?" he cried. "Has anything happened to her?"

Reynolds didn't answer. Instead he asked a question of his own,
"When did you see Mrs. Griffin last?"

"Look, you guys, if something's happened . . . Yesterday afternoon at her house . . . How about telling me . . ."

"What time?"

"Oh, two o'clock, three o'clock maybe. I'd been in town to pick
up some typing paper. I was nearby, so I stopped. She said she
had a headache and still had her shopping to do at the supermarket. I offered to go for her, but she said no. I left right away."

"She was worried, afraid?"

"Afraid? Hey, what is all this anyway! Will you please tell . . ."

"How did you happen to meet Mrs. Griffin?"

"You mean make her acquaintance?"

"That's what I mean," Reynolds said.

"First time I saw her was right here. She was using Shady Oak as a cutoff between her place and Fairhill turnpike."

"What's on Fairhill?" Reynolds said.

"Dudley Loudermilk," I said. "A fellow who does yard work for us now and then."

"That's right," Randy said. "She did say something about seeing a yard man. Anyhow, she was in trouble. The fanbelt had snapped on her car. People never think of a fanbelt until it breaks, and that's usually a million miles from nowhere. Damn it, you've got to tell me . . ."

"Her car was on Shady Oak?" Reynolds broke in.

"Yes, about half a mile from the house. Steaming like a calliope. She was afraid to try driving it farther and had remembered passing a cottage, my cottage. She wanted to use a phone to get a tow car. I didn't have a phone, but I had a car and of course offered to help her.

"She was tired from the hike, especially since she'd made it in spike-heeled shoes, and I offered her something to drink. She accepted a glass of water and we chatted for a few minutes. She saw the typewriter and a play manuscript on my desk and the talk switched to the theater. In five minutes or so we were old friends.

"Now for the last time will you tell me what this is all about?"

"Mrs. Griffin is dead," Reynolds said.

"Dead?" Randy said in a thin whisper. "When? How?"

"Last night. She was run over by a car on Timmons Street."

The boy stood perfectly still; the day was suddenly so quiet the insects outside could be heard. Then Randy's face began to twist. It became the face of a tortured boy; and the mustache and Vandyke became incongruous, almost ridiculous.

Tears came to his eyes. Then he covered his face with his long, thin, sensitive hands and ran out of the room. A bedroom was off the front room. He went in there and flung himself across the bed. His hard, choking sobs convulsed his shoulders, his entire body.

He tried to control himself and succeeded after awhile. He

pulled himself around on the bed and sat up. Tear streaks ran down his cheeks to his mustache. He knuckled tears out of his eyes with both hands.

Then he dropped his hands in his lap and sat staring at us, intermittent sobs snubbing his breath.

"How could it have happened to her?" he said. "How could it?"

His eyes begged for an answer, but Reynolds had none and neither did I.

Then a new thought came to Randy, causing him to sit straighter. "Timmons Street . . . What was she doing there?"

"We think she was taken there," Reynolds said.

"Deliberately? *Forced* to go?"

Reynolds nodded.

"Who did it? Who *would* do it?"

"We don't know yet." Reynolds stood with his hands in his pockets. "Whoever he was, he made two previous attempts on her life. Did she mention that to you?"

"No, but I had the feeling something was bothering her. I asked, but she just said she hadn't been feeling well for some time. So I let it drop."

"Where were you last night, Price?"

Randy stood up. "You think that I . . ."

"I'm just asking."

"I was here."

"Alone?"

"Alone. If I'm supposed to have an alibi, I'm out of luck. I didn't know I'd need one." He turned to me. "When will the funeral be?"

"Day after tomorrow, I think."

"I'll be there. If you need me for anything, let me know."

"Thanks."

He followed us to the front door. When Reynolds and I drove away, he was sitting on the sagging front steps of his cottage, staring into the distance.

We rode in silence. Then Reynolds said, "I don't like him."

I glanced across the car seat at him. "Why not?"

"I don't know. I see a person now and then who makes me think, 'I wouldn't want you coming up behind my back.' Too long a cop, I guess. Too much watching for opposites in people."

Reynolds shook his head somberly. "Even while that boy was crying, I kept picturing him in my mind with his lips curled in contempt of everything beneath his own fancied genius. His sobs filled my ears, Griffin, but the echo was faint, distant laughter, and I knew he would have a certain way of moving through the dark. Quickly, decisively, without the slightest hesitation."

The remainder of the morning fled, consumed at police headquarters where there were papers for me to sign okaying an autopsy. The autopsy was to be held that afternoon. Reynolds said Maureen's body would be released to me tomorrow or the next day.

Reynolds talked with the two men who'd spent the morning on Timmons Street. They'd learned nothing new. There had not been any witnesses to the killing.

Reynolds said he would send me home in a squad car. "Can you take some more legwork?" he asked.

"If it's necessary."

"I think it is. I want you as close to the investigation as possible. A chance word or action might crop up somewhere that would seem okay to us, but which you—knowing her—would spot as being out of line."

"I'll get some lunch. You can pick me up at the house."

A young, fresh-faced cop drew the assignment of taking me home. He was respectful, sympathetic, and silent. And he seemed to understand, when I said I wanted to detour by Timmons Street.

I recognized it as a morbid impulse. But there was also the wish to have been there at the very end, to have been able to do something to avert the end.

Timmons Street had about it an air of desertion and decay. The big warehouses loomed dirty and silent, backs to the street, faces to the turgid river.

There were a couple of poolrooms, with lean teenage boys lounging in the doorways, and a greasy restaurant or two.

The only sign of real activity was the mooring of a scabrous barge at the end of an old dock built to service a warehouse which belonged, according to a weathered sign, to Kukolovitch & Sons. Seamen made the barge fast and the tug that had brought it moved downriver with a hoot of the horn.

"Right over there, Mr. Griffin," the young cop said.

He'd stopped the car for me. I got out and walked a few steps. The police had made some chalk marks on the cracked asphalt. Other than that, there was no sign of the terrible thing that had happened there. She might never have existed so far as the street was concerned. There were not even skid marks, because he hadn't been trying to stop; he'd been trying to hit her.

I turned away, got in the squad car, and went home to lunch.

■ ■ ■

Vicky Clayton and Penny were the only people in the house. Vicky explained that Will had left a half hour earlier after calling his office.

Vicky had the table spread with sandwiches, tossed salad, coffee and cake. Penny was finishing lunch, talking between bites about her delightful morning. Then Vicky took Penny upstairs for her afternoon nap.

Vicky returned as I finished my coffee. We cleared the table together and as Vicky stacked dishes in the sink she gave me a direct look. "I'm looking for work, Steven."

"Thought you teach."

"I do. But there's no school now; it's summer. I have loads of time and have been wondering what to do with myself. I've attended summer sessions at the university for the past three summers in a row. I'm tired of that." She ran hot water into the sink, added detergent. "You haven't had a chance to think about it yet, but finding the right person to keep house and take care of Penny is going to be a sizable problem. Please, let me help. For a few days. Until you have a chance to start setting your life in order again."

I nodded, granting her request. "In many ways you're like her."

"Maureen?"

"Yes," I said. "The same sort of kindness. The same impulsive generosity."

■ ■ ■

Reynolds arrived in a police car. When we were in the car, I said, "Where are we going?"

"Plant nursery. Then the supermarket."

The trip to the plant nursery consumed time without returning a dividend. No one there had seen a woman almost hit by a car two days ago.

Reynolds and I got back in the car and drove from the suburban nursery to the supermarket south of Meade Park. There, the manager polished his glasses. "Sure, I remember some of the employees talking about a woman almost getting hit."

"Who saw it?" Reynolds asked.

"Why, I don't know."

"Someone did, or they wouldn't have been talking about it. Let's find out."

The third employee we talked to was a plump, brunette girl. She was a checker and stood with her back to her cash register. Customers with food buggies in nearby lines watched curiously.

"Gee, yes, she was almost killed!"

"You saw it?" Reynolds asked.

"No, but I was the first one he told about it."

"Who?"

"Tommy. Tommy Haines. He saw it."

Reynolds glanced at the manager.

"Tommy is a stock clerk," the manager said. "When we have long lines out here, he bags purchases and carries them out to our customers' cars. He's in back now helping unload a shipment of tomatoes."

The stockroom was cool and dim, cluttered with crates and baskets. It smelled of earth and winey apples.

Tommy was a tall, thin boy with a shock of sandy hair. He walked over to one side of the stockroom, wiping his face on the tail of his large, white apron.

He looked at Reynolds' badge, then at Reynolds' face. "Yeah, I saw the lady almost get hit. She trying to locate the driver?"

"Something like that. Is this the lady?" From his inside pocket, Reynolds produced a picture. It was of Maureen, a smaller reproduction of the picture of her DeCoster had taken with him the night before. I wondered how many of those small pictures were scattered about town in the pockets of men who were out asking questions.

"That's her," Tommy said. "I'd know her anywhere, even if she was so scared she looked a little different yesterday."

"Tell us exactly what you saw," Reynolds said.

"Well, it was right at closing time and we had a last-minute rush. I'd taken a double armload of groceries out to a customer's car. I was headed back across the parking lot when I saw this lady come out. She was carrying her own, only a small package.

"I didn't pay too much attention, except to notice she was worth a second look. She stepped off the curb to cross the street—sometimes they park over there, because if you want to turn left it's hard to get out of the parking area when traffic is heavy.

"She must have been past the middle of the street when she screamed. Not loud. But loud enough. I wasn't watching, because I'd started back into the store. But I turned around when I heard her yell like that.

"She'd caught a good break in traffic, to make her crossing. But there was this car that must have whipped out of the intersection. Whoever was driving was driving too fast, and when she saw him and yelled, he must have lost his head."

"What do you mean, Tommy?"

"Well, she dropped the groceries, and she was getting out of the way. And fast. But instead of cutting away from her, the guy got rattled and cut toward her. Then right at the last second, he shifted the wheel away from her. Lucky thing she was young and quick. If she'd been an old lady, it would have been curtains. She never would've got out of the way in time. I ran out and helped her get up. She said she was okay. Didn't want a doctor. Going home, she said. When she saw her husband, she said, everything would be all right."

"She got in her car and drove away then?"

"Yeah. And the funny thing, she was driving a twin to the car that nearly hit her."

"How about the license number, Tommy?"

"Golly, I didn't even think about it until the guy had gone around the next corner and was out of sight."

"You're sure a man was driving?"

"Looked like a man."

"Could it have been a woman with, say, an Italian haircut?"

"Never thought of that. Could have been. Just figured it was a man."

"Did she say anything to you about the car or driver?"

"Nope. She was crying a little. That didn't surprise me. She was mumbling something that didn't make sense. Just words."

"Remember them?"

"Well, she was crying. And she said she wanted her husband. She said she had to reach somebody and let him know he was wrong, that she hadn't meant it. Just words. Kind of hysterical, you know."

"Thanks, Tommy."

"Sure," he grinned. "Glad to get away from them tomatoes for a few minutes. I guess the lady was okay once she got home to her husband."

Reynolds and I walked out of the store, got in the police car, and drove away. I thought of the way he'd tortured her and then of the way he'd succeeded at last on Timmons Street. I began to picture him dead. I didn't want Reynolds or the state to get him. I began wanting to pronounce sentence myself and see that that sentence was carried out.

Reynolds was a deft, swift driver. We threaded through traffic.

"How about that car he was driving," Reynolds said, as if speaking to himself. "Odd that it was a twin to yours, Griffin. She remarked on it. So did Tommy Haines."

"Coincidence?" I asked.

"Maybe. But a broad one. That shade of green isn't too common in that make of car."

"No, we bought it for that reason, among others," I said. "Maureen wanted something unique. Not flashy. Just a bit unusual."

"I think we're dealing with a nut," Reynolds said. "Everything points to it. He took a long chance on somebody seeing him well enough for future identification or getting his license number when he tried that stunt in front of a busy supermarket. That isn't a man thinking in normal patterns.

"Suppose for a minute that he *is* a nut with the fixation in his garbled mind that the job had to be done with a certain kind of car—a car like yours. Why? What would lead him to think like that?"

I stared at Reynolds.

His face was tight. "I suspect you're a jump ahead of my reasoning. The car, in his mind, must be tied in with his reason for wanting to do what he did. But why the car—unless your car had done something to him?"

"Maureen would have reported an accident."

"Maybe. Maybe not. If she hurt someone, she might have panicked. Anyway, I didn't say she was driving. Do you ever loan the car?"

"We never have. But we wouldn't turn down a friend if he made a request."

"Has the car been repaired recently? Bent fender, broken headlight, anything like that?"

"Not that I know of."

"We'll find out. It'll take time. He's built himself a tight house, Griffin. Nobody knows him. Nobody saw him. Nobody knows his reason. The car is the one loose brick."

. . .

There were hushed, taut people at the house again. Will was there. I endured the barrage of murmured sympathy. The people filtered away and Will said, "You look peaked. You need some coffee. Vicky Clayton left a fresh pot, anticipating the need. Smart girl, that Vicky."

"Where is she?"

"Took Penny downtown. Too many people in and out, she said. They would communicate their feelings to Penny, Vicky said."

We had coffee and I thought of a loose end or two of business. But Will wouldn't let me mention them.

"Forget the business for a month. Or as long as necessary. The business won't suffer. Wouldn't be what it is if it hadn't been for you in the field, anyway."

"I spent too much time in the field, Will."

"I know."

"A month or two out. Weekend at home. No good."

He put his hand on my shoulder. "You can't unwind the past. What's Reynolds found out?"

I told him of Reynolds' idea about the car.

"Reynolds is no genius," Will said, "but he's a tough, shrewd cop, and he has experience. He's accustomed to looking for patterns. Maybe he's found one. Something was bothering Maureen, as I mentioned last night. And it didn't start two days ago, when the first attempt was made, either."

"You'd noticed it before?"

He shifted his weight in the breakfast-nook chair. "I first noticed it one afternoon about three weeks ago. I ran into her downtown. She was coming out of a florist shop, looking like she'd lost her last friend."

He helped himself to a second coffee. "I thought she was ill. She said she was feeling okay and brightened somewhat. Then I guessed she was just tired, maybe lonely. I invited her to have something tall and cool and she said she had to get home. Then I made a bright crack. I thought maybe it would cheer her up, that she might smile. I said, 'Rich uncle kick off and you're getting some flowers for the funeral?' I knew of course that no one we knew had died. But she didn't laugh. She almost burst into tears."

I pushed my coffee cup aside. "You remember the florist?"

"Sure. The little place on the corner of Second and Park."

Will accepted my abrupt departure without ruffled feelings. I remembered a lesson I'd learned from Reynolds. I went upstairs and got a small picture of her before I started out.

The florist was a slender, smiling, soft-spoken woman of middle age; her gray hair was cut short.

"You want some flowers for a lady, sir? Roses? You appear to me to be the rose-buying type."

"I want a funeral wreath."

Her smile vanished. "Please forgive me!" She came from behind the long glass case that held baskets and sprays. "That was extremely untactful of me, but you are young and . . ." She spread her hands. Then gently, "Your mother perhaps?"

"My wife."

"Oh, I *am* sorry."

I accepted most of her suggestions about the wreath, paid her, told her where it was to be sent and that the services were tentatively set for day after tomorrow.

"I'll attend to everything, Mr. Griffin. Rest assured that everything regarding the flowers will be taken care of."

"She was in your shop about three weeks ago," I said. "You might recall her."

"There are so many people . . ."

She broke off to take the picture of Maureen I was holding out to her.

"So young and lovely," she said. "But I'm sorry, Mr. Griffin, I don't recall the name. The picture . . ." she tilted her head, holding it before her. "Yes, it strikes a memory. Someone very like her came in. I remember a face like hers. An interesting face, one you notice. But I do not remember her for that. I recall her nervousness. She upset a basket beside the door and insisted on paying for it. But the name . . . it means nothing."

"She might have given a different name."

The florist handed back the picture, shrugged.

"May I use your phone?"

She nodded toward a phone that sat on a desk in the far end of the shop.

I dialed police headquarters. "This is Steve Griffin. Is Lieutenant Liam Reynolds there?"

He was out. He was, I guessed, probably checking auto-body repair shops.

"I want to see him right away," I said. "I think I have something important."

"We can radio him in."

"Radio him to the florist at the corner of Second and Park."

I hung up. The florist was standing close to me when I turned. Her face was rigid and pale. "Really, Mr. Griffin, I have no idea what this is all about. But for you to call the police on me . . ."

"Don't misunderstand," I said. "My wife has been killed. The name she used here, the flowers she bought might help the police find who did it."

"Oh." She exhaled a good, long breath. When she raised her face, her eyes were again clouded with sympathy. "Of course, I'll help in any way I can."

She opened a steel file beside the desk, pursed her lips and touched her chin with a fingertip. She spent several moments remembering. Then she began going through the file.

She was still at it when Reynolds arrived about five minutes later.

She acknowledged my brief introduction—"How do you do, Lieutenant?"—without turning from her file.

"This is it—I think." She drew a daily sales sheet from the file. "Jane Brown. I recall thinking that it was odd, such a common, lackluster name for a striking woman."

Reynolds said, "Do you always put down the customer's name?"

"Oh, no. But when we sell flowers for special occasions, weddings, big parties, funerals, we of course ask for the name of the sender and recipient."

"Where'd she have you send them?"

"She didn't have them sent any place. She bought a large funeral basket. When I asked for the name she gave it. Then when

I asked where the flowers were to go, she hesitated and said she'd take them."

I felt as if all the air had suddenly been pressed out of my lungs. Maureen had bought flowers for an unknown person's funeral, but she'd been afraid she might be traced through the florist who had seen and could identify her. Maureen had thwarted us. But not him, not the nut in the green sedan.

Reynolds asked the florist a few more questions. The answers added to nothing. Maureen had left the shop to get her car. She stopped and chatted with some man on the sidewalk—that would have been Will. Then she had gone on down the street. A few moments later she appeared in the car, tapped the horn, and double-parked long enough for the florist to hurry out with the basket and put it in the back seat of the car. Reynolds asked a final question and we learned that Maureen had been alone during all this, except for the few seconds she'd spoken to Will.

The florist followed us to the doorway. We thanked her, and I noticed the gilt lettering on the window of the shop for the first time. The Blossom Shoppe, Elda Dorrance, prop.

The gray squad car was in a loading zone in front of a store a short distance down the block. My own car was in a parking lot around the corner.

Reynolds and I stopped beside his car. "Don't let it get you down, Griffin. It happens like this all the time."

"I thought it was a good lead."

"It was. It gave us one thing. She bought flowers for somebody's funeral, and she didn't want anyone to know about it. We've got the date of purchase—twenty-three days ago today. The flowers would have been used within two or three days at the most. So we check funerals. Every funeral for three days beginning twenty-three days ago."

"Will you know which one it is?"

"The one with an automobile as a contributive cause."

"My automobile," I said. "Driven by Maureen."

"Take it easy, Griffin."

My shoulders dropped. "Okay. I think I'll go home now."

I wasn't fooling him. When I was three steps away, he spoke my name. I stopped and looked back.

He gave me a level smile. "You did the right thing. It was a good lead, and it belonged to the police. Keep doing it that way,

Griffin. You've got a good head. You might run onto something. Don't try any solo flights. You might find him—and they lock you up just as fast for killing nuts."

"I don't know what you're talking about."

"Fine," he said. "I'll keep in touch."

• • •

No one was at the house when I arrived there. I went in the living room and sat down on the couch. Then I swung my feet and lay prone. Fatigue came to me like an opiate, making my limbs heavy, my mind dull. I put my hands over my face and drifted into troubled sleep.

I sat up suddenly. The sound that had awakened me was the front door opening. It was Penny and Vicky.

Penny was eager to impart news of her shopping trip and show me the hankies she'd bought. Vicky's calm eyes didn't miss the way I was feeling. She reminded Penny to go upstairs and change clothes so she could help prepare dinner.

When Penny raced out of the room, Vicky sat on the edge of a chair opposite me. "Would it help to talk about it, Steven?"

"I hate even to think about it. Reynolds is on a bloody scent. He thinks Maureen killed someone and then someone else, close to the first someone, set out to kill Maureen in revenge."

"You knew her, Steven. Could she have killed?"

"Accidentally, yes. She might have and then run in panic. But then for this, whoever it is, to plot her death coldly and deliberately . . ."

"Perhaps his mind was unhinged by grief."

I stood up. "So I should forgive him, wish him well?"

Her fingers were gripping the arms of her chair. She said in a choked tone: "Right now you're wearing the same shoes he wore, feeling the same things he must have felt."

"And he didn't forgive Maureen!"

"But if there is never any forgiveness, where is there any hope?" She began crying. She made no display of it. Tears simply started running down her cheeks.

The next day I decided to send Penny away for a few days. The shadow over the house was communicating itself to her as hushed people came and went. Will Burke offered to loan his lake cottage. We'd been out there on weekends. Penny loved the lake, the tall, cool pines, the birds and the rabbits that hopped across the sage field. Vicky insisted on going along as governess. It would mean staying at the cottage night and day, but she was staying at a hotel now because her relatives were in a small apartment, she explained.

I rented a car, loaded it with groceries, and drove my car out ahead of them, guiding Vicky, who was driving the rented car.

The cottage was made of logs, overlooking a pier and boat dock. Inside was a beamed living room with fieldstone fireplace, kitchen, dining nook, two bedrooms and bath.

"Pardon my pioneering instincts," Vicky said when she saw the interior, "but how does one manage out here? Deep freeze, electric stove, telephone—and look at the couches and chairs in the living room. Even a bearskin rug."

"There's a small outboard cruiser in the boathouse. Want me to get it out for you?"

"Thanks, but my sea legs are none too steady. Anyway, Penny might fall overboard."

Vicky insisted I stay long enough for coffee. Then I drove back to town.

■   ■   ■

Reynolds was parked in front of the house in the gray police car.

I stopped the sedan in the driveway. Reynolds and I met in the yard and entered the house.

"No suspicious funerals," he said. "I checked them for five days, beginning twenty-three days ago. She may have taken the flowers out of town."

"How about repairs on the car?"

"She might have taken that to a neighboring town also." Reynolds pitched his hat on a chair, sat on the couch, and exhaled. "Busy morning. And we still have several garages to go. Some of the small ones in the suburbs." He stretched his legs before him and looked at his shoes. A hard, icy sheen came to his eyes. "It's got to work. There has to be a garage."

"Otherwise?"

"We're up a stump. We'll have to back up and find a new tack."

"Or fail."

"We won't fail. His crime isn't perfect. No crime is."

"How about the unsolved ones?" I said.

"Not one that isn't studded with mistakes," he insisted. "A

crime in itself is a foolish, illogical act, contrary to the good of the group of which the criminal is a part. An unsolved crime means only that a dull, disinterested cop slipped up."

"Perfect enough from where the crook sits," I said. "Nothing to stop him from growing old, dying in bed, and having grandchildren honor his grave with a bouquet of posies."

Reynolds jumped to his feet. "Griffin, you're remarkable!"

"What did I say?"

"The flowers. Why assume they were for a funeral? Why not a bouquet to honor a grave—a grave several days old? I looked in the wrong direction. Instead of starting twenty-three days back and working down the calendar, I should have worked up."

He strode into the hallway. I heard him telephoning.

While Reynolds was still on the phone, an express truck stopped before the house. The expressman got out of the truck with a flat, oblong package in his hand. It was for Maureen, collect.

I paid, took the package, and closed the door on the departing expressman's back. I opened the package. The contents were two Randy Price play manuscripts and a letter from Hull and Jordan, Author's Representatives.

Dear Mrs. Griffin,

Pursuant to our correspondence of a month ago, we have had both Mr. Hull and Mr. Jordan read the enclosed manuscripts. While the plays indicate the author has promise, they also unfortunately reflect immaturity and inexperience. However, the return of these efforts does not mean that we are averse to seeing more of his work. On the contrary, we wish to assure Mr. Price that he definitely has talent, a feeling for people, a crude but promising way of expressing his unique ideas about life. Please be assured that anything else of his will receive a sympathetic reading here and that all our resources will be used to his advantage the moment he produces something that is a bit more professional than these two.

Yours sincerely,
Roger W. Hull

P.S. I certainly do remember you, Maureen, from my days as an actor's agent. So now you're married and have a little girl?

Congrats, many times over. I was in service, briefly, and began handling authors instead of actors when I donned civvies again.

RWH

The postscript was jotted in pen and ink, an afterthought when Hull's secretary had laid the letter on Hull's desk for signature.

I slid the manuscripts and letter in a table drawer. Then Reynolds came into the room and I quit thinking of the hope and encouragement Randy Price would get from the letter. I knew Reynolds had something. It showed in his face.

"You want to go?" he said. "I'll tell you about it in the car."

We walked out of the house, got in the police car, and Reynolds pulled away from the curb with a short cry of rubber.

"Twenty-eight days ago," he said, "at eight-fifty-five in the evening, a young woman with a little boy in her arms stepped from the curbing on West End Avenue. A car swung an intersection wide. It was moving fast and skidded. Out of control, it bore down on the mother and child. The mother tried to throw her small son to one side, but she wasn't in time and the car couldn't stop. Both were buried two days later."

A shiver passed over me. Reynolds' voice seemed to recede. Maureen behind the wheel of a car, a mother and child looming before her . . . Maureen frozen with sudden terror, unable to stop the hurtling mass . . . No, no! It couldn't be!

"Hit-run told me," Reynolds was saying, "that they're still looking for the car. It slowed, but it didn't stop. It fled in blind panic. The boys on the detail got the usual conflicting descriptions of the car. They could be certain only that it was a heavy sedan, dark gray, or one of the new shades of pastel blue—or green. Nobody got the license number."

"Who were the people?" I asked, and had a hard time saying the words.

"Martin's the name. He owns a hole-in-the-wall grocery over on West End. We'll learn more about him. Bill Ravenel is meeting us. He's been on the case."

■ ■ ■

At the turn of the century, West End had been an address of distinction. Genteel quiet had reigned over large, impressive houses. Fine carriages reposed in the carriage houses or were pulled along the street by matched teams. Proper good mornings were exchanged on a sidewalk dappled by sunlight and the shade of maple trees.

Today, the quiet was no more than a lingering memory. West End seethed with people, noisy people, at this hour of the afternoon, tailend of the work day. The houses were gabled, gingerbread monstrosities, needing paint, gloomy in outlook, chopped into crowded, dreary apartments. Only a few of the trees remained and these were bedraggled from the onslaughts of climbing children. Laundries, fixit shops, pawnbrokers and garages had wedged between the houses, desecrating every final inch of space.

Reynolds parked near a fire hydrant, and a few moments later a gray twin to Reynolds' car swung in ahead of us. A man got out and walked back to us.

"Bill Ravenel," Reynolds said.

I reached across Reynolds to shake hands through the open window of the car. Ravenel was young and tall with a boyish face and crew cut. His blue eyes were cold. He made the handclasp short.

"A little family has been wiped out of existence, Griffin," he said. "I hope it wasn't your wife driving the car."

"Ravenel . . ." Reynolds said in a curt tone.

Ravenel looked at him, then at me. "Sorry," he said stiffly. "But I'm close to this case. I know what the Martins were like. Good people. Poor people. People in love—until a thoughtless, drunken couple came barrelling along."

A shiver crawled down my back. "A couple?"

"Man and woman."

"And drunk?"

"They must have been, way they were moving along."

We got out of the car to stand beside Ravenel. For a moment, I wondered if my legs were going to hold me.

Ravenel pointed to a spot near the center of the street. "There's where it happened. The Martin woman was killed instantly. Child lingered a few hours."

We crossed the street. As Ravenel and Reynolds talked to people who'd known the Martins and showed Maureen's picture around, my first instinctive hatred of Ravenel was tempered. I glimpsed the case as he saw it.

Alec Martin had soldiered three years in the Pacific theater during World War II before succumbing to battle fatigue. He'd talked about his time in the hospital readily with friends, as if it were something he wished to get off his mind.

A product of West End, he'd married a school-days girl friend, Sally. They'd lived in a small second-floor apartment, sharing a bath at the end of the dark hallway with a second couple. Alec had bought a small grocery store half a block away, a year before the birth of their son.

"They used to go to the store to meet Alec every night he stayed open late," Sally's father told us. He was a gaunt, gray, grizzled man, sitting in a stuffy, ancient living room next to his wife, a bony woman whose eyes were set in hollow craters of grief.

"The mother and boy," the old man said. "They used to walk over to the store and Sally would help Alec close up. He was staying open late almost every night. They wanted to buy a small place away from West End. On the edge of town where there was sunshine and air.

"He saw it happen. He was expecting them, watching for them. Sally saw him and was waving to him. Maybe that's why she didn't see the car in time."

The woman beside the old man closed her eyes; it took all life from her face.

"It almost killed Alec," the old man said. "Nearly drove him crazy. He didn't sleep and he couldn't eat—just sat in that apartment and stared at the walls, not even bothering to turn on a light when it got dark. I tried to talk him out of it, but nothing you could say helped. He just had to start living again on his own accord. A week ago he sold out the grocery. Said he couldn't stand to live on West End any longer. Promised he would write and let us know where he was, what he was doing, but we haven't heard from him."

Ravenel stood up, his gaze resting on the old man. "We'll try not to bother you again," Ravenel said. "If you hear from him, let us know."

The old man went with us to the door. "You find out who was driving the car yet?"

"We're working on it."

The old man glanced at the three of us, one by one. I wanted to turn away. I wondered what his eyes would hold if he knew what Ravenel and Reynolds suspected. The old man shook his head. "What terrible hell they must be living in, that man and woman. The woman especially. She was driving. You learned that, didn't you?"

"Yes," Ravenel said softly, "some kids playing told us that much."

"But nobody got the license number," the old man said. "Nobody thought fast enough. And then the car was gone."

∎ ∎ ∎

We went back into the noise and grime of West End.

"Sally Martin and the kid," Ravenel said, "were buried in Memorial Park. Let's have a look."

We drove to the cemetery in one of the gray cars. The graves were side by side on a sloping hillside. The sod over them had not yet taken good hold.

A weathered, decaying floral basket stood at the head of Sally's grave. Ravenel walked around the grave carefully, kneeled, and examined the basket.

He looked up at me, and the silence of the cemetery oozed over me like a living, tangible thing. I walked to the head of the grave and saw what Ravenel had seen, a tiny sticker on the base of the basket. It had been almost obliterated by rain and weather, but Ravenel had knocked dirt aside and the faded letters were still visible: The Blossom Shoppe.

"This is where she brought the basket," Ravenel said. "Now we can picture most of it. Martin did see the license number of the car that killed his family. He was standing right there in the doorway of his store. He denied seeing it because he didn't want us to get to Maureen Griffin. He wanted to get to her himself."

"You don't have any proof she brought it!" I pointed at the basket. "Coincidence has hung innocent people in the past."

"True, but the occasions have been rare," Ravenel said. "The pattern here fits together too well. The pattern is so complete that I'll stick my neck out and fill in a few more of the details. Martin saw the license. He went to the registration bureau and found out who owned the car. He was an essentially decent human being, but he was thinking in a sick manner. Then he sold his store. But I'll bet he didn't leave town. I'll bet he bought himself a big, green car—a weapon."

Ravenel turned from the graves. Then he stopped and looked at me. "By the way, Griffin, where were you the evening Sally Martin and the boy were killed?"

I was stunned. It seemed like a lot of time was going by and I wasn't saying anything. "I was out of town," I said.

"Can you prove it?"

"I might be able to."

"You might have to. After all, there was a man in the car with Mrs. Griffin."

That night I stayed with Will and Carla Burke. I couldn't face the silence of my own house. The three of us sat and talked until late, Carla on her best behavior, not criticizing Will once.

Finally, I didn't have the ill grace to keep them up longer. I went to bed in the guest room. But sleep wouldn't come. Maureen had been good, gentle, kind. She might have panicked after the accident, any human being might have. But she wouldn't have run far. She'd have gone back, offered assistance—unless the man had forced her not to.

I slipped into the bathroom, found Will's sleeping pills. It took two of them to put me under.

■ ■ ■

Being in Will's and Carla's company helped me get through the funeral the next morning. After a gloomy lunch, I went home. I had to go back to the house sometime.

I called the lake cottage. Vicky said everything was okay. Penny was minnow fishing from the shore with a string and bent pin.

Next I called Reynolds. His news was anticlimactic. A clerk in the license bureau remembered that a man of Martin's description had asked about a plate number. And a used-car dealer remembered the sale of a big, green car a week ago. The buyer, again, answered Martin's description, his manner and insistence on a certain type of car causing the dealer to recall the sale. Martin had registered the car in his own name.

"We know the how and why," Reynolds said. "Now we've got to find Martin."

I came from the phone alcove into the living room. The front door was open. Randy Price was peering in the screen.

"Hi, Steve," he said glumly.

"Oh, hello, Randy. Come in."

He sat down in a club chair and clasped his hands and cracked his knuckles. "I had to see somebody, talk to somebody," he said. "I was at the funeral."

"Yes, I saw you. How about some coffee?"

"Sure."

We went into the kitchen.

"That Reynolds," he said. "He doesn't like me. Had a man on my neck off and on since you two came out to my place. Thinks I was taking Maureen for a ride or something. You don't think that about me, do you, Steve?"

He stood before me, nervously pulling his Vandyke. I saw the same catlike quality Reynolds had seen, and a light lurking deep in his eyes made me wonder if his talk was just so much soft soap.

"I don't know what to think about you, Randy."

"Okay, if that's the way you feel about it."

"Don't be a spoiled brat."

Anger flashed hot in his eyes; then it died. "Sure, this is a lousy time for you, Steve. And I won't ask you."

"Ask me what?"

"For a small loan. You see, Maureen loaned me a bit and I thought that if you . . . Well, after all, it isn't as if the money was being thrown away. Believe me, Steve, you'll be helping genius along."

I thought of those checks written to cash in Maureen's checkbook. Now I knew where the money had gone. It didn't matter. It was rather a relief. I knew how Maureen would have felt toward this boy. His work, not the guy himself, would have been the important thing in her mind.

"Don't make it sound so much like a privilege, my lending you money," I said.

"Thanks, Steve." He grinned and accepted coffee. And twenty dollars.

Not until Randy was driving away did I remember his play manuscripts. I went out the front door, but he was already turning the corner.

The postman was coming down the sidewalk. He turned in, offered his sympathy, and handed me a letter.

I went inside. The envelope was plain, white, with a local postmark. There was no return and the address was printed in ink. I ripped the end off the envelope and drew out a single sheet of white paper. It bore the same neat hand printing. No salutation, no signature, a single line of words marching across the otherwise blank page:

You owe me the kid too, Griffin.

The words blurred. I crushed the paper in my hand. The very air of the house was suddenly charged with the terror, the tension of a scream.

I forced myself to walk, not bolt, to the phone. My hands were shaking so badly I misdialed once and had to start over.

"Reynolds speaking."

"Steve Griffin. For God's sake, get out here right away."

"What's happened?"

"He's after Penny!"

"How do you know?"

"A note. He sent a note. Reynolds . . . you know Lake Apopka?"

"Yes."

"Will Burke owns the cottage at the northern end. Get a man out there, will you? She's there with Vicky Clayton."

"It's as good as done. Hold yourself together, Griffin. I'm on my way."

I hung up and stood perfectly still. I'd been afraid before. Overseas, I'd been afraid. I'd been more than afraid when Maureen's phone call had brought me through a hundred miles of night and rain. But this fear was different.

I went upstairs and opened the top drawer in the chest of drawers in the master bedroom. Up high, beyond Penny's reach, was the gun I'd brought home when I'd decided to go on the road.

Maureen had laughed. "I don't know which I'm afraid of most, the gun or a prowler."

I checked the gun. It was loaded. I slipped it in my inner coat pocket.

When Reynolds arrived, I had the outward, visible part of the shakes under control.

He examined the note. Common dimestore paper and envelope. Nothing there to help us. No lead toward Alec Martin anywhere. When he'd bought the big green car, the city had swallowed him, taken him like a diseased cell, a germ, into its teeming bloodstream.

During the drive to the lake, Reynolds said that Ravenel had gone out after my call. With the Griffin case and Martin case consolidated, the two detectives were working together.

Penny saw our arrival and came from the lakeshore at a run.
She jumped into my arms and I held her so tightly she winced.

She wriggled to the ground, telling me what fun she was
having, and I walked with her to see the tiny fish she'd caught.
After baiting her pinhook, I left her at the water's edge and followed Reynolds up the clearing to the cottage.

Ravenel was sitting on the peeled log railing of the porch smoking a cigarette and looking at Vicky Clayton. She sat in a rawhide
and rattan chair, huddled in it, tensed as against cold.

Ravenel threw away his cigarette and stood up as Reynolds and
I mounted the porch. I glanced at Vicky. Her lips trembled and
she looked away. Her demeanor was certainly puzzling. It struck
me now that it was that of a guilty person.

"Nothing out of the ordinary out here," Ravenel said, "except
her."

He glanced at Vicky and she flinched.

"I saw her coming out of Martin's apartment one evening when
I went over to talk to him," Ravenel said. "I asked him who she
was. She's his sister."

Vicky jumped to her feet. She crossed the porch, stopping a
few feet from me.

"Don't judge me too quickly, Steven," she said in a strangled
tone. "What he says is true. Alec is my brother. Our parents
divorced years ago and I lived with my mother while Alec stayed
with father, who later remarried. I didn't know Alec very well, but
we corresponded from time to time. His final letter was a rather
incoherent account of the tragedy that had befallen his family,
written to me about twelve days ago, several days after the burial
had taken place.

"When I got to him, he was in a state of acute mental distress.
He would sit in the apartment and stare at the walls for hours.
Then he would go out without saying where he was going or when
he would be back."

Her voice broke. It was a moment before she could go on.

"I might have suspected," I said. "You never said anything
specific about Maureen or your friendship. And that one time
you defended Martin and begged me to forgive him."

Her head moved from side to side, slowly, as if the movement
took great effort. "Defended him—no, Steven. Pleaded for him,
yes."

Vicky was looking directly at me. The plea in her eyes was humble and eloquent.

"Alec," she went on, "sold the store and said he was going away for a while, to forget everything. I had hopes he was snapping out of it. I helped him pack a few things in his apartment that were to be stored. There were some notes he'd made . . . Maureen's name and address . . . brief bits of information about her . . . a license plate number."

"Shadowing her," Ravenel said, "in those times when he was out. Stalking her."

A visible shiver crossed Vicky's shoulders. "He seized the notes, said they meant nothing, and tore them up. Then he went away, and I decided to stay on in town for a few days with my father. Actually, he was a stranger to me, but he'd suffered a great loss and he needed me.

"I was making plans to go home when I saw that news item the other morning. The name leaped out at me. I tried to tell myself that it couldn't be the woman whose name I'd seen in Alec's notes, that her accident could have had nothing to do with the accident that had cost him so much.

"But rationalization wouldn't satisfy me. I went to her neighborhood—Meade Park. It was easy to pick up general information about her. I stopped in the corner drugstore and everyone was talking about it.

"I learned she had a child. Alec had had a child, too. I couldn't bear to think of the implication."

She closed her eyes and fastened her lower lip between her teeth, fighting for strength to continue talking.

"Right then you should have come to the police," Ravenel said.

She was silent a moment longer. Then she said, "He was my brother. Perhaps—I was a fool."

Reynolds glanced at Ravenel and said, "Miss Martin, if I'd had a brother in a terrible jam, I might have been the same kind of fool myself."

"I had no real proof that he had killed Maureen," she said. "I still can't quite believe it—unless he has gone completely mad. If you had known him, you'd understand. He was quiet, gentle, kind. He might have plotted such a thing, wished for it, but the actual killing would have been against his grain.

"If he were innocent and I caused his arrest, I was afraid it would finish what the tragedy he'd suffered had begun. But I realized, too, that I might be wrong. If he were guilty, he might try to get to Maureen's child. Then I would be guilty too, for not having done anything."

Reynolds shot a glance at Ravenel, who was about to speak. "So Miss Martin," Reynolds said, "you decided to do something on your own. Namely, to assume the responsibility for the protection of the child."

"You do understand!"

"I didn't say that. I'm merely asking if that's what was in your mind when you knocked at the door of the Griffin home and introduced yourself as a friend of Mrs. Griffin?"

"You've stated it exactly," Vicky said.

Her eyes were still on my face, dark and deep.

"If you had wanted to harm Penny," I said, "you've had ample opportunity."

"I agree," Reynolds said.

Vicky choked on a sob and turned away quickly.

"The important question is still a-begging," Ravenel said irritably. "How about Martin? He's still at large with his threat against the little girl."

Reynolds looked toward the lake where Penny was trailing her fishline in the water. Then he glanced over the clearing around the cabin.

"This is our best natural defensive terrain," he said. "A hit-run killing couldn't be arranged and a stranger can't come within a quarter of a mile of the place without being seen. Wherever we might try to hide her in the city, there'd be risks. Any face in a crowd might be his. Any footfall on a fire escape or in a corridor.

"I'll keep three shifts of well-armed men out here until we run him to earth. I think I can guarantee the safety of the little girl that way, Griffin."

"How about her?" Ravenel said with a nod toward Vicky.

Reynolds waited for me to speak.

"She stays," I said, "if she will."

"Thank you, Steven, thank you!" Vicky said.

We remained at the cottage until the arrival of two, big, capable-looking plainclothesmen. Penny, we decided, would be told they were friends of Will's, and there for the fishing.

I planned to ride back to town with Reynolds, pack a few things in an overnight bag, and return to the cottage after dinner that night.

■ ■ ■

At home I finished packing the bag and securing the house. The day was almost gone, and I wondered how many days I would have to live through until Penny was out of danger.

I was ready to leave the house to have dinner when Reynolds called.

"It's over," he said.

For a moment, I stood holding the phone as though petrified. "What?"

"We've found Martin."

My knees wanted to fold. I sat down in the chair beside the telephone stand. "Where?"

"In the river. He's dead. He was in his big, green weapon, sitting there on the bottom of the river."

"Reynolds, wait a minute. . . . I've got to take this a word at a time."

He gave a short laugh of relief. "Okay. One word at a time. Here it is. There is a wharf on Timmons Street, near the spot where Maureen was killed, belonging to Kukolovitch & Sons. It's low and old, with a ramp to the driveway so trucks can load and unload. Martin drove himself right off the end of the dock, Griffin. The spot must have haunted him. Who knows what goes on in a diseased mind? He must have gone back to look at the place where he'd killed Mrs. Griffin. And then an impulse grabbed him and he turned into the alley and hurtled the car off the dock. Must have happened at night. At any rate, no one saw it. Some teenagers were spearfishing off the dock this afternoon. One of them took a very deep dive—and there in the depths below him was the shadowy outline of a car. Martin's green weapon—with Martin in it."

"How about the barge that was tied up there?"

The line crackled. Then Reynolds said, "What barge?"

"I was down there the morning after Maureen was killed," I said. "Seamen were docking a barge. I remember the name of the dock because it was peculiar and because of the lonely sound of the horn as the tugboat pulled away and went downriver. Reynolds, the barge was light. The seamen left it there—like it would be loaded eventually from the warehouse. Now if kids are in the habit of fishing or swimming from the dock and the car wasn't discovered until this afternoon . . ."

"You don't have to draw me a map," he said. "Sit still. I'll call you back."

I sat still. As still as Alec Martin must have sat after the death of his wife and child. I stared at the wall, and I saw the same things Alec Martin must have seen.

The phone roused me.

Reynolds said, "You're right! The barge was there from the morning after her death until this afternoon. Martin's car was under it the whole time."

"Then he went in the drink the same night Maureen was killed."

"He must have."

"He couldn't have written the note threatening Penny," I said. "Somebody was being real cute, writing that note. Somebody thought he was being real smart."

"A crackpot . . ."

"Crackpot, hell," I said. "The man who wrote the note had a good reason for doing so. The car hadn't been found, and the man who put the car there began to breathe again, began to believe that the water was deep enough, that the car would never be found. The note clinched the case against Martin. With the police running in circles, trying to find a man who was at the bottom of the river, the man who wrote the note was perfectly safe. Only he didn't know about the barge—and he didn't realize fully what it does to a man to have life smashed out of his wife."

"Listen, Griffin, if you know anything . . ."

"I'll see you around."

"Griffin!"

I hung up. Seconds later I was driving away from the house.

■　■　■

He sat perfectly still in a quiet room, and the last red rays of the sinking sun came through a window at my back and struck him in the face. But he didn't blink. He looked at the gun in my hand and he listened to me talk.

"This guy Martin," I said, "decent, gentle, kind. He sees his wife and child killed and he gets a license number and he knows the name of the woman who was driving. He plans to kill her. He wants to kill her, wants it more than anything. He does it a thousand times over in his mind—and yet after making two attempts, at a nursery and again at a supermarket, he fails. Why? Because he wasn't cut of the stuff of which killers are made. Because something deep in his character caused him to fail at the final instant each time.

"Does he wait and try a third time? No. After his failure at the supermarket, he must have realized he couldn't do it—not that way. Instead of stalking Maureen like the hunter, which he isn't, he goes to the house. He's there long enough to smoke a cigarette and leave the stub in an ashtray. He had her dead to rights, and Maureen knew it. She must have told him everything, including the name of the man who was with her the night Martin's family was killed.

"Martin wants this man, too. He forces Maureen to leave the house with him. He confronts the man, but he isn't dealing with a woman now. He's facing a man, a selfish, desperate, heedless, merciless man.

"The man is a little too tough for Martin. He gets the best of Martin. He dumps Martin in Martin's own car. He tells Maureen that she has no choice but to play the string to its end.

"The man heads for Timmons Street, for one reason alone. He's going to use the river to get rid of Martin. But at the final moment, Maureen breaks. She has some measure of decency, too—though the man would never understand that. She gets out of the car, Martin's car, and the man hits her. He's lucky. Nobody sees it. Then he runs the car into the river with Martin in it.

"Duck soup. The man is safe now. Nobody will ever know that he was party to a hit-run and subsequent criminal conspiracy. Not one breath of this kind of scandal is going to touch the man's name, mar his future. Not one moment of his precious time is going to be spent in a courtroom and behind bars.

"How does it read, Randy? Like a play?"

He moved then. He stood up, and he smiled contemptuously.

"A very lousy play. But, of course, you're not insinuating that I'm this mysterious and criminally brilliant man?"

"I think you are. You were very lucky, but you made two mistakes. You wrote that note, without knowing a barge was at the dock over the car. That diverted the pointing finger from Martin. And you lied to me—and that swung the finger at you, Randy."

He stood loose-jointed, almost relaxed. A faint breeze fluttered the pages of some of the magazines piled around the living room of the cottage.

"I'm beginning to get a little sore, Steve," he said. "After all, I've known you only a few days and you're assuming a lot to come here and . . ."

"You've known Maureen longer."

"A couple of weeks."

"You're repeating yourself," I said. "Maureen was a discreet woman, almost timid in some ways. She told you she wanted you to meet me. And I strongly suspect that, when she introduced you to our crowd, it would be in my company, as a mutual friend."

"That much I'll admit."

"So when you were together, it was the two of you alone. After she was dead, how could she contradict you?"

"She couldn't very well, could she?"

"But you're wrong; she could. Two weeks ago was after the accident, but you've known her longer than that. A month ago— before the accident—she wrote an agent about your work. She sent him a couple of plays."

Color began leaving his face.

"It would have been a nice surprise if she could have got some good news from the agent for you, wouldn't it, Randy?"

"Now look, Steve, let's not build mountains. Maybe I did meet her more than two weeks ago. Maybe I said a couple of weeks without thinking . . ."

"Because you didn't want to be connected with her at a time prior to the accident. Why else should you lie? You must have known about the accident, in which a woman and a child were killed. To have known, you must have been there.

"You were great in the execution of the grandiose lie, Randy, being the egotist that you are. It was the little one that you loused up."

His face was gray. Behind his eyes, his thoughts were scurrying, darting, searching for a way out.

"The Martin woman and child were killed at eight-fifty-five," I said. "That's right after dinnertime. You were coming from dinner, weren't you, when you headed for West End? There are certain kinds of restaurants Maureen favored. I know them, Randy. If I wanted to waste the time, I could take you to them. They're not limitless in number. You and a picture of Maureen. Both of you would be easily remembered, especially you with the mustache and Vandyke on that boy face."

"What do you mean by wasting time, Steve?"

"I'm certain you're the man. I'm certain it happened just as I said. Her blood was all over the scum of Timmons Street, Randy. You shouldn't have done it. You should never have done it at all."

He backed away. His face glistened with sweat.

"You can have a little more time," I said, "if you want to tell me about it."

"Can I have a beer?"

"Go ahead."

I followed him into the kitchen. He opened a can of beer and drank half of it in one gulp.

"They'll get you, Steve," he said. "The way Martin caught up with her and the way you caught up with me."

"Try and scare me!" I shouted, daring him.

He dropped the beer can. It spewed foam on the floor. He leaned on the kitchen table, gripping its edge. "You can't do it! Remember what you said about decency, Steve! You're decent, too. Your decency won't let you do it!"

"My decency screams for me to do it."

He began crying, but it wasn't an act this time as he'd put on when Reynolds and I had come here the first time and told him about Maureen.

He cried in rage and desperate frustration. "She treated me like a kid," he cried. "Like a baby brother. That night—after dinner—she was lecturing me. I was young. Don't rush yourself. Get a part-time job. I laughed at her. It made her angry. She whipped into West End. She was turned to say something to me. Then all of a sudden, they were there in the middle of the street, the woman and kid.

"Maureen didn't have time to stop. The woman had blundered into the street, looking and waving at her husband, who was standing in the doorway of his grocery store. The woman lost her head when she saw the car. She jumped the wrong way, right in the direction that Maureen had whipped the car.

"There wasn't much sound. Just like somebody had pitched an overripe melon into the front of the car. Maureen took her foot off the gas, but I slammed down on the accelerator and told her to get out fast, and she obeyed automatically."

"Then she hadn't been drinking?"

"No. She was fighting the car to keep it under control. Once we were away, I told her we didn't dare go back. It was too late to help them, anyway. My talk scared her. We came to the cottage and she sat on the front steps and cried all the time I was cleaning the front of the car. I took her home and the next day I took the car to a grubby garage and had the fender and headlight repaired. To play it extra safe, I stole a set of license plates before I went to the garage. I took the plates off and threw them away after the car was fixed.

"Then she showed up here with Martin. I didn't mean any of it, Steve! I just wanted a loaf of bread and a chance to write my plays. It wasn't my fault. One thing after another was forced on me from the moment that fool woman and her kid wandered into the street."

He dried his eyes on the sleeve of his shirt. "I need another beer."

He opened the ice box, took out the beer, and came around the table.

His back was half-turned to me. He'd talked all he could. He figured his time was up and that he had nothing to lose. He struck hard and fast, spinning on his toes and hurling the can of beer with his tall, lean body like a willow whip behind it.

The edge of the can laid open my left cheek. It almost knocked me down. I heard the gun in my hand go off, but the bullet missed him.

The screen slammed, and he was outside. Out in the dying afternoon. Red was still streaking the sky, like blood.

He was moving down the driveway like a broken field runner when I got outside. But my car was parked behind his and I was behind him with the gun. He ducked and changed direction when he glanced back and saw me.

He moved out across the wide, empty field that stretched east of the cottage. Beyond was timber, safety. He was a zigzagging, running target, and he knew that he had a chance, that it would be hard to put a pistol bullet in the right place in such a target.

Blood was washing down the side of my face from the cheek cut. He was fast, a lot faster than I.

But he wasn't faster than the car. The same kind of big, green car that had killed Maureen and carried Martin to the bottom of the river.

He'd reached the middle of the field when he heard the surge of the car's power. He looked over his shoulder. Through the windshield I could see his face, his mouth a round hole, laboring for breath.

He yelled hoarsely. He leaped to one side, and the car veered past.

I twisted the wheel. The car slewed around like an enraged bull and started for him again.

He ran in the opposite direction. Long, strong legs flashing, head pulled into his shoulders.

He timed the car by the sound of the motor, and again he leaped and the car missed by inches.

He had slipped. Then he was up again and running, but his legs were wobbling. He went to his knees and got up again.

The car skidded as I brought it around. He flung another glance over his shoulder. His face was drawn, his eyes jutting.

He tripped. And this time he didn't have reserve to get up. He quit. He quit cold, and covered his face with his hands and huddled on the ground, waiting for the car.

I stopped the car, got out, and walked toward him. I stood over him, watching the violent tremors cross his shoulders, seeing the gray blotch of his face as he finally looked up at me.

"You're . . . not going to . . ."

"No, Randy," I said wearily. "For a moment I thought I could, but I guess you were right. If I'd been trying the way I thought I was trying, I could have made it on that first pass."

The day, I noticed, had changed. The redness had gone out of the rays of the sinking sun. There was twilight—and silence. It made me think of my child, Penny. I wanted to go to her. I looked down at Randy, glad I hadn't done it.

Donald E. Westlake

AN EMPTY THREAT

From *Manhunt,* February 1960

A *recent issue of* Mystery Scene *magazine noted that "page for page, Donald E. Westlake is the best crime writer of his generation." While probably best known for his comedic crime novels (notably his Dortmunder series), Westlake has also given new life to the moribund caper novel. His books as by Richard Stark strike the perfect tone for the modern noir. Westlake's masterpiece is his latest novel,* The Ex, *which must certainly be a benchmark in contemporary novels about crime.*

E. G.

AH, THE SOUTH SEAS. MAUGHAM HEROES AND THE YOUNG NA-tive girls, buxom and burgeoning at eighteen, so warm, so soft, so simple and oh, so willing. Ah, the South Seas and simple youth and the soothing, sun-tanned sirens of Samoa. Ah, for romance with the charming native girls, who never never never, it seems, give birth.

And ah, the daydreams in the cold, cold winter air. With all the car windows closed, Frederick Leary shriveled in the dry warm air spewed from the heater beside his knees, and the windshield misted over. With a window open, the cold air outside reached thin freezing fingers in to icily tweak his thin nose, and the vulnerable virgins of the South Pacific receded, waving, undulating, growing small and indistinct and far, far out of reach.

And Frederick Leary was only Frederick Leary after all. Manager of the local branch of the Bonham Bookstore chain. Well-read, through accretion. A husband, but not a father. Thirty- two, but not wealthy. College-trained, and distantly liked by his employees.

Irritated, annoyed, obscurely cheated, Frederick Leary turned into his driveway, and the car that had been following him pulled to the curb three houses away. Frederick pushed open the car door, which squeaked and cracked, and plodded through the snow to push up the garage door, an overhead, put in at great expense and a damned nuisance for all the cost. And the car that had been following him disgorged its occupant, a pale and indecisive youth, who shrunk inside his overcoat, who stood hatless in the gentle fall of snow, who chewed viciously upon a filter-tip cigarette and fondled the gun in his pocket, wondering if he had the nerve.

Returning to his car, Frederick drove it into the garage. Armed with a brown paper sack containing bread and milk, he left car and garage, pulled down the damned overhead behind him, and slogged through the new-fallen snow toward the back porch. And the youth threw away the soggy butt and shuffled away, to walk around the block, kicking at the drifts of snow, building up his courage for the act.

The back porch was screened, and the slamming of the screen door made an odd contrast to the snow collapsing from the sky. Frederick maneuvered the brown paper bag from hand to hand as he removed his overshoes, then pushed open the back door and walked into a blast of heat and bright yellow. The kitchen.

Louise had her back to him. She was doing something to a vegetable with a knife, and she didn't bother to turn around. She already knew who it was. She said, "You're home late."

"Late shoppers," Frederick told her, as he put the milk in the refrigerator and the bread in the bread-box. "You know Saturday. Particularly before Christmas. People buy books and give them to each other and nobody ever reads them. Didn't get to close the store till twenty after six."

"Supper in ten minutes," Louise told him, still with her back to him, and brushed the chopped vegetable into a bowl.

Frederick walked through the house to the stairs and the foyer and the front door. He put his coat and hat in the closet and trotted upstairs to wash his hands, noticing for the thousandth time the places where the stair treads were coming loose. From his angle of vision, it seemed at times as though everything in the world were coming loose. Overhead doors, screen doors, stair treads. And the cold water faucet. He left the bathroom, refusing to listen to the measured drip of cold water behind him.

And outside, the youth completed his circuit of the block. He paused before the Leary house, looking this way and that, and a phrase came to him, from somewhere, from a conversation or television. "Calculated risk." That's what it was, and if he played it smart he could bring it off. He hurried along the driveway to the back of the house. He could feel his heart beating, and he touched the gun in his pocket for assurance. A calculated risk. He could do it.

On Saturday and Sunday, Frederick and Louise dined in the dining room, using the good silver, the good dishes and the good tablecloth. It was a habit that had once been an adventure. In silence they sat facing one another, in silence they fed, both aware that the good dishes were mostly chipped, the good silverware was just slightly tarnished. In pouring gravy on his boiled potatoes, Frederick spotted the tablecloth again. He looked guiltily at his wife, but she ate stolidly and silently, looking at the spot of gravy but not speaking. In the silence, the cold water dripped in the sink far away upstairs, and the tarnished silver clinked against the chipped dishes.

■ ■ ■

Stealthily, slowly, silently, the youth pushed open the screen door, sidled through, and gently closed it once again. He crept to the back door, his long thin fingers curled around the knob, soundlessly he opened the door and gained entrance to the house.

Louise looked up. "I feel a chill."

Frederick said, "I feel fine."

Louise said, "It's gone now," and looked back at her plate.

In the yellow warmth of the kitchen, the youth stood and dripped quietly upon the floor. He opened his overcoat, allowing warmth to spread closer against his body. The uncertainty crowded in on him, but he fought it away. He took the pistol from his overcoat pocket, feeling the metal cold against the skin of his hand. He stood there, tightly holding the gun until the metal grew warmer, until he was sure again, then slid forward through the hall to the dining room.

He stood in the doorway, looking at them, watching them eat, and neither looked up. He held the pistol aimed at the table, midway between the two of them, and when he was sure he could do it, he said, "Don't move."

Louise dropped her fork and pressed her palm against her mouth. Instinctively, she knew that it would be dangerous, perhaps fatal, for her to scream, and she held the scream back in her mouth with a taut and quivering hand.

Frederick pushed his chair back and half-rose, saying, "What—?" But then he saw the gun, and he subsided, flopping back into the chair with his mouth open and soundless.

Now that he had committed himself, the youth felt suddenly at ease. It was a risk, a calculated risk. They were afraid of him, he could see it in their eyes, and now he was strong. "Just sit there," he ordered. "Don't make any noise. Do like I tell you, and you'll be all right."

Frederick closed his mouth and swallowed. He said, "What do you want?"

The youth pointed the pistol at Frederick. "I'm gonna send you on a little trip," he said. "You're gonna go back to that bookstore of yours, and you're gonna open the safe and take out the money that's in it. You got Friday night's receipts in there and you got today's receipts, all in there, maybe five or six grand. You're gonna take the money out of the safe and put it in a paper bag. And then you're gonna bring it right back here to me. I'll be waiting right here for you. With your wife." He looked at his watch. "It's just about seven o'clock. I'll give you till eight o'clock to get back here with the money from the store. If you don't come back, I'll kill your wife. If you call the cops and *they* come around, I'll kill her for that, too."

They stared at him, and he stared back at them. He looked at Frederick, and he said, "Do you believe me?"

"What?" Frederick started, as though he'd been asleep.

"Do you believe me? If you don't do what I tell you, I'll kill your wife."

Frederick looked at the hard bright eyes of the youth, and he nodded. "I believe you."

Now the youth was sure. It had worked, it was going to pay off. "You better get started," he said. "You only got till eight o'clock."

Frederick got slowly to his feet. Then he stopped. "What if I do what you tell me?" he asked. "Maybe you'll kill the both of us anyway."

The youth stiffened. This was the tough part. He knew that might occur to them, that he couldn't let them live, that they could identify him, and he had to get over it, he had to make them believe a lie. "That's the chance you got to take," he said. He remembered his own thoughts, out in front of the house, and he smiled. "It's what they call a calculated risk. Only I wouldn't worry. I don't think I'd kill anybody who did what I told them and who gave me five or six grand."

"I'm not sure there's that much there."

"For your sake," said the youth softly, "I hope there is."

Frederick glanced at Louise. She was still staring at the youth, and her hand was still pressed against her mouth. He looked back at the youth again. "I'll get my coat."

The youth relaxed. It was done, the guy had gone for it. "You only got till eight o'clock," he said. "You better hurry."

"Hurry," said Frederick. He turned and walked to the hallway closet and put on his coat and hat. He came back, paused to say to his wife, "I'll be right back," but the sentence sounded inane, said before the boy with the gun. "I'll hurry back," he said, but Louise still stared at the youth, and her arm was still bent and tense as she tightly gripped her mouth.

Frederick moved quickly through the house and out the back door. Automatically, he put on his overshoes, wet and cold against his ankles. He pushed open the screen door and hurried over to the garage. He had trouble opening the overhead door. He scraped between the side of the car and the concrete block wall of the garage, squeezed behind the wheel, backed the car out of the garage. Still automatically, he got out of the car and closed the overhead door again. And then the enormity of it hit him. Inside there was Louise, with a killer. A youth who would murder her, if Frederick didn't get back in time.

He scurried back to the car, backed out to the street, turned and fled down the dark and silent, snow-covered street.

Hurry. He had to hurry. The windshield misted and he wiped impatiently at it, opened the window a bit and a touch of frost brushed his ear. The car was cold, but soon the heater was working full-strength, pumping warm dry air into the car.

His mind raced on, in a thousand directions at once, far ahead of the car. Way in the back of his mind, the Samoan virgins swayed and danced, motioning to him, beckoning to him. At the front of his mind loomed the face of the youth and the functional terror of the pistol. He would kill Louise, he really would.

He might kill her anyway. He might kill them both. Should he call the police? Should he stop and call the police? What was it the youth had said? Calculated risk. Calculated risk.

He turned right, turned left, skidded as he pressed too hard on the accelerator, barely missed a parked car and hurried on. His heart pounded, now because of the narrow escape from an accident. He could kill himself in the car, without any youths with pistols and sharp bitter faces.

Nonsense. Even at thirty miles an hour, bundled up in an overcoat the way he was, hitting a parked car wouldn't kill him. It might knock him out, shake him up, but it wouldn't kill him.

But it would kill Louise, because he wouldn't get back in time.

Calculated risk. He slowed, thought of a life without Louise. The snow collapsed from the sky, and he thought of Samoa. What if he didn't go back?

What if he didn't go back?

But the boy might not kill her after all. And he would return, tomorrow or the next day, and she would be waiting for him, and she would know why he hadn't come back. She would know that he had hoped the boy would kill her.

But what if he *couldn't* go back?

Calculated risk. With sudden decision he accelerated, tearing down the empty residential street. He jammed his foot on the brakes, the tires slid on ice, he twisted the wheel, and the car hurtled into a telephone pole. The car crumpled against the pole with a squealing, jarring crash, but Frederick was lulled to unconsciousness by the sweet, sweet songs of the islands.

Lawrence Block

PACKAGE DEAL

From *Ed McBain's Mystery Book #3,* 1961

Lawrence Block is the pro's pro. When you look at the work he's done since 1958, you realize that here is a true master of popular fiction. He works in a sleek, streamlined style that can be comic (his Bernie Rhoden- bahr novels) or urban dark (his Matt Scudder novels). He is also an excel- lent short story writer and has been since his earliest days as a professional writer. Here is a fine example of how good Block was even at the start of his career.

E. G.

"IF I WERE YOUNGER," JOHN HARPER SAID, "I WOULD DO THIS myself. One of the troubles with growing old. Aging makes phys- ical action awkward. A man becomes a planner, an arranger. Re- sponsibility is delegated."

Castle waited.

"If I were younger," Harper went on, "I would kill them myself. I would load a gun and go out after them. I would hunt them down, one after another, and I would shoot them dead. Baron and Milani and Hallander and Ross. I would kill them all."

The old man's mouth spread in a smile.

"A strange picture," he said. "John Harper with blood in his eye. The president of the bank, the past president of Rotary and Kiwanis and the Chamber of Commerce, the leading citizen of Arlington. Going out and killing people. An incongruous picture. Success guts a man, Castle. Removes the spine and intestines. Ties the hands. Success is an incredible surgeon."

"So you hire me."

"So I hire you. Or, to be more precise, *we* hire you. We've had as much as we can take. We've watched a peaceful, pleasant town taken over by a collection of amateur hoodlums. We've witnessed the inadequacy of a small-town police force faced with big-town operations. We've had enough."

Harper sipped brandy. He was thinking, looking for the right way to phrase what he had to say. "Prostitution," he said suddenly. "And gambling. And protection—storekeepers paying money for the right to remain storekeepers. We've watched four men take control of a town which used to be ours."

Castle nodded. He knew the story already but he wasn't impatient with the old man. He didn't mind getting both the facts and the background behind them. You needed the full picture to do your job properly. He listened.

"I wish we could do it ourselves. Vigilante action, that type of thing. There's a precedent for it. Fortunately, there's also an historical precedent for employing you. Are you familiar with it?"

"The town-tamer," Castle muttered.

"The town-tamer. An invention of the American West. The man who cleans up a town for a fee. The man who waives legality when legality must inevitably be abandoned. The man who uses a gun instead of a badge when guns are effective and badges are impotent."

"For a fee."

"For a fee," John Harper echoed. "For a fee of ten thousand dollars, in this instance. Ten thousand dollars to rid the world and the town of Arlington of four men. Four malignant men, four little cancers. Baron and Milani and Hallander and Ross."

"Just four?"

"Just four. When the rats die, the mice scatter. Kill four. Kill Lou Baron and Joe Milani and Albert Hallander and Mike Ross. Then the back of the gang will be broken. The rest will run for their lives. The town will breathe clean air again. And the town needs clean air, Mr. Castle, needs it desperately. You may rest assured of that. You are doing more than earning a generous fee. You are performing a service for humanity."

Castle shrugged.

"I'm serious," Harper said. "I know your reputation. You're not a hired killer, sir. You are the twentieth-century version of the town-tamer. I respect you as I could never respect a hired killer. You are performing an important service, sir. I respect you."

Castle lit a cigarette. "The fee," he said.

"Ten thousand dollars. And I'm paying it entirely in advance,

Mr. Castle. Because, as I have said, your reputation has preceded you. You'll have no trouble with the local police, but there are always state troopers to contend with. You might wish to leave Arlington in a hurry when the job is finished. As I understand it, the customary method of payment is half in advance and the remaining half upon completion of the job at hand. I trust you, Mr. Castle, I am paying the full sum in advance. You come well recommended."

Castle took the envelope, slipped it into an inside jacket pocket. It made a bulge there.

"Baron and Milani and Hallander and Ross," the old man said. "Four fish. Shoot them in a barrel, Mr. Castle. Shoot them and kill them. They are a disease, a plague."

Castle nodded. "That's all?"

"That is all."

The interview was over. Castle stood up and let Harper show him to the door. He walked quickly to his car and drove off into the night.

■   ■   ■

Baron and Milani and Hallander and Ross.

Castle had never met them but he knew them all. Small fish, little boys setting up a little town for a little fortune. They were not big men. They didn't have the guts or the brains to play in Chicago or New York or Vegas. They knew their strengths and their limitations. And they cut a nice pie for themselves.

Arlington, Ohio. Population forty-seven thousand. Three small manufacturing concerns, two of them owned by John Harper. One bank, owned by John Harper. Stores and shops. Doctors and lawyers. Shopkeepers, workers, professional men, housewives, clerks.

And, for the first time, criminals.

Lou Baron and Joe Milani and Albert Hallander and Mike Ross. And, as a direct result of their presence, a bucketful of hustlers on Lake Street, a handful of horse drops on Main and Limestone, a batch of numbers-runners and a boatload of muscle to make sure everything moved according to plan. Money being drained from Arlington, people being exploited in Arlington, Arlington turning slowly but surely into the private property of four men.

Baron and Milani and Hallander and Ross.

Castle drove to his hotel, went to his room, put ten thousand dollars in his suitcase. He took out a gun, a .45 automatic which could not be traced farther than a St. Louis pawnshop, and slipped the loaded gun into the pocket which had held the ten thousand dollars. The gun made the jacket sag a bit too much and he took out the gun, took off the jacket and strapped on a shoulder holster. The gun fit better this way. With the jacket on, the gun bulged only slightly.

Baron and Milani and Hallander and Ross. Four small fish in a pond too big for them. Ten thousand dollars.

He was ready.

■ ■ ■

Evening.

A warm night in Arlington. A full moon, no stars, temperature around seventy. Humidity high. Castle walked down Center Street, his car at the hotel, his gun in its holster.

He was working. There were four to be taken and he was taking them in order. Lou Baron was first.

Lou Baron. Short and fat and soft. A beetle from Kansas City, a soft man who had no place in Kerrigan's K.C. mob. A big wheel in Arlington. A man employing women, a pimp on a large scale. Filth.

Castle waited for Baron. He walked to Lake Street and found a doorway where the shadows eclipsed the moon. And waited.

Baron came out of 137 Lake Street a few minutes after nine. Fat and soft, wearing expensive clothes. Laughing, because they took good care of Baron at 137 Lake Street. They had no choice.

Baron walked alone. Castle waited, waited until the small fat man had passed him on the way to a long black car. Then the gun came out of the holster.

"Baron—"

The little man turned around. Castle's finger tightened on the trigger. There was a loud noise.

The bullet went into Baron's mouth and came out of the back of his head. The bullet had a soft nose and there was a bigger hole on the way out than on the way in. Castle holstered the gun, walked away in shadows.

One down.

Three to go.

* * *

Milani was easy. Milani lived in a frame house with his wife. That amused Castle, the notion that Milani was a property-owner in Arlington. It was funny.

Milani ran numbers in St. Louis, crossed somebody, pulled out. He was too small to chase. The local people let him alone.

Now people ran numbers for him in Arlington. A change of pace. And Milani's wife, a St. Louis tramp with big breasts and no brains, helped Milani spend the money that stupid people bet on three-digit numbers.

Milani was easy. He was home and the door was locked. Castle rang the bell. And Milani, safe and secure and self-important, did not bother with peepholes. He opened the door.

And caught a .45-caliber bullet over the heart.

Two down and two to go.

* * *

Hallander was a gunman. Castle didn't know much about him, just a few rumbles that made their way over the coast-to-coast grapevine. Little things.

A gun, a torpedo, a zombie. A bodyguard out of Chi who goofed too many times. A killer who loved to kill, a little man with dead eyes who was nude without a gun. A psychopath. So many killers were psychopaths. Castle hated them with the hatred of the businessman for the competitive hobbyist. Killing Baron and Milani had been on the order of squashing cockroaches under the heel of a heavy shoe. Killing Hallander was a pleasure.

Hallander did not live in a house like Milani or go to women like Baron. Hallander had no use for women, only for a gun. He lived alone in a small apartment on the outskirts of town. His car, four years old, was parked in his garage. He could have afforded a better car. But to Hallander, money was not to be spent. It was chips in a poker game. He held onto his chips.

He was well protected—a doorman screened visitors, an elevator operator knew whom he took upstairs. But Hallander made no friends. Five dollars quieted the doorman forever. Five dollars sealed the lips of the elevator operator.

Castle knocked on Hallander's door.

A peephole opened. A peephole closed. Hallander drew a gun and fired through the door.

And missed.

Castle shot the lock off, kicked the door open. Hallander missed again.

And died.

With a bullet in the throat.

The elevator operator took Castle back to the first floor. The doorman passed him through to the street. He got into his car, turned the key in the ignition, drove back to the center of Arlington.

Three down.

Just one more.

■ ■ ■

"We can deal," Mike Ross said. "You got your money. You hit three out of four. You can leave me be."

Castle said nothing. They were alone, he and Ross. The brains of the Arlington enterprise sat in an easy chair with a slow smile on his face. He knew about Baron and Milani and Hallander.

"You did a job already," Ross said. "You got paid already. You want money? Fifteen thousand. Cash. Then you disappear."

Castle shook his head.

"Why not? Hot-shot Harper won't sue you. You'll have his ten grand and fifteen of mine and you'll disappear. Period. No trouble, no sweat, no nothing. Nobody after you looking to even things up. Tell you the truth, I'm glad to see the three of them out of the way. More for me and no morons getting in the way. I'm glad you took them. Just so you don't take me."

"I've got a job to do."

"Twenty grand. Thirty. What's a man's life worth? Name your price, Castle. Name it!"

"No price."

Mike Ross laughed. "Everybody has a price. Everybody. You aren't that special. I can buy you, Castle."

Ross bought death. He bought one bullet and death came at once. He fell on his face and died. Castle wiped off the gun. He had taken chances, using the same gun four times. But the four times had taken less than one night. Morning had not come yet. The Arlington police force still slept.

He dropped the gun to the floor and got out of there.

■ ■ ■

A phone rang in Chicago. A man lifted it, held it to his ear.

"Castle," a voice said.

"Job done?"

"All done."

"How many hits?"

"Four of them," Castle said. "Four off the top."

"Give me the picture."

"The machinery is there with nobody to run it," Castle said. "The town is lonely."

The man chuckled. "You're good," he said. "You're very good. We'll be down tomorrow."

"Come on in," Castle said. "The water's fine."

Marcia Muller

ALL THE LONELY PEOPLE

From *Sisters in Crime I*, 1989

By now, it is a cliché to note that Marcia Muller is the "founding mother" of the female private eye. If the names Paretsky or Grafton mean anything to you, you'll also likely know that both these writers acknowledge their debt to Marcia. To many, Marcia is the best of them all: a better plotter, a better stylist, a sounder psychologist than any of her peers. Acknowledging her own debt to the late Ross MacDonald, Marcia's novels grow deeper and richer with each succeeding title—and explore much the same geographical and spiritual milieus that MacDonald himself did. Here is one of her very best stories.

E. G.

"Name, Sharon McCone. Occupation . . . I can't put private investigator. What should I be?" I glanced over my shoulder at Hank Zahn, my boss at All Souls Legal Cooperative. He stood behind me, his eyes bemused behind thick horn-rimmed glasses.

"I've heard you tell people you're a researcher when you don't want to be bothered with stupid questions like 'What's a nice girl like you . . . '"

"*Legal* researcher." I wrote it on the form. "Now—'About the person you are seeking.' Age—does not matter. Smoker—does not matter. Occupation—does not matter. I sound excessively eager for a date, don't I?"

Hank didn't answer. He was staring at the form. "The things they ask. Sexual preference." He pointed at the item. "Hetero, bi, lesbian, gay. There's no place for 'does not matter.'"

As he spoke, he grinned wickedly. I glared at him. "You're enjoying this!"

"Of course I am. I never thought I'd see the day you'd fill out an application for a dating service."

I sighed and drummed my fingertips on the desk. Hank is my best male friend, as well as my boss. I love him like a brother—

sometimes. But he harbors an overactive interest in my love life
and delights in teasing me about it. I would be hearing about the
dating service for years to come. I asked, "What should I say I
want the guy's cultural interests to be? I can't put 'does not matter' for everything."

"I don't think burglars *have* cultural interests."

"Come on, Hank. Help me with this!"

"Oh, put film. Everyone's gone to a movie."

"Film." I checked the box.

The form was quite simple, yet it provided a great deal of
information about the applicant. The standard questions about
address, income level, whether the individual shared a home or
lived alone, and hours free for dating were enough in themselves
to allow an astute burglar to weed out prospects—and pick times
to break in when they were not likely to be on the premises.

And that apparently was what had happened at the big singles
complex down near the San Francisco–Daly City line, owned by
Hank's client, Dick Morris. There had been three burglaries over
the past five months, beginning not long after the place had been
leafleted by All the Best People Introduction Service. Each of the
people whose apartments had been hit were women who had
filled out application forms; they had had from two to ten dates
with men with whom the service had put them in touch. The
burglaries had taken place when one renter was at work, another
away for the weekend, and the third out with a date whom she
had also met through Best People.

Coincidence, the police had told the renters and Dick Morris.
After all, none of the women had reported having dates with the
same man. And there were many other common denominators
among them besides their use of the service. They lived in the
same complex. They all knew one another. Two belonged to the
same health club. They shopped at the same supermarket, shared
auto mechanics, hairstylists, dry cleaners, and two of them went
to the same psychiatrist.

Coincidence, the police insisted. But two other San Francisco
area members of Best People had also been burglarized—one of
them male—and so they checked the service out carefully.

What they found was absolutely no evidence of collusion in
the burglaries. It was no fly-by-night operation. It had been in
business ten years—a long time for that type of outfit. Its board

of directors included a doctor, psychologist, a rabbi, a minister, and a well-known author of somewhat weird but popular novels. It was respectable—as such things go.

But Best People was still the strongest link among the burglary victims. And Dick Morris was a good landlord who genuinely cared about his tenants. So he put on a couple of security guards, and when the police couldn't run down the perpetrator(s) and backburnered the cases, he came to All Souls for legal advice.

It might seem unusual for the owner of a glitzy singles complex to come to a legal services plan that charges its clients on a sliding-fee scale, but Dick Morris was cash-poor. Everything he'd saved during his long years as a journeyman plumber had gone into the complex, and it was barely turning a profit as yet. Wouldn't be turning any profit at all if the burglaries continued and some of his tenants got scared and moved out.

Hank could have given Dick the typical attorney's spiel about leaving things in the hands of the police and continuing to pay the guards out of his dwindling cash reserves, but Hank is far from typical. Instead he referred Dick to me. I'm All Souls' staff investigator, and assignments like this one—where there's a challenge—are what I live for.

They are, that is, unless I have to apply for membership in a dating service, plus set up my own home as a target for a burglar. Once I started "dating," I would remove anything of value to All Souls, plus Dick would station one of his security guards at my house during the hours I was away from there, but it was still a potentially risky and nervous-making proposition.

Now Hank loomed over me, still grinning. I could tell how much he was going to enjoy watching me suffer through an improbable, humiliating, *asinine* experience. I smiled back—sweetly.

" 'Your sexual preference.' Hetero." I checked the box firmly. "Except for inflating my income figure, so I'll look like I have a lot of good stuff to steal, I'm filling this out truthfully," I said. "Who knows—I might find someone wonderful."

When I looked back up at Hank, my evil smile matched his earlier one. He, on the other hand, looked as if he'd swallowed something the wrong way.

■　■　■

My first "date" was a chubby little man named Jerry Hale. Jerry was *very* into the singles scene. We met at a bar in San Francisco's

affluent Marina district, and while we talked, he kept swiveling
around in his chair and leering at every woman who walked by.
Most of them ignored him but a few glared; I wanted to hang a
big sign around my neck saying, "I'm not really with him, it's
only business." While I tried to find out about his experiences
with All the Best People Introduction Service, plus impress him
with the easily fenceable items I had at home, he tried to educate
me on the joys of being single.

"I used to be into the bar scene pretty heavily," he told me.
"Did all right too. But then I started to worry about herpes and
AIDS—I'll let you see the results of my most recent test if you
want—and my drinking was getting out of hand. Besides, it was
expensive. Then I went the other way—a health club. Did all
right there too. But goddamn, it's *tiring*. So I then joined a bunch
of church groups—you meet a lot of horny women there. But
churches encourage matrimony, and I'm not into that."

"So you applied to All the Best People. How long have
you—?"

"Not right away. First I thought about joining AA, even went
to a meeting. Lots of good-looking women are recovering alco-
holics, you know. But I like to drink too much to make the sac-
rifice. Dear Abby's always saying you could enroll in courses, so I
signed up for a couple at U. C. Extension. Screenwriting and
photography."

My mouth was stiff from smiling politely, and I had just about
written Jerry off as a possible suspect—he was too busy to burglarize anyone. I took a sip of wine and looked at my watch.

Jerry didn't notice the gesture. "The screenwriting class was
terrible—the instructor actually wanted you to write stuff. And
photography—how can you see women in the darkroom, let alone
make any moves when you smell like chemicals?"

I had no answer for that. Maybe my own efforts at photography
accounted for my not having a lover at the moment. . . .

"Finally I found All the Best People," Jerry went on. "Now I
really do all right. And it's opened up a whole new world of dating
to me—eighties-style. I've answered ads in the paper, placed my
own ads too. You've always got to ask that they send a photo,
though, so you can screen out the dogs. There's Weekenders, they
plan trips. When I don't want to go out of the house, I use the
Intro Line—there's a phone club you can join, where you call in

for three bucks and either talk to one person or on a party line. There's a video exchange where you can make tapes and trade them with people so you'll know you're compatible before you set up a meeting. I do all right."

He paused expectantly, as if he thought I was going to ask how I could get in on all these eighties-style deals.

"Jerry," I said, "have you read any good books lately?"

"Have I . . . *what?*"

"What do you do when you're not dating?"

"I work. I told you, I'm in sales—"

"Do you ever spend time alone?"

"Doing what?"

"Oh, just being alone. Puttering around the house or working at hobbies. Just thinking."

"Are you crazy? What kind of a computer glitch are you, anyway?" He stood, all five-foot-three of him quivering indignantly. "Believe me, I'm going to complain to Best People about setting me up with you. They described you as 'vivacious,' but you've hardly said a word all evening!"

■　■　■

Morton Stone was a nice man, a sad man. He insisted on buying me dinner at his favorite Chinese restaurant. He spent the evening asking me questions about myself and my job as a legal researcher; while he listened, his fingers played nervously with the silverware. Later, over a brandy in a nearby bar, he told me how his wife had died the summer before, of cancer. He told me about his promise to her that he would get on with his life, find someone new, and be happy. This was the first date he'd arranged through All the Best People; he'd never done anything like that in his life. He'd only tried them because he wasn't good at meeting people. He had a good job, but it wasn't enough. He had money to travel, but it was no fun without someone to share the experience with. He would have liked to have children, but he and his wife had put it off until they'd be financially secure, and then they found out about the cancer. . . .

I felt guilty as hell about deceiving him, and for taking his time, money, and hope. But by the end of the evening I'd remembered a woman friend who was just getting over a disastrous love affair. A nice, sad woman who wasn't good at meeting people; who had a good job, loved to travel, and longed for children . . .

■ ■ ■

Bob Gillespie was a sailing instructor on a voyage of self-discovery.
He kept prefacing his remarks with statements such as, "You
know, I had a great insight into myself last week." That was nice;
I was happy for him. But I would rather have gotten to know his
surface persona before probing into his psyche. Like the two previous men, Bob didn't fit any of the recognizable profiles of the
professional burglar, nor had he any great insight into how All
the Best People worked.

■ ■ ■

Ted Horowitz was a recovering alcoholic, which was admirable.
Unfortunately, he was also the confessional type. He began every
anecdote with the admission that it had happened "back when I
was drinking." He even felt compelled to describe how he used
to throw up on his ex-wife. His only complaint about Best People—this with a stern look at my wineglass—was that they kept
referring him to women who drank.

■ ■ ■

Jim Rogers was an adman who wore safari clothes and was into
guns. I refrained from telling that I own two .38 Specials and am
a highly qualified marksman, for fear it would incite him to passion. For a little while I considered him seriously for the role of
burglar, but when I probed the subject by mentioning a friend
having recently been ripped off, Jim became enraged and said the
burglar ought to be hunted down and shot.

■ ■ ■

"I'm going about this all wrong," I said to Hank.

It was ten in the morning, and we were drinking coffee at the
big round table in All Souls' kitchen. The night before I'd spent
hours on the phone with an effervescent insurance underwriter
who was going on a whale-watching trip with Weekenders, the
group that god-awful Jerry had mentioned. He'd concluded our
conversation by saying he'd be sure to note in his pocket organizer
to call me the day after he returned. Then I'd been unable to
sleep and had sat up hours longer, drinking too much and listening for burglars and brooding about loneliness.

I wasn't involved with anyone at the time—nor did I particularly want to be. I'd just emerged from a long-term relationship
and was reordering my life and getting used to doing things alone

again. I was fortunate in that my job and my little house—which I'm constantly remodeling—filled most of the empty hours. But I could still understand what Morton and Bob and Ted and Jim and even that dreadful Jerry were suffering from.

It was the little things that got to me. Like the times I went to the supermarket and everything I felt like having for dinner was packaged for two or more, and I couldn't think of anyone I wanted to have over to share it with. Or the times I'd be driving around a curve in the road and come upon a spectacular view, but have no one in the passenger seat to point it out to. And then there were the cold sheets on the other side of a wide bed on a foggy San Francisco night.

But I got through it, because I reminded myself that it wasn't going to be that way forever. And when I couldn't convince myself of that, I thought about how it was better to be totally alone than alone *with* someone. That's how *I* got through the cold, foggy nights. But I was discovering there was a whole segment of the population that availed itself of dating services and telephone conversation clubs and video exchanges. Since I'd started using Best People, I'd been inundated by mail solicitations and found that the array of services available to singles was astonishing.

Now I told Hank, "I simply can't stand another evening making polite chitchat in a bar. If I listen to another ex-wife story, I'll scream. I don't want to know that these guys' parents did to them at age ten that made the whole rest of their lives a mess. And besides, having that security guard on my house is costing Dick Morris a bundle he can ill afford."

Helpfully Hank said, "So change your approach."

"Thanks for your great suggestion." I got up and went out to the desk that belongs to Ted Smalley, our secretary, and dug out a phone directory. All the Best People wasn't listed. My file on the case was on the kitchen table. I went back there—Hank had retreated to his office—and checked the introductory letter they'd sent me; it showed nothing but a post-office box. The zip code told me it was the main post office at Seventh and Mission streets.

I went back and borrowed Ted's phone book again, then looked up the post office's number. I called it, got the mail-sorting supervisor, and identified myself as Sharon from Federal Express.

"We've got a package here for All the Best People Introduction Service," I said, and read off the box number. "That's all I've got—no contact phone, no street address."

"Assholes," she said wearily. "Why do they send them to a P. O. box when they know you can't deliver to one? For that matter, why do you accept them when they're addressed like that?"

"Damned if I know. I only work here."

"I can't give out the street address, but I'll supply the contact phone." She went away, came back, and read it to me.

"Thanks." I depressed the disconnect button and redialed.

A female voice answered with only the phone number. I went into my Federal Express routine. The woman gave me the address without hesitation, in the 200 block of Gough Street near the Civic Center. After I hung up I made one more call: to a friend on the *Chronicle*. J. D. Smith was in the city room and agreed to leave a few extra business cards with the security guard in the newspaper building's lobby.

■   ■   ■

All the Best People's offices took up the entire second floor of a renovated Victorian. I couldn't imagine why they needed so much space, but they seemed to be doing a landslide business, because phones in the offices on either side of the long corridor were ringing madly. I assumed it was because the summer vacation season was approaching and San Francisco singles were getting anxious about finding someone to make travel plans with.

The receptionist was more or less what I expected to find in the office of that sort of business: petite, blond, sleekly groomed, and expensively dressed, with an elegant manner. She took J. D.'s card down the hallway to see if their director was available to talk with me about the article I was writing on the singles scene. I paced around the tiny waiting room, which didn't even have chairs. When the young woman came back, she said Dave Lester would be happy to see me and led me to an office at the rear.

The office was plush, considering the attention that had been given to decor in the rest of the suite. It had a leather couch and chairs, a wet bar, and an immense mahogany desk. There wasn't so much as a scrap of paper or a file folder to suggest anything resembling work was done there. I couldn't see Dave Lester, because he had swiveled his high-backed chair around toward the window and was apparently contemplating the wall of the building next door. The receptionist backed out the door and closed it. I cleared my throat, and the chair turned toward me.

The man in the chair was god-awful Jerry Hale.

Our faces must have been mirror images of shock. I said, "What are *you* doing here?"

He said, "You're not J. D. Smith. You're Sharon McCone!" Then he frowned down at the business card he held. "Or is Sharon McCone really J. D. Smith?"

I collected my scattered wits and said, "Which are you—Dave Lester or Jerry Hale?" I added, "I'm a reporter doing a feature article on the singles scene."

"So Marie said. How did you get this address? We don't publish it because we don't want all sorts of crazies wandering in. This is an exclusive service; we screen our applicants carefully."

They certainly hadn't screened me; otherwise they'd have uncovered numerous deceptions. I said, "Oh, we newspaper people have our sources."

"Well, you certainly misrepresented yourself to us."

"And you misrepresented yourself to *me*."

He shrugged. "It's all part of the screening process, for our clients' protection. We realize most applicants would shy away from a formal interview situation, so we have the first date take the place of that."

"You yourself go out with *all* the women who apply?"

"A fair amount, using a different name every time, of course, in case any of them know each other and compare notes." At my astonished look he added, "What can I say? I like women. But naturally I have help. And Marie"—he motioned at the closed door—"and one of the secretaries check out the guys."

No wonder Jerry had no time to read. "Then none of the things you told me were true? About being into the bar scene and the church groups and the health club?"

"Sure they were. My previous experiences were what led me to buy Best People from its former owners. They hadn't studied the market, didn't know how to make a go of it in the eighties."

"Well, you're certainly a good spokesman for your own product. But how come you kept referring me to other clients? We didn't exactly part on amiable terms."

"Oh, that was just a ruse to get out of there. I had another date. I'd seen enough to know you weren't my type. But I decided

you were still acceptable; we get a lot of men looking for your
kind."

The "acceptable" rankled. "What exactly is my kind?"

"Well, I'd call you . . . introspective. Bookish? No, not exactly.
A little offbeat? Maybe intense? No. It's peculiar . . . you're peculiar—"

"Stop right there!"

Jerry—who would always be god-awful Jerry and never Dave
Lester to me—stood up and came around the desk. I straightened
my posture. From my five-foot-six vantage point I could see the
beginnings of a bald spot under his artfully styled hair. When he
realized where I was looking, his mouth tightened. I took a per-
verse delight in his discomfort.

"I'll have to ask you to leave now," he said stiffly.

"But don't you want Best People featured in a piece on singles?"

"I do not. I can't condone the tactics of a reporter who mis-
represents herself."

"Are you sure that's the reason you don't want to talk with
me?"

"Of course. What else—"

"Is there something about Best People that you'd rather not
see publicized?"

Jerry flushed. When he spoke, it was in a flat, deceptively calm
manner. "Get out of here," he said, "or I'll call your editor."

Since I didn't want to get J. D. in trouble with the *Chron*, I
went.

■ ■ ■

Back at my office at All Souls, I curled up in my ratty armchair—
my favorite place to think. I considered my visit to All the Best
People; I considered what was wrong with the setup there. Then
I got out my list of burglary victims and called each of them. All
three gave me similar answers to my questions. Next I checked
the phone directory and called my friend Sandy in the billing
office at Pacific Bell.

"I need an address for a company that's only listed by number
in the directory," I told her.

"Billing address, or location where the phone's installed?"

"Both, if they're different."

She tapped away on her computer keyboard. "Billing and location are the same: two-eleven Gough. Need anything else?"

"That's it. Thanks—I owe you a drink."

■   ■   ■

In spite of my earlier determination to depart the singles scene,
I spent the next few nights on the phone, this time assuming the
name of Patsy Newhouse, my younger sister. I talked to various
singles about my new VCR; I described the sapphire pendant my
former boyfriend had given me and how I planned to have to
reset to erase old memories. I babbled happily about the trip to
Las Vegas I was taking in a few days with Weekenders, and promised to make notes in my pocket organizer to call people as soon
as I got back. I mentioned—in seductive tones—how I loved to
walk barefoot over my genuine Persian rugs. I praised the merits
of my new microwave oven. I described how I'd gotten into col-
lecting costly jade carvings. By the time the Weekenders trip was
due to depart for Vegas, I was constantly sucking on throat lozenges and wondering how long my voice would hold out.

■   ■   ■

Saturday night found me sitting in my kitchen sharing ham sandwiches and coffee by candlelight with Dick Morris' security guard,
Bert Jankowski. The only reason we'd chanced the candles was
that we'd taped the shades securely over the windows. There was
something about eating in total darkness that put us both off.

Bert was a pleasant-looking man of about my age, with sandy
hair and a bristly mustache and a friendly, open face. We'd spent
a lot of time together—Friday night, all day today—and I'd pretty
much heard his life story. We had a lot in common: he was from
Oceanside, not far from where I'd grown up in San Diego; like
me, he had a degree in the social sciences and hadn't been able
to get a job in his field. Unlike me, he'd been working for the
security service so long that he was making a decent wage, and
he liked it. It gave him more time, he said, to read and to fish.
I'd told him my life story, too: about my somewhat peculiar family, about my blighted romances, even about the man I'd once
had to shoot. By Saturday night I sensed both of us were getting
bored with examining our pasts, but the present situation was
even more stultifying.

I said, "Something has *got* to happen soon."

Bert helped himself to another sandwich. "Not necessarily. Got any more of those pickles?"

"No, we're out."

"Shit. I don't suppose if this goes on that there's any possibility of cooking breakfast tomorrow? Sundays I always fix bacon."

In spite of my having wolfed down some ham, my mouth began to water. "No," I said wistfully. "Cooking smells, you know. This house is supposed to be vacant for the weekend."

"So far no one's come near it, and nobody seems to be casing it. Maybe you're wrong about the burglaries."

"Maybe . . . No, I don't think so. Listen: Andie Wyatt went to Hawaii; she came back to a cleaned-out apartment. Janie Roos was in Carmel with a lover; she lost everything fenceable. Kim New was in Vegas, where I'm supposed to be—"

"But maybe you're wrong about the way the burglar knows—"

There was a noise toward the rear of the house, past the current construction zone on the back porch. I held up my hand for Bert to stop talking and blew out the candles.

I sensed Bert tensing. He reached for his gun at the same time I did mine.

The noise came louder—the sound of an implement probing the back-porch lock. It was one of those useless toy locks that had been there when I bought the cottage; I'd left the dead bolt unlocked since Friday.

Rattling sounds. A snap. The squeak of the door as it moved inward.

I touched Bert's arm. He moved over into the recess by the pantry, next to the light switch. I slipped up next to the door to the porch. The outer door shut, and footsteps came toward the kitchen, then stopped.

A thin beam of light showed under the inner door between the kitchen and the porch—the burglar's flashlight. I smiled, imagining his surprise at the sawhorses and wood scraps and exposed writing that make up my own personal urban-renewal project.

The footsteps moved toward the kitchen door again. I took the safety off the .38.

The door swung toward me. A half-circle of light from the flash illuminated the blue linoleum. It swept back and forth, then up and around the room. The figure holding the flash seemed satisfied that the room was empty; it stepped inside and walked toward the hall.

Bert snapped on the overhead light.

I stepped forward, gun extended, and said, "All right, Jerry. Hands above your head and turn around—slowly."

The flash clattered to the floor. The figure—dressed all in black—did as I said.

But it wasn't Jerry.

It was Morton Stone—the nice, sad man I'd had the dinner date with. He looked as astonished as I felt.

I thought of the evening I'd spent with him, and my anger rose. All that sincere talk about how lonely he was and how much he missed his dead wife. And now he turned out to be a common crook!

"You son of a bitch!" I said. "And I was going to fix you up with one of my friends!"

He didn't say anything. His eyes were fixed nervously on my gun.

Another noise on the back porch. Morton opened his mouth, but I silenced him by raising the .38.

Footsteps clattered across the porch, and a second figure in black came through the door. "Morton, what's wrong? Why'd you turn the lights on?" a woman's voice demanded.

It was Marie, the receptionist from All the Best People. Now I knew how she could afford her expensive clothes.

■　■　■

"So I was right about *how* they knew when to burglarize people, but wrong about *who* was doing it," I told Hank. We were sitting at the bar in the Remedy Lounge, our favorite Mission Street watering hole.

"I'm still confused. The Intro Line is part of All the Best People?"

"It's owned by Jerry Hale, and the phone equipment is located in the same offices. But as Jerry—Dave Lester, whichever incarnation you prefer—told me later, he doesn't want the connection publicized because the Intro Line is kind of sleazy, and Best People's supposed to be high-toned. Anyway, I figured it out because I noticed there were an awful lot of phones ringing at their offices, considering their number isn't published. Later I confirmed it with the phone company and started using the line myself to set the burglar up."

"So this Jerry wasn't involved at all?"

"No. He's the genuine article—a born-again single who decided to put his knowledge to turning a profit."

Hank shuddered and took a sip of Scotch.

"The burglary scheme," I went on, "was all Marie Stone's idea. She had access to the addresses of the people who joined the Intro Line club, and she listened in on the phone conversations and scouted out good prospects. Then, when she was sure their homes would be vacant for a period of time, her brother, Morton Stone, pulled the job while she kept watch outside."

"How come you had a date with Marie's brother? Was he looking you over as a burglary prospect?"

"No. They didn't use All the Best People for that. It's Jerry's pride and joy; he's too involved with the day-to-day workings and might have realized something was wrong. But the Intro Line is just a profit-making arm of the business to him—he probably uses it to subsidize his dating. He'd virtually turned the operation of it over to Marie. But he did allow Marie to send out mail solicitations for it to Best People clients, as well as mentioning it to the women he 'screened,' and that's how the burglary victims heard of it."

"But it still seems too great a coincidence that you ended up going out with this Morton."

I smiled. "It wasn't a coincidence at all. Morton also works for Best People, helping Jerry screen the female clients. When I had my date with Jerry, he found me . . . well, he said I was peculiar."

Hank grinned and started to say something, but I glared. "Anyway, he sent Mort out with me to render a second opinion."

"Ye gods, you were almost rejected by a dating service."

"What really pisses me off is Morton's grieving-widower story. I really fell for the whole tasteless thing. Jerry told me Morton gets a lot of women with it—they just can't resist a man in pain."

"But not McCone." Hank drained his glass and gestured at mine. "You want another?"

I looked at my watch. "Actually, I've got to be going."

"How come? It's early yet."

"Well, uh . . . I have a date."

He raised his eyebrows. "I thought you were through with the singles scene. Which one is it tonight—the gun nut?"

I got off the bar stool and drew myself up in a dignified manner. "It's someone I met on my own. They always tell you that you meet the most compatible people when you're just doing what you like to do and not specifically looking."

"So where'd you meet this guy?"

"On a stakeout."

Hank waited. His eyes fairly bulged with curiosity.

I decided not to tantalize him any longer. I said, "It's Bert Jankowski, Dick Morris' security guard."

Ed Bryant

DOING COLFAX

From *Night Visions 4*, 1987

Ed Bryant has written some of the most innovative and stunning science fiction and horror of his generation. While still in his early twenties, he was already something of a legend in science-fiction circles; and he became equally important to the "urban horror" movement a decade later. Much of his more recent fiction falls into the "dark suspense" category—fiction too dark to be called merely "mystery" but lacking the supernatural touches that would make it true "horror." Here's a good example: a short tale that gives us a photograph of the urban zombies that scare the hell out of all us sensible and God-fearing citizens—and with damned good reason.

E. G.

YOU WANNA EAT?" SAID JEFFIE.

Kin stared out the passenger's window of the big old Chevy at the neon dazzle of Colfax Avenue. "I want to do someone."

"Aw, come on." Jeffie put his free hand on Kin's wrist, let the fingers lie there lightly. "Let's eat. I'm buyin'. Burgers okay?"

Kin started to turn away from the night. "Yeah, burgers are—hold it. Look at that one."

That one was what looked to be a teenaged girl standing by a bus bench with her thumb out. Short dark hair, shorter suede skirt, defiant stance. She stared directly into the windshield of the Chevy and smiled.

"I want to do *her*," said Kin.

"Burgers—" Jeffie protested.

"*Her*."

Jeffie braked the sedan to a stop. Kin reached back over the seat and unlatched the rear door.

The girl climbed in, set a canvas book-bag down beside her and said, "Hi. Hey, thanks—I don't think the R.T.D. ever stops here. Not ever."

"How far you headin'?" said Kin.

"As far east as you're going. Anywhere on Colfax. I live out in Aurora."

"We're going that far," Kin said.

"That's really great," said the girl. She leaned forward, forearms on the seat divider. "You guys got names?"

They told her. Neither asked the girl her name. She told them anyway. Neither Kin nor Jeffie remembered it.

The Chevy cruised along through the night. Jeffie scrupulously obeyed each speed sign. He ran no yellow lights. The girl told them about night school at Auraria. She was going to be a psychiatric social worker, or maybe just a psychologist. She had a part-time job at a Burger King. Jeffie perked up briefly when he heard that. The girl talked and talked, and finally they crossed under I-470. Though there were still plenty of lights, Jeffie sensed that the eastern plains lay close ahead. Nebraska. Kansas. He felt the oppressive freedom of all that space.

"Anywhere along here," said the girl. She started to arrange her canvas bag.

"Naw," said Kin, and then he was over the seat and in back with her.

"What are you—" she started to say. Kin slapped her hard across the jaw and her head fetched up solid against the window on Jeffie's side. The driver's shoulders hunched when he heard that meaty sound.

"She's just out," said Kin. He extracted a length of coarse baling twine from under the seat ahead, let the girl's body slump over his lap, twisted her arms behind her, and bound the wrists tight. He set her upright again, wedged back into the corner between seat and window.

"Jesus, I'm starved," said Jeffie.

Kin said, "You just keep driving." While he waited for her to wake up, he explored the girl's body with his hands. His fingers went up under her skirt and rolled the dark pantyhose down off her hips and legs, and finally off her feet after he pulled her flats loose. "It's her time of the month," he said, grimacing. "Guess nothing's goin' right for her."

The girl screamed. Startled, Kin jerked upright and cracked his head against her chin. He muttered something and slapped her again, but this time not as hard as before. "Listen," he said. "Hey, listen to me."

The girl stared at him and listened. Kin picked something up off the car floor and showed it to her. "Know what this is?"

She shook her head.

"It's a tennis ball, dummy. I don't want you to scream. And I don't want to hit you again. If you keep on yellin' like that, I'm gonna have to put this in your mouth and keep it in there with some tape. You understand?"

Her eyes widened, but she didn't say anything at all.

And she didn't scream. Her eyes looked like they were all wide, dark pupil.

"If I have to do that," said Kin, "then maybe too I'll go on and pinch your nose shut, or maybe tape it altogether. You know what'll happen then?"

She slowly nodded, eyes still fixed on his.

"Okay," said Kin. He started touching her again. The girl struggled against him, but almost silently. Little whimpers came out.

"How you gonna do her?" said Jeffie.

Kin looked thoughtful.

The girl briefly stopped struggling. Her eyes glistened with tears, but she seemed to pull herself together visibly. She said, "*Do* me?"

The two men stared back at her.

"Listen, you bastards. You're going to kill me, say it. Don't talk like I'm not really here." She paused. "I'm here. I'm real."

They didn't say anything.

"You're not going to *do* me—you're going to *kill* me."

Jeffie and Kin stared at each other in the rearview.

After a long pause, Jeffie said again, "How you gonna do her?"

"This way," said Kin. "Best I know how." He used the pantyhose he had tugged off the girl earlier. She struggled silently, as though using all her strength to twist away from him. Somehow she got her chin between the taut loop and her throat. Her eyes never left Kin's.

"Give me the screwdriver out of the jockey box," said Kin hoarsely, trying to hold her body still with one arm, attempting to draw the noose tight with his other hand.

"Phillips or the other one?" said Jeffie, rummaging.

"Don't matter. Just a screwdriver."

"Here you go." Jeffie passed the steel tool over the seat. He winced as either Kin or the girl kicked the backrest.

Kin put the screwdriver shaft between the loop of pantyhose and the nape of the girl's neck, and began to twist. The nylon stretched, then tautened. The noose crept along the point of the girl's chin, then snapped free, digging into the flesh of her throat.

"That's it," said Kin.

And it was.

The girl's eyes never did close, so Kin finally had to twist her head around so that she looked accusingly out at the neon night.

"We gotta dump her," said Jeffie.

It was like Kin didn't hear him. "I'm hungry now," he said. "I feel good and I'm hungry."

"We got to—"

"I heard you, buddy. We'll do it. But I want a burger. I'm starvin'."

"Guess it'll have to be a drive-up."

"Guess so," Kin agreed.

The old Chevy ghosted through the dark.

"I'm hungry too," Jeffie finally said.

"Yeah," said Kin. "Let's just do some burgers."

C. B. Gilford

THAT STRANGER, MY SON

From *Manhunt*, October 1954

The name C. B. Gilford appeared on many good stories in the digest magazines of the fifties and sixties. At least one of those stories deserves classic status: the story we have here, "That Stranger, My Son." Every once in a while, a writer reaches up into the sky and grabs lightning—writes above his usual level of skill and talent. Such is the case here, in this sad and chilling little story which writers of every station should envy.

E. G.

IT WAS DARK WHEN THEY ARRIVED. AT THE DOOR THE MAN FUMbled with the keys. But because his hands were shaking, he could not seem to find either the keyhole or the correct key. Finally the boy took the keys. They went inside. The boy found the light switch.

"It's like an oven in here," the man said.

But the boy refused to abandon his smile. "We're home, Dad," he answered. He started making the rounds of the windows, unlatching them, heaving them upward.

The man did not join in the homecoming chores. He looked all around him, taking inventory of the familiar walls and furniture. The close, hot atmosphere of the room quickly brought beads of perspiration to his face. But he was too unaware of it even to apply a sleeve to his forehead.

"Dad, make yourself at home!" The boy had returned, the persistent smile with him. He crossed the room to the man and hugged him briefly, without embarrassment.

The man made no motion to return the show of affection. "Are all the windows open?" he asked.

"Sure thing, Dad."

The man peered closely at his son. The boy was not much shorter than his father, and though he lacked the man's mature heaviness, he showed promise of future hardihood and power.

"You're a strong boy for thirteen, Paul," the man said.

"Yes," the boy agreed proudly. "I'm like you, Dad."

"And Davey wasn't like me. Is that it?"

"Don't talk about Davey, Dad . . ."

"He was my son!"

"But he's dead!"

A gray shadow of worry flitted across the boy's face. Like his father, he had begun to perspire. The wetness glistened on his smooth, tanned skin.

"We're alone now, Paul. For the first time since it happened." The man walked back to the door and closed it, shutting out a portion of the small breeze. "Sit down. I want to talk to you."

"You're pretty tired, Dad. Can't we talk tomorrow?"

"Now, Paul. Sit down."

Obediently the boy sat in a chair. The expression on his face was blank, submissive.

"What happened to Davey, Paul?" the man began.

"Dad, I've told you a hundred times. I've told everybody."

"I don't mean that, Paul. I want you to tell me what really happened."

"I've told you everything I remember," the boy answered cautiously.

"You said it was Davey's own idea to go swimming?"

"Yes, he said this summer he wanted to become a real good swimmer."

"You encouraged him?"

"No, I told him he was too little. And he wasn't very strong."

"Because you knew that would make him want to become a good swimmer all the more? He always envied his big brother, didn't he, Paul? . . . So like a big brother should, you went out with him?"

"Yes, we swam out together. Not very far. Then I said to Davey, 'We better swim back now.' I thought he heard me. So I started back, and I thought he was with me. When I was halfway in, I looked up and he wasn't there. He was out toward the middle. He'd been swimming away from the shore all the time. And he was calling for help."

"Then what happened, Paul?"

"Dad, I've told you . . ." The boy stood up. He wiped across his eyes with the back of his hand. But his hand was wet too.

"Sit down, Paul. Tell me again."

The boy was accustomed to obedience. He sat down again. "I knew I couldn't swim clear out to where Davey was and then swim all the way back with him. The only thing to do was to come the rest of the way in and get the boat. That's what I did."

"Did the motor start right away?"

"Not right at first. But it was only a minute. Then I steered right out to where I'd seen Davey figured he'd gone down but he'd be up again. I went to the place and stopped the boat and jumped into the water. But I couldn't find him . . ."

The boy could see that his father had not moved, except for the big hands which kept closing into fists and then opening again. In the ensuing silence he watched the hands.

"Is that all?" the man asked finally.

"Yes."

"It's not all!" Almost in one stride the man was across the room and standing over the boy's chair.

The boy waited. Not daring to look into his father's eyes, the boy watched the fists instead.

"There's one thing I've never asked you, Paul." The man's words came thickly. "If you really loved your brother, Paul, why did you take the time to go back for the boat? If you loved him, why didn't you swim out there and do your best . . . even if you drowned with him?"

The boy lifted his head, daring to meet the wild look in his father's eyes. He spoke finally, his voice steady and clear.

"I'm glad I didn't do that, Dad," he said. "If I'd have drowned with Davey, you'd have been left here all alone."

The man's rage ebbed out of him with a terrible suddenness, leaving him white and shaking. He groped his way unsteadily to the door, threw it open, and sucked in the cooler, reviving air of the outdoors.

Without going to him, the boy stood up and explained himself simply. "I love you, Dad," he said.

The man did not turn back. "Go to bed, Paul," he ordered finally.

"All right, Dad. See you in the morning."

"Yes, in the morning."

The sun rose early, and the day was hot before it was half an hour old. The boy, accustomed to waking at dawn, slept a few minutes later this morning, because he was tired from the motor trip. But the heat and light eventually roused him. He dressed sketchily, and found his father already up, standing in front of the fireplace, staring at the photograph perched above it.

But the boy did not go to him. He moved instead to the open door, breathed the morning air with great satisfaction. "The lake looks fine this morning," he began.

"I never noticed until just now," the man answered, "how strange that picture really is. Come here and look at it, Paul. There are you and I on the left. We have our arms around each other. And your mother and Davey on the right. Their arms are around each other. It isn't a group picture at all. It's divided right down the middle."

The boy came obediently. "That's the way it was, Dad," he said. "I belonged to you. Davey belonged to Mother."

"Davey was my son too!" It was a protest.

"Sure, Dad. I mean that I was like you, and Davey wasn't. We did things together, and we liked the same things. Davey liked what Mother liked, books and pictures and things . . . And now we're together, and they're together. Maybe it's better, Dad . . . for Mother, I mean."

The man listened, strangely fascinated. In the end he turned away, and stood with sagging shoulders, looking at nothing. When he went finally to a chair and sat with his face hidden in his hands, the boy followed and knelt beside him.

"Sure you loved them, Dad," the boy said, soothing, comforting. "You stayed in town and worked when you really wanted to be out here. You bought Mother all the medicine she needed, and you paid for the operations. And I took care of the house. But they're gone now. Thinking about them won't bring them back and it'll spoil things for us."

It was an impassioned speech, and a long speech for a boy. It was the manifesto of a mind matured before its time by unusual responsibility.

"You said, Paul," the man answered finally, "that I loved Davey. What about you, Paul?"

"Me? Of course, Dad."

"You hated Davey, didn't you, Paul?"

The question surprised the boy. He rose from his kneeling position and backed away. For a long time he stood, thinking. Then he replied, "No, I didn't hate him, Dad. But I loved you more."

The simple confession went unanswered. The man continued to stare at the floor, lost in some secret sorrow. After a while the boy turned away. The conversation or trial or whatever it was, he knew, was over.

The boy's mind was of the very practical sort. And he was only thirteen. He went to the kitchen. He went about the task of preparing breakfast with the confidence and sureness which only a motherless boy can learn.

And when breakfast was finished, he followed his father down to the dock, keeping worshipfully close to him. They stood together there for a while, watching the lake. The sun was hot on their heads. The water looked inviting to the boy, but he refrained from mentioning it.

The boat was sitting sluggishly beside the dock, its bottom heavy with rain water. Absently the man noted its condition.

"Somebody has stolen the motor," he concluded, but without dismay or alarm.

"No, Dad," the boy assured him. "I took it in the house."

"When?"

"Three days ago. Before we left."

"Just after we brought Davey in?"

"Yes. The motor's dry and safe."

The man seemed to shiver, as if hit by a sudden cool wind.

"Did you want to go out in the boat, Dad?" the boy asked eagerly.

"No, Paul. Not now."

The boy looked longingly at the water once more, but he did not argue. Together they walked back up to the house.

The boy loved the water. Every day, when he had finished his chores, he stripped to his swimming trunks and went down to the dock. There he would let the warmth of the sun possess him and, as time passed, his healthy tan deepened. Often, when it was very hot, he would sit on the dock with his legs dangling over the side. Then, by stretching a little, and pointing his feet downward, he could manage to get his toes into the water. But beyond this small delight he did not go. He did not swim.

The boy was, in fact, so supremely happy that no petty diffi-culty could touch him. His happiness was not even disturbed for very long when his father discovered the absence of the photo-graph.

"I was dusting," the boy explained easily. "It fell off and broke the glass. I put it away in a drawer until we could get another glass. I thought you'd want me to take good care of it."

The man did not argue. The fire that had begun to smoulder in his eyes died slowly. The boy's answer had been so open, frank, without mischief or guile.

And the boy passed the next test too, on the following day, at dinnertime.

"I've been looking around," the man told him. "Everything's gone. Everything of Davey's. His books, his stamp collection, his brushes and paints. Even his clothes. The house doesn't look as if Davey ever lived here."

The boy was calm but wary. "I took care of it, Dad," he an-swered simply.

"Who told you to?"

"No one. But I thought it would be easier for me to do than for you. So it was my job."

The man stood up. He cast a long shadow over the table, and in the shadow the boy remained seated.

"None of the things I got rid of were any good. Davey was little and skinny. I couldn't wear any of his clothes. I didn't want his books or stamps or paints. If the things stayed around, they'd just remind you of Davey, and you'd be sad. So I burned everything."

The man walked away, walked to the open door and stared out.

From the table the boy said, "When Mother died you got rid of everything of hers. You said it wasn't right to have a house seem like it was lived in by somebody who didn't live there any-more."

The man was wrestling with his thoughts. It was in his face, in the twitching of his mouth, in the look of intense concentration he turned toward his son.

He spoke at last, slowly, with great difficulty. "I've had terrible thoughts, Paul. Maybe I've been wrong."

"About what, Dad?"

"It doesn't matter now."

The boy went to him then, and they hugged each other, unashamedly. There were tears in the man's eyes, but the boy was too happy to cry.

"You're all I have left, Paul. I can't lose you. If I lose you, there's nothing."

It was enough for the boy.

■   ■   ■

In the morning the boy was up before his father. The day was warm and sticky like its predecessors. He went immediately to look out at the lake. The sight fascinated him. A soft, early breeze came through the door and caressed his bare skin. He felt exhilarated.

He checked first to make sure his father was still asleep. Then he donned his swimming trunks and went down to the dock. Even there he hesitated, the victim of grave doubts and his natural caution. But the attraction was too strong. He sat on the side at first and dangled his legs, wetting only his toes. A moment later, however, he had lowered his whole boy into the beckoning, cooling, delightful water.

Then he commenced to swim, at first close by the dock, slowly, without exerting great effort, enjoying the water's touch and feel. Occasionally he plunged his head below the surface for a few seconds and then, coming up, he shook moisture from his face and eyes, blew spray out of his mouth, and laughed aloud from the sheer joy of the experience.

Finally he began swimming in earnest, making a straight course away from the dock. His strokes were long and churned the water furiously. He was the kind of swimmer whose progress could be noted and computed from quite a distance. He did not know how far he swam, but when his first burst of energy had been spent, he turned about and headed back toward shore. On this return journey he proceeded more slowly, stopping now and then to rest, floating on his back or treading water, even though he wasn't exhausted he conserved his strength in this way, so that when he finished, he was breathing easily and still felt good. And he was happier than he had been for a long time . . .

Until he climbed back on the dock, and found his father standing there, and saw his father's face. The face was hard and pale, the eyes in it cold, deadly.

"I saw you out there," the man said. "I saw you through the

window. Don't you suppose I know the spot where they found Davey? I know exactly where it is, where your little brother drowned. And just now, you swam to that place, and you swam back again!"

The boy could not speak. He stood transfixed, his tanned, well-muscled body clean and still gleaming from the water.

The man's face had grown even paler as he spoke. It was a wet clammy pallor, composed of equal parts of horror and perspiration. The eyes spelled a hatred that the boy could read.

"Dad!" The boy screamed finally, the cry of a wounded animal. He rushed to the man, threw himself at him, encircled him with groping arms.

"Dad, I love you. Whatever you think of me, I love you." The words came sobbing out of him, as he clawed and hugged his father, and struggled to prove his words by the strength of his embrace.

But the man was stronger. He seized the boy's arms in his big hands, and thrust the smaller body away from his own. The boy's feet slipped on the puddle-wet dock and he fell.

"What are you going to do with me, Dad?" he asked, without daring to move.

The man's voice was toneless and dead when he answered. "That's what I've been trying to decide," he said and turned away to stare out at the lake.

Not even then, and not till minutes later, did the boy venture to lift himself up. His father paid no attention to him. So he trudged silently back to the house.

He did not eat any breakfast. Instead he lurked at the window. He saw his father continue to stand motionless, hands thrust deeply into his pockets, his gaze fixed, never straying from the lake. He saw too the gathering of the clouds and the disappearance of the sun, and at last the rain itself, which began softly, stealthily, scarcely more than a drizzle at first.

It was the rain which finally impelled the boy to action. He saw his father oblivious to it, standing in it, getting chilly and wet. For with the arrival of the rain, the air had cooled. The boy felt the change on his near naked body.

So he left the house finally and went part of the way down toward the dock. From a distance of twenty feet or more he called out, "Dad, come inside."

The man turned to face him, but made no move to come in. "We're going out in the boat," he announced.

"But, Dad, it's raining and getting colder."

"You wanted a boat ride, didn't you?" The words came clipped, fierce, unarguable. "Well, that's what we're going to do . . . Bring down the motor."

The boy was puzzled, but he obeyed. The man let him do everything. He bailed with a tin can. He carried down the heavy outboard motor. He brought the fuel can, filled and primed the motor, got it started.

"Ready to go, Dad."

"You in front, Paul."

The man steered. The course he followed was perpendicular to the shoreline, and they ran at full speed. The rain pursued them. The boy shivered a little, but it was mere reflex, and he was not conscious of it. They rode almost to the middle of the lake, and there the man stopped the motor. Their world, which had been so full of rasping sound, became suddenly and completely quiet. The boy looked about him. The water was clear and unobstructed, the boat being the only visible object on its surface. He looked then to his father. They regarded each other across six feet of silence.

"How far from our dock would you say we are?" The question came suddenly, from nowhere.

It surprised the boy, but he looked around calmly before he answered. "Almost a quarter of a mile."

"Davey was a hundred yards offshore when he drowned. If you could have swum in with him that day, it would be about equal to swimming from here to our dock, wouldn't it?"

The boy was thinking, and he spoke very solemnly. "A swimmer who could swim in from here ought to be able to pull in a drowning person from a hundred yards."

The man nodded. "There's been a question about how far you can swim, Paul. We'll settle it now. Get into the water."

His father was acting very strangely and the boat was small, so the boy seemed almost glad to escape its narrowness. He slipped over the side easily, disappearing briefly beneath the surface, then coming up again. Shrugging moisture from his eyes, he looked to his father for instructions.

"Go ahead, Paul. See if you can make it to our dock."

The boy turned away quickly, put his face into the water, and began to swim. He started strongly, as if pursued, making great splashes with his flailing arms.

The man watched the swimmer for a little while. Finally he started the motor. The boat quickly overtook the boy. By throttling the motor to idling speed, the man was able to keep just abreast of the swimmer.

They had covered perhaps a third of the distance to shore, moving thus together, when the boy stopped. His head bobbing up and down, now above, now under the surface, he began to tread water. The boat pulled slowly away from him.

"You're only pretending you're tired, Paul," the man called out.

Stung by the rebuke, the boy commenced swimming again, with greater effort even than before. For a few seconds he managed to gain on the boat. But he could not maintain such a pace. He began once more to fall behind. The great splashes he made, and which marked his progress so well, diminished quickly in size and vigor.

The man watched intently. Once he dipped a hand into the water. The coldness of it surprised him. But its surface, except for the imprint of the rain and the foaming course of the swimmer, was smooth and untroubled. The boat continued toward the dock, and the interval between it and the boy lengthened.

Man and boat were more than two-thirds of the way to their destination when the call first came. It was clear and certain, a single, shrill, piercing word carrying across the water.

"Help!"

The splashes were there, but they were moving slowly. So the man did not turn the boat, nor did he cut the motor.

"Dad, help!"

The man craned his neck to look. He blinked against the rain, which was coming down quite heavily now. He could not see too well, but he was nevertheless sure that he still saw the splashes.

"Dad, come back!"

But the splashes were there . . .

When the boat reached the dock, the man moored it, and climbed out. He stood there then, and faced toward the lake, watching still. The splashes were not more than fifty yards away, and they were still coming closer.

But quite suddenly they stopped. A hand reached out of the

water, groping upward, grasping air. When it disappeared, the lake closed over it, and the rain came down.

He knew the truth then, because he got back in the boat and raced it furiously to that empty place on the water. And he circled round and round it, till the motor ran out of fuel and the boat began to drift aimlessly.

And he kept calling into the unresponsive depths, "Paul . . . Paul . . . son . . . my son . . ."

Stephen Marlowe

TERRORISTS

From *Accused,* January 1956

Stephen Marlowe's series of literate, fast-paced paperback originals featuring Washington D.C.-based private detective Chester Drum was one of the longest-running of its era; it spanned a total of 20 novels, beginning in 1955 with The Second Longest Night *and ending with* Drum Beat—Marianne *in 1968. Part of the series' ongoing appeal was that Drum was the first successful globetrotting private eye, his cases taking him to such farflung locales as Iceland, India, Russia, Spain, France, Italy, and South America. "The Terrorists," one of several Drum short stories, takes place on his home turf—and although it was first published more than forty years ago, its political theme is as applicable to the world of the 1990s as it was to the world of the 1950s.*

B. P.

FROM THE SIDEWALK OF F STREET IN DOWNTOWN WASHINGton, D.C., I could see a light on in the window of my office in the Farrell Building. It surprised me. It was a very hot night, a typical August night in Washington, D.C., and while they say anything can happen in Washington in the dog days of August, when Congressmen are hunting whatever Congressman hunt in the Minnesota woods or in Canada, I still wanted to know about that light in my window.

"Evening, Mr. Drum," the night operator said as I went through the dark lobby to the bank of elevators. There was the greensoap smell of pine and antiseptic on the newly washed floor and the dragging sound of a cleaning woman's footsteps out of sight beyond the elevators. "That's all right, Mr. Drum," the night operator said. "You don't have to sign the night book."

"Are the cleaning women finished on my floor?" I asked.

The night operator looked at his wristwatch. "Yes, sir. Couple of hours ago, I guess."

"They never leave the lights on?"

"No, sir. The first thing they learn."

I pressed the elevator buzzer and waited. I watched the dial over the doors of the one elevator in service, but the hand did not move.

"That George," the night operator said. "Asleep up there, I guess. Always asleep at night like that. Better lean on it a bit, Mr. Drum."

I leaned on the buzzer and soon the elevator started down. George, the other night operator, looked as if he *had* been sleeping. I went into the elevator car and he smiled at me mechanically and took it up. "Damn hot night," he said.

I nodded.

"They ought to air-condition the building."

I said I thought that would be a good idea. I got off on the fourth floor. After the elevator doors had slid shut, I removed my shoes and padded down the hall in my stocking feet. The dark offices on either side of the hall housed C.P.A.s, lawyers and a real estate man or two. A light was on, as I had seen from the street, behind the pebble-glassed door of suite 424. The black-lettered sign said: *Chester Drum—Confidential Investigations*. Evidently the adjective did not bother whoever was snooping in there.

I leaned against the wall and slipped my loafers back on. I tried the handle carefully, but the door was on the snaplock. The key went into the lock silently. I turned the handle, pushed the door suddenly and said, "All right. What the hell are you looking for?"

A startled cry came from the inner office and I reached the archway in three strides. I began smelling greensoap again. There was a pail of water on the floor with a mop handle protruding from the mechanical wringer. A plump woman in a polka-dotted dress looked at me with round white eyes. She had dark glossy hair with a streak of gray at either temple. I placed her age at anything from forty-five to sixty. Somehow, I got the impression she was Latin.

"Hoping," she said.

"What?" I said.

"I already finished up here two hours ago, Mr. Drum. I was hoping."

"All right," I said. "I'll bite."

"I am Mrs. Arbolis-Nunez," she told me. The Spanish accent became more noticeable when she pronounced her name. "Are you angry?"

I shrugged and let that one ride. It was too hot to be angry and too hot to say it was too hot to be angry.

"I imagined myself in fine clothing," said Mrs. Arbolis-Nunez. "I imagined I came to your office as a client and we talked long into the night about Miguel. There, you see? It was very foolish of me."

Mrs. Arbolis-Nunez picked up the pail by its handle and trudged toward the archway and the outer door. She looked like she was carrying more on her shoulders than Atlas ever carried. She turned around and said, "What time is it, please Mr. Drum?"

I looked at my watch. "Eleven-thirty."

"Already? Please listen. He is coming here."

"Who's coming here?"

"Miguel."

"Listen, Mrs. Arbolis-Nunez—"

"Mr. Drum. He is coming here. At eleven-thirty, I told him. I said you would be here." She spoke very quickly. She did not look at me. She was watching the door. "I knew, of course, you would not be here. I was going to give him a message from you. Did you know you are his hero? He worships you. We have only been in Washington four years from Puerto Rico, you see, Mr. Drum, and a boy like that needs a hero, like a modern *El Cid Campeador*. You are his hero. If you could tell him this of the terrorism is wrong, all wrong, if you could say that. . . ." She clapped a hand to her mouth. There was the sound of the elevator doors opening on this floor and then the brisk tap-tap-tap of leather-soled shoes approaching the office.

■ ■ ■

A gentle shove would have nudged Mrs. Arbolis-Nunez to tears, to laughter, or to flight. The door opened. Miguel was about eighteen and of a very dark olive complexion. His hair was glossy black like Mrs. Arbolis-Nunez's and he had a handsome, arrogant face. His eyes softened when he saw Mrs. Arbolis-Nunez and became wary when they saw me.

"Señor Drum," he said. We shook hands. "I thought my mother, she was joking. But you are here."

"Yeah," I said.

"Puerto Rico should have its independence," Miguel said abruptly. "You cannot tell me otherwise."

"I wouldn't try," I said. "It's just like what happened to the

Philippines. When they were ready, they were given independence."

Mrs. Arbolis-Nunez looked at me gratefully, as if somehow I
had said the right thing. But Miguel looked at my height and my
blond hair and said, "You are Filipino?"

"No," I said.

"Then you would not know. It is not the same thing."

He waited for me to refute that. Mrs. Arbolis-Nunez was watching me steadily, the hope fading from her eyes. She said, "Tell
him what you said about the Secretary of State, Mr. Drum."

"*Madre!*" Miguel said harshly. "You were to tell him nothing,
nothing of the details. Do you think we are playing games? We
are children pretending? You merely wanted me to meet Mr.
Drum and—"

"Tell him, Mr. Drum," Mrs. Arbolis-Nunez persisted, "what
you told me. Tell him it would be foolish to assassinate the Secretary of State when he arrives in Washington tomorrow."

I said nothing. I looked at Mrs. Arbolis-Nunez. At first I
thought she was pulling my leg, but her dark expressive eyes said
she was not. I looked at Miguel. His dark, big eyes, solemn face
suddenly split in a grin. "My mother is joking," he said.

Mrs. Arbolis-Nunez shook her head. Her lips were trembling.

"A joke," Miguel said.

"Tomorrow afternoon," Mrs. Arbolis-Nunez recited *sotto voce*,
"the Secretary of State returns from a brief stay in Puerto Rico,
where he was vacationing after the recent Latin American conference. Although colonialism and Communism were condemned
by the conference, no mention of Puerto Rico was made. I have
seen the people my son calls his friends *Cabrones!* They are terrorists, Mr. Drum. And their leader—*una perra*.".. . .

"Don't talk about Gabriella like that," Miguel said. "Don't ever
talk like that."

"By the Virgin, I swear it," Mrs. Arbolis-Nunez said. "Gabriella.
The name of an angel, but the heart of a dog. She is a Red, Mr.
Drum."

"You lie!" Miguel cried

"A Red. Do you think she cares about the Puerto Ricans or
their independence movement? But it would be a feather in the
Red propaganda cap if young American colonials shot and killed

the American Secretary of State on his return from the Latin American conference. Well, wouldn't it? Wouldn't it, Miguel?"

"You would not understand, *madre*." He had the incongruously patient but cynical voice of a teenager in violent disagreement with a dogmatic parent. "This is all my life and my reason for living. This is my mission, given me by God as he has given me hands and feet—oh, what's the use? I shouldn't have come here." He turned toward the door.

"Miguel," his mother said.

He came back abruptly and with fluid athletic grace took a switchblade knife from his pocket. The blade snicked out and hovered in air a couple of inches from my face. Miguel said, "You remember nothing. You heard nothing."

His hand was rock-steady. Yellow light gleamed on the knife blade.

I reached up. It was close. It was very close. The point of the knife nicked the skin over my collarbone. Miguel's face went white as my fingers closed on his wrist. I swung away from him and clamped a double wristlock on his arm. The knife clattered to the floor.

"You'll break my arm," Miguel wailed. "See? I let go of the knife. Let go of my arm."

Mrs. Arbolis-Nunez began to cry, but that wasn't a good enough reason to let go of her son's arm. "Don't go to the police, Mr. Drum," she said. "I could have gone there. I did not. I was like Miguel. I had faith in you. Faith, Mr. Drum. Both of us, the young terrorist and the old . . . fool." Her voice broke. Miguel glared at me.

"He could prove nothing to the police," Miguel said. He squirmed a little and winced as he applied pressure to his own wrist.

"Who's Gabriella?" I asked Miguel. He didn't answer me until I forced his forearm up a few inches. His mother was whimpering and looking out of the dark window at the black, faceless night.

"All right," Miguel said at last. Something in his elbow made a cracking noise.

When he told me Gabriella's full name, I said, "I don't believe you."

He shrugged and cursed me in Spanish. Then he laughed. "I

am a terrorist," he said, "and you can believe that. But not Gabriella, for you don't believe an important person like Gabriella can be a terrorist, too."

"You are no terrorist," Mrs. Arbolis-Nunez said. "You talk as if with the voice of a terrorist. And Gabriella, she too is no terrorist. She is *una roja perra*. A Red insect."

I let go of Miguel's arm. He rubbed it for a few moments. His mother came over and massaged the wrist. I picked up the switchblade knife and went over to my desk. I opened a drawer and stuck the point in about an inch of its length, then shut the drawer. I yanked the knife handle down and away from the desk and the blade snapped off and then I gave what was left of the knife back to Miguel. He did not say anything. He had mentioned Gabriella's last name once and at first I had not believed him, but I looked at his face and at Mrs. Arbolis-Nunez's face and I believed him now.

Which meant that the Red leader of the self-styled terrorists was the sister of the Ambassador to the United States of one of the largest and most influential South American republics.

"What about her brother?" I asked Miguel.

He sneered at me. He went to the door and opened it. "Why don't you ask her?" he said, and went out into the hall. We both listened to his footsteps fade away and then Mrs. Arbolis-Nunez said:

"You must not condemn him. He has no father. He knows the wrong people."

I said nothing.

"If you go to the police, what is left in life for me? I work for him. I live for him. I wanted him to go to college. I have saved the money. He is very good in school, his teachers say. In history he is excellent. He loves history. Please, Mr. Drum. I beg you: do not go to the police."

The police. The police could do nothing. The Secret Service would do something, all right, but you don't have to warn the Secret Service. Every working day, which is seven days a week, the Secret Service assumes assassination is afoot. It's their job.

"I won't go to the police," I said.

"You will forget this?" She was one part happy and one part sad.

"I'll see what Gabriella thinks," I said.

Mrs. Arbolis-Nunez and I entered the elevator together. She got off with her mop and pail on the second floor without looking back at me. The presence of the elevator operator made us strangers.

It was pushing one A.M. when I reached my apartment near the Uline Arena. A long freight rolled through the railyards beyond the arena, rattling my windows. I found a bottle of beer in the icebox, but it wasn't cold enough. It was too hot to sleep. In the apartment next door, a man and a woman were arguing steadily, monotonously. I sat down on the floor in front of the radio, because they say heat rises. I stripped to my shorts and heard the one o'clock news summary. The radio told you what kind of beer to drink. It happened not to be my brand. The radio told you there was trouble off Formosa, trouble in Southeast Asia, trouble in Palestine and murder in Fargo, North Dakota. Washington was slumbering for the summer, the radio said, but there were indications of next fall's fireworks. The radio waxed poetic and said you could see these indications in the heat lightning which surrounded the city. And the radio said the Secretary of State was returning from his Puerto Rican vacation today. His special plane was expected at Washington International Airport at three in the afternoon. His motorcade would hit Pennsylvania Avenue by four-thirty and stop at number 1600 by five. He had an early dinner date with the man at that address, who happened to be the President of the United States. Good night, the radio said.

But it was still too hot to sleep.

I thought of a would-be terrorist named Miguel. I wondered if it were far-fetched. But terrorists are usually young, for the same reason that the Japanese kamakazi warriors were young. And they're usually bright kids because, right or wrong, they need an ideology. Their heads can usually be turned by a man on horseback, by an impassioned orator, or by a beautiful woman.

Like Gabriella. I had seen pictures of Gabriella in the newspapers and I had met her once at a cocktail party at Senator Hartsell's in Georgetown. She was beautiful. She was Washington's number one bachelor girl.

It was much too hot to sleep.

• • •

In the morning, I remembered a few odds and ends which needed cleaning up at my office. F Street was different now. F Street was alive. The men in wash-and-wear summer suits watched the girls in sun-back dresses. Traffic moved in fits and starts. Horns hol-

lered at each other. I picked up a newspaper in the lobby of the
Farrell Building and because nothing else was happening in
Washington the headline told me about the impending arrival of
the Secretary of State.

"Hot," said the elevator operator. A car full of workbound
white collar workers nodded. The small fan over the elevator operator's head circulated stale air, perfume and body heat. I
thought it was a very good day for terrorists, a day when the heat
frays tempers and magnifies cockeyed ideologists, a red day if days
have color, a day for dying.

She was waiting in the hall outside the pebble-glass door of my
office. It was very hot in the hall and I could already feel the
sweat plastering my shirt to my shoulders, but she looked as cool
as an iceberg would in the Persian Gulf. She was tanned the color
of coffee with about twice the amount of cream I like. Her long
sleek dark hair was braided and the braids were coiled up over
her head. Her eyes were big and set wide apart, the irises a gold-
flecked green. Her eyes were smiling at me. She wore a dark green
sun-back dress which made the smiling eyes seem greener. The
dress exposed her shoulders, throat and collar bones and the
tanned skin was stretched tight as a drumhead.

"Hello, Chet," she said.

"Hello, Gabriella."

"Well, I'm glad. I didn't know if you'd remember me."

"I remember you."

"It was the party Senator Hartsell gave when his son returned
from France."

"Yeah."

"We had a drink. You said if ever I needed a detective. . . ."

"Do you?" I asked, and opened the office door. "I say that to
all the beautiful girls."

"Is it your theory that most of them eventually need private
detectives?"

"You found me out," I said.

We went inside together, and through the archway with the
peeling paint to my inner office which has three battleship gray
filing cabinets, rarely used, a water cooler, a desk, a swivel chair
for me and an armchair for the client. Gabriella sat down in the
client chair and crossed her legs. She took a cigarette case out of
a small buckskin pouch of a handbag. I lighted her cigarette and

one of my own and, even when she moved, what skin you could see still looked tight as a drumhead and you knew somehow without seeing the rest of her that there was not a wrinkle, not a blemish, not an imperfection on her.

"Yes," she said.

"Yes what?"

"Yes, I need a private detective."

I thought about Mrs. Arbolis-Nunez. *Una roja perra*, Mrs. Arbolis-Nunez had said. "I'm listening," I said.

"I have a study group for boys, Chet. Maybe you've heard of it?"

"I don't think so."

"To promote good neighbor relations between the hemispheres. It was my brother's idea and at first I thought I wouldn't like it, but I do. I like it a lot. I feel I'm doing something. Oh, it's a small thing but in its own way it is important. You understand?"

She was the daughter of a rich coffee planter in South America. She had been educated here in this country, in an exclusive finishing school and at Bryn Mawr. Her life could have been that of the idle rich and the beautiful. I said I thought I understood.

She leaned forward and put her cigarette out. She looked at me. Her lips were moist and very red against her tanned skin. "But there's no telling about such a study group," she said. "They're young. I like to give them a free hand. There was a Puerto Rican boy named Miguel Arbolis-Nunez——"

"All right," I said. "Good."

"I'm afraid I——"

"I was waiting for you to get around to Arbolis-Nunez. Did he see you last night? Or this morning? About me."

"Why, no. No, Chet. Why should he see me about you?"

I got up and walked to the archway and peeled off a scab of paint, powdering it between my fingers. I turned around and pointed a finger at Gabriella. "Because I saw him last night."

"Are you serious?" Gabriella said. "This is a coincidence."

"I don't think it is. Miguel Arbolis-Nunez and his mother were both here last night."

"Somehow, you never think in terms of their parents. All the boys in my study group, and I never thought about their parents. What is the señora like?"

"She called you *una roja perra*. She said you had incited Miguel and some other Puerto Rican lads to assassinate the Secretary of State on his arrival in Washington today."

Spots of color appeared on her cheeks. The green eyes smouldered, became darker, as dark as the green of her dress. She said, "*Puta!*" which is Spanish and does not merit translation. Then, slowly, she smiled. "Forgive me," she said. "But I was startled. You didn't believe her, Chet, did you?"

"Show me a reason why she should lie?"

Gabriella laughed. It was a lovely sound, but I thought of Ulysses and the siren song. "I didn't say the señora was lying. I haven't met her. But Miguel: it's why I came to see you."

"All right, what about Miguel?"

"Well, in the first place, he probably lied to his mother."

"About you?"

"If that's what his mother told you, yes."

"Why did you come to see me about Miguel? Is he why you need a P.I.?"

"Yes. Miguel and some other Puerto Ricans in our study group became fascinated by the implications of the Latin American revolutionary movements of the last century. They substituted Puerto Rico for South America and this century for last in their minds. They decided that political ends are attained through violence chiefly. Chet, do you know what sort of person makes the best revolutionary, the best terrorist?"

"I've already thought about it," I said.

"Miguel Arbolis-Nunez has a crush on me. I'm ten years older, but it doesn't matter to him. So he confided in me. He said they are going to kill the Secretary. He boasted. He said. 'Isn't it as you have taught us?' He is confused, but he's not basically bad."

"Why did you come here? Why didn't you go to the Secret Service?"

"Because he may be just talking. It would be a shame for them to arrest him. Because basically he's good."

"So you came to me?"

"Yes." She leaned forward and put her hand over mine on the desk. She had long, cool fingers. She stood up and came around behind me and leaned over my shoulder and scribbled an address on the pad in front of me. "Miguel's," she said. "The other

Puerto Rican boys are nothing. If you stop Miguel, you stop everything. You'll do it?"

I tore the sheet off the pad and put it in my pocket. "Yeah,
I'll do it."

"Chet, I don't know how to thank you. Do you get a retainer
first or do I pay you afterwards? I never did business with a private
detective before."

I shook my head. "It's on the house."

"But that isn't fair. Just because we met once. . . . Don't you
get most of your business like that?"

"Yeah," I said. "But this time it's on the house."

She looked at me. She said, "Please stand up."

I did so. She came against me gently as a feather and brushed
her lips against my lips. She was out of reach before I could blink
my eyes. "Goodbye," she said from the archway. A moment later
she added, "I trust you, Chet. I have faith in you." Then I heard
the door close behind her.

■ ■ ■

I lit a cigarette. I found Nuncia Arbolis-Nunez's name in the
telephone book and it matched the address Gabriella had given
me. I called the number and heard three buzzes and then Mrs.
Arbolis-Nunez's voice. "Miguel?" she cried eagerly.

"Uh-uh," I said. "It's Chester Drum."

"*Madre de Dios*, Mr. Drum. He was not home all night. He
did not sleep in his bed. But no, it is not entirely right. He was
here before I came home. He took his father's gun. His father
was a scout with a Puerto Rican Army unit in Hawaii. He died
at Pearl Harbor. Miguel hardly remembers him, but the gun is a
memento. Miguel oils it and polishes it and——"

"Is there a hangout where he goes with some of his friends?
His Spanish friends?"

"The other Puerto Rican boys, you mean? *Sí*. Yes, Mr. Drum.
The luncheonette of Rafael Lopez." She gave me the address,
which was about half a mile from 1600 Pennsylvania Avenue.
"Shall I go to him?"

"No," I said. "Stay home. Everything's going to be all right.
You'll stay home?"

"*Sí*. Oh, *Sí*! I trust you, señor. Oh, *sí*."

I hung up. Everybody trusted Chester Drum. I shook my head

and wished I had taken up Senator Hartsell's offer to hunt with him in Alaska. It would be very cool in Alaska now and if a Kodiak bear came at you you could shoot him in the face and hope for the best. I wished Mrs. Arbolis-Nunez was a cleaning woman in some other private eye's office building. I sighed and made another telephone call.

"Hello, Phil," I said. "This is Chet Drum."

"Real life's answer to Mike Hammer," he said.

"How's the Secret Service?"

"A lot of service, not many secrets. But don't tell my boss."

"The Secretary of State thing got you hopping?"

"I guess. Routine motorcade coverage. Which means a few score ops en route and a dozen or so with the convoy and a lot of sweating in the hot sun. What for, I don't know."

"I do," I said. "Phil, is this call being monitored?"

"Not unless you hear a faint beep."

I heard no beep. I said, "It may be the real thing this time, Phil. Assassination attempt."

"Are you kidding?"

"No."

"O.K. What the hell do you know?"

"That's all," I said. "No names."

"No names?" he shouted.

"In case I'm wrong. I'll work on the names."

"Then what the hell did you call me for?"

"So the coverage is more than routine. It's only a bunch of crazy kids, Phil. Maybe they won't try anything."

"Maybe, he says. At least tell me——"

But I didn't. I hung up. The telephone started ringing almost immediately. I let it ring. I opened the bottom left hand drawer of my desk, which was locked. I took out the Magnum .357 and the shoulder rig. I opened the magazine and checked the clip, then slid the gun in the rig and strapped the rig under my left arm. It was uncomfortable and it meant I'd have to wear my jacket. I checked Rafael Lopez' address in the phone book and went downstairs to my car. The shoulder holster rubbed and rubbed.

■   ■   ■

It was a long two-story brick building with apartments upstairs and stores down. I parked the De Soto convertible outside Rafael Lopez' luncheonette, which was second from the corner. Two little girls outside were skipping rope. They wore sunsuits and didn't mind the heat and a lady poked her head out of the florist's next to Rafael Lopez' luncheonette, looked at the girls, and smiled.

I went inside and told the man behind the counter, "Iced coffee."

He was a short fat fellow and got the ice out of a bucket with his hand. He poured the hot coffee over it in a glass and the ice became slush. "Miguel Arbolis-Nunez," I said.

There was no one else in the small luncheonette. There were voices coming faintly from the kitchen, though. Eager voices. Boy voices.

"That's your name?" the short fat fellow asked me.

"That's who I'm looking for."

"Try the phone book in the corner," he said.

I tasted the coffee. It was sour. "Maybe I'll try your kitchen, Señor Lopez," I said.

I got up and walked toward the back of the narrow store.

"Hold it," he said. I heard him coming around the counter in a hurry. I turned around fast. He had a sawed off oarblade in his hands. He was holding it over his shoulder like a baseball bat. The wooden blade was stained brown from years of service in the coffee urn. I reached inside my jacket because I wanted to see if he would use the oarblade. He began to swing it like a batter who was waiting to see if the pitcher's delivery would be a curve ball.

I ducked under the blade and he fanned, his short fat body twisting in the follow through, exposing his right side. I sliced the edge of my left hand against it, not hard but hard enough. I caught the kidney and he screamed like a woman before he fell down.

Miguel came out of the kitchen. Two other boys were behind him. Just then two matronly women entered the luncheonette. Rafael Lopez was getting up, but his back was toward them. "We're closed," I said.

"But——"

"We're renovating. Goodbye."

They turned around and got out of there. "Lock the door from the inside," I told Miguel. "Pull down the shade." He just looked at me. "Hurry up," I said. I took out the Magnum .357.

Miguel went to the door and locked it and pulled down the shade. "When the neighborhood cop comes by he'll know something's the matter," Rafael Lopez said. He was rubbing his side gingerly.

"Yeah," I said. "Something's the matter. Where's your father's gun, Miguel?"

"I don't have a father."

"Give me the gun."

He shoved his hands deep in his pockets and spat on the floor in front of my feet. I remembered his mother's words. *Did you know you are his hero? He worships you.* This was a new kind of hero worship.

"Is this the whole gang of you?" I said.

There were two boys behind Miguel. They were probably his age, but looked younger. And there was Rafael Lopez, who was old enough to be his father. "Look," I said. "Wise up. The police don't have to know. Just give me your guns and we'll all climb into my car and take a drive down into Virginia. We'll spend the day out in the country, how about it?"

Rafael Lopez called me a name in Spanish. Rafael Lopez was old enough to know better. I thought I would have liked to take the boys out into the country, but not Rafael.

"You can go scratch yourself," Miguel said.

I grabbed his arm and swung it behind him, pivoting his body. I found the gun, a .45 automatic, tucked under the tail of his shirt and in the waistband of his trousers. I lifted it clear and shoved him away from me.

And then someone else came out of the kitchen.

It was Gabriella. Miguel's two boyfriends were between us. Gabriella said, "I have a gun, Chet. I can shoot you but you'll only shoot these boys. Drop your gun."

■　■　■

"So they just got out of hand," I said.

"Drop it!" she said.

"Basically, they're good boys."

She shrugged her bare shoulders. "I didn't know if you believed me or not. I thought I could keep you busy with Miguel, but he's not that dedicated. Are you Miguel?"

"I want to be where I am of most value," he said.

"He could have been a red herring," Gabriella said. "He could have led you all over town, while the others——"

"They lack strength," said Miguel. "I am needed."

"Now what am I going to do with you?" Gabriella asked me. I shrugged. She said, "For the last time, drop it."

The boys were still between us. I dropped the Magnum and Miguel picked it up. "Give me my gun also," he said. I gave it to him.

"You're a Red, aren't you?" I asked Gabriella. "Mind telling me why?"

"Why are you a private detective, Chester? You were in the F.B.I., weren't you?"

"Yeah."

"It didn't thrill you enough?"

I wondered why she thought my current occupation was thrilling. I said nothing. She said, "You wouldn't understand. You couldn't possibly understand. Being a Red is like—like a sexual thrill."

"You're cold," I said. "Aren't you? Otherwise, you're completely cold."

She walked between the boys and came very close to me and slapped my face. For some reason, Miguel winced. "I'll bet you stay up nights thinking about Puerto Rico," I told Gabriella.

"That's enough," she said. She looked at Miguel. Miguel did not look at her.

"I am no Communist," Miguel said.

"Just a label," Gabriella told him. "We fight for the same thing—for freedom, against colonial rule. Don't we?"

"It is a hard and ugly thing," Miguel said. "It is not like a thrill. It is bitter."

"Shut up, *hijo*," Rafael Lopez said.

"If it is like a thrill to you, that is all wrong."

"Listen to him," Rafael Lopez said. His voice sounded amused but his eyes were ugly.

"Here," Miguel told me, offering me the Magnum.

Before I could take it, Gabriella hit him, bringing the .38 revolver she carried down against the side of his head, the barrel slashing across his ear and ripping it, the ear splitting blood in a sudden torrent and Miguel falling forward on his face. I dropped on my hands and knees for the Magnum, which Miguel was still clutching instinctively. Gabriella kicked me in the face, jarring me. But I grabbed her calf and twisted and she came tumbling down on top of me. Her revolver went off and I felt the powder burn my face and the roar deafened me. Her mouth was open and she was probably laughing, but I heard nothing.

I wrestled the revolver from her and began to get up. Something nudged my back from behind and I fell away quickly to the left, against the luncheonette counter. It was Rafael Lopez' foot which had nudged me. Rafael Lopez tried to check himself but could not. He brought the sawed-off oarblade down, edge foremost, and it slammed across Gabriella's face. I was beginning to hear again. I heard the oarblade crunch against the bones of her face and her skull.

Rafael Lopez held the oarblade and looked at what he had done. He lifted the oarblade in a gesture of defense, but I took it from his hands. It was like taking it from the hands of a baby. He looked down at Gabriella and he was suddenly, violently sick.

Miguel was crying. The other two boys were standing near the doorway to the kitchen. Their faces were very white.

The front door rattled. A voice called: "Hey, Rafe! What's going on in there?"

"Cop," Miguel said.

I went to the door and opened it. The cop was a young fellow with a pleasant face. I had seen him around one of the precincts, but I didn't remember which one.

"There's a dead girl in there," I said.

He closed the door and locked it again. He took me by the arm and led me back inside. I didn't mind and when he saw I didn't, he let go of my arm. He would make a good cop.

Gabriella was dead. Maybe she deserved to die, I don't know. I'm no judge. My De Soto was waiting at the curb outside, but there would be no ride in the country for Miguel and his friends today. I tried to tell myself it was better this way, that if they were the kind of kids they were they were learning their lesson today the way it had to be learned. However they learned it, or even if they failed to learn it entirely, today would be just routine motorcade coverage for the Secret Service. That was something.

The young cop looked at the boys. He looked longest at Miguel. Then he studied Rafael Lopez' face. He bent down and picked up Gabriella's wrist and dropped it. He stood up and said to Rafael Lopez, "All right, Rafe. Suppose you tell me how you did it?"

I was right. He would make a good cop.

Vin Packer

HOT SNOW

From *Justice*, January 1956

In the early sixties The New York Times Book Review *called Vin Packer (Marijane Meaker) "consistently the most sensitive and illuminating writer of paperback originals," an opinion anyone who has read such singular and entertaining novels as* The Evil Friendship, The Twisted Ones, *and* Something in the Shadows *is certain to share. It has also been said that Packer's novels are totally devoid of either heroes or villains, for her protagonists and secondary characters alike are all conflicted, maladjusted, and beset by personal demons of one sort or another (often to the point of psychosis). The same is true of the unnamed young man in "Hot Snow," one of only two short stories to carry the Packer byline—a dark little cautionary tale about a life damaged beyond repair.*

B. P.

I LOVE ONLY THE WHITE SNOW," HE SAID ALOUD TO HIMSELF, looking beyond Tony into the long mirror behind the bar.

Tony said, "Yep. Yeah," and went on washing glasses.

Besides the two of them in that place there was this girl. She was on her third drink; rye on the rocks; and she was nice. What is meant by "nice" is good to look at, a fresh and pretty face, and hair that was soft and very black, and eyes green-changing-blue. She was twenty-eight? . . . Probably thirty. She wore a trench coat; her legs were slender, and she did not smile—but her expression was pleasant all the same, and she had been minding her own business until he had said that about the snow.

He had not said it to attract her attention, nor had he said it to Tony. In his small square hands he held a glass of gingerale, and he looked at no one in particular; at his reflection in the mirror, maybe—but that was all. Then his round dark eyes glanced down to study his wrists, the watch on the left one, and the cuffs of his white shirt below the sleeves of his worn tweed jacket. He was a gaunt young man; he had a sad and tender handsome face; a melancholy air; and dark brown hair, strands of which fell to his forehead while he shoved them back mechanically.

She spoke to him then. She was shy, so that her words were followed by a slight chuckle of embarrassment. She said, "There's not much snow around this time of year."

"Not much," he agreed, and turned sideways to see her.

She blushed and lowered her eyes to her drink; then raised the glass and swallowed some of the rye.

"Do you like it when it's Winter?" he asked her.

"Oh, yes," she said. "Yes, I do."

"Do you *really?*" he said. His tone was too earnest for the question. A puzzled look came on her countenance.

"Y-yes," and then, "but I like Spring too. Spring is nice."

He said quietly, "I see."

He started to stare again at his wrists, without talking, and she watched him momentarily with a thin smile tipping her lips, and then she murmured wonderously, " 'S funny, you know?"

"What is?"

"I mean, I never heard a fellow in a bar talk like you do. You talk different. Do you know?"

"How so?" he said.

"I don't know. Like—well—mysterious."

"I'm a very mysterious guy," he said, snickering sardonically, "Ah, yes."

She said, "You college?"

"Uh-uh. . . . Nope. . . . But I read a lot. . . . I teach myself."

"I been in a lot of bars," she said, "but I never heard someone just blurt out about loving snow and all. 'S funny."

Tony shuffled back into the kitchen with a tray of glasses, and she glanced out the window of the bar.

"Still raining out, I guess," she said.

The young man said, "You ought to get out of here."

"Why?"

"What are you doing here anyway?"

"The same as you. Having a few drinks," she answered, and her eyes fell to the glass of gingerale in his hands.

He said, "Don't you have anything better to do?"

"What's the matter with it? Is there anything the matter with it?"

"You look like you ought not to be in a grubby bar having drinks by yourself," he said. "Don't ask me why. You just look like you ought not to be here."

"I moved down here," she said. "I live around here. I moved down here yesterday."

"So why do you come to a bar?"

"For drinks!" She sounded angry now.

The young man shrugged. He said, "Some people are lushes, some aren't. I didn't figure you for a lush."

"Look, mister," she said, "Is there anything wrong with a couple of drinks in a neighborhood bar?"

"What are you—all alone or something? Don't you have anyone?"

"No," she said flatly.

"I'm sorry."

"That makes it worse," she said.

■   ■   ■

They sat there drinking silently then, and the young man began to notice her in a careful, interested way, his eyes fixed on her. Tony came back and stood behind the bar.

"What time's the plane coming in?" he asked the young man.

The young man's face turned from the girl to Tony, becoming suddenly tired. "Lord, I wish I knew!" he sighed.

She asked, "You waiting for a plane?"

She finished the rye in her glass and pushed it forward, stretching to get Tony's eye. "Another here, please," she said, and for the first time it was obvious that she was a little high; not drunk; but just a little high. She swayed slightly atop the stool she was perched on.

"Sure," the young man answered her. "A plane from Alaska. From snow land."

"Here?"

"Sure," he said. "Right here."

She picked a cigarette out of her pack, dropped it, reached for it and dropped it again. After she got it into her mouth and lit it, she offered the pack to the young man.

"No," he said, "I don't smoke."

"Nor drink?"

"Nor drink."

"A man who talks about snow," she said with intoxicated thoughtfulness, "white, white snow."

"White, white snow," he said. "That's right."

He faced her once more, studying her profile as he asked, "What's your name?"

"Florence?"

Tony walked wearily to the end of the bar and picked up a magazine and a pencil. He started to work the crossword. He drank coffee and stood back there scratching his head and biting on the eraser of the pencil, frowning down at the open page.

She looked into the young man's eyes:

"What's yours?"

"Ben," he answered, "Ben."

He moved closer to her, getting off the stool and walking over to her, his arm resting beside hers, barely touching hers. He said, "Why didn't I know you before?"

"And if you had?"

"I don't know."

"Things would be different?"

"Maybe I could still—" his voice trailed off. "Now I don't want you to go," he said. "That's funny, isn't it?"

"I wasn't going anyway, Ben."

"I'm glad," he said, "I'll buy you a drink."

He did, and they stood quietly together; and he kept watching her. "I might not meet that plane," he said.

"Oh?"

"I might not."

"If you're supposed to, you'd better," she said.

"I'm not supposed to."

"You talk all mixed-up," she said. "You don't make much sense."

"I love you," he said.

She didn't look at him. He was standing very close to her.

"Take me to your place," he said. "With you."

"No, Ben."

"I don't know how it happened. I just fell in love with you. Can't something crazy like that happen? All of a sudden?"

A breeze blew in from the door; and a heavy man stood in the entranceway. Momentarily he looked about him; then he went to the back of the bar. He called to Tony, "Kitchen open?"

"Sure," Tony said.

"Hamburger?"

"Sure."

He followed Tony to the back room. He was saying, "I got to use the phone, o.k., isn't it?"

The girl looked up at the young man. "You're not in love with anyone," she said. "You just like to talk."

"No," he shook his head adamantly. "Other times maybe you could say that about me, but not now. Something happened to me, Florence. You. You're better than snow," he grinned at her. "How do I know that?"

"You're just talking, Ben," she said.

"Take me to your place, will you?"

"No."

She could not look at him now.

"I ask you to."

"No."

"I'll wait for you," he said, "until you're finished lushing. I'll wait."

"And the plane?"

"I love *you*," he said emphatically.

Tony called out at him then: "Ben? Can you watch the burger a second? I got no help."

"What for?" the young man asked, but already he moved away from the girl. He stood uncertainly at the bar, eyeing Tony.

"C'mon, sport," Tony said. "Be big about it!"

The young man touched the girl's hand; then his fingers curled around her wrists tightly. "I'll be back. I'll be right back. Do you believe that? Will you wait, Florence?"

She nodded without looking at him, and he stood like that for a moment, holding her arm, and then he let go. And he went to the back room.

■   ■   ■

The heavy man back there took a teaspoon from the pocket of his overcoat. The handle was broken off and the bottom was charred from the matches which had been lighted under it. From an envelope he took a capsule and opened it, and emptied powder into the spoon.

Then he took a hypodermic needle and an eyedropper from his breast pocket and laid them on the table. There was a water tap at one side of the room and he went over and dripped water into the spoon. Back at the table he struck a match and held the flame under the spoon.

The young man watched him.

"How'd you like blue-grassing?" the heavy man asked. "Did you get the cold turkey treatment, Benny?"

The young man could not take his eyes from the flame.

"We missed you," the heavy man said. "No one could push decks like you could, Benny, when you were hooked. Then you had to go soft." He shook his head. "Well, now you're back. It'll be Winter again, Benny."

"I kicked it, Ace," the young man said, standing transfixed, staring at the spoon, and then at the eyedropper the older man used to suck up the milky fluid. "I just came down for one bang. Period! I kicked it, Ace."

"Sure, you did. This is just a skin-pop, Benny, for past services faithfully rendered. White snow on the house, Benjamin. For being a good boy, ah?"

"I never told, Ace. Sometimes I thought I'd go crazy if they wouldn't shoot me with the stuff, but I never told."

"That's right," Ace said. "Stick the leg out."

The heavy man jabbed the needle through the young man's trousers into the thigh of his left leg. He placed the eyedropper over the needle, and pressed the fluid into the flesh. As he did this, he said, "But someday you would have, Benny—you're a weak kid. You would have got hooked again and then kicked it again, and you would have kept on like that until you had to rat, Benny."

"*Would* have?" Suddenly the young man's eyes became alert.

"Tony says you fell in love again tonight. While you were waiting for the plane. You see what I mean, Benny? You're impressionable, kid."

"No," the young man said. "I really—" and then he leaned back against the wall. "You said I *would* have, Ace."

"I've got to cut out now, Benny. It's Winter again, kid. It'll be Winter all the time now."

"Is it hot, Ace? Is it a hot shot? I don't deserve that, Ace! Ace, is it? Am I going to—"

The young man's question was not answered. Noise came; men with it; two in uniform and two in street clothes; and there was this girl.

The young man saw her. "I told you, Florence," he said, "you didn't belong here." He leaned back against the table, *pushing* the strands of brown hair back on his forehead; he was perspiring.

The policemen had the heavy man by the arms and collar. They pulled him out of there.

The girl said, "You were right, Ben."

"C'mon, hophead," a man in a brown overcoat said to the young man. "C'mon."

"The girl didn't do anything," the young man said, holding his head with his hands, unmoving.

"It's all right, Ben," she told him. "We'll go together."

He said, "I—c-can't, Flor—" and he lurched forward suddenly while the two men caught him. His body sagged in their arms; his mouth quivered. He said her name uncertainly: "Florence?"

The girl's hands tightened to tense fists as she watched, the fist of her right hand cradling her silver policewoman's badge, the edges of it cutting into the flesh of her palms. She murmured, "I never thought it would be as rough as this," to the man beside her.

"You'll get tough," he answered. "First time's like no other."

"Hot shot," the other said. "I guess he got one, all right."

"Florence," the young man said, "I love—" she bent near his face, her fingers loosening his collar and he looked at her through his dark eyes—"only the white snow," and died.

Marthayn Pelegrimas

I'M A DIRTY GIRL

Marthayn Pelegrimas has quickly been making her reputation as a writer of uniquely dark stories that bridge the old-fashioned kind of horror with the new-fangled, urban variety. Here is a hardboiled suspense story that shows her considerable talents at her very best. She is presently at work on a novel that will bring her the wider audience she so clearly deserves.

E. G.

> "I'm a flasher at heart.
> I'm a dirty girl."
> . . . Deborah Harry

GUYS NEVER LIKED ME. WHY SHOULD THEY? I WAS ALWAYS THE scrawny kid. There I sat, in every damn class picture, third from the left, first row. Mousy hair, skinny arms stickin' out of home-made sleeves, buck teeth. Lookin' down at the floor cause I was always too shy or too scared to face the camera. They never took the time to know me—not even the girls—until I improved my-self.

I took acting lessons while all the other girls were pissin' away their time in some snotty sorority house. And after they graduated and got forced into the real world, lookin' around all frantic for a job in their "chosen field," I took modeling classes. In between the classes and lessons I pulled double shifts tendin' bar at the VFW. But it wasn't until the night of my twenty-fifth birthday that my learned skills and natural talents all started workin' to-gether for me.

One of my regulars, a guy named Petey Lindstrom, came up to me with a big box, all wrapped in shiny red paper.

"Petey," I said, "you didn't have to get me nothin'." I see the other guys laughin' and I figured it was one of them gag gifts and decided to play along. So after he goes on and on about how it's just a little somethin' he wants me to have, just a token, I said thanks and started unwrappin'.

When I lifted the lid off the big box, there was another box, and then another, until I got down to the last one. Finally, after all the paper's off, what did I spy but one of them Wonder Bras, black lace.

Well, the guys all howled so I played along and acted like I was embarrassed. They got a big charge out of the whole thing, kept shoutin' for me to "Put it on! Put it on! PUT IT ON!"

"Jesus!" I shouted. "Okay, anything to shut you idiots up."

The mirror in the bathroom was cracked right across the middle but I could see I looked hot. The bar went ape shit when I sashayed out with my tee-shirt tied tight under that push-up bra. And it was at that exact moment I realized the time was as right as it was ever gonna be for me to get my boobs done.

Oh, I know, it takes a hell of a lot more than a pair of 38Ds, and a tight ass to make it big. And you better believe I intend on makin' it bigger than big. Gigantic even. Cause I know the secret; I know it's all in timin' and preparation. You gotta know when to be flashy or classy. When to coo and when to howl.

Well, Doctor Roseman said I should take a few days off to recuperate. TV got boring, so I cleaned out some closets. I read all the Cosmos that had been layin' around for months. There were lots of hours to think about what I'd done. All of a sudden I found myself with the bod and the talent but not the cash to get me to New York, to one of those fancy modeling agencies. I had to come up with somethin' to feed my bank account if that was ever gonna happen.

That's where Jess came in.

About a year ago my friend Jess, moved to this po-dunk town outside of Omaha, over on the Iowa side, near the river. The place's crawlin' with porn shops, and strip clubs. She called out of the blue (see what I mean about timin'?) and while I went on and on 'bout my surgery and how I didn't have no money, she told me the real reason she'd called—her old man had split. Then she had one of her brainstorms, said that I should come out there an' we could get a great place, rents were dirt cheap. Hell they should be in the middle of who knows where. An' she could get me a job at the club she worked at. Well, it was time to take my girls out for a test run and I figured, why not?

So I moved into the Riverview apartment complex. River view my ass! You gotta drive half a mile just to see some water and before you even see it, you smell it. But who needs a view anyway, I figured, as long as the place was cheap. But it wasn't. It seemed every day I spent at the Riverview, I found one more lie I had to swallow.

Like for instance, the "gentlemen's club" turned out to be a joint called "Tit-illations." Get it? Tits? Jess thinks it's real clever and that I'm stupid or somethin' when I don't bust a gut every time she laughs at the cleverness.

And the money sucks. Oh, on a good night, a Saturday, I can pull in four, maybe five hundred, but the rest of the time I'm prancin' 'round up there on that joke of a stage for a few drunks. Leon, the owner, he's tryin' to get a lunch crowd but as long as I been there—four and a half weeks—there's never much of a line in front of Leon's Chinese buffet. Buffet, that's another lie. I think you need to have more than one gigantic big bowl of rice, some Chop Suey an' egg rolls to consider what he puts out to be a buffet.

I was bitchin' to Jess one night, complainin' that things just weren't turnin' out the way I expected. She said that I had to give it more time.

"It?" I asked her, "Which *it* are you referrin' to? The rent *it*, the pissy job *it* or the shit heads that come in here *its*?"

"All of *it*!" she said in that scolding way that made me really mad.

"One more month an' I'm outta here. End of conversation."

"You're just pissed because you're lonely. So stop taking it out on me because you need a man." Then she flipped that long blonde hair of hers.

We were sittin' in the back room at the Tit, waitin' for our next set. My chair was wicker and I knew it was gonna leave those criss-cross marks all along the back of my thighs, but I didn't give a shit. I leaned down to pull the sags out of my fishnets; if I looked at her face I'd puke.

"I can have any man I want—whenever I want. I just happen to have certain requirements. Unlike you who'll sleep with anything."

"A girl, such as yourself, is gonna get very lonely each night, all alone with her precious requirements."

I could hear my music startin' up; I stood and yanked at that ugly spangled bra Leon made me wear. An' then I said the only thing I could in a situation like that, "Up yours, Jess."

■   ■   ■

When opportunity knocks you right in the head, you gotta answer . . . or at least take notice. So when I walked out onto the stage that night, it wasn't the three burned out bulbs my eyes kept starin' at but the guy at a back table. His hair was styled with just the right amount of gel. He wasn't wearin' any jewelry, not even a pinkie ring like most all of Leon's friends, even Leon himself wore. An' the very best thing about that guy was that killer suit of his. Some kind of tweedy stuff like from one of them fancy shops in England. He didn't smoke; didn't even have a beer bottle in front of him. He just sat there, eyein' me like I was bein' interviewed for a job instead of grindin' my bare ass against a brass pole.

As the last few notes of "I will Survive" screeched out of the monster speakers, I bent down to pick up my clothes, real slow, gave the guys one last good look while I watched that dude, out of the corner of my eye. Before I got backstage, Leon came up to me, grabbed my arm and told me that Killer Suit wanted a lap dance.

"Let me go put on my Daisy Dukes first."

"He said now, he has an appointment and can't wait."

Leon was holdin' my arm real tight so I jerked away from him, gave him that look of mine. The one that said if he touched me again I'd knock those gold teeth right out of his mouth.

I walked slow. Sashayed my hips as I went. It don't matter what a girl's wearin', it's how she carries herself that really counts. But clothes do help and I snapped that bra back on just so I had somethin' to take off.

Before I could introduce myself, the guy holds out his hand. I didn't want to embarrass the poor sap so I shook it but I could feel he was tryin' to keep me away from him.

"My name's John," he said.

"An' I bet your last name's Doe, or maybe Jones?" I laughed.

"Neither."

"Well, John, I'm Mandy. Did my boss tell ya it's twenty bucks? An' no touchin' my tits."

"That's fine."

I dumped my things on top of the table next to him an' sat down. "The next song should start up in a minute. You want to get your money's worth. If I start now you only get five minutes instead of ten."

"Five minutes should do it," he said, so serious.

"Fine with me, John." I stood up. "Night Train" was playin'. I moved the table away from him so I could get closer and started runnin' my hands across his shoulders. He looked me square in the eyes, sized me up. I leaned over and shook my 38s in his face and he glanced down at 'em, sizin' them up. I turned around, unhooked my bra and lowered myself nice and ladylike into John's lap. The music was slow an' moody; I closed my eyes, feelin' the beat drivin' down my spine and nuzzled his face along my neck. When I leaned back John pushed me away an' started takin' somethin' out of his wallet. I guessed it was my money but instead of cash, he slapped a business card down on the table. An' that's when his face lit up, not from anything I done.

"You're perfect."

"Well . . . I've been told . . ."

"I'd like to offer you a job."

"What the hell do you think I'm doin' here?" He was pissin' me off, treatin' me like that.

"Sit there." He pulled a chair over for me. "I'm an investigator, I specialize in matrimonial discord cases."

"Matrimonial what?"

"When a wife, or husband—mostly wives—have a suspicion that their spouse is cheating on them, they hire me. I send out a decoy, who tries to nail the guy, or gal, in the act."

"Wait a minute. I don't take money to let guys . . ."

"No contact will ever be made. What we do is wire you up and send you out to entice . . . make the guy ask you out on a date. Then you inquire if he's married. He'll say no . . ."

"But you told me these were married guys."

"They always say no. Then you arrange to meet him and get as much on tape as you can. We deliver the evidence to the missus all neat and clean. No fuss, no mauling, no problem."

"And how much do I get paid for bein' a prick teaser?"

He tried to hide his grin by lookin' down into his lap a minute.

Then he looked back at me all serious like. "A hundred a job."

"I'll have to think about it," I told him as I scooped up his card an' then my stuff. "Don't call me, I'll call you."

■   ■   ■

The guy's card said that he was really named John. But his last name wasn't as simple. It was long an' Polish, started with a D, had three i's an' seemed to run for miles along the top of the card. First thing I did, as soon as I got home that night, was call the number printed in big red letters, in the bottom right hand corner. I figured there would be some sort of answerin' machine hooked up to the other end an' I wanted to hear how professional it sounded. After five rings I got this woman an' she told me she was the agency's "service." I made up some phony name an' hung up.

The next day I decided to call the Better Business Bureau. They said John had a license registered but they didn't have any complaints against him so they couldn't tell me much more. That afternoon I drove down to check out the address on his card. Sure enough, there was this dinky place stuck between Scotties Market an' Blockbusters with his name painted on the door.

When I told Jess all about it that night, in the back room of the Tit, she practically exploded all over the place.

"A hundred bucks? Just for flirting with some schmuck? That's all you gotta do?" Then she got this scared look, leaned closer in to me an' said in a quiet voice, "Are ya sure there won't be any danger to yourself?"

"How dangerous can it be? We'll be sittin' in a public place. Hell, it sounds safer than most the dates I been on."

I thought about it all that night, through all my sets. When I spotted Leon I asked him about John. All he knew for sure was that the guy wasn't a regular. But after all my thinkin' an' checkin' the thing that cinched it for me appeared in the newspaper like a sign from God.

It was another one of them price wars. Fares to New York were cheaper than I had ever seen before. With the money I made strippin' an' the extra I could make decoyin' I figured I could be in the Big Apple inside a month. So I booked myself a one-way from Omaha (the biggest airport near Council Bluffs) to New York City. The very next day I called John and told him to "sign me up." He promised there'd be at least two jobs a week. It took some jugglin' but by Thursday night, my regular day off, I was workin' my first decoy job.

■ ■ ■

Like I said before, a girl's got to know when to be flashy and when to be classy. I been in the lounge at the Best Western, over by the dog track before. And as I stood in front of my closet, trying to decide the perfect outfit to wear for my new job, I knew the leopard print spandex would work. The top's cut low and my black lace bra peeks, just a little bit out of the sides. John looked me over real good when I got there. We met at the bar for a drink.

"Maybe next time you could wear something more conservative?" He frowned but I didn't give a shit what he thought so I acted as though I couldn't hear him with all the talkin' in the room. "Now don't think this is the way it'll go down before each job. Because tonight's your first time out, I thought you might be a little nervous so I'm here for you."

I crossed my legs, ran my hand up the shiny black hose on my right leg. "Need I remind you what I do for a living?"

"Need I remind you," he said shooting me such an attitude, "that stripping for a bunch of drunks who know they can't touch you, with bouncers in every corner of the room, ain't exactly the same as being out on your own without any protection?"

I poked my finger down inside my bra. Even though the microphone he'd taped to me was the tiniest thing I'd ever seen, I kept thinkin' it would cause some trouble.

"Okay, okay, I'll watch myself."

"Good." John tossed back what was left of his scotch, slammed the glass down on the bar an' said, "Now, slap me."

"What?"

"Your mark, Albert Coral, just arrived. He's standing by the door, watching us. Make a scene so we can get his attention."

The actress in me kicked in. "You son of a bitch!" I screamed. Then I slapped John so hard even I was surprised. "I can't believe you did this to me! Get outta here! You make me sick."

He wasn't bad himself, as far as actin' ability goes. He looked real hurt, rubbed his cheek a little, stood up an' threw a ten at me. "It's been real." Then he walked outta there like we'd just had a real lover's spat.

I didn't turn to see if anyone was watchin' me, just swiveled my stool back to face the bartender who was askin', "You okay lady? Anything I can do?"

"Yeah, how about another drink." I slid my empty glass across to him.

"Sure thing." He hurried off, glad that I hadn't asked him to do somethin' more difficult.

I admired my nails while I waited. I'd splurged on one of them fancy manicures. I had the girl press little gold stars into the red polish, right on the tip of each nail. I clicked them on the bar as I looked up to watch Mr. Coral in the mirror.

"Hey, you okay?" A young kid, probably just old enough to get his ass into the place plopped down next to me.

"Yeah, I'm fine." I never made eye contact, didn't want him thinkin' I was invitin' him to get any closer.

He straightened the Cornhusker cap on his head, I saw the shine of a big class ring on his fat finger. "Well, I'm glad to hear it. A gorgeous redhead like you shouldn't be sitting here . . ."

"Go away." I didn't have time to dick around.

"Pardon me?"

"Look, kid, go away now while you can still move. Because, if you don't haul your flabby ass offa that stool, I will stab you."

He got that look on his face, sorta like he wanted to laugh but didn't cause he wasn't sure he heard me right. "You'll what?"

I picked up my purse and reached inside. "I will stab you with my nail file; it's very sharp. An' it's so dark in here. What if I missed your leg on account of I'm so upset? I'm sure a stud like you plans on havin' some kids someday."

"You're one crazy bitch," he said right before he walked away.

Albert was still standin' by the door. I had to do somethin' to get him to move.

"There you go." The bartender was back. "One screwdriver for the pretty lady. That'll be three fifty."

I handed him the ten John had given me and asked, "Could you please have the waitress take a martini over to that guy by the door? With my compliments."

The bartender grinned. "You mean Bert? Sure."

John had filled me in on this Mr. Coral. He owned a small jewelry store in town. Mrs. Coral told John that her husband wanted to expand, open another store at the big mall in Omaha. But what he really wanted to do with his life was sing. So he came to the Best Western every Monday and Thursday night cause that's when they had Karaoke competitions. He even had a followin', she said. And oh how he loved martinis.

I watched as Mr. Coral took his drink from the waitress and saw him talkin' to her, no doubt askin' who it was from. She pointed across the room to me. I stared straight ahead, watchin' it all in the mirror. When he waved to me, I looked down, like I didn't see. Ignore a guy and he's yours. It always works. Treat 'em like shit, he'll never leave.

"Ahh, Miss?" Albert Coral tapped me on the shoulder.

I swiveled around, brought my bodacious self right up into clear view. "Yes?" I tossed back my head like Jess does.

"I'd like to thank you for the drink."

"My pleasure," I said it with such fuckin' sincerity I almost made myself sick.

"Mind if I join you?"

I patted the stool next to me. "Please do."

"I couldn't help but notice the guy you were with."

"The asshole I smacked or the jerky kid?"

"The asshole." He twirled the olive speared to a toothpick around in his drink and a diamond ring sparkled on his right hand. It was just big enough to be tasteful lookin'.

He wasn't bad. Medium height, longish straight, dark hair, just brushed his collar in the back. He was wearin' black jeans, a white shirt, a black suede vest an' he smelled great. His face was nice—not too friendly, in that phony way—with just the right amount of teeth so's he didn't look horsey. His eyes were dark and he spoke kinda slow, like he was makin' sure I would catch each word, like it was real important. That's the way he listened, too.

The usual amount of crap got flung around. I told him I was an actress and model. What a coincidence, he said, he was an entertainer. "Really?" I said all impressed and breathless. "By the way, I didn't catch your name." I held out my hand all dainty like. "I'm Mandy. Mandy Monroe."

"Extremely nice to meet you, Mandy." He kissed my fingers. "I'm Bert Coral."

I had to give the bastard credit. He looked me straight in the eye and told me his real name. I'd really expected an alias, like in the movies. Either the guy was too lame to think of somethin' more excitin' or thought he was too slick to get caught. Some guys are like that, think they're wearin' some kinda protective coatin'.

"So, what kind of entertainin' do you do?"

He smiled, so full of himself. "Guess."

Seein' as how I already knew the answer and didn't feel like wastin' too much time, my second guess was, "Singer?"

Typical man, he was really pumped that the conversation revolved around him and his dreams and his talent. I nodded an' smiled, tryin' not to yawn while he went on an' on an' fuckin' on. How he wanted to get a singin' contract but first had to sell off some property. I guessed he meant his store. How he had to get to L.A., out where the music industry was. He talked about half an hour, non-stop, until ten o'clock when some guy announced that the Karaoke would begin.

Bert asked me what my favorite song was.

"Oh, gee, I like 'em all."

"No," he insisted, rubbin' his hands together, "your all time favorite."

"New York, New York," I waited for him to ask why, but he didn't. He was suddenly hoppin' off the bar stool an' dashin' up to some DJ guy.

"First up tonight is a favorite here at the Bluffs Run Best Western, Bert Coral!" The microphone gave out with a shrill screech. "Bert's gonna do 'New York, New York' for us."

The lights got dimmer and the stage got brighter. Bert walked up there like a real pro. He held the microphone in his right hand and the cord in the other, just like I seen Dean Martin do it. He pointed toward me and said, "This one's for the lovely Mandy."

The music switched on an' Bert started off real soft an' gentle. He never took his eyes off me; I could feel all the women there were wishin' they was me. He looked handsome in that light. It was a nice picture: him singin' an' all of us admirin' him up there. By the time he got to the middle part, he got a little louder. I could see why he had some fans, he knew how to work the crowd, just like I do when I dance. By the end, he was beltin' those words out. Each time he got to the New York part it all seemed new an' excitin'. I knew then that he had every freakin' one of us in the palm of his hand. It was truly a breathtakin' experience.

The applause went on forever. The DJ had to hold the next singer back awhile until Bert finished takin' a few more bows. As he made his way to me, people slapped his shoulder, tellin' him how great he was.

"Well? What did you think?" he asked, as if he had to ask.

"I am truly impressed." And I was.

"So then you'll have some dinner with me? To celebrate? After they announce the winner, that is."

John's only instructions had been that I shouldn't let the guy touch me, he didn't say nothin' about eatin' with him.

"Sure, why not."

■   ■   ■

The trophy sat on the table between us like a big gold centerpiece.

"How many of these things do you have?" I asked after we ordered our steaks.

"Twenty-four. But enough about me; we've been talking about me all night. What's your story?"

So I told him a few lies—little ones—but mostly I told him the truth.

"Why do you have to go to New York? I thought you said you were already into modeling."

"Small time. To make it big ya gotta be in new York, or Europe."

"Well, I'm sure you won't have one bit of trouble. I mean, just look at yourself."

"Oh, I ain't worried about my looks." I stretched a little, just enough to pull the front of my dress tighter. His eyes went right in the direction I wanted them to go. "It's gettin' noticed. It's gettin' some hot shot at some big time agency interested."

"Don't worry. I've seen the toothpicks they have in those fashion magazines. I'll let you in on a secret. Men want something to grab onto, know what I mean? A woman with some womanly flesh on her bones." Then he brushed his fingers down my arm.

I thought the time was right so I straightened up an' asked, "So, Bert, tell me, are you married or what?"

"Why do you want to know?" He looked a little angry, kinda suspicious. I didn't want to blow it just when things were goin' so well.

"I just figured a gentleman like you would certainly have somebody."

"Yeah," he said, "I'm married."

I waited for him to add somethin' like . . . but we're separated, or we don't get along . . . some kind of bullshit excuse why he was sittin' at a table with me. But he didn't say another thing about it. Even though I admired his bein' so honest, I did have a job to do. So I figured I should play it like I was upset. Maybe it would force him to say somethin' incriminatin' into my cleavage.

"Then why the hell are you here with me?"

"Good question, I was asking myself the same thing. All I can tell you is that I don't have a good reason; I've never done this before. But I just couldn't resist you. And when you get right down to it, we're only having dinner. After I walk out of here, it's back to my wife. And you'll go back to . . . ?"

"Me? I ain't married."

"There isn't even a fiancé or boyfriend somewhere?"

"Nope, just me an' my roommate Jess in our shitty little apartment." I couldn't believe how goddamn pathetic I sounded. It made me embarrassed thinkin' that John was listenin', back in his office, to my sorry ass self. I could only hope he thought I was connin' the guy.

"Sometimes life sucks, doesn't it? But sometimes it's great, like right now." Then Mr. Albert Coral leaned over an' kissed me. Oh, I heard about those kinds of kisses in songs an' on "The Young and the Restless." But that was the very first time I had one planted on my own lips. I know how sickening it sounds but it was like our souls melted down. The heat rushed through me an' made my heart throb an' my pants wet. I couldn't help myself from takin' a second one an' then a third.

When our food finally came, my appetite was long gone. All I wanted to do was crawl into bed and then all over that sexy man. But instead I worked on my prime rib an' thought. So far Bert hadn't said nothin' that his wife could use. He hadn't lied about bein' married, even said how he was goin' home to her. So what if he told me he was a singer an' left out the jeweler part? There sat the trophy in front of us to prove he was honest about performin'. What had he done so wrong, I asked myself, 'cept have dinner with me? An' steal a few kisses. Why I bet that with all the noise around us the mike hadn't even picked the kissin' part up. We didn't moan or nothin'.

While I was thinkin' through it all Bert opened his mouth like he was gonna say somethin'. Before he could get a sound out, I

said real quick, "Excuse me a sec." Then while he sat there
lookin' all confused, I high tailed it to the Ladies. I didn't have
a plan when I ran into that flowery room, but I sure as hell had
one when I came out.

I stood there by the table with Bert lookin' me up an' down, his
eyes finally stoppin' to check out the paper towels bunched in my
hands. If I read him right, and I was pretty sure I had, he'd go along
with me. If not, I knew it wouldn't take much to convince him.

After plantin' my butt, I laid down the piece of towel I had
written on with my eye liner, in the bathroom. I watched as his
lips mouthed: YOUR WIFE HIRED SOMEONE TO TAIL YOU.
SHE WANTS THE JEWELRY STORE FOR HERSELF. OUR
TABLE'S BUGGED. THE BALD GUY BY THE PHONE TOLD
ME. READ WHAT I WRITE OUT LOUD. When he was done,
Bert looked at me. I knew he believed it cause he hadn't told me
about the store an' there was, in fact, a scary lookin' bald dude
standin' by the phone, who I had picked just because he was there
. . . convenient.

Then I started. "So, I guess there's no chance for us, huh? You
bein' married an' all?"

I wrote frantic like and Bert read: "No, I'm sorry. I love my
wife too much to ever hurt her." He did it real convincin'. But
then I knew him bein' a spotlight junkie like me, he'd do good.

"You won't even meet me back here for one lousy drink tomorrow night?"

He read as I wrote. "No, I'm not gonna risk losing my store for
a one night stand." When he saw those words his eyes got sad
and he turned red.

"You're a real asshole, ya know that?" I stood up, made a lot
of noise so the mike in my bra would get it all. His hands reached
over to grab me but he stopped himself. I smiled that I understood and it was okay. Then I told him, loudly, "You can't just
invite me out an' insult me like this. I have feelins ya know."
Then I handed him a shred of paper with my phone number on
it and a message: GIVE ME AN HOUR THEN CALL ME.

In the car, on the way home I talked to myself, like I forgot
that John was listenin' to every word. I sniffed a little here an'
there for realism. "That's it! I've had it! I don't need this shit;
who the hell does he think he is?" I screamed into my breasts.

■ ■ ■

I was soakin' in the tub when the phone rang—just like I knew it would. I reached over an' picked up the cordless sittin' on the toilet. "Yeah?" I made my voice sound good an' pissed.

"Mandy, considering it was your first time out, you did just fine. But you gotta stop taking the whole thing so personal. Remember, it's just a job."

"It's kinda hard on my ego, ya know? I thought you said these guys always say yes."

"Well," John sputtered like he was runnin' outta gas, "almost always. Who'd a thought you'd find the only saint in Iowa? Forget it. Stop by my office on Monday, I'll cut you a check and set you up with another job."

"Sure thing," I said and hung up.

I couldn't help laughin' as I dried off and got into my robe. "Gee, Johnny, a whole hundred bucks, all for myself. How 'bout you keep your chump change? I got me some serious money to worry about.

I was pourin' myself a vodka when the phone rang. Right on time. I picked up the receiver and cooed like a love bird. "Thank God you're okay, honey. Yeah, your wife's out to get ya alright. But listen, I know just what we should do." If I said it once, I'll keep sayin' it forever—it's all in the timin'.

And the preparation . . . don't forget that part. Boy was I prepared to talk Albert Coral into blowin' that pop stand with me after we grabbed some of wifey's inventory, of course. She'd never be expectin' it an' I figured that good report she was gonna pay John for would keep her off our ass a few days. Then we could fly to New York an' get me interviewed at the Ford Modeling agency. After I signed a contract with them, we'd head for L.A. to get Bert an agent to work on his singin' career. We sure as hell both had more than our share of talent.

"What, honey? Yeah, I felt it too. We got somethin' special." He bought into the whole bad bald guy routine and I hung on the other end of his conversation smellin' like a rose. No one would ever be able to convince him I was really such a dirty girl.

David Goodis

THE PLUNGE

From *Mike Shayne Mystery Magazine,* October 1958

Along with that of Jim Thompson, the fiction of David Goodis was the bleakest, most existential of all the post-World War II noir writers. Early in his career Goodis wrote voluminously for the Mystery/Detective, Air-War, and Weird Menace pulps and produced five fairly well-received but undistinguished suspense novels, most notably Dark Passage (1946) *which was filmed with Humphrey Bogart and Lauren Bacall. Three years in the Hollywood script mill in the late '40s seem to have soured Goodis's outlook to the point of nihilism; the thirteen paperback originals he penned in the '50s and early '60s, beginning with the bestselling* Cassidy's Girl *in 1951, are dark, bitter sagas of lives lived at the edge of common decency, fraught with violence, alcoholism, paranoia, debilitating poverty, failure, and hopelessness. The handful of short stories he published during this period, of which "The Plunge" may be the least known, are likewise grim yet undeniably powerful dramas.*

B. P.

SEVEN OUT OF TEN ARE SLOBS, HE WAS THINKING. THERE WAS no malice or disdain in the thought. It was more a mixture of pity and regret. And that made it somewhat sickening, for he was referring specifically to the other men who wore badges, his fellow-policemen. More specifically still, he was thinking of the nine plainclothesmen attached to the Vice Squad. Only yesterday they'd been caught with their palms out, hauled in before the Commissioner, and called all sorts of names before they were suspended.

But, of course, the suspensions were temporary. They'd soon be back on the job, their palms extended again, accepting the shakedown money with the languid smile that seemed to say, *It's all a part of the game.*

He'd never believed in that cynical axiom, had never let it touch him during his seventeen years on the city payroll. From rookie to Police Sergeant and on up to Detective Lieutenant he'd stayed away from the bribe, rakeoff and conniving and doing favors for certain individuals who required official protection to remain in business.

Of course, at times he'd made mistakes, but they were always clean mistakes. He'd been trying too hard or he was weary from nights without sleep. It was honest blundering and it put no shadows on his record. In City Hall he was listed Grade-A and they had him slated for promotion.

His name was Roy Childers and he was thirty-eight years old. He stood five-feet-ten and weighed a rock-hard one-ninety. It was really rock-hard because he was a firm believer in physical culture and wholesome living. He kept away from too much starches and sweets, smoked only after meals, had a beer now and then, but nothing more than that, and the only woman he ever slept with was his wife.

They'd been married eleven years and they had four children. In a few months Louise would be having the fifth. Maybe five was too many, considering his salary and the price of food these days. But, of course, they'd get along. They'd always managed to get along. He had a fine wife and a nicely arranged way of living and there was never anything serious to worry about.

That is, aside from his job. On the job he worried plenty. It was purely technical worriment because he took the job very seriously and when things didn't go the way he expected, he'd lose sleep and it would hurt his digestion. When he'd been with the Vice Squad, it hadn't happened so frequently. But a year ago he'd become fed up with the Vice Squad, with all the shenanigans and departmental throatcutting and, of course, the never-ending shakedown activity he saw all around him.

He'd requested a transfer to Homicide, and within a few months his dark brown hair showed grey streaks, pouches began to form under his eyes, the unsolved cases put creases at the corners of his mouth. But mostly it was the fact that Homicide also had its slobs and manipulators, its badge-wearing bandits who'd go in for any kind of deal if the price was right.

On more than one occasion he'd been close to grabbing a wanted man when someone tipped off someone who tipped off someone else, with the fugitive sliding away or building an alibi that caused the District Attorney to shrug and say, "What's the use? We've got no case."

So that now, after eleven months of working with Homicide,

there was a lot of grey in Childers' hair, and his mouth was set tighter, showing the strain of work that demanded too much effort and paid too little dividends.

He was sitting at his desk in Homicide, which was on the ninth floor of City Hall. His desk was near the window and the view it gave him from that angle was the slum area extending from Twelfth and Patton Avenue to the river. Along the riverfront the warehouses looked very big in contrast to the two-storey rat-traps and fire-traps where people lived or tried to live or didn't care whether they lived or not.

But he wasn't focusing on the slum-dwellings that breeded filth and degeneracy and violence. His eyes sought out the warehouses, and narrowed in concentration as they came to rest on the curved-roof structure labeled "No. 4" where not so very long ago there'd been a $15,000 payroll robbery, with one night-watchman killed and another permanently blinded from a pistol-whipping.

He'd been assigned to the case three weeks ago, after coming to the Captain and saying it looked like a Dice Nolan job. For one thing, he'd said, Dice Nolan was a specialist at payroll robbery, going in for warehouses along the riverfront and using a boat for the getaway. Nolan had used that method several times before they'd caught up with him some ten years ago.

They gave him ten-to-twenty, and according to the record he'd been let out on parole this year—in the middle of March. Now it was the middle of April and that just about gave him time enough to get a mob together and plan a campaign and make a grab for loot.

Another angle was the pistol-whipping. Dice Nolan had a reputation for that sort of thing, always going for the eyes for some weird reason planted deep in his criminal brain. Childers had said to the Captain, "What makes me sure it's Nolan, I've checked with the parole officers and they tell me he hasn't reported in for the past ten days. He's on a strict probation and he's supposed to show them his face every three days."

The Captain had frowned. "You figure he's still in town?"

"I'm betting on it," Childers had said. "I know the way he operates. He wouldn't be satisfied with a fifteen-grand haul. He'll stick around for a while and then go for another warehouse. He knows every inch of that neighborhood."

"How come you're wise to him?"

"It goes back a good many years," Childers had said. "We were raised on the same street."

The Captain was quiet for some moments. And then, without looking at Childers, he'd said, "All right, go out and find him."

So he'd gone out to look for Nolan and the search took him along Patton Avenue going toward the river, past the rows of tenements where now they were strangers who'd been his childhood playmates, past the gutters where he'd sailed the matchbox-boats, unmindful of the slime and filth because it was the only world he'd known in that far-off time of carefree days.

Days of not knowing what poisonous roots were in the squalor of the neighborhood. Until the time when ignorance was ended and he saw them going bad, one by one, Georgie Mancuso and Hal Berkowski and Freddie Antonucci and Bill Weiss and Dice Nolan.

He'd pulled away from it with a teeth-clenched frenzy, like someone struggling out of a messy pit. He'd promised himself that he'd never breathe that rotten air again, never come near that dismal area where the roaches thrived and a switchblade nestled in almost every pocket. He'd gone away from it, telling himself the exit was permanent, feeling clean. And that was the important thing, to be clean, always to be clean.

He'd been acutely conscious of his own cleanliness as he'd questioned the men in the taprooms and poolrooms along Patton. They looked at him with hostile eyes but were careful to keep the hostility from their voices when they told him, "I don't know" and "I don't know" and "I don't know."

And some of them went so far as to state they were unacquainted with anyone named Dice Nolan. They'd never even heard of such a person. Of course he knew their lying and evasive answers were founded more on their fear of Nolan than on their instinctive dislike of the Police Department.

It told him his theory was correct. Nolan had engineered the payroll heist, and certainly Nolan was still in town.

But that was as far as he'd got with it. There were no further leads, and nothing that could come to a lead. Night after night he'd come home with a tired face to hear his wife saying, "Anything new?" And he'd try to give her a smile as he shook his head.

But it was getting more and more difficult to smile. He knew if he didn't come in with something soon, the Captain would take him off the case. He hated the thought of being taken off the case, he was so very sure about his man, so acutely sure the man was hiding somewhere near. Very near—.

The ringing phone sliced into his thoughts. He lifted it from the hook and said hello and the switchboard girl downstairs said to hold on for just a moment. Then a man's voice said, "This Childers?"

Instantly he had a feeling it was something. He could almost smell it. He said, "Yes," and waited, and heard the man saying, "I'm gonna make it fast before you trace the call. Is that all right with you?"

He didn't say anything. For a moment he felt awfully weary, thinking: It's just some crank who wants to call me some dirty names—.

But then the man was saying, "It's gonna be good if you wanna use it. I got some personal reasons for not liking Dice Nolan. Thing is, I can get you to his girl friend."

Childers reached automatically for a pencil and a pad. The man gave him a name and an address, and the pencil moved very rapidly. Then the call hung up, and Childers leaped from the desk, ran out of the office and down the hall to the elevator.

■　■　■

It was a seventeen-story apartment house on the edge of Lakeside Park. He went up to the ninth floor and down the corridor to room 907. It was early afternoon and he doubted she'd be there. But his finger was positive and persistent on the doorbell-button.

The door opened and he saw a woman in her middle-twenties, and his first thought was, a bum steer. This can't be Dice Nolan's girl.

He was certain she couldn't be connected with Nolan because there was nothing in her make-up that indicated moll or floosie or hard-mouthed slut. She wore very little paint and her hair-do was on the quiet side. There was no jewelry except for a wrist-watch. Her blouse was pale grey, the skirt a darker shade, and he noticed that her shoes didn't have high heels. Again he thought, *Sure, it's a bum steer*. But anyway, he said, "Are you Wilma Burnett?"

She nodded.

"Police," he said, turning his lapel to show her the badge.

She blinked a few times, but that was all. Then she stepped

aside to let him enter the apartment. As he walked in, the quiet neatness of the place was impressed upon him. It was simply furnished. The color motif was subdued, and there wasn't the slightest sign of fast or loose living.

He frowned slightly, then got rid of it and put the official tone in his voice as he said, "All right, Miss Burnett. Let's have it."

She blinked again. "Let's have what?"

"Information," he said. "Where is he?"

"Who?" She spoke quietly; her expression was calm and polite. "Who are you talking about?"

"Dice." He said it softly.

It seemed she didn't get that. She said, "I don't know anyone by that name."

"Dice Nolan," he said.

For a moment she said nothing. Then, very quietly, "I know a Philip Nolan, if that's who you mean."

"Yes, that's him." And he thought, *Let's see if we can rattle her*. His voice became a jabbing blade, "I figured you'd know him. He pays your rent here, doesn't he?"

It didn't do a thing. There was no anger, not even annoyance. All she did was shake her head.

He told himself it wasn't going the way he wanted it to go. The thing to do was to hit her with something that would throw her off balance, and while he groped for an idea he heard her saying, "Won't you sit down?"

"No thanks," he said automatically. He folded his arms, looked at her directly and spoke a trifle louder. "You're doing very nicely, Miss Burnett. But it isn't good, it just can't work."

"I don't know what you mean."

"Yes you do." And he put the hard smile of law-enforcement on his lips. "You know exactly what I mean. You know he's wanted for robbery and murder and you're trying to cover for him."

That'll do it, he thought. *That'll sure enough break the ice*. But it didn't work that way, it didn't come anywhere near that. For a few moments she just stood there looking at him. Then she turned slowly and walked across the room. She settled herself in a chair near the window, folded her hands in her lap, and waited for his next remark. Her calm silence seemed to say, *You're getting nowhere fast*.

He said to himself, *Easy now, don't push it too hard.* Yet his voice was somehow gruff and impatient, more demand than query. "Where can I find him? Where?"

"I don't know."

"Not much you don't." He took a step toward her, his mouth tightening. "Come on, now. Let's quit playing checkers. Where's he hiding out?"

"Hiding?" Her eyebrows went up just a little. "I didn't know he was hiding."

"You're a liar."

She gazed past him. She said, "Tell me something. Is this the only way you can gather information? I mean, does your job require that you go around insulting people?"

He winced. He knew she had him there, and if this was really checkers, she'd scored a triple-jump. But then he thought, *It's only the beginning of the game, we can get her to talk if we take our time and play it careful—.*

Again he smiled at her. This time it was an easy pleasant smile, and his voice was soft. "I'm sorry, Miss Burnett. I shouldn't have said that. I apologize."

"That's quite all right, Mister—" she hesitated.

"Childers," he said. "Lieutenant Childers—Homicide." He pulled a chair toward hers, sat down and went on smiling at her. "It'll help both of us if you tell me the truth. I'm looking for a crook and a killer, and you're looking to stay out of prison."

"Prison?" Her eyebrows went up again. "But I haven't done anything—"

"I want to be sure about that. I'm hoping you can prove you're not an accessory."

"Meaning what?"

"Meaning if you're helping him to hide, you're an accessory after the fact. That's a very serious charge and I've known cases when they've been sent up for anywhere from three to five years."

She didn't say anything.

He leaned forward slightly and said, "Of course you understand that anything you say can be held against you."

"I'm not worried about that, Lieutenant. I haven't broken any laws."

"Well, let's check on it, just to be sure." His smile remained pleasant, his voice soft and almost friendly. "Tell me about yourself."

She told him she was a free-lance commercial artist. She said her age was twenty-seven and for the past several years she'd been a widow. Her husband and two children had died in an auto accident. There was no emotion in her voice as she talked about it, but he saw something in her eyes that told him this was genuine and she'd been through plenty of hell. He thought, *She's really been hit hard.*

■　■　■

Then all at once it occurred to him that she was something out of the ordinary. It wasn't connected with her looks, although her looks summed up as extremely attractive. It was more on the order of a feeling she radiated, a feeling that came from deep inside and hit him going in deep, causing him to frown because he had no idea what it was and it made him uncomfortable.

He heard himself saying, "I owe you another apology. That crack I made about Nolan paying the rent. I guess that wasn't a nice thing to say."

"No, it wasn't." She said it forgivingly. "But I know you didn't mean to be personal. You were only trying to find out—"

"I'm still trying," he reminded her. His manner became official again. "I want to know all about you and Nolan."

For a long moment she was quiet. Then, her voice level and calm, "I can't tell you where he is, Lieutenant. I really don't know."

"When'd you last see him?"

"A few nights ago."

"Where, exactly?"

"Here," she said. "He came here and we had dinner."

He leaned back in the chair. "You cooked dinner for him?"

"It wasn't the first time," she said matter-of-factly.

He pondered on the next question. He wasn't looking at her as he asked, "What is it with you and Nolan? How long have you known him?"

"About a month." And then, before he could toss another question, she volunteered, "We met in a cocktail lounge. I was alone, and I think I ought to explain about that. I don't usually go out alone. But that night I felt the need for company, and although I drink very little I really needed a lift. I'd been going with someone who disappointed me, one of those awfully nice gentlemen who leads you on until you happen to find out he's married—"

"Rough deal." He looked at her sympathetically.

She shrugged. "Well anyway, I must have looked very lonesome and unhappy. I don't know how we got to talking, but one word led to another and I didn't know where it was leading. But to be quite truthful about it, I really didn't care. He told me he'd just been released from prison and it had no effect on me, except that somehow I appreciated the blunt way he put it. Then he asked me for my phone number and I gave it to him. Since then we've been seeing each other steadily. And if you're curious as to whether I sleep with him—"

"I didn't ask you about that."

"I'll tell you anyway, Lieutenant." There was a certain quiet defiance in her voice, and it showed in her eyes along with all the pain and suffering that had been too much to take, that had led to the breaking-point where a woman grabs at almost anything that comes along.

She said, "Yes, I sleep with him. I sleep with the ex-convict you're looking for. I know what he is and I don't care. And if that makes me a criminal, you might as well put the handcuffs on me and take me in."

Childers stood up. He turned away from her and said, "You shouldn't have said all those things. It wasn't necessary."

She didn't reply. He waited for her to say something, but there was no sound in the room, and after some moments he moved toward the door. As he opened it, he glanced at her. She sat there bent far forward with her head in her hands. He murmured, "Goodbye, Miss Burnett," and walked out.

■   ■   ■

His wife and four children were looking at him and he could feel the pressure of their eyes. Their plates were empty and on his plate the pot roast and vegetables hadn't been touched. He gazed down at the food and wondered why he couldn't eat it. There was an empty feeling inside him but it wasn't the emptiness of needing a meal. It was something else, something unaccountable. The more he tried to understand it, the more it puzzled him.

"What's wrong with you?" his wife asked. It was the fifth or sixth time she'd asked it since he'd come home that evening. He couldn't remember what answers he'd given her.

Now he looked at her and said wearily, "I'm just not hungry, that's all."

The children began chattering, and the youngest, five-year-old Dotty, said, "Maybe Daddy ate some candy bars. Whenever I eat too much candy bars, I can't eat my supper."

"Grown-ups don't eat candy bars." It was Billy, aged nine.

And Ralph, who was seven, said, "Grown-ups can do anything they want to."

No *they can't*, Childers said without sound. *They sure as hell can't.*

Then he asked himself what he meant by that. The answer came in close, danced away, went off very far away and he knew there was no use trying to reach for it.

He heard six-year-old Agnes saying, "Mommie, what's the matter with Daddy?"

"You ask him, honey," his wife said. "He won't tell me."

"What's there to tell?" Childers said loudly, the irritation grinding through his voice.

"Don't shout, Roy. You don't have to shout."

"Then lay off me. You've said enough."

"Is that the way to talk in front of the children?"

His voice lowered. "I'm sorry, Louise." He tried to smile at her. But his mouth felt stiff and he couldn't manage the smile. He said lamely, "I've had a bad day. It's taken a lot out of me—"

"That's why you need a good meal," she said. And then, getting up and coming towards him, "Tell you what. I'll warm up your plate and—"

"No." He shook his head emphatically. "I don't feel like eating and that's all there is to it."

"I wonder," she murmured.

He looked at her. "You wonder what?"

"Nothing," she said. "Let's skip it—"

"No we won't." He heard the suspicion in his voice, couldn't understand why it was there, then felt it more strongly as he said, "You started to say something and you're gonna finish it."

She didn't say anything. Her head was inclined and she was regarding him with puzzlement.

"Come on, spill it," he demanded. He rose from the table, facing her. "Tell me what's on your mind."

"Well, all I wanted to say was—"

"Come on, come on, don't stall."

"Say, who're you yelling at?" Louise shot back at him. She put her hands on her somewhat wide hips. "You're not talking to some tramp they've dragged in for questioning. I'm your wife and this is your home. The least you can do is show some respect."

"Mommie and Daddy are fighting," little Agnes said.

"And maybe it's about time," Louise said. She kept her hands on her hips. "I knew we had a show-down coming. Well, all right then. You told me to say what's on my mind and I'll say it. I want you to drop this Nolan case."

He stared at her. "What's that you said?"

"You heard me. I don't have to repeat it. I know your work is important, but your health comes first."

She pointed to the untouched food on his plate. "I had a feeling it would come to that. I've seen you walking in at night looking as if you were ready to drop. I knew it would reach the point where you wouldn't be able to eat. First thing you know, you'll have an ulcer."

He felt a thickness in his throat, a wave of tenderness and affection came over him, and he reminded himself he was a very fortunate man. This woman he had was the genuine article, an absolute treasure. His health and happiness and welfare were her primary concern. In her eyes he was the only man in the world, and after more than a decade of marriage, the knowledge of her feeling for him was something priceless.

He looked at her plump figure that was now over-plump with pregnancy, look at her disordered hair that seldom enjoyed the luxury of a beauty parlor because she was too busy taking care of four children. Than he looked at her hands, reddened and coarse from washing dishes and doing the laundry and scrubbing the floors. He said to himself, *She's the best, she's the finest.* And he wanted very much to put his arms around her.

But somehow he couldn't. He didn't know why, but he couldn't. He stood there paralyzed with the realization that she was waiting for his embrace and he could not respond.

All at once he felt a frantic need to get out of the house. He groped for an excuse, and without looking at her, he said, "I told the Captain I'd see him tonight. I'm going down to the Hall."

He turned quickly and walked toward the front door.

*   *   *

But his meeting was not with the Captain, his destination was not City Hall. He walked a couple of blocks, climbed into a taxi, and said to the driver, "Lakeside Apartments."

"Right you are," the driver said.

Am I? he asked without sound. *Am I right?* And there was no use trying to answer the question, his brain couldn't handle it. Yet somehow he knew that from a purely technical standpoint this move was the logical move, and he was making it according to the book. It amounted to a stake-out, going there to watch and wait for Dice Nolan. The thing to do, of course, was plant himself across the street from the apartment-house and keep an eye on the front-entrance.

Twenty minutes later he stood in the darkness under a thickly leafed tree diagonally opposite the Lakeside Apartments. A car was parking across the street and instinctively he reached inside his jacket to check his shoulder-holster. But there was nothing there to check. He'd forgotten to put on his holster and the .38 it carried.

You've never done that before, he thought. And then, with a slight quiver that went down from his chest to his stomach and up to his chest again, *What's the matter here? What the hell is happening to you?*

Across the street someone was getting out of the car. But it wasn't Nolan, it was just a tiny middle-aged woman with a tiny dog in her arms. She walked inside the apartment-house and the car moved away.

Childers leaned against the tree. For a moment he wished the tree-trunk were a pillow and he could sink into it and fall asleep. It had nothing to do with weariness. It was simply and acutely the need to get away from everything, especially himself. The thought brought a blast of anger, aimed at his own eyes, his own mind, and in that moment he fought to think only in terms of his badge and the job he had to do.

*   *   *

He glanced at his wristwatch. The hands pointed to seven forty-five. Assuming that Nolan would be coming to see her tonight, assuming further she'd be cooking dinner for Nolan, the chances were that Nolan hadn't yet arrived. In Nolan's line of business, dinnertime was anywhere from eight-thirty to midnight. So it figured he had time to hurry back home and get his gun and come back here and—

His brain couldn't take it past that. Before he fully realized what he was doing, he'd crossed the street and entered the apartment-house.

In the elevator, going up to the ninth floor, he wasn't thinking of Nolan at all. Somewhat absently, he straightened his tie and smoothed the hair along his temples. There was a small mirror in the elevator but he didn't look into it. He knew that if he looked at himself in the mirror, he'd see something that he didn't want to see.

The elevator was going up very fast, going up and up, and there was something paradoxical and creepy about that. Because it wasn't the way going up should seem or feel at all. It was more like falling.

■   ■   ■

He pressed the doorbell-button. A few moments passed and then the door of 907 opened and she stood there smiling at him. He wasn't surprised to see the smile. He had a feeling she'd been expecting him. It wasn't based on anything in particular. It was just a feeling that this was happening the way it had to happen, there was no getting away from it.

"Hello, Wilma," he said.

She went on smiling at him. She didn't say anything. But her hand came up in a beckoning gesture that told him to enter the apartment. In the instant before he stepped through the doorway, he noticed she was wearing a small apron. And then, as she closed the door behind him, he caught the smell of cooking.

"Excuse me a moment," she said, walking past him and into the kitchen. "I have something on the stove—"

He sat down on the sofa. He looked down at the carpet. It was a solid-color broadloom, a subdued shade of grey-green. But as he listened to her moving around in the kitchen, as he visualized her hands preparing a meal for Dice Nolan, the color he saw was an intense green, a furious green that seemed to blaze before his eyes.

Before he could hold himself back, he'd lifted himself from the sofa and walked into the kitchen. His voice was tight as he said, "When is he due here?"

She was pouring seasoning into a pot on the stove. "I'm not expecting him tonight."

He moved toward the stove. He looked into the pot and saw it was lamb stew and there was only enough for one person.

Again she was smiling at him. "You don't put much trust in me, do you, Lieutenant?"

"It isn't that," he said. "It's just—" He didn't know how to finish it. Then, without thinking, without trying to think, "I wish you'd call me Roy."

Her smile faded. She gave him a level look that almost seemed to have substance, hitting him in the face and going into him, drilling in deep. For a very long moment the only sound in the kitchen was the stew simmering in the pot.

And then, her voice down low near a whisper, she said, "Is that the way it is?"

He nodded slowly. His eyes were solemn.

"Are you sure?" she murmured. "I mean—"

"I know what you mean," he interrupted. "You mean it can't be happening this fast. You want to tell me it's impossible, we hardly know each other—"

"Not only that," she said, her eyes aiming down to the thin band of gold on his finger. "You're a married man."

"Yes," he said bluntly. "I'm married and I have four children and my wife will soon have another."

She looked past him. She seemed to be speaking aloud to herself as she murmured, "I think we'd better talk about something else—"

"No." He came near shouting it. "We'll talk about this. Can't you see the way it is? We're got to talk about this."

She shook her head. "We can't. We just can't, that's all. We'd better not start—"

"We've started already. It was started as soon as we met each other."

His voice became thick as he went on, "Listen to me, Wilma. I tried to fight it the same as you're fighting it now. But it's no use. It's a thing you can't fight. It's like a sickness and there's no cure. You know that as well as I do. If I thought for a minute it hasn't hit you the same as me, I wouldn't be saying this. But I know it's hit you. I can see it in your eyes."

She tried to shake her head again. She was biting her lip. "If only—" she couldn't get it out. "If only—"

"No, Wilma." He spoke slowly and distinctly. "We won't have any *ifs* or *buts*. A thing like this happens once in a lifetime. It's more important than anything else. It's—"

He hadn't heard the sound of the key turning in the lock. He hadn't heard the door opening, the footsteps coming toward the kitchen. But now he saw her staring eyes focused on something behind his back. He turned very slowly and the first thing he saw was the gun.

Then he was looking at the face of Dice Nolan.

■   ■   ■

Nolan said very softly, "Keep talking." His lips scarcely moved as he said it, and there was nothing at all in his eyes.

The prison pallor seemed to harmonize with the granite hardness of his features. Except for a deep scar that twisted its way from one eyebrow to the other, he was a good-looking man with the accent on strength and virility. He was only five-nine and weighed around one-sixty, but somehow he looked very big standing there. *Maybe it's the gun*, Childers thought in that first long moment. *Maybe that's what makes him look so big*.

But it wasn't the gun. Nolan held it loosely and didn't seem to attach much importance to it. Now he was looking at Wilma and his voice remained soft and relaxed as he said, "You fooled me, girl. You really fooled me."

"Maybe I fooled myself," she said.

"Could be," Nolan murmured. He shifted his gaze to Childers. "Hey you, I told you to keep talking."

"I guess you heard enough," Childers said. "Saying more would make no sense."

Nolan grinned with only one side of his mouth. "Yeah, I guess so." Then suddenly the grin became a frown and he said, "You look sorta familiar. Don't I know you from someplace?"

"From Third and Patton," Childers said. "From playing cops and bums when we were kids."

"And playing it for real when we grew up," Nolan murmured,

his eyes sparked with recognition. "You put the pinch on me so many times I lost count. I guess ten years in stir does something to the memory. But now I remember you, Childers. I damn well oughta remember you."

"You're a bad boy, Dice. You were always a bad boy."

"And you?" Dice grinned again, his eyes flicking from Childers to Wilma and back to Childers. "You're the goodie-goodie—the Boy Scout who always plays it clean and straight."

Suddenly he chuckled. "Goddam, I'm getting a kick out of this. What're you gonna do when your wife finds out?"

Childers didn't reply. He wasn't thinking of his wife, nor of Wilma, nor of anything except the fact that he was a Detective Lieutenant attached to Homicide and he'd finally found the man he'd been looking for.

"Well? What about it?" Dice went on chuckling. "Tell me, Childers. How you gonna crawl outta this mess?"

"Don't let it worry you," Childers murmured. "You better worry about your own troubles."

The chuckling stopped. Nolan's eyes narrowed. The words seemed to drip from his lips. "Like what?"

"Like skipping parole. Like carrying a deadly weapon."

Nolan didn't say anything. He stood there waiting to hear more.

Childers let him wait, stretching the quiet as though it was made of rubber. And then, letting it out very slowly, very quietly, "Another thing you did, Dice. You pulled a job on the waterfront three weeks ago. You heisted warehouse number four and got away with fifteen thousand dollars. You murdered a night-watchman and the other one is permanently blinded. And that does it for you, bad boy. That puts you where you belong. In the chair."

"You—" Nolan choked on it. "You can't pin that rap on me. I didn't do it."

Childers smiled patiently. "Don't get excited, Dice. It won't help you to get excited."

"Now listen—" The sweat broke out on Nolan's face. "I swear to you, I didn't do it. Whoever engineered that deal, they fixed it so the Law would figure it was me. When I read about it in the papers, I knew what the score was. I knew that sooner or later you'd be looking for me—"

"It sounds weak, Dice. It's gonna sound weaker in the court-room."

Nolan's features twisted and he snarled, "You don't hafta tell me how weak it sounds. I wracked my brains, trying to find an alibi. But all I got was zero. I knew if I was taken in for grilling, I wouldn't have a chance. That's why I skipped parole. That's why I'm carrying a rod. I ain't gonna let them burn me for something I didn't do."

Childers frowned slightly. For an instant he was almost ready to believe Nolan's statement. There was something feverishly convincing in the ex-con's voice and manner. But then, as he studied Nolan's face, he saw that Nolan's eyes were aimed at Wilma, and he thought, *It's not me he's talking to, it's her. He's trying to sell her a bill of goods. He wants her to think he's clean, so when he walks out of here she'll be going along with him.*

And then he heard himself saying through clenched teeth, "She won't buy it, Nolan. She knows you're a crook and a killer and no matter how many lies you tell, you can't make her think otherwise."

Nolan's eyes remained focused on Wilma. His face was expressionless as he said, "You hear what the man says?"

She didn't reply. Childers looked at her and saw she was gazing at the wall behind Nolan's head.

"I'm telling you I'm innocent," Nolan said to her. "Do you believe me?"

She took a deep breath, and before she could say anything, Childers grabbed her wrist and said, "Please—don't fall for his line, don't let him play you for a sucker. You walk out of here with him and you're ruined."

Her head turned slowly, her eyes were like blades cutting into Childers' eyes. She said, "Let go of my wrist, you're hurting me."

Childers winced as though she'd hit him in the face. He released his burning grip on her wrist. As his hand fell away, he was seized with a terrible fear that had no connection with Dice Nolan's presence or the gun in Nolan's hand. It was the fear of seeing her walking out of that room with Nolan and never coming back.

His brain was staggered with the thought, and again he had the feeling of falling, of plunging downward through immeasurable space that took him away from the badge he wore, the desk he occupied at Homicide in City Hall, his job and his home and his family. *Oh God*, he said without sound, and as the plunge became swifter he made a frantic try to get a hold on himself, to stop the descent, to face this issue and see it for what it was.

He'd fallen victim to a sudden blind infatuation, a maddened craving for this woman whom he'd never seen before today. And that didn't make sense, it wasn't normal behavior. It was a kind of lunacy and what he had to do here and now was—

But he couldn't do anything except stand there and stare at her, his eyes begging her not to leave him.

And just then he heard Dice Nolan saying, "You coming with me, Wilma?"

"Yes," she said. She walked across the kitchen and stood at Nolan's side.

Nolan had the gun aiming at Childers' chest. "Let's do this nice and careful," Nolan said. "Keep your hands down, copper. Turn around very slowly and lemme see the back of your head."

"Don't hurt him," Wilma said. "Please don't hurt him."

"This won't hurt much," Nolan told her. "He'll just have a headache tomorrow, that's all."

"Please, Philip—"

"I gotta do it this way," Nolan said. "I gotta put him to sleep so we'll have a chance to clear out of here."

"You might hit him too hard." Her voice quivered. "I'm afraid you might kill him—"

"No, that won't happen," Nolan assured her. "I'm an expert at this sort of thing. He won't sleep for more than ten minutes. That'll give us just enough time."

Childers had turned slowly so that now he stood with his back to them. He heard Nolan coming toward him and his nerves stiffened as he visualized the butt of the revolver crashing down on his skull. But in that same instant of anticipating the blow he told himself that Nolan would be holding the barrel instead of the butt, Nolan's finger would be away from the trigger.

In the next instant, as Nolan came up close behind him, he ducked going sideways, then pivoted hard and saw the gun-butt flashing down and hitting empty air. He saw the dismay on Nolan's face, and then, grinning at Nolan, he delivered a smashing right to the belly, a left hook to the side of the head, another right that came in short and caught Nolan on the jaw. Nolan sagged to the floor and the gun fell out of his hand.

As Childers leaned over to reach for the gun, Nolan grunted and lunged with what remaining strength he had. His shoulder made contact with Childers' ribs, and as they rolled over, Nolan's hands made a grab for Childers' throat. Childers raised his arm, hooked it, and bashed his elbow against Nolan's mouth. Nolan fell back, going flat and sort of sliding across the kitchen floor.

Childers came to his knees, and went crawling very fast, headed toward the gun. He picked it up and put his finger through the trigger-guard. As his finger came against the trigger with the weapon aiming at Nolan's chest, a voice inside him said, *Don't— don't—*. But another voice broke through and told him, *You want that woman and he's in the way, you gotta get rid of him.*

Yet even as he agreed with the second voice, even as the rage and jealousy blotted out all normal thinking, he was trying not to pull the trigger. So that even when he did finally pull it, when he heard the shot and saw Nolan instantly dead with a bullet through the heart, he thought dazedly, *I didn't really mean to do that.*

He lifted himself to his feet. He stood there, looking down at the corpse on the floor.

Then he heard Wilma saying, "Why did you kill him?"

He wanted to look at her. But somehow he couldn't. He forced the words through his lips, "You saw what happened. He was putting up a fight. I couldn't take any chances."

"I don't believe that," she said. And then, her voice dull, "It's too bad you didn't understand."

He stared at her. "Understand what?"

"When I agreed to go away with him—I was only pretending. It was the only way I could keep him from shooting you."

He felt a surge of elation. "You—you really mean that?"

"Yes," she said. "But it doesn't matter now." Her eyes were sad for a moment, and then the bitterness crept in as she pointed toward the parlor and said, "You'd better make a phone call, Lieutenant. Tell them you've found your man and you've saved the State the expense of a trial."

He moved mechanically, going past her and into the parlor. He picked up the phone and got the P.D. operator and said, "Get me Homicide—this is Childers."

The next voice on the wire was the Captain's, and before Childers could start talking, he heard the Captain saying, "I'm glad you called in, Roy. You can stop looking for Dice Nolan. We got something here that proves he's clean."

"Yeah?" Childers said. He wondered if it was his own voice, for it seemed to come from outside of himself.

"We got the man who did it," the Captain said. "Picked him up about an hour ago. We found him with the payroll money and the gun he used on those night-watchmen. He's already signed a confession."

Childers closed his eyes. He didn't say anything.

The Captain went on, "I phoned you at your home and your wife said you were on your way down here. Say, how come it's taking you so long?"

"I got sidetracked," Childers said. He spoke slowly. "I'm at the Lakeside Apartments, Captain. You better send some men up here. It's Apartment nine-o-seven."

"A murder?"

"You guessed it," Childers said. "It's a case of cold-blooded murder."

He hung up. In the corridor outside there was the sound of footsteps and voices and someone was shouting, "Is everything all right in there?" Another one called, "Was that a shot we heard?"

Wilma was standing near the door leading to the corridor and he said to her, "Go out and tell them it was nothing. Tell them to go away. And keep the door closed. I don't want anyone barging in here."

She went out into the corridor, closing the door behind her. Childers walked quickly to the door and turned the lock. Then he crossed to the nearest window and opened it wide. He climbed out and stood on the ledge and looked down at the street nine floors below.

I'm sorry, he said to Louise and the children, *I'm terribly sorry.* And then, to the Captain, *You'll find the gun on the kitchen table. His fingerprints and my fingerprints and I'm sure you'll believe her when she tells you how it happened, how someone who's tried so hard to be clean can slip and fall and get himself all dirty.*

But as he stepped off the ledge and plunged through empty darkness, he began to feel clean again.

Dorothy B. Hughes

THE BLACK AND WHITE BLUES

From *New Copy—A Book of Stories and Sketches*, 1959

The novels of Dorothy B. Hughes are taut and disturbing set pieces, conveying a fine sense of place and character—one of the reasons such outstanding titles as In a Lonely Place, Ride the Pink Horse, *and* The Fallen Sparrow *were made into successful films starring such major actors as Humphrey Bogart, Robert Montgomery, and John Garfield. A noted critic, Hughes also wrote insightful reviews of mystery fiction for many years and penned the definitive biography of Erle Stanley Gardner,* The Case of the Real Perry Mason *(1978). She produced relatively few short stories during her esteemed career—none better than this haunting, beautifully stylized tale of jazz music, extortion, and racial hatred which originally saw print in a Columbia University Press mainstream anthology.*

B. P.

HERE IS HOW THEY PLAYED IT. REAL DRAGGY AND LOUD. A LOT of brass and tin and shouting and snapping fingers. "I wanna be with you f'jes 'n hou-ah . . ." Big buck Negro waving his trombone and shouting it. A lot of sweat on his lip and a big diamond on his finger. "I wanna be with you jes al-ways . . ."

Here is where the two girls were standing. Little white girl with a blur of black hair sticking in her eyes. A blot of scarlet felt on the back of her head. Hands dug in the pockets of a scarlet jacket. Talking up to the big white girl with the nearsighted eyes and ugly ankles.

" 'F I had any money I could look as good as her. I could have a new dress every Sat'day night and a marcel and have all the fellas dancing with me. Where does she get all her dough? Tha's what I'd like to know. Where does she get it?"

Nearsighted girl says she's a manicurist. Gets big tips.

"Where does she get it, tha's all I wanta know. Every Sat'day night, a new dress. Him taking her home in his big car."

Big girl says to keep quiet. He's coming up to ask her to dance.

"I'm sicka dancing with that little squirt. I'm sicka going home in his rattletrap. Her riding in big cars and having a marcel every Sat'day night."

Little boy with sweaty shirt asking her to dance.

"Who? Me?"

"Come on, le's dance. You don't care, do you, Lil?"

Girl with ugly ankles don't care. Go on and dance with him.

Little girl wraps her red arm around his neck. Bobs the scarlet blob on the back of her head.

"You're a swell dancer, kid. Le's do some fancy stuff."

Little girl's red shoes slide and kick and hop.

"C'n I take you home tonight? There's room for Lil, too. C'n I take you home?"

"I d'know. I guess so. Wait out at the side. Dance up by the orchestra. I like to hear them sing. Lookit the diamonds those Negroes wear. I bet they make a lot of money playing in an orchestra."

"You bet they do. They make a lot of money. You oughta see the swell cars they drive."

"Big cars?"

"You bet. Real cars."

■ ■ ■

Fat black Negro plays the drums. Silk shirt sticking to his fat black arms. Little skinny light-faced Negro plays the horn. Diamond stickpin in his tie. Buck Negro plays the old trombone. Diamonds and sweat on him. Three yellas playing three saxophones. One looks like the white guy taking tickets downstairs. One's got on a linen suit and he's got a straight nose and a little mouth, hardly any kink in his hair. Nice-looking Negro, looks almost white. He stands up on a chair and plays the clarinet and the other Negroes shout and smack their hands together. Woman playing the piano, black straight oily bob, lots of rouge on her brown cheeks, lots of rouge on her big mouth. Earrings in her ears, pink silk dress and a big rope of pearl beads. Got a voice like a crazy crow. Got a voice like a hell's imp sitting on her tongue. Shouting up at the clarinet player, shaking their fingers at each other and smiling at each other. Swaying her shoulders at the clarinet Negro.

"Tha's real music. Clap hard. Play it again. Go on play it again."

"I wanna be with you all night long . . ."

Red blot nodding. "Dance close up to the orchestra. I wanta hear it."

Little boy's sweaty arm tight around the belt of the red jacket. "That Negro's looking at you. Come on, le's go out in the middle and do some fancy stuff."

"No, I wanta dance up close to the orchestra. I wanta learn the words."

"That Negro's looking at you."

"Don't be dumb. You don't own me. I wanta hear the words."

Lights up on the balcony changing from yellow to blue to red. Electric stars twinkling through the blue ceiling. Feet shuffling. Hot Missouri air coming cool out of the ventilators.

"Let me take you home, will you? I got the car outside."

"Wait out at the side. I gotta talk to Lil."

"There's room for Lil, too."

Little girl looks over his shoulder at a new green, flowered dress.

"I d'know. I think Lil's got a date. You wait out at the side."

Here is how they played Home Sweet Home. Real slow and brassy. Little girl goes up to big girl standing under the Spanish arch.

"Lissen. I got a date to go home."

Big girl twists her hands. "Will there be room for me?"

Red blob shakes. "It ain't with him t'night. I'm sick'n tired of riding in his rattletrap. You ain't scared to go home alone, are you?"

"No, I ain't scared. What'll I tell your mother? Who's it with?"

"You don't know him. Don't tell her nothing. I'll be in early. I'm gonna ride in a real car t'night."

■　■　■

Big girl goes on down the steps. Little girl watches all the dancers going down the steps. Shirt sleeves and marceled hair and new dresses. She stands where he can't help seeing her. He brushes right by. He's looking at that marcel and new green, flowered dress with the cherries on it. He don't even see the red jacket. He goes right by without speaking or anything. All the dancers go pushing downstairs to get their hats and coats out of check. Buck Negro and Negro woman going out together. Negro orches-

tra pushing through the white crowd. Pretty soon the Negro in
the linen suit comes along. Little girl smiles at him.

He sets down his black instrument case. He pulls down his
Panama and straightens his tie. She smiles at him again.

"Was the music all right tonight?" He says it easy-like.

"You bet. It was wonderful. It was wonderful a'right. I had a
wonderful time."

He picks up his case getting ready to go downstairs.

"'F I could only find the gennleman that ast to take me home.
I lost him in the crowd after the dance."

He sets down the case. "Maybe I could find him for you. It's
thinning out some down there."

She shakes her head. "Nev' mind. I guess I'll get home a'right.
My girl friend I come with had to go home early. I thought I'd
get home a'right but I missed him in all the crowd. I guess I'll
get home a'right though. Don't you bother."

He fingers his tie. "Do you live far?"

She pulls the red blob back on her head. "Not so far. I gotta
transfer, that's all. It's kinda hard transferring and the street cars
don't run so often this time o'night." She looks up at him and
smiles again.

He turns the big diamond on his finger. "Would you—would
you want me to give you a lift?"

She looks quick at him. "Have you got a car?"

He nods his head.

"What kind of a car you got?"

"Chrysler 2. Pretty good car. I git it bran' new when I come
on this job here. I drove here in it. It runs pretty good."

Little girl looks downstairs. Most everybody's gone. "Sure
you can give me a lift. I guess my gennleman friend missed
me."

Negro looks around, but everybody's gone downstairs. "I'll get
my car and drive around to the side door and you can come out
and get in. Then you won't have to walk none to where it's
parked."

She brushes the black blur out of her eye. "Come to the front
door. The's a fella that's jealous of me always watches the side
door. He might start a fight. He's that kind. He's jealous. Come
to the front door with it."

There is a Chrysler painted cream color with green lines on it.
A big open car. Little girl slides into the front seat.

"Gee, this is grand. This is sure a swell car. It musta cost you
a lot of money. You must make a lot of money in that orchestra
to have a swell car like this. You must make a lot of money."

"Make enough. Make more than most of them 'cause I double.
I play saxophone and clarinet both and I can play the horn too,
and the drums. Makes you more money when you can double."

▪ ▪ ▪

Little girl sighs. "It must be grand to have a lot of money and a
car like this. I could ride forever in a car like this."

"You'd get pretty tired of it. Riding forever."

Little girl laughs. "I wouldn't get tired. I might get hungry,
though. Don't dancing make you hungry, though? It makes you
starving, actually starving."

"Playing does too. I'm hungry now."

"So'm I. I'm starving."

Negro drives kinda slowly. "You haven't told me which way
you live. Or would you like to eat something first?"

"You bet I would." Little girl nods her head. "You bet I would.
Le's drive out to Swope Park. They got barbecues out there. It's
a swell drive out, too. You know where it is?"

He points. "It's south out there, isn't it? That big park where
the zoo is."

"Tha's where."

"Do you live out that way?"

She shakes her head. "I live the other way. But they got swell
barbecues out there. If we went someplace around here, you
might see that fella that's jealous of me and always trying to start
a fight."

"Maybe he might be out to Swope Park."

She shakes her head. "No, he won't. You won't see nobody out
there this time o'night. You won't have to worry about seeing
nobody. Everybody out there's minding their own business, not
trying to start fights."

It's a long drive out to Swope Park from the dance hall. Swope
Park is big and dark and winding roads through it and a lot of
trees. Down at the end of one road right by the Raytown bridge,
there's a whole bunch of barbecue stands. All you got to do is
honk your horn and a boy with a white cap on his head ambles

over and gets your order. Then you can eat it in the car or you can drive away to one of the roads and eat it. Only you got to bring back the pop bottles.

∎   ∎   ∎

Chrysler don't park up under the lights. Parks over at the side and honks the horn. Boy comes over for the order.

"I wanta barbecue chicken and some cherry pop."

"Le's have two chickens and two pork. Sure you want pop? We got some of this left." He pats the pocket of his coat.

"I want pop." Boy goes off to fill orders. "I don't like gin much. I don't care much for it."

"It's good gin. I paid seven dollars a quart for it."

Little girl shakes her head. "I don't like the taste of it much. It tastes funny. I like pop better."

He pulls out the bottle and looks at it. Shakes it. "Tha's good. Ain't near enough for two. Ain't hardly enough for one."

"What would you done if you'd taken her home? Then what would you a done?" Little girl laughs at him.

He scowls. "I tell you I don't take her home none. I tell you I don't never take her home—hardly ever."

Little girl shakes her head. "Bet she'd like to have you take her home. Bet she likes you best of any of you. Lookit the way she looks at you and shakes her finger at you."

∎   ∎   ∎

He tilts his hat to the back of his head. "Tha's just part of the business. I tell you tha's part of the business, her and me looking at each other. It don't mean nothing."

Little girl tilts her nose. "I bet it does."

"No sir, it don't! I tell you she's married. She's married to that fella she goes home with. She's married to Jim, the trombone player. She used to be married to Fritz, the big fat fella playing the drums. They got separated and now she's married to Jim. She don't want me none."

Little girl pushes a dimple in her chin. "I bet she'd like you. You're the best-looking one of you. I bet she'd like you to take her home."

He laughs kind of apologizingly. "You're just talking."

She looks up at him with her black eyes. "No, I ain't. I mean it. I c'n tell the way she looks at you. What kind of a car has Jim got?"

"It's a Chevvie."

"Only a Chevvie?"

Tilts his hat over his eyes again. "He can't 'ford no better. He got a wife to s'port. He can't 'ford nothing but a Chevvie."

Boy with the white cap coming with the order.

"Bet she'd rather ride in your Chrysler than Jim's Chevvie."

Two big hot chicken-barbecue sandwiches wrapped up in paper napkins. Two big hot pork barbecues wrapped up in greasy paper napkins. Ice cold bottle of cherry pop.

"Here's your money. Keep the change." He waves the bill aside with his hand and the big diamond sparkles. The bill comes off a big roll he can't hardly close his hand around.

Little girl sucks at the bottle. "Le's drive on one of them other roads where there won't be nobody to bother us. We c'n bring back the pop bottle after while."

" 'Fraid somebody might see you with me?" He lets the car out easy-like, big Chrysler moving smooth and easy-like.

"I ain't afraid of nobody seeing us. Only it's nicer out on the roads where nobody is. Too many bugs flying around the lights.

Big car slips quietly onto a road where there's trees and no lights or nothing.

"In Chi you wouldn't have to be afraid of nobody saying nothing. In Chi, colored gennleman can go any place he wants to. In Chi, I goes out with white girls all the time. Goes any place. Downtown to the movies and to dancing places. In Chi it's different."

Little white girl wipes the grease off her mouth. "I bet it's a real town. I ain't never been there. I ain't never been any place much."

Negro takes a bite out of his second barbecue. "It's a real place. Sometimes I gets kinda lonesome for it and seeing nice people. Here in this town, you can't get acquainted with hardly no one. Here in this town, there ain't no chance to get acquainted."

Little girl laughs. "You got acquainted with me all right. Did you honest notice me dancing out on the floor?"

"I say I did. I saw that little red hat of yours and your red coat. I been noticing you every Sat'day night since we came. Didn't you see me noticing you?"

·　·　·

Little girl takes her last drink of pop and throws the bottle out of the car. "I didn't know. Sometimes I thought you were and sometimes I thought you were looking at that yellow-haired girl with the new dress every Sat'day night."

"Which one do you mean?"

Little girl looks hard at him. "Go on. You know who I mean. Laura Pearl. That girl with the marcel every Sat'day night. She lives on my street. She has a date every Sat'day night. My mother won't let me have a date to go. She makes me go with Lil, the girl friend I was with tonight. Lil, she lives in our house. I bet I could have a date and ride home in a big car if I had a new dress and a marcel every Sat'day night. She's a manicurist and she gets tips. I work in a store. I'm a stock girl. I don't get no chances to get no tips. I don't get a new dress hardly ever."

He wipes his fingers on a white silk handkerchief. "You don't need new dresses, little white girl. You're pretty enough as you is. You don't need no new dresses."

She tosses the red blot on her head. "Now you're just talking."

"No I ain't. I means it. I been noticing you ever since we come here."

He takes off his Panama hat and lays it careful-like in the back seat. His hair's got a little tiny kink in it, brushed down with lavender water.

"Wouldn't you like a little taste of gin to wash down those sandwiches?"

She shakes her head. "I don't like the taste of it. It tastes funny."

He tilts up the bottle. "Mmm. It's good gin. It costs seven dollars a quart. It's 'most as good as the gin you get in Chi."

. . .

He puts his arm around the back of the seat. Little white girl sits down in the far corner from him.

"Bet you're rich to pay seven dollars a quart for gin. That's 'most as much as I make all week. That roll of bills you got. Bet you're rich."

He laughs. "I ain't rich. I ain't got much." He takes out the roll of bills and puts his fingers around it and they don't hardly meet. "I ain't got so much, but there's plenty more where it comes from."

She touches the roll and her eyes shine. "How much in there? I've never seen so much money, not even in banks. How much you got there?"

He ruffles it. "Maybe four hundred—maybe five. I been playing with the other fellas in intermissions tonight. I been shooting a little bit. Luck's been with me tonight." He puts the roll back in his pocket. He smiles. "Luck's sure enough with me tonight. Your fella missing you and me coming along." He touches her shoulder. She moves around kind of sideways.

"Is that a real diamond?" She points to his hand on the back of the seat. "Is that diamond real?"

■ ■ ■

He puts his arm down where she can see it. "Sure it's real. Sure it's real."

"It's the biggest diamond I ever seen. It's a whopper."

"It's good enough. Ain't so big as some of the fellas got, but it's a real one. Cost me five hundred dollars. Got it offen a friend of mine in Chi."

"It must sure be grand to have a lot of money and diamonds and a Chrysler and live in a big place like Chicago."

He puts his arm round back on the seat again. "It ain't so bad. It ain't so bad when I c'n get acquainted with somebody like you." He drops his arm onto her shoulders. He edges over to her.

"Don't."

"What's the matter? I likes you a lot. You're so pretty and sweet. Don't you like me none?"

■ ■ ■

She tries to move farther in the corner but there's no farther.

"You better take me home. It's time I went home."

"What you want to go home for? It's nice out here. Nice and quiet and ain't nobody around. Nobody round but you and me, little pretty white girl." Negro's voice is slow and soft and easy-like.

She can't get no farther away. "You take me home. Now! Quick! Don't touch me. Don't you dare to touch me. Don't—" She can't get away.

■ ■ ■

"You dirty nigger!" She wipes at her mouth with the back of her hand. "You dirty nigger. They'll lynch you for this. They'll lynch you!" She scrubs at her mouth.

He laughs easy-like. "What you getting mad about? What you talking that way for?"

"It ain't talk." Her eyes are like bullets. "You ain't in Chicago now. You're in Missouri. In Missouri they lynch niggers for what you done. They'll lynch you, you dirty nigger."

He looks around over his shoulder. He laughs, not so easy-like. "Ain't nobody around here. You say so yourself. Ain't nobody knows."

She scrubs at her mouth. "They're gonna know. Ain't no nigger can kiss me and get away with it." She spits. "They'll lynch you. This is Missouri. Niggers can't take out white girls in Missouri."

He looks over his shoulder. He leans toward her. "Nobody'll know lessen you tell. And you ain't gonna tell!"

She looks scared over her shoulder. She's moving away and he's leaning towards her. She throws back her head and laughs and laughs.

"Ain't I the only one what knows? What about Lil? She didn't go home early. I just told you that so I'd get a good ride home for once instead of in that little squirt's rattletrap. Lil never goes home till she sees me start out. She was standing there outside when we drove off. And what about the boy at the barbecue? Didn't he see us? What about the pop bottle I threw away here? Why d'ya think I threw it away instead of taking it back? Just so's that boy would remember. You c'n stop me from telling maybe, but they'll get you just the same, you dirty nigger. They'll lynch you sure."

He wipes his forehead with his white silk handkerchief. "You ain't gonna tell nobody, are you? I didn't hurt you. I didn't mean to do anything. Honest. I didn't think you'd care. You ain't gonna tell anybody?" He wipes his forehead again and his handkerchief is damp.

"You bet I'm gonna tell. Just because you're rich with a big car and diamonds and I ain't got nothing, you thought you could insult me. You bet I'm gonna tell, you dirty nigger. They'll lynch you."

He looks over his shoulder and twists the white silk handkerchief. "Maybe—maybe I could fix things up. Maybe you wouldn't tell nobody and make me lose my job and get in trouble."

"They'll lynch you."

He pulls the diamond ring off his finger. "Wouldn't you like to have this? I didn't mean nothing. Would you like this ring for your finger?"

She slants a glance at it. She doesn't touch it.

"Wouldn't you like it? I don't need all that money. I don't need none of it. Wouldn't you like to have it maybe and not say anything to nobody? Wouldn't you like to buy you a pretty new dress and have this ring for your finger? Wouldn't you like it? I didn't mean nothing. I wouldn't want you to say nothing to nobody."

She takes the ring and looks at it. She takes the bills. "You drive me home quick. I'll think about it."

The car goes so easy and fine. It rolls up quiet on a dark street before a sagging frame house. The engine keeps going.

Negro whispers, "You won't say nothing. You'll keep those and not say nothing. I didn't mean no harm. I wouldn't want you telling nobody. You won't say nothing."

"Is this diamond real?"

■　■　■

Here's the way they play those Negro blues. Blowing on horns and hitting cymbals and pounding on the piano and everybody shouting. Woman with rouge on her brown face smiling up at the new clarinet Negro, big tall Negro with gold in his mouth. She smiling up at him and shaking her finger and him standing on a chair and blowing hard on the clarinet. Big buck Negro with sweat on his face and diamonds on his hands shouting it out. "I wanna be with you f'jes 'n hou-ah . . ."

Here's the Spanish arch where the girl with the big ankles and nearsighted eyes stands. The little squirt of a boy in his sweaty shirt stands beside her. They both look out on the floor where new red shoes are doing fancy steps with a different partner every time. Black hair with a marcel in it, keeping it from blurring her eyes. And a new red dress with red flowers on the shoulder.

Manager is pretty mad. That good clarinet-playing Negro went back to Chicago. Gave up his job and went back. Didn't say why, just acted kinda nervous. Didn't want to stay no more. Fritz, the orchestra owner, was pretty mad. Clarinet Negro borrowed some money offa him to go on. That Negro woman wailed and said she wouldn't stay neither, but she did.

"I wanna be with you f'jes' 'n hou-ah . . ."

John Lutz

HIGH STAKES

From *The Saint,* June 1984

A *few years ago, John Lutz published* Single White Female, *a suspense novel so good it should be studied seriously by anyone attempting the form. Hollywood turned it into* SFW Seeks Same, *a very good movie that critics and audiences loved. Over a three-decade career, Lutz has written virtually every kind of crime story, and done well by all of them. His continuing characters are a diffident man named Fred Carver, and a troubled man named Alo Nudger. Both rank among the most vivid creations of our time. Look for such Lutz titles as* Hot *and* Ride the Lightning, *stories on the cutting edge of contemporary crime fiction.*

E. G.

ERNIE FOLLOWED THE BELLHOP INTO THE CRUMMY ROOM AT the Hayes Hotel, was shown the decrepit bathroom with its cracked porcelain, the black-and-white TV with its rolling picture. The bellhop, who was a teenager with a pimply complexion, smiled and waited. Ernie tipped him a dollar, which, considering that Ernie had no luggage other than the overnight bag he carried himself, seemed adequate. The bellhop sneered at him and left.

After the click of the door latch, there was thick silence in the room. Ernie sat on the edge of the bed, his ears gradually separating the faint sounds outside from the room's quietude—the thrumming rush of city traffic, a very distant siren or occasional honking horn, the metallic thumping and strumming of elevator cables from the bowels of the building. Someone dropped something heavy in the room upstairs. A maid pushed a linen cart with a squeaky wheel along the hall outside Ernie's door. Ernie bowed his head, cupped his face in his hands, and stared at the worn pale blue carpet. Then he closed his eyes and sought the temporary anonymity of interior darkness.

Ernie's luck was down. Almost as low as Ernie himself, who stood a shade over five-foot-four, even in his boots with the built-up heels. Usually a natty dresser, tonight he'd disgraced his slender frame with a cheap off-the-rack brown suit, a soiled white shirt, and a ridiculous red clip-on bow tie. He'd had to abandon his regular wardrobe at his previous hotel in lieu of settling the bill. Ernie had a face like a conniving ferret's, with watery pinkish eyes and a long, bent nose. His appearance wasn't at all deceptive. Ernie ferreted and connived.

He had spent most of his forty years in the starkly poor neighborhood of his birth, and if he wasn't the smartest guy around, he did possess a kind of gritty cunning that had enabled him to make his own erratic way in the world. And he had instinct, hunches, that led to backing the right horse sometimes, or playing the right card sometimes. Sometimes. He got by, anyway. Getting by was Ernie's game, and he just about broke even. He was not so much a winner as a survivor. There were people who resented even that.

One of those people was Carl Atwater. Ernie thought about Carl, opened his eyes, and stood up from the sagging bed. He got the half-pint of rye out of his overnight bag and went into the bathroom for the glass he'd seen on the basin. He tried not to think about Carl and the thousand dollars he owed Carl from that card game the last time he'd been here in his home town. He poured himself a drink, sat at the nicked and scarred plastic-topped desk, and glanced around again at the tiny room.

Even for Ernie this was a dump. He was used to better things: he didn't always slip into town on the sly and sign into a fleabag hotel. If he hadn't needed to see his sister Eunice to borrow some money—not the thousand he owed Carl, just a couple of hundred to see him down to Miami—he wouldn't be here now, contemplating how he would bet on the roaches climbing the wall behind the bed if someone else were here to lay down some money on which one they thought would be first to reach the ceiling.

He smiled. What would Eunice think of him betting on cockroaches? She wouldn't be surprised; she'd told him for years that gambling was a sickness, and he had it bad. Maybe she was right, harping at him all the time to quit betting. But then, she'd never hit the big one at Pimlico. She'd never turned up a corner of a hole card and seen a lovely third queen peeking out. She'd never . . .

The hell with it. Ernie got two decks of cards from a suit coat pocket. He squinted at the decks, then slipped the marked one back into the pocket. Ernie always made it a point to carry a marked deck. A slickster in Reno had shown him how to doctor the cards so that only an expert could tell, and then only by looking closely. He broke the seal on the straight deck and dealt himself a hand of solitaire. He always played fair with himself. Two minutes after he'd switched on the lamp, tilting the yellowed shade to take the glare off the cards, he was lost in that intensity of concentration that only a devout gambler can achieve.

After losing three games in a row, he pushed the cards away and rubbed his tired eyes.

That was when someone knocked on the door.

Ernie sat paralyzed, not only by fear of Carl Atwater but by fear of what all gamblers regard as their enemy—the unexpected. The unexpected was what gave the dice a final unlikely tumble, what caused the favorite horse to stumble on the far turn, what filled inside straights for novice poker players. This time what the unexpected did was the worst it had ever done to Ernie; it delivered two very large businesslike individuals to his hotel room. They had a key, and when their knock wasn't answered they opened the door and walked right in.

They were big men, all right, but in the tiny room—and contrasted with Ernie's frailness—they appeared gigantic. The larger of the two, a lantern-jawed ex-pug type with a pushed-in nose and cold blue eyes, smiled down at Ernie. It wasn't the sort of smile that would melt hearts. His partner, a handsome dark-haired man with what looked like a knife scar down one cheek, stood wooden-faced. It was the smiling man who spoke.

"I guess you know that Carl Atwater sent us," he said. He had a deep voice that suited his immensity.

Ernie swallowed a throatful of marbles. His heart ran wild. "But . . . how could anyone know I was here? I just checked in."

"Carl knows lots of desk clerks in hotels all over the city," the smiler said. "Soon as you checked in, we heard about it and Carl thought you rated a visit." He grinned wider and lazily cracked his knuckles. The sound in the small room was like a string of exploding firecrackers. "Don't dummy up on us, Ernie. You know what kind of visit this is."

Ernie stood up without thinking about it, knocking his chair over backward. "Hey, wait a minute! I mean, Carl and I are old buddies, and all I owe him is an even thousand bucks. I mean, you got the wrong guy! Check with Carl—just do me that favor!"

"It's precisely because you only owe a thousand dollars that we're here," the dark-haired one said. "Too many people owe Carl small sums, welshers like yourself. You're going to be an example for the rest of the petty four-flushers, Ernie. It will be a bad example. They won't want to follow it. They'll pay their debts instead, and that will add up to a lot of money."

"There ain't no good ways to die," the smile said, "but some ways is worse than others."

Both men moved toward Ernie, slowly, as if wanting him to fully experience his dread. Ernie glanced at the door. Too far away. "Just check with Carl! Please!" he pleaded mindlessly, back-pedaling on numbed legs. He was trembling. The bone-crushers kept advancing. The window was behind Ernie, but he was twelve stories above the street. The fleabag room wasn't air-conditioned, so the window was open about six inches. Corner a rat and watch it instinctively choose the less immediate danger. Ernie whirled and flung himself at the window. He snagged a fingernail in the faded lace curtain, felt the nail rip as he hurled the window all the way open. The smiler grunted and lunged at him, but Ernie scampered outside onto the ledge with speed that amazed.

A gargantuan hand emerged from the open window. Ernie shuffled sideways to avoid it. He pressed his quaking body back against the brick wall and stared upward at the black night sky, the stiff summer breeze whipping at his unbuttoned suit coat.

The smiler stuck his huge head out the window. He studied the narrowness of the ledge on which Ernie was balanced, stared down at the street twelve stories below. He exposed a mouthful of crooked teeth and laughed a rolling, phlegmy rumble. The laugh was vibrant with emotion, but not humor.

"I told you some ways to die was worse than others," he said. "You're part worm, not part bird." He pulled his head back inside and shut the window. Ernie got a glimpse of sausage-sized fingers turning the lock.

Be calm, he told himself, be *calm!* He was trapped on the ledge, but his situation was much improved over what he had been a few minutes ago.

Then he really began to analyze his predicament. The concrete ledge he was poised on was only about six inches wide—not the place to go for a walk in his dress boots with their built-up slick leather heels. And just to his right, the ledge ended four feet away where the side of the building jutted out, and there were no other windows Ernie might be able to enter. To his left, beyond the locked window to his room, was a window to a room that did have an air conditioner. The old rusted unit extended from the window about three feet. Not only would that window be firmly fastened closed against the top of the unit, but there was no way to get around or over the bulky, sloping steel squareness of the air conditioner to reach the next window.

Ernie glanced upward. There was no escape in that direction either.

Then he looked down.

Vertigo hit him with hammer force. Twelve stories seemed like twelve miles. He could see the tops of foreshortened street lights, a few toylike cars turning at the intersection. His mind whirled, his head swam with terror. The ledge he was on seemed only a few inches wide and was barely visible, almost behind him, from his precarious point of view. His legs quivered weakly; his boots seemed to become detached from them, seemed to be stiff, awkward creatures with their own will that might betray him and send him plunging to his death. He could see so far—as if he were flying. Ernie clenched his eyes shut. He didn't let himself imagine what happened to flesh and bone when it met the pavement after a twelve-story drop.

He shoved himself backward against the security of the wall with what strength he had left, his hands at his sides, his fingernails clawing into the mortar. That rough brick wall was his mother and his lover and every high card he had ever held. It was all he had. He was hypocrite enough to pray.

But the terror seeped into his pores, into his brain and soul, became one with him. A thousand bucks, a lousy thousand bucks! He could have gone to a loan shark, could have stolen something and pawned it, could have begged. He could have . . .

But he had to do something now. Now! He had to survive.

Not looking down, staring straight ahead with fear-bulged eyes, he chanced a hesitant, shuffling sideways step to his left, back toward his window. He dug his fingertips into the bricks as he moved, wishing the wall were soft so he could sink his fingers deep into it. Then he was assailed by an image of the wall coming apart like modeling clay in his hands, affording no support at all, sending him in a horrifying breathless arc into the night. He tried not to think about the wall, tried not to think about anything. This was a time for the primal raw judgment of fear.

Ernie made himself take another tentative step. Another. He winced each time his hard leather heels scraped loudly on the concrete. The material of his cheap suit kept snagging on the rough wall at his seat and shoulders, the backs of his legs. Once, the sole of his left boot slid on something small and rounded— a pebble, perhaps—with a rollerlike action that almost caused him to fall. The panic that washed over him was a cold dark thing that he never wanted to feel again.

Finally, he was at the window. He contorted his body carefully, afraid that the night breeze might snatch it at any second, craned his neck till it hurt, and peered into his room.

It was empty. The bonecrushers had left. The threadbare furniture, the bed, the hard, worn carpet, had never looked so sweet. One of Ernie's hands curled around the window frame, came in contact with the smooth glass. He could see the tarnished brass latch at the top of the lower frame, firmly lodged in the locked position.

He struck at the window experimentally. The backward force of the blow separated him from the brick wall. Air shrieked into his lungs in a shrill gasp, and he straightened his body and slammed it backward, cracking his head on the wall, making him dizzy and nauseated. He stood frozen that way for a full minute.

Gradually, he became aware of a coolness on his cheeks—the high breeze drying his tears. He knew he couldn't strike the glass hard enough to break it without sending himself in an unbalanced lean out over the street to death waiting below.

Carl's bonecrushers were probably already having a beer somewhere, counting Ernie as dead. They were right. They were professionals who knew about such things, who recognized death when they saw it. Ernie's lower lip began to tremble. He wasn't an evil person; he'd never deliberately done anything to harm anyone. He didn't deserve this. *No one deserved this!*

He decided to scream. Maybe somebody—one of the other guests, a maid, the disdainful bellhop—would hear him.

"Help! Help!"

He almost laughed maniacally at the hopelessness of it. His choked screams were so feeble, lost on the wind, absorbed by the vast night. He could barely hear them himself.

As far back as he could remember, desperation had been with him as a dull ache in the pit of his stomach, like an inflamed appendix threatening to burst. If it wasn't a friend, it was surely a close acquaintance. He should be able to deal with it if anyone could.

Yet he couldn't. Not this time. Maybe it inevitably had to come to this, to the swift, screaming plunge that had so often awoken him from dark dreams. But tonight there would be no awakening, because he wasn't dreaming.

Ernie cursed himself and all his ancestry that had brought him to this point. He cursed his luck. But he would not let himself give up; his gameness was all he had. There was always, for the man with a feel for the angles, some sort of edge against the odds.

His pockets! What was in his pockets that he might use to break the window?

The first object he drew out was a greasy comb. He fumbled it, almost instinctively lunged for it as it slipped from his fingers and dropped. He started to bow his head to watch the comb fall, then remembered the last time he'd looked down. He again pressed the back of his head against the bricks. The world rocked crazily.

Here was his wallet. He withdrew it from his hip pocket carefully, squeezing it as if it were a bird that might try to take flight. He opened it, and his fingers groped through its contents. He explored the wallet entirely by feel, afraid to look down at it. A few bills, a credit card, a driver's license, a couple of old IOU's that he let flutter into the darkness. He kept the stiff plastic credit card and decided to drop the wallet deliberately. Maybe someone below would see it fall and look up and spot him. The odds were against it, he knew. This was a bad neighborhood: there were few people on the sidewalks. What would happen is that somebody would find the wallet, stick it in his pocket, and walk away. Ernie started to work the bills, a ten and two ones, out of the wallet, then decided it wasn't worth the effort and let the wallet drop. Money wouldn't help him where he was.

There was a slight crack between the upper and lower window frames. Ernie tried to insert the credit card, praying that it would fit.

It did! A break! He'd gotten a break! Maybe it would be all he'd need!

He craned his neck sideways to watch as he slid the credit card along the frame and shoved it against the window latch. He could feel warmer air from the room rising from the crack and caressing his knuckles. He was so close, so close to being on the other side of that thin pane of glass and safe!

The latch moved slightly—he was sure of it! He pressed harder with the plastic card, feeling its edge dig into his fingers. He could feel or see no movement now. Desperately, he began to work the card back and forth. His hands were slick with perspiration.

The latch moved again!

Ernie almost shouted with joy. He would beat this! In a minute or five minutes the window would be unlocked and he would raise it and fall into the room and hug and kiss the worn carpet. He actually grinned as he manipulated his weakened fingers to get a firmer grip on the card.

And suddenly the card wasn't there. He gasped and snatched frantically, barely feeling the card's plastic corner as it slipped all the way through the crack into the room. He saw it slide to the bottom of the window pane, bounce off the inside wooden frame, and drop to the floor. From where he stood, he could see it lying on the carpet. Lying where it could no longer help him.

Ernie sobbed. His body began to tremble so violently that he thought it might shake itself off the ledge. He tried to calm himself when he realized that might actually happen. With more effort than he'd ever mustered for anything, he controlled himself and stood motionless.

He had to think, think, think! . . .

What else did he have in his pockets?

His room key!

He got it out and grasped it in the palm of his hand. It was affixed to no tag or chain, simply a brass key. He tried to fit it into the narrow crack between the upper and lower window frames, but it was far wider than the credit card: he couldn't even insert the tip.

Then he got an idea. The putty holding the glass in its frame was old and chipped, dried hard from too many years and too many faded layers of paint.

Ernie began to chip at the putty with the tip of the key. Some of it came loose and crumbled, dropping to the ledge. He dug with the key again and more of the dried putty broke away from the frame. He would have to work all the way around the pane, and that would take time. It would take concentration. But Ernie would do it, because there was no other way off the ledge, because for the first time he realized how much he loved life. He flexed his knees slightly, his back still pressed to the hard bricks, and continued to chip away at the hardened putty.

After what seemed like an hour, a new problem developed. He'd worked more than halfway around the edges of the window pane when his legs began to cramp painfully. And his knees began trembling, not so much from fear now as from fatigue. Ernie stood up straight, tried to relax his calf muscles.

When he bent to begin work again, he found that within a few minutes the muscles cramped even more painfully. He straightened once more, felt the pain ease slightly. He would work this way, in short shifts, until the pain became unbearable and his trembling legs threatened to lose all strength and sensation. He would endure the pain because there was no other way. He didn't let himself consider what would happen if his legs gave out before he managed to chip away all the putty. Cautiously he flexed his knees, scooted lower against the wall, and began wielding the key with a frantic kind of economy of motion.

Finally, the putty was all chipped away; lying in triangular fragments on the ledge or on the sidewalk below.

Ernie ran his hand along the area where the glass met the wood frame. He felt a biting pain as the sharp edge of the glass sliced into his finger. He jerked the hand back, stared at his dark blood. The finger began to throb in quick rhythm with his heart, a persistent reminder of mortality.

His problem now was that the pane wouldn't come out. It was slightly larger than the perimeter of the window frame opening, set in a groove in the wood, so it couldn't be pushed inward. It would have to be pulled out toward the street.

Ernie tried fitting the key between the wood and the glass so he could lever the top of the pane outward. The key was too wide.

He pressed his back against the bricks and began to cry again. His legs were rubbery; his entire body ached and was racked by occasional cramps and spasms. He was getting weaker, he knew, too weak to maintain his precarious perch on the narrow ledge. If only he still had the credit card, he thought, he would be able to pry the glass loose, let it fall to the sidewalk, and he could easily get back inside. But then if he'd held onto the card he might have been able to force the latch. The wind picked up, whipped at his clothes, threatened to fill his suit coat like a sail and pluck him from the ledge.

Then Ernie remembered. His suitcoat pocket! In the coat's inside pocket was his deck of marked cards! His edge against the odds!

He got the cards out, drew them from their box and let the box arc down and away in the breeze. He thumbed the top card from the deck and inserted it between the glass and the wooden frame. He gave it a slight twist and pulled. The glass seemed to move outward.

Then the card tore almost in half and lost all usefulness.

Ernie let it sail out into the night. He thumbed off the next card, bent it slightly so that it formed a subtle hook when he inserted it. This time the glass almost edged out of its frame before the card was torn. Ernie discarded that one and worked patiently, almost confidently. He had fifty more chances. The odds were with him now.

The tenth card, the king of diamonds, did the trick. The pane fell outward top first, scraped on the ledge, and then plummeted to shatter on the street below.

On uncontrollably shaking legs, Ernie took three shuffling sideways steps, gripped the window frame and leaned backward in a stooped position, toward the room's interior.

Then he lost his grip.

His left leg shot out and his shoulder hit the wooden frame. Gravity on both sides of the window fought over him for a moment while his heart blocked the scream in his throat.

He fell into the room, bumping his head on the top of the window frame as he dropped, hitting the floor hard. A loud sob of relief escaped his lips as he continued his drop, whirling into unconsciousness.

■ ■ ■

He awoke terrified. Then he realized he was still lying on his back on the scratchy, worn carpet, on the motionless, firm floor of his hotel room, and the terror left him.

But only for a moment.

Staring down at him was Carl Atwater, flanked by his two bonecrushers.

Ernie started to get up, then fell back, supporting himself on his elbows. He searched the faces of the three men looming over him and was surprised to see a relaxed smile on Carl's shrewd features, deadpan indifference in those of his henchmen. "Look, about that thousand dollars . . ." he said, trying to ride the feeble ray of sunshine in Carl's smile.

"Don't worry about that, Ernie, old buddy," Carl said. He bent forward, offering his hand.

Ernie gripped the strong, well-manicured hand, and Carl helped him to his feet. He was still weak, so he moved over to lean on the desk. The eyes of the three men followed him.

"You don't owe me the thousand anymore," Carl said.

Ernie was astounded. He knew Carl; they lived by the same unbreakable code. "You mean you're going to cancel the debt?"

"I never cancel a debt," Carl said in an icy voice. He crossed his arms, still smiling. "Let's say you worked it off. When we heard you checked in at the Hayes, we got right down here. We were in the building across the street ten minutes after you were shown to this room."

"You mean the three of you? . . ."

"Four of us," Carl corrected.

That was when Ernie understood. The two bonecrushers were pros; they would never have allowed him to escape, even temporarily, out the window. They had let him get away, boxed him in so that there was no place to go but out onto the ledge. The whole thing had been a setup. After locking the window, the two bonecrushers had gone across the street to join their boss. Ernie knew who the fourth man must be.

"You're off the hook," Carl told him, "because I bet a thousand dollars that you'd find a way off that ledge without getting killed." There was a sudden genuine flash of admiration in his smile, curiously mixed with contempt. "I had faith in you, Ernie, be-

cause I know you and guys like you. You're a survivor, no matter
what. You're the rat that finds its way off the sinking ship. Or
off a high ledge."

Ernie began to shake again, this time with rage. "You were
watching me from across the street. The three of you and whoever
you placed the bet with . . . All the time I was out there you were
watching, waiting to see if I'd fall."

"I never doubted you, Ernie," Carl told him.

Ernie's legs threatened to give out at last. He staggered a few
steps and sat slumped on the edge of the mattress. He had come
so close to dying; Carl had come so close to backing a loser. "I'll
never place another bet," he mumbled. "Not on a horse, a football game, a roulette wheel, a political race . . . nothing! I'm
cured, I swear it!"

Carl laughed. "I told you I know you, Ernie. Better than you
think. I've heard guys like you talk that way hundreds of times.
They always gamble again, because it's what keeps them alive.
They have to believe that a turn of a card or a tumble of the
dice or a flip of a coin might change things for them, because
they can't stand things the way they are. You're like the rest of
them, Ernie. I'll see you again sooner or later, and I'll see your
money."

Carl walked toward the door. The bonecrusher with the knife
scar was there ahead of him, holding the door open. Neither big
man was paying the slightest attention to Ernie now. They were
finished with him, and he was of no more importance than a
piece of the room's worn-out furniture.

"Take care of yourself, Ernie," Carl said, and they went out.

Ernie sat for a long time staring at the floor. He remembered
how it had been out on that ledge; it had changed him permanently, he was convinced. It had wised him up as nothing else
could. Carl was wrong if he thought Ernie wasn't finished gambling. Ernie knew better. He was a new man and a better man.
He wasn't all talk like those other guys. Carl was mistaken about
him. Ernie was sure of it.

He would bet on it.

Robert J. Randisi

COP WITHOUT A SHIELD

From *Mystery Monthly*, August 1976

While much of Robert J. Randisi's early crime work was overlooked, his recent novels such as The Turner Diaries *and* Alone with the Dead *have brought him the kind of attention he's long deserved. Randisi is one of those writers who improves year by year, each novel truer to character and theme, and even more skillfully paced than the previous one. Here is a memorable example of Randisi's work.*

E. G.

THE "TRIAL ROOM" HAS BEEN DESCRIBED BY COPS AS THE PLACE where "the department tries its best to lower the boom on some dumb cop who was just trying to do his job."

On this particular occasion, the hearing involved Jonas Quarterman, a not-so-dumb sergeant of detectives.

"Sergeant Quarterman? Have you anything to say before I give my decision in this case?" asked the trial commissioner. He was a big-bellied—what they liked to call "well-fed"—desk jockey of about fifty-five who hadn't seen the street in the line of duty since Eisenhower was president. He was also a full inspector.

Quarterman, a large, big-boned man of thirty-five, a veteran of twelve years in the department, knew when he rose from his chair what the decision would be. It didn't matter that a court of law had found him innocent of any "willful, criminal act." In the eyes of the department, that did not make him innocent. A cop was innocent only when it decided you were innocent—and vice versa.

So, knowing full well what the trial commissioner's decision would be, Quarterman knew he had nothing to lose by speaking his mind.

"Inspector, when was the last time you were on the streets?"

"I fail to see how that——" the inspector began, but Quarterman went on.

"I mean, as a cop. When was the last time you opened your eyes, a cop's eyes, to what is going on out there, to what we have to go through? Do you really expect us to defend this city against the fifth——"

"Sergeant Quarterman——"

"——the animals, the human disease that exists out there? Do you really expect us to be able to defend the city against all that with our hands handcuffed behind our backs by decisions like Miranda, forcing us to respect the rights of criminals while they in turn respect no one's rights; by 'revolving-door' courts that turn them loose as fast as we arrest them?" Quarterman's voice rose until he was yelling at the inspector. "You've put restrictions on us——"

The inspector slammed his gavel and snapped, "That will be quite enough, Sergeant!"

"——that we simply cannot operate efficiently under, and when we try to do our job the way it should be done, we get hauled into the trial room. I don't see how you can justify——"

"That will be enough, Sergeant!" the trial commissioner shouted over the sound of his banging gavel. "I'm warning you——"

"No!" Quarterman shouted back, pointing a finger at the older man. "I'm warning you! You are going to have every cop in the city too frightened to do his job! You'll have a police force of scared little boys who won't be able to control and contain the disease that contaminates this city!"

"Officers! Remove this man from the room!" the inspector ordered the two court officers at the door. "Carry him if you have to!"

"No, wait!" Quarterman shouted, but in a different tone from his previous shouting. He held up one hand to the officers and addressed the trial commissioner.

"Inspector, please, I know I'm out of line, but you're going to take my shield from me. At least let me say what I have to say," he said, almost pleading.

When the two officers took him by the arms he did not resist, but merely watched the man behind the desk. As they began pulling him towards the door, the inspector told them. "Wait."

Then he addressed Quarterman. "All right, Sergeant, I'll let you finish, but in a less boisterous manner. Another outburst and I *will* have you removed." He waved the court officers away and they retreated to their posts.

Quarterman continued. "I know what your intentions are, sir," he said, his tone subdued. "You will find me guilty. You will take from me my gun, my shield, my job, and my pension. I'll be an ex-cop, with no way to make a living. This is punishment for not doing my job the department's way. But let me tell you something: you can't make me an ex-cop. What makes me a cop—a damn good cop—is not the shield, or the gun. It's what's in here," and he tapped his chest. "And you can't take that away from me. The very worst you can do is make me a cop without a shield."

With that Sergeant Quarterman turned on his heels and strode from the trial room.

■ ■ ■

They were waiting for Quarterman outside his apartment house when he got home that night. As he approached the front door he heard them in the shadows, but pretended he hadn't. He tried to anticipate the first blow, to soften its effect, but he still caught most of it on the back of the head. He was knocked off his feet and kicked while he was down.

"Well, if it ain't Detective Sergeant Quarterman himself," a voice said from out of the shadows. "Oh, pardon me, I should say ex-Sergeant Quarterman. You ain't a cop anymore, are you, Sarge?" the voice mocked. The question was followed by another kick. He could have caught the foot, but he allowed it to land, grunting as it caught him in the ribs. He decided he would have to make the next one look better than this, so next time he made a clumsy grab for the foot, missing deliberately.

Two hands reached down, grabbed his jacket front and hauled him to his feet. The second man, idle until now, stepped in and pushed a short punch to his right kidney. Quarterman groaned and was thrown back to the ground by the first man. He lay there.

"He ain't so tough no more, is he?" asked the first man. He began to laugh, a wheezing laugh, but was cut short by his partner.

"Why don't you stop talking so much?"

The first man didn't like being spoken to like that so he took it out on Quarterman. He reached down and pulled him to his feet again and smashed him in the face. Quarterman felt his lower lip split and tasted blood. He remained limp in the man's hands.

"Hell, all the fight's gone from him," the first man complained. "He ain't even a man anymore."

"Let's finish it," the partner suggested.

There were many more punches and kicks after that.

■ ■ ■

"Don't turn on the light."

"Oh, Jonas," she whispered when she opened the door. If she hadn't caught him he would have fallen. He was tall, but, surprisingly, not very heavy. She was a big girl and that helped. She half carried, half dragged him to her bed and let him drop on it. When he groaned, she apologized.

" 'S'alright," he told her. "I'm all right."

She went to the bathroom, came back with a damp cloth, and began cleaning him up.

"Didn't you even fight back? I know you, you'd've had to fight back."

"No," he croaked, "No, couldn't. . . ."

"All right, shut up and let me clean you. I should call a doctor."

He started to protest, but she cut him off. "Don't worry, I won't. I'm just saying what I should do—if I were sane." Shaking her head she said, half to herself, "You and your crazy ideas."

Telly Jennings, tall, copper-haired, and thirty, was a prostitute. She had met Quarterman five years back when he was in plainclothes working the Times Square area. He'd busted her but they had hit it off anyway and become good friends. During those five years she had become used to his crazy ideas, but this, she thought, was the craziest of them all. And she was crazy for letting him talk her into helping him—not that he'd had to do that much talking. He'd come running too many times in the past to help her out; she couldn't turn him down the first time he ever asked for something.

She finished cleaning his face and helped him off with his shirt. She sucked in her breath when she saw the bruises on his torso.

"You *are* crazy," she told him in an awed voice.

Later, when she had treated his cuts as well as she could, she asked him how the department trial went.

"They told me they disapproved of the way I had conducted myself in this matter," he told her, able to speak a bit easier now.

"They said my conduct was unbecoming that of a police officer. They took my gun, my ID, and my shield."

"Oh, Jonas——"

"But they can't make me stop being a cop. I told them that!" He was hissing.

"Jonas——"

"Anyone come around?" he asked, changing the subject.

She shook her head. "No, not that I could see." Her hair was cut in a shag. It framed a face that, though not lovely, showed a lot of character. It was a good face, a strong face.

"You got that gun I gave you?"

She hesitated.

"Telly——"

"Yes, I have it!" she snapped. He sat up in bed, groaning.

"Get it," he told her.

"Jonas——"

"Stop saying 'Jonas' every time I tell you to do something! Get it."

She rose and walked across the room to a bright purple vase and stuck her hand in it. It took her a while and she finally had to upend the vase to get it out. She brought the gun to him.

"That's a great place for it," he told her. "What if you had to get to it in a hurry? What if someone——"

"I would have broken the damn vase over his head! Then I wouldn't have had to shoot him. That's your way," she said, scolding him. "That's what got you into this mess. You and your guns and your stupid ideas." She pushed the gun into his hands.

It was a .38-caliber Smith and Wesson Chief's Special, one of three guns he owned—or two, now that they'd taken his "on-duty" gun from him. He would have to turn in his off-duty gun also. This one they didn't know about. Best of all, it couldn't be traced back to him. He swung the cyclinder out to make sure it was loaded and snapped it back into place gently.

Holding the gun in his right hand, he extended his left hand to her and said, "Help me up." She grasped his big hand in her two and pulled him to his feet. She could see the pain on his face; but he said nothing.

The room was still dark, as it had been since he arrived. He wanted it that way so anyone watching the apartment would not be aware of his presence. He had come by way of the rooftops, and he was fairly certain he hadn't been seen.

Now he stepped next to the window and peered out, careful not to show himself.

"Do you think they'll come tonight?" she asked.

"Are you afraid?" Quarterman asked.

"Hell, yes," she admitted without hesitation.

He nodded. "So am I." He turned from the window and said, "No, I don't think they'll come tonight. They'll want to be sure that what those two goons found out tonight is true; they'll want to find out if what Darcy said tonight is true." Darcy was the first man, of that he was sure. That wheezing laugh gave it away. The second man was probably Darcy's shadow, Lampkin.

"What did he say?"

"That I wasn't even a man anymore."

Neither of them said anything more after that. They slept together on the bed, she in her robe, he fully dressed, just in case.

• • •

He woke in the morning, the sun in his eyes. He quit the bed without disturbing her. In the bathroom mirror he inspected the damage Darcy and Lampkin had inflicted on him the night before. His body was stiff, splattered with bruises from the size of a nickel to one the size of a grapefruit. The split lip was the only sign of damage to his face.

He dressed in some old clothes he'd left at Telly's place weeks ago, before this whole thing started, and left the apartment.

Up to the roof, across three more, and down to the street. That had been his route for the past two weeks. He had left the gun with Telly. He didn't like to leave her alone, but it was necessary at times. He was reasonably certain they would wait until at least tonight.

He went back to his own apartment and used the phone.

"Lieutenant Mehias, please," he said when the headquarters operator answered. A few clicks and Lew Mehias' deep, resonant baritone came on the line. Mehias and Quarterman had gone through the police academy together. Mehias, with a touch more ambition, had made lieutenant a few years before, but that was probably as far as he would go. He was a good cop, but not much of a politician.

"Jonas, Lew."

"Hey, Quart. How are you?" His friend's voice was a bit unsure.

"The judge advocate was a little rough, Lew."

"He, uh, had his reasons, Jonas."

"I'd be interested in hearing them. Anyone else know?" he asked.

"No, it hasn't come over the teletype yet. I, uh, spoke with the inspector yesterday. He wanted to know if I thought you were psychotic."

"What'd you tell him?" Quarterman asked with real interest.

Mehias laughed. "I told him you weren't, of course." He paused. "Quart?"

"What?"

"Are you?"

"Probably," he answered.

Mehias paused again. "You'll appeal, of course."

"No, Lew, I won't."

"What do you mean, you won't? Of course——"

"If they want my damn shield that bad, Lew, they can have it; I don't want it."

"Hey, Jonas, that doesn't sound like you."

"It's not me, Lew. I'm not me anymore," Quarterman told him, and hung up.

Before leaving his apartment he picked up his off-duty gun, a short-nosed .38-caliber Colt Detective Special. He clipped the holster to his belt just above the right hip. He felt better immediately. He grabbed a jacket to cover the gun and left.

He stopped by a small grocery and picked up some cold cuts, bread, lettuce, milk, pickles, potato chips, and some cake he knew Telly liked. He made his way back to her apartment by way of the rooftops.

"Goodies," he told her, holding up the bag when she opened the door to his prearranged knock.

"Good, I'm starved." She was delighted when she saw the cake. "You'll make me fat," she said.

"More to pinch," he told her, demonstrating. He moved to the window.

"Anyone?"

"No," she answered. She busied herself putting away the groceries in the apartment's other room, a kitchenette.

"Where's the gun?" he asked.

"In the vase."

"Damnit!" he snapped, but said nothing further. He could smell the coffee she had put on. He watched her move about the small kitchenette, dressed now in a yellow sweat shirt and tight blue jeans, and thought about the mess he was getting her into. . . .

 ▪   ▪   ▪

They'd killed Willie Molesco and dumped him in an alley.

Molesco had been an inoffensive little runt, a part-time stoolie for Quarterman. He had been knocked off, Quarterman was sure, because he had agreed to help Quarterman nail Walter Resnick, this year's local "Mr. Big." What had made Willie decide to help Quarterman was not that he owed Quarterman—which he did—and not that Quarterman had something on him—which he did—but the mere fact that he liked Quarterman—which he honestly did.

What Quarterman had never let Willie know was that he had liked the mousy little runt, too. It was the chief reason for Quarterman's decision to nail Willie's killers.

An autopsy of Willie's body by the medical examiner indicated that there had been more than one killer. Willie had been beaten and then shot. The lab found four bullets of two different calibers in Willie's body. That meant two separate guns, which usually meant two people.

Quarterman figured Darcy and Lampkin had to have been there because they were Resnick's "main men," and Willie had been killed not long after he began helping Quarterman get the goods on Resnick.

Quarterman presented his "evidence" to his superiors, even though he knew he'd get nowhere. They rejected it as even less than circumstantial. His superiors argued that it didn't matter worth a damn that Quarterman "knew" who killed Willie, he had to "prove" it, and the best way to do that was to find a witness.

Quarterman looked for a witness who might have seen someone dump Willie's body in the alley. He spent two days canvassing the area but could find no witness.

So he invented a witness.

First he had to find someone he trusted enough to set up as a witness. Someone who would have a reason for being by the alley to see the body being dumped.

He chose Telly Jennings. Who would have a better reason for being on the streets than a streetwalker?

With his witness recruited, Quarterman proceeded to "pass the word" on the streets that he had found a "witness" to the Molesco killing. But he didn't inform his superiors of his plan, so that when two men broke into Telly Jennings' apartment and were killed in a shootout with Detective Sergeant Jonas Quarterman, who "just happened to be visiting her at the time," the department took a dim view of the incident. In fact, they took such a dim view that even after Quarterman was acquitted of any "intentional wrongdoing" by a court of law, the department tried him. The judge advocate built a strong case for his dismissal.

Quarterman, who knew that this might happen, refused legal counsel and chose to defend himself. The only attempt he made at a defense was to say that he "knew" these men were guilty, and so did the department.

"Their guilt or innocence is not the point here," replied the judge advocate. "Whether or not Sergeant Quarterman's actions followed department guidelines is the only point in question here." The judge advocate faced the trial commissioner and went on very dramatically, "It is not in the proper performance of duty for an officer to decide who is innocent and who is guilty and then act as their executioner. What Sergeant Quarterman has done here is attempt to commit the perfect crime and escape the penalty usually connected with murder!"

The judge advocate went on to say that Quarterman had indeed been acquitted by a court of law, but he did not think that the department should let him remain in a position where he could continue to use the fact that he was a police officer to his own advantage.

"The department," he finished, "does not need vigilantes."

The judge advocate had argued well. Quarterman was dismissed from the force.

■ ■ ■

Quarterman's departmental trial had been covered by every newspaper in the city. After his dismissal the department prepared a press release explaining just what Quarterman's "crime" had been and why he had been dismissed. They also made a statement that, as far as was known, there were no witnesses to the Molesco killing, that it had been a fabrication on Quarterman's part to justify the actions for which he was dismissed.

Quarterman knew, however, that Resnick would take no

chances. As long as there was a chance that Telly might have been a witness, he would send Darcy and Lampkin to take care of her; and he would send them thinking she would be unprotected, since Quarterman was the only one who might consider her in danger and he, according to Darcy, "ain't even a man anymore.".

Which was just what Quarterman wanted them to think. It was why he had accepted the beating from Darcy and his partner; why he had gone to and from Telly's apartment via the rooftops; why he even told Mehias he would not appeal the decision. He wanted everyone to think that having his shield taken from him had broken him.

He wanted Darcy and Lampkin to make a move, and with him seemingly out of the picture, they would. He'd be waiting.

"Coffee?" Telly asked behind him.

He turned. "Sure." She brought him a cup and a piece of cake and watched as he nibbled at it absently.

Shaking her head she said, "Look at you. You haven't been eating right, you've lost weight and you're tearing yourself up inside. Jonas," she knelt before him, hands on his knees, "since this thing began you've gone against everything you believed in the twelve years you were a cop. Look what it's doing to you. Is it worth it?"

He hesitated before answering. "I really don't know, Telly. I don't know if it's worth it now or if it will be when I'm finished, but I can't think about that now. I've started this thing and I have to finish it. When it's done, then I'll think about whether it was right or wrong. If I stop to think now, I could end up dead."

"You don't have that shield anymore, Jonas," she reminded him.

"Maybe not, but I'm still a cop. There are certain things I can do now that I couldn't do when I had the shield."

She shook her head. "Not even you believe that, Jonas." Rising, she looked around her, at the apartment that had become a prison for her and Quarterman. "Oh Jonas, what's it all for?" she asked. She had never asked him for reasons before this, she had been content simply to help him. But now she was tired and scared, and for the first time she wished she had never met him.

"What's it for?" he repeated. He smiled at the irony of his answer. "For justice." He got up and paced the room, careful not to appear in the window.

"During the last year I've had at least half a dozen arrests thrown out of court because I'd violated my prisoner's rights. But what about the rights of the people these punks are ripping off? Don't they count for anything? We can't do our job without some smart lawyer coming up with a right we violated and getting his client off free so he can rip somebody else off. Do you know they've got a judge, Judge Lee, they call him 'Set 'em free, Lee' because he sets them free as fast as we bring them in? If it's not because we violated some punk's rights it's because the punk cops a plea and gets off with a fine. Or maybe he cries 'police brutality' and we end up in front of the Civilian Complaint Review Board. We end up the defendant instead of him.

"I couldn't take it anymore, Telly. The fact that it was Willie who was killed was only half of it. I think I might have done it no matter who it was. I just can't see Resnick and his boys getting off because I don't have enough 'hard' evidence to bring them in even for questioning. Damnit, ten years ago you could bust a case wide open with a gut feeling, a hunch. Now you need evidence you can trip over before you can move——"

There was a knock at the door. She looked at him quickly and he motioned her to sit on the bed. He drew his gun and walked to the door, careful not to stand in front of it.

"Who is it?" he asked.

"Lew Mehias, Jonas. I want to talk to you."

Quarterman was puzzled at how Mehias had found him here. But he relaxed a bit, and opened the door.

"C'mon in, Lew," Quarterman said, backing away from the door and holstering his gun. "You know Telly." Mehias had met Telly when he was Quarterman's Times Square partner. Though Telly and Quarterman had hit it off, Mehias considered her just another whore, another piece of filth on the street. Now he nodded to her. She smiled tentatively.

"How did you know I'd be here?" Quarterman asked.

Mehias shrugged, still standing in the open doorway. "I figured you had to come here. You know Resnick won't take any chances. He's got to hit the girl," he answered, speaking as if Telly weren't even in the room.

"And you came to back me up?" Quarterman asked. Mehias just smiled and raised his hands, palms up.

"Partners again, eh, Lew?" Quarterman said, pleased that he wouldn't be alone. "How about a drink, partner?"

"Fine," Mehias answered.

Quarterman went to the cabinet where Telly kept her liquor, on the wall opposite the front door. Mehias was still standing in the open doorway. Telly remained seated on the bed.

"C'mon, shut the door, Lew," Quarterman told the lieutenant. His hands were outstretched, one reaching for the bottle and the other for a glass. He heard Telly's sharp intake of breath.

"Keep your hands just like that, Jonas, where I can see them."

Quarterman turned his head and saw Mehias standing with his service revolver pointed at him.

"Turn around, Jonas, and move to your left. That's it, stop right there," Mehias ordered. Quarterman was standing opposite Mehias.

"What's this all about, Lew?" Quarterman asked. He felt both confused and afraid.

"It's about you, Willie, and Resnick. The eternal triangle. You wanted to use Willie against Resnick, so Resnick had him offed. Then you started to dig, deep, and you came up with a witness, so Resnick got nervous——"

"You're in Resnick's pocket, Lew?" Quarterman asked in disbelief. "For God's sake, why, Lew? What for?"

"For a future, Quart. You know me, I'm no politician, and there's no future for a cop who's not a politician. No future as anything but a lieutenant, shuffling papers, dealing with pimps, pushers, and whores," he explained. He jerked the gun in Telly's direction. She flinched as if struck. "That's not for me, Quart," he continued, shaking his head. "I can't go any further than I already have in the department——"

"So Resnick made you a better offer and you took it," Quarterman said.

Mehias' knuckles whitened as he squeezed the gun in his hand. Quarterman sucked in his breath, but the weapon did not go off.

"I should have known better," Mehias said. "You had them fooled, Jonas. Resnick's boys were going to waltz right in here, just like the two that you killed, but I knew you'd be here. You'd have to be here to protect your whore."

"So you told Resnick, 'Let me do it, Walt. Let me go up and

take care of my old buddy Jonas.' Is that why you came here, Lew? To kill me?"

"I'm sorry, Jonas, but I can't let you bust Resnick."

Quarterman hissed and lowered his hands.

"Do what I tell you, Jonas," Mehias warned.

Quarterman stopped with his hands half lowered.

"Take your gun from your holster and drop it on the floor," Mehias ordered. "Now kick it."

Quarterman did as he was told, his eyes on Mehias' gun the whole time. He was sweating and beginning to feel nauseous as fear crowded all other emotions away.

"Are you going to do it, Lew? Or do we wait for Darcy? Ah, I think I see," Quarterman went on, eyeing the purple vase on the coffee table to his right from the corner of his eye. "You're going to hold me here until he gets here and he'll do it. How long did you tell him to give you? Three minutes? Five? It's almost time, isn't it?"

At the mention of the time, Mehias glanced reflexively towards his watch. In the fraction of a second that he took his eyes off Quarterman, the ex-detective lunged for the vase and threw it at Mehias. But Mehias ducked in time, the vase smashed against the wall, the shards spraying the right side of the room and Telly.

"Okay, Jonas!" Mehias shouted, and they both knew he was going to shoot. Quarterman's mouth went dry. Stupid idea, he thought, goddamn stupid idea. . . .

For Telly Jennings time seemed to stand still. Right in front of her, on the bed, was the gun she had been keeping in the vase so she wouldn't have to look at it. Now it had fallen from the smashed vase on the bed. She knew Mehias was about to kill Quarterman. But that wasn't what made her pick up the gun and shoot him. It was the realization that after he killed Quarterman, he would most certainly kill her.

Her shot took Mehias in the chest. An instant before his shot, intended for the heart, hit Quarterman in the left shoulder. Both men were thrown backwards, Mehias through the still-open door and into the hallway. He lay still.

Quarterman knew Darcy and Lampkin were on their way up. Grabbing the gun from Telly's nerveless fingers, and taking his own gun from the floor, he propelled himself into the hallway just as Darcy was clearing the top step of the stairway with Lampkin right behind him. Both men had their guns out. Quarterman didn't hesitate: he pulled the triggers of both his guns. The bullets hit Darcy in the stomach, driving him back into Lampkin and sending them both down the stairs.

Quarterman walked to the head of the stairs and stared down at Lampkin, entangled in the arms and legs of the dead Darcy.

The ex-detective aimed a gun at Lampkin's head. Lampkin's gun was halfway up the stairs, where he'd dropped it when Darcy collided into him.

Quarterman's finger tightened on the trigger. Three men, he thought. I've already killed three men. Why not four?

"Jonas!" Telly called from behind him. Her voice broke the spell he felt himself under. He lowered the gun shakily. He had just begun to feel the pain in his left shoulder.

"It's okay, Telly. It's all over."

■　■　■

"It weighs in your favor that you did not kill Lampkin as he lay helpless before you," the trial commissioner told him. "He confessed to the Molesco killing and also implicated his employer, Walter Resnick. Both are being arraigned accordingly.

"As for the charges previously filed against you by the department, because of Lampkin's confession, which proved the guilt of the three men you shot, and also taking into consideration that you were acquitted by a court of law"—which had no bearing on the case in the beginning, Quarterman remembered—"the department sees no reason why you should not be reinstated at your former rank and pay scale." Indicating Quarterman's shield, gun, and ID which lay on the table before him, the trial commissioner said, "You may pick up your shield, Sergeant."

Quarterman stared at the shield, wanting to leave it there, wanting to say, "Forget it, Inspector. Keep it." He thought about Mehias, whose real role he could not keep a secret from the department after Lampkin had squealed. He couldn't change the way he felt about what the department had done to Mehias, what it had led Mehias to do, and what it had made Quarterman himself do. With its restrictions and "decisions" and "rulings," it had made him go outside the law he had believed in for twelve years.

Sure, he thought, leave it there. Walk away. And then what will you do? How will you live?

He picked it up. It didn't mean to him what it once meant, and it would always be a little tarnished, but it was all he had.

L. J. Washburn

LYNCHING IN MIXVILLE

From *Lethal Ladies,* 1996

L. J. (Livia) Washburn manages to make fresh every genre and sub-genre she writes in. The following story is a good example. Back in the early part of the century, a lot of real-life cowboys came to California because large parts of the West were experiencing an economic depression. In L.A., they became stunt men and extras in the growing silent film industry. This is the setting for the following story and for three excellent novels about her cowboy detective.

E. G.

"BUT WERE WE SCARED?" ASKED THE MAN IN THE CREAMY white Stetson and fancy beaded shirt. "No, sir, not one damn bit. There were at least thirty desperadoes holed up in that cabin, and me with a force of ten deputies. Well, hell, three-to-one odds ain't nothin'. We charged that cabin, guns a-blazin', and killed upwards of twenty of them owlhoots. As for the rest . . ." Tom Mix shrugged. "Well, we hung 'em. Figured it was best just to save the state the expense of a trial."

The reporter from the movie magazine was eagerly making notes as Mix spun the yarn. She glanced up from time to time, clearly overwhelmed by the charm of the handsome cowboy actor.

"What about Tony?" the girl asked breathlessly.

Mix patted the big white horse who stood patiently next to him. "Right there with me every step of the way, of course. Man couldn't want a better hoss than ol' Tony here, could he, boy?"

The horse shook his head from side to side, long white mane flying.

The girl broke out laughing. "How precious! Such a smart horse."

Several yards away, one man dressed in range clothes muttered to another, "Horse is smarter than Mix, if you ask me."

They were on the back lot at Mixville, the large studio complex in Glendale where Tom Mix, the King of the Cowboys, made the motion pictures that were thrilling the whole country. The sun was almost directly overhead, and Mix and his crew and actors were taking their lunch break. Never one to shun publicity, Mix was also taking advantage of the break to grant an interview.

Even on a break, the place was busy. Men and women scurried around after finishing the box lunches provided by the studio. Producers conferred with directors, directors conferred with scenarists, scenarists conferred with their own private muses and tried to come up with something else exciting for Tom Mix to do in front of the cameras. There were props to be arranged, lights to be moved, horses to be saddled. The respite would be over before long, and then it would be back to the serious business of creating fantasies.

The only people who didn't seem to be in a hurry were the cowboys.

They were the riding extras and the stuntmen, the horsemen who made up all the posses and outlaw gangs and cavalry troops. All shapes and sizes, they had one thing in common—they were cowboys, and to them a job you couldn't do on horseback usually wasn't worth doing.

They were used to Mix's bragging, and they put no stock in the phony flamboyant biography that somebody—either the studio publicity department or Mix himself—had dreamed up for the star. Mostly, they didn't pay a whole lot of attention to him. He paid well and offered steady work to good riders, and that was the main thing. There was no point in challenging any of the whoppers he told. That would just make him mad, and that was like cutting your nose off to spite your face.

Lucas Hallam had found some shade under a tree, and he was polishing off his lunch out of the hot sun. A big man dressed in buckskins and a floppy-brimmed felt hat, Hallam had the same look of authenticity about him that the other cowboys did. The reason was simple. Like the others, he looked like what he was— an old cowboy.

There was something different about Hallam, though. There

was a sharpness in his blue-gray eyes, set deep in the craggy face. They were the eyes of a manhunter.

In his time, he had been sheriff, Ranger, Pinkerton man. He had skirted the fence on the other side of the law, too, as a hired gun. The West had still been wild when he was a young man, and he had been wild along with it. Then the times had changed, and so had he. Like a lot of others, he had found a home of sorts here in Hollywood, doing the sort of work he had done all his life, only now it was for a camera. And he had a license from the state that said he could work as a private investigator when he wanted to, so the skills he had developed as a lawman weren't wasting away from lack of use.

He wasn't thinking about any of that on this hot summer day, though. He was thinking about finishing his lunch and then maybe tipping his hat down over his eyes to catch a snooze before the director called them back to work.

That plan got spoiled.

A high, querulous voice said, "And I'm callin' you a damn liar, Mix! I don't care how big a star you are, boy."

Hallam looked over to see Tom Mix and that gal reporter standing close by Mix's private trailer. He had heard that the girl was interviewing Mix for her magazine, but he hadn't paid much attention to what was going on. Publicity was a common thing on a Mix picture.

There were several cowboys standing close to Mix and the girl, and it was one of them who had done the shouting. He was an old man, stringy thin, and Hallam recognized him as Hank Daniels. As Hallam climbed to his feet and started to amble in that direction, Daniels went on, "No, you're a liar *and* a coward! I'm tired o' listenin' to it, Mix."

"You know what you can do, then," Mix said with a cold stare on his face as Hallam walked up. "You can get the hell off this picture."

"Don't think I won't!" Daniels railed. "I'm gettin' my stuff and clearin' out! But I'm goin' to tell this gal the truth first."

There were three other men standing with Daniels, and they looked uncomfortable. Jack Montgomery, Roy Norwood, and a waddy Hallam knew only as Shorty were all cowboys, and while they didn't want Daniels making Mix mad, they weren't going to stick their noses in another man's business, either. Hallam nodded to Montgomery, who was one of his closest friends in Hollywood, and watched while Daniels continued his ranting.

"Thirty outlaws, my foot!" Daniels snapped. "Twernt but five of 'em, and they put up about as much fuss as a pack o' newborn pups. And there was at least twenty of us in the posse. When them boys in the cabin seen us ridin' up, they throwed out their guns and come out with their hands in the air. I been hearin' you tell about leadin' the posse that caught the famous Ghost River Gang for years, Mix, but you don't know the first damn thing about it. You weren't there!"

Mix had listened to the old man with little change of expression. There was a fire burning in his dark eyes as he said in a low voice, "Are you through, Daniels?"

Daniels spat into the dust. "Reckon I am." He leered at the girl. "One more thing, missy. Mix got one part of it right by accident. We hung them bastards, all right, ever' one of them."

The girl glanced back and forth between Mix and Daniels, obviously torn about which one to believe. Like all the other fans, she wanted to believe Mix and his dashing stories. But there was no denying the sincerity in the old man's voice.

"But why?" she asked. "What did they do?"

"They tried to rob the Ghost River bank," Daniels said. "Can't let folks get away with things like that. So we hung 'em. Boyd and Devers, Schaefer and Newcomb and the Palo Duro Kid. Hung 'em, every one."

Daniels laughed, a cracked quality to his voice. The girl looked at him, aghast.

This had gone on long enough. Hallam stepped over to Daniels, put a hand on his arm, and said, "Come on now, Hank. You've had your say."

Daniels nodded. "Damn right I did. Had enough o' that fancy dan."

With gentle pressure, Hallam started to lead the old man away. The other three cowboys fell in behind.

Mix suddenly rapped out, "Hallam."

Hallam looked over his shoulder. There was no fear in his eyes as they met Mix's. "What is it, Tom?"

"I meant it when I said I want that old man off the lot."

Hallam nodded. "Know you did."

Daniels was still muttering as the little group headed for the long clapboard bunkhouse that served as a dormitory for the cowboys who had no other place to stay. It was set off away from the soundstages, and there were always at least a dozen men staying there to answer the early morning call of "Roll out or roll up, you sons of bitches!"

As Daniels started up the short flight of steps that led into the bunkhouse, he paused and grabbed at the railing, swaying slightly. Hallam caught his arm and steadied him. "You all right, Hank?" he asked.

"Shore, shore," Daniels said. "Reckon I been out in that hot sun too long. Not as young as I used to be, you know."

Montgomery, Norwood, and Shorty all expressed concern, but Daniels waved them off. "You boys go on back to work," he said. "I'll round up my gear and get out o' here, like Mix wants, soon's I rest up a mite."

Hallam suddenly realized that he didn't know just how old Hank Daniels was. Judging by appearances, he was probably in his late sixties, but when a cowboy got old and leathery, the years probably didn't show up as much. Daniels could have been in his eighties, and that was a lot of years to be carrying around in weather like this.

Hallam knew about carrying around a lot of years. He'd passed the half-century mark himself. And Daniels' talk about the Ghost River Gang had brought back some memories for *him*, too.

As he followed Daniels into the shadowy interior of the bunkhouse, Hallam heard the assistant director bawling for the riding extras to get back to work. Again, Daniels told them to go on, assuring them that he'd be all right. Montgomery, Norwood, and Shorty went, but grudgingly. The cowboys stuck together, because they were the only ones who really understood the reality behind all the playacting.

Hallam stood in the doorway and watched Daniels make his shaky way to his bunk. As the old man sank down on the hard mattress, Hallam said, "You sure you're goin' to be all right, Hank?"

"Dammit, I told you to quit your worryin'!" Daniels barked. "Get back to work, boy. I'll just sit here for a spell. Mix won't mind too much, I reckon."

Hallam nodded slowly. "All right, Hank. Reckon I'll see you

around the Waterhole," he said, referring to the Hollywood speakeasy where most of the riding extras gathered to wet their whistles.

"Reckon so," Daniels said. Sitting down, he suddenly looked smaller to Hallam, almost like somebody had stolen his old bones.

Hallam went back out into the glaring sunlight, and as he walked toward the bustling back lot, he thought about his own connection with the Ghost River Gang. He had been a deputy U.S. marshal at the time, and he had ridden into the town of Ghost River on the trail of the Palo Duro Kid. The kid came from a good family in East Texas, according to the information that Hallam had, but that hadn't stopped him from following the lure of a desperado's life. Hallam had arrived too late in Ghost River, though; the aborted bank robbery had occurred the day before, and by the time he caught up with the posse, the members of the youthful gang were already dangling from hemp ropes. Hallam had never held with lynch justice, but in this case there was nothing he could do about it.

He had known, of course, that Tom Mix hadn't had a thing to do with the capture of the Ghost River Gang. At that time, Mix had probably still been back in the coal mines of Pennsylvania. But it made a good story for the actor to tell, especially after it had been fancied up some, and Hallam wasn't one to begrudge a man his tall tales.

Before he could reach the back lot, he saw Mix's big car roaring toward him. Mix brought it to a halt beside Hallam, kicking up a cloud of dust in the process, and said over the smooth purring of the big engine, "Did you get rid of that old coot?"

"He's goin'," Hallam said. "He wasn't feelin' so good, so he's restin' up in the bunkhouse for a little bit. But then he'll be off the lot."

"He'd better be," Mix grunted angrily. "He showed me up in front of that pretty little gal, and I don't like that. Not one damn bit."

Hallam said nothing in reply, and after a moment, Mix gunned off in the direction of the bunkhouse and the offices beyond. He must not have been in any of the next scenes on the shooting schedule, Hallam supposed, or he wouldn't be leaving at a time like this. Usually, he was on the set even for scenes he wasn't in, just so that he could keep an eye on things and make sure that the finished product had his stamp on it.

Once Hallam got back to work, a couple of hours went by quickly. He rode up and down the streets of the back lot town, whooping and hollering and shooting off his big Colt along with the rest of the boys. They were supposed to be an outlaw gang terrorizing the town, and Mix was going to put a stop to that soon enough. He showed up again about an hour after roaring off in his car and went right to work on the next scene that called for his presence. Hallam had just about forgotten the altercation between Mix and Daniels.

Until one of the studio flunkeys came running from the bunkhouse, yelling at the top of his lungs.

The director bounced out of his chair and spun around, livid at the interruption. But then everyone on the set heard the words "Dead! He's dead!"

Hallam wheeled his horse and put the spurs to it. He was the first one in motion, but the other cowboys were right behind him. He covered the two hundred yards to the bunkhouse in a matter of moments and yanked the horse to a stop in front of the steps. Hallam swung down from the saddle, took the steps two at a time, and burst into the bunkhouse.

He stopped just inside the door, his face hard as granite. He had expected to find Hank Daniels dead, all right, but most likely from a heart attack or a stroke or just plain old age.

He hadn't expected to find him strung up from a ceiling beam, a noose tight around his neck and his booted feet dangling two feet off the floor.

Hank Daniels had been lynched. Just like the Ghost River Gang. . . .

■ ■ ■

Police investigations were nothing new to Hallam, seeing as how he was in the detective business himself. But to most of the people on the set, being involved in a murder case was a brand-new and not very pleasant experience.

And it *was* murder. That much was plain right off. Nobody could tie their own hands behind their back and then hang themselves.

It was late afternoon before the cops got through questioning everyone. A detective lieutenant named Ben Dunnemore was in charge of the investigation. Hallam knew him fairly well, and the two of them stood under the same tree where Hallam had eaten his lunch.

"Well, Lucas," Dunnemore said, "what do you think?"

Hallam studied the lieutenant a moment before replying. Dunnemore was stocky and middle-aged, with a world-weary look about him, and there was no point in trying to read his expression. He was probably the best poker player Hallam knew.

"About what?" Hallam asked innocently.

"Don't play games with me, Lucas. You were here all day, you know the people involved. Who do you think killed this old man?"

Hallam shook his head. "The city don't pay me to have opinions on things like that, Ben. Reckon that's your job."

Dunnemore glared at him. "In other words, you don't want to say."

"Most of these folks are friends of mine, Ben."

"What about Daniels? Wasn't he your friend?"

Hallam said nothing.

Dunnemore was right, though; Hallam had his own ideas about what had happened today and why, but he didn't want to say anything about them. This whole business had put him in a damn sorry position.

"All right, then," Dunnemore went on after a moment, "if you don't want to say anything, I'll just tell you how it looks to me." He paused again, but Hallam kept his mouth shut. Dunnemore sighed. "Daniels and Tom Mix had an argument earlier this afternoon. Daniels called Mix a liar, and Mix ordered the old man off the lot. A little later, you told Mix that Daniels was still here, and he drove off in a huff. I've got all this from other witnesses besides you, Lucas, so there's no point in denying any of it."

"You're doin' the talkin'," Hallam said.

"Daniels didn't have any other enemies around here, not according to what I've heard. Nobody seemed to know him real well, because he kept pretty much to himself, but he hadn't had any run-ins with anybody else on the lot. That leaves me with only one good suspect, Lucas."

Hallam shook his head. "You ain't tryin' to say that you're goin' to charge Tom Mix with murder?"

"What choice do I have?" Dunnemore shrugged. "Unless you've got a better idea for a suspect?"

Hallam stared off at the sunlight and rubbed his bristly jaw. Unfortunately, he had come to the same conclusions that Dunnemore had.

As far as opportunity went, a lot of people could have lynched Hank Daniels. He had been alone in the bunkhouse when Hallam left him, and as far as anybody knew, no one else had entered the bunkhouse until the studio man had gone in to post the next day's tentative shooting schedule on the bulletin board. The schedule hadn't gotten posted, because the fella had been too busy running back out and hollering about the dead man.

Around a busy place like a movie set, though, there was almost no way to account for every minute that a person spent. It would have been simple enough for someone to slip into the bunkhouse unseen. Hank Daniels was a tired old man; it wouldn't have taken long to overcome any fight he might have put up. Then it was a matter of seconds to lash his hands behind him, put the noose around his neck, and haul him up to die.

All told, the killer might have been in the bunkhouse only three or four minutes.

And Mix had been off the set for at least an hour.

"Well?" Dunnemore said.

"What's Mix say he was doin' while he was off the set?" Hallam asked.

Dunnemore jerked his head in the direction of the offices and bunkhouse. "He says he was in the offices talking to some of the studio executives. They confirm that he was there, and I've got plenty of witnesses who saw his car parked there. But nobody can swear where Mix was every minute he wasn't on the set. He could have walked over to the bunkhouse, killed the old man, and come back to the set without anybody noticing anything out of the ordinary."

Hallam nodded. Dunnemore was no fool. He had considered the possibilities and come up with the most logical suspect—Tom Mix.

"Seems like a mighty weak motive," Hallam said stubbornly. "They had a few words, but I've heard a heap worse on movie sets."

"Daniels embarrassed Mix in front of a reporter," Dunnemore

pointed out. "Publicity's food and drink to that man, and you know it. Besides, the reporter was a pretty girl. I'm sure that didn't help any."

"You're goin' to take him in?"

"I don't see as I have any choice, Lucas. I at least have to take him in for further questioning."

"You do what you think best, Ben," Hallam told him. He knew that Dunnemore didn't want to believe that Tom Mix was a murderer any more than he did. If Mix was arrested, it would shock the whole country. Clean-living cowboy heroes didn't go around killing old men in cold blood.

Not to mention the effect that such a thing would have on the movie industry. This was going to be a bad day, sure enough.

Ben Dunnemore wasn't going to shirk his duty, though. Hallam was as sure of that as he was of anything.

"I told Mix to wait in his trailer," Dunnemore grunted. "Guess I'd better go tell him he'll be coming along with me."

Hallam nodded but didn't say anything. He watched the lieutenant start walking slowly toward the trailer where the King of the Cowboys waited.

Jack Montgomery and Roy Norwood had been lounging in the shade of another tree nearby, and now they came over to Hallam with anxious expressions on their faces. "What's up, Lucas?" Montgomery asked. "What's that lieutenant goin' to do?"

"What he has to," Hallam replied as he saw Dunnemore vanish into the trailer. "He's goin' to arrest Tom Mix."

Shocked exclamations came from both of the other cowboys. "He can't do that!" Norwood moaned. "That'll shut down production, and we'll be up Salt Creek."

"Nothin' else he can do," Hallam said. "Mix is the only suspect he's got."

Montgomery shook his head regretfully. "Damn, I wish we'd put a stop to it when ol' Hank started in on Mix. Me and Roy and Lawson shoulda hustled him away from there."

Hallam frowned. "What?"

"I said we shoulda just got Hank away from Mix."

Hallam's eyes had narrowed in concentration. "You and Roy and who?" he asked, a strange intensity in his voice.

Montgomery stared at him in puzzlement. "Shorty Lawson,"

he said. "What's the matter with you. Lucas? You losin' your hearin'?"

"Reckon I never heard him called by his full name," Hallam mused. "Just knew him as Shorty."

"I don't for the life of me see why you're worryin' about that," Norwood said impatiently. "I don't know about you, but I *needed* this job."

"Maybe you'll still have it," Hallam said. "Either o' you fellers seen Shorty here lately?"

"He was amblin' down toward the corral last time I saw him," Montgomery said. "What's gotten into you, Lucas? You look a little spooked."

"Just doin' a little rememberin', Jack," Hallam said. "Just a little rememberin'."

He walked off toward the corral, his long legs carrying him along at a good clip, the limp in the right one hardly slowing him down.

He hoped he wasn't too late already.

As he neared the corral, he saw a short, stocky figure hefting a saddle and getting ready to swing it up on the back of a horse tied to the fence. Hallam called out, "Howdy, Lawson. Gettin' ready to do some ridin'?"

Shorty Lawson turned around quickly, holding the heavy saddle between himself and Hallam. There was a startled look on his face that was replaced by a quick, friendly grin.

"Lordy, you spooked me, Lucas," Lawson said. "Didn't know anything was around."

Hallam didn't return the grin. He gestured at the saddle with a big hand. "Asked if you was goin' to be ridin'," he rumbled.

Lawson shrugged. "Anything wrong with that?" The grin was rapidly melting off his face.

Hallam ignored the question and asked another of his own. "You wouldn't be one of the East Texas Lawsons, now would you, Shorty?"

"Could be," Lawson said curtly. He made no pretense of being friendly now. "What's it to you?"

"Well, it's a funny thing. I got to rememberin' another fella name of Lawson. Theodore Lawson, his name was. Young fella, probably not more than twenty or so. Came from a respectable family in East Texas, but goin' into the family business wasn't enough for Theodore. He thought the money would be better and the gettin' it more fun on the owlhoot trail. He picked out another name to go by, so as not to shame the folks back home. Got to give him credit for that. Called himself the Palo Duro Kid."

Lawson took a deep breath. "Mind tellin' me why you're spinnin' this yarn, Hallam? Maybe you should go into the book writin' business, like Zane Grey."

"This is no yarn," Hallam said. "It's the truth, Lawson. There's more to it, though. This young fella, the Palo Duro Kid, came to a bad end. Got himself hung by some vigilantes. I was on his trail at the time, and I wanted to bring him in alive. So I was mighty upset when I found out he'd been lynched. Reckon I wasn't as upset as the boy's older brother, though. I didn't remember the Kid's real name right off, not until I was reminded of it. I don't reckon his brother ever forgot that lynchin', though."

There was about ten feet between the two men. Hallam could see the muscles twitching in Lawson's face. Lawson's voice shook slightly as he said, "They had no right to string him up like that. He was only a kid, goddamn it! And they didn't even get any money from that bank."

Hallam stood with his feet spread wide, his thumbs hooked in his belt. "Why'd you come here, Shorty? Had you heard about Mix claimin' to have been one of the posse?"

Lawson nodded. "Word got back to me a couple of years ago. Somebody who'd worked on a Mix picture heard him tell the story about the Ghost River Gang. I was workin' on a spread in Oklahoma at the time, so as soon as I could, I drifted on out here and got into the picture business." He smiled again, but it wasn't a pleasant expression this time. "I been waitin' for the right time ever since."

"Until today you found out you were after the wrong man," Hallam said. "You heard the truth of it from Hank Daniels."

Lawson's lips pulled back from his teeth even more. "Hell, I knew Mix had to be colorin' it up some. I knew the straight of it, how it happened and all, I just didn't know all the men who were involved." He paused, then said, "I found some of 'em, though. Enough to make a start on payin' 'em back for Teddy."

Hallam felt a chill go through him. He knew what Lawson

meant. There were other dead men behind him besides Hank Daniels, men who, over the years, had paid a blood debt to Shorty Lawson.

"Couldn't pass up the chance when ol' Hank confessed right in front of you, could you?" Hallam said. "You knew he was by himself up there in the bunkhouse, so you slipped up there while we were all busy and strung him up. Findin' a lariat around there was no problem. Musta seemed fittin' to you, killin' him that way."

"And I watched him kick his life out," Lawson said savagely. "I watched his eyes and his tongue bulge out just like Teddy's must have when they hung him from that tree. And I laughed, Hallam. It was a damn funny sight."

Hallam sighed and took a step toward him. "You'd best come with me, Shorty. We'll go talk to the lieutenant."

"The hell we will," Lawson grated. "I had a score to settle. Nothin' wrong with that."

"Maybe not in the old days. But times have changed, Shorty."

"Not for me."

He threw the saddle at Hallam as hard as he could.

Hallam tried to duck, but the heavy saddle slammed into him and staggered him. He caught his balance as he went down on one knee.

Lawson jerked the reins of his horse loose and vaulted onto its back in one smooth motion. His heels dug into its sides and sent it spurting away from the corral.

With a muttered curse, Hallam yanked the corral gate open and caught the first horse he laid hands on. There was no time to saddle up, no time for a bridle and bit. All he could do was grab the animal's mane, swing onto its back, and kick it into motion just as Lawson had.

Lawson had a good start, and he was lighter than Hallam. Hallam leaned forward over the neck of his horse, patting it and talking to it in low tones and communicating with it as only a man could who has spent most of his life in partnership with a horse. As they pounded back toward the soundstages, Hallam's mount put on a gallant burst of speed, but he could see that it wasn't going to be enough. Lawson was pulling away.

Lawson flashed past Mix's trailer just as Dunnemore stepped out with the cowboy actor right behind him. Mix looked upset, and both he and Dunnemore leaped back, startled, as Lawson rode by and left a cloud of dust.

"What the hell?" Mix yelled.

Hallam was on them by that time, heeling his horse around and racing past them. "He killed Daniels!" he shouted over the uproar of galloping hooves, and then he was by them.

He heard a faint whistle behind him and glanced over his shoulder to see Mix leaping into Tony's saddle. The big white horse took off like a flash of light, leaving Ben Dunnemore behind to yell, "Hey! Come back here!"

Hallam grinned. Tom Mix was joining the chase.

Lawson's horse was lining out across open country now, having gone past the soundstages, the offices, and the bunkhouse where Hank Daniels had met his Maker. They filmed a lot of chase scenes out here on this back lot, and Hallam knew it well. Still he had to watch close to keep his horse from stepping in a hole.

He heard the pound of hooves beside him and looked over. Mix had caught up with him. That Tony was some horse, and despite his faults, there was one thing you could say for his rider.

Tom Mix rode like the wind.

Lawson looked over his shoulder and saw them coming. Mix was pulling ahead of Hallam now. He was lighter, a better rider on a better horse. It was only a matter of time until he caught up with Lawson. The fleeing man kept looking back, fear visible on his face even at this distance.

And then Lawson's horse went down.

It was probably the most spectacular horse fall Hallam had ever seen, more brutal than any Running W. The horse must have stepped in a hole, because he went hooves over head with a wild scream. Lawson came off his back and landed hard, and then the horse rolled clean over him.

Miraculously, the horse clambered to its feet as Hallam and Mix rode up and leaped out of their saddles. It seemed to be unhurt, just walleyed and shaken up, which was more than you could say for Lawson.

Lawson was screaming in a high thin voice as Hallam knelt beside him. It took only a second for Hallam to see what had happened. "Back's broke," he said. "No tellin' how bad he's busted up inside. But he'll live long enough to make sure you don't go to jail, Tom."

Mix knelt beside Hallam, the late afternoon sun sparkling on his hat and shirt. "You said he's the killer?"

"That's right. Story goes back a long way, but it can all be checked out, even if Lawson don't confess. He's got a hell of a lot better motive than you, so I don't think you'll be goin' to the hoosegow just yet." Hallam leaned forward and put a calloused hand on the shoulder of the writhing Lawson. "Take it easy, Shorty," he said. "Help's on the way."

Lawson's eyes suddenly rolled up in his head and he went limp. Hallam knew he had fainted from the pain.

Mix and Hallam stood up and watched the crowd of people who were running toward them across the back lot. Mix looked down at Lawson and shook his head. "Hell of a way for a man to end up," he said. "Even a killer."

"So's dancin' at the end of a rope," Hallam said.

Lawson had been right about one thing. The times had changed, but he hadn't. And just like in the old days, the story of the Ghost River Gang had finally come to a violent end.

Norbert Davis

MURDER IN TWO PARTS

From *Black Mask*, December 1937

Norbert Davis was one of the few pulp writers of the '30s and '40s to successfully blend the hard boiled story with farcical humor. The more than 100 short stories and novelettes he published in such magazines as Double Detective, Detective Fiction Weekly, Detective Tales, *and* Black Mask *(where the atmospheric non–series tale which follows first appeared) are fast-paced, action-jammed, occasionally lyrical in a hard-edged way, and often quite funny. The same qualities infuse his three novels,* Mouse in the Mountain, Sally's in the Alley, *and* Oh, Murderer Mine!, *all of which feature the screwball adventures of Doan, a boozy private eye who looks fat but isn't, and Carstairs, an aloof, fawn-colored Great Dane whom Doan won in a crap game.*

B. P.

BRENT STOOD ON THE STATION PLATFORM LOOKING UP AT THE conductor. The lights from the end coach outlined his long hard jaw, the square-cut spareness of his face. His eyes were a light blue, deep-set under heavy brows. His mouth was wide, thin-lipped. His features were homely and irregular, but still they were attractive in a hard-boiled, reckless way.

"All right," he said. "Throw him down. Careful. He's fragile. Don't break him."

The conductor let go of Fuller, and Fuller dove gracefully and limply out into space. Brent caught him under the arms.

"Yi," said Fuller in a faintly pleased voice without opening his eyes.

"Good-bye!" said the conductor emphatically. "And good riddance!"

Brent nodded up at him. "Thanks. Same to you."

The conductor swung his lantern and the engine pulled the three dinky coaches out of the station. Then Brent looked down at Fuller.

"Come on," he said wearily. "Stand up, will you?"

"No," said Fuller. He was smiling peacefully. He was small and slight. His round, smooth face was flushed now, and his blond hair was rumpled down over his forehead. He kept his eyes shut tight, and his legs wavered loosely, bending outward at the knees.

There was a rumble of iron wheels on the platform, and a man came shuffling toward them hauling a hand baggage truck. He stopped and examined Fuller and Brent dispassionately.

" 'Evening," he greeted gravely. "Your friend's kinda drunk."

"Him?" Brent said. "Oh, no. He never drinks. It must be something he ate. How's for giving me a hand with these?" He nodded toward the two leather suit-cases sitting on the platform beside him.

The old man pushed the baggage truck in against the wall of the station. "Sure. Want a taxi?"

"Yes," said Brent. "To the hotel."

The old man picked up the bags. "Come on, then. Ira's sleepin' inside."

He led the way to the waiting room of the small station. A fat stove filled one corner, and a man sat in a chair beside it, tipped back against the wall with his hat pulled down over his eyes. He was snoring enthusiastically.

"Ira," said the old man. "Ira. Here's a couple fellows want a taxi."

One of Ira's snores stopped in the middle, and he said, "Taxi," in a blurred voice. He shut his mouth and pushed his hat back, revealing a long, sad face with high cheek-bones and a long, inquisitive nose. He looked Brent and Fuller over carefully and then nodded.

"Drunk?" he asked, pointing to Fuller.

"No," said Brent. "Walking in his sleep."

"Oh," said Ira. He considered gravely for a moment and then nodded again. "Well, I've heard it can be done. You wanta go to the hotel right now?"

"Sometime in the near future," Brent answered. He was still holding Fuller up, and he shifted the man around now, getting a new grip. "If it isn't too much trouble."

"Nope," said Ira. "No trouble. Business is business. Come on."

He picked up the bags, and Brent hauled Fuller after Ira. Fuller's feet trailed loosely on the floor.

Ira's taxi was a big, old-fashioned touring car. The top was down. Brent heaved Fuller into the back seat.

"Whoops," said Fuller, bouncing on the cushions.

Brent climbed in after him, and sat him up. Ira piled the bags into the front seat, got in himself. The motor kicked over with a sudden battering roar.

Ira's thin shoulders heaved as he turned the wheel. The headlight wavered across a road-bed that was six inches thick with a mixture of sand and soft white dust. The breeze felt cool in Brent's face, and he took off his hat and wiped his face with his handkerchief, sighing wearily.

The lights of the short main street gleamed small and pale ahead of them. The car's lights showed a vacant lot on their left, grown high with brown, dusty weeds. Brent thought he saw vague, dark movement there, but before he could locate it or define it, flame spurted at them in a bright rippling slash. All in the same instant there was a whanging report and the left side of the windshield dissolved in a misty spray of shattered glass.

Ira yelled frantically and went down out of sight under the steering wheel. With his left arm Brent knocked Fuller off the seat and on to the floor. At the same time he drew the big revolver from his waist-band, leveled it over the door.

The car hit the curb, jumped it. The head-lights flicked up high for an instant, and Brent saw a thin, black figure standing erect in the vacant lot with the weeds waist-high around it. Blued steel gleamed in its hand, and the face was a white blur. The head-lights flicked down again, and the figure was gone.

Brent swore in a tense whisper. He didn't dare fire. He didn't know what was in back of the vacant lot, and his revolver was a .38–40, powerful enough to punch right through the wall of an ordinary house. He leaned over, jerked the steering wheel around. The car banged down off the curb again. Brent caught Ira by the shoulder, hauled him up.

"Drive, damn you! Get us out of here!"

"S-shot!" Ira wailed. "Shot right at us!"

"Yes, and he missed!" Brent said savagely. "You want to stick around here while he tries again?"

"No!" Ira denied emphatically. He grabbed the steering wheel, and the sound of the engine ascended to a screaming howl.

The car rattled and banged over the bumpy road. Brent knelt on the back seat, his gun leveled. Brent expected another shot, and his shoulders crawled with the tenseness of waiting for it. But nothing happened. The car rocked into the narrow main street. Then Ira bumped hard into the curb in front of a long, low brick building that had a sign in front with the word "Hotel" painted on it. The sign had a red Neon border, and in its light Ira's long face looked queerly yellow staring at Brent.

"That—that fellow back there. He shot at us! He hit the windshield. Right in front of me."

"Right in front of me, too," said Brent. "Did you see him?"

"No," said Ira. "I didn't see him, and I don't wanna. I don't want no more to do with you, neither. This is the hotel. Now you get out. Both of you. You get right out."

"With pleasure," Brent said. He got out and, reaching back in again, seized Fuller by the coat collar and hauled him out on the sidewalk.

"Let's fight," Fuller suggested pleasantly, waving his arms around. His eyes were still tightly shut.

"Quit it!" Brent snapped.

Ira dumped the suit-cases over the door. "Look!" he said plaintively. "Look at my windshield. Just look at it. All smashed." He shook a bony finger at Brent. "And I might have been killed! You understand that? That bullet might have gone right through me!"

"Don't blame me," Brent advised. "I didn't shoot it."

Ira glared at him. "That don't fix my windshield."

Brent extended a five-dollar bill. "Maybe this will."

Ira snatched the bill. "Well. . . . But you ain't got any right to get shot at while you're ridin' with me! And you ain't gonna ride with me no more, either! Not even if you give me ten dollars! Now! How do you like that?"

"Fine," said Brent.

"And I'm gonna go right and tell the police, too! I'm gonna tell the police all about it!"

"Go ahead," said Brent.

Ira swallowed hard. "Say. Do you suppose that fella is around here, anywhere close?"

"Sure," said Brent. "He's probably hiding behind that barber pole across the street. Better move on before he starts shooting again."

Ira's head swiveled around hurriedly. His hands groped for the gear shift lever, and the big car jerked away from the curb with a sudden grinding clash.

Brent had put the big .38–40 back in his waist-band, but his right hand was inside his coat touching its grip now. He held Fuller up with his left arm, and his eyes were steady, alert, watchful.

After a moment, Brent backed slowly across the sidewalk. He went up two worn cement steps, still walking backwards, and pushed the door of the hotel open with his shoulders. He went inside and closed the door carefully in front of him. Some of his tenseness relaxed, then, and he breathed deeply. Fuller sagged over his left arm.

The lobby was small and square, and it looked dusty and unused. There was no one in sight anywhere.

"Hey!" Brent called loudly.

A head came up slowly over the top of the desk. It was a round head, white and glistening and hairless, and it had bloodshot little eyes pouched deeply in folds of white, smooth fat.

"What?" said the head sourly.

"We want a room," Brent said. "Keep an eye on this for me." He dumped Fuller on a long couch covered with faded red plush.

He went to the door again, then, and opened it a little. After watching the empty street for a moment, he dodged quickly outside and retrieved the two bags Ira had dumped on the sidewalk. He came back in the lobby carrying them and kicked the door shut behind him.

"Give us a double with a bath," he said.

The head had risen above the level of the desk now, revealing a dumpy torso covered with a faded expanse of pink silk shirt. The man leaned heavily on fat elbows and glared at Fuller.

"He's drunk," he said accusingly, pointing.

"Oh, no," Brent denied. "He's in a trance. I just hypnotized him."

"He's drunk," said the fat man, unconvinced.

Brent sighed. "Do we have an argument, or do you give us a room?"

The fat man opened a register with a sharp slap. "All right. But I'm not gonna have any scandalous goings-on in this hotel. Understand that. This is a respectable place. See that you sign your right names."

"I forget how to spell mine," Brent said. "Can't I just put down the number they gave me the last time I was in prison?"

Without waiting for an answer, he seized the register, picked up a dilapidated pen, and wrote: James Brent, New York. Hugh Fuller, New York.

The fat man spun the register around again and examined both names suspiciously. "All right," he said at last. "But just remember—no goings-on. I won't have it." He waddled around the desk on short legs that stretched a pair of white duck trousers to the bursting point. "Come on." He picked up the two bags and hefted them calculatingly.

Brent lifted Fuller up off the couch. He followed the fat man along the scuffed path in the carpet to the stairs, up them, and along a narrow, dark hall. The fat man opened a door and went through it, snapping on an electric light.

"Only double I got. Ain't used very much."

■　■　■

It was a small room, square, and the air was close and hot and musty. The paper on the ceiling was stained with water in brown, dappled spots. There were two narrow beds, a couple of straight-backed chairs, a white-painted dresser, and an enormous old-fashioned wardrobe that loomed ugly and grotesque, filling all of one corner of the room.

"Bath," said the fat man. He went over and opened a door and snapped on another light.

Brent put Fuller down on the bed and got his wallet out. "All right. Now I want some ice."

"Huh?" said the fat man.

"Ice. You know, frozen water. I want a dishpan full of chunks about this size." Brent held up his doubled fist to illustrate.

"All right," the fat man said. He took the dollar bill Brent was extending, went out of the room, and slammed the door behind him.

Brent went into the bathroom and ran the tub half-full of water. Then he came back in the room and began to undress Fuller. He was interrupted by a knock on the door. It was the fat man with a dishpan full of chopped ice.

Brent took it from him and shut the door in the fat man's face. He carried the ice into the bathroom, and dumped it into the bath-tub. He stirred it around for a moment and then went back in the other room and finished undressing Fuller.

Naked, Fuller looked slight and small and boyish at first glance.

A second look revealed that most of the slightness was flat, lithe muscle. He was small-boned, but quick and amazingly strong.

Brent examined the belt around Fuller's waist curiously. It was the first he had ever seen just like it, and it interested him. It fitted tight and flat, making no bulge under Fuller's clothes when he was dressed. The outside layer was soft, black leather. Under that, Brent knew, there was a layer of thin, pliable strips of chrome steel, interlaced. Under the steel was a layer of chamois-skin to protect the jewels Fuller carried. The belt had a lock in the front about four inches long. The lock was chrome steel, too, and it was part of the steel strips under the leather. There was a small, flat key hole in the center of the lock. Brent picked up Fuller's trousers and felt along the cuff of the right leg until he found the flat lump that was the key, sewn tightly into it.

The belt was as thief-proof as ingenuity could make it. It was too small to slip over Fuller's shoulders or over his hips. It would be impossible to cut through it.

Leaving the belt on him, Brent picked Fuller up and carried him into the bathroom and slid him gently into the tub. Fuller kept on snoring peacefully. Brent propped him up and left him sitting there, while he went back in the front room.

He took off his coat and vest and threw them over the foot of the bed. He was dead tired, and his arms and shoulders ached with the strain of carrying Fuller. He opened his suit-case and took out a bottle of Scotch. He held it up and shook it, calculating the amount of liquor that was left, and then took a small sip. He sat still for a moment, relaxing.

There was a sudden heaving splash of water from the bathroom. Fuller screamed, a blood-curdling howl that rattled the pictures on the wall. Brent didn't pay any attention. He merely lit up a stubby, battered pipe.

Fuller howled again and again, and there was more splashing of water. He appeared abruptly in the doorway of the bathroom, dancing up and down and shuddering violently.

"You—you—" he yelled incoherently. "That was a hell of a thing to do!"

"I got tired of you," Brent said. "I've been carrying you around for two days and nights. I want a rest."

Fuller disappeared and came out again with towels in each

hand. He began to dry himself, rubbing hard. He was grinning cheerfully now.

"Well, I had a good time, anyway."

"I didn't," said Brent.

"Sorry," said Fuller. "How's for a drink?"

"No," said Brent. He took another swallow of the Scotch, corked it carefully, and put it back in the suit-case. "This is the time when you sober up for a while, at least until you sell somebody those diamonds."

Fuller patted the belt around his waist, lit a cigarette and sat down on his bed. "Never you mind, pally. After I sell these little babies in the belt, me and you will go on a bust that is a bust."

"Thanks just the same," said Brent. "But I'll do my busting in private. You're a little too strenuous for me."

The door of the room shook under a sudden thunder of hammering blows.

Brent jerked his head around. "Who is it?" he demanded, pulling the .38–40 out of his waist-band.

"Open in the name of the law!" a voice bellowed defiantly.

Fuller's blue eyes were very wide, staring at Brent. "What—" he whispered, "what's the idea?"

Brent shook his head. "I don't know. You answer it. Jerk the door wide open and then get out of my way."

Fuller swallowed. He nodded reluctantly and got up and tip-toed to the door, approaching it at an angle. He jerked the door wide open, flattening himself against the wall.

Brent was still sitting on his bed, the big revolver held easily in his hand. "Come on in," he invited. "But don't crowd. I'm nervous." The hammer of the revolver clicked coldly.

■　　■　　■

All three of the men standing in the doorway looked like they wished they weren't there. The one in front was small and spindling and bow-legged. He wore a black sombrero and a long black coat, and his trousers were tucked into high, dusty boots. His face was grayish, as though it, like his boots, was covered with dust. His colorless eyes stared at Brent's gun with stupefied surprise. Crowded close behind the little man, trying to hide behind his skinny body, were the cab-driver Ira and the fat proprietor of the hotel.

"Come on in," Brent repeated.

The little man moved his hands, as if he didn't quite know what to do with them. "I—I'm the town marshal. My name is Lapswich." His voice wasn't a bellow, and it wasn't defiant, either. He looked and sounded apologetic.

"Glad to know you," said Brent. "My name is Brent, and the gentleman in the shorts over there is Hugh Fuller. We've already met your two stooges."

"Well," said Lapswich, edging inside the door and watching Brent's gun narrowly, "Ira, here, he come to me with some story about somebody shootin' at him or you or somethin' when he was bringin' you from the train. We come down to see Dade, here," he nodded to indicate the fat proprietor, "and while we was talkin' to him, why we heard some awful screamin' and takin' on."

"My friend was taking a bath," Brent said. "He always yells when he takes baths. He's afraid of water. Doesn't even like to drink it. Isn't that right, Fuller?"

"Sure," said Fuller quickly. "Now listen, Brent, if this gentleman is a policeman, you don't want to threaten him."

"*If*," Brent said meaningly. "Can you prove it?"

"You bet!" said Lapswich. He flipped the lapel of his coat back expertly, revealing a big metal shield. "And you can ask Dade or Ira, here, or anybody."

Brent grinned. He dropped the gun on the bed. "Sorry to be suspicious, but you see Fuller is carrying a quarter of a million dollars' worth of diamonds on him, and I'm guarding him and them."

The three men turned with one accord to stare at Fuller.

"A quarter of a *million!*" Dade said in an awed tone.

"Diamonds," Ira said. "Oh, my."

Fuller nodded cheerfully. "Right here." He tapped the leather belt around his waist. "Want to see 'em?"

"No!" said Brent. "You don't show those to anybody but the man who is going to buy them!"

"No, no," said Lapswich hurriedly. "I should say not! Two hundred and fifty thousand dollars! Whew! I'm glad *I'm* not responsible for 'em! Who—who is gonna buy 'em?"

"Man by the name of Carruthers," Fuller told him.

Ira, Dade, and Lapswich looked at each other, wide eyed.

"Whew!" said Lapswich. "Eli Carruthers, huh?"

"Gosh," said Ira. "Boy, oh, boy."

"What's that old cuss buyin' 'em for?" Dade demanded. "His daughter, I bet you."

"Nope," Fuller denied. "He's buying them for an investment."

"Gee whiz," said Ira, still awed. "Two hundred and fifty thousand dollars. That there's a lot of money."

"I told you he had it," Dade said, nodding his bald head. "You remember, Ira, I said just the other day that old Eli, the stinking old miser, had plenty salted away if the truth was known."

Lapswich blinked his colorless eyes at Brent. "Say! That guy that shot at you and Ira! I bet he was gonna try and steal them diamonds!"

Brent shook his head. "No. I don't think so. He wouldn't have gone about it that way. Probably he wasn't even shooting at Fuller and me. Remember, Ira was in that car, too."

"Ira?" said Lapswich incredulously.

"Sure. Maybe somebody doesn't like him. Got any rivals in the taxi business, Ira?"

"Shucks, no," said Dade. "Ira's the only one dumb enough to try and run a taxi around here."

"Yeah," Ira agreed, not resenting the implication. "Everybody likes me."

"Well, look here, now," Lapswich said seriously. "I don't want you gettin' robbed in my town. I don't want that at all. All the big city papers would be makin' fun of me and callin' me a hick constable, and I'd lose my job, like as not.

"I better keep an eye on things," he continued after a pause.

"Thanks a lot," Brent told him.

Lapswich drew himself up importantly. "I'll start out by just takin' a good look right in this room to see there ain't nobody hidin' and lurkin'. You can't tell about these city crooks. They're smart and they're sly."

"Go right ahead," Brent invited. "If you find any pink elephants crawling on the ceiling, don't pay any attention to them. They belong to Fuller. He keeps quite a menagerie. Carries them around with him in bottles."

Lapswich looked carefully under both beds and explored the bathroom. He pulled up the curtains on the two windows and tested the locks with an air of important efficiency.

"What's that thing?" he demanded suddenly, pointing at the huge, grotesque wardrobe.

"Don't ask me," Brent said.

"It's a thing to hang clothes in," Dade explained. "I put it in here because there ain't no closet in this room."

Lapswich fiddled with the catch, finally solved it. He jerked and one of the big, carved doors swung wide open. Lapswich stood there stiffly, with his hand still out, and finally he made a little wordless squeaking sound.

"Oh," said Ira in a sick voice.

Fuller drew in his breath in a long gasp, and Brent reached down quietly and picked up his big Colt.

"It's Mrs. Miller," Dade said stupidly. "Why, this ain't her room. Why, she ain't supposed to be here at all."

The woman was standing against the back of the wardrobe with her knees bent laxly under her. Her head was canted sideways, her face turned toward the wall. She stayed there without moving at all, and it was obvious that she was quite dead.

She was blond and not very old. She had a slim, straight body, and she must have been pretty. It was difficult to tell now whether she had been or not because her face was a dull purple, terribly distorted.

She was wearing a pair of green silk pajamas. Whoever had killed her had slipped her arms out of the sleeves of the pajamas, tied the sleeves together, and fastened them over one of the hooks in the top of the wardrobe. That held her in her awkwardly upright position with the pajama jacket bunched around her neck. She had been stabbed three times over the heart. The wounds were dark, thin slits in the smooth whiteness of her skin.

"See?" Dade yelled suddenly. "I told you! I told you they was crooks! They murdered her! That's what they done! That was her screamin'! I told you!"

"Now just what in the devil is all the row?"

Every man in the room turned around to look at the speaker. He was standing in the doorway, glaring ferociously. He was a short man, barefooted, dressed only in a night-shirt that was so short it revealed knobby knees and thin, hairy calves. His grayish wiry hair was standing up on end. His bony face was twisted into an expression of outraged indignation.

"Answer me!" he yelled. "You, Dade! I
and I demand some consideration around
Don't you know I've got the room above t
think I ever want to sleep? Just because I'm a d
I want to lie awake all night and listen to yo
hyenas down here?"

Dade waved his arms to stop the outburst.
Look! Mrs. Miller—dead! Right there! Killed!"

"Who's Mrs. Miller?" Ralph demanded, not pacified.

"You know, the one that is staying in 203."

"Oh!" said Ralph. "That one. No wonder. Who did it?"

"Them," said Ira, pointing at Fuller and Brent. "Them two."

"I did not!" Fuller shouted, panic stricken.

Ralph looked at him and then at Brent, taking due note of the
big revolver Brent was holding casually on his lap. "Huh!" said
Ralph. "Well, where is she?"

"Right in there," Lapswich told him, pointing.

"Well, what's she doing in there? Get her out!"

"Me?" said Lapswich doubtfully.

Brent got up, slipping the revolver back into his waist-band.
"I'll help. Come on."

Together, he and Lapswich disentangled the knotted pajama
arms, got the woman out of the wardrobe, laid her carefully down
on one of the beds. Ralph leaned over her for a second and then
straightened up, shrugging callously.

"She's dead, but I suppose you knew that. Killed instantly with
three knife blows that all touched her heart. She's been dead at
least twenty-four hours."

"Twenty-four hours!" Dade echoed incredulously. "Why, that
can't be! These guys just came in."

Ralph looked at him. "I said she'd been dead at least twenty-
four hours. If you think you're better capable of judging the phe-
nomenon of rigor mortis than I am, just go right ahead."

"No, no," said Dade hastily. "I didn't mean—But, these guys
didn't get here until tonight. They came in on the 11:02."

"Then they didn't kill her," Ralph said. "She was murdered
about this time last night."

"We were on the Limited last night," Brent put in quietly.
"We can easily prove that we were and that we stayed on the
train all the time."

...re now, Dade," Lapswich said placatingly. "See, you just
...t the wrong idea about these gents." ——

Dade was reluctant about admitting it. "Well, well, I guess
maybe I did at that."

"Don't take my word for this," Ralph said. "Go get the coroner
and ask him. He's a fool and shouldn't be allowed to practice
medicine on anything with a more complicated structure than a
glow-worm, but even he knows enough to tell you I'm right."

"Sure," said Lapswich. "We know you're right, Doc. And we
apologize to you, Mr. Brent and Mr. Fuller. You see, we was kinda
excited and all. . . ."

Brent smiled. "Forget it. How long has she been staying here?"

" 'Bout a week," Dade answered. "She owes me for the whole
business and all her meals, too. I hope she left some money."

A telephone rang lustily somewhere—two short rings and then
two long ones.

"That's your ring, Dade," Ira informed him.

Dade nodded his bald head. "Yeah. Wonder what somebody
wants this hour of the night?" He trotted out of the room on his
fat, short legs. He was back in a moment, puffing hard. "It's for
you, Mr. Fuller."

Fuller whipped a bathrobe out of his case and started for the
door.

"Not so fast," Brent warned. "I'm coming right along. You're
not getting out of my sight until I deliver you and the diamonds."

Brent followed Fuller along the hall, down into the stuffy lobby.
The telephone was fastened to the wall next to the desk. Fuller
picked the receiver up.

"Hello," he said. "Fuller speaking."

Brent put his ear close enough to the receiver to hear the
burred rasping voice of the other man.

"This is Eli Carruthers."

Fuller raised his eyebrows at Brent. "Oh, yes. How do you do,
Mr. Carruthers? It's a pleasure to talk to you again."

"Never mind that. I want you to come over to my house now—
at once. Hire a car or a taxi. I want to conclude that deal of ours
just as soon as possible."

Brent shook his head violently at Fuller and pointed at the old-
fashioned alarm clock sitting on top of the desk.

"Well," said Fuller into the telephone, "it's a little late, Mr. Carruthers, and I hadn't planned—"

"I want to conclude that deal at once!"

"Surely," said Fuller. "I'll be right over. Thank you for calling, Mr. Carruthers." He hung up the receiver.

"What's the idea?" Brent demanded. "Don't you know it's after one o'clock? I don't like the idea of wandering around this late with those diamonds. Why didn't you stall him?"

Fuller shrugged. "I tried. But I'm telling you, he's a hell of a crusty old cuss. No use arguing with him."

"I don't like it," Brent said. "It's taking needless chances. He could just as well have waited until morning."

Fuller slapped him on the shoulder. "What're you worrying about, Brent? Those diamonds are plenty safe in this belt of mine. Nobody can get the belt off, without the key, unless they cut me in two."

Brent nodded slowly. "That wouldn't be altogether impossible either, you know."

∎   ∎   ∎

Ira had refused directly and emphatically to drive Brent and Fuller anywhere, but he had consented to rent them his taxi. Brent was driving it now. The engine labored noisily as the car took the sharply curving ascent of the road. Wind came through the shattered windshield, cool and strong with the rank salt smell of the ocean.

Brent leaned forward, both hands clamped tightly on the top of the steering wheel, carefully examining everything that was revealed in the jiggling glimmer of the head-lights. Fuller lolled easily beside him, his head back on the cushions.

"Lot of stars tonight," he said casually. "Bright, too. Almost as bright as these little babies in my belt."

"Yeah," Brent said. His thin face was drawn. He looked worried and tired and uneasy.

The graveled road curved upward in another long sweep. This short section of the coast was cold, rocky, forbidding. High cliffs jutted out bleakly into the ocean.

"Gonna be foggy pretty quick," Fuller said. "It's coming in now from the ocean. Does every night about this time. Hell of a climate around here."

They swung around another curve and were at the top of the hill. The road followed the shore-line closely here, and the smell of the ocean was stronger; even over the engine sound Brent could hear the sullen mutter of the waves pounding themselves against the rocks somewhere far below in the darkness.

"Around the next curve," Fuller directed. "There's a driveway that goes up to your right."

Brent turned around the next corner, and headed the big car into a narrow road that twisted sharply back and up.

"There," Fuller said. "See it?"

There were dim spots of light in the windows, and the house itself was square and gaunt and ugly against the misty blackness of the sky. The stunted shrubbery and trees around it, bent by the constant unchanging push of the wind, seemed to accentuate its grim loneliness. The car coasted to a stop even with the steps of the high front porch.

"Hell of a cheery place, isn't it?" Fuller asked. "I wonder what he wants to live here for? Must be swell for his daughter. She's a good-looking gal, by the way, but a little bit on the stand-offish side, or maybe she just doesn't like salesmen. She certainly didn't warm up to me at all. Come on."

The sound of the sea was a sullen, ugly mutter that was like a giant voice talking in an undertone. The wind pushed and hauled at them in quick, gusty puffs. Their feet grated on the fine sand strewn on the porch, and Fuller hammered with the bronze knocker on the door. A light above them snapped into sudden radiance. The door opened a crack, cautiously, then swung wider.

"Hello, Mr. Carruthers!" Fuller greeted cheerfully. "Here we are."

"Who's that with you?"

"His name is Brent," Fuller explained easily.

"What's he doing here? What right had you to bring him?"

The man was enormously tall and gaunt, with thin shoulders that were hunched forward grotesquely. The skin on his face looked yellowish and moist, unhealthy. His mouth was a straight lipless line, and there were deep, semicircular creases in his sunken cheeks. His eyes were wide-set and so coldly expressionless that they looked artificial.

"I didn't bring him," Fuller said. "He just came. Brent, this is Mr. Carruthers."

Brent nodded. "How do you do?"

"Get out," Carruthers said. "Get out of here. I'm dealing with Fuller and no one else. I don't want people prying into my business. I won't have it."

"Now wait a minute," Brent advised. "Take it easy. I'm not going to interfere with your business. These diamonds that Fuller is carrying, the ones he is going to sell to you, are insured for full value. I'm a special agent hired by the insurance company to guard Fuller and them. The insurance company is perfectly within its rights, sending me along. That was part of the contract of insurance. Fuller's employers agreed to it."

"Ridiculous!" Carruthers said violently. "Can't Fuller take care of himself? What kind of a diamond salesman is he, if he can't?"

"Why not be reasonable?" Brent asked. "I'm not going to bother you. My job was to deliver the diamonds and Fuller here safely. I've done it."

Carruthers jerked his stick-like arms. "All right! All right! I suppose there's nothing I can do about it, but I'm dealing with Fuller and not with an insurance company."

"That's fine with me," Brent said. "Park me somewhere nearby, and you and Fuller can deal with each other to your heart's content. Personally, I don't care if he sells you the diamonds for a dollar. That's not my business. All I want is to see that no one steals them, until after the title has passed to you, at least. Go ahead and bargain with Fuller."

Carruthers watched him unblinkingly for a moment. "All right. Come in."

Brent and Fuller went into a narrow, high-ceilinged hall lighted by a shaded bulb that hung down on a long chain. It was swinging a little now, turning in the thrust of the wind that came through the open door, sending shadows creeping slyly and noiselessly in dark corners.

"In here," Carruthers said, indicating a doorway.

It was a long, low room, surprisingly comfortable and modern looking with deep leather chairs and a long couch. There was a big smoke-stained stone fireplace at the far end, and flames glinted and snapped brightly in it.

"My daughter," said Carruthers. "You've met Mr. Fuller, my dear. And this is Mr. Brent, a detective assigned to guard the diamonds."

She was a tall girl, straight and lithe and strong. Her hair was blond, bleached slightly by the sun, combed back smoothly from a wide, high forehead. She wore a sleeveless sweater, a short woolen skirt. Her features were widely spaced, even, and a little arrogant. She had an air of calm self-confidence. She nodded at Fuller indifferently and said: "How do you do?" to Brent.

"That is my study," Carruthers said, pointing to a door at the side of the room. "Mr. Fuller and I will go in there and conclude our bargain, if you'll excuse us."

Brent could see almost all of the interior of the room Carruthers had indicated. It was small, lined with bookshelves that stretched from ceiling to floor. There was a wide, flat desk with a reading lamp on it.

Carruthers nodded jerkily at his daughter. "Please entertain Mr. Brent for a few moments, Joan."

He and Fuller went into the study, and the door closed softly behind them.

■   ■   ■

"Sit down?" the girl asked Brent.

Brent nodded and seated himself on the couch, sighing a little. He extended his hands toward the bright warmness of the fire. She was sitting a little back from the fire, and the shadows moved soft, black fingers across her face. ,

She said in a careless voice, "Would you care for a drink? Whiskey and soda?"

"Thanks," Brent said. "A very small one."

He was listening hard. He could hear the faint murmur of voices behind the study door, but he couldn't distinguish words. He was uneasy, and he shifted nervously on the couch, watching the girl get up and move in her gracefully lithe way to the silver decanter and glasses on the table.

"Your father's face seemed slightly familiar to me," he said.

"Did it?"

"Yes. A resemblance to someone I know, I suppose. Has he always lived here?"

"No," she said.

"He was in business somewhere?" Brent asked.

"Yes."

"Where?"

"Several places," she said.

"What kind of business?"

She handed him one of the tall glasses.

"Father said you were a detective, didn't he, Mr. Brent? That must be an interesting life. Dangerous too, I suppose?"

"Sometimes," Brent answered. "Especially when you're dumb like I am. What business was your father in?"

"He had quite extensive interests. Did I make your drink correctly? I don't drink myself, and it's rather hard for me to get the right proportions."

"It's fine," Brent said. He hadn't tasted the drink. "What kind of interests?"

She raised her eyebrows. "I beg your pardon?"

"What kind of interests did your father have?" Brent repeated patiently.

She stood up again. "I really don't know. I've never been interested enough to inquire. Something boring, I expect. Now, will you pardon me for a moment? I have a telephone call to make."

Without waiting for him to answer, she walked out of the door through which Brent and Fuller had entered. Brent sat still, staring moodily into the fire. After a moment, he glanced up at the squat clock on the mantel. It was a little after two and Brent wondered about the phone call excuse. He stared at the door into the study. He could no longer hear the low murmur of voices inside, and it bothered him.

He looked back at the door through which Joan Carruthers had disappeared, listening carefully. He couldn't hear anything but the muffled whoosh of the wind outside, and ghost-like scurry of sand across the bare boards of the front porch. After a moment, he put his drink down carefully on the floor and got up.

He walked in quiet, short steps toward the door of the study. He was half-way there when all the lights went out. Brent felt as though a thick black bandage had suddenly been slapped across his eyes. He couldn't see anything, and he wavered sideways two steps, clawing instinctively at the air to regain his balance.

Glass tinkled sharply behind him. There were three sharp, slamming reports. Little pencils of flame winked at him from the window nearest the fireplace. Brent heard the bullets hit the wall behind him, and one of them came so close to his face that he felt the cold, quick breath of it passing. Feet drummed on the porch, running.

Brent jerked the big revolver out of his waist-band and made for the window. He stumbled over a chair, righted himself, knelt in front of the shattered glass, peering out. There was a vague figure, dark and blurred against the white sand, running up the slope of the hill. Brent fired at it once, and then it was gone, disappearing like magic into the shadow of the stunted shrubs.

Brent turned and blundered back across the room. He felt his knees hit the couch, and then he got his direction and headed straight across for the study door. He ran against it with his shoulder, and he raised the revolver and struck the panels twice with the short barrel.

"Fuller!" he called. "Fuller! Carruthers!"

His voice echoed emptily, and he swore to himself in a tense whisper, groping for the knob. He found it, and it turned easily and silently in his fingers. The door swung back.

There was no more light in the study than in the living-room, and Brent stood crouched in the doorway, squinting painfully, trying to make out some outline in the darkness.

"Fuller," he said.

He fumbled in his pocket, found a match. The flame made a bright yellow waver. Brent held it up over his head. He was expecting a shot, expecting anything, and he tensed himself instinctively.

The study was empty. There was no sign of any disturbance. The furniture was placed just as Brent had seen it before. There was two empty chairs sitting on either side of the flat desk, and there was nothing on the desk except a dull spatter across the slickness of its surface.

Brent lowered the match slowly. He saw that the spatter consisted of small rounded splashes that were red and wet. It was blood.

The match burned his fingers, and he dropped it. He had marked the position of the window in back of the desk, and he moved quietly to it now. It was a French window, extending from the ceiling almost to the floor. The latch clicked under his fingers, and Brent stepped through. He was on a long, low porch. He kept in the deep shadow close to the wall, edging slowly toward the back of the house. The porch stopped at the corner of the house, and Brent stood there for a long moment, watching, trying to make out some form in the stunted tangle of shrubbery that moved and whispered softly in the wind.

Twice his eyes passed over one little clump of bedraggled brush before he could distinguish the man who was crouching there. The man was on his knees, leaning forward, and he had a gun in his hand. It was the blued glitter of the barrel that had attracted Brent's eyes.

Brent stood still. He didn't think the other man had seen him. The white blur of the face was turned to one side, and the gun barrel wasn't pointing in Brent's direction. The man was listening and watching, just as Brent was, and now he got to his feet in slow, cautious jerks. He came running on tiptoe toward the house, hunched over.

Brent let him get within about two yards, and then he said softly:

"Stand still and drop that gun."

The other man straightened with a jerk. The gun spun out of his fingers, chucked softly into the sand.

"D-don't shoot. I'm a policeman."

"Lapswich!" Brent exclaimed.

Lapswich turned his head. His teeth were chattering.

"H-huh? Oh! It's Mr. Brent! What—"

"Back up," Brent said.

Lapswich went cautiously backwards.

Brent took two steps forward, bent over, and picked up Lapswich's gun. It was a Luger automatic with a disproportionately long barrel. Brent felt the breech with his fingers, sniffed at the muzzle. The gun hadn't been fired recently, and Brent relaxed slightly.

"What're you doing here?" he asked.

"Well—well, I was worried, what with that woman gettin' herself murdered and them diamonds. I sort of snuck along behind you and Mr. Fuller just to see that none of them crooks got after you. I was scoutin' round outside, and I heard shots—"

"Little out of your territory, aren't you?" Brent asked. "I thought I heard you say you were town marshal."

"Sure. Sure, I am. But I'm a deppity sheriff, too. This here is part of the county."

Brent held the Luger up by its long barrel. "This the only gun you've got?"

"Sure!" said Lapswich. "Ain't that enough? That's a mighty fine gun, Mr. Brent! I sent to New York for that, and it cost me a month's salary. It's got a special eight-inch barrel—"

"All right," Brent said, handing it to him. "Sorry I jumped you. You can help, now you're here. Fuller's disappeared."

Lapswich's mouth opened. "Disappeared! And the diamonds? But Mr. Carruthers—"

"He's gone, too. And so is his daughter. And somebody tried to make me disappear. That was the shooting you heard. Come on. We'll look for them now. Keep even with me about ten feet away. Don't shoot unless I do."

They went slowly up the slope of the hill in back of the house, crouching low to keep in the cover of the shrubs. They reached the top of the slope. They were in the full sweep of the wind now, and Brent could feel the moist, salt taste of it on his lips. He could see plainly down the slope toward the house. There was no movement, no light.

"What's that?" Brent asked, pointing to something square and low sitting on the sand twenty-five yards away. In the night it looked like an enormously magnified building block.

"Oh," Lapswich said, and let his breath out in a sigh. "That. That's just some boards nailed together in a square. It's where Joan Carruthers takes her sun baths. She don't wear any clothes when she's in there. Not any clothes at all."

"Come on," Brent said.

He walked slowly toward the dark loom of the board square. It was about seven feet high and possibly twelve-by-twelve in length and width. Brent circled a little, approaching it, located the narrow flap of heavy canvas that served as an entrance and an exit.

"If you're in there," he said, "you'd better come out."

"You bet," Lapswich echoed feebly. "You—you're under arrest."

The canvas flap moved slowly and gently in the wind, but there was no answer. Brent jerked the flap aside. There was no floor inside the structure except the soft whiteness of the sand. The only furnishing was an army cot with a few pillows heaped on it.

Brent looked at something in the far corner, then. Something that was half buried in the sand, glinting a little. He stepped over to it, moved it with his foot. It was an ax. He struck a match and knelt down in the sand. The blade of the ax was crusted with coagulated blood. Even the handle was thick with it.

"Gaah!" Lapswich said, choking.

Brent's mouth tightened, and his face looked hard and white in the flicker of the match flame. He struck another match and, putting his revolver in his waist-band, began to sift through the sand gingerly with his fingers. He touched rough cloth, spread the sand away from it.

It was a flattened burlap sack. Something in it clinked softly when Brent moved it.

"Hold a light for me," Brent asked in a low voice.

Lapswich was shivering so violently he had difficulty holding a lighted match. He finally holstered the Luger and used both hands, bracing them one against the other. Brent reached very slowly inside the burlap sack. He brought his hand out holding a tubular leaden sash-weight. He dropped it on the sand.

"There's a couple more in the sack," he said absently.

Brent went carefully over the sand, touching it with his fingers. Beside the cot he stopped, still kneeling, brushed with quick little flicks of his hand. The soft sand was only a thin layer here. Underneath it was packed hard. It was gummy, caked with something that glinted red.

"Oh," said Lapswich.

Brent wiped his fingers carefully on his handkerchief and stood up.

"B-blood?" Lapswich inquired.

"Yes," Brent said.

"What—what's it mean? The sack, everything—"

"You saw Fuller's belt," Brent said slowly.

Lapswich dropped the matches. "Sure. Looked like a money belt."

"On that idea," Brent agreed. "That belt was made out of steel strips interlaced. It couldn't be cut through. It had a lock on it that couldn't be picked. It was too small to slip over Fuller's hips. There was only one way to get it off him in a hurry if you didn't have the key."

"How?" Lapswich asked.

"Cut him in two."

Lapswich repeated, uncomprehending, "Cut him—you mean—oh!"

"Yes," said Brent. "This is the place to do it. The ocean is nice and handy. Put the parts of the body in burlap sacks weighted down, throw them over the cliff. I guess we bothered the murderer. He didn't have time to finish the job. That's why one burlap sack was left here."

"Oh," said Lapswich. He swallowed with a gulp. "Say! Say! Where's Carruthers?"

"That's what I'm wondering."

"He done it!" Lapswich exclaimed. "It's a plot! I see it all, now! He never meant to buy them stones! He meant to steal 'em! And he got your friend to bring 'em clear out here and—and then he done it!"

She hadn't made any noise, but she was there suddenly, in the entrance of the board square, holding the canvas flap aside and looking in at them. Her head was back, and she was straight and erect and defiant. Brent couldn't see her face in the darkness, but her voice was a little uncertain, fumbling with the words.

"I heard—what you said. . . ."

"Where is your father?" Brent asked.

"I don't know. The lights went out. I couldn't find him." She drew in a deep breath. "You think he killed that conceited fool of a Fuller, don't you?"

"Well, now," Lapswich said uneasily. "Well, Miss Joan, I wouldn't want to go hurting you, but now what's a man to think?"

"You fool!"

"Well," Lapswich said, "it looks to me like your father wanted those diamonds without payin' for 'em."

"Faugh! Those diamonds! Do you think my father would do what you think he did for trash like they are?"

"Trash?" Lapswich said. "Well, now, I dunno about that. A quarter of a million dollars—"

"He didn't do it!"

"Well," said Lapswich. "Well, Miss Joan, I sure hope he didn't. But if didn't, where is he? Why don't he show up and explain himself?"

Her hand clenched on the canvas. She was still erect and defiant, but she was holding herself up by sheer will-power.

"He didn't do it!"

She whirled away blindly and ran stumbling down the slope toward the dark, gaunt house.

Lapswich coughed. "I gotta call the sheriff."

∎ ∎ ∎

It was almost daylight when Brent got back to the hotel, and he was so tired that his body was one great ache and it took a conscious physical effort to keep his eyes open. Dade had assigned him a new room, and he went there and tried to sleep. After an hour he gave it up. He got up and got dressed.

The wind hadn't risen yet, and the night fog was still thick over the village. Outside the window of Brent's room it was a gray, moist blanket, unmoving and dead, veiling everything. He put the big Colt in his waist-band and went down to the lobby.

Dade was behind the desk, busily writing, and there was another man sitting in a chair opposite the desk, reading a newspaper that concealed his face and upper body.

"'Morning, Mr. Brent," Dade greeted, looking up. "Gettin' around kinda early for a city feller, ain't you?"

Brent nodded. "Yes. Where's Lapswich's office?"

"Down the street to the next corner and turn right. It's the second building. Say, I heard what happened last night. Say, that's terrible, that is. That's gonna give the town a bad reputation."

"It's going to give me one, too," Brent said.

"Well, wait a minute," Dade requested. "I wanta talk to you about this. I got some ideas, I have. Maybe I could give you some new angles. Just as soon as I get Mr. Carson's bill made out, I'll be with you."

Brent glanced casually at the man sitting in the chair. The man moved a little, adjusting the opened paper, and Brent caught a little wink of green from a big stone in the ring on the middle finger of his right hand. Brent's eyes narrowed alertly. The man was wearing a neat pin-stripe blue suit and pearl gray spats.

"There!" said Dade, straightening up. "All fixed now, Mr. Carson. I'll just get your bags—"

"Stay there," Brent said. He was standing rigidly still at the bottom of the stairs, and now he held the .38–40. "Hello, Faro," he said.

The seated man didn't move, didn't speak. He kept the paper up in front of his face.

"That's Mr. Carson," Dade said. His voice trailed away faintly, and he swallowed with an audible gulp.

"Hello, Faro," Brent repeated.

The silence grew thicker, heavy with strained menace. The seated man didn't move in his chair.

"I think you've got a gun in your lap, Faro," Brent said. "Don't try to use it. Drop the paper, but keep your hands just where they are now."

The seated man's fingers loosened, and the paper fluttered to the floor. He was slender, dapper, small. His face was smooth and round, and his features were very small and even. His eyes were a wide limpid brown. There was a .45 automatic lying in his lap, and it was cocked.

"Hello," he said. His voice was low and soft. "I don't think I know you."

"You don't," Brent answered. "But I know you. I spotted the green ring and the spats. You shouldn't wear things like that, Faro. Not in your business. Stand up. Let the gun fall on the floor."

"No," said Faro. "Better think it over. There's no reward on me."

"Stand up," said Brent.

"No. You're not taking me in. You know why. There's two murder raps on me."

"Three, now," Brent said. "And maybe four. Counting the dame upstairs and that business last night at Carruthers'."

"Yeah," Faro said. "So I'm not going in. Better just drop the idea. I'll down you, you know I will. You'll get me, too, maybe. But that won't do you much good when you're dead. Let's call it off. Put the gun away."

"No," said Brent. "Stand up."

"I didn't do anything at Carruthers' last night."

Running feet made a sudden echoing pound outside. The front door slammed open, and Lapswich burst into the lobby. He was waving a yellow slip of paper in his hand.

"Dade!" he yelled. "Look! I just heard—"

He walked between Faro and Brent. Faro moved like a striking snake. He came out of the chair with the automatic in his right hand. His left arm went around Lapswich's neck, choked off Lapswich's voice in a sputtering gurgle.

"All right," Faro said. His voice was still soft, but it had a thin, snarling viciousness in it. "I'm dealing now." He was holding Lapswich close against him, and only his eyes were visible, peering at Brent over Lapswich's rigid shoulder. "Drop the gun."

Brent's lips twisted desperately. Dade had disappeared down behind his desk. Lapswich's face was a queer lemon color, and his eyes rolled wildly.

"Drop it," Faro said. "If you don't I'll put a bullet right through this old boy's spine."

"S-shoot!" Lapswich gurgled desparately. "Mr. Brent, don't let him—" His voice choked off again as Faro tightened his grip.

"You win," Brent said. His gun thudded on the floor.

"That's right," Faro commended. "Now I'm going out of here. I'm taking the old boy along. If you don't push me too close I won't hurt him. I'll dump him out down the road. Keep right close to me, pop. You behind the desk, come on up."

Dade's bald, shining head slid up into sight an inch at a time.

"Go out and see where that car is. Don't get funny. Remember, the old boy gets it right where it'll hurt the most if anybody tries to stop me."

"Y-yes, sir," said Dade.

Ira's lean, gangling form appeared in the doorway behind Faro and Lapswich. He stared at the scene with eyes that bulged in unbelieving amazement.

Brent saw him. "Wait!" he said quickly to Faro. "You can't get away from here. The sheriff's got deputies blocking off every road out of this district, looking for Carruthers."

"I've got a hostage," Faro said. "They'll let me through. Just stand right where you are."

Ira's throat moved as he swallowed. "Mister," he said in a shaky voice. "You put that gun down, or I'll shoot you. I sure as hell will."

Faro jerked around and fired at him. His grip loosened on Lapswich, and Lapswich twisted violently, fell sprawling on his back. Brent dove for his gun.

Faro spun around lightly, fired at Brent. Brent saw the carpet twitch six inches in front of his face, and then his desperately clutching fingers closed on his revolver. He pulled the trigger three times.

Faro's smooth features disappeared in a purple smear. He

slammed head-first over the chair he had been seated in, landed in a limp pile in the corner. His legs moved a little, and then he was still.

Brent sat up on the floor. He took out a handkerchief and wiped his forehead.

Lapswich coughed, holding his throat tenderly, and Dade's bald head rose slowly from behind the desk.

Lapswich got up and leaned over Faro. "Dead, all right. Who was he, Mr. Brent?"

"His name was Faro," Brent said wearily. "He's a jewel thief. One of the very best, or worst. He was a killer. He's wanted in two States for murder."

"He killed Mrs. Miller!" Dade exclaimed.

Brent nodded. "Yes. There was something familiar about her face. I couldn't place it. But I remembered when I saw that green ring of Faro's. He always wore it. Thought it was good luck. The Miller woman used to be an accomplice of his. He worked that way. She sometimes got a job as a maid in some big place, spotted the layout for him and told him when to pull the job. He stabbed her and hid her in the room Fuller and I had because it wasn't very often used. He thought she wouldn't be found for a while—until he had time to get out himself."

"Gosh!" said Dade. "Right in my hotel." He scowled at Lapswich. "A fine constable you are, letting such things happen!"

"Yeah," Lapswich said meekly. "I guess I ain't very smart."

"What was you yellin' about when you come in?"

"Oh!" Lapswich said, suddenly remembering. "Look, Mr. Brent! The sheriff's fingerprint man went over the room where Fuller and Mr. Carruthers was talkin' last night before they both disappeared. The sheriff sent the prints into Washington, and I just got this telegram." He picked it up off the floor. "And what do you think? Eli Carruthers was a crook!"

"That old stinker," said Dade.

Lapswich continued: "Just like this here Faro. A big jewel thief, only he quit about five years ago and disappeared, and they ain't never been able to lay hands on him! His real name was Reynolds. And Joan phoned the sheriff last night for help!"

"You sure of this?" Brent demanded.

"You bet! They sent a description. It's right here. It matches old Eli Carruthers right to a T. He was hidin', see? That's why he was livin' clear out here. But he was still thievin', see, and that's why he had Fuller bring them diamonds out here, pretendin' he wanted to buy 'em, just so he could kill Fuller and steal 'em. But you come along with Fuller and spoiled things."

"And that Faro was in it, too," Dade added. "Him and his woman that he killed. I knew there was somethin' wrong with him. He was always actin' funny. Just this mornin' he wanted Ira to drive him out to Foster's Point so he could fish! Hah! If that ain't crazy!"

"Where did you say?" Brent asked.

"Foster's Point. Why, everybody knows you can't fish there. There ain't nothing to catch."

"He was going there this morning?" Brent inquired.

Dade nodded. "Yup. He said he wanted another try at fishin' before he left, but I told him—"

"Wait," Brent interrupted. "Can you land a boat at Foster's Point?"

"Sure," said Lapswich, "you can, but it ain't a very good place for it."

"Then I think I'll go fishing, too," Brent said. "I wonder where Ira went?"

"Shucks," said Dade. "You ain't gonna get Ira to drive you no place this mornin', not if I know Ira. If you was to look, you'd probably find him in the back of Potter's Pool Hall workin' on a quart of corn whiskey."

"Then I'll borrow his car," Brent decided.

"Could I come along?" Lapswich asked. "Honest, Mr. Brent, I won't do nothing dumb this time."

Brent started for the door. "Come on, then."

"Here!" Dade protested violently. "What about this body? You can't leave that in my lobby!"

"Call the coroner," Lapswich advised. "Me and Mr. Brent is too busy to bother now."

■   ■   ■

The motor of Ira's car rumbled monotonously in the fog that surrounded it like a soft wrapping of woolly, wet cotton. Lapswich was driving. Brent, sitting beside him, couldn't see more than ten feet beyond the car's radiator, but Lapswich seemed to find his way by instinct. The car skidded going around a curve, tires chewing vainly at soft, damp sand. Brent felt a little chill along his spine, listening to the sullen sound of waves invisible somewhere far below them. The car jerked, straightened out.

"How close are we to the ocean?" he asked.

"Quite a ways—down," Lapswich answered absently. "This road runs along them high cliffs south of town."

"It's pretty narrow," Brent said. "Aren't we liable to meet another car unexpectedly?"

"Nope," said Lapswich. "Nobody uses this road. It's been condemned. It runs too close to the cliff edge. Keeps crumbling off all the time."

He jerked the wheel suddenly. The car swerved, and Brent caught a glimpse of a crevice three feet wide that extended into the center of the road.

"That's a bad place," Lapswich said. "I was lookin' for it, but I come on it a little sooner than I expected."

Brent looked over his side of the car and found that the side of the road was no longer there. He could see nothing but fog rolling dimly.

"Hey!" he said, breath catching in his throat.

Lapswich turned the wheel, and the side of the road appeared again. "Pretty close there," he said. "Oughta put up a rail or something. We're almost there now. What do you think we'll find out here?"

"I don't know," Brent said. "I'm just hoping."

"Why do you suppose that Faro killed that Miller woman if she was his accomplice?"

"Faro specialized in jewels," Brent answered. "The insurance people kept pretty close track of him, as close as they could. There was a rumor that he and his accomplice had split up. That must have been true. He probably ditched her. She didn't like it, and she followed him down here to declare herself in on this job. He wasn't having any. I told you he was a killer. He was already wanted for two murders. One more wouldn't make any difference to him. So he just got rid of her. He didn't figure on her being found so quickly."

"You think he was the one that shot at you and Ira and Fuller when you was comin' into town?"

"No. And he wasn't the one that shot at me last night."

"How do you figure?"

"The man that shot at Fuller and Ira meant just to scare us.

That must have been the reason. Otherwise it doesn't make sense. Faro wouldn't want to scare us. And if he had been the one that shot at me last night, he'd have hit me. Faro's a dead shot, and he doesn't get excited. The fellow that shot at me was all in an uproar. He cut the light wires by the window—and then shot when it was dark and he couldn't see. Faro would have shot me first."

Lapswich turned off the road suddenly, and the car bumped and rocked over rough ground and stopped with a jar.

"This is as close to Foster's Point as we can drive. It's a couple hundred yards over yonder," Lapswich said.

"We're probably too late," Brent said, getting out of the car. "I've got an idea that Faro had arranged for a boat to come in and pick 'em up here."

"Then we ain't too late," Lapswich said. "You couldn't get a boat in here this morning. The tide's comin' in, and it's too foggy. Lots of rocks and surf."

The sandy ground underfoot grew damp, and bare wet rocks protruded here and there as the two walked down the road. Lapswich stopped suddenly.

"Look," Lapswich requested. He pointed to a scuffed place in the soil. He knelt down, touched it with his fingers. His face was a little strained when he looked up at Brent. "Fresh. Somebody just come along here. They ain't far ahead."

"Good," Brent murmured. He drew his Colt, balanced it in his hand. They went forward slowly, watching the roll and shift of the fog.

"There," said Lapswich. "Stairs."

Brent saw a sagging wooden railing, slick and black with moisture.

"They go down the face of the cliff," Lapswich said. "There's an old wharf down at the bottom. Go careful. These stairs ain't very safe."

Brent looked at the crooked stairway clinging precariously to the bare rock. He couldn't see more than a few yards down, but the sense of a long drop was there just the same, and he could hear the sullen, hungry sound of the surf far below. He started down the stairs, and he could feel them sway and move under him. He walked down slowly, settling his weight evenly on each step, sliding one hand along the wet railing. The fog grew thicker,

seeming to close in on him as he went. He didn't look back, but
he knew Lapswich was keeping just a step behind him.

He had descended an interminable number of steps, and his
knees were beginning to feel numb under him when he heard the
soft muttering of voices below. He stopped short, listening. The
voices went on talking, but the words were indistinguishable. Lapswich grunted behind him, and Brent heard the soft click of the
safety on the long barreled Luger.

"Watch that gun," Brent whispered. "I'll tell you when to use
it."

He went cautiously down more steps, and then he could see
the wet, sagging boards of the platform at the bottom of the
stairs. A person was standing there. Brent saw brown, bare legs,
slimly rounded. He went down another step, and then he could
see the rest of Joan Carruthers. She was wearing a bathing suit
with a heavy white sweater over it. She had her back toward
Brent, and she was talking to a man who was a vague gray shape
in the fog. He was on the wharf below the platform, farther away.

Brent took another step, and the rotten board cracked under
his weight. He stumbled, caught himself with a frantic clutch at
the railing. Joan Carruthers whirled with a sharp, frightened cry.

"Hold it!" Brent shouted.

But the vague gray man-shape was gone. He had whirled back
on the wharf, jumped off. Brent heard the sucking thud of his
feet landing on wet sand, and then the slash-slash-slash of water
as he ran.

Brent jumped down the remaining steps, landed hard on the
platform. He brushed past Joan Carruthers, hurdled from the
platform to the wharf, jumped off. His feet hit hard on packed
sand and water sucked at his ankles. He caught his balance and
ran forward blindly. Lapswich was floundering noisily behind him.

The ground sloped away under Brent, and the water came up
coldly around his waist. He felt himself falling, and then Lapswich's hand seized his shoulder, dragged him back.

"Shore zigzags here," Lapswich panted. "That girl—you want
me to get her?"

"No," Brent said. "Let her go. Come on."

They were running ahead again, blindly.

"Wait," Lapswich said breathlessly. "Low place here. Cave
washed out of the cliff."

Brent slowed cautiously, saw the wide black fissure.

"Look," said Lapswich. He pointed to small parallel streaks shoulder high on the rough rock beside the cave entrance. "Fingers. Someone's grabbed the rock here and turned."

"Went in the cave," Brent said. "Can he get out the other end of it?"

"No. Ain't no other end."

"How far back does it go?"

Lapswich shook his head. "I dunno. Ain't never been in it. Quite a ways, I reckon. Dangerous place. There's always water coverin' the bottom. Might be some deep holes. What we gonna do?"

"Go in after him," said Brent.

"In there?" Lapswich asked uneasily. "It's kinda dark."

"All the better," Brent said. "He can't see us. Keep close to the wall until you get inside so he can't spot us against the light."

Brent slid along the wetness of the rock wall. Inside the cave the air was suddenly damper and heavy. The sound of the waves outside echoed like the muffled boom of drums. Water sloshed around Brent's ankles. He waited until he felt Lapswich close behind, and then he started forward in the dark, misty gloom, his left hand extended in front of him. He could catch a faint, slick reflection from the walls that closed in on either side. Lapswich slipped suddenly and went down with a floundering splash.

Instantly there was a dull boom ahead of them, and then two more in quick succession. Brent leaned over Lapswich, picked him up.

"We've got him," he whispered. "He's right around that turn ahead, and he's scared. He was shooting blind then. He can't see us."

"I'm scared, too," Lapswich said, shivering. "I'm damned scared."

"Stay here, then, I'll get him."

"N-no, I'll come."

Brent went forward step by step. He could see a little better now. There was the jut of a wet, smooth shoulder of stone ahead, a turn in the jaggedly narrow corridor. Brent stopped there, listening, and then deliberately splashed in the water with his foot.

The unseen gun boomed out again, and a ricocheting bullet

screamed weirdly. Brent poked his gun around the corner and fired.

"No!" a voice wailed. "Don't shoot! Don't kill me!"

"Throw the gun down," Brent ordered.

There was a quick splash.

"All right," Brent said. He slid around the corner. Behind him Lapswich gulped noisily and then followed.

There was a little niche in the rock wall, and a dark figure huddled there, arms wound tightly around its head. It moved, and its face was a white, distorted smear, peering at them.

"Hello, Fuller," Brent said.

"Fuller!" Lapswich exclaimed. "Fuller! Why, he's dead!"

"No," Brent said. "Not very. Carruthers didn't kill him. He killed Carruthers. Carruthers—or Reynolds—had retired from the diamond stealing business, but either Fuller or Faro found him, and the two of them decided to put the squeeze on him. They'd worked together before. Fuller held a job with a very reputable firm of diamond brokers—his present employers. But he has expensive tastes. He wanted more money. So on the side, he acted as tip-off man and fence. His job gave him a swell front for that, and in the past he's always dealt with the company very honestly, because he wanted to keep the front."

He tightened his hold on the trembling Fuller and went on:

"But this was too good a chance to stay even that honest. He and Faro told Carruthers that Carruthers would have to buy a quarter of a million dollars' worth of diamonds from the company Fuller represented, or they'd squeal on Carruthers and turn him up for some of his past jobs. The idea, so they told Carruthers, was to give Fuller the commission he would get from the company for making the sale, which would be plenty. But actually Fuller and Faro intended to steal the diamonds from the company and the money for their purchase from Carruthers. Then they'd both conveniently disappear and let Carruthers take the blame. It was quite an elaborate plan, but they were playing for a stake of a half-million dollars in cash and diamonds. That's worth going to some trouble for. Carruthers suspected something—he was no fool."

"He's a dead fool now," Fuller blurted.

Brent said, "Shut up, you rat." Then to Lapswich: "That's why Carruthers shot at us in the car. He meant to scare Fuller, show him he wasn't going to take it lying down if Fuller meant to pull anything. He knew Fuller was yellow. But, as it happened, Fuller was too drunk at the time to know much about it."

The three of them sloshed through the water to the cave's entrance.

"Gosh," said Lapswich. "How was they gonna do all this?"

"Just like they did. Kill Carruthers and make it look like he had killed Fuller. Fuller stabbed him last night as soon as they were alone in the study. The burlap sack, the ax, the bloodstains were all left on purpose. They'd been planned ahead of time. Fuller and Faro didn't actually cut Carruthers up, I don't think. They just killed him and threw him in the ocean. Fuller'll hang for that."

"But the girl," Lapswich said. "Miss Joan?"

"She must have known Fuller was at the bottom of this. She found him here. When we came he was trying to stall her off long enough for Faro to get here. Faro would have fixed her just like he did the other one."

Fuller had straightened up slowly, even leaned against the gun Brent had pushed in his back. His blond hair was plastered wetly over his forehead. His lips were pinched with the cold, but they twisted into a sarcastic sneer.

"So you think that's the way it happened, huh? Maybe you think you can prove it, too. But you won't. Oh, no! You'll accept my story. Faro did it all by himself. I just got scared when he killed Carruthers and hid here. I didn't even know he had killed that woman in the hotel until—"

"You liar," said Brent. "You knew who she was just as soon as you saw her, and you knew why Faro killed her. You knew he had ditched her and that she was trying to do him dirt."

"You won't prove that, either," Fuller said. "Why? I'll tell you why. Because of those diamonds. I haven't got them on me. They're hidden. And you won't find them. That's why you'll accept my story. Because if you don't the insurance company you work for will be out two hundred and fifty thousand. Get the idea?"

"Roughly," said Brent. "And it might be a good one if I didn't know where the diamonds were. But I do."

"You don't!" Fuller shouted.

"Sure, I do. Right here." Brent unbuttoned his vest and shirt and indicated a small leather pouch that hung on a fine steel chain around his neck. "Hell's bells! Do you think I'm crazy? Do you think I'd let you run around on a train as drunk as you were with a quarter of a million dollars on you? Of course not. The first time you passed out, I ripped the stitches in your pants' cuff with a razor blade and got the key to your belt. I took the diamonds out, put in some imitations I carried with me for just such a purpose. Then I sewed the key back in your pants again with a needle and some thread I borrowed from the porter. I did a pretty good job, too, even if I did stick my finger seventeen times while I was at it. You didn't spot it. I would have told you what I did when you sobered up, only by that time things began to look pretty fishy to me."

"You lie!" Fuller screamed hysterically.

He jumped around and leaped straight at Brent with both his hands crooked into claws, raking at Brent's eyes with his fingernails. Brent stepped back, ducking, and Lapswich swung the long barrel of his Luger in a swishing arc. The steel made a slapping sound on Fuller's head. He went down face foremost in the shallow water of the beach.

"Got him!" said Lapswich proudly. "I did do something after all, darn it!"

"Good work," Brent commended. "Pick him up before he drowns. You can take him back to town. I'm going to stay here and get acquainted with Joan. I think she needs some consolation."

He walked off through the fog.

James Reasoner

DOWN IN THE VALLEY

From *Mike Shayne Mystery Magazine,* September 1979

Author of innumerable novels in innumerable categories, James Reasoner is best known—under his real name, anyway—as the author of Texas Wind, *one of the great cult hardboiled novels of our time. Somebody really ought to bring it back into print, and very soon. One other thing: Reasoner is as good a short story writer as he is a novelist. Here is an example of what a master can do in just a few perfectly chosen words.*

E. G.

FORTY-THREE MEN HUDDLED IN THE BACK OF THE TRUCK, COLD and afraid. There was no moon, and the canvas flaps on the side cut out what little starlight there was. It was pitch black inside, and none of the men knew where they were headed.

Ramon didn't care. He was in the United States now, and that was all that mattered to him. Now he would never have to go back to the little village in the hills. He shifted his shoulders against the wall of the truck and closed his eyes.

There were whispered conversations all around him, as the nervous men tried to ease the tension. No one talked to Ramon, though. He had always been a quiet one, preferring to let his knife speak for him when it had to. That was why he was here now; his knife had one day been too eloquent and left a dead man on the floor of the cantina. Now he was on his way to a new life in a new country.

Up in the cab, the driver rubbed his neck and squinted down the path of the headlights. He was a big man named Flood who thought about neither the past nor the future, but only about the money he had coming when he got his load of wetbacks to

San Antonio. Flood didn't care about the legality of what he was doing. The men who had set up the pipeline paid well.

Farther down the road, two men sat drowsily in a parked car. It was a battered old Plymouth, and anyone passing by on the highway wouldn't have given it a second look. The two men inside had been sitting there for four hours, waiting.

Ramon felt sleep easing into his head as the truck rolled along. He let it come in gladly. The last seventy-two hours had been busy.

In his dream, he woke up. He got out of bed and went to the door of his hut. Down at the end of the valley, the sun was creeping up over the hills. Ramon enjoyed watching the sunrise; he liked the pretty colors. But he did not like going to work in the fields, and that was the thing that the sunrise signaled.

"Ramon?" It was a sleepy murmur from the bed. He returned to it and stroked the glossy black hair spread out on the pillow. It was hard for him to make his hand be gentle.

"Go back to sleep, Elena," he said quietly.

". . . love you," the woman said, and snuggled back down into the covers. Ramon went outside, wondering briefly why he could not say it as easily as she could.

■   ■   ■

While Ramon slept and dreamed, Flood felt his own eyelids getting heavier. He was glad the truck had a radio, even if it could only get one station. He switched it on and turned it up loud, not caring if it disturbed his passengers.

The twangy chords of country music made him more alert and even brought back some memories. He wasn't one for reminiscing, but there was one moment he liked to relive every now and then.

He had come home from the oilfield covered with dirt and grease, as usual, and announced, "I'm not goin' back to that place. I've had it with roughneckin'."

His wife was feeding the baby and watching the Grand Ole Opry on TV. She looked up at him and pushed the hair out of her face. "Then how are we supposed to eat from now on?"

He opened a can of beer and said, "That's your problem, not mine." Before she could start screaming, he went on, "I'm getting out of here."

"You're leavin' me?" she shrilled. "Leavin' the baby?"

"You got it, ace. You always were real quick on the uptake."

She put the baby down and it started to cry. She ignored it and caught at his arm. "You can't do that! What'll we do?"

He shook her hand off and headed for the bedroom to pack. She followed close behind, face mottled with fury. She yelled, "Just where do you think you're goin', anyway?"

He pivoted and started to slap her, but he stopped the blow when she cringed back. "I'm going far away from here, just as far as I can get from your whining and nagging. I want something better." His voice lowered, became more intense. "I want plenty of money and fancy women and good whiskey, and I won't ever have none of that if I stay here!"

Tears rolled down his wife's face as she sobbed, "But what about me and the baby? What about your responsibilities?"

He had to laugh. "Honey, we don't even speak the same language anymore!"

Well, he had more money now, but the whiskey and the women still weren't always that easy to come by. He chuckled to himself in the dark cab. Anything was better than living with that woman.

He barely glanced at the old Plymouth as he barreled past it.

* * *

Inside the car, one of the men suddenly nudged the other and said, "There he goes, Dave. Right on time."

The man called Dave wasn't sleepy anymore. He reached under the dash and picked up a microphone. "This is Unit 101. Suspect vehicle just passed our position, proceeding north. You can start closing the net, Barney. We'll be right behind him."

Even while he was speaking, the other man had started the car and pulled out onto the highway. The Plymouth started to pick up speed.

* * *

The truck bounced slightly as it went over a rough spot in the road. Ramon woke up, and in that split-second when he didn't remember where he was, he almost cried out. His fingers instinctively sought the handle of his blade. But then he recognized the rocking motion of the truck and settled back into a more comfortable position.

He wondered what the Fates held for him in the big American city. What should he become? He didn't know yet; all he knew was that he didn't want to work in the fields, long hours of labor that made the body ache so. He had had enough of that.

Up front, Flood moved around on the seat, trying to find a new way to sit. He had been driving for several hours and was getting tired. His right leg hurt from trying to maintain a constant pressure on the gas pedal. His employers had made it clear. He was to be very careful not to break any traffic laws.

Flood's eyes moved all the time, from the mirror to the panel and back again. This time, when they flicked to the mirror, they saw a pair of lights behind him in the night.

The radio in the Plymouth crackled and said, "One-oh-one, this is one-oh-four. We're all in position, Dave. He's your baby now, and you can goose him any time you want."

Dave acknowledged the transmission and then said, "Okay, Jack, let's move up on him." The Plymouth put on more speed.

■   ■   ■

Flood kept glancing uneasily at the mirror as the lights drew closer. He was tempted to speed up, but he was already going the speed limit, and he had his orders. Then a red light suddenly flashed into existence on top of the following car, and Flood felt his breath catch in his throat. His foot automatically tromped down on the accelerator.

Ramon felt the lurch as the truck picked up speed and wondered what had happened. He hoped there was nothing wrong. The man to whom he had given all his money had promised that there would be no trouble.

Flood was cursing to himself as he gripped the steering wheel tight. This was supposed to be a perfect setup. Someone along the pipeline must have fouled up and spilled the whole operation to save his own skin.

This was a flat stretch of road, sided by plains covered with scrubby growth. Flood was pushing the truck as hard as he could, but it had been built to be useful and inconspicuous, not fast. The car behind was steadily closing the gap.

A smaller road crossed the highway about a mile ahead. Lights blazed on at the crossroad as the truck approached. Police cars clustered in the middle of the intersection.

Flood groaned. There went his last real chance. All he could do now was get the truck off the road, abandon it, and hope he could slip off into the brush on foot.

The men in the back of the truck were gabbling chaotically. They asked each other what was going on, but no one had any answers. A few of them yelled in fright as the truck suddenly swung off the highway and started bouncing wildly across the rough ground.

Flood had to fight the wheel as it tried to tear itself out of his hands. Sweat dripped down his face. It would take a miracle to get him out of this.

■   ■   ■

Dave stood beside the Plymouth and watched the taillights of the truck. A searchlight lanced out from one of the police cars and pinned it momentarily in a bright beam. The driver had to realize the hopelessness of his situation.

Ramon could feel his heart pounding inside his chest as he was thrown back and forth by the gyrations of the truck. There was bedlam all around him now. Something was very wrong, and he was afraid that he would never be a rich man.

Brush slapped against the fields. Flood had decided that he would jump and take his chances, letting the truck go on by itself. He was fumbling for the door handle when the front wheels suddenly dropped off into empty air. Flood screamed.

The drop lasted only a split-second as the truck landed right-side-up on a narrow dirt road that sliced through the fields. Flood fought down his panic and spun the steering wheel desperately. This was an unexpected chance, and he was going to grab it if he could. The wheels suddenly caught in the soft dirt and sent the truck shooting down the road.

Dave heard the truck's engine roar, saw its lights pick up speed. He struck the fender of the Plymouth with a fist and said bitterly, "Damnit! Where's that helicopter they promised us? Get some men over on that other road!"

Flood reached down and cut his lights off. It was a good gamble. The road seemed to be flat and straight. Running dark would make him that much harder to find.

Ramon's heart was tripping wildly. When the truck had lurched downward, his spirit had plummeted along with it. His ambitions had vanished, leaving only a frantic desire for life. Now that the truck was running more smoothly, he was drawing slow, deep breaths and trying to calm himself. His companions were still in

an uproar around him. His nerves were so tight that it was all he
could do not to strike out at them.

· · ·

Four hours later, the truck rolled down a back street between
dark warehouses in San Antonio. Flood had eluded the pursuers,
getting lost in the process, but he had finally found his way back
to a road he knew. He was behind schedule, but he had delivered
his cargo.

The men in the back of the truck were quiet now, some of
them sleeping an exhausted sleep. Others, like Ramon, were still
awake, beginning again to think about their new lives in this
country.

Flood found the warehouse he was looking for. He pulled up
in front of the big doors and tapped his horn in a signal. A moment later, the doors swung open. The truck rolled forward into
the darkness.

The doors swung shut behind it. Lights came on. Flood shut
the engine off and dropped to the concrete floor.

Two men in business suits walked toward him. They had bland
faces and very hard eyes. One of them said, "You're late. Is the
freight in good condition?"

"Yeah," Flood replied. "We had some trouble, but nothing was
hurt. Some cops were waiting for me down south of here, but I
got away from 'em. I think you got a leak in your pipeline."

The two men exchanged glances while Flood went to the back
of the truck and unlocked it. He rolled the door up and snapped,
"Okay, you lousy wetbacks, get outta there."

Ramon didn't understand the man's words, but he was very
glad to see light again. With the others, he climbed out of the
truck and stood uneasily on the hard floor.

Men in suits, magnificent suits like none Ramon had ever seen,
looked the group over. He wondered if they were there to hire
workers. He would like to work for men like this.

The man who had spoken turned to Flood and said, "This will
have to be the last load. If our setup is compromised, we can't
afford to keep on with it. We'll have to cover our trail."

Flood shrugged. "Okay by me, although I hate to see it go.
Until tonight, it was easy money."

"You don't understand, Flood. You know too many things. You
know too much about us."

The second man started to reach inside his coat.

Ramon still didn't understand what was being said, but he knew the look of fear that suddenly sprang into the eyes of the man who had driven the truck.

Flood didn't wait to see what was coming. He knew what kind of men these were, and he knew what would happen next unless he got away. With a yell, he bulled between them and started to sprint toward the warehouse doors, past the group of huddled aliens. One of the men behind him yelled, "Stop him!"

Ramon understood looks of fear and anger and desperation. And he knew when one man had more power, more to offer, than another.

Flood saw the dark-faced figure step out in front of him, and he started to shout, "Outta my way, damn y—"

Ramon's knife spoke silently and interrupted him, flickering in and out brightly as it laced three neat holes in Flood's body.

The cold concrete rasped on Flood's face as he fell. He hugged himself, feeling the roughness, and then, for him, there was nothing more.

Ramon put his knife away. Everyone was looking at him, even the two men in the wonderful suits. One of them knelt by the body on the floor, while the other began to speak in Ramon's language.

"You are very gifted with a blade, my friend. Such talent is rare."

Ramon bowed his head in honest humility.

"Talent should not be wasted," the man went on. "Would you like to work for me? I can find many such jobs for you to do." He looked at the body as he said it.

There were the beginnings of a smile on Ramon's face as he nodded shyly.

This was a wonderful country, after all!

Jay Flynn

THE BADGER GAME

From *Guilty*, November 1956

The score of paperback originals which appeared between 1958 and 1976 under the bylines Jay Flynn and J. M. Flynn were the work of a writer who had much in common with his protagonists, nearly all of whom were tough, hard-living, heavy-drinking, women-chasing, blarney-spouting, scatter-brained, occasionally inept, and yet completely likable Irishmen. Five of Flynn's novels feature an off-the-wall San Francisco bar owner and secret agent named McHugh—a sort of poor man's James Bond who blithely brawls and blusters his way through dizzy plot-swirls involving, among other things, missing Navy flyers, Mafia hit men, a Caribbean island dictator and his army of thugs, and a fortune in hidden Nazi loot. One of his best works, The Action Man, *a caper novel about a bank heist that goes awry, was filmed in France. "The Badger Game," his first published fiction and only published short story, first appeared in the* Manhunt *clone,* Guilty, *in 1956.*

B. P.

COPS HATE THE SUCKER-SQUEEZING BOYS AND GIRLS WHO WORK the old badger game. There are assorted reasons for this. The skilled practitioners are smooth, hard to catch as an oiled eel. On the average, a cop is as lazy as the next joe, and for the effort that goes into catching a couple of badger artists cold, bank robbers can be had.

And cops, having practical minds, will usually admit privately if not publicly that the suckers get about what they deserve. Most of the marks don't squeal, because it means spilling what they paid to keep buried in the first place.

So keeping an ear to the grapevine turns up most of the leads that find their way to Headquarters and the precinct houses. The word comes in on some team that's been making one big score after another. The trap is set carefully, and maybe one time in ten or twenty a badger gets caught. Then—if the pigeon who's been taken doesn't wing out—the fall is good for a year in the bucket.

So you try to set up an extortion or grand theft rap, and if you can tie it up the way the D.A. likes, your boy and his girl may hit the big book for five years.

There are leaks in any cop shop, so you make noises like a clam when you're setting the trap. The files on Gus and Lynn Wahlberg were locked in the desk in my apartment, and the boys in Headquarters didn't know these files existed, any more than they knew the trap was set.

■   ■   ■

It was just across the county line, up in the North End, one of the "intimate" places that get a big play from married characters who want to be intimate with people they're not married to. When the phone rings, the barman picks it up and mutters, "Gene's," grunts once or twice and says, "No—no, lady, he hasn't been around a couple of days now." Then he walks to one of the curtained booths and gives the guy inside the word that his everloving has the dragnet out.

Lynn showed when I was working slowly on the third scotchon-the-rocks, filling the ashtray with half-smoked cigarettes. Gene's was almost empty, and she stopped just inside the door, eyes adjusting to the gloom. What light the management allowed burnished her ash-blonde hair. Tall girl. Sleek. The finest, if you like them built long in the leg and tight in the sweater.

No sweater this time. She wore a simple black dress worth a couple of hundred of somebody's bucks, cut low and wide across high, tilted breasts. She walked toward me, just putting one long, nylon-sleek leg in front of the other, but it was enough to make the barman stop polishing glasses. I held a chair for her.

"Hi. You're late. Have a hard time with Gus?" I signaled for a round of drinks.

"Don't—don't mention him, Bart. I might get an attack of conscience." She reached for my hand, eyes dark and moist, and I could almost believe it. Believe this spectacular woman was skipping out on a well-set-up husband for the unspectacular likes of Bart Corey. Her hand was cold and damp when it should have been warm and eager, and when the drinks came she put half of hers away before speaking again. "He's at the office. Specs for a new building. We'll have four or five hours."

■   ■   ■

"Enough time to finish our drinks." I tried the scotch again, letting her know I wasn't a hurry-up boy.

"Do we go to your place, Bart? Or were you thinking of something else?"

■   ■   ■

"My apartment. I dropped a couple of hints around and Sharon took the bait. Decided it was time to take in the theatah. She'll pubcrawl later, so we're okay there." If I'd suggested a hotel or motel, Lynn's end of the game would have been complicated because she'd have had to (1) find out where and (2) get the word to Gus.

■   ■   ■

We drank up and walked into the chill of a California night. Lynn moved close to me in the car while the top climbed out of its well, wrapping us in a deeper darkness. There was a hesitation when I kissed her but it was a long kiss, deep, and both of us got a little shook up. We were still that way when I parked the Caddy in front of the apartment house. It's one of those with a panoramic view of San Francisco and the Bay.

Lynn was in my arms before the door closed, trembling a little. "There's still time to back out, hon. If it's not good for you, it won't be for me either," I whispered.

"It'll be good, Bart." She pressed the full length of her body against me, and small, sharp teeth nibbled my ear. "It's just the first time cheating. I'm jumpy."

"Okay. There's something black and lacy in the bedroom closet if you want to try it for size."

She did. I poured more scotch while the record player went to work on a stack of hi-fi longhair. The bedroom door was shut. I got the .25 automatic from the desk in the study. Not much of a gun, but effective if used right and you can carry one with the muzzle shoved into your watch pocket and the butt out of sight under a wide belt. I wear wide belts.

Lynn waited on the bed, moved over to make room for me when I brought the drinks. The black lace business slipped a little along the rippling, tanned thighs. She said, "Is the door locked? Just in case Sharon . . ."

"I forget. I was busy kissing you when we came in." The door has a spring lock, and Lynn had to be sure it would open when the time came.

"I'll see." The light shone through the negligee as she went to make sure. I kicked my shoes off and wondered how much time I had before Gus Wahlberg would bust in and start Act Two.

*   *   *

I shoved my hand between the mattress and box spring. The handcuffs, steel-hard and cold, were still there. I'd need them. Gus was a big Swede, wide in the shoulders and muscles all over. And kitten-soft Lynn might make like a wildcat when the show-down came.

Gus was in his early thirties. Tall and lean without being bulky. The files said he posed usually as an engineer or architect, but he could do an artist or corporation executive bit just as easily. No big bites had been put on him so far. A few pickups here and there but no convictions on his rap sheet.

We hadn't met. But we would, before the hour ran out.

Lynn was his wife, either legal or common-law. And all woman, somewhere in her early or middle twenties. The record showed she'd taken up with Wahlberg after getting not much of any-where in show business.

Their operation was high-class. They picked the guys who could pay, and who could be put in the position of having to pay. Like me. I had a wife. Or they thought I did, which was just as good. To put the long arm on them I needed the plush apartment, the hi-fi, the Caddy convertible and scotch-on-the-rocks.

I wondered about the bankroll. The files said they kept their loot with them at all times, because if you have to blow a town in a hurry, twenty grand in the bank won't help if you've got only two bucks in your pocket. That should be about it, twenty grand, judging from the grapevine reports. It figured to be on Gus, be-cause Lynn's end of the job called for putting up with explora-tions from little hot hands.

*   *   *

Lynn came back, stood there with her breasts half out of the negligee. I knew who and what she was.

I wanted her anyway.

"You're careless, lover. It wasn't locked," she said.

"It is now. Come here, doll."

She came to me, warm and soft and completely desirable.

She saw the picture on the nightstand. "Wait, Bart." She turned it face down. The girl in it had dark eyes and dark hair that curled above them in bangs, a mouth wide enough to be interesting but too wide to be really beautiful. I didn't know who she was, but across the portrait was scrawled *"Sharon loves Bart"* and in our little drama she was playing the role of absent and about-to-be-wronged wife. "I don't want her watching," Lynn murmured. Her hands sought me.

There you are. You spend three months trying to put two illegal types in the sneezer and it looks like you've made it. The girl is with you, hot and exciting, making the animal sounds of love, and you forget about little things like doors that aren't locked.

Gus came in on cue but I didn't hear him because her mouth was on mine, hungry, demanding, and the negligee had somehow come untied. I came out of it when she was yanked from my arms and heaved across the rumpled bed.

"Tramp!" The file said Gus stood six-two, but from where I was lying he looked bigger, up around eight feet somewhere, and he was moving fast. One of the big hands exploded against her mouth and blood spurted.

I got the idea maybe Lynn had put more of herself into this caper than necessary. The hand swung back, slammed into the side of my head, made bright lights blink while I measured the distance between my foot and his crotch. But the two savage clouts seemed to satisfy him. He glared at us.

"Slut. You think I go to the office. But I followed you and I waited, and I see what I expected to see," he rumbled. He hit her again, hard. Tears filled the deep grey eyes and more blood seeped from her full lips.

That was my cue. I kicked, but I was still flat on my back and there wasn't much authority to it. For my trouble I got a judo cut across the throat. I watched the ceiling and walls jump up in the air and come down again. When I could talk I demanded to know what the hell it was all about, who this guy thought he was, breaking in on me and my girl. I got real outraged about it.

■ ■ ■

From there the script has long whiskers. Lynn crept away from me and pulled the negligee over the lush curves, sobbing and moaning about how it was all a big mistake and I'd got her drunk. Wahlberg told me in much detail how he was going to beat me to a mass of dog meat, then get me heaved in the can for making off with his wife if I didn't die.

I rode with it, pleading, telling him finally I had a wife of my own and something like this could foul me up if she found out because she was looking for a chance to divorce me and take every dime I had anyway. He wasn't interested until I got around to offering him money, two thousand dollars worth, and all he had to do was forget the whole thing and take his chippy wife out of my happy home and beat the hell out of her. I showed him the two grand.

He muttered something about killing both of us, then said, "Maybe this'll teach you a lesson, you bastard."

He grabbed the money. That was it.

My hand had been lying across my belt, just over the watch pocket, and Wahlberg's eyes popped when he saw the little .25 muzzle pointed where his brows met between them. He froze, and stayed that way long enough for me to get the handcuffs out and snap one on his wrist.

Lynn, still breathing hard, stared at us. I pointed to a hot-water radiator. "Shag on over there, beautiful. Do it slowly so I don't get excited and plug friend Gus here."

She got it then. Disbelief and hatred twisted her face as she gathered the black lace around her and walked slowly to the radiator. I tugged Gus across the room, passed the free end of the cuffs around the inlet pipe and locked them together.

"A stinking cop!" she snarled.

"That's what it says here." I pulled a small leather case from beneath the mattress and showed them what was inside. A badge, and a card identifying one Bart Corey as a sergeant of detectives. I let them think about it while I shook Gus down, and now Lynn's tears were for real.

■ ■ ■

Gus was clean, except for a wallet that held just under twenty thousand bucks, including my two grand. The grapevine had been right. It was a fat bankroll, and all sucker money. I put the wallet in my pocket. "Evidence."

"Smart cop," Lynn snarled. "What's it prove? Money's money. How do you tell the jury we took some of it away from you?"

I pulled my jacket on, and I could feel the swelling in my face where Gus had clipped me. "Easy, doll, easy. There's a chemical on those bills. It doesn't show yet, but when Gus washes his hands, they turn green. A real crazy dark green. Believe me, a jury will buy it. Now I go to call the bastille taxi."

I walked out, and the eyes of the badgers I'd worked so long to trap followed me through the door. The fog had churned in off the bay, softening the city lights, and the Caddy's windshield was silver-white with the stuff. In my pocket, the twenty grand made a nice bulge. I was wondering when they'd catch on and start yelling for someone to cut them loose from that radiator.

So I didn't see the two boys in topcoats and Homburg hats until they moved in on me from the shadows by the steps.

"Bart, we've been waiting for you," one of them said. His right hand was in the pocket of the topcoat, so I didn't try for the .25 automatic.

■   ■   ■

Steel chattered against steel and the second guy had bracelets on me before I could make a break for the Caddy. They shoved me into a sedan parked at the curb and the one who'd done the talking shoved something in my face.

A small leather folder with a star and a card inside.

"Inspector Milt Johns. Bunco detail, Bart. This is Officer Denton. Now we'll go to headquarters."

Denton took the wheel. The motor rumbled and the car gathered speed, ploughing into the billowing fog. The initial shock was gone already, and I was in no big sweat. My pigeons couldn't put up a squeal without making the can themselves. Johns had spotted me, figured my game. But figuring and proving it in court are different.

"What's the charge?" I asked.

"Let's start with grand theft of this, Bart," the inspector said. He jerked Wahlberg's wallet from my pocket. His hand probed a little more and he came up with the gun, then the fake badge and credentials. "Also impersonating an officer and carrying a gun while committing a felony. That'll do," Johns told me.

I ran over it fast. Lynn and Gus couldn't testify without implicating themselves. The gun I had a license for. The badge wasn't an exact replica and the only one I'd pulled it on was Wahlberg.

"Won't stick. You know it," I told him. I pointed out why.

The car squeaked its tires in front of the police station. Johns turned on the dome light. "It'll stick. Look in back."

I looked. There was a box about suitcase size on the seat, a tape recorder.

My pad had been bugged. It would all be on the tape. I'd had it. Johns lit cigarettes for the three of us. "Okay. I'll cop out. No trial necessary."

"Good," Johns said. "Now we'll go back and get your pals. Three badgers in one trap is a fair haul, Bart. You should have been a cop."

Jack Ritchie

DON'T TWIST MY ARM

From *Manhunt,* April 1958

From the mid–'50s to the mid–'80s, Jack Ritchie was one of the two or three best writers of the criminous short story. He published several hundred in a broad range of magazines and anthologies, some of the best of which can be found in his three collections: A New Leaf and Other Stories, a 1971 paperback original, and two hardcovers, The Adventures of Henry Turnbuckle and Little Boxes of Bewilderment. All of Ritchie's work is distinguished by what Anthony Boucher called "an exemplary neatness— no word is wasted, and many words serve more than one purpose." Much of it is light and humorous in tone, but early in his career he published several much harder-edged tales, of which "Don't Twist My Arm" is among the most effective.

B. P.

POP TOLD ME TO ROLL UP THE SLEEVE OF MY SHIRT. "YOU CAN see for yourself," he said. "The kid's arm is all bent. He can't use it hardly at all now and it'll get worse year by year."

Mr. Ward leaned forward to look and the eyes in his heavy face showed nothing.

Pop waved a hand. "We'll hit them for all we can get. I don't care who pays. Either Peterson or his insurance company."

Mr. Ward rolled the cigar in his mouth a couple of times and then reached for his pen.

"Henry Peterson is the guy's name," Pop said. He watched Mr. Ward write. "Senator Henry Peterson."

Mr. Ward and Pop looked at each other for about ten seconds, and then Mr. Ward got a little smile on his face. "All right," he said. "Go on."

"My kid was crossing the street when he was run down by the senator's car," Pop said. "A big job in the five thousand dollar class."

I cleared my throat. "I was playing ball in the street."

Mr. Ward's eyes went over me without finding anything interesting. "Shut up, kid," he said.

"I was sitting on the stoop and I saw the whole thing," Pop said. "I picked up Freddie and took him to a doctor."

Mr. Ward played with his pen. "How come you didn't take the kid to a hospital? That's what usually happens in cases like that."

Pop shrugged. "The doc was nearer."

Mr. Ward smiled and rubbed his chin. "You were excited. That's natural. A father's first concern is for his kid and he's got the right to lose his head. What did Peterson do?"

Pop crossed his legs. "He came along."

I remembered the look on Senator Peterson's face when he saw how dirty Dr. Miller's office was.

Mr. Ward looked at my arm again. "When did all this happen?"

Pop shifted in his chair. "About two years ago."

Mr. Ward chuckled very softly.

Pop got a little red. "I figured the arm would turn out all right. But the kid kept yammering about it day and night. I finally took him to another doctor."

Mr. Ward puffed his cigar and waited.

Pop ran his tongue over his lips. "They'll have to break Freddie's arm and put it back together again. Even then it might never grow any longer than it is now."

Pop shook his head and looked down at his hands. "The kid's future is ruined. And look at him. He's lost maybe twenty pounds. He can't get no sleep nights because of the hurt."

Mr. Ward studied me. "How old is he?"

"Fifteen," Pop said. "He's always been a runt."

Pop took a cigarette out of a crumpled pack and lit it. "I signed a paper with Peterson's insurance company and got five hundred dollars. I needed the money. But that don't mean a thing now. Not when the arm turned out this way."

Mr. Ward looked at the ceiling. "Why not sue the doctor?"

"You can't get blood out of a stone," Pop said.

Mr. Ward chuckled again and looked Pop over. "When we get together with Peterson, it might be a good idea if you shaved. Wear a necktie too."

We left Mr. Ward's office and walked down three flights of stairs to the street.

When we got near Danny's Bar, Pop slowed down and rattled the change in his pocket. He licked his lips, but I knew he wasn't going in there. Danny charges thirty-five cents for a drink. At O'Brien's you get the same stuff for twenty.

At Thirty-eighth, we crossed the street so that we wouldn't have to go past Ricco's. Pop doesn't go near there ever since he had that fight with Louie Milo who hangs out there.

Pop went into O'Brien's and I followed him.

Mr. O'Brien waited until Pop put money on the bar before he poured a drink. Then he looked at me. "Get the hell out of here, kid."

Pop yawned. "You heard him, Freddie."

"I'm not doing anything," I said.

Mr. O'Brien leaned over the bar. "Move before I put a boot in your rump."

Pop downed his drink and put some more change on the bar.

I looked at him for a few seconds and then I left and started walking home.

My arm hurt pretty bad. It gets that way when it's damp.

I went upstairs to the place where Pop and I live. There was half a bottle of olives in the refrigerator and some butter. There was a tomato too, but it was rotten. I found some bread and ate a little before I went outside again.

Turk and Pete and Gino were hanging around Harrigan's Grocery and they were wearing their Red Hawk jackets.

Once I nearly got one. I had eight dollars, but that was gone now.

They didn't pay no attention when I came up and leaned against the building next to them.

Pete got out his cigarettes and passed the pack to Turk and Gino. I put out my hand, but Gino gave the pack back to Pete.

Pete lit up for all three of them.

"I once read how that got started," I said. "You know, that business about three on a match being unlucky. It was in the First World War and if you kept a match lit long enough for three lights, a German sniper was liable to get a bead on you."

They didn't look at me and so I guess they didn't care about the story.

I waited a little while and then said, "I saw a couple of the Goldens today. I went through their territory."

Gino looked at me. "You beat their heads together? Is that it, Freddie?"

I changed my mind about what I was going to say. I shrugged. "I didn't want to start nothing there. I would've been mobbed."

"I'm surprised at you, Freddie," Turk said. "You're the brave type. It runs in the family."

Gino coughed on some cigarette smoke. "I thought I'd bust a gut when I seen little Louie chase Freddie's old man out of Ricco's. He's sure got speed when he's scared. Ain't that right, Freddie?"

I looked at the Poulos girls passing across the street and tried to quick think of something to say about the way they swung their hips. But I couldn't think of nothing.

Red Kelly's chromed-up Chevvy pulled to the curb and Pete, Turk and Gino got inside. I thought there was room for one more, but Gino shut the door after him.

They took off and I watched them turn the corner.

Pop came home around ten o'clock with Willie Bragan. They had a pint with them and they began talking about the job they were going to do on Saturday night. I asked if I could be lookout, but Pop told me to shut up.

When they settled everything and finished the pint, Bragan went home.

Before Pop went to bed, he looked under the kitchen clock. He always does that ever since he found the eight dollars I set aside for the jacket.

I fixed myself some butter bread and went to the window and looked down. It was getting quiet outside and the traffic was thinning.

Pop woke at twelve. When he was through, I got the mop and cleaned up. Then I went to bed.

Senator Peterson was at the meeting and Mr. Jenkins, the lawyer from his insurance company, and Mr. Ward.

Pop looked mad. "You seen the X-rays. The kid's crippled for life."

Mr. Jenkins shuffled some of the papers on his lap. "This Dr. Miller who set the boy's arm. He lost his license several months ago for unethical practices."

"How the hell was I supposed to know what kind of a doctor he was?" Pop said. "The sign on the door said 'Doctor.' Am I supposed to drop the kid on the floor and check with the Medical Society first?"

Mr. Jenkins' voice was dry. "How did you happen to select him?"

Mr. Ward cleared his throat. "As my client explained, Dr. Miller was the nearest aid available."

Senator Peterson had grayish hair and he was about Pop's age. But his skin was clear.

He studied Pop. "It would seem that this Dr. Miller is the man to sue."

Mr. Ward smiled. "Dr. Miller disappeared shortly after losing his license. We've made an extensive search, but we've been unable to find a trace of him."

Pop pointed to Senator Peterson. "You're the one who's responsible. It was your car that hit the boy."

Mr. Jenkins sighed. "I fail to see that you have any case at all. At the time of the accident you absolutely refused to have the boy taken to a hospital. You refused to allow our doctors to examine him. In addition, you signed an agreement waiving all future claims, for which you received five hundred dollars. Under the circumstances, neither my company nor Senator Peterson can be held responsible for the mistakes of this Dr. Miller."

It was quiet for a while and then Mr. Ward took the cigar out of his mouth. "Perhaps we don't have an iron-bound case, from the legal point of view." He looked at Senator Peterson. "I believe you are running for the Senate again? Do you suppose the publicity might be harmful?"

Mr. Jenkins and Senator Peterson looked at each other.

"I see," Mr. Jenkins said. He put his paper back in his briefcase and got to his feet. "Are you coming, Senator?"

Senator Peterson didn't look at him.

Mr. Jenkins smiled tightly. "At any rate, my company is not running for the Senate."

He went to the door and left.

But Senator Peterson stayed.

■ ■ ■

It was evening and I didn't feel like going to the movies. I got some candy bars instead and went back home. I went up the fire escape and sat down outside our window.

I heard voices inside the kitchen and shifted over a little so I could take a peek inside.

Dr. Miller and Pop were drinking from a bottle on the table. I could see the label and it was a real expensive brand.

Dr. Miller filled his glass. "The kid around?"

Pop lit a cigar. "No. I gave him a buck and told him to take in a movie." He slapped the table. "That bastard Ward took forty percent. He even said we were lucky he didn't take more."

Dr. Miller was bald and he wore glasses that made his eyes twice as big as anybody else's. He shrugged. "It's robbery, but there's nothing we can do about it. We still got twelve thousand out of the deal and we split that even."

I threw away the candy bar. I could feel sweat begin all over my body.

Pop's face was dark red. "I get a lousy six thousand. That's all I get for listening to that kid whimper for two years."

I shook my head. That was all wrong too. I didn't whimper.

Dr. Miller took a cigar out of the box on the table. "We had to wait at least a couple of years. I told you that in the beginning. We had to give that arm time to get real bad."

Pop pounded the table. "By rights, I'm entitled to more than a fifty-fifty split. I'm the one who got the idea for the whole thing the second I seen what a high price car hit Freddie."

Dr. Miller laughed. "Hell, all the kid got out of it was a trip to the movies. Be satisfied that he don't know what you did to him. He might get the notion to cut your throat one of these nights."

I gripped the cool railing of the fire escape hard with my good hand. There was a big knife in the drawer of the kitchen table. I'd wait until Dr. Miller was gone and Pop was asleep. Then I'd do it.

Dr. Miller stayed for another hour before he left. I settled down on the fire escape, waiting and watching Pop drink. I figured that he'd probably have enough by eleven o'clock.

Then I remembered that this was Saturday and he and Bragan were supposed to do a job.

I wondered if Pop could get out of it. He wouldn't want to take any chances with small stuff, now that he had the six thousand. But he couldn't tell Bragan that he had the money. You don't do something like that with Bragan if you want to keep it.

Willie Bragan came at ten and Pop looked surprised. I guess he forgot that it was Saturday.

Bragan looked at the bottle of whiskey and then at the cigars. "I thought you was broke."

Pop licked his lips. "A guy paid me back fifty he owed."

Bragan grunted. "Since when you been lending money?"

Pop laughed nervous. "An old friend."

Bragan wasn't buying that, but he shrugged. "We'll talk about it later. Let's get going. I got the truck downstairs in front."

Pop's voice had a whine in it. "Let's put it off, Willie. I'm not feeling so good tonight."

Bragan smiled a little and took a handful of cigars out of the box.

Pop didn't like that, but Bragan is a big man and you don't complain.

"Honest, Willie," Pop said. "I've been feeling rotten all day."

Bragan smelled one of the cigars. "Take a couple aspirins."

I watched them get in the truck down below and then I went down the fire escape.

It was cool in the streets and I began walking. Pop wouldn't be back for three or four hours and I couldn't sit still that long. Not with what was going on in my head.

I don't know how long it was, but after a while I was in a long empty street and there were mostly warehouses on both sides. I was a little surprised to be there. But now that I was, I sat down in a doorway and watched the warehouse near the end of the block.

A cop turned the corner far down the street. He walked slow, shining his flashlight into the doorways.

And then he stopped in front of the warehouse I was watching. He seemed to be listening and then he took the gun out of his holster. He moved on his toes to the doors of the warehouse and he listened for another half a minute.

I wondered if I should do something, but then I remembered what I'd heard on the fire escape and I kept quiet.

The cop pulled open one of the sliding doors fast and jumped inside. The light poured out and I could see the cop's shadow stretching all the way across the road.

I waited a while and then I got up and walked toward the open door.

The cop had his back to me and he was standing just inside the door with his gun.

Pop and Bragan were facing him with their hands over their heads. Pop's face was white and Bragan was scowling. They were standing next to Bragan's big truck and it was about half loaded with automobile parts and new tires from the warehouse.

Bragan's eyes shifted in my direction and he saw me.

The cop noticed that and he jumped to one side like a scared cat. His gun swung back and forth between us. "Get over there with the rest of them."

I shook my head. "I don't have anything to do with this. I was just passing by."

The cop had a hard laugh. "At two o'clock in the morning, kid? Like hell." His gun jerked again. "Get your hands up."

I put up my right arm. "I can't lift the other one."

He looked at my short arm and his lips twisted. "So you got a cripple for the lookout work. Maybe that's all he's good for. He wouldn't be much help wrestling tires into your truck."

I looked at the cop and I saw that he had the kind of yellow brown eyes that Pop has.

Pop swallowed hard. "Look, we can fix this up."

The crop grinned. "That's right. I'm just a poor cop. I don't earn too much."

I could tell from his voice that he was just playing, but Pop kept trying anyhow.

"Five hundred bucks," Pop said. "I can raise five hundred."

The cop kept grinning. "Keep going."

Pop was sweating. He had a record and it wasn't going to be easy for him if he got in front of a judge. "A thousand," he said. "I can get it to you in a day."

Bragan was looking at Pop now too and I guess he was wondering whether Pop was faking it or whether he really had the money. Maybe he was thinking about the whiskey and the cigars.

The cop's eyes flicked around the big room and he saw the wall phone.

Pop's voice got high. "Two thousand," he said. "Three."

For a second the cop looked interested. But then I guess he took another look at Pop and figured that he couldn't have that kind of money.

The cop couldn't keep his eyes on everything. Not on Bragan, and Pop, and me, and the wall phone. I guess he decided I was the least important.

He took his eyes away from me for a few seconds when he started edging for the phone.

Pop looked at me now and he was asking for help.

There wasn't much time and I had to make up my mind. I hesitated for a second and then I stooped down and grabbed a tire iron leaning against the wall. I swung with all my might and the iron bit deep into the cop's skull.

Bragan came out of the shock first. He went to the door and pulled it shut. Then he knelt down beside the cop. After a while, he looked up. "He's dead."

I nodded and tossed the tire iron aside.

Pop was shaking. "The kid done it. We got no part of this."

Bragan got to his feet. "We're in it as deep as the kid is. We're in the big league now."

He picked up the tire iron and wiped my fingerprints off with his handkerchief. "All right," he said. "Let's go."

He went to the big doors and slid them open.

I stood to one side and watched them get into the truck. Pop put his head out of the cab. "Damn it," he yelled to me. "Get in."

I stood there for a few seconds, uncertain. I was sick with what he was. I didn't know if I wanted to stick with him anymore—I didn't even know why I'd stuck with him this long . . .

"For God's sake, kid, get in," he said again. And I saw his frightened eyes dart over in the direction of Bragan.

Pop would have trouble with Bragan about the six thousand. *He might need me.* And as I thought it, I realized why I'd stuck with him, because no one else on earth had ever needed or wanted me for any reason, and, jeez, how I needed to be needed . . .

"All right," I said. "All right, Pop, I'm coming."

Richard S. Prather

THE GUILTY PARTY

From *Come Seven/Come Death*, 1965

Richard S. Prather's Shell Scott novels were the best-selling books pub-
lished by Gold Medal in the fifties. Few writers in this century have given
readers as much pleasure as Prather. Shell Scott's adventures were parodies
of the private eye formula, and were also witty (and inventive) novels on
their own. At present, Prather is working on a very long novel, and looking
forward to publishing novels again after a long hiatus. Here is a gem of a
Shell Scott tale.

E. G.

THERE ARE DAYS WHEN YOU FEEL EUPHORIC FOR NO PARTICULAR
reason; and there are babes who make you feel euphoric for particular reasons. Put them both together and anything can happen.

Maybe that's why it happened. Who cares why it happened?

She came into my office like a gal out in the woods in one of
those sexy movies, smiled at me, flowed across the room with the
fluidity of hot molasses, sank into the big leather chair opposite
my desk, and crossed her legs slowly, gracefully, gently, as though
taking care not to bruise any smooth, tender flesh.

I rose to my feet, walked clear around the desk and sat down
again.

"Lady," I said, "whatever it is, it's eight to five I'll do it."

She smiled, but still didn't say anything. Maybe she couldn't
talk. Maybe she was an idiot. I didn't care. But if curves were
convolutions, she had an IQ of at least 37-23-36, or somewhere
in that neighborhood, and that's the high-rent district.

Moreover, if some faces can stop a clock, hers would have made
Big Ben gain at least forty minutes an hour. A lot of black hair,
somewhat tangled, as if a horny Apache dancer had just wound
his hands in it, preparatory to flinging her across the room. Nar-

row dark brows curving hotly—yeah, whether you think so or not, they curved hotly—over tawny brown eyes the indefinable shade of autumn. Lips that would burn holes in asbestos. And then that genius body. Man, whatever she had, it should be contagious.

She was looking me over, still silently. I leaned forward, waiting. And I started hoping she wasn't really, truly an idiot.

Finally she said, "So you're Shell Scott?"

"That's me. And you? You?"

She didn't tell me, darn her hide. Instead she cocked her head on one side and said, "I almost hate to take up your time with this little difficulty of mine. I mean it's nothing big and exciting like murders or gangsters—"

"Now, don't you worry, it's big and exciting enough already, and I don't care how little—"

"I mean, I've heard stories about the big cases you've handled and all. I hardly believed them. But I do now. You certainly look capable."

"Yeah? Of . . . what?"

"Anything. You really do." She smiled. "You look as if you just got back from an African safari. After shooting lions and tigers and things."

Well, it was a new approach. So to hell with the old approaches. Maybe she was serious. Or maybe she was pulling my leg. But I'll go along with a gag. Besides, I was feeling pretty wild.

"That's me," I said. "Just got back from darkest Zuluongo, where the pygmies are nine feet tall. Braved the poison swamps, the burning heat, the creeping goo—"

"Goodness! It sounds dangerous."

"Dangerous? Why, it's not even in the UN. But nothing daunts me when I'm on a trek." I shrugged. "Killed a couple elephants this trek."

She chuckled. "With your bare hands, of course."

"Of course not. I . . . used a rock. But enough about me. You said something about a—a little difficulty?"

"Yes. It's a bit embarrassing. And I wanted to get to know you a little first."

"OK by me. In fact, you can get to know—"

"You see, there's a thing under my bed, Mr. Scott."

"Shell. A what?"

"A thing under my bed."

"A thing? I don't—is it alive? Hell, I'll kill it. You came to the right place—"

"No, nothing like that, Mr. Scott."

"Shell."

"It's a little funny metal thing. I thought it was a bomb at first. But probably it isn't. When I got out of bed this morning I heard it fall from the springs or somewhere—that's how I found it—and it didn't go off. It's sort of square, about three or four inches long, and has a small doodad on it. Can you guess what it is?".

"I couldn't guess. What is it?"

"I don't know. That's why I came here. I told you it wasn't anything important." She sighed. "I knew you wouldn't be interested."

"But I am! It's just that your description . . . Could you sort of narrow it down a little more? I mean, I can think of a million things it isn't. But if we're going to pin this thing down, we've—we've got to pin it down."

I stopped. This wasn't me. Or wasn't I. It wasn't either of us. This gal had me thinking with a stutter. I shook my head, remained silent, waiting.

She described the thing again, in more detail this time. Finally her description rang a bell.

"Ah-ha," I said. "I think I've got it. I think your bed has been bugged."

"It's a bedbug?"

"No—look, a 'bug' is a term for a microphone, or listening device. The item in question sounds like a small radio transmitter. Though why in the world anybody would put a portable transmitter under your . . ."

I let it trickle off, as suspicion trickled in. The same trickle got to her at about the same moment.

"No!" she cried.

"You're wrong, I'm afraid," I said. "I'm afraid the answer is Yes!"

"But why?"

"Well, possibly somebody—" I started over. It was kind of delicate. "Do you talk in your sleep?"

"How would I know?"

"How indeed? Well, that's out." I paused. "OK, let's be logical, what? Usually people plant them to hear or record conversations—for blackmail purposes, to catch crooks, get inside information, business secrets and so on. Now, who might benefit in some way by hearing your conversations?"

"In the bedroom?"

"Well . . ." She had a point. And it stimulated my thinking.

I said, "We've been going at this all wrong. We have assumed the bedroom bug is the only one. The place may be lousy with them. They may be all over the joint—living room, dining room, attic, everywhere. Where do you live, anyway?"

"I've a suite in the Montclair." The Montclair was a swank hotel only three or four blocks away.

We attacked the problem from all angles for a few minutes. She was a lingerie model—it figured—and thus didn't have any big business secrets to discuss in her suite. She didn't dictate important letters or help plan union strikes, didn't know any criminals, and so on. She didn't even entertain anybody in her suite, although she did mention one name, which obviously I heard incorrectly.

All in all, there seemed no reason whatsoever for anybody to bug her rooms. It was a puzzler.

Finally I said, "OK, you live in the Montclair. And your phone number?"

"Will that help?"

"It'll help me."

She smiled. "Oxford 4-8096, that's the Montclair's number. And I'm in number Twenty."

"And your name?" I said, all business.

"Lydia Brindley. At least until next week."

"It won't be Lydia next week?"

"It won't be Brindley. It will be Fish."

"I don't believe it."

"Oh, you do too. Stop joshing me. That's the name of my fiancé."

"Your—*oh*."

I got a sharp shooting pain, in an area which it is impolite to mention. An area, in fact, which it is ghastly to mention.

I went on, "Say what you said again. About—about you won't be Brindley."

"It's nothing, really. My fiancé is Rothwell Hamilton Fish, and we'll be married next Friday."

"Nothing, huh? Maybe to *you* it's nothing. Rothwell Hamilton Fish, huh? I never heard of him."

"I mean it's nothing to do with my difficulty. And Rotty hasn't lived in Los Angeles until just lately. He's from Las Vegas. That's where we'll be married."

"Uh-huh. So he's from . . . wait. He's not—*he's not Rotty Fish!*"

"Yes. You do know him, then?"

"My God, no." I paused, closed my eyes. "That's what you said before. Rotty Fish. I thought it was a cat food or something. You remember. When we were wondering who might benefit from recording anything you might say, you mentioned that there was hardly ever anybody in your suite except you and Rot—Rothwell. Right?"

"Right."

"Uh-huh. Uh-huh. Where does Rot—Rothwell live?"

"At the St. Charles in Hollywood."

"Way out there? That makes it tougher. He doesn't live at the Montclair, then."

"No, but he was visiting a friend there one day, and that's how we met. In the elevator. It was so romantic—he kissed my hand and everything."

"No!"

"He's very polite and polished, a real gentleman."

"Uh-huh. He's at the St. Charles now?"

"No, he's out of town for a few days. Wrapping up business affairs and things before we get married."

"Uh-huh. I see. Yeah. I've solved it. He did it. He bugged you."

"What? That's preposterous. And why?"

"Why not? He's bugging me—and I don't even know him. Besides, we eliminated everybody else."

"Oh, we did not."

"Maybe you didn't. Well, he won't get away with it! I'll catch him." I stood up. Then I sat down again. "Tell me," I said, "about Rothwell. All about Rothwell."

They had met two months ago in that romantic spot, the elevator. Love or something blossomed, a marriage date was set. Rotty, Lydia said, was tall and slim and dark and divine, and had a little thin black moustache. He danced like a dream, and when they'd met in the elevator, as she'd said, he had kissed her hand, like those fruity Continental bounders.

"He sounds like a con-man to me," I said.

I was all steamed up. In this life, a man has to fight for what he wants. The Government can't give you everything. Some things a man has to do for himself, no matter what you've heard. Fight fair, yes; but *fight*.

"Why, Mr. Scott," Lydia said, blinking the big brownish eyes hotly at me. "How can you say that?"

"Easy. Call me Shell, huh?"

"Shell. But how can you say such a thing? He's priceless. And he's horribly jealous, isn't that wonderful?"

"No, that's horrible. Either he trusts you or he doesn't. It's as simple as that."

"Well . . ."

"You see? He's horribly jealous. That means he doesn't trust you. Besides, he has a little thin black moustache—you said so yourself."

"But you don't even *know* him."

"Lydia, give him up. We'll all be happier—"

"Why are you talking like this? What do you care—"

"Well, I'm jealous."

"But you just said—"

"Never mind what I said. Tell me more about Rotty."

There wasn't a great deal more. They had dined and danced and had wine and crepes suzette—he could even order in French.

"He sounds like a con-man to me," I said.

"He's not, either. Oh, at first I thought maybe he was only after my money, but now I'm sure it isn't that."

"That's clear thinking. . . . You've got money, too?"

"Yes, my father was the Brindley of Brindley Nuts—canned pecans, almonds, cashews and so on. He left me several million."

"Nuts?"

"No, dollars, silly. I'm—well, I guess you'd say loaded."

"That's what I'd say." I paused, thinking, considering all angles. Then I stood up.

"Let's go."

"Where are we going?"

"To the Montclair."

■   ■   ■

Lydia's suite was composed of living room, sitting room, kitchenette, bedroom and bath. I cautioned Lydia to be very quiet and we went in silently. I then spent half an hour going over the place, but all was in order except for the "thing" she'd mentioned finding under the bed. It was a compact portable transmitter, all right. I left it under the bed, undisturbed, then joined Lydia in the front room.

As far as I could figure it, there were only two probabilities, especially since there were no other transmitters to be found. First, the culprit was a hi-fi bug, one of those cats who sit around listening to trains hooting and crickets cricketing and wild bird calls and such. Second . . . that was the one I liked.

But how to prove it? I could call all the people in town who sold electronic eavesdropping equipment, trace the men who'd recently bought such items. That could take days, though. Or, if the receiver were here in the Montclair I could start knocking on doors—a method that also failed to strike me as speedy or efficient. And nothing would really be proved even if I found a receiver. Besides, the little transmitter had power enough to broadcast on its special frequency for several blocks.

Or I could . . . I had it.

I whispered, "When did Rot—Rothwell leave on his trip?"

"Let's see. This is Friday, so it was Tuesday. Three days ago. He'll be back Monday."

"He may be back today."

I started to tell Lydia about it, but decided not to. It was eight to five she'd think I was nuts, and ten to one she wouldn't cooperate anyway. I would simply let it happen, and trust in my fairy godmother or whatever it is that watches over me. It might even work better this way. Moreover, the other way Lydia might get confused. There was a pretty good chance she'd get confused anyhow, but in this case to think was to act.

I jumped up, walked to the front door, opened it and slammed it shut again, careful that it didn't lock. Then I thumped over the living room carpet.

"Well, here we are!" I bellowed. And I thumped across the living room to the bedroom and whacked the door open.

Lydia, a puzzled expression on her face, walked up behind me.

"Here we are," I said loudly, "alone at last."

"Shell," she said, "we have been alone for—"

I interrupted. "Let's have some more of those hot martinis!"

Lydia was starting to look a bit unnerved. "Hot martinis!" she said.

"That's the ticket," I shouted.

"What's this?" she said, peering at me dubiously. "Why hot?"

"Yes, why not? Let's try something *new*. Let's not be hidebound by static old conventions. I'm tired of that static. Let's be different, let's be gay. Oh, Lydia, Lydia!"

"Huh?" she said.

I trotted back and forth over the bedroom carpet, stamping my feet. "No, you don't!" I roared. "You won't get away from me now. Ha! Got you!"

Lydia stood motionless in the bedroom doorway, staring at me. A slow paralysis seemed to be creeping over her. Except for her head, which was wagging back and forth.

"Here we go!" I yelled, and sprang through the air and landed with a thump in the middle of the bed. Then I got my feet under me and started springing about. I was beginning to have a few misgivings about this; if it didn't work, Lydia and I would be all washed up. But it was too late to stop now, I had burned my bridges, cast the die, flung the gauntlet. Too late. So I kept bouncing.

"Shell!" she cried.

"Lydia!" I cried.

"What are you doing?" she yelled frantically. "What are you *do*ing?"

Lydia was doing marvelously, I thought, even without coaching. I bounced up and down on the bed as if it were a thick trampoline, the springs wailing and shrieking, letting out noises actually un-bedlike. I was going higher and higher now, getting the hang of it.

"Shell!" Lydia wailed, "have you lost your mind, are you mad?"

"Yes! This is madness—"

"What happened? This is crazy."

"—madness!"

I bounced almost to the ceiling, and when I came down, some springs let go with the twanging sound of coiled ricochets.

Lydia almost screamed. "Stop it, Shell, *stop it*, STOP IT!"

"DARLING!" I yelled.

"STOP!"

"DARLING!"

"Cops—murder—*help!*" she yelled, all unstrung.

I lit on the edge of the mattress and the bed broke, the frame splintering with a crashing sound that blended with the grating and twanging of springs giving up and letting go. I figured this had gone far enough, and stopped bouncing.

Lydia had just spun about as if preparing to sprint for miles. "Wait," I called to her. "Don't leave. Listen."

She stopped, looked back over her shoulder at me. "But—"

"Shh. Listen."

There had been, I thought, the sound of a distant crash. Like a door slamming maybe. Fifty feet or so away? Then came faint thumpings. Was it . . . ? Yes, more thumpings, feet pounding, pounding nearer, getting louder. And a high, keening sound out there: "Lyyyydia! *Lyyyyydiaaaa!*"

I climbed down off the slanting bed.

"What's—what happened to you? What's going on?" Lydia asked me.

"We'll soon know. We stirred something up. I'll explain later—"

That was all there was time for.

The thumping and keening sounds were almost upon us now. The front door crashed open.

Feet thumped across the living room, reached the bedroom.

He was tall, slim, dark, moustached, and very speedy. He took one step into the room, left his feet and flew four yards through the air straight toward the bed, without even looking. He landed atilt and bounced and wound up in a heap over at the intersection of the walls.

But he was up in an instant, head snapping about, teeth gnashing, eyes rolling.

"Hoo!" he snorted. "Hah!" He lamped Lydia, then focused on me and sprang again. At me this time. He came at me like a windmill, arms flailing.

I grabbed his arms, got my fingers around his biceps as Lydia yelled, "Rotty! Stop it!"

"Yeah, Rotty," I said. "Stop it."

But he was swinging and snorting, completely out of control. I'd managed to ward off all the blows so far, but there were so many it was quite an operation. I was sort of winded from all that bouncing anyway.

"Look," I said. "It's all right, pal. Relax. Just a little trick."

"A *trick!*" he roared. "I'll trick you!"

"Dammit," I said. "If you don't watch out, you're going to hit me, and then there'll be hell—"

I knew it. Right then he sneaked a hand loose and got me a good one on the eye.

There was no help for it then. I stopped trying to hold him, ducked a roundhouse right and tapped him one. It wasn't an especially hard blow, but it landed on his kisser, which for at least a week was going to be of no use to him for kissing.

He sailed back and landed on his rear pants pockets and sat there with a pained look on his face.

Lydia raced over to him, knelt by him and said, "Rotty, darling, are you all right? Where did you come from? Oh, I'm a nervous wreck!"

He blinked at her. "*You're* a nervous wreck!"

"What happened?" she said. "What happened?"

He said, "I'll ask the questions. What happened?"

Then, as he stared at her, his brows pulled down and down and down, until he appeared to have very hairy eyes, and he looked her over carefully, and he looked me over carefully. Then he said in a dull voice, "Something is cuckoo here."

"Lydia." I cleared my throat. It was time for the explanation, and I wasn't exactly sure how Lydia would take it. "This will require your undivided attention for half a minute," I said. "A sort of generous, what-the-hell attitude would help, too."

She straightened up and stood looking at me, a puzzled expression on her face. Not that her expression had changed much during these last few minutes.

"You see," I went on, "the problem was to find out who planted that item under your bed, who was the guilty party. There were several long-drawn-out ways to check the thing, but I had a feeling the villain was Rotty dear, here. I had a hunch he didn't trust you to the ends of the earth, and his 'business trip' might merely be an excuse to check into the Montclair where he could keep a beady eye—or ear, if you'll accept the phrase beady ear— on you. So I cooked up this little episode on the fifty-fifty chance it would pop him out of hiding." I paused. "I had no idea it would shoot him out of a cannon."

"I don't . . ." She frowned. "I don't quite understand."

"You will. Just take your time. And remember I did only what you employed me to do. If I'd told you what I was up to, you wouldn't have believed me in the first place; and in the second place, you sure as fate wouldn't have cooperated with me in the gambit. So I just played it by—by ear. Incidentally, Lydia, you did splendidly. In fact, I hope he really has it recorded."

"Recorded?" It sank in part of the way then. She glared at me. "Why, you beast. The very idea! You beast—"

But then it sank the rest of the way in. The first part had been merely my deviltry—or whatever Lydia might have preferred to call it. But the second part was the Rotty part.

Slowly she swung her gaze from me to him, then finished what she'd started to say. Only this time she was speaking to Rothwell Hamilton Fish. "You *beast!*" she cried. *"The very idea!"*

Rotty was just struggling to his feet, poor chap, when she hauled off and socked him right in the chops. Not just once, but several times, moving with much agility.

Rotty went down again, clear onto his back this trip.

Slowly, very slowly, he clambered to his feet. He knew the jig was up, but at the last there he said something that almost got him onto my good side.

He glanced at Lydia and shrugged, then looked at me.

"Hell," he said. "I can lick her. She just hit me with eight or ten lucky punches."

Then, without another word, he turned and walked out of the bedroom and through the living room and out the front door, never, I felt sure, to be seen in these parts again.

For maybe a minute Lydia and I stood there in the bedroom, not saying a word. We gazed around the room, at chairs, the dresser, at the broken bed, at each other.

I waited.

But finally the suspense was too much. I was, after all, greatly interested in what her reaction would be. So at last I said, "Remember, I did only what you employed me to do. So, baby, you'd better not try socking me."

And at last she smiled. Gently at first. But then a little more warmly. And with this tomato, a little more warmly was like the house burning down.

"Shell," she said, "I'll bet you did kill those elephants with rocks."

I sighed, and relaxed, and grinned. "Not really," I said. "In fact, elephants scare the devil out of me."

"They certainly didn't scare it *all* out." She kept smiling.

"Well, they were small elephants. Hardly more than babies. The worst part was the burning swamps and creeping—"

"Shell," she interrupted me, "I suppose you did me a favor."

"Time will tell." I grinned. Not for any special reason. I just felt like grinning.

"But what made you think it was Rotty?"

"Oh, a lot of things—mainly you." I grinned some more. "But just his name alone should have warned you, Lydia. Imagine going through life with a name like Rotty Fish. Bound to mix a man up. He was irrevocably doomed on the day when he failed to insist that you call him Rothwell."

Lydia walked over to the dresser and peered into the mirror, patted the tangled black hair, smoothed a hotly curving eyebrow. "This must seem like an odd case for you, Shell. Different, anyway. No murder, no kidnaping—nothing even criminal."

"I wouldn't say that. Bugging bedrooms must be at least a misdemeanor. Besides, what I did to Rotty—*that* was criminal."

She smoothed the other brow.

I said, "Well, I suppose I'd better get back to the office. I suppose. Feed the fish or something. I have guppies, you know. Uh . . ."

She turned, leaned back against the edge of the dresser, fixed the tawny brown eyes on me. "You've done enough work for today, haven't you?"

"Why, if you want the truth, I've done enough work for a week." I cleared my throat. "Besides, my office guppies are very well fed. Almost obese."

"Stay a while, then," she said. "We'll talk a little."

"OK."

Her brows creased slightly. "That reminds me," she said.

She walked to the bed, bent down and reached under it, stood up holding the little transmitter. Without a word she went to an open bedroom window, peered out and looked down, apparently to make sure nobody was below, then tossed the transmitter vigorously out the window. I heard it crack on the cement.

Then Lydia turned around, smiling, and walked toward me.

"There," she said. "Now we can talk. Or—Shell, what would *you* like to do?"

She stopped in front of me, looking up at me, close enough to scorch, those incandescent lips slightly parted.

I grinned down at her. "Well," I said, "for a start—how about a hot martini?"

Wade Miller

WE WERE PICKED AS THE ODD ONES

From *The Saint Mystery Magazine,* July 1960

The writing team of Bob Wade and Bill Miller was both prolific and accomplished at a variety of different types of crime fiction from the mid-'40s to the early '60s. As Wade Miller, they produced six excellent hard-boiled private eye novels featuring San Diego-based Max Thursday; the first, Guilty Bystander (1947), *has been favorably compared to Spillane's* I, the Jury *and was filmed in 1950 with Zachary Scott. As Whit Masterson, they published numerous non–series suspense novels, including* Badge of Evil, *the basis for the outstanding Orson Welles film,* Touch of Evil. *(For several years after Miller's premature death in 1961, Wade continued to write top quality suspense fiction under the Masterson name.) The pair wrote relatively few short stories, of which this deceptively simple short-short from* The Saint Mystery Magazine *is among the select. You may think you know exactly what's going on as you read it, but chances are you won't quite be prepared for the quiet little stinger in its tail . . .*

B. P.

HE WASN'T USED TO BEING NOTICED AND THAT WAS WHY HE SO strongly felt her eyes poring over him. He was sitting alone on the loveseat when she came through the archway and caught her first glimpse of him. He imagined that, to her, he looked huddled and forlorn but he considered himself as merely bent contemplatively over the highball he held, nearly hidden, in both big hands.

She was already breathing heavily as she drifted nearer through the music and the happy-voiced clusters of conversation and the faintly secretive pall of cigarette smoke. Then her gaze trailed along the mark on the side of his neck and she moved more quickly to him.

She said, "The Longleys throw a nice party, don't they?" She smiled broadly, plainly wanting to make the most vivid impression possible.

"Sure thing," he replied, looking up at her suspiciously. He saw a pale gaunt girl, eyes bright for him. She wore a wool skirt and a long-sleeved sweater buttoned to the throat, and her figure seemed good enough although not exactly on display. Finally, he gave her his short shy smile.

"Well, I'm going to sit down whether you ask me or not," she informed him. She did, and her hip was soft where it touched him. "My name's Janis."

He told her his was Ray Turrebon. "Sorry if I'm a little slow at this. First, you surprised me, and then I was looking at you, and then I was remembering to check if your drink needed refurnishing . . . Janis what?"

"That's a multiple choice question. I've had at least two short marriages that were utter failures. Do you want to bother with a choice? Oh, I'm shocking you, Ray."

"Not really," he decided. "Still merely surprised. At being descended upon."

She bowed her head to him graciously. "You make me sound like a harpy." Experimentally, she suggested, "There's dancing out in the playroom, you know."

"Certainly, I know. But isn't this cosy enough right here and now?"

"Definitely. I'm just feeling you out." She clinked her glass against his and drank as if toasting something. "You didn't arrive until so late and the instant I saw you I tabbed you as the modest type. Indrawn and with secrets."

His laugh was little more than a humorless puff as he glanced down at his business suit. "I barely consider myself presentable, if that's what you mean. In this gathering."

"Then you haven't been here often?"

"Once before."

She seemed delighted, which bothered him. He felt it necessary to explain his position as a junior accountant in Longley's firm. He told her about the degree and three year apprenticeship necessary to qualify as a CPA. About the four part exams, far more rigorous than bar exams, offered twice yearly. Pass one and you got no credit for it. Pass two and then you only had to worry about the remaining two. Well, this last time he had passed three which left only one part to go—Theory—and the dread semi-annual was now rolling around again, inexorably, and he was studying with all his might. One more river to cross, and a few months to work out on his apprenticeship, and then he would be entitled to call himself a Certified Public Accountant. Some where along the line he told her that he was a bachelor.

She was an excellent listener. Indeed, he had an uncomfortable feeling that he was being studied. "The whole thing sounds extremely confining," was her judgment.

Telling the story of the climb toward his career had stimulated him. He cautiously slipped his hand onto her nearest one. Her fingers were icy from tightly clasping her drink.

She leaned her head back on the loveseat, pretending a relaxation he knew she didn't feel. "I'm merely an assistant to Mrs. Longley's interior decorator. This is my first party here, Ray. I guess I looked interesting to someone." Before he could get his tongue around a gallant reply, she said, "I guess we were picked as the odd ones."

"What do you mean by that?"

"For the party. So that everyone can be coupled up neatly in case some character of either sex begs off at the last minute. The hostess needs one odd boy and one odd girl, just in case. See?"

"Don't you think we're a little mature to be referred to as boy and girl?"

She was pleased again. "Okay, dear. So we're man and woman. That better? What's troubling you so? You can tell me."

"Your excitement. You've been excited from the very moment you walked up to me. Now don't try to kid me about it and tell me I radiate something or other. Women have never taken this kind of interest in me before."

She dropped her lashes, a shy pose of her own that wasn't intended to fool anybody. "The news excites me, always, news of what's happening to other people. Just before I met you, I sneaked out on the party. Not that I left the house or anything. I tiptoed into the children's room and turned on their television set, real low so they wouldn't wake up. I wanted to watch the ten o'clock news."

He chuckled. "A news program—you must have a low boiling point. So what's going on in the world?"

"Right here in the city." She leaned her shoulder closer to his, her breath warm on his cheek. "That icepick fellow is still running loose. He attacked another woman again tonight. That's the fourth one in three weeks."

Her intimate closeness, a nakedness of spirit, touched him deep inside but he frowned at her, nevertheless. "I don't know what you're talking about. I'm afraid I'm not very good about keeping up with the newspapers and such like."

"Oh, Ray, how could you have missed this? He hasn't killed anybody yet but he's got every female in town scared to go out alone at night. For fear they'll be leaped out at and get their precious skins punctured a few times."

"Very interesting." He released her cold hand. She let it slide, with all naturalness, onto his leg. He said, "You know, if you have a deep abiding interest in crime, I happen to know that there's a deputy district attorney here tonight."

"Oh, him! I hate officials. I like real people, without positions to uphold. What's so wrong in wanting to make friends with you? You're real people." Her logic, he had to agree, was beautiful. At her request, he went to the bar in the playroom and had their drinks refilled. When he returned, she was waiting pleasantly on the loveseat, room for two only.

"There's a contagion to crime," was her first remark, "especially sex crimes. It gets everyone to talking about it, thinking about it. Every living soul must have a streak of depravity, I suppose."

"Drink your drink," he said. "You've got a talking streak."

"That's what makes me so allfired fascinating." Then she glanced at him and obeyed. He gulped down some of his, too. She said, "Not that I entirely blame the poor guy. Have you ever thought about life, the monotony of life, as a real slow dripping torture? I mean, agony is a cinch, misery is easy, but nothingness must be unbearable. Oh, Ray, the very thought makes me want to cry."

"For God's sake, don't." He slipped an arm around her shoulders and she made herself comfortable against him. She wanted, at that point, to know what he was thinking about and he let her know he didn't intend to tell her. "Except that you feel very good in this position."

"Interior decorating," she murmured, "gives one a practical eye for detail. All the people at the party, I didn't see you. You came late."

"I was studying that damn Theory. I lost track of time."

"Don't interrupt me, dear. The very first thing I noticed about you was that scratch along the side of your neck. As if a woman had clawed you with her fingernails. Have you been fighting with a woman?"

He snorted. "I can't remember one ever taking that much notice of me."

"So you'd like to get back at them?"

He liked to hold her; he could almost feel the flow of her blood through her slim body. But he said, not releasing her, "Pal, you're getting drunker and drunker."

"Sheerly on emotion, sweet."

"There's a rosebush right by the front steps of where I live. If the landlady doesn't trim it tomorrow, I cut her throat. It was the rosebush that nearly clawed my head off tonight when I was rushing out to this party."

"So glad you made it." With the slightest turn of her face, she kissed the corner of his mouth. "Do you have your car here?"

"It's laid up. I took the bus."

"Good. I have my car out front, a real flashy convertible. The payments are breaking me and it's pure torture on cold nights but it's transportation to and from."

He was acutely conscious of her heavy heartbeat and hoped it covered the telltale boyish throb of his own. "To and from where?"

"My apartment, darling, what else? At least, it's mine in the sense that my roommate's positively gone for the whole weekend. I can mix better drinks than these caterers and it wouldn't be too horrible if we slipped out of here and over there where we could be alone, would it? I mean, I gather you live in some sort of a rooming house and wouldn't it be fun for you to spend a little time in an all girl apartment? Everything guaranteed feminine?"

He controlled his voice with extreme care. "I want nothing more than to kiss you where there isn't a crowd passing back and forth."

"I'll get my things." She wriggled out of his arms and they stood up together, gazing into each other's eyes. "I'll make you forgive what I wore tonight, this sweater and skirt. I've watched you watching some of the other girls milling around, their bare shoulders, bare backs, bare whatnot. Well, the truth of the matter is I didn't feel very sexy tonight, not until I spotted you." She started away, turned back. "You know, even the symbolism of the icepick fascinates me. Did you ever give that much thought?"

"The only thing that occurred to me was where in hell this guy managed to procure an icepick in this day and age. I've begun to think of them as antiques. Oh, I suppose you must still be able to buy them in hardware stores."

She grinned and disappeared. Out of a sense of responsibility to Longley, he mixed with the nearest group, thinking of little else but the swaying grace of her body, the cute twists and turns of her mind. The group happened to contain the deputy district attorney who was being called away from the party on business. Suddenly, he began to listen attentively.

Janis skirted into view again, a cloth coat over her arm. He took the arm possessively, pointing her toward the door. He said, "Just to make your evening complete, I've got a late news flash for you. Your icepick fellow has just been picked up, full confession and everything. A laborer on a construction gang, wife and four kids. Find the symbolism there."

Her face went rigid. "You're lying. Not nice lying. Deliberate."

"Don't be silly. I just helped bid goodbye to the deputy DA. Case closed."

She stared at him for a long moment, then pulled her arm free. "Excuse me. I forgot to go to the little girl's room."

She vanished again. After a while he went browsing for her. He even went outside but any car that could be described as a flashy convertible was gone by now. He paid his respects to Mrs. Longley but she didn't know Janis' address and couldn't remember her last name. He didn't feel like making an issue of it.

At the bar he talked to the caterer's man, gazing all the time into his big container of broken ice. "You don't still use icepicks in your business, do you?"

"Not on your life. Ice comes in cubes, or I don't think I'd stay in this work. We've got these ice-crushers here for some types of cocktails, mostly those things ladies drink . . ." He held up a small pair of tongs with metal boxes at the crushing end. "Oh, and we've got this electric pulverizer when we need ice that's shaved real fine."

"I see. I thought maybe if you had an icepick you'd let me buy it from you."

"Afraid not. It wouldn't even be mine to sell."

"You're right. It was just an idea, and not a very good one." He ordered another drink instead and drifted into the mainstream of the party.

Day Keene

NOTHING TO WORRY ABOUT

From *Chase*, 1945

Day Keene was the prototypical commercial writer. He started out writing radio dramas in the '30s, switched to pulps in the '40s, and became a mainstay of the new paperback original field in the '50s. During the last years of his life, he ended up well published in hardcover, with at least two of his novels becoming bona fide bestsellers, one of them, Chautauqua, being an exceptionally well-done book. He wrote too much, he could be sloppy and occasionally trite, but even in his minor books you see a fine, wry intelligence at work. In recent years, his work has come back into vogue, as well it should—he was a very good writer. Some people have complained about the "pen-name" sound of the name Day Keene—you'd use a pen name, too, if your real name was Gunard Hjerstedt.

E. G.

IF THERE WERE ANY LETTERS OF FIRE ON ASSISTANT STATE'S Attorney Brad Sorrel's broad and distinguished brow they were invisible to his fellow passengers in the lighted cabin of the Washington-Chicago plane, as it circled the Cicero Airport at fifteen minutes to midnight. The stewardess, appraising his broad shoulders, graying temples and hearty laughter, considered the woman to whom he was returning very fortunate indeed. His seat mate had found him intelligent and sympathetic.

At no time during the flight, or during the hours preceding it, had there been anything in Sorrel's voice or demeanor to which anyone could point and say, "I knew it at the time. He was nervous. He couldn't concentrate. His conversation was forced. He talked and acted like a man about to kill his wife."

It was no sudden decision on Sorrel's part. He had considered killing Frances, often; only a firm respect for the law that he, himself represented had deterred him. He had, in the name of the state, asked for, and been given, the lives of too many men to be careless with his own. Intolerable as his marital situation had become it was preferable to facing a jury whom he had lost the right to challenge.

The *No Smoking* and *Please Fasten Your Seat Belt* panels over the door of the pilot's compartment blinked on. The lights of the field rushed up to meet the plane.

This is it, Sorrel thought. *In twenty minutes, thirty at the most, Frances will be dead. Poor soul.*

His seat mate wound up the telling of the involved argument and verbal slug-fest in which he had just engaged with the Office Of Price Administration. Sorrel gave him one-half of his mind, sympathizing hugely, assuring him he had been right, that it couldn't last forever, and agreeing that it seemed that private business was headed for a boom.

The other half of his mind considered the thing that he had to do. It would not be pleasant. In his search for a solution to his problem he had inspected, weighed, and judged, the none-too-many means by which murder could be done. The alleged clever methods—accidental death, suicide, death by misadventure—he had rejected almost immediately. They left too many loopholes for failure; few of them ever succeeded. There was a reason. No matter how brilliant a killer might be he was seldom, if ever, a match for the combined technical, executive, and judicial branches of the law.

Crime detection, trial, and judgment, had become akin to an exact science.

The art of killing, the three M's, means, method, motive, had changed little in the known history of man. To take a life one still had to shoot, knife, drown, strike, strangle, or poison the party of the unwanted part. And, as with most basic refinements to the art of living, the first known method of murder used—that of striking the party to be removed with whatever object came first to hand—was still the most difficult of detection, providing of course that the party who did the striking could maintain a reasonable plea of being elsewhere at the time.

■ ■ ■

It was, after mature consideration, that method that Sorrel had chosen. He had even chosen his weapon, one of the heavy cutglass candlesticks that stood on Frances' dressing table.

"Murphy. J. P. Murphy is the name," his seat mate identified himself. He shook Sorrel's hand vigorously. "It's been a pleasure to meet you, Prosecutor. And if you decide to enter the senatorial race, as I've seen hinted at in the papers, you can count on my vote as certain."

Sorrel's hearty laugh filled the plane. "Thanks. I'll remember that, Murphy."

His only luggage was his briefcase. The stewardess insisted on getting it down from the rack for him. He tucked a forbidden bill in the breast pocket of her uniform. "Nice trip," he smiled. "And thanks."

"Thank *you*, Mr. Sorrel!" She beamed. One met such few really nice men. Most tipping hands brushed or hovered, seeking a partial return on their investment.

■ ■ ■

Sorrel stood in the open door of the plane a moment sniffing the night air. The fine weather was still holding. It was neither too hot nor too cold.

He descended the steps and lifted a hand in greeting to the pilot as he passed the nose of the plane. He did so habitually on his not infrequent trips. There must be no departure from the norm, no errors of omission or commission, no nervously spilled milk in which the bacteria of suspicion might breed.

He, John Sorrel, assistant state's attorney, was returning from Washington with nothing on his mind but the successful conclusion of the business that had taken him there. He wasn't nervous. He felt fine. He assured himself that he did.

In the doorway of the terminal, Murphy touched his arm. "I'm taking a cab to the Loop. If you'd like to share it, Sorrel . . ."

"Thanks, no," Sorrel said. "My car should be waiting." He managed to edge his words with the proper amount of innuendo without being vulgar. "You see, I—well, I'm not going directly home."

The other man winked. "I—see."

■ ■ ■

They parted after shaking hands again. He was, Sorrel realized, running the risk of being slightly too clever. But the more people who knew, or who thought they knew, that he had gone directly from the plane to Evelyn's apartment the stronger would be his alibi.

He had never kept their affair a secret. He doubted that any prosecutor, judge or jury—if it should come to that—would question so embarrassing an alibi as a husband's being forced to admit that, while his wife had been killed, he had been with another woman, railing against the deceased, because she had refused to divorce him.

Despite the lateness of the hour the terminal was crowded. He saw three or four men whom he knew and nodded cordially to as he passed through the terminal.

■ ■ ■

Jackson was waiting behind the wheel of a department car. Sorrel tossed his case into the back seat and slid in beside him. "So you got my wire."

"And why not?" Jackson asked. "You wanna go home, the office, or . . .." He left the question open.

Sorrel sighed. "Home, I suppose. But let's drop by the Eldorado first."

"I figured that," Jackson said.

Sorrel rode, the night wind cool on his cheeks, eager to be done with what he had to do, wishing that Frances had been reasonable. If she had been, if she had been willing to divorce him, none of this would have to be.

In front of the building he told Jackson, "I won't be long, I think."

Jackson fished in his vest pocket for a toothpick, found one. "Take your time."

He meant it. He liked Sorrel. He liked Evelyn, too. For all of her good looks she was a lady. Frances Sorrel wasn't, what with her calling a spade a dirty shovel and her drinking and her fighting—she was no wife for a man who soon might be a senator. Although, at that, he reflected, he had heard someone say that she had worked like a dog for the money that had put Sorrel through law school, and she had always sworn she hadn't started to drink and chase until he had gone lace curtain Irish on her.

Under the marquee of the building the colored doorman grinned whitely at Sorrel. "Glad to see you back, Mister Smith. Been missin' you for a week now."

Sorrel creased a five dollar bill and slipped it into his hand. "I've been in Washington saving the nation."

The doorman chuckled, hugely amused. "He say he been in Washington savin' the nation," he confided to Jackson.

Jackson continued to pick at his teeth. "Yair."

■ ■ ■

Inside the lobby, Sorrel paused briefly, suddenly short of breath. This was murder. He, John Sorrel, an assistant state's attorney who would have been state's attorney had it not been for his wife, and who was being considered by the party as a senatorial candidate, was proposing to steal into his own home by stealth and remove the sole obstacle who stood in the path of his political success.

That angle would not enter the case, however. It would not be considered a motive. None of the powers-that-were had ever mentioned Frances. But he knew, there was the feminine vote to consider. And what with things as they were, the party couldn't afford to take a chance. Frances' scenes were too well known. She drank; she cursed; she was unfaithful. Not that he had ever been so fortunate as to obtain proof that would stand in a court of law.

■　■　■

He closed his eyes and saw his wife as he had seen her, fat, slovenly dressed, her face puffed with drink, during the last public scene that she had made. That had been in the lobby of the Chalmer's House, before a delighted ring of onlookers.

"Sure I'm drunk. An' I'm a tramp," she had taunted while he had tried vainly to hush her. "An' don't you tell me to shut up. Wash a hell. I'm human. The trouble with you is that you've got too big for your bed. You're one of them whitened sepelcurs like Father Ryan wash always talking about." She had turned to the crowd, her voice suddenly gin-throaty, maudlin tears spilling down her cheeks. "I'm not good enough for him anymore. Me, who put him through school, who loved him when he didn't have a dime." She had attempted to embrace him. "Cansha understand? I still love you, Johnny." The tears had dried as abruptly as they had come. "An' I'll shee you in hell before I'll let some painted young tart make a bigger fool of you than you are. Now go ahead an' hit me. I dare you to, you blankety blankety blank."

Sorrel opened his eyes, his moment of weakness gone. There was only the one thing to do. But at least in one respect she was wrong. He was very human. He wanted to feel Evelyn's arms soft and cool around his neck, hear her assure him again that some day everything would be all right, if only they were patient.

His jaw muscles tightening, he opened the door of the self-service elevator and punched the twelfth floor button. He was finished with being patient. He had been patient for ten years. It was not his fault, it was her own fault, that Frances had not grown with him. One thing he knew, he could no longer stand the sight or sound or touch of her.

Tonight must end it.

■ ■ ■

In front of Evelyn's door he slipped his key from his pocket, paused at the realization that if he saw her now he would make her a party to his crime. More, she would attempt to dissuade him. It was best that she know nothing about it, until the affair was over.

Light streamed out from under her door. Her radio was playing softly. He could hear the sound of movement, a drawer being opened and closed. It was enough to know that she was home, that she had received his wire and was waiting. Good girl. Evelyn was a brick. Whatever happened, he could count on her.

He descended to the second floor, left the elevator and walked down the service stairs and out of the side door. The coupe was parked where he had left it. His one fear had been that he might find it stripped.

The motor started easily. He glanced at his watch in the dash light. Five of the thirty minutes that he had allotted himself were gone. Driving at forty miles an hour, the three miles he had to travel would take him two minutes each way. It was fifteen minutes of one. Allow even six more minutes for mishaps and he still had plenty of time to do what he had to do and be back in Evelyn's apartment within a half hour from the time that he had left Jackson. At one-fifteen he would phone down to the doorman and ask him to have Jackson bring up his briefcase and the bottle of rye it contained.

■ ■ ■

He had no fear that Frances would not be at home. His telegram had stated that his plane was arriving at midnight. Clinging to the tattered remnants of their marriage she always made it a practice to be home and more or less sober whenever he returned.

"You'll never catch me that way," she had told him once. "I'm a good wife to you, Johnny, see? And I'm willing to be a better one if you would only let me. Why can't we start all over?"

There were a dozen answers to that one, the best of which was Evelyn. The two women had never met. Frances knew that she existed, that was all. That was enough.

As he slowed for the intersection at 63rd Street, Sorrel smiled wryly at a suggestion that Evelyn, intrigued by the fact that they had never met, had made.

"We know she's not true to you, Johnny," she had pointed out. "She has no right to point a finger. She doesn't know me. So why can't I strike up a drinking acquaintance with her, or take a job as her maid, or something, and get some concrete proof that would stand up in a divorce court?"

Sorrel had refused to hear of it. Frances was shrewd. A scene between the two was unthinkable. Frances fought as they fought in back of the yards, where both of them had been born—for keeps. Then, too, a sense of guilt had assailed him. His own hands were not clean. He, and he alone, was responsible for Frances' infidelities. She was merely reaching out for the love that he denied her. He had told Evelyn at the time that whatever was done, he would do. He was keeping his word now.

There were few cars on 63rd Street. There were none on the darker residential street onto which he turned. He drove for another quarter mile and parked a half a block and across the street from his home.

There were lights in both the kitchen and in Frances' bedroom. The shades of the bedroom were drawn, but, as he watched, a vague figure crossed the room, too far back of the shade to seem more than a passing shadow.

■   ■   ■

His eyes felt suddenly hot and strained. His throat contracted. His mouth was dry. His hands felt cold and clammy on the wheel. He sat a moment longer, wondering at himself, revolted by the thing he had come to do. This was murder. This was what other men had done for reasons no better than his own and he, in his smug superiority, safe in the law's ivory tower, had thundered against them and denounced them as cool-blooded conniving scoundrels.

He stepped from the car with an effort and crossed the street. He had come a long way in his climb up—he intended to go still further. With Frances dead and Evelyn beside him, there was no goal to which he might not aspire.

He stopped under a spreading elm tree in the yard and cursed his shaking hands. There was no reason to be afraid. The law would never touch him. He had planned too well. There would be no insurance angle. Frances had none. His only gain would be peace of mind and that wasn't considered a motive for murder. A few of the boys in his own office might suspect him but no one would be able to prove a thing.

* * *

Frances' failings were well known. She had come home drunk. She had left the door unlocked. A night prowler had entered and killed her. No one would be more surprised and shocked than he when he returned with Jackson an hour from now and found her—dead.

He slipped his key in the front door. The inner bolt was shot and it refused to open. He considered ringing the bell and killing her in the hall. He decided to stay, as far as possible, with his original plan. There was no convenient weapon in the hall. A single scream would shatter the stillness of the sleeping street. What he had to do must be done in silence.

The back door leading into the kitchen was open but the screen door was locked. He slipped on a pair of gloves and fumbled in one corner of the porch where he had remembered seeing a rusty ice pick. His luck was holding. The pick was there. He probed it through the screen and lifted the hood from its eyes.

* * *

The door open he waited, listening, hearing nothing. There was a half emptied bottle of milk, a clouded glass, and the remains of a peanut butter sandwich on the kitchen table.

Frances, he decided, was playing the sober and repentant wife this time.

Believe me, John. I love you. I'll stop drinking. I'll do anything you say. You're all that matters to me. Why can't we start all over?

He had heard it so many times that he could play the record by heart. He noted that the kitchen shade was up. Anyone entering the kitchen would be visible from the darkened windows of the house next door. Sweat beading on his forehead, he slipped in a hand before him and snapped the switch, thankful that he had noticed the shade in time. It was the little things of murder that sent men to the chair.

The darkness magnified his strain. His mouth grew even drier.

He heard, or thought he heard, the pounding of his heart. He had to force himself to cross the kitchen, feeling his way along the wall to the rear stairs.

Now he could hear sounds in the bedroom. She seemed to be opening and closing drawers, probably in search of one of the bottles she was always hiding from herself.

He crossed the dark hall toward the closed bedroom door and his weight caused a board to creak. The light in the bedroom went out and the door opened. They stood only feet apart in the black hallway, aware of each other but unable to see.

The blood, Sorrel thought suddenly. *It will splatter. I'll be covered with blood. Damn it! Why didn't I think of that!*

Then he realized he still was clutching the rusted ice pick in his hand. It was as good a weapon as any, better than most. Murder Incorporated had used them as the chief tool of their trade. An ice pick had been used in the case of the State versus Manny Capper. The sweat on his brow turned cold. Manny had gone to the chair.

Galvanized by his own terror, crying out hoarsely, Sorrel sprang forward. His groping hand felt teeth in time to clamp his palm over the welling scream. It died still-born as he plunged the pick in his hand repeatedly into the yielding flesh. The body he held ceased squirming and sagged limply. He allowed it to fall to the floor, relieved to be rid of it.

■ ■ ■

The ice pick fell from his nerveless hand. He tried to fumble a match from his pocket and could not. His hands were shaking too badly. Afraid of the dark, afraid of the woman whom he had killed, he squatted beside the body and felt for a pulse with the back of his wrist, where flesh gaped between glove and coat cuff. There was no pulse. It was over, done with, *finis*. He was free.

He crept back down the stairs and out through the kitchen to the porch. Then he remembered the pick. It would have no fingerprints on it. He considered returning for it and his stomach rebelled.

So there were no fingerprints on the death weapon. So what? Most house prowlers with the sense of gnats wore gloves. It was nothing for him to worry over.

He walked silently, unseen, back to his car and examined his gloves in the dash light. One was slightly splattered with blood but there seemed to be none on the cuffs of his suit. All that remained to be done was to rid himself of the gloves.

It was over, done. He was free. There was nothing to stop him now, nothing to stop the boys from running him for whatever office they pleased. Frances had made her last scene. He was young, under forty. His new life was just beginning.

As he drove the horror of the thing that he had been forced to do left him. He wanted to sing, to yell, to shout to the stars that he was free. He contented himself with a grin.

It had been a relatively simple matter, after all. He wadded the gloves into a ball and tossed them out the car window. They could not be traced to him. There was nothing to tie him to the murder but the fact that he and Frances were married. Back at the Eldorado he parked the coupe in the same space it had occupied before and glanced at his watch, before switching off the lights. It was eleven minutes past one. He was four minutes ahead of schedule.

He expended them by walking to the corner and peering around it cautiously. The doorman and Jackson were deep in some discussion. Satisfied that he had not been missed he entered the side door.

Telling Evelyn would take some doing. She would be horrified at first, but she was quick-witted enough to realize that no other course had been open to him. It didn't matter now. All that mattered was that the thing was done.

His throat and mouth were normal again. In the bright light of the cage he could see no bloodstains on his suit. He had been fortunate. He was whistling softly, almost cheerfully, as he inserted his key in the door.

■   ■   ■

The radio was still playing softly. A bottle of his best scotch beside her Frances was sitting in one of Evelyn's easy chairs. "I knew you'd come here first," she said. "What's a matter? Was your plane late?"

He stared at her open-mouthed, screams he was unable to utter tearing at his throat.

"You poor damn fool," his wife continued. "Why didn't you let me meet her? Why didn't you make me realize what a swell kid she really was? Why didn't you tell me that the boys wanted to run you for senator? You should have known me better, John.

You're my man. You always will be. No tramp was goin' to take you from me. But a sweet kid like that is another matter." She fluffed at her frowsy hair. "I feel kind of honored like."

Sorrel managed to gasp one word, "Evelyn . . ."

▪ ▪ ▪

Frances nipped at the scotch. "Oh, you didn't know. Well, she showed at the house this morning and gave me a song and dance about being a maid out of work, her with fingernails that long." She laughed, shortly. "So I hired her and I pumped her. She's probably goin' through all my things right now, spyin' on me." Frances picked an oblong scrap of yellow paper from the table. "She never even got a chance to see her telegram because I copped her key from her purse and come over here shortly after I got the telegram that you sent me. Mine was all right. But after I read this one I kinda wondered." She read it aloud, " 'Sweetheart. Be in your apartment at twelve tonight. Don't leave it for any reason. And don't let anyone in but me. This is important, more important than you realize.' "

His voice sounding strange to himself, Sorrel asked. "You—knew?"

Frances Sorrel smiled thinly. "I know you," she admitted. "But don't worry. Think nothing of it. As long as your plane was late, you've got nothing to worry about."

Fredric Brown

CRY SILENCE

From *Black Mask*, November 1948

Like so many of his contemporaries, Fredric Brown learned his craft in the pulp magazines of the '30s and '40s. The more than 100 stories he published in Detective Tales, Dime Mystery, *and other periodicals were stepping stones to the production of an impressive array of crime novels— detective stories featuring the Chicago team of Ed Hunter and his uncle Am (a series that began in 1947 with the Edgar-winning* Fabulous Clip-joint*) and such memorable non–series thrillers as* The Screaming Mimi *and* Knock Three-One-Two. *"Cry Silence" is one of dozens of Brown's mordant short-shorts, a demanding form at which he proved himself a master—and also his only story to appear in the king of the mystery and detective pulps,* Black Mask *(November 1948).*

B. P.

IT WAS THAT OLD SILLY ARGUMENT ABOUT SOUND. IF A TREE falls deep in the forest where there is no ear to hear is its fall silent? Is there sound where there is no ear to hear it? I've heard it argued by college professors and by street sweepers.

This time it was being argued by the agent at the little railroad station and a beefy man in coveralls. It was a warm summer evening at dusk, and the station agent's window opening onto the back platform of the station was open; his elbows rested on the ledge of it. The beefy man leaned against the red brick of the building. The argument between them droned in circles like a bumblebee.

I sat on a wooden bench on the platform about ten feet away. I was a stranger in town, waiting for a train that was late. There was one other man present; he sat on the bench beside me, between me and the window. He was a tall, heavy man with an uncompromising kind of face, and huge, rough hands. He looked like a farmer in his town clothes.

I wasn't interested in either the argument or the man beside me. I was wondering only how late that damned train would be.

I didn't have my watch; it was being repaired in the city. And from where I sat I couldn't see the clock inside the station. The tall man beside me was wearing a wrist watch and I asked him what time it was.

He didn't answer.

You've got the picture haven't you? Four of us; three on the platform and the agent leaning out of the window. The argument between the agent and the beefy man. On the bench, the silent man and I.

I got up off the bench and looked into the open door of the station. It was seven-forty; the train was twelve minutes overdue. I sighed, and lighted a cigarette. I decided to stick my nose into the argument. It wasn't any of my business, but I knew the answer and they didn't.

"Pardon me for butting in," I said, "but you're not arguing about sound at all; you're arguing semantics."

I expected one of them to ask me what semantics was, but the station agent fooled me. He said, "That's the study of words, isn't it? In a way, you're right, I guess."

"All the way," I insisted. "If you look up 'sound' in the dictionary, you'll find two meanings listed. One of them is 'the vibration of a medium, usually air, within a certain range,' and the other is 'the effect of such vibrations on the ear.' That isn't the exact wording, but the general idea. Now by one of those definitions, the sound—the vibration—exists whether there's an ear around to hear it or not. By the other, the vibrations aren't sound unless there is an ear to hear them. So you're both right; it's just a matter of which meaning you use for the word 'sound.'"

The beefy man said, "Maybe you got something there." He looked back at the agent. "Let's call it a draw then, Joe. I got to get home. So long."

He stepped down off the platform and went around the station. I asked the agent, "Any report on the train?"

"Nope," he said. He leaned a little farther out the window and looked to his right and I saw a clock in a steeple about a block away that I hadn't noticed before. "Ought to be along soon though."

He grinned at me. "Expert on sound, huh?"

"Well," I said, "I wouldn't say that. But I did happen to look it up in the dictionary. I know what the word means."

"Uh-huh. Well, let's take that second definition and say sound is sound only if there's an ear to hear it. A tree crashes in the forest and there's only a deaf man there. Is there any sound?"

"I guess not," I said. "Not if you consider sound as subjective. Not if it's got to be heard."

I happened to glance to my right, at the tall man who hadn't answered my question about the time. He was still staring straight ahead. Lowering my voice a bit, I asked the station agent, "Is he deaf?"

"Him? Bill Meyers?" He chuckled; there was something odd in the sound of that chuckle. "Mister, nobody knows. That's what I was going to ask you next. If that tree falls down and there's a man near, but nobody knows if he's deaf or not, is there any sound?"

His voice had gone up in volume. I stared at him, puzzled, wondering if he was a little crazy, or if he was just trying to keep up the argument by thinking up screwy loopholes.

I said, "Then if nobody knows if he's deaf, nobody knows if there was any sound."

He said, "You're wrong, mister. That man would know whether he heard it or not. Maybe the tree would know, wouldn't it? And maybe other people would know, too."

"I don't get your point," I told him. "What are you trying to prove?"

"*Murder*, mister. You just got up from sitting next to a murderer."

I stared at him again, but he didn't look crazy. Far off, a train whistled, faintly. I said, "I don't understand you."

"The guy sitting on the bench," he said. "Bill Meyers. He murdered his wife. Her and his hired man."

His voice was quite loud. I felt uncomfortable; I wished that far train was a lot nearer. I didn't know what went on here, but I knew I'd rather be on the train. Out of the corner of my eye I looked at the tall man with the granite face and the big hands. He was still staring out across the tracks. Not a muscle in his face had moved.

The station agent said, "I'll tell you about it, mister. I *like* to tell people about it. His wife was a cousin of mine, a fine woman. Mandy Eppert, her name was, before she married that skunk. He was mean to her, dirt mean. Know how mean a man can be to a woman who's helpless?

"She was seventeen when she was fool enough to marry him seven years ago. She was twenty-four when she died last spring. She'd done more work than most women do in a lifetime, out on that farm of his. He worked her like a horse and treated her like a slave. And her religion wouldn't let her divorce him or even leave him. See what I mean, mister?"

I cleared my throat, but there didn't seem to be anything to say. He didn't need prodding or comment. He went on.

"So how can you blame her, mister, for loving a decent guy, a clean, young fellow her own age when he fell in love with her? Just *loving* him, that's all. I'd bet my life on that because I knew Mandy. Oh they talked, and they looked at each other—I wouldn't gamble too much there wasn't a stolen kiss now and then. But nothing to kill them for, mister."

I felt uneasy; I wished the train would come and get me out of this. I had to say something, though; the agent was waiting. I said, "Even if there had been, the unwritten law is out of date."

"Right, mister." I'd said the right thing. "But you know what that bastard sitting over there did? He went deaf."

"Huh?" I said.

"He went deaf. He came in town to see the doc and said he'd been having earaches and couldn't hear anymore. Was afraid he was going deaf. Doc gave him some stuff to try, and you know where he went from the doc's office?"

I didn't try to guess.

"Sheriff's office," he said. "Told the sheriff he wanted to report his wife and his hired man were missing, see? Smart of him. Wasn't it? Swore out a complaint and said he'd prosecute if they were found. But he had an awful lot of trouble getting any of the questions the sheriff asked. Sheriff got tired of yelling and wrote 'em down on paper. Smart. See what I mean?"

"Not exactly," I said. "Hadn't his wife run away?"

"He'd murdered her. And him. Or rather, he was *murdering* them. Must have taken a couple of weeks, about. Found 'em a month later."

He glowered, his face black with anger.

"In the smokehouse," he said. "A new smokehouse made out of concrete and not used yet. With a padlock on the outside of the door. He'd walked through the farmyard one day about a month before—he said after their bodies were found—and noticed the padlock wasn't locked, just hanging in the hook and not even through the hasp.

"See? Just to keep the padlock from being lost or swiped, he slips it through the hasp and snaps it."

"My God," I said. "And they were in there? They starved to death?"

"Thirst kills you quicker, if you haven't either water or food. Oh, they'd tried hard to get out, all right. Scraped halfway through the door with a piece of concrete he'd worked loose. It was a thick door. I figure they hammered on that door plenty. Was there sound, mister, with only a *deaf* man living near that door, passing it twenty times a day?"

Again he chuckled humorlessly. He said: "Your train'll be along soon. That was it you heard whistle. It stops up by the water tower. It'll be here in ten minutes." And without changing his tone of voice, except that it got louder again, he said: "It was a bad way to die. Even if he was right in killing them, only a black-hearted son of a bitch would have done it that way. Don't you think so?"

I said: "But are you sure he is—"

"Deaf? Sure, he's deaf. Can't you picture him standing there in front of that padlocked door, listening with his deaf ears to the hammering inside? And the yelling?

"Sure, he's deaf. That's why I can say all this to him, yell it in his ear. If I'm wrong, he can't hear me. But he can hear me. He comes here to hear me."

I had to ask it. "Why? Why would he—if you're right."

"I'm helping him, that's why. I'm helping him to make up his black mind to hang a rope from the grating in the top of that smokehouse, and dangle from it. He hasn't got the guts to, yet. So every time he's in town, he sits on the platform a while to rest. And I tell him what a murdering son of a bitch he is."

He spat toward the tracks. He said, "There are a few of us know the score. Not the sheriff; he wouldn't believe us, said it would be hard to prove."

The scrape of feet behind me made me turn. The tall man with the huge hands and the granite face was standing up now. He didn't look toward us. He started for the steps.

The agent said, "He'll hang himself, pretty soon now. He wouldn't come here and sit like that for any other reason, would he, mister?"

"Unless," I said, "he *is* deaf."

"Sure. He could be. See what I meant? If a tree falls and the only man there to hear it is maybe deaf and maybe not, is it silent or isn't it? Well, I got to get the mail pouch ready."

I turned and looked at the tall figure walking away from the station. He walked slowly and his shoulders, big as they were, seemed a little stooped.

The clock in the steeple a block away began to strike for seven o'clock.

The tall man lifted his wrist to look at the watch on it.

I shuddered a little. It could have been coincidence, sure, and yet a little chill went down my spine.

The train pulled in, and I got aboard.

Donald Wandrei

TICK, TOCK

From *Black Mask,* November 1938

Donald Wandrei is best known for his weird fantasy stories and as co-founder, with August Derleth, of the highly regarded Arkham House publishing imprint in 1939. But in the '30s he published more than thirty mystery and detective short stories and novelettes, nearly all of them in two pulp magazines, Clues and Black Mask. *Far and away the best is "Tick, Tock," which must have both startled and disturbed* Black Mask's *readers when it was published in 1937. Even by today's standards it remains an effectively tense, bone-chilling, and explosive (literally) tale of homicidal obsession.*

B. P.

JUD KERRUN WRAPPED THE BOX CAREFULLY WITH PAPER CUT from a grocer's brown sack and tied it with ordinary white string. He took a stencil from the top of the work bench, laid it across the lower right surface of the package, and briskly rubbed a black wax crayon across the stencil. When he moved the stencil, the package had an address in bold, block letters: LESLIE GRAMM, 307 FRONT ST.

He held the package tight against his ear. It said, in a whisper so faint that he was not absolutely certain he had heard it:

Tick, tock.

Jud put the package into a cardboard box on a layer of old newspapers. He added a red sweater to the package, and rolled the two items with the newspapers, and tucked the bundle under one arm.

Then he pulled his gloves off and tossed them aside.

That was the way to do it. Even if everything went wrong, the cops wouldn't find fingerprints, clues, or handwriting.

He rubbed the back of a hand across the stubble on his chin as he opened the door. Sunlight of late afternoon slanted briefly inside the combination workshop and garage. The light touched on a battered six-year-old machine and the work bench beside it, its top littered with pieces of wire, lengths of metal, and a few spilled flakes of black powder. All that stuff could be cleaned up later. Time counted, now. Time was saying:

Tick, tock.

Jud closed and locked the door as he went out. He squinted his eyes till they became used to the sun. He rubbed his chin again, nervously, with the back of his clenched fist. Then he looked at the fist and scowled. He let his arm hang loose as he walked around the side of a two-story frame house badly in need of paint.

A caterpillar was crawling at the edge of the grass beside the path. Jud went three steps out of his way to mash it.

He angled back to the path again with a loose, shambling gait. His shoulders slouched. His whole body had a kind of slouch. Even his soiled brown hat slid down over the ridge of his forehead as though trying to escape. He walked with a kind of hesitant weakness, a furtive pacing; yet strength ran in his thick chest and shoulders, his long, powerful arms, and a sultry, avid hotness nestled in his pale blue eyes.

"Jud!"

His jaws twitched. Damn that snooping woman!

"Jud, you going downtown?" She was a thin, tired woman, once pretty, but the years had taken the hope out of her face. An apron at her waist, she stood on the porch fluttering a slip of paper in the bird-like claw of her hand.

"Jud," she called, "I need some things from the grocery."

"Send the kid."

"Pete's out playing somewheres."

Jud kept going. "Wait'll he gets back."

"But I need these for supper."

"Whatta ya think I am, a horse?"

"Jud, where you going?"

He answered in a surly voice, "Never mind. It's none of your damn business." He turned on the sidewalk with never a backward glance.

He hardly saw where he was going. The hatred of Leslie Gramm that filled him churned in his brain like a sullen sea of fire. It was Gramm, the plant superintendent, who had kept him from getting to be a floor boss, or even boss of his section. Every year, some other guy got promoted, but not Jud Kerrun. Leslie Gramm didn't like him. Leslie Gramm had it in for him. Leslie Gramm would see to it that Jud never did get a better job at better pay.

The only way for Jud to fix that was to fix Leslie Gramm. Then there'd be a new foreman, and a step-up all down the line. Jud had the seniority right. He ought to be made at least a section boss this time.

The beauty of it was, nobody had any reason to suspect Jud. He and Leslie had never done more than exchange a few words at the plant. Nobody would dream that Jud had a motive. The cops would be off on a wild-goose chase. Labor troubles, strikes, clashes between rival unions had beset the plant all summer. The unions or strikers would get the blame.

The section of dilapidated old frame houses dropped behind him. The road turned, following a long hill to his left. An empty field stretched to his right. Some kids were playing sand-lot ball on its hard surface. A cluster of onlookers, their backs to Jud, watched the game. Nobody saw him. Anyway, they were all too far out in the middle of the field to notice him.

The road curved. Jud came to a path and started climbing the hill. Halfway up, he stopped, listened to make sure he was alone, and plunged into the dense underbrush and trees.

When he stepped out into the path again several minutes later, his hat was gone, he wore the red pullover sweater, and instead of the bundle under his arm he carried only the parcel, the size of a big cigar box, the parcel that had a faint voice:

Tick, tock.

He loitered. He had passed this path often on his way to the plant. Another section of houses lay across the hill. He knew that only youngsters used the path, children going down to the field to play.

A little girl came down the path. She had stringy, taffy-colored hair, and wore a faded blue playsuit. Her bare arms and legs and back were chocolate brown from the sun. She glanced at him with the frank curiosity of the very young, but mostly her eyes strayed to his blazing red sweater.

Jud said, "Wanna earn two bits, kid?"

She stopped, eying the package that he held out. "Watcha got in there, mister?"

"Uh, a present for a guy. It's a clock. I want him to get it right away."

"Oh." She wrinkled her nose. "Mummy told me I could only stay out for a little while."

"This won't take a half-hour, and you'll have two bits to spend. All you have to do is deliver this. The address is 307 Front Street. It's a corner house. It's sort of a green color."

She nodded. "It's got a funny stone lion in front."

"Sure, sure, that's right. All you gotta do is leave this package there. Just ring the bell, and put it inside the screen door. You don't need to wait. It's a birthday present, and they'll know who it's from when they open it."

He held out two coins. "Here's fifteen cents. Hurry right back and I'll give you the other dime."

She looked dubious. "My mummy said—"

"You'll get home in plenty of time. It ain't far, nine or ten blocks. You can make it there and back in a half-hour, easy."

"My mummy doesn't want me to take things from grownups. She said so. She told me to keep away from strange men."

Jud cursed under his breath. He forced a toothy smile. "There, there, that's all right. Your mother's right about that." He jangled the two coins. "I just thought a bright little girl like you'd like to earn a quarter, is all. It wouldn't hardly take twenty-thirty minutes."

She couldn't take her eyes off the coins. She said, with that exasperating, iron-clad, unanswerable logic of the very young and the very innocent, "Why don't you go? If you're going to wait for me here, you could bring the clock yourself, and come back here, and it wouldn't cost you a quarter."

Jud felt like spanking the infernal brat. He jangled the coins once more. "Guess I will, though I'm kinda tired walkin'. Run along. I'll find somebody that's smart and—"

He started to put the coins away. He was getting jittery. Somebody else might be coming along the path soon.

The receding money won her over. She thrust her hands out. "Gimme the quarter. I'll go."

Hesitantly, as though he, too, was changing his mind, Jud gave her the parcel and fifteen cents. "I'll give you the other dime soon as you're back."

She shook her head obstinately. "No. I want it now. How do I know you'll really wait for me?"

Jud could cheerfully have thrashed her. But he was almost in a panic. He couldn't stand here and argue with the little fool. The minutes were slipping by.

"All right. Here's the other dime. Now hurry! It's pretty near six-thirty. You gotta get the clock there by seven sharp. And hang onto this, don't drop it!"

"Why?"

Jud nearly yelled, "It's the guy's birthday and he won't be home tonight, see? He's gotta have this by seven o'clock! Run along, now, hurry! It's liable to get busted if you drop it!"

She went skipping down the path. Jud watched, his face working, till she was out of sight around a bend. He rubbed the back of his fist tightly across the stubble on his chin. Then he faded into the woods.

He took off the red sweater, stuffed it in the empty shoebox, and rolled it up in the newspapers. The bundle looked the same as before. He put his battered brown hat on again.

A few minutes later, he strode down the path with the bundle under his arm. He savagely kicked a couple of loose stones out of his way. When he reached the sidewalk, he rolled a cigarette and stuck it in a corner of his mouth. It dribbled sparks as he sauntered homeward.

■   ■   ■

The two dimes and the nickel made the little girl's palm sweat. After a while, she put a dime and a nickel in a handkerchief, made a ball out of it, and pushed it down in the pocket of her jumper suit. She kept the other dime in her hand.

She trudged along the path at the base of the hill. After the equivalent of a couple of long blocks, the hill came to an end. The field across the road also ended. In the near corner a group of boys was playing softball.

By the time she came back this way, it would be getting dark and the game would be over. It was more fun watching a game than carrying a funny old package that went:

Tick, tock.

Anyway, she had only seven or eight more blocks to go, and it wouldn't take long to get there. She could easily make it by seven o'clock. And what if she was a few minutes late? She couldn't see that it made any difference if the man got his darn old clock at seven or whenever, so long as he got it. The thing was, she couldn't stay out late. But she'd be home before dark. There was plenty of time.

She crossed the road and dawdled, watching the game. She knew several of the boys. They yelled at her and she talked back fliply. Other boys, a few girls, and a couple of men watched the game. They were sitting along a bench made of weather-stained two by fours.

They moved over to make room for her. She sat holding the package in her lap, the package with a voice that whispered ever so faintly:

Tick, tock.

It was a funny kind of birthday present to give, she thought. She took the package and jiggled it against her ear, but it didn't rattle. It must be a pretty big clock. An alarm clock, maybe. Then she put the package back in her lap and forgot about it. Her thoughts strayed to the game.

Jimmy Roth was at the plate, jumping and yelling at the pitcher. The pitcher threw the ball underhand and Jimmy swung with all his might. Wham! The ball flew out over the infield, dropped between left and center, and went bounding away with both fielders hot after it.

Everybody was yelling at everybody else, somebody on second came tearing home, and Jimmy scooted around the bases so fast that he slipped and fell at third. The ball sailed in toward home plate. Jimmy picked himself up and raced for the bag. The ball beat him, but the catcher couldn't hold on to it. Jimmy crossed the plate with a home run as the ball bounced off the catcher's glove and spurted toward the bench.

It was lots of fun. The side went down.

"What's the score?" the little girl asked a man next to her.

"Sixteen to twelve."

"What inning?"

"Last of the fourth."

The game went on, and grew more exciting. The other side tied it up at sixteen to sixteen in the next half-inning.

The man beside her started to leave, and jostled her in doing so. The package slid off her lap. She grabbed for it. It teetered on her knees, almost dropping to the ground before her fingers got hold of the string.

She held the package against her ear, but the jiggling didn't seem to have hurt it any. The voice inside still murmured:

Tick, tock.

She jumped to her feet. Absorbed in watching the game, she had forgotten all about delivering the package.

"What time is it, mister?" she asked the man who was moving away.

He looked at a wrist watch. "Quarter of seven."

She hurried off, half skipping, half running, for a couple of blocks before she slowed down. Seven o'clock, seven o'clock, kept repeating in her head. That was when he had told her she must deliver the package. No, he had said to deliver it before seven. Before seven. Ring the bell and leave it before seven. But running made her lose her breath. She was panting. Why hurry? Why run your legs off for a darn old clock? A clock that couldn't say anything but:

Tick, tock.

She came to a small candy store and looked in the window longingly. Licorice sticks, taffy, horehound, chewing gum, candy bars, chocolates, caramels, mint wafers, all day suckers, jelly drops, lozenges, marshmallows, crackerjack, and other sweets lay temptingly spread out. The dime itched her palm moistly. What to buy? Five cents worth of mixed candy and a box of crackerjack? Or an all day sucker and a vanilla ice cream cone? Or a big double cone, chocolate and strawberry?

A swinging movement caught her gaze. Her eyes strayed to a wall clock with a pendulum. The hands stood at twelve minutes of seven. Every time the pendulum swung, she fancied she could hear it, and such a big clock would make a bigger noise than the clock she was carrying, a great big:

TICK, TOCK.

Twelve minutes to seven. Six blocks to go. It really hadn't ought to take more than ten minutes. But it would be longer, it would be after seven, if she stopped now and went in the store to buy a double ice cream cone, chocolate and strawberry.

She reluctantly turned away from the windowful of candies. Her nose felt funny where she had held it against the glass. She rubbed it until the tingle went away.

A block farther, she reached a corner drugstore. The window had another one of those big clocks with a pendulum. The hand stood between ten and nine minutes of seven. She guessed she'd better hurry a little faster, or she wouldn't quite make it.

Before she could start running, a boy caught up with her and began to pass her, walking at a brisk, crisp clip. He was taller than she, and perhaps a year older. His tousled head sprouted from a scrawny neck. His hands were thrust deep into his pockets so that his elbows flapped as he moved. His stubby nose hung like a round little marble over his short upper lip. It gave his face a nasty look as though he had been caught in the act of stealing pennies from a playmate. She vaguely remembered seeing him on the bench at the ball game.

He looked at the little girl, and slowed up beside her. "Whatcher name?"

There was no answer, except that she hurried more.

"Watcher name?" He kept pace with her.

"You leave me alone!"

"Watcher hurry? You ain't scared or nothin', are you?"

She clenched the package tighter under her arm. She could almost feel its faint sound of:

Tick, tock.

The dime slid around in her damp palm. She wedged it between thumb and forefinger. "I'm not scared of *you*."

"Watcha scared of then, 'fraidy cat?"

"I'm not scared at all."

"Then watcha runnin' for, huh?"

"I'm in a hurry. I have to bring this to a man. He has to have it by seven o'clock."

"Why?"

"It's his birthday. He just has to have it by seven. That's what the man said."

"What's in it?"

"None of your business. You leave me alone!"

He persisted, "What's his name? How far does he live?"

"It's written down on the box. Go away!"

But he wouldn't leave. His eyes fastened on the coin that she held. "Watcha holdin' that for? What's he gonna give you for bringin' him the box?"

She began, "He paid me already—" and broke off, fearing she shouldn't have told him.

They were passing a grocery store. A light over the counter inside shone on the face of an alarm clock. The hands pointed to seven minutes of seven. Four blocks to go; she'd have to hurry.

She started across the street. He stayed at her side. He said, "Gimme that. I'll take it to him."

She shook her head, and brought her hand up to drop the dime into the single pocket of her playsuit. Her foot tripped on the curb. She stumbled forward, throwing her hands out to save herself. The package slid loose and began dropping to the sidewalk.

It happened fast. He grabbed her, tore the dime from her grasp, and snatched the package. He deliberately gave her a hard shove that sent her sliding along the cement on hands and bare knees. Then with a taunting yell he flew down the street.

She burst out crying. She picked herself up and took a few steps after him, but he was far ahead, and gaining. Her knees hurt. She looked down, and saw them scratched and bleeding with bits of sand imbedded in the skin.

She cried harder. She fumbled around for the handkerchief in her pocket and wiped her eyes. She felt the sharp edges of the other dime and the nickel through the cloth.

After a while she stopped crying. She tied a knot in the handkerchief and put it back in her pocket. She turned around, trudging back toward the candy store and a double ice cream cone, strawberry and chocolate.

■　■　■

He looked over his shoulder after he had run half a block. The little girl wasn't chasing him. She was standing still, bawling. He ran hard for another block just to be safe.

Then he read the address on the package, his lips moving, "Leslie Gramm, 307 Front Street. Gee, that's only, let's see now, one, two, two and a half blocks more. Hey, old lady, got the time?"

An elderly woman stared down at him. She said, "Yes, my dear young fellow, I do have the time," and walked away indignantly.

He made a face at her back and went on down the street. It couldn't be seven yet, but close to it, maybe. The radio in a car parked at the curb spoke: "At this time every day, six fifty-five P.

M., the baseball scores are brought to you through the courtesy of—"

He didn't hear the rest. Five minutes to seven. Two and a half blocks to go. Shucks, that was a cinch. Anybody could cover two and a half blocks in five minutes.

In fact, why hurry? Why go at all? He had the dime. Nobody knew that he had the package. Maybe there was something valuable in it. Nobody would ever know the difference if he just walked off with it.

He shook the package against his ear. It didn't rattle, but it made a sound like:

Tick, tock.

He looked at the package in disgust. A clock! It couldn't be anything else but an alarm clock, not in a package the size of a big cigar box. Most likely one of those cheap alarm clocks that you see in drugstore windows for eighty-nine cents. It wasn't worth even two cents to him. He couldn't use it. He couldn't eat it. He didn't want it. He'd have the dickens of a time trying to trade it off or sell it.

He trudged glumly along. He had half a notion to chuck it into the road and forget about it. Let somebody else take care of the package. The dime was in his pocket. It was silly to go any farther. The dime. . . .

"Girls don't play fair. They always lie," he mumbled.

The dime. She *said* she had already been paid. That didn't mean anything. She was lying. It was her dime to begin with. She wanted to get rid of him. She was afraid he'd steal the clock and get the money she was hoping for. Her dime. He could take the clock to the man, and the man would pay him another dime at least. That would make twenty cents.

He might as well take the package to where it was going. He might as well try to get there by seven. Things were different now.

He turned left at the corner of the jeweler's shop. The window was full of time-pieces—wrist watches and fob watches and clocks. Some of them weren't running. All of them showed different hours. But a cuckoo clock in the middle had a swinging pendulum. Its hands pointed to three minutes of seven. Two blocks to go. Two short blocks. Shucks, he could make it in no time. The sooner the better, and he'd have another dime to spend. The man would give him something if he got there on time. The package itself kept reminding him to hurry, with its insistent sound of:

Tick, tock.

He legged it for the next block. He could see the house, now, with a gray stone lion out in front. The lion squatted in the middle of the lawn. His back had a hollow place full of water, where the robins and sparrows took baths.

There were lights in the house. Cars stood along the curb. As he drew nearer, he heard quick, harsh blasts from a radio in the house. Someone was twirling the dial from station to station. He eyed the cars, all five of them. It looked like a party.

Cars. Unwatched. His steps slowed. He remembered the time he had swiped a robe from a car on Center Street. And the purse he snatched from the seat beside a lady who stopped for a traffic light. Cars. Loot. The clock suddenly became small in his eyes. At most he'd get a dime for it. But the line of autos. . . .

He didn't see anyone around. He entered the second car. For a few moments he peered out the windows, ready to jump and run. But nobody had seen him. He was safe. It was a cinch. He opened the dashboard tray, looked at the back seat, and poked into the side pockets. No luck. The only thing he found was a yellow case half full of powder. Girl stuff. The case might be gold. He put it in his pocket.

He took the package and slid out.

The radio in the house blared: "See the new Meridian watch at your jeweler's, the gift of the century. All styles, all prices, beginning at only thirteen ninety-five. If it's Meridian it's standard, the watch of the world. The time is thirty seconds before seven o'clock, Meridian watch time. We now bring you a special bulletin from the Radio News Service. . . ."

He hesitated. Thirty seconds to seven o'clock. The third car looked black and shiny. The package under his arm was marking off the seconds:

Tick, tock.

■ ■ ■

Jud Kerrun watched his newspaper-wrapped bundle go up in flames. The red sweater made a smell of burning cloth. His wife didn't know about it. She wouldn't even remember it. He had told her months ago that he gave it away.

He liked the stealth, the leisure, the casual way he had worked. Phrases ran through his head, bits of information that he had picked up at the plant simply by keeping his ears open. Leslie Gramm saying, "Friday's fine. But don't be late. We always have dinner at seven on the dot." And another time, "The seventeenth of next month? Afraid I can't make it, old chap. That's my birthday and I'll be spending the evening at home."

A blast echoed hollowly in the distance.

Jud hadn't realized how tense he was until the explosion came. He didn't start nervously. He didn't react at all. He had been expecting it all the time. But something inside him snapped.

The fire smouldered down to ashes.

He went back in the garage. He put into a box all the shotgun shells from which he had emptied the powder. The next thing to do was bury them.

Jud wondered just how it had happened. He had built the bomb to go off at seven, or whenever the package was opened. Maybe Leslie Gramm was having a birthday dinner. Maybe he waited till he had all his presents before opening them.

Jud finished with the shotgun shells. He was getting hungry. Any minute, now, his wife ought to call him to supper.

He started cleaning up the pieces of metal, wire, and materials on the work bench. A few minutes more, and he'd be through by seven-thirty.

The noise of the opening door made him whirl around, his face twitching. Damn that snooping woman! He'd ordered her never to interrupt him when he was in the garage. She'd never dared cross him before. He'd smack her for this!

But it wasn't his wife in the doorway. It was a cop. The cop looked at the work bench, the betraying pieces, and the telltale flakes of spilled powder.

Jud made a wild dive for the alley door of the garage. A powerful grip seized his shoulder and swung him around. Then fists like exploding dynamite were smashing his face, beating his features to pulp, breaking him in a kind of deliberate fury.

Through the pain and body concussions of those blows, Jud heard the cop's voice, harsh and murderous, in snatches of phrase:

"Don't care what they do to me down at H. Q. Stand up, guy, and take it. You've got lots more coming. Hash is all you'll be when I'm through. . . . Told your wife and she fainted dead in her tracks. Said you were out here.

"This paper in my fist, it's the biggest piece of anything we found after the blast. . . . List of groceries and the name they were to be charged to—Kerrun. She sends the kid off to get the groceries and you give him a bomb to deliver, only he didn't get there in time.

"God, your own kid. . . ."

William Campbell Gault

CONSPIRACY

From *Alfred Hitchcock's Mystery Magazine,* August 1957

Bill Gault made his first professional sale in 1936; his last published work, the novel Dead Pigeon, *was published fifty–six years later. In his long and distinguished career his byline appeared on more than 300 short stories and novelettes—mystery, fantasy, science fiction, sports—and some sixty novels, half of them mystery/suspense and the other half juvenile sports books. His debut novel,* Don't Cry for Me, *was awarded an MWA Edgar as Best First Novel of 1952. Gault was particularly good when writing about young people; his understanding of and insight into the adolescent mind was unerringly accurate. "Conspiracy" offers ample evidence of this, and of the solid plotting, believable characters, and honest human emotion that also marked the best of his fiction.*

B. P.

JOHNNY AND I WERE TRYING TO DROWN OUT A GOPHER WHEN we first saw this car just tearing around the big bend above Nestor's cornfield. Wow, that car was really going; you could hear the tires screech where we were standing and we must have been a half mile away.

Johnny put the tin can full of water he was pouring into the hole down next to him and stared at the car as though he was waiting for it to go over.

"Crazy, huh?" I said. "Man, he's moving."

Johnny nodded without looking at me. "I'll bet he won't make that next one; it's harder."

I didn't want to look, but I couldn't take my eyes away. There was a straight stretch after the big bend and then a little hill and right by our stand of timber, this side of the hill, there was a real sharp curve and a culvert. You couldn't see the turn from the other side of the hill, though there was a big sign up there warning everybody. Before they put the sign up, a lot of guys hadn't made that turn by our timber, most of them because they were drunk and coming back from a dance somewhere. It isn't a main road and we don't get any strangers driving it much.

From where we stood, on the bluff above the creek, we could see this speeding car coming to the hill now and he wasn't slowing none at all.

"He's not going to make it," Johnny whispered. "Watch this, Steve!"

The car came over the top of the hill and we heard the tires screeching again as the driver tried to swing it around the sharp turn. He was good, that guy. He almost made it.

And then the car was drifting toward the culvert and the front end of it crashed with a horrible clang and we saw it go up on its nose. It was like a slow motion picture, almost, as it went end for end down the bank of the creek and one door flew open and we saw a guy falling out and then we couldn't see the car anymore.

We just stood there.

In a couple seconds, Johnny said, "The water's deep there. If there was anybody else in the car, they could drown, Steve."

"We'd better go over to Nestor's and call the Sheriff," I said.

We don't have a phone. Pa says they're a waste of money. Ma wants one, but Pa says they're a waste of money.

"I guess we'd better," Johnny said, and then he pointed. "Hey, look!"

A man was climbing up over the bank. He had cotton army pants on and a light blue sweater and a gray cap. He was carrying a suitcase.

The way I figured right then, he was maybe a bum the guys in the car had picked up and he was getting out of there so he wouldn't be questioned by the Sheriff. He was limping. I figured he'd head down the road toward us, but he didn't.

He went trotting and limping toward our little stand of timber that runs along the road.

"He's running away," Johnny said. "Why didn't he head for Nestor's, for a phone?"

"I don't know," I said.

"It's damned funny."

"Pa says you shouldn't swear, Johnny."

"To hell with Pa. It's damned funny."

"Maybe he's a bum, Johnny."

He turned to face me. "With that suitcase? That was heavy. Did you see the way it dragged him?"

I didn't say anything. I was watching the other end of the woods, the end that runs along the other road, the road to Saugus.

Johnny said, "We'd better get to Nestor's. I guess we're the only ones that saw it happen."

"Look," I said, and pointed at the far end of the woods.

The man in the army pants was coming out from there now, heading for the other road. And he wasn't carrying the suitcase.

Johnny looked at me and I looked at Johnny. I don't know what we were thinking as we looked at each other. And then we heard the siren and we could see the Sheriff's car coming down the road from Ridgeland.

It was like we were in the balcony watching a play or something; the whole thing was spread out below us, the Sheriff's car storming from where the other car had come and the man walking out of the woods without the suitcase and remembering that car we couldn't see down in the creek and the whole day so bright and peaceful around us. I got the shivers.

The Sheriff knew about the sharp turn and his car slowed up before it came to the top of the rise. And from there, he must have seen the car in the creek, because he slowed more and pulled over on the side of the road and stopped.

And I could recognize him, him being so fat, but I wasn't sure who the other guy was that got out of the car on the other side.

Johnny said, "Let's go down there. C'mon, Steve, I'll race you down there."

Johnny's thirteen, a year older than me, and bigger, and he knows he'd beat all right. But I raced him anyway because I wanted to get down there to see what the Sheriff had to say.

By the time we got there, the thinner man had gone down to the creek and come up again and I could see it was Jess Laurie, one of the deputies.

I was puffing like a steam engine and Johnny, too. Johnny took a couple of real deep breaths and asked, "What happened, Mr. Laurie?"

"Three men robbed the bank in Ridgeland," he said. "Did you boys see this car tip over?"

I nodded. Johnny looked at me and frowned. Then Johnny said, "We were just on the way to Nestor's, to phone you. Boy, was that car ever moving." He took another deep breath. "Is anybody in it, Mr. Laurie?"

Jess Laurie looked at him sharply. "Of course. You don't think the car got all the way out here by itself, do you? Why did you ask that? Did you see somebody walk away from the wreck?"

Johnny looked at me and I knew we were both thinking of the suitcase. Johnny looked real steady at Mr. Laurie and said, "Yes, sir, we did. We saw a man with a suitcase."

Jess looked over the bank and said, "Hey, Sheriff, we got a lead. Better come up; maybe we can still catch the third man."

Old, fat Sheriff Taggart came puffing up the bank. "I don't know as we ought to leave here until we get an ambulance out, Jess. One of those men looks like he's still alive."

I was watching Johnny and I could tell his mind was racing. Mine was, too.

Johnny didn't wait to be asked. He said, "We saw this man come up the bank and then a car came along, and the car stopped and this man with the suitcase got into it. It sure looked funny to me, the way that car came along."

Jess said quickly, "What kind of car?"

"It was a brand new Pontiac," Johnny said slowly. "It was dark green and it had white-wall tires and it went straight down the road toward Center City."

"How about the man with the suitcase? Could you see him?"

"Not his face," Johnny said. "He had blue pants on and a blue denim jacket and no hat. He was kind of fat and short."

I kept looking at Johnny as he lied. I couldn't look at Mr. Laurie or the Sheriff. Johnny can think fast and move fast; that's where he's got it all over me. And when he lies, he smiles, like he knows you're not believing him, but he doesn't care if you do or not.

Jess looked at the Sheriff and the Sheriff said, "I'll stay here for the ambulance. You take off."

"Alone, Tom?" Jess asked. "He's armed, you know."

The Sheriff said grouchy, "Okay, *I'll* go and you phone for the ambulance."

Jess said, "I'll go, I'll go—" He started for the car. He turned and said, "And don't forget to send out an all points for that Pontiac."

"Yes, Jess," Sheriff Taggart said, tired-like. "Of course, Jess." He went toward the Nestor's place as Jess Laurie drove off.

We were alone.

Johnny looked at me and said, "I'll race you to the woods. Why didn't you tell Jess Laurie I was lying, tattle-tale? How come you didn't tattle? You always do."

I didn't say anything.

"I'll race you to the woods," he said again.

I shook my head.

He laughed. "A little nickel-nurser like you and you won't even run for all that money? What's the matter, you worried?"

I nodded.

"What's there to worry about?" He laughed again. "We're just kids, Steve. Just a couple kids was drowning out a gopher and saw an accident. We didn't rob no bank."

"I'm worried about you," I said. "No patience, that's what's the matter with you. You got to run all the time. With the Sheriff there where he can see the woods, and the Nestors sure to be out here in a minute, you got to run for the money."

He laughed again. "You're not fooling me. Patience means you want me to wait for you. You want some of that money."

I nodded. "I want half."

He stared at me. "Maybe you want a poke in the yap, too, huh? Who did the lying? Who got the idea? Half, huh!"

I said patiently. "Just half, that's fair. Or I tell the Sheriff you lied to him. Decide right now, Johnny."

"I ought to poke you in the yap," he said. "I think I will. If you tell the Sheriff anything, you'll be sorry, Steve."

"Decide, Johnny. Half?"

He stared at me for what seemed a long time, but probably wasn't. "Okay. I guess there'll be enough." He patted my shoulder. "I guess there'll be *plenty*, huh, old Stevie-boy?"

That's Johnny for you. He can't stay sore. He can get so mad he'd darn near kill you and then be so sorry you want to cry for him. He's a crazy guy.

I said, "That man that left the suitcase ain't going to be back for a while, you can bet. We got time, Johnny. We can at least wait until it's dark."

He nodded and smiled. "A green Pontiac with white-wall tires, that was pretty good, huh, Steve? Maybe we ought to buy one, huh? With a radio and a heater and four carburetors and—"

"Shut up," I said. "Here comes the Sheriff."

He winked at me. "Right. Patience. Old patient Steve, the nickel-nurser; this is the time to listen to him."

We could hear another siren now, probably the ambulance. And over the top of the rise a wrecker was coming from Chopko's garage in Ridgeland.

The Sheriff said, "This isn't going to be anything you boys should see. Run along and play now. That's what vacations are for."

"It won't bother me," Johnny said. "I watched Pa stick pigs, and this won't bother me. Steve better take off, though, huh, Sheriff?"

Sheriff Taggart waved at us with the back of his hand. "Both of you take off right now. Scat!"

"Okay," Johnny said. "C'mon, Steve, let's go play in the woods."

I couldn't have said that. Johnny's got the guts to say anything. And he's a fast thinker. I would have to be careful and watch him or I'd never see any of that money.

We went over to the woods and climbed a tree, so they'd think we were playing. Johnny went up real high, where he knew I'd be scared to follow and he yoo-hooed like Tarzan and the men who were running the hoist line down to the car looked our way and one of them waved. The ambulance was turning around in Nestor's driveway, getting ready to back down to the culvert.

And then Johnny said. "They won't be watching us now, Steve. Let's go down and look around."

"Take your time," I said.

"C'mon, sissy," he said, "before I forget you're in for half."

We climbed down and started walking around in there, looking for hiding places that a man in a hurry might see. It was Johnny who found it, a hollowed out place under a ledge overhanging with Johnson Grass and weeds. We could just see the handle of the suitcase in there.

Johnny started to reach, and I said, "Not yet. We know it's there, but we don't know who's watching. Not yet. Patience, remember."

He looked at the handle of the suitcase and I could almost see him tremble. He said, "Tonight, as soon as it's dark."

"As soon as it's dark," I agreed.

We went back to where we'd been pouring water down the

gopher holes. It was high up there and we could watch the woods and the car being pulled out of the creek. It was almost all the way up, now, full of mud and all bent out of shape.

From the corner of the barn, Pa and Ma were looking over at the wreck and then Pa called us.

Johnny said, "You go. Somebody's got to watch that woods."

"He's mad," I said. "We were supposed to hoe corn this afternoon. We'd better both go."

When we got to where they were standing, Pa said, "What happened over there at the turn?"

"Some bank robbers went into the ditch," I said, "but one of them got away."

Ma said, "You boys were supposed to work this afternoon. Your father promised you a penny a row for hoeing." She smiled at me. "That wouldn't mean much to Johnny, but I can't see you forgetting it, Steve."

Johnny said, "The Grange is offering ten cents each for gophers and we were going after them."

That was a lie, I knew, but I didn't say anything. I didn't want Johnny mad at me, not with that suitcase still in the woods.

Pa said, "Well, forget the gophers and get out into that corn. Both of you, *right now!*"

"Yes, sir," Johnny said, and winked at me. "C'mon, money-bags."

When we were where the folks couldn't hear us, I said, "You're too mouthy. Did you have to mention money?"

"I meant the ninety dollars you saved," Johnny said. "Any guy that can save ninety bucks on the green nickels Pa hands out is a real money man. I'll bet you'll be rich some day, Steve."

I nudged him. "We're rich already, maybe, Johnny. But let's be careful. Don't go sounding off all the time."

"*Right,*" he said, and picked up a hoe. "C'mon, I'll race you."

C'mon, c'mon, c'mon—that was all I ever heard from Johnny. And I followed him around like he was a general or something. I was dumb to follow him all the time, to take his dares and let him lead me around by the nose.

"I don't want to race," I said. "A penny a row—who needs it?"

He laughed. "Oh, Steve, that sure didn't sound like you. You're starting to think like a rich man now instead of a miser, huh? You got big ideas."

"Lay off," I said. "You've always got your big mouth on me. Lay off."

He stood there with the hoe in his hand, studying me. "What you all wound up about? The money? Boy, that's got you real nervous, ain't it?"

I looked right back at him. "Darn right. You know there could be thousands of dollars there? You know what that could mean when we grew up and invested it?"

"Grew up? You crazy? As soon as I get to high school this fall, I'll be in town where I can use that money. I ain't going to wait until I grow up."

"You start spending this fall, Johnny, and you'll wind up in jail. Remember, we're *stealing* that money."

He shook his head. "They stole it. We found it."

"It's not ours, either way. Jeez, Johnny, for the first time in your life, use your head."

He studied me a couple seconds more and then he started to hoe. "You sound like an old man," he said. "You sound like you're a million years old."

We paired off and worked down the rows. I kept thinking about the money, what a big lucky break it had been and how Johnny would probably ruin it. He just didn't have any sense at all. He talked fast and thought fast, but that's different than having sense. Why hadn't I been alone when that car went over the bank?

I wasn't working any harder now than I had been climbing that bank to get water for the gopher hole, but this was different; this wasn't doing what I wanted to do. I thought about Pa, who'd worked like this since he was my age, and Ma, who didn't have anything she wanted, not even a telephone. When I was their age, would I be living like they did? Would I work as early and late as there was sun to see by?

If Johnny started spending that money in town, we'd be in trouble. Worse than that, we'd lose the money. Of course, if Johnny hadn't lied to the Sheriff . . .

■ ■ ■

Chopko's tow car had already hauled away the wreck, and nobody was standing down on the road anymore. I looked over toward the woods and nobody was there, either. Maybe he'd come back for the money tonight. We had better get there the minute it got dark. Or maybe he'd been caught . . . ? Not if the police were looking for a fat, short man wearing a denim jacket.

Around five-thirty, we heard the bell clang up at the house, and both of us stopped right where we were, without finishing the row.

As we walked to the house, I said to Johnny, "We'd better get to the woods the *second* it gets dark."

He nodded.

"That guy might be back," I explained.

He nodded.

"You're sure quiet," I said. "You haven't said a word since we started hoeing."

"I don't want to be mouthy." He stopped walking. "Steve, does it bother you when I razz you? I didn't know it bothered you that much."

I smiled. "No. I guess I'm just nervous."

He put a hand on my shoulder. "Because remember we *are* brothers, Steve. I give you a rough time, huh?"

"It's okay," I said, and kept walking.

What was he planning now? What was he being so buddy-buddy about? That Johnny, he scared me.

While we were washing up, Pa said, "Those two crooks in the car are dead. But they didn't find the other one. And he's got the money." He shook his head. "Forty-eight thousand dollars!"

Johnny looked at me and at Pa. "Forty-eight thousand? Where'd you hear that?"

"Len Nestor heard it on his radio." Pa picked up a carrot and started to chew it. "Makes an honest man sick, don't it?"

Neither of us said anything. I started to tremble. Then Johnny laughed. "Gosh, a guy would have to hoe a lot of corn to earn forty-eight thousand dollars, huh, Pa?"

Ma laughed, but Pa didn't seem to think it was funny. Johnny is supposed to favor Ma and I'm supposed to be more like Pa. I don't know about that, but I know Ma favors Johnny. He's her pet. She thinks he's as funny as Red Skelton.

I guess Pa don't favor anybody, but he admits I'm more sensible. That don't mean he liked me any more.

While we were eating, I figured it in my head. Forty-eight thousand dollars at six percent came to two thousand, eight hundred and eighty dollars a year. Gosh, a guy wouldn't have to spend his principal, just rent it out. Half of that would be mine, and half would be one thousand, four hundred and forty dollars a year. That's a lot of corn at a penny a row.

After supper, Johnny said, "Steve, what do you say we do a little more hoeing before it gets dark? At least we could finish those rows."

Both Pa and Ma looked puzzled; that wasn't the kind of thing Johnny would say. But I knew he wanted to be sure we could get out of the house when it was dark. We could go right to the woods from the cornfield.

Pa said, "Well, our oldest is finally getting some money sense. I'm glad to see it."

Johnny smiled and said, "It's about time, Pa?" And then he winked at me.

Outside, as we walked back to the field, I said, "You're a funny guy; you ought to be on television, you're so funny. Keep talking funny and lose forty-eight thousand dollars."

He laughed. "We got out of the house, didn't we? You never thought of that. I had to think of it. And I had to lie to the Sheriff and if that guy comes back for the money, old sissy Steve will be so scared he'll run and get it for him."

"I suppose you wouldn't be afraid of no bank robber? Not much!"

"Not me," he said. "Wait'll we get the money; you'll see." He laughed. "I wonder if old Jess Laurie is still looking for that fat man in the Pontiac."

He had to keep reminding me about that, letting me know that if it hadn't been for his big mouth we wouldn't have no chance at the money at all. He thinks he's smart. And maybe he is, but he sure hasn't got any sense.

I never saw the sun go down so slow, or the rows look so long. I worried about Pa; he must think it was queer for Johnny to want to work after dinner. Pa would be in the barn now, milking the one cow we kept just for our own milk and butter. And he could see us from the barnyard. I kept hoeing away and so did Johnny.

Then we saw Pa go up to the house with the pail, and it was almost dark, and Johnny said, "Maybe we'd better not wait any longer, huh?"

"Let's go," I said. I was trembling again and my voice shook.

Johnny was smiling. "If it's still there, we'll bring it back to the barn and find a place to hide it."

"What do you mean, if it's still there? Where could it be?"

"Maybe the man came back when we weren't watching."

"Don't be crazy," I said. "It's there. It's got to be there." I started to run.

But Johnny passed me up before I'd gone twenty steps and we ran like fools down the slope to the culvert and over it into the woods.

"Wait," I hollered. "What's your hurry?"

But he kept running and laughing and I hated him for it and I tried to run faster, but my lungs were burning already and my legs were aching and tightening up.

And then Johnny stopped running and laughed louder. "Oh, Steve—take it easy. I scared you, huh? C'mon, brother, let's walk. We're partners."

I didn't say anything. I sucked in all the air I could and didn't look at him as we walked over to where the suitcase had been that afternoon.

Johnny put his hand in under the overhang and looked at me with his eyes wide. "It's gone!"

My stomach gave a lurch and I started to reach past him to feel around in there. But he pushed me back and laughed—and swung the suitcase out.

My stomach settled down then and I felt better than I had all day. Forty-eight thousand dollars in one package without even an hour of work.

Johnny said, "Once we find a place to put the money, we'll get rid of the suitcase, right?"

"Right," I said. "Let's take it to the tool shed; we can lock that door from the inside and there's a flashlight in there."

The tool shed was on the other end of the barn from the house and Pa had let Johnny and me use one end of it for a clubhouse.

Johnny said, "Remember that old hole we dug under the floor? That's big enough to hide this. We'd better not stay out tonight, though, Steve. Pa will wonder what we're doing."

"We can open it, at least," I said, "and look."

"Sure," he said.

The suitcase bumped against me as we walked along in the dark. "Is it heavy?" I asked.

"Plenty," he said. "But I can carry it."

We could see the lights in the house now, but no light in the barn. We walked up the back way, keeping the barn between us and the house.

"Pa's going to be looking for us soon," I said. "What'll we do?"

"Like you said, take it into the tool shed and lock the door."

"But he'll come down there for sure."

"The door will be locked. And we can hide this before we unlock it."

I was getting nervous again. Johnny was so crazy and careless. He didn't have any sense and any patience and he didn't realize how much more important it was to be sensible now. To Johnny, money was just something to spend.

We came to the tool shed, and I went ahead to open the door and find the flashlight. When he came in, I closed the door behind him and put the two-by-four across it to lock it.

Johnny put the suitcase down in the middle of the floor and I turned on the flashlight and he opened the suitcase.

Green, green, green . . . All the bills were stacked in hunks with a strip of brown paper around each hunk. Fives and tens and twenties. Johnny lifted one package out, and there were hundred dollar bills underneath.

"Man!" he said. "Oh, Steve!"

My stomach was fluttering and I was listening for a sound outside. "Let's hide it. Quick!" I said.

He didn't seem to hear me. "Look, how neat they stacked it. Man, they must have been cool guys, huh? Stacking this stuff so neat right in the bank full of people. Boy, if—"

"Hurry," I said. "Let's get it hid."

He looked up and smiled. "Scared, Steve? Your voice is shaking."

I stood there, glaring at him—and then came a knock at the door. And Pa said, "You boys in there? What's going on in there?"

I couldn't talk. The trembling went through me like a sickness and my mouth was brassy and I was glaring again at Johnny.

Johnny called out, "We're having a meeting of the club, Pa, a secret meeting. We'll be through in a couple minutes."

A silence, and then Pa said, "All right, all right. But you be up at the house in five minutes. I don't like you out in the dark like this."

"We'll be there, Pa," Johnny said, grinning at me.

Silence again, and then Johnny said, "Old gutless Steve. Man, you were green."

"You're crazy," I said, "absolutely crazy. You ought to be in a nuthouse."

He wasn't smiling anymore. "I'm crazy? Who lied to the Sheriff? Who got us out of the house? Who stalled Pa? I'm crazy, all right, forty-eight thousand dollars crazy. What'd you do? You're a penny-a-rower, that's your speed."

"It's half mine," I said. "You promised it's half mine."

"I promised. And it is. But you'd better get some guts, Steve. This ain't corn-hoeing money."

"I've got guts, don't worry. You'll see. I got plenty of guts now."

We moved the old cream separator that we'd used when we had cows, and moved out the loose plank flooring under it, and put the suitcase full of money underneath, in the hole. Then we put the flooring back and put the separator on top of it.

"We'll think of a better place later," I said. "That ought to be good enough now."

He didn't say anything. I put the flashlight back and we unlocked the door and went out.

We walked to the house and he didn't say a word. What was he thinking about? Maybe he finally got some sense. Or maybe he was remembering I really didn't do anything to help get the money.

Len Nestor and his wife were in the kitchen when we got to the house, and they were talking to Ma and Pa about the robbery. They'd brought the *Ridgeland Courier* along; we don't get a newspaper. Pa says they're a waste of "good" money. What other kind of money is there?

Len Nestor was saying, "The men wore paper bags over their heads, with holes punched out to see through. Wilderson said it was some sight." Then he looked up and saw us. "Well, you boys made the paper, all right."

Johnny smiled. "No kidding? Could I see it, Mr. Nestor?"

Mr. Nestor handed Johnny the paper and we took it over to the table and he spread it out. We read how "two sharp-eyed youngsters at play in a field" had given Sheriff Taggart a "surprisingly complete description" of the robber who had escaped in the green Pontiac.

Johnny nudged me. "We're famous, Steve." And then he whispered real low, "Famous and rich."

I didn't say anything.

Pa said, "What's that, Johnny?"

Johnny looked up. "I said that we were famous, Pa."

"And then you whispered something. It sounded like cussing to me."

"I didn't cuss, Pa. Honest."

Ma said, "We're going to have coffee. Would you boys like some cocoa?"

"Not me," Johnny said. "I'm tired; I'm going to bed."

"Me, too," I said.

As we went up the steps, I heard Mr. Nestor say, "That Johnny, he's a funny one. I'll bet he'll be a comedian, that kid."

"I wish he'd get some sense," Pa said.

Johnny said to me, "Sense—like he's got. Lost all our cows and wound up with nothing."

"Pa didn't lose 'em," I said. "He just found out there wasn't enough money in dairy farming."

"Sure," Johnny said. "Oh, sure."

We went into our room and he went over to stand by the window, looking out at the barn. "We're in trouble, Steve."

"How?" I said.

He turned around to stare at me. "Think. That robber that got away, he can read, can't he? He's going to read that cock and bull story about the Pontiac, ain't he? And won't he know it's a lie and won't he wonder why we lied?"

I sat down on the bed. "Yeah. Oh, God!"

He smiled. "How are the old guts, now, Steve? I mean the new guts."

"Don't' worry about me," I said. "What can he prove? What can he do?"

"I don't know," Johnny said. "Do you? You're the sensible one."

I didn't say anything.

"Well," Johnny said, "it don't do us any good to worry now. For all we know, the guy might be in China, right now. Maybe he's still running."

Because of that forty-eight thousand dollars that he'd hid for himself, I didn't think the guy would keep running and Johnny didn't either. A guy that's cool enough to stack that money so nice wasn't going to panic. Nobody had seen his face; he could come back any time.

Johnny opened the little drawer in the bureau to put away the junk in his pockets and then he put his hand in the drawer and took out the hunting knife he'd earned, selling salve.

He took it out of the scabbard and held it up. "I could give him this, right in the belly, huh, Steve?"

I didn't say anything. The knife was real bright and it sent reflections running around the room. Johnny touched the tip with one finger, and winked at me.

But he wasn't fooling me. When we used to trap, I had to open all the traps. Johnny couldn't handle a dead or wounded wild animal. A pig, now, that was different. Or a hen. But anything wild, Johnny was soft about.

"Put it away," I said. "You're talking foolish."

"For a hundred thousand, I might," he said, and laughed. "But not for a crummy forty-eight thousand." He put the knife back into the scabbard. "I sure sold that salve. I bet I could sell anything."

He'd forgotten about the man already. If the man came, Johnny would think up some more lies, but he wasn't planning ahead. He never did.

If the man came, if the man came . . . *When* the man came. Oh, he'd come, all right . . .

Long after Johnny was asleep, I kept thinking about the man and hoping something would happen that would keep him from coming back.

In the morning, Pa had to go to town to see about a note at the bank and Johnny told Ma he thought we ought to clean up the barn. She thought that was a good idea, and mighty thoughtful.

The way Johnny explained it to me, he didn't want to be out in the corn if that man came back. He wanted to be around where he could keep an eye on him.

So we swept and dusted and washed windows and hosed down all the stanchions that weren't being used anymore. And in the corner, where the old milk cans were stacked, Johnny got his idea.

"We could put that money in one of these and bury it," he

said. "We could bury it someplace where nobody'd ever think of looking."

"When would we get the chance?" I said. "The folks are always here."

"Not always. They go away every once in awhile. To town, or over to see Uncle George."

"And we go along."

"Not next time."

"They'd wonder why we wanted to stay home."

He nodded. "You don't expect to keep that money in the suitcase, do you? The first rain, and the water seeps under that floor and it's ruined. We've got to keep it dry and safe."

I smiled. "I thought you were going to spend it when you went to school this fall."

"That was before," he said. "Before I knew how much there was. Forty-eight thousand, that makes it different."

"Even half, your half, makes it different."

He grinned at me and started to answer, and then stopped, looking past me.

I turned and looked out the barn door toward the road. A man was coming up the road. He was wearing cotton army pants and a blue sweater and he was limping. He carried a small bag.

That brassy taste was in my mouth again. I said, "The other man wore a cap, a gray cap. Remember?"

"Anybody can throw away a cap," Johnny said. "I'll bet you a dime he turns in here, Steve."

I didn't answer.

"I'll bet you twenty-four thousand dollars he turns in, Steve. C'mon, be a big gambler."

It sounded like he was talking through a tunnel. And the man got so big he seemed to hide everything behind, the trees and the road and the cornfield. I promised myself if he turned in or not, he'd *never* get a smell of that money. He wouldn't scare anything out of me.

He turned in. And went up the dirt driveway toward the house. I could see Ma in the back yard.

"C'mon, Steve," Johnny said. "Let's go and see what he wants."

"Maybe he'll go away," I said. "Ma's in the back yard and she might not hear him knock."

"He's not going away. C'mon, sissy."

I followed him out of the barn and out to the front yard. The man was on the porch, standing in front of the door.

Johnny said, "My Ma's in the back yard. What do you want?"

He was a kind of thin man, about as tall as Pa, with bushy black eyebrows and gray eyes that seemed to look right through Johnny and me. He said, "I want to talk to your Pa, boy. Run and get him or tell me where he is and I'll go there."

"He's in town," Johnny said. "He won't be back for a while. What do you want?"

"I'll wait," he said.

"Stay here," Johnny told me, "and keep an eye on this bum, Steve. I'll get Ma."

"I'll get her," I said quickly, and I ran around the end of the house to the back yard.

Ma said, "What are you so pale about? Maybe he's just selling something, Steve. You don't have to get all excited." She put a hand on my forehead. "You're feverish, son."

"No," I said. "I've been working hard. The man looks like a bum, Ma."

She frowned and went around the side of the house and I followed. The man was off the porch now, standing on the grass near Johnny. Johnny was grinning and the man was smiling.

Ma said, "What is it you want, mister?"

"I'm looking for work," he said. "I need it bad, ma'm. I'd work for my keep, or I had another idea."

"What idea?"

"That timber, down on the turn, that's yours, isn't it?"

Ma nodded.

"It could stand some thinning," he said. "I figured I could cut it up the right size and we could sell it for firewood on shares."

"There's not much money in firewood," Ma said.

"If a fellow goes around to the right districts with a truck, ma'm, it's surprising the price you can get for fireplace wood."

Nobody said anything for a second. And then Ma said, "Well, you can wait until my husband comes home. Come into the kitchen and I'll fix you a couple of eggs."

"Thank you, ma'm," he said.

They went around to the kitchen door and Johnny and I stayed in front. Johnny was still grinning.

"What's so funny?" I asked him.

"That guy," Johnny said. "He's a cool one, huh? He told me I shouldn't call him a bum. He said he was proud to be a hobo, but he wasn't no bum."

"You call that funny? He's going to sleep in the tool shed. Laugh that one off."

He kept grinning. "Steve, the way you worry, a guy would think that was your money."

"It's half mine. And how about a bank robber sitting in the kitchen with Ma? Is that funny?"

"I guess not, Steve. Why don't you run right in and tell her he's a bank robber?"

I felt something bitter in my throat and it came up into my mouth. There was a red haze all around Johnny. He's so awful smart. He'd learn how smart he was if he ever tangled with that gimpy guy in the kitchen. I almost wished the money wasn't half mine, so I could be glad when Johnny got outfoxed.

"What's the matter with you," Johnny said. "You look like you've lost your mind."

I couldn't say anything.

"I wish I had a mirror," he said quietly. "You should see your eyes."

The haze grew around him and the house behind him began to tilt. I wavered on my feet, and he came over fast and put an arm around me. "Are you sick, Steve? What the hell's the matter?"

"I'm all right," I said. "Don't touch me."

Then I heard the pick-up rattling along the road and Johnny said, "Here comes Pa."

I took a deep breath and held it. I said, "Don't say anything about me being sick. We got to stay on our feet. And you've got to get some sense."

He moved a step away from me. "I'll tell you something. I worry more about you than I do about me. I worry about your guts."

Pa stopped the pick-up right next to us and cut the engine. He said, "What were you boys doing, wrestling? With all the work to be done around here?"

"We weren't wrestling, Pa," Johnny said. "I was just hugging my loving brother. You should see the barn, if you think we haven't been working."

"I'll do that right now," he said, and climbed out of the truck.

"There's a man in the kitchen wants to see you," I said. "A bum looking for easy work."

"I'll see him first," Pa said.

When he went through the front door, Johnny said, "That was all right, that crack about easy work. You're learning."

"Don't worry about me," I said.

"If he stays here," he said, "you know what we ought to do? We ought to go out tonight, after everybody's asleep, and get that money and bury it in one of those milk cans."

"That's risky," I said. "And Pa would miss the can."

"So? What's he going to do, dig up the whole hundred and sixty acres looking for it?"

"But if we get caught out late at night—"

"All right," he said. "You think of a better idea. I'm going into the kitchen and listen to that crook out-smart Pa."

I went back to the barn when Johnny went into the kitchen. One corner of it was clear and clean, the corner near a window, and there were some beams overhead.

I got a hammer and some nails and a couple of worn-out tarps. I got a ladder and hung the tarps to the beams, so that the corner was just like a room now, with the tarps making the walls.

I was just putting the ladder away again when Johnny came down to the barn. He looked at the tarps and shook his head. "Oh, boy, you're really giving it away."

"I don't get you, Johnny."

"Look, the guy will figure the money's in the barn or the tool shed, right? So when you fix him up a place in the barn, what's he going to think?"

"Let him think. We'll get it out of the tool shed before he gets a chance to look in there. I didn't want him to sleep there tonight."

Johnny shrugged.

I asked, "Is he going to stay?"

Johnny nodded. "He's going to cut the timber on shares. You know what him and Pa were talking about?"

"The robber?"

"That's right. He was talking to Pa, but he meant it for me to hear, about how he'd read we saw the man with the suitcase and what smart boys we must be to remember about the kind of car and all. Man, he put it on, all for me."

"And what'd you say?"

"I kept my mouth shut." Johnny rubbed the back of his neck. "And then Pa said, 'Do you really think there's any money in that timber?' And the guy looked *right at me* and said, 'There used to be. Maybe there still is.' I tell you, Steve, this guy's not scared of nothing."

"Forty-eight thousand dollars don't grow on trees, Johnny. That kind of money builds up a guy inside."

He looked past me, over at the woods, not saying anything.

I said, "Maybe tonight we'll bury it in a milk can? We ought to take one outside now, so we don't have to come in here where he's sleeping tonight."

"All right," he said. "You'll have to wake me tonight, though. I always sleep right through until morning."

So we took the can outside and then got a cot out from the tool shed and dusted it and set it up behind the tarps and even put some nails in the walls for him to hang his clothes on.

When Pa saw it all, he shook his head. He looked around the clean barn and the room I'd made and almost smiled. "And I didn't offer you a dime for all this work."

Johnny said, "You can offer it now, Pa, if you want."

He shook his head. "You boys aren't fooling me. You fixed this up so you wouldn't lose your secret meeting place."

Johnny laughed. "You're too smart for us, Pa. If we help the man with the timber, would he pay us, you think?"

"Maybe," Pa said. "I'll talk it over with him and maybe we can work something out. You got the key to the tool shed? I got to get those saws sharpened up."

"I'll get 'em, Pa," Johnny said. "Don't forget to tell him what good workers we are, huh?"

Johnny went to the tool shed and I went up to the house. I could see the man sitting on the front porch, smoking, so I went in through the kitchen door.

I wasn't scared anymore; I just didn't want to talk to him.

Mom said, "Where have you been? Everybody's eaten but you."

"I was fixing a room for the man."

"For Frank?"

"If that's his name. I'm not hungry, Ma."

"Come here," she said. "Let me feel your head."

I came over and she put her hand on my forehead. She said, "It seems all right. But maybe you'd better take a little nap."

"Maybe," I said. "I'll try, anyway."

"You worked hard this morning," she said. "You're probably tired."

I nodded, and went up the steps to our bedroom. I wasn't tired. I just wanted to be alone, to think. I had to think this all out careful because there was more at stake than there probably ever would be in my life again. I'd bet there wasn't a farmer in the township that ever saw forty-eight thousand dollars in one hunk.

Pa had been paying me for chores for three years now, and I'd saved every penny of it and had ninety dollars, including Christmas money from Uncle George.

Johnny was right about me, in a way. He had more chance of protecting that money because he had more guts and was older and he had more gab. And he thought fast, when he had to.

I went over to the window and looked out and everything was green, the color of money. Johnny thought fast; I'd have to think careful. And once I decided what the surest way was to protect that money, I'd have to find the guts to go through with it.

I was laying on the bed when Johnny came up. He said, "We ought to get rid of the wrappers on that money. That shows it's the bank's money. With those gone, who could prove it?"

"I've been thinking of that," I said.

"What else you been thinking?"

"Everything. Like building up my guts."

He laughed and lay down on his bed. "Well, old Frank's down starting on the timber and Pa's working on the fence near the Saugus road and Ma's going over to Nestor's. Why don't we get rid of those brown wrappers as soon as she goes?"

"A good idea," I said. "And something else—why don't we spike down that tool shed floor until we get a chance to bury the money in the milk can?"

"You're thinking, Stevie boy," he said. "You're hitting on all eight."

Ma left in a couple minutes and we went down to the tool

shed. We took all the wrappers off and put them in a paper sack and put the money back and spiked the floor down good.

Johnny said, "We ought to burn these wrappers, but where?"

"Give 'em to me; I'll get rid of 'em," I said. "You keep a watch on Frank until I come back."

He smiled. "Brave Stevie boy."

When I came back, he said, "Why don't we go swimming, like fun-loving kids? I'll bet this new Steve would even dive off the bank, now."

"Any time," I said.

"Remember, Pa said he'd skin us if he caught us diving off that bluff."

"Pa can't see us from the Saugus road," I said. "I'll bet you a dime I'll dive closer to the rock than you will."

"It's a bet," he said. "C'mon, I'll race you to the house for our trunks."

The bank was maybe twenty feet high and the water was deep enough below it, but there was this sharp rock near the middle that came almost to the surface. Pa said if we ever hit that, diving, it would split our head wide open and I guess he was right. But Johnny used to dive real close to it until Pa caught him one time. And then he said we couldn't dive from the bank at all.

Johnny beat me to the house and got into his trunks faster and went racing out ahead of me. But when I came down there, he was still standing on the bank.

"The bet's off," he said.

"All right, you owe me a dime."

"All right, I owe you a dime. You know why the bet's off?"

I shook my head.

"I was never worth forty-eight thousand dollars, before. I can't take chances with myself, now, huh, Stevie?"

"You're getting some sense," I said, "but you're only worth twenty-four thousand dollars."

He laughed. "I just said that to heckle you." He looked over toward the woods. "That Frank's sure working. I wonder how long he'll work before he gives up?"

"How long would you," I asked, "for forty-eight thousand dollars?"

Johnny didn't answer. He just stood there, looking at the

woods. If it hadn't been Johnny, I would have said he looked scared. For the first time in my life, I felt bigger than Johnny.

Around four o'clock, we got tired of swimming and went up to the house for some milk. Then Johnny said he was going to take a nap. I put on some clothes and went over to where Pa was stringing new fence. I helped him out there until Ma rang the bell for supper.

Frank ate with us. He sat next to me and didn't talk much, except to Pa, about the timber. Johnny didn't talk at all and that was maybe a new record. After supper, Johnny went upstairs to read, he said.

Frank stretched and looked out through the kitchen window and said, "I've got a couple axes to sharpen. How much would you charge me to turn the grindstone, Steve?"

"Ten cents an axe," I said.

He looked at me sort of half smiling. "Make it a nickel."

"Ten cents," I said. "I don't need the money."

Pa laughed and Ma smiled. Frank said, "All right. You drive a hard bargain, Steve."

"He's got ninety dollars saved," Pa said. "Steve will never wind up on the poor farm."

Frank and I went out to the barn with a can of water to wet down the grindstone. He had a hand axe and the big double-edged axe with him and I should have been scared, but I wasn't, much.

He poured some of the water into the container that dripped on the stone, and said, "I've been thinking about those robbers. I read where they got away with forty-eight thousand dollars. If I had that kind of money, I know where I could double it in six months."

"Gee," I said, "it's too bad you don't have that kind of money, then."

He stood there with the hand axe in his hand, staring at me. "How old are you?"

"I'll be thirteen next month," I said.

He shook his head. "Well, I'll be——"

"You'd better not let Pa hear you swear," I butted in, "or you won't be cutting any more timber. Pa don't hold with swearing."

He took a deep breath. "I'd better be careful, then. I wouldn't want to get cheated out of all that money."

I didn't say anything.

"The money I'm going to make on the timber," he explained.

"Sure," I said. "What else? You want me to start turning now?"

"Any time," he said. He took another breath. "I'm a patient man."

"Me, too," I said, and started to turn the grindstone.

He sure knew how to sharpen an axe, that Frank. Slow and easy until he had the edge sharp as a razor. He wet some of his whiskers with spit and shaved 'em right off with that hand axe while I stood there.

Then he took the big axe and I started to turn again. He said, "We work pretty good together, Steve. I bet we could make out all right, working together."

"Maybe," I said. "Who knows?"

"I've kicked around a lot," he said. "I think I've learned how to turn a buck by now."

I didn't say anything.

"I wouldn't have to rob a bank, if I had a stake," he went on. "I'd know how to make it grow."

"Pa says it takes money to make money," I said.

"And he's right. The way things are these days, a guy with a nest egg could fix himself up for life."

"Not a nest egg of ninety dollars," I said.

He smiled. "I guess not."

"If I knew a place to get more," I said, "you could tell me how to make it grow, I'll bet."

"You're dead right, kid. You think about it. A kid needs help when it comes to getting rich. I could show you lots of angles."

"I'll think about it," I said. "Maybe Johnny knows a place where we can get some money."

He nodded and kept working the big axe lightly over the turning stone. He looked awful pleased with himself, I'd say.

He gave me twenty cents when we were finished and I went up to the house. It was getting dark now. We don't have daylight saving time on the farm. We don't have much of anything on the farm.

I thought about those two guys that had been killed trying to get away from the robbery and Johnny's lie about the Pontiac and the way he was acting since we went swimming this afternoon.

Johnny was losing his guts, maybe. It wasn't a big funny lie, any-more, a wise guy's game. This Frank had changed it from a game.

In the kitchen Pa said, "Well, you've had a full day, haven't you?"

"Yes, sir," I said, "I sure have."

"Maybe you'd better hit the hay early."

"I'm going to," I said. "I'm going up now. Good night, Pa."

In our room, Johnny was reading an auto racing book. That's about the only kind he likes. He looked at me and asked, "What'd he say?"

"He said if he had a stake, he knew how to make a million."

"What'd you say?"

"I told him it was too bad he didn't have a stake, then."

Johnny stared at me for seconds. "Man, you've changed."

"You, too," I said.

"Don't worry about me."

"I'm not," I told him, "not anymore."

He kept staring at me without talking. Then he looked back at the book. I laid down on the bed and thought.

In a little while he got up and took off his clothes and climbed under the covers. "Steve," he said, "I think I'm getting scared."

"Don't," I told him. "Don't think about it. Nobody can prove nothing on us, *nothing*, unless we get scared and blab."

After a few seconds, he said, "That's right. You're right. Well, they'll never get anything out of me, I promise you that."

I didn't answer him.

In a little while, he fell asleep and I went over to sit by the window and look out at the bright moonlight.

■   ■   ■

In the morning, I heard Ma in the kitchen and she sounded half crazy and then Pa came charging up the steps, and I closed my eyes. Johnny's bed is closest to the door and Pa shook Johnny until he woke up.

Then Pa said, "Run right over to Nestor's and tell them to call Sheriff Taggart. Tell them to send the Sheriff here right away, this second."

"What's the matter, Pa?" Johnny asked. "What happened?"

"Never mind what happened. Get some shoes and pants on and get over there right away. I got to stay with your Ma; she's half crazy, she's so scared."

Pa left and Johnny came over to shake me. "Steve, something's happened."

I sat up. "What?"

"I don't know. But I got to run to Nestor's to call the Sheriff. Steve, it must be about Frank. What could it be?"

"I don't know," I said. "Maybe one of his buddies came here and they had a fight. How do I know what happened?"

He put some pants on and a pair of shoes and went running out, without a shirt. I got up and dressed.

When I came down to the kitchen, Ma was sitting in the rocker, rocking and hanging on tight to the arms. "I had to call him," she said. "I had to call him for breakfast."

"Who, Ma?" I asked. "What happened?"

Pa came in from outside. "Never mind, boy," he said rough. "Your ma's had a shock. Better go out in the front and wait for the Sheriff. Tell him to go down to the barn."

I went out and stood on the front porch to wait for the Sheriff.

· · ·

"Stabbed three times in the throat," Sheriff Taggart said, "and four times in the chest. And these money wrappers scattered all over the floor. How would you figure it, Jess?"

Jess Laurie just shrugged his shoulders. They were standing in the front yard, waiting for the Coroner from Center City. I was standing in the bushes at the side of the house. Pa and Ma were in the house with the Nestors and I didn't know where Johnny was.

"I'll tell you how I figure it," the Sheriff said. "I figure this was the guy that drove that Pontiac. And he swindled the money from that fat guy in the denim jacket and came back here to hide. Only the fat guy found him, that's what I figure."

"It don't make sense," Jess said, "for the guy to come here to hide. Why would he come here?"

"Use your head," Sheriff Taggart said. "Where would be the last place in the world the fat guy would look for him?"

I came out from the bushes. "Sheriff, I heard something funny last night."

"Funny?" He frowned at me. "What—what do you mean?"

"I woke up," I said, "and heard talking in the barn. And then I heard a big thump, and then a little later, I heard a car start, up the road aways. I went to the window, but I couldn't see any lights."

Jess Laurie stared at me. "You heard talking in the barn and didn't go out there? Why not?"

"I thought maybe it was Pa talking to Frank. I didn't know what time it was. And I thought maybe the car was neckers, you know."

"Was it your Pa's voice?" Jess asked.

"I couldn't make out the voices," I said. "I didn't think nothing of it until after what happened this morning."

"You didn't see the car?" Sheriff Taggart asked.

"No, sir. I just heard the starter and then it driving away."

"It was a bright night," Jess Laurie said.

Sheriff Taggart looked down the road. "Where's your window, Steve?"

I pointed to it.

"The car could've been around the bend," he said. "The guy could've come up to the barn without being in sight of the house. I'd bet ten dollars those weren't no neckers. I'd bet it was a green Pontiac parked down there."

"You mean the robbers, Sheriff?" I asked.

He looked at Jess. "Who else?"

"I'm scared, Sheriff," I said. "I don't want no robbers coming around here."

Sheriff Taggart smiled. "Don't worry, boy; they won't be around. They got no reason to come here anymore."

"Is there anything else you heard or saw?" Jess Laurie asked me.

I shook my head. "No, sir, that's every bit of it."

Then the Coroner's car was coming up the road and they went out to wave him down and I went looking for Johnny. I could have told them I'd seen a green Pontiac, but if they ever found out the Pontiac had been a lie of Johnny's, I'd be in trouble. The way I'd told it, they couldn't ever prove what I'd said wasn't true.

In the back yard, Pa and Mr. Nestor were talking. Pa was saying, "I guess the other one came back for the money. Gosh, Len, could you kill a man for money?"

Mr. Nestor said, "All of us have done mean things for a lot less than forty-eight thousand. I guess murder's just another step up the ladder, John."

Pa said, "What are you doing out here, Steve? I told you to stay in the house."

"I'm looking for Johnny," I said.

"He's in the house. Get in there, now, until I tell you to come out."

I went into the house. Ma and Mrs. Nestor were in the front room. I went up the steps and there was Johnny on his bed. He was laying on his back, just staring at the ceiling.

He didn't look at me. "Where'd you put my knife? Where is it?"

"You crazy, Johnny? What would I do with your knife?"

"Don't be funny. Where is it, Steve?"

I sat down on the bed and looked at him. For the first time in my life, he didn't seem bigger to me. For the first time, he seemed like an equal, no more. I had proved myself.

I said, "Let's not talk about your silly old knife, Johnny. You can buy another one. Think of the money we've got."

He sat up. "What's happened to you? You've changed."

"Everybody changes," I said, "sooner or later, right?"

He took a deep breath. "I know you killed him, Steve. Because of the wrappers."

"What wrappers, Johnny?" I asked.

"The ones you were going to get rid of." His voice dropped. "The ones that were all over the floor in Frank's room."

I said, "Maybe the guy with the green Pontiac put them there. That's what the Sheriff thinks."

He sat there staring at me and I stared right back. He laid down again, frowning at the ceiling.

"You told me I had no guts, Johnny," I reminded him. "I had to prove myself, you told me."

He closed his eyes. "You're crazy. It was too much money. It put you over the edge. You're crazy as a loon, Steve."

"No," I said. "Don't talk like that. Think of the money and don't talk like that."

He didn't answer. He opened his eyes again, but didn't look at me. I laid down on my bed.

His voice was almost a whisper. "It was the way you were heading. You were always money-crazy. This just brought it on faster."

"Everybody is," I said, "everybody with any sense."

"Not everybody," he said. "Not me."

"When you're old enough," I told him, "you can buy a big Cadillac. You can even buy a racing car. There won't be any smart crook looking for you, figuring a way to steal your money back."

"Shut up!" he said. "You're loony, I tell you."

"Be sensible, Johnny. *Think!* All right, I'll shut up."

Silence. I closed my eyes and I could hear the voices of Ma and Mrs. Nestor below and the Sheriff out in the front yard talking to somebody. I saw Frank's face smiling in his sleep, and I got sick to my stomach, but I fought it, and changed my mind from that to thinking of the money, all that money.

I said quietly, "I wonder how many guys Frank killed in *his* life." I licked my lips. "A dirty old bank robber like that."

Johnny didn't say anything.

"Maybe he had getting killed coming to him."

Johnny still didn't say anything.

I stretched and kept my eyes open, so I wouldn't see any more ugly pictures. I heard a couple of car engines start out in front and then I heard Pa coming up the stairs. Johnny sat up, as though he'd been waiting to tell Pa something.

Pa came in and said, "Your mother's going over to your Uncle George's and Aunt Jane's for a couple of days. I'm taking her over now. You boys afraid to stay here?"

I shook my head.

Johnny said, "I'll stay, too. How soon will you be back, Pa?"

"In a couple hours. Why?"

Johnny started to talk, stopped, and then said, "I just wondered." He laid back again, looking very thoughtful.

"Maybe you ought to get out of the house," Pa said. "Why don't you go swimming? It's hot today."

Johnny nodded. "Maybe I will."

"If you dive off that bluff," Pa said, "stay clear of that rock. I guess I can trust you to do that, can't I?"

Johnny nodded again. "Don't worry. I'll be careful, Pa."

Pa went out and we heard him talking to Ma. Ma never came in to say good-bye. I guess she was still in shock. I heard the pickup rattle out onto the road and then it was suddenly so quiet I could hear Johnny breathe.

I said, "Why did you want to know when Pa was coming back? Were you going to tell him—? I mean, about the—knife and the wrappers?"

He didn't answer.

I got up and went to the window. "It started with *you*, remember," I said. "With that story about the Pontiac. That started the whole thing."

"I'm remembering that," he said.

I turned around to face him. "You did something. I did something. So now we got the money. I did something, didn't I? I thought you'd be—well, I thought—" I stopped. I wasn't going to tell him I wanted him to be proud of me.

He wasn't listening to me, anyhow. "Maybe," he said, "I haven't got the guts to tell the Sheriff I lied about that Pontiac, and maybe I have. That's what I've been thinking about."

"Now why would you do that? That would be foolish."

He didn't answer. I didn't know what he was thinking about; I hoped it was the money, that big bunch of money and what it would buy. I was actually wishing he'd get back to talking bigmouthed, like he did before.

After a couple seconds, I said, "You could give your half away, if you didn't want it. You could give it to the Salvation Army."

He didn't answer and he didn't look at me. I said, "I'm going swimming. I'm not going to argue with you if you don't at least argue back."

Still nothing from him.

I put on my trunks and a pair of shoes and went out without saying any more. I was worried about him. He was unpredictable. I went down to the bluff and stood there, looking at the rock. It looked big.

What would I gain by trying to prove myself twice in twenty-four hours? What could I gain, by seeing how close to the rock I could dive?

I was rich now; I had too much to lose. Getting myself killed now would be a big waste.

But it came to me in a strange way that when you've got a lot to lose, you have to be sure you're not gutless. I don't mean you got to be reckless, but you can't be gutless. Because there would be a lot of guys wanting to take that money away from me.

So I stood there, measuring the distance, and made the dive, as close to the rock as I had guts for. I skinned my hand, going down, rubbing it along the sharp edge of the rock.

I came up feeling sick again, but good, too, because I'd made the dive. I looked up and there was Johnny on the bluff above.

"That was close," he said.

I smiled and nodded.

Then he came down, in one of his beautiful, clean dives and it looked for sure like he was going to hit right on top of the rock. But at the last, he twisted away, and his body seemed to scrape as he hit the water.

He came up and I said, "Closer. You're a better diver."

"Let's go over to the bank," he said. "I want to talk to you."

We came up on the bank and we were right at the place where Frank had stacked the cordwood. He could sure handle an axe and saw, that Frank. I got a funny feeling thinking of him dead, and his firewood still stacked there, wood he'd cut only yesterday.

"You're shivering," Johnny said.

I didn't answer. I looked at my scraped hand. It wasn't bleeding anymore.

He sat on the cordwood. His voice was very soft. "What was it like? Was it hard to do? How did you get the guts?"

"It was—scary," I said. "After—well, after the first—cut, it was easier." I looked at him steady. "I could do it again—I think. He probably killed people, lots and lots of 'em, so—"

"Was it only the money, Steve? Is that why, or was there another reason, too? Was any of it my fault, the way I called you gutless and like that—?"

"The money mostly," I said. "Everything—but the money mostly."

"What do you mean—everything?"

"Oh, Pa grubbing and—well, Ma favoring you and the way you always looked down at me. You don't act like no brother, Johnny. You act like a big bully, most times."

He nodded. He kept nodding, like he was remembering a lot of things. Then he said, "You give that money to the Salvation Army or the Red Cross, and there'll never be a word out of me to Pa or Sheriff Taggart or anybody else in the whole world."

I stared at him. "How could I do that? Where would I tell 'em I got it?"

"I don't mean now. Later, I mean. You could just send it in a package with no return address. It would be easy."

I sat down and looked at the water. "And Pa keeps grubbing

and Ma, too. And the whole thing was for nothing. Your lying and my—doing what I did, and nobody gets nothing out of it but the lousy Red Cross. It's not sensible, Johnny."

He sat there, frowning. I sat there looking at the water. It seemed like a long time before he said, "Well, maybe we could fix some way to let Ma and Pa get some of it. They sure can use it better than the Red Cross. And we owe them something."

"Sure," I said. "They could at least get a halfway decent car, right?"

He nodded, and I could see his eyes flash when I said *car*. *Racing car*, I figured he was thinking.

He sucked in the hot, bright air. "The money's safe, huh?"

"Oh, yeah," I said, "plenty safe."

He looked up at the bluff and over at the rock and down at the ground, everywhere but at me. "Maybe, we got some of that money coming, too, don't you think? It was like we did a service, getting it and all, you know."

"And we ought to by rights get paid for our time, that what you mean?"

"Yeah. Sure."

"You're the boss, Johnny," I said.

But I knew he wasn't, really. Not now.

And I think he knew it, too.

Then I said, like I was giving an order, "We won't take any more of that money than what's coming to us. But that's quite a bit, come to think of it."

Craig Rice

SAY IT WITH FLOWERS

From *Manhunt,* September 1957

Funny doesn't always get you much respect from critics—few people wrote as funny as Craig Rice, at least not in the mystery genre. In such comedic landmarks as Having Wonderful Crime *and* Trial by Fury, *Rice displayed wit, warmth and wiles in a way that had never been seen before in the crime story. True, she used the then-familiar conventions of the screwball comedy in much of her writing, but she made the conventions very much her own, especially when showing off her inebriated Irish attorney, John J. Malone.*

E. G.

"YOU WOULDN'T REFUSE TO HELP POOR LITTLE ME?" THE BEAU-tiful blonde said. She leaned over the desk and fluttered her eye-lashes at John J. Malone.

Malone sighed and looked away. He gazed, apparently fasci-nated, at the row of filing cabinets that lined one wall of his office. Turning his head slightly, he stared with the same fixity of expression at the tiny shelf which Maggie had put up against the adjoining wall. It held a small potted plant which was begin-ning to overflow its pot and creep down the dingy wall, a mini-ature brass teapot and a particularly repulsive porcelain rabbit. "Cheer up the place," Malone muttered to his cigar. "Add a little atmosphere." He sighed again, bitterly this time.

"What?" said the beautiful blonde.

Malone waved negligently at the shelf. "What do you think of it?" he asked. "Do you think it adds a cheery atmosphere?"

The blonde stared for a second. "I think it's horrible," she said decisively. "But, listen, Malone, I didn't come here to talk about decorations. I want you to—"

"I know," Malone said. "You told me. Your uncle Jasper McIlhenny—"

"Jabez," the blonde murmured.

"It doesn't matter," Malone said grandly. "Your uncle has disappeared, and you want me to find him."

"Yes, Malone," the girl said. "And you will do it, won't you? For me, Malone?" She batted her eyelashes again. Malone turned resolutely away and tried to think of something else.

"I don't need money," he said at last, expansively. "I'm on my way to Havana. Havana, Cuba," he added, in case there had been a misunderstanding. "And, besides, what can I do that the police force of Chicago can't do better?" He hoped that Miss McIlhenny didn't know the answer to that one.

"It's been two weeks, Malone," she said. "I went to the Missing Persons Bureau and they say they're working on it, but two weeks is a long time. I've heard about you, and I just know you can find Uncle Jabez, if anyone can."

"The fact remains," Malone began, and wondered what else he had been going to say. "The fact remains. And moreover, I am on my way to Havana, Cuba. If I see your uncle there I'll give him a message from you. I can't be fairer than that, can I?"

"Malone," the girl said, "you are heartless. Absolutely heartless." She stepped back to give the rumpled little lawyer the full benefit of her gaze. It was a gaze that spelled murder, Malone thought. It spelled several other things, too. Reluctantly, Malone removed his mind from the brink of temptation.

"Miss McIlhenny," he began, in what he hoped was a fatherly tone, "I'm sure that—if you have a little patience—the police will be able to find your uncle. I really couldn't do a thing except send you bills. Exorbitant bills."

"Money doesn't matter," the girl said. "We have plenty of money." She dug into a black leather handbag and produced a sheaf of bills. She removed three of them and placed them carefully on Malone's brown desk. "Will that do for a retainer?"

Malone stared at the three one-hundred-dollar bills. "It would be fine," he said sadly. "But I have tickets. My boat leaves on Friday. This is Thursday morning—early Thursday morning," he amended. "I just can't do a thing. I'm very sorry."

"Ha," the girl said. She picked up the money with one sweeping motion, and went to the door. She opened it, turned and said: "Heartless. Absolutely heartless." She banged the door behind her and went out.

Malone sat behind his desk. Missing Persons would turn up Uncle Jabez, he told himself. So, it was obvious that there was no use in thinking about the blonde Miss McIlhenny anymore. He might as well pretend she had never existed. Instead, he could think about the poker game, the wonderful poker game to which Judge Touralchuck had invited him the night before. The game had given him enough money to buy tickets for a Havana cruise, and assure himself of a couple of weeks of fairly riotous living— and no girl was going to take all that away from him, even if she was beautiful, and seemed so lost, and murmured at him.

Perhaps thinking about the poker game wasn't such a good idea. He would stare at the shelf. The porcelain rabbit stared back unwinkingly. That was one good thing about the shelf, Malone thought vaguely; it gave a person something to think about when times were rough. Just because a beautiful blonde came to your office early Thursday morning and begged you to help her, that didn't mean . . .

Malone sighed.

I am going to forget all about her, he told himself firmly. "She wasn't even here," he said, and listened to his voice echoing in the room. It had a very satisfactory sound, a firm, no-nonsense tone to it that appealed to him.

"She wasn't even here," he said again. "Ladies and gentlemen of the jury, I defy you to prove that my client ever knew this woman. I defy you to prove that she ever came to his office."

The office door opened and Malone looked up guiltily. But the girl standing on his threshold was raven-haired and petite. "Now, Malone," she said. "What are you practicing for? You should take it easy. You're going to Havana for a nice rest."

"That's exactly where I'm going, Maggie," John J. Malone said in his firmest voice. "And not even all the blondes in Chicago— not even all the blondes in the United States—" he added recklessly—"are going to stop me."

■   ■   ■

"So you're leaving for Havana," Joe the Angel said, a little while later. He put a double rye in front of the little lawyer.

Malone looked around the musty precincts of Joe the Angel's City Hall Bar. Only the City Hall janitor inhabited the room, and he sat silently at the other end of the bar, nursing his beer. Malone picked up his glass and looked at it reflectively.

"Havana, Cuba," he said. "And when I'm nice and warm there, just lying on the beach with nothing to do, I'll think of you, Joe. By the way," he added anxiously, "do I owe you anything?"

"Just a couple of bucks on the bill, Malone," Joe the Angel said. "It'll keep until you get back."

"I'll pay you now," Malone said. He dug into his pocket and fished out a collection of crumpled bills. Carefully unwrapping two of them, he laid them on the bar. "Now we're all square," he said. He looked around the empty room. "This deserves a celebration."

Joe the Angel hesitated only a second. "Have one on the house, Malone," he said grandly. Malone downed his first drink and Joe poured again. "We're going to miss you around here," he said.

"I'm not going to miss Chicago," Malone announced. "People always coming to you with problems they won't let you not solve or . . ." He considered for a minute and drank deeply. "Anyhow, I won't miss it. It's all water under a burning bridge. Or walking on water before you come to it."

"Sure, Malone," Joe the Angel said sadly.

"Listen," Malone went on, "when I get to Havana, the first thing I'm going to do . . ."

The telephone rang. In a dark corner of the bar the parrot screamed: "Ring! Ring!"

"Excuse me, Malone," Joe the Angel said. He went to the telephone, turned and scowled fiercely at the bar parrot. It shut its beak and looked at Malone disapprovingly. Malone stared back belligerently.

"Okay," Joe the Angel was saying. "Yes, sure he's here. You just wait a minute, he'll talk to you." He cupped the receiver against his chest and shouted: "Malone!"

"I'm not here," Malone said without taking his eyes off the parrot. "I went home hours ago."

"It's Captain Von Flanagan," Joe the Angel said. "He sounds pretty mad."

Malone almost said: "I don't care how mad he sounds." He reconsidered just in time. After all, Von Flanagan was an old friend.

"Hello?" he said tentatively.

A torrent of profane abuse scorched his ear. Malone held the receiver a little away from him and heard Von Flanagan's voice screaming: ". . . Just because you're too busy to help, I've got to talk to the Commissioner! He wants to see me now, and what am I going to tell him, Malone? This is what I get for helping you all these years . . ."

"Wait a minute," Malone said. "Wait a minute. Suppose you tell me what you're talking about?"

"Don't pretend you don't know," Von Flanagan said. "Don't play innocent with me this time. I've got you dead to rights and you're going to wish you'd never been born. The next parking ticket you come to me with . . ."

"Von Flanagan." Malone's reasonable tone seemed to enrage the police officer even further, but after another shriek or two he subsided, muttering. "Now," Malone said, "what are you talking about? What did I do to you?"

"McIlhenny," Von Flanagan moaned. "The Commissioner's own niece by marriage."

A horrible light began to dawn on Malone. "You mean that blonde," he said.

"That blonde. She can't find her uncle, and we're working on it. Malone, you know we're working on it." Von Flanagan's voice was breaking.

"Of course you are," Malone said. "That's what I told her."

"But she wants a report every five minutes," Von Flanagan said. "I can't do any work with her bothering me every time I turn around. Malone, I swear to you, I suggested your name in all innocence. Not that you could do anything we can't . . ."

Malone thought of a number of things, and said none of them.

". . . but she'll pay you for being bothered, and then she'll come to you and we can get some work done."

"Why not just tell her you're working?" Malone suggested. "I've seen you brush people off before."

"*Malone,*" Von Flanagan sobbed. "*The Commissioner's niece by marriage.*"

"Oh," the lawyer said. "I see."

"And then you refuse to help her. You tell her you're going away, some wild story like that. Malone, I swear to you, the next time there's an unsolved murder in Chicago, I'm going to pin it on you. I'm going to fake evidence if I have to, and bribe witnesses. I don't care. When you refuse to help an old friend . . ."

Malone thought quickly. On the one hand, he *was* going away, where Von Flanagan couldn't reach him. On the other hand, he might want to come back some day, even if he couldn't imagine why. And Von Flanagan was an old friend, after all, regardless of how he treated Malone.

And besides, his boat didn't leave until Friday, and it was only Thursday afternoon. That left almost one whole day.

"All right, Von Flanagan," Malone said. "But this is the last time . . ."

The voice on the other end became silk-smooth. "Anything you want, Malone. Just ask me."

"Don't worry," the little lawyer said. "I will."

                              * * *

Malone went back to his office, humming *St. James Infirmary* under his breath. He got Maggie busy finding a Miss McIlhenny in the telephone book, relaxed, lit a fresh cigar, and thought about the situation.

There wasn't much to think about, he discovered. He had reached the point of deciding to look for Jabez McIlhenny in Havana, where any man with enough money and a little common sense would prefer to be found, when Maggie announced that a Miss McIlhenny was on the line.

Malone picked up the receiver and said in his most official tones: "This is Malone."

"I hoped you'd call," said the sultry voice he remembered. "You will look for Uncle Jabez, won't you? And I'm sure you'll do ever so much better than those old police . . ."

"I'll take your case," Malone said sternly. "The retainer will be . . . ah . . ." He paused for thought.

"If three hundred isn't enough," the voice said, "we'll make it five. You darling man, you!"

A little had been attractive, Malone decided, listening to the cooing of his new client, but too much was definitely enough. He wondered briefly exactly what he'd meant by that, decided to forget it, and said instead:

"Five hundred will be fine. But I'll have to talk to you . . ."

"Clues," said the voice. "I'll be down right away."

There was a dull click. Malone held the receiver in his hand, shrugged, and went back to puffing at his cigar.

He put in fifteen minutes staring at the china rabbit on his new shelf before Maggie entered. "A Miss McIlhenny to see you, Mr. Malone," she said.

"Can't you see I'm busy with these papers?" Malone growled. He grabbed a few papers from his desk and rustled them, convincingly, he hoped. "Oh, all right," he said, "send her in."

The beautiful blonde swayed in and sat, without invitation, on the chair next to Malone's desk.

"I had to make a check," she said. "I hope you don't mind." She put a folded piece of paper on the desktop. Malone did not pick it up.

"I'll have to ask you a lot of questions," he said.

"All right," she said.

"You may not like some of them."

"If they'll help you find Uncle Jabez . . ." She blinked back a sob. "I don't mind." She looked like a brave little girl. Malone refrained from patting her hand, and wondered just how much of her was play-acting. All of her, he decided savagely.

"Did your uncle have any enemies, that you know of?" he said after a second.

Miss McIlhenny thought. "Everybody liked Uncle Jabez. He was such a sweet old man."

"Was?" Malone said.

"I mean . . . well, he still is, I suppose."

"He might be dead," Malone pointed out, and watched the blonde's face for a reaction.

Her expression didn't change. She took a handkerchief from her black handbag and held it near her eyes without using it. Then she put it down on the desk. "If he's dead, I'd like to know about it," she said. "The police can't find out anything . . ."

"I know," Malone said. "You told me. They're doing the best they can."

He thought for a minute and went on:

"When did you see him last?"

"He was just leaving the house, early Tuesday morning. Two weeks and two days ago. He lives in the big McIlhenny—well, I suppose you'd call it a mansion—near the Drive. I live with him."

"Anyone else in the house?" Malone asked. He remembered the place: a turreted pile of stone with Gothic windows and a general air of crumbling decay. It sat alone near the Lakefront, brooding out on the water. The place had always given Malone cold shivers. He didn't like the idea of going there.

"Only the servants," the blonde said. "And when he left the house I asked . . ."

"Servants," Malone said. "Who are they?"

"Oh, a man named Paul Finn," the blonde said. Servants, Malone imagined, were beneath her dignity. One never mentioned servants. "He's Uncle's secretary. And my maid Rose. Rose Billington."

"Were they both in the house?"

"When Uncle left? Oh, no. Tuesday is their day off. I suppose they were out somewhere—smooching."

. . .

Malone tried to remember the last time he'd heard that word, and failed. He marked the fact down in his mind. The male secretary and the maid were having a romance. It sounded important. The lawyer didn't know why, and he told himself he might just as well be wrong.

"What did you say?" he asked, discovering that the blonde had gone right on with her paragraph.

She looked a little startled. "I said that I was all alone. I asked Uncle where he was going, and he said he had to see someone on business."

"What kind of business?"

"I don't know," she said. "I just didn't think about it at the time—you know the way a sentence just doesn't register on your mind—but when the police asked me I realized how strange it was. Uncle inherited a great deal of money, and it's been invested in very safe bonds. There's really—no business at all he'd have to attend to."

"He didn't say anything else?" Malone asked.

"He walked down to the corner and I went back in the house."

"Walked?"

"Uncle like to walk," the blonde said. "He said it was good exercise for him."

"Where did he usually go when he went for a walk?" Malone asked.

The blonde thought. "Sometimes he went down to Eve's," she said. "And then there was Martine. Oh, yes, Martine."

The little lawyer began to feel confused. The conversation

seemed to be traveling in a fog. "Eve and Martine," he said. "Girls he knew?"

"Well," the blonde said, "Martine was, anyhow. A girl. A—chorine? But he certainly wouldn't go to see her on *business*. Oh, goodness, no."

"I see," Malone said.

"Eve—that's Eve Washington—you've heard of her."

Malone considered. "No," he said at last.

The blonde shook her head. "Chicago's best-known ceramicist," she said, "and you say you've never heard . . ."

"Miss McIlhenny," Malone said softly. "I'm a lawyer and I spend a lot of time in court. Sometimes I don't read the science page in the newspaper. You're going to have to tell me what a ceramicist is."

"Really," the blonde said. "Now you're just fooling little old me."

"No," Malone said.

"Oh." The blonde appeared to consider carefully, and Malone hoped for some reason that she wouldn't take the folded check from the desk, put it in her bag and leave. He would feel insulted. It wasn't a criminal offense not to know what a ceramicist was, he thought. He couldn't help it if he didn't know everything.

"Clay," the girl said. "She makes clay objects."

"Like mud pies," Malone said thoughtfully.

"More or—less," said the girl slowly. "She's very well-known and very expensive." She turned her head and seemed, for the first time, to catch sight of the brooding porcelain rabbit. "She might have made that," she said. "Though she wouldn't, of course."

"Doesn't like rabbits?" Malone suggested.

"It's too cheap, mass-produced. Not at all her type of thing."

"But," said Malone delicately, "Jabez McIlhenny was her type of thing?"

"Not the way you're thinking," the girl said. "Uncle Jabez likes clay sculpture. He bought pieces from Eve every so often. They were—just good friends."

"Maybe that's what he meant by business," Malone said. "You go home. I'll call you later."

"What are you going to *do?*" the blonde said.

"I'm going to start earning that money," Malone said. He reached for the check and unfolded it.

"All right," the blonde said. She was out the door by the time Malone had read the line on the check that read: "Five Hundred and 00/100 Dollars," and long before he drew his gaze down to the bottom line, where her name was signed:

"G. G. G. McIlhenny."

Malone realized he didn't know his client's first name. He didn't know any of her first names. The bank must, though, he told himself cheerfully as he pocketed the check, stood up, and left his office.

■ ■ ■

The sign outside the door read, in a curlicued script: *Eve Washington: Ceramics.* There was a tiny buzzer underneath.

Malone pressed it. He wondered briefly what a mud-pie maker was doing on the tenth floor of Chicago's most exclusive set of apartments, but decided that there must be more to the business than met the eye. He was congratulating himself on his fairness when there was a click and the door swung open.

Malone stepped into a room which reminded him of some of the worst scenes from *Bertha, The Sewing Machine Girl,* the scenes that showed Bertha's life in her poverty-ridden home. Old grey jugs and shapes were everywhere, along with a fantastic litter composed of straw, sawdust, wood shavings and ancient yellow newspapers. Over everything hung a cloud of dust.

From a long way off Malone heard a whirring sound which reminded him of a sawmill. He called, tentatively: "Hello?"

"Just a minute," a voice called back. Malone stared around him at the mess, and waited. When the minute was up, and had taken two or three more with it, a very dusty woman in an old smock appeared at the inner entrance of the room. "Yes?" she said.

"I've come to see Miss Washington," Malone said. "My name is John J. Malone."

"You'd like to buy something?" the dusty woman said. She was only a little shorter than the little lawyer; her face was heart-shaped and her hair, as much of it as wasn't covered by dust, was a very dark brown. She might have been, Malone thought, twenty-eight.

"I'd like to see Miss Washington," he said. "I've got a few questions for her."

"I'm Eve Washington," the woman said. "But I'm quite busy now, I'm afraid. I really don't have time for interviews . . ."

"It's about Jabez McIlhenny," Malone said.

The woman stepped back. "You're with the police?"

Malone shook his head. "Just a friend," he said. "I understand he's disappeared, and I'd like to ask a few questions."

"I told the police everything," Eve Washington said. "Why don't you ask them?"

"This will only take a minute," Malone said. "Besides, I might be a customer. You never know."

"So you might." Surprisingly, Eve Washington laughed. The sound, like her voice, came from low in her throat. "Come in to my studio. McIlhenny was the only man I allowed back there, but you're a friend of his. Besides, you look as crazy as I am." She turned and went through the entrance again. Malone followed her.

They went through a long hall, and came out into a large airy room which seemed even more cluttered than the entrance room. Malone noticed four ashtrays, all made of baked clay, piled on a littered couch which, he estimated, had originally cost something over a thousand dollars. One of the ashtrays had three lipsticked cigarettes and a dusty cigar butt in it. The others were empty, but filmed with powdery dust. Malone felt as if he needed a bath.

In one corner a square box sat and whirred to itself quietly. "Kiln," Eve Washington said, noticing Malone's stare. "It bakes clay. Up to three thousand degrees in that furnace, so I wouldn't get too close if I were you."

Malone backed even farther away from the box. "Jabez McIlhenny disappeared just over two weeks ago," he said. "On a Tuesday." Somehow, that approach didn't sound right. "He was coming to see you when he left home, and his niece hasn't seen him since," he said after a pause.

The dusty woman waited, and finally said: "Yes?"

"When did he leave here?" Malone asked.

"He never arrived here," she said. "You say he was coming to see me?"

"That's right."

"He always called me in advance," Eve Washington said. "Every few weeks he would call, and I'd have a new piece ready for him to look at. He had fine taste, Mr. Malone. He always knew just what he wanted—and let me tell you, after some of the batty old ladies who come up and want little presents for their nephews . . ."

"I'm sure," Malone said sympathetically. "But this Tuesday—the day he disappeared he didn't call?"

"No," she said. "I was expecting him to call me—it was about time, you know—and I had this all ready for him." She produced an object from the litter. Malone stared at a light-green vase about a foot and a half tall. "I've still got it, in case he does show up, you know. He'd want to have this." She patted the vase fondly. "And a real bargain, too," she said. "Only three hundred dollars."

Malone nodded absently. "Miss Washington," he said. "Do you know of any enemies Mr. McIlhenny had?"

"Had?" she said. "You mean he's dead?"

Malone thought it over. There seemed no harm in admitting the truth. "He's been missing for two weeks," he said, "and his niece hasn't gotten any ransom notes, or any word from him. He's probably dead. I'm looking for the person who killed him."

"Maybe he just got tired and went away," the woman said. Under the smock, Malone noticed, she was really very pretty. Maybe the vase was worth three hundred dollars. After all, Malone thought, he was no judge of vases. Three hundred dollars might even be a bargain. Maybe he could take Eve Washington out to dinner, and they could talk it over.

He reminded himself sternly that he was investigating what was almost certainly a murder, and that he had to leave Chicago the next day anyhow.

"People don't get tired and go away," he said. "Not without leaving some kind of note."

"Maybe the note hasn't been found yet," Eve Washington said.

Malone looked around the room. If the McIlhenny home looked anything like the Eve Washington Ceramics Studio, the note might not be found for months. But he doubted it.

"Did he have any enemies?" Malone asked again.

"Not that I know of," Eve Washington said. "He was such a sweet old man."

"I know," Malone said.

"He discovered me, you know. I was just another ceramicist, struggling to get along—you know how it is."

Malone tried to imagine a struggling ceramicist, but the image wouldn't come. He couldn't even pronounce the phrase, let alone go any farther.

"Well," she was saying, "I showed some of my work at a small gallery, and Mr. McIlhenny dropped in one afternoon—and that was that. He bought several pieces, and word got around, you know. I feel quite grateful to him. I'd be terribly broken up if anything happened to him."

"You haven't—heard from him since the Tuesday he disappeared?" Malone said.

"Of course not," she said. "I still have the vase, don't I?" She seemed to realize that she was still holding it, and suddenly smiled dazzlingly at Malone. "Here," she said. "You take it. I can't hold a piece forever, you know. People might see it and want it. But if you see Mr. McIlhenny, you can give it to him."

Malone refrained from pointing out, again, that her client was probably beyond any interest in green vases. He didn't, he told himself, want to see Eve Washington all broken up, even though it would be nice to hold her head on his shoulder and dry her tears. He had, he thought sternly, too much to do, and almost no time to do it in.

He took the vase. "If I see him," he said.

"He'll pay me, of course," Eve Washington said. "You don't even have to mention money to him. He'll call me right up and send me a check."

The vase weighed a little over two pounds. Malone decided he'd better put it in his office safe before going on to his next suspect. Martine would just have to wait, he thought.

Somehow, he managed to get to the street with the green vase clutched firmly in his arms. He hailed a cab with difficulty, gave the driver directions to his office, and sat back in the leather seat. The vase was propped next to him.

Maybe I can put it on the shelf, Malone thought. Next to the rabbit. It might go nicely.

■   ■   ■

Back in his office, Malone admired the vase some more. It really was nice, he thought. It gave dignity to his office, right up there on the shelf. He could put it in the safe, but it was too pretty to be in a safe. And the cleaning woman wouldn't knock it over. He'd warn her about it.

On second thought, if he mentioned it she'd be self-conscious about it and knock it over trying to be extra-careful. He'd just have to let nature take its course.

Now, he told himself, for Martine.

It was at that point that he discovered he didn't know Martine's last name. He called a friendly night-club owner hurriedly.

"Girls named Martine?" the club-owner said. "Malone, they're all named Martine, or Sybil, or Fritzi. You find me a nice chorus girl named Bella, Malone, it'll be a big relief to me. Always Sybil or Martine or Fritzi. I mean it, Malone."

"You don't know a particular Martine who was friendly with Jabez McIlhenny?"

"None of them are particular, Malone. They're slobs. A bunch of slobs. I tell you, for one chorus girl named Bella—she doesn't even have to dance, I'll just keep her around the club to tell people about. Look, Malone . . ."

With difficulty, Malone sidestepped an invitation to a "friendly little party" after hours. He promised the owner: "I'll do the same for you some time," and hung up.

He could, of course, ask Von Flanagan. But somehow, he told himself, he didn't want to go to the police. They'd given him the case and he was going to solve it for them and show them. Vaguely, he wondered just what he was going to show them, but didn't get very far with the idea.

He remembered the servants. Paul Finn and Rose Billington. If he went to the McIlhenny home now, the servants would be there and he could talk to them, and find out Martine's last name from Miss McIlhenny at the same time. Maybe Miss McIlhenny's first name was Georgette. Georgette Georgina—er—Georgie McIlhenny. It had a nice ring to it, Malone thought.

The servants were having a romance, he remembered suddenly. That had sounded important, but it probably wasn't. He had the impression that he'd heard something that hadn't sounded important, but really had been. He tried to think of it, without success. Maybe, he told himself, it had been something he'd seen, and not something he'd heard at all.

When he found himself muttering: "Servants should be seen and not heard," he gave up. On the way out of the office he told Maggie:

"Put some flowers in the vase. And don't wait up for me. Just leave a light burning in the window."

"You take care of yourself, Malone," Maggie told him.

He thought of the crumbling McIlhenny mansion, and shivered. Then he told himself not to be silly.

And he wondered what was silly about being afraid of a house which almost certainly had ghosts—and one ghost, in particular, who'd just joined the crowd in the last two weeks or so.

• • •

The cabbie looked up at the stone steps winding up to the mansion. "Some rich place," he said.

"Some people think it's pretty," Malone said defensively.

"Me," said the cabbie, "I think it's haunted."

Malone paid him with trembling hands. "Everybody to his own opinion," he said. He started up the steps, feeling as if ominous organ music followed him at every turn. Far, far below him, he heard the cab clash its gears and speed away, and he felt very lonely.

He climbed grimly to the top of the steps and faced the old oaken door. There was a silver knocker projecting from its center. Malone reached out, pulled his hand back, told himself not to be silly, and knocked once, timidly.

After a minute he tried again, a little louder.

The door opened with a creak, and Malone paled. A cadaverous face looked out at him. The face had eyes that burned right through Malone, and bushy black eyebrows. The eyebrows raised, slowly.

"Yes?" the face said.

Malone said: "I'm here to see Miss McIlhenny." He congratulated himself on remaining so calm.

"Whom shall I say is calling?" said the face in sepulchural tones.

"Me," Malone said. "I."

"Your name?" said the face.

Malone gave it, hurriedly. The door banged shut again.

Many years passed before it opened again. Malone was sure that his hair was white, if he had any hair left at all. He passed an experimental hand over his scalp and felt, but he couldn't tell the color. He chewed on his cigar, nervously.

Finally the door swung slowly open, and a familiar face peered out. "Oh, Malone," the blonde said. "Come in. Paul didn't know—I didn't mention your name to him when I went out . . ." Malone entered.

"That was Paul Finn," Malone said in the hall. "The—man who opened the door." He was beginning to feel better. The blonde had offered to mix him a drink, and he lit a fresh cigar. He really hadn't been afraid at all, he told himself. All that was just silliness.

"Of course," she said. "A friend of yours is here."

"Really?" Malone said.

"A policeman. I told him there was no need for him to do anything at all, now that you've agreed to take over, but he insisted on being here when you arrived. He said he wanted to ask you some questions."

Malone felt a cold knot in his stomach. "Von Flanagan," he said.

"He said that was his name, Malone. He's waiting in the living room. Come on, and you'll have that drink, and we can talk." She paused. "Have you found out anything yet?"

"I've found out your uncle had an enemy," Malone said savagely. He thought of Von Flanagan, and Eve Washington, and his ship tickets, and wondered why he had ever let himself get involved in the case.

"Who was his enemy, Malone?" the blonde said anxiously.

"Me," the lawyer snapped, and marched past her into the living room.

■　■　■

The blonde (Georgina? Malone thought. Gertrude? Gwendolyn?) went off to see about the drinks, and Malone and the police captain were left alone.

"It's murder, you know, Malone," Von Flanagan said.

"I thought it was," Malone said. "Two weeks is a long time."

"He didn't have any motive to disappear. Everything was going fine for him, just the usual way. Only he didn't have any enemies."

"That's what I found out," Malone said.

"Every rich man has enemies," Von Flanagan said sagely. "Even I have enemies, and what have I got?"

"Enemies," Malone suggested.

"I mean money. If I have enemies, Jabez McIlhenny had enemies. Somebody killed him, after all."

"Maybe it was an accident," Malone said. "Maybe he walked into the path of a car."

"We've checked every hospital and morgue record for the last two weeks," Von Flanagan said sourly. "Somebody managed to dispose of his body perfectly. That was no accident."

"Maybe jumped in the river."

"In this weather?" Von Flanagan said. "It's cold out. He'd have to be crazy—and he wasn't any crazier than usual."

"How do you know?"

"Questioning the niece," Von Flanagan said. "Unless she knocked off the old man . . . she could lie about it, I suppose, just to make things tough for me."

Miss McIlhenny returned with the drinks, and there were several minutes of meaningless conversation before Von Flanagan said: "Look, Miss, I'd like to talk to Malone privately. Can we . . ."

"Of course," she said. "You stay right there. I've got work to do in the kitchen, anyhow."

When she was gone, Malone said: "What motive would she have for killing her uncle?"

"That's what I can't figure out," Von Flanagan admitted. "The old guy left his money to an animal home. He never had any pets, and he felt guilty about it. He left a couple of thousand apiece to the servants, but nothing at all to his niece except a fund that would bring her about ten grand a year. She was getting more than that when he was alive."

"Maybe he threatened to stop giving her any money," Malone said.

"I talked to the servants myself," Von Flanagan said. "They didn't hear anything like that. Everything was peaceful."

Malone said: "She didn't do it. She's my client."

"Now, Malone . . ."

"I know she didn't. I don't know why I know, but I know. Does that make sense?"

"No," Von Flanagan said. "And you couldn't take it into court."

"She mentioned a chorus girl named Martine," Malone said.

"Martine Vignette," Von Flanagan said. "That's her name. We talked to her. It seems she and old McIlhenny were just good friends. Sure. She's got kind of a temper, Malone. Maybe she got mad one night and bashed his head in."

"And made him disappear like a ghost," Malone suggested. "You searched her home, and the night club she works at, didn't you?"

"Sure we did," the police captain said bitterly. "People just go out of their way to make things tough for me, Malone. I never wanted to be a cop . . ."

Malone sat back, closed his eyes and waited until Von Flanagan was finished with his complaint. Then he said: "How about somebody else?"

"There isn't anybody else," Von Flanagan said. "Some crazy sculptor, this Martine Vignette, and the niece herself."

"Von Flanagan," Malone said. "What's her name?"

"The niece?"

"That's right."

"McIlhenny," Von Flanagan said.

"I mean her first name."

A blank look passed over the police captain's face. "You know," he said, "I never asked."

"Neither did I," Malone said.

"I only waited for you, Malone, because I wanted to talk to you before we pulled the niece in. Just in case. Not that I think you have anything . . . I mean, you can't go up against the Chicago police force . . . but . . ."

"Wait a minute, Von Flanagan."

"I called your office and that girl of yours said you were on your way down here. Malone, can you think of one reason why we shouldn't take her in?"

"She didn't do it," Malone said. "I saw something—or heard something—"

"What, Malone?"

"I don't know," the little lawyer admitted. He sighed deeply. "I'll find out, though, sooner or later."

"I can't sit on my hands forever," Von Flanagan said. "The Commissioner . . ."

"Give me an hour," Malone said. "Just one hour."

"Malone, it's illegal . . ."

"One hour, Von Flanagan, or I'll . . . tell your wife about that poker game."

"One hour," the officer said sadly. "Malone, I don't like this any more than you do. The Commissioner's niece by marriage . . ."

"Don't worry, Von Flanagan," Malone said grandly. "I'll get you out of the fix."

The police captain's voice turned a violent purple. "Look here, Malone . . ."

"One hour," Malone said. "You promised."

■   ■   ■

Rose Billington's story was a simple one. Malone looked at her long, sad, horselike face and thought what a perfect match she and the cadaverous Paul Finn would make. They looked like two Charles Addams creations, he thought. He cocked a sympathetic ear.

"I told the story already three times, to the police. Now you want me to tell it all over again. I wasn't even here, me and Paul went out. We went to the movies. I told the police already three times what we saw."

"Did you notice anything unusual when you left the house?"

"It was just like always," Rose said. "Old Mr. McIlhenny, he was dressing up to go out, but he didn't say where, so don't ask me."

"I won't," Malone said.

"Miss McIlhenny, she was sleeping, like sometimes she sleeps late. Me and Paul, we went to a movie. You want to know what we saw?"

"No," Malone said, "that won't be necessary." He wished he had another drink. "Mr. McIlhenny's will leaves you each a little money. Enough to get married on."

"Oh, we don't want to get married," Rose said.

"You don't?"

"Paul, he's married already, so we don't want to break the law or anything. He married some woman in New York, and he can't get a divorce or anything because that would make her feel he didn't want her anymore and that's bad for you, Paul says. He reads psychology."

"Doesn't she . . . doesn't she feel he doesn't want her anymore now that he's in Chicago?"

"That's different, Paul says. He reads a lot. So we just go out like to the movies. I could tell you all about the movie, what we saw."

Malone felt his head whirling rapidly. "I don't need to know," he said. "As a matter of fact, I don't want to know. It would spoil things."

"It was a pretty good movie," Rose said.

"I'm sure," Malone said.

• • •

Paul's story backed up the maid's. "We went to see a film," was the way he put it. Malone refrained from asking about the first Mrs. Finn. There was no sense in complicating things any further.

That left only Martine Vignette. But Von Flanagan had searched for McIlhenny's body and found nothing at all. You could trust Von Flanagan to conduct a search like that, Malone thought.

All the same, G. G. G. McIlhenny hadn't committed any murders.

But if she hadn't, who had?

Or had her uncle Jabez just gotten tired and gone away, the way Eve Washington had suggested?

That didn't sound right, either.

The whole thing was a mess, Malone thought.

A mess.

Suddenly his head came up and he marched to the living room. Von Flanagan was sitting in an overstuffed chair, looking uncomfortable.

"I'll be right back," Malone said. "Don't go away."

"Where are you going?" the police captain asked.

Malone chewed on his cigar with satisfaction. "To bring you back a killer," he said. "Now don't go away."

"Malone . . ." Von Flanagan began, but the little lawyer was out of the front door and running down the steps as if he didn't even care about breaking his neck.

Von Flanagan sighed and settled back in the chair.

• • •

"All right," the killer said, a half-hour later in Von Flanagan's office. "I did it. He deserved to die!"

Gadenski took the murderer away. Von Flanagan tipped his feet up on the desk and said to Malone: "I was sure it was the niece."

"It had to be somebody else," Malone said. "If she'd killed her uncle, she wouldn't have come to me to find him. I've got a reputation, after all."

"But why . . ."

"Well, I found this note in her couch, slipped under the cushions. Probably fell there by accident. The trouble with Eve Washington was, she never cleaned house."

"You didn't know about the note when you went there."

"No, but it gives you a motive," Malone said. "It's from McIlhenny, and it tells her he's not going to marry her. It seems they were a little more than good friends after all—and when he came over to tell her in person she blew up and hit him with whatever was handy. That studio of hers has lots of things to hit a man with."

"But . . ." Von Flanagan shook his head.

"The cigar butt in the ashtray," Malone said. "I saw it there the first time I came to her house. And she said nobody but McIlhenny ever came to her studio. I didn't think she would smoke cigars. So, she must have been lying. If she'd ever cleaned up that studio of hers, she might have been safe forever."

"They always slip up somewhere," Von Flanagan said gravely. "But how did she dispose of—how'd she get rid of him?"

Malone lit a fresh cigar and blew a cloud of smoke. "She's confessed, and I'm not going to take her case, because I'm going to Havana," he said. "So you don't need to know how she got rid of Jabez McIlhenny, and that'll just be our little secret."

"Malone!"

"I've got good reasons," the little lawyer said.

"I'd think you could trust me by this time. After I've solved a case for you."

"You solved it?" Von Flanagan said. "She confessed here. Right in this office."

"Listen, Von Flanagan," Malone said. "One more word out of you, and I—I won't even send you a card from Havana."

"You listen to me, Malone," the officer began, but the little lawyer was gone.

■   ■   ■

At the bank, he cashed G. G. G. McIlhenny's check. "Incidentally," he asked a teller, "what do the initials stand for?"

"You mean you don't know?" the teller said.

"That's right," Malone said.

"You ask her," the teller said. "She gave you a check, you must know her."

Malone hunted up a phone booth and put in a call.

"Oh, you darling man, I knew you could solve it . . ." the blonde cooed at him from the other end of the wire.

Malone decided that too much was, very definitely, even more than enough. "Your uncle's dead," he said sternly.

"Oh, Malone, I can't even think of Uncle Jabez now that I know you're so handsome and clever . . ."

Malone muttered something impolite. "Miss McIlhenny, I have a question to ask you."

"Oh," she said. "Oh. The answer is—yes, Malone. Yes."

"The question," he said grimly, "is: what do the initials stand for?"

There was a long silence on the other end of the wire. "My friends call me G-G," she said. "Like the French name."

Malone waited.

"Well," she said, "father and mother both wanted a boy, but they were resigned to God's will. So when I arrived I was christened God Giveth Girls. God Giveth Girls McIlhenny."

"Oh," said Malone. Very slowly, he hung up. Then he picked up the receiver again and dialed his office.

Maggie answered at once. "Malone, there's a man here with a bill for the telephone, and . . ."

"I'll be there in the morning," Malone said. "I'll pay everything before I leave. Oh, and Maggie . . ."

He thought for a second of the square humming box in Eve Washington's studio, and of the kiln that could heat up to three thousand degrees. It could reduce a body to nothing but ash, and you could mix the ash with clay and never worry that anyone would find traces of the man you'd killed . . .

"Yes, Malone?" Maggie said.

"Don't forget to put some fresh flowers in Mr. McIlhenny before you leave."

He hung up. After all, he told himself consolingly, it was a *very* pretty vase . . .

John Jakes

GUILT

From *Hunted,* October 1955

John Jakes spent a lot of years writing excellent crime, science-fiction, and historical novels that not a whole lot of people read. But the people who did read them loved them. Jakes spent his early years writing for the last of the pulps. He learned his craft very, very well. Consequently he was ready when a book packager offered him a chance to write longer books that a whole lot of people would be inclined to read. Jakes did so well with the books—bringing historical novels about America back into vogue again—that the public bestowed upon him the title bestseller. He hasn't stopped writing bestsellers since 1975. Here's a short, snappy Jakes with a serpent swimming just below the surface of the dark water.

E. G.

DEAR LARRY:

Now that it's all over for me—well, even though I'm still here to write this, I know it's all over because tomorrow night's the night—I wanted to sit down and write you and say I'm sorry. A lot of good that does, I know, but I can't help writing this any more than the doctor tells me I could help what I did to your wife, because I hated you.

That's right, I've been talking to the doctor a lot lately. Every afternoon from two to two-forty-five. The doctor is a pretty nice guy. He smokes a pipe and looks like one of those college professors, but he does not try to act smart. I've told him a lot about the past, and he's explained it to me in a way that makes pretty good sense. I guess you probably understand too. Seems like I'm the only one who didn't, but I think I do now. Maybe it would be a lot better if they put me into the electric chair. I could forget sort of automatically. But tomorrow night they're going to take me to that place downstate. The doctor says that in time I may be well enough to be released, but I've heard some talk about the place and it sounds pretty nice. They have a wood shop, and I'll probably stay in the place the rest of my life. Somehow I don't

expect I'll live much longer. I'm not sick, physically. But tomorrow night I'm just going to forget everything, that's all, as well as
I can. My life will be over. I want it that way, Larry, because I'm
pretty tired.

If I had thought ten years ago I would go that far, and do what
I did, I would have thought I was crazy. (Excuse rambling—it's
just coming out the way I think it. Also excuse the bad writing,
but you know I never had a very good hand.) As I say, ten years
ago, you didn't know Beth, and I didn't either. Then when you
came home from the service, and she came with you as your new
wife, I began to get the idea. She was a beautiful girl, Larry. I
can still remember that October day you two drove up County
Street to the house, her blonde hair blowing out behind and the
sun flashing on the fenders of your new Pontiac. When you
opened the door on your side and ran around to help her out on
her side, I could tell from the way you looked at her that she was
the one thing in your life you'd really wanted and gotten. I could
tell she was happy, too, by the way she tugged your arm.

She was always nice to me. So you see I didn't hate her. I hated
you. And not just because you had a girl, but because she was—I
guess they call it a symbol—of what it took to make you really
happy. I know you didn't want to come over and eat dinner with
me too often, because maybe then you knew, deep down, how I
felt, but you came anyway, and each time the three of us sat
eating my pizza or fried onion rings or whatever, I hated you more
because I saw how happy you were together.

It wasn't sex, Larry. Believe me it wasn't. I know she was beautiful, and had that incredible figure, and the newspapers made
something pretty dirty out of it. I know I did it, but it wasn't just
because I wanted her. It was because she made you so happy. If
I'd just wanted a girl, I could have gone out on the street and
followed some flippety teen-ager home some night, and done the
same thing to her.

Then, last Christmas Eve, when you two came over and
brought me that cigarette lighter and told me about the baby on
the way, it got worse. Christmas Day you went to Beth's folks in
Molene and I sat home, just watching television. I sat there in
the dark, with the blinds down, and once in a while laughing
people crunched by in the snow outside, and the Willets next
door had all their relatives in for dinner. I thought of how happy

you probably were in Molene, eating dinner with her family, while
I didn't have anybody to keep me company. Her face had shone
on Christmas Eve, and so had yours. You were happier than you
had ever been, that night, and it made me hate you all the worse.

Still, I only saw Beth every other week or so, and that way, I
didn't keep feeling my hate all the time. I mean, the cause wasn't
always there, where I could see it. When I didn't see you both, I
didn't feel it so hard. So maybe it never would have happened at
all if you hadn't asked me to build your new house for you. I
imagine it's going to be pretty lonely for you now, and I'm sorry
about that too. But you knew I was the best contractor in Lake
County, and I guess it was only natural for you to ask me. When
you did, that day over lunch, I had a sudden feeling: 'I wish he
hadn't asked me.' But I knew I'd do it, because right then, the
idea was beginning to form, although it was still pretty vague.

When spring came, and we started work on the place, I saw
you and Beth more often. You remember how you came out to
see how work was progressing, almost every evening, and the more
I saw Beth, and how happy you were over the idea of the new
house and the new baby in it, the worse it got for me.

You know, Larry, that I've never really had the chance to tell
you what happened that Tuesday night. I've told the doctor how
I felt, but all the court heard were the dirty facts, and—I don't
know how to say it to make you believe it—it wasn't that way at
all, not at first. When we were in court you never would talk to
me, or even look at me, and I guess I don't blame you. But I have
to try to make you understand how it happened. I didn't want to
hurt Beth. Now I've got to be careful how I say this, because I
know what I planned at first was bad, but you've still got to
understand how I felt. I was going to kill her. But quickly, and
cleanly. So she wouldn't feel any pain. I wanted to hurt *you*.

The hate built up in me, each night you came to look at the
house, and when the house was finished and you moved in, I
couldn't stand it any longer. Your business trip to Indianapolis
gave me the opportunity. I knew you'd be out of town that Tuesday night. I drove out to the subdivision and parked about a block
from the house. With the subdivision on the edge of town, and
the houses pretty far apart, I had it easy. I'd been out at Hank's
drinking whisky, if I remember, from around six-thirty or so until

nine-thirty, and I drove to the spot near the house around a quarter of ten.

I crept across the ravine, the back way, and sneaked around the side of the house. My head was going around, and I had a choking feeling in my throat. I could only see in a crack through the venetian blinds, but I saw Beth sitting in front of the TV, and you know she didn't have on—well, only underthings. Something crazy started thittering in my head. It was a damp night, and I had a slicker on, and the tire iron under it, the one I dropped right then on the new-seeded lawn, the one they found. It all seems fuzzy and far away now, because I feel empty and all burned out. Suddenly I saw another way to hurt you, even worse than killing Beth clean.

I went around to the back again and knocked on the door. There were no lights on in the nearest house. Beth came to the door in a green wrapper. She seemed glad to see me. "Why, hello!" she said. I could smell beer on her breath. "Larry's not home." She laughed. "But of course you knew that. Come on in." I went in. She wanted to get me a beer, but I said no. She turned from the icebox and kind of looked at me funny, as if she was thinking, Well, what did he come for?

She looked at me hard, and I think she knew. She put one hand up to her mouth. I don't remember what I said, though I guess it was pretty terrible. She started to scream, and I put my hands around her throat and held on. She kicked me, but I'm pretty strong. I pushed her into the hall and into the bedroom. Believe me, Larry, I didn't even think of how beautiful she was while I—you know. All I was doing was hurting you. She whimpered for a while, but I kept one hand over her mouth. Then, when I was through with her, I looked at her eyes and I knew she was dead.

I got sick. You'll never know how sick. Then I sat down and cried. Oh, I know you won't believe all this. You think I'm crazy and I suppose maybe I am, or I'd be electrocuted instead of sent downstate. But you know what I did after that. I called up Sam Firebaugh at the police station and told him what I'd done. I was blubbering like a baby.

I guess there was no avoiding it, Larry. I can say I'm sorry a million times and it won't do any good. Now, I wish it would.

Before, I didn't care. I guess it had to come spilling out some time. I tried to hurt you before. I criticized your playing on the high school football team, when you were good, to make you feel bad. The senior prom, when you wanted to borrow my car, and I said you could, and then called up to tell you I had a flat tire and couldn't get into town in time. You were counting on the car to make an impression, I know. I didn't really have a flat. I was out drinking at Hank's that whole evening. All the extra money you asked for, that you needed, when you were at Champaign—I said I didn't have it but I really did. I could tell you a hundred more examples, but you'd only hate me more. Now, I wouldn't blame you.

Martha was the most beautiful woman in the world, to me, and when the doctor saved your life instead of hers, I never forgave you. Now, I guess I can. It doesn't do anybody much good, though. I'm sorry I've hated you, but that doesn't help either. All of a sudden this letter looks pretty lame. I guess I can't change things. Well—

I know you'll never come to see me downstate, but I hope someday you can forgive me a little. Goodbye, Larry.

Sincerely,
Dad

Gil Brewer

BOTHERED

From *Manhunt,* July 1957

With the help of former Black Mask *editor Joseph T. Shaw, Gil Brewer
sold his first short story in 1949 and his first novel in 1950.* 13 French
Street *was a million-copy bestseller in 1951, and throughout the '50s his
noir crime tales for Gold Medal, Avon, and other paperback houses were
consistently successful. His strongest work,* A Killer Is Loose *(1954), is a
truly harrowing portrait of a psychopath which comes close to rivaling the
nightmare visions of Jim Thompson; it was filmed in France. During that
highly prolific decade Brewer also contributed scores of short stories to a
wide range of digest-size mystery magazines and men's magazines, of which
"Bothered"—one of his ten* Manhunt *tales—is a typically dark example.*
B. P.

FOR A TIME HE KNELT ON THE RED HASSOCK BEHIND THE TALL
glassed windows of the sun porch, looking across the bright afternoon into Mrs. Welch's back yard. Mrs. Welch was out there,
snipping at the branches of a plum tree. She called it "pruning,"
but Kenneth could never understand why a person would prune
a plum tree. You certainly wouldn't plum a prune tree.

"Kenny?" his mother called from the kitchen.

He had never even seen prunes except in those red boxes with
the pretty-eyed girl painted on them.

"Kenneth? Didn't you hear me?"

"Yuh."

Watching the window, he stuffed into his pocket a small note-
book and pencil stub he'd been holding. Just then Mrs. Welch,
across the yards, turned her bitter-mouthed face and stared directly at the sun porch. He knew she couldn't see him, but something inside his chest curdled with a wild, trapped feeling.

His mother appeared suddenly behind him, wiping her hands
on a red- and white-striped hand towel. She looked somewhat
harried, and whatever sensitivity the shape of her mouth revealed,
was negated by the despotic steadiness of her chilly blue eyes.

"Why don't you run along and play?"

He shrugged off the hassock, started out past his mother; lean, tow-headed, in skinny dungarees and a clean T-shirt.

"Kenny," his mother said, touching his shoulder. "It's high time you answered when spoken to. You're ten years old now. The rest of the kids are over in the lot, playing ball. Why aren't you with them?"

"Don't want to play ball."

"Why not run out into the yard, then?" She gave an exasperated sigh. "Is *something* the matter?"

"It's that Welch," he said, whirling to point through the sun-razed windows. "She's after me."

His mother *tsked* faintly, and shook her head.

"She hates me," Kenneth said. "Watches me all the time."

"Well, don't pay any attention to her. She *likes* you, Kenny. I'll admit, she is a little *abrupt*—but she's alone so much. Her husband away with his trucks, and all."

He marched swiftly off through the house.

"You get outside in that sun, Kenny."

The side screen door slammed behind him, as he stepped into the garage areaway. Lately he had spent a lot of time going over the countless things Mrs. Welch had done to him. Calling him "Babyface", the first time she saw him, and all the rest, till everything loomed monstrous. The very thought of her made him clench his eyes.

He heard his mother in the kitchen, and drifted along the side of the garage to the rose trellis, where he leaned in the brambled shadows, craning his head toward the Welch rear yard.

It was getting so he hated week-ends. Friday afternoons, the long Saturdays that once had been filled to brimming with a kind of blazing splendor, and the slow Sundays after church and dinner, when everybody sat around—these had been *his* days. No school. Freedom. Only not anymore—not with *her* over there.

"You snot-nosed little brat, don't look at me that way!" she'd said. "You trampled my flowers!" Her face like on TV in one of those murder programs, young and pretty and golden-haired, red-mouthed and mean. *"Your father ought to give you a good whipping. You think I don't know who wrote all over my car with soap last Halloween? Think I don't know who dumped that garbage can*

on my porch? It was you—you little sneak! If I had you, I know what I'd do!"

Leaning against the side of the garage, he jammed his hands against his ears, making noises in his throat. He hadn't been able to tell anybody. Somehow he couldn't get it out past his lips. Nobody would believe him. If he told his mother, or father, that he hadn't done any of those things, they would believe *her*.

"Ken?"

He looked up. From the open window of the house next door, a boy of his own age watched. It was Jimmy Decks.

Kenneth said nothing.

"What you doing?" Jimmy asked.

"Nothing."

"I got to stay in."

"How come?"

"I carved the dining room table."

"Oh."

"She says I got to stay in all day."

Kenneth's mind wasn't on Jimmy's troubles. He flapped his hand, and stepped around to the back of the garage.

"Why don't you come on over?" Jimmy called.

Kenneth didn't answer, peering through a snow-ball bush over toward Mrs. Welch in her back yard. A red handkerchief hooded her hair, and she wore black shorts, and a white apron.

"Hey, Ken!"

Kenneth made a wry face, and hunched down by the snow-ball bush, watching Mrs. Welch. He wished Jimmy would shut up. He glanced further up, toward Mrs. Willowtrot's greenly hedged yard, then over at Mrs. O'Donnell's bird houses in the apple tree. Then he turned back to Mrs. Welch.

There was only the short expanse of the yard separating him from the woman across the way. She knelt down and began pulling weeds in a small flower bed.

"I see you," she said quietly, not even looking toward him, pulling the weeds. "Think I don't know you're watching, you dirty little sneak? I think I'll tell your mother."

He did not move. Neither did she, except to continue pulling weeds. He watched her, watching her through a kind of haze now, because this had gone on for as long as he could remember, and he knew he couldn't stand it anymore. Weeks, it had gone on. Months. He couldn't explain it to anybody. They'd believe her, and so he was trapped, only he had to do something.

"When my husband gets home today," she said. "I'm going to have *him* do something about you."

Kenneth recalled how her husband was as bad as she was, and the one reason he'd been able to bear up as long as he had was because Mr. Welch was away most of the time.

She nodded her head above the flowers, pulling weeds, not looking toward him, smiling to herself. "I've got it all worked out." She lowered her voice. "A secret plan. Just what to do with you. He'll fix you good." She kept on nodding to herself, and Kenneth listened to her speaking in the warm sunlight, and he couldn't have said anything if he'd wanted to. He couldn't move. He could hardly breathe. "That's right," she said. "I know just what to do about you." She turned and looked squarely at him, speaking softly. "In the middle of the night," she said. "When it's all dark outside, when you're asleep in your bed. When it's real dark, with no moon. We'll get you."

The warm yellow sunlight filtered through the air, and somewhere a bird sang once above the silence.

"Won't do any good to tell your mother," she said softly, staring at the snow-ball bush behind which Kenneth crouched. "She won't believe anything you say, you sneaky little brat."

They watched each other that way. Then she picked up the pruning shears, and started snipping at the dead stalks of flowers, clearing the bed.

"We'll get you," she said. "Some time when you're home at night, all alone. We'll get you."

He stood up slowly and walked across to the edge of his yard, watching her. She did not rise, snipping and snipping. He stood there, watching her. She laid the pruning shears down, and grubbed in the dirt, loosening roots.

"In the dark," she said. "When you're asleep."

"No," Kenneth said.

"Oh, yes."

"No," Kenneth said.

"You'll never even know," she said, very softly. "Just the sound of something there in the dark, behind you."

"No," Kenneth said.

His face was very pale, his eyes like glass, and all around inside him was a painful void. He stepped across onto Mrs. Welch's lawn and picked up the pruning shears.

"You get back over there."

He looked at her.

"Didn't you hear me?"

She was still kneeling, her face turned up to him, the apron stretched taut between her bare thighs. She was breathing hard, and she was mad.

He started walking toward her house.

She stood up and came after him.

"Give me those shears—you thieving little monster!"

"No."

He ran around the back of the house and down the sidewalk. He stopped, then suddenly grabbed at the screen door, swung it open, and dodged into the cellar entranceway. Steep stairs led up into the kitchen. He scrambled up there, just as Mrs. Welch came inside.

The screen door slammed, spring shrieking.

"You give me those shears! This is the last! Damn you, you—!"

She cursed and ran violently up the stairs at him. He turned and scurried through the house, sliding on unfamiliar throw rugs across polished floors, smelling unfamiliar smells, bumping unfamiliar furnishings, his heart thickly yammering, and the trapped feeling big now, really big.

What was he doing here?

He halted, panting, on the edge of two broad steps leading down into a rattan-furnished sunken porch, where a radio softly played.

"I'll call the cops," Mrs. Welch snapped. She stood there, drawing long breaths, then ran at him, grabbing for the shears.

Kenneth jumped aside.

"Brat!" Mrs. Welch said. She slipped flying past Kenneth, and sprawled with a rattling thump onto the porch floor.

Suddenly he knew she would scream. He knew she mustn't scream. He had to stop her from screaming, so he could get out of here. Her mouth was open, her eyes wide, all ready to yell, as he leaped on her and smashed at her mouth with the shears.

The sharp steel-bright blades ripped into her face, her mouth, her throat. Panting, he drove the shears into her with a sudden savage elation.

"No more," he gasped. "No, you won't. Lied!"

She bubbled something redly.

"Trying to scare me," he sobbed, jabbing. "I ain't scared of you—of nobody!"

Finally she ceased. She did not move at all. She just lay there on the floor, with the curtain puffing a little at the window, and the radio softly playing distant music.

He heard the sound of a truck in the driveway. He dropped the shears, scrambled up the two steps, and ran to a window. Mr. Welch was climbing from the truck.

Kenneth turned wildly. He ran out onto the porch again, nearly stepping in it, and heard Mr. Welch at the front door. He climbed over the sill of the open window and let himself down into the crisping flower beds, crouching.

The man had entered the house. He lumbered down the hall, through the living room.

"Honey? Hey—where the hell you at?"

Then he saw her.

Mr. Welch ran to his wife, kneeling, and said, "God—what?" He swept her into his arms, blood and all, rocking back and forth. "God," he said. He clutched up the pruning shears.

Kenneth ran across the yards. Jimmy Decks and his mother were beside the garage.

"Mom let me come out after all," Jimmy said.

"What's the matter, Kenneth?" his mother said.

"Welch," Kenneth said, gasping. "He killed her. Killed his wife—over there. I seen him do it."

He turned his face away. His mother would think he was turning so she wouldn't see him crying, but Kenneth wasn't crying. He was smiling, a wonderful secret smile.

He'd done it, he told himself. He'd thought about fixing that Mrs. Welch and her husband, lots of times, but he'd never known for sure if he had the courage to go through with it. Now it was over, and the police would believe Kenneth. They'd take Mr. Welch away. Imagine the way she tried to frighten me, Kenneth told himself. Nothing can frighten me. I fixed them good.

And now he knew what would happen next, too. The next one

would be that Mrs. O'Donnell down the block. She'd slapped him in the face once, for writing with chalk on her sidewalk.

But Kenneth knew just how to fix her, now, just how to fix them all . . .

Herbert D. Kastle

GAME

From *Ed McBain's Mystery Book #3*, 1961

A prolific writer of both novels and short stories, Herbert D. Kastle devised mysteries, dark suspense, Westerns, science-fiction, and mainstream fiction with equal aplomb. His crime novels include the paperback originals Countdown to Murder *and* Hot Prowl *and the psychothriller* Cross-Country. *"Game," which was originally published in the regrettably short-lived* Ed McBain's Mystery Book *in 1960, may well be the best of his shorter works—a truly harrowing chiller that lingers in the memory long after reading.*

B. P.

ED GAINES WAS A MAN IN HIS THIRTIES, TALL AND SLIM, WHO had lost the excitement, the drive, the verve of life during the past ten years. Working in Margaret's father's shoe store had done it; living with Margaret herself had done it. So he was running, fleeing down the two-lane highway which stretched over the Texas Big Bend country like a dark ribbon.

He'd left the Fort Worth store at one, saying he had an appointment at the doctor's after lunch. That would hold his father-in-law. And the call he'd made at 5 P.M. from the gas station on the highway would hold Margaret. "I've run into an old friend, dear . . ."

Now it was almost nine and he'd penetrated deep into the near-desert. His lights tunneled a path through the blackness; a path which could end in Mexico, Argentina, Brazil—he had enough money to go anywhere, to start fresh when he got there. Eight thousand seven hundred dollars: his life's savings; Margaret's, too, for that matter. He had emptied their joint bank account at one thirty this afternoon. He had taken it in cash, and put it in the money belt fastened around his waist under his clothing. Now he was driving toward the Rio Grande, about three hours away. Now he was heading for a renewal of brightness and youth. Or so he hoped, and the hope was strong enough to keep him smiling and humming.

Until shortly after the gaudy Cadillac hard-top passed his Lark sedan, passed it so quickly that he failed to catch even a glimpse of the occupants. It shot ahead some hundred feet, slowed, and stayed there, matching his own sixty to seventy miles per hour. Together they streaked along the smooth, straight road, through the cloudy-night darkness, deeper into arid country.

Five minutes later, the Cadillac swerved far to the left, across the white line and into the opposite lane of the two-lane road, to smash a jack rabbit that was attracted by its lights.

Ed Gaines was immediately sickened. He'd lived in Texas all his life; he'd traveled its roads and knew the habits of the jack rabbit and had no particular love for the stupid creature which often ran mothlike into the lights of the night-traveling autos. But he'd never met anyone who *deliberately* ran them down. What was more to the point, he had never been so captive an audience to the results—his eyes and senses were offended by the red-and-brown splotch streaming on the night-cool pavement. And within the next sixty seconds, the driver of the Cadillac swung even farther to the left to destroy a second rabbit. And again the bloody mess came under Ed's headlights.

He turned on the radio, made himself hum, made himself go back to planning the good life. A store of his own. A beautiful woman to arouse and satisfy passion. Leisure time . . .

Twenty minutes later, the road bulged around a huge malpais rock formation, then straightened. During that brief turn, Ed glimpsed the interior of the car before him—a split-second view of two shadowy shapes in the front seat.

He wondered what it was like to be traveling with the kind of man who enjoyed smashing out life at seventy miles per hour. He wondered if the second shadow was a wife, and felt quick pity.

They approached a gas station, small, dark, dead, with a dim light showing from behind drawn shades on the second floor. Someone lived up there; and someone's dog ran out barking to meet the Cadillac. Ed never did see what sort of dog it was, only that it was small. And while it was a foolish mutt to chase after cars, it wasn't quite so foolish as to cross in front of the hurtling vehicles. But the driver of the Cadillac swung hard right as soon as the dog appeared. The dog tried to reverse field, but the Cadillac plunged off the road, churning up hard-packed sand and scrub grass, hunting it down. The dog was sent spinning up and over the hard-top's roof to land in a mangled, intestine-smeared clot near the pavement.

Ed shouted and pounded his horn and pressed his gas pedal to the floor boards, raging to catch the Cadillac and do something to the man who was driving. But the Cadillac swung back onto the road and shot out ahead, picking up speed much faster than the six-cylinder Lark could. And continued to streak away at what must have been close to a hundred miles an hour, its taillights dwindling rapidly in the darkness, until Ed was again alone on the road to Mexico—except for a bloody little clump some five miles farther on.

It was a few minutes to ten when he pulled off the road onto the black-top of the Green Circle Tavern, which maintained a dozen cabins in addition to its wine-and-dine facilities. He turned left to park within white guide lines, radiator first against a low wire fence. Walking back toward the road and the entrance to the tavern, he counted four other cars beside his own. The last one made him stop. It was the Cadillac hard-top.

The Green Circle's taproom held three separate couples at three separate tables. Ed Gaines walked to the bar, took a stool and glanced into the long mirror. To his right, near the door and just visible past the barrier of his own reflection, were two middle-aged women chatting over the remains of a meal. To his left was the greater part of the room, and the other two couples. The one nearest him—just a few feet away—immediately claimed his attention. The man was big and heavy and graying, but it was his face that made Ed feel a swift return of the rage he'd experienced on the road. He quickly cautioned himself about judging people by their looks, and moved his eyes to the woman. She created another quick surge of emotion. She was slender, yet fully fleshed; small-boned and curved and catlike; a dark, sleek girl with wide-set eyes. And those eyes rose, as if in response to his and searched his face in the mirror. They looked at each other a moment, and in that moment, Ed knew she was full of sickness, full of despair. As if to point to the reason for this despair, her glance flicked to the man beside her. The man laughed, and said quite distinctly, "Would you like *him* for your Prince Charming, Cecily?" She paled, picked up a cocktail glass and drank. The man laughed and drew on a cigarette and looked at Ed in the mirror. Ed's first impulse was to drop his eyes, but he controlled it. He stared back at the thick-faced, hard-faced, cruel-faced man. And something made him move his eyes slowly, deliberately, to the lovely woman and smile at her. The man laughed again.

Ed examined the last couple—youngsters; honeymooners, probably; wrapped up in each other. He made himself consider the possibility that they, or the middle-aged women now rising from their table, were the occupants of the Cadillac. Or a person or persons not present. But then he returned his eyes to Cecily, and she was again looking at him, and her sickness, her *hatred* of the man beside her, again came through. And the soft, thick laughter again sounded, and the deep, taunting voice said, "He's definitely the Prince Charming type, Cecily."

Ed turned and looked at the lovely girl. "You and your friend driving to Mexico?"

The man laughed. "I told you, Cecily." He nodded at Ed. "We are. Or we were. But we've had a few discussions, my lovely wife and myself, and we're undecided now."

The bartender finally made his appearance. Ed ordered beer and a ham sandwich. His heart was pounding wildly, and he wondered why he was doing this. And said, "That your Cadillac in the parking lot?"

Cecily's eyes remained on the table; her face remained deathly pale. Her husband looked surprised. "That's right." Then his smile grew and a note of vindictive delight entered his voice. "You're the one we passed, aren't you? You're the one who blew his horn." He slapped his hands on the table. "He's the one, Cecily. I tell you—"

She jumped up, whispering, "Let me go, Carl! *Let me go!*" She stopped then. The young couple was staring.

Ed's mouth was dry, but he said, "My name's Ed Gaines. Mind if I join you?"

Cecily looked at him. There was surprise in her face, which was quickly replaced by a childish surge of pure hope.

"By all means," her husband said, and he was shaking his head and laughing heavily, consistently.

Ed walked to their table. As he sat down, one clear thought emerged. *This girl was the beauty and passion he'd wanted all his life!*

Cecily was still standing. Ed examined her, openly, not hiding a thing from the heavy-set man. She wore a simple, tight sheath; pale-blue, sleeveless, perfect because her body was perfect. He smiled at her. She sat down.

The bartender came with his beer and sandwich. He raised his glass, and cleared his throat. "It might help to tell me what the trouble's all about."

Carl lighted a fresh cigarette. His voice was heavy with sarcasm. "Why certainly, Ed. Cecily wants me to give her a divorce. She wants to get away from me as soon as possible—tonight; tomorrow morning; just as soon as she can." He smiled, his hard face genuinely amused. "But I won't allow it. I like having her."

"Having me," Cecily whispered.

Carl nodded, looking at her. "I spent thousands feeding, clothing and entertaining you. That proves I like having you, doesn't it?"

Her face flamed.

Ed sipped his beer. He looked at that wide, cruel face, at the smirking lips, at the amused but cold eyes, and felt a sudden chill. Dogs and rabbits weren't the only things that man could kill. Yet he said, "Are you sure you want to leave your husband, Cecily?"

She put her hands to her cheeks and whispered hoarsely, "God, I've never been so sure of anything in all my life! If you asked me whether I'm more sure of that or of wanting to live, I couldn't answer."

"Then I offer you transportation."

"I accept."

He nodded, the blood pounding in his temples. "Would you like to leave now?"

"Yes, but . . ." Her eyes broke away.

"I really feel bad about mentioning it," Carl said, "but I still want her around. At least for a while yet." He shook in laughter.

"This is the United States," Ed said. "You can't force a woman—"

Carl's laughter ended. "You're wrong, Prince. I *can*."

This was the part Ed feared; the part where the claws would begin to show. "How, if we just drive away?"

Carl rose slowly. "I have money, and money can buy all sorts of services, and I also have the will—" his smile was pure malice as he looked down at his wife— "and the contacts to carry out that will. If you doubt me, leave with Cecily while I'm washing up. I won't follow. I'll just use the phone." He walked away.

Ed raised his glass, but his hand was trembling and he put it down again. "Want to leave?" he asked.

"He means what he says!" And then, face and voice suddenly shy, "Why in the world would you want to . . ." She didn't finish.

"I'm running away myself," he murmured. "We could run together."

Her hand came across the table and touched his. His fingers reacted as if with a will of their own, meshing in hers. The trembling flowed through both of them, merged, and stilled. Her eyes blinked back tears. "So quickly—yet we both feel . . ." She shook her head. "But it's a waste, Ed. Only when he dies . . ."

"It can happen." He heard himself say it, and didn't wonder. He only *wanted*. He'd wanted to leave the old life, and had done so. Now he wanted to gain the most important single component of his new life—a woman to arouse and satisfy passion—and would do so. He stood up, jerking his head at the archway. "Just for a minute, Cecily, please?"

She flushed at the hunger in his voice, and rose. They went along the central corridor to the doors, where it was dark. He touched her arms, and she turned. A second later, she was tight up against him, her lips parting moistly under his. Then her breath tingled his ear. "Money and possessions, that's all he ever thinks of! That's why I hate him. *Feelings*—excitement and warmth and human feelings—they don't mean a thing to him. But you, Ed! You're what I've wanted. You're doing this, even though you heard what he said."

He backtracked. "He wouldn't actually try to—"

"He would! He's not just an ordinary businessman. He manufactures games—pinballs and one-armed bandits and dice cages and roulette wheels. He has contacts with all sorts of people. He'd have me killed—you, too." Her head jerked; she made sure her husband wasn't returning. She whispered. "He's had others—at least one I know of—taken care of. Please don't doubt that, Ed! He can kill without a thought!"

Ed nodded slowly. Thinking of that dog, he believed her. And for a moment, he wanted to walk away. But in the next moment, her lips returned to his; her kiss was pure fire; they rocked together, burning. He spoke to her, and learned they were staying the night, and got the number of their cabin. And said, "If it's the only way, so be it." She trembled against him. They spoke again, whispering frantically, interrupting each other frequently. Then it was settled.

When Carl came to find them, they were sitting on straight-backed chairs, smoking. Carl laughed. "For a minute I thought I'd have to make those calls. But Prince Charming's sensible, isn't he? Try again in a year or so, Prince Charming. I might be ready to dump her."

Cecily left. Carl laughed. Ed returned to the taproom, just as the honeymoon couple was leaving. His sandwich and beer were still waiting. He ate slowly, alone in the room. The bartender began cleaning up. Ed finished, paid, and said, "Well, back to the road." He went outside. Hugging the building shadows, he moved toward the line of twelve cabins a hundred or more feet back. And noticed that only the Lark and Caddy remained in the parking lot, and that no other car was visible at the cabins. Still, he moved carefully, quietly, as he approached the one lighted cabin. When he reached the door marked with a brass FOUR, he put his hand on the knob and turned. Cecily had done her part. The door opened and he stepped inside. And from then on was in mortal danger, because the important part of his plan was that there be no plan at all when it came to this.

Carl was standing near the bed, fastening a blue silk dressing gown around his thick body. Cecily was on the other side of the bed, face twisted, saying, ". . . . never again!" They both turned to Ed. Carl's mouth dropped open in surprise. Cecily said, "On your right, Ed." Ed saw the table, and the two full bottles of whisky. He took one by the neck. It felt heavy in his hand. He was terribly afraid.

Carl said, "Get out of here, *fast!* You can still save your life!" He stepped forward, fists rising.

Cecily moved then. She picked something up off the lamp table—a long nail file. Carl glanced at her. Ed moved forward with the bottle.

Carl jumped back. His face changed. He was afraid. He said, "Now just a minute. Now hold it a minute. Maybe—"

"He'll have us killed," Cecily whispered. "If he ever gets to a phone, we're dead."

Carl laughed—a braying, panicked sound. "That was just talk. Big talk with nothing—"

Cecily was near enough to jab his shoulder. Carl said, "No, please!"

Ed didn't want to do anything to this frightened man. But then Carl grabbed Cecily's wrist and the nail file clattered to the floor. "Silly broad!" he said, triumphant and threatening again.

Ed hit him with the bottle. It broke. Whisky flooded the graying hair, soaked the blue dressing gown. Carl sat down on the floor, hands over his head. "Stop," he murmured. He fell over on his side and his eyes rolled back. He said something else. Ed bent, trying to hear. "Again," Cecily said, and put the other whisky bottle in his hand. "Again, Ed, again, or he'll kill us!" So he hit him again, and yet again, as Cecily directed.

They worked hard, cleaning the cabin of everything but liquor, moving Carl and their luggage to the Caddy. Ed didn't allow himself to think of what he'd done. He merely walked to the Lark as Cecily went to the restaurant-bar. It was 2 A.M.

Ten minutes later, he was parked at the side of the road, waiting. Cecily was to tell whoever was on night duty that she and her husband were getting an early start for Mexico. She was to ask for a bottle of bourbon, and pay as much as necessary to get it. She was to act drunk, and intimate that her husband was even drunker. If she heard Ed pulling out of the lot, she was to raise her voice to cover his exit. Failing that, she was to say it was a car on the highway. Then she would go to the Caddy and drive off.

If everything went well, that is.

The Caddy pulled up behind him. He got out. Cecily ran over. "The bartender was the only one there," she said. "He didn't hear you." He nodded and went to the Caddy. She went to the Lark and pulled onto the highway. He followed her, refusing to glance at the body propped up beside him.

Eight or ten miles farther, he saw the sign on the right reading ARROYO NEGRO—BLACK CANYON. Cecily pulled over and waved her hand at car tracks packing down the sandy soil. He drove carefully, though moon and stars gave plenty of light. And saw the low picket fence and second sign—a warning to stop here as the canyon commenced within fifty yards. He went off the car tracks and around the brief fence and saw the change in land ahead; saw the black gash in the earth which was Arroyo Negro. Cecily had been here before, on her honeymoon.

He opened the Caddy's door. He stepped on the gas. As he'd

seen so many times in movies, he sent the car spurting forward and leaped clear. It went over, hit the side with a tremendous rending of metal, bounced, and continued down to the bottom, about three hundred feet at its deepest point. There it settled with a chittering of smashed parts. There it lay in the moonlight, even more of a wreck than he'd hoped.

Cecily stood beside him, brushing at his clothes, examining him for cuts and bruises. There weren't any, except for a mildly skinned wrist. "We're all right," she said. "It'll be found, but not soon. They'll think I got out and died in one of those caves. Or wandered into the desert. Or maybe wasn't in the car when it crashed. Anyway, we'll be in South America. Far away. We'll be together. Forever. We'll be so happy . . ." She was gripping him about the waist. He felt her body pulsing against his. But he was very tired now; very dull and drained and tired.

They returned to the Lark. He asked if she minded driving. He just had to rest for a while. She kissed him and said of course she would drive. She would do whatever he wanted from now on. Weren't they bound together by the strongest of ties—blood?

They pulled onto the road. He slumped low in the seat and put his head on her shoulder. Her fragrance came to him, soft and delicate. After a while, he slept.

He awoke, knowing something was wrong. It was still dark, and he was still in the car, and she was still driving. Nothing had changed from the time he'd fallen asleep, so nothing could be wrong. And yet he *knew* there was.

His thoughts came to an end as he squinted up at her. She was sitting—or crouching—over the wheel, lips parted, eyes wide and fixed, dampness covering her forehead, face and neck. And even as he stared, a new and terrific tension entered her body.

He moaned once—a sound embodying his sudden and complete loathing for this terrible stranger to whom he was tied forever; this stranger who might yet cost him his life. She didn't hear him. She was too engrossed in swinging the wheel hard left, peering intently at the road directly in front of the swerving, hurtling car, and then releasing her pent-up breath in a gasp of pure delight as the thump and sodden, squishing sound filled his ears and all the world.

Leigh Brackett

I FEEL BAD KILLING YOU

From *New Detective*, November 1944

Leigh Brackett's relatively small output of crime fiction—three novels and a dozen or so short stories—reflects her admiration for Raymond Chandler and the Black Mask school. Her 1944 mystery, No Good from a Corpse, *a Southern California tale featuring private detective Edmond Clive, is so Chandleresque in style and approach that it might have been written by Chandler. Brackett was so completely versed in his work, in fact, that in 1946 she co-authored the script for* The Big Sleep, *and twenty–five years later wrote the screenplay for the Robert Altman-Elliot Gould film version of* The Long Goodbye. *The mean–streets novelette which follows might also have carried Chandler's byline, and might have been published in Black Mask—a magazine in which Brackett didn't appear even once—instead of the lesser known* New Detective.

B. P.

1
Dead End Town

LOS ANGELES, APR. 21.—The death of Henry Channing, 24, policeman attached to the Surfside Division and brother of the once-prominent detective Paul Channing, central figure in the Padway gang-torture case, has been termed a suicide following investigation by local authorities. Young Channing's battered body was found in the surf under Sunset Pier in the beach community three days ago. It was first thought that Channing might have fallen or been thrown from the end of the pier, where his cap was found, but there is no evidence of violence and a high guard rail precludes the accident theory. Sunset Pier was part of his regular beat.

Police Captain Max Gandara made the following statement: "We have reliable testimony that Channing had been nervous and despondent following a beating by *pachucos* two months ago." He then cited the case of the brother, Paul Channing, who quit the force and vanished into obscurity following his mistreatment at the hands of the once-powerful Padway gang in 1934. "They were both good cops," Gandara said, "but they lost their nerve."

Paul Channing stood for a moment at the corner. The crossing-light, half a block along the highway, showed him only as a gaunt shadow among shadows. He looked down the short street in somber hesitation. Small tired houses crouched patiently under the wind. Somewhere a rusted screen door slammed with the protesting futility of a dying bird beating its wing. At the end of the deserted pavement was the grey pallor of sand and, beyond it, the sea.

He stood listening to the boom and hiss of the waves, thinking of them rushing black and foam-streaked through the pilings of Sunset Pier, the long weeds streaming out and the barnacles pink and fluted and razor sharp behind it. He hoped that Hank had struck his head at once against a timber.

He lifted his head, his body shaken briefly by a tremor. *This is it*, he thought. *This is the deadline.*

He began to walk, neither slowly nor fast, scraping sand under his feet. The rhythm of the scraping was uneven, a slight dragging, off-beat. He went to the last house on the right, mounted three sagging steps to a wooden porch, and rapped with his knuckles on a door blistered and greasy with the salt sweat of the sea. There was a light behind drawn blinds, and a sound of voices. The voices stopped, sliced cleanly by the knocking.

Someone walked heavily through the silence. The door opened, spilling yellow light around the shadow of a thick-set, powerful man in shirtsleeves. He let his breath out in what was not quite a laugh and relaxed against the jamb.

"So you did turn up," he said. He was well into middle age, hard-eyed, obstinate. His name was Max Gandara, Police Captain, Surfside Division, L.A.P.D. He studied the man on the porch with slow, deliberate insolence.

The man on the porch seemed not to mind. He seemed not to be in any hurry. His dark eyes looked, unmoved, at the big man, at him and through him. His face was a mask of thin sinewy flesh, laid close over ruthless bone, expressionless. And yet, in spite of his face and his lean erect body, there was a shadow on him. He was like a man who has drawn away, beyond the edge of life.

"Did you think I wouldn't come?" he asked.

Gandara shrugged. "They're all here. Come on in and get it over with."

Channing nodded and stepped inside. He removed his hat. His dark hair was shot with grey. He turned to lay the hat on a table and the movement brought into focus a scar that ran up from his shirt collar on the right side of his neck, back of the ear. Then he followed Gandara into the living room.

There were three people there, and the silence. Three people watching the door. A red-haired, green-eyed girl with a smouldering, angry glow deep inside her. A red-haired, green-eyed boy with a sullen, guarded face. And a man, a neat, lean, swarthy man with aggressive features that seemed always to be on the edge of laughter and eyes that kept all their emotion on the surface.

"Folks," said Gandara, "this is Paul Channing." He indicated them, in order. "Marge Krist, Rudy Krist, Jack Flavin."

Hate crawled into the green eyes of Rudy Krist, brilliant and poisonous, fixed on Channing.

■   ■   ■

Out in the kitchen a woman screamed. The swing door burst open. A chubby pink man came through in a tottering rush, followed by a large, bleached blonde with an ice pick. Her dress was torn slightly at the shoulder and her mouth was smeared. Her incongruously black eyes were owlish and mad.

Gandara yelled. The sound of his voice got through to the blonde. She slowed down and said sulkily, to no one in particular, "He better keep his fat paws off or I'll fix him." She went back to the kitchen.

The chubby pink man staggered to a halt, swayed, caught hold of Channing's arm and looked up at him, smiling foolishly. The smile faded, leaving his mouth open like a baby's. His eyes, magnified behind rimless lenses, widened and fixed.

"Chan," he said. "My God. Chan."

He sat down on the floor and began to cry, the tears running quietly down his cheeks.

"Hello, Budge." Channing stooped and touched his shoulder.

"Take it easy." Gandara pulled Channing's arms. "Let the little lush alone. Him and—that." He made a jerky gesture at the girl, flung himself heavily into a chair and glowered at Channing. "All right, we're all curious—tell us why we're here."

Channing sat down. He seemed in no hurry to begin. A thin film of sweat made the tight pattern of muscles very plain under his skin.

"We're here to talk about a lot of things," he said. "Who murdered Henry?" No one seemed particularly moved except Budge Hanna, who stopped crying and stared at Channing. Rudy Krist made a small derisive noise in his throat. Gandara laughed.

"That ain't such a bombshell, Chan. I guess we all had an idea of what you was driving at, from the letters you wrote us. What we want to know is what makes you think you got a right to holler murder."

Channing drew a thick envelope from his inside pocket, laying it on his knee to conceal the fact that his hands trembled. He said, not looking at anybody, "I haven't seen my brother for several years, but we've been in fairly close touch through letters. I've kept most of his. Hank was good at writing letters, good at saying things. He's had a lot to say since he was transferred to Surfside—and not one word of it points to suicide."

Max Gandara's face had grown rocky. "Oh, he had a lot to say, did he?"

Channing nodded. Marge Krist was leaning forward, watching him intently. Jack Flavin's terrier face was interested, but unreadable. He had been smoking nervously when Channing entered. The nervousness seemed to be habitual, part of his wiry personality. Now he lighted another cigarette, his hands moving with a swiftness that seemed jerky but was not. The match flared and spat. Paul Channing started involuntarily. The flame seemed to have a terrible fascination for him. He dropped his gaze. Beads of sweat came out along his hairline. Once again, harshly, Gandara laughed.

"Go on," he said. "Go on."

"Hank told me about that brush with the *pachucos*. They didn't hurt him much. They sure as hell didn't break him."

"Flavin, here, says different. Rudy says different. Marge says different."

"That's why I wanted to talk to them—and you, Max. Hank mentioned you all in his letters." He was talking to the whole room now. "Max I knew from the old days. You, Miss Krist, I know because Hank went with you—not seriously, I guess, but you liked each other. He liked your brother, too."

The kid stared at him, his eyes blank and bright. Channing said, "Hank talked a lot about you, Rudy. He said you were a smart kid, a good kid but headed for trouble. He said some ways you were so smart you were downright stupid."

Rudy and Marge both started to speak, but Channing was going on. "I guess he was right, Rudy. You've got it on you already—a sort of greyness that comes from prison walls, or the shadow of them. You've got that look on your face, like a closed door."

Rudy got halfway to his feet, looking nasty. Flavin said quietly, "Shut up." Rudy sat down again. Flavin seemed relaxed. His brown eyes held only a hard glitter from the light. "Hank seems to have been a great talker. What did he say about me?"

"He said you smell of stripes."

Flavin laid his cigarette carefully in a tray. He got up, very light and easy. He went over to Channing and took a handful of his shirt, drawing him up slightly, and said with gentle kindness, "I don't think I like that remark."

Marge Krist cried, "Stop it! Jack, don't you dare start trouble."

"Maybe you didn't understand what he meant, Marge." Flavin still did not sound angry. "He's accusing me of having a record, a prison record. He didn't pick a very nice way of saying it."

"Take it easy, Jack," Gandara said. "Don't you get what he's doing? He's trying to wangle himself a little publicity and stir up a little trouble, so that maybe the public will think maybe Hank didn't do the Dutch after all." He pointed at Budge Hanna. "Even the press is here." He rose and took hold of Flavin's shoulder. "He's just making a noise with his mouth, because a long time ago people used to listen when he did it and he hasn't forgotten how good that felt."

■ ■ ■

Flavin shrugged and returned to his chair. Gandara lighted a cigarette, holding the match deliberately close to Channing's sweaty face. "Listen, Chan. Jack Flavin is a good citizen of Surfside. He owns a store, legitimate, and Rudy works for him, legitimate. I don't like people coming into my town and making cracks about the citizens. If they step out of line, I'll take care of them. If they don't, I'll see they're let alone."

He sat down again, comfortably. "All right, Chan. Let's get this all out of your system. What did little brother have to say about me?"

Channing's dark eyes flickered with what might have been malice. "What everybody's always said about you, Max. That you were too goddam dumb even to be crooked."

Gandara turned purple. He moved and Jack Flavin laughed. "No fair, Max. You wouldn't let me."

Budge Hanna giggled with startling shrillness. The blonde had come in and sat down beside him. Her eyes were half closed but she seemed somehow less drunk than she had been. Gandara settled back. He said ominously, "Go on."

"All right. Hank said that Surfside was a dirty town, dirty from the gutters up. He said any man with the brains of a sick flea would know that most of the liquor places were run illegally, and most of the hotels, too, and that two-thirds of the police force was paid to have bad eyesight. He said it wasn't any use trying to do a good job as a decent cop. He said every report he turned in was thrown away for lack of evidence, and he was sick of it."

Marge Krist said, "Then maybe that's what he was worried about."

"He wasn't afraid," said Channing. "All his letters were angry, and an angry man doesn't commit suicide."

Budge Hanna said shrilly, "Look out."

Max Gandara was on his feet. He was standing over Channing. His lips had a white line around them.

"Listen," he said. "I been pretty patient with you. Now I'll tell you something. Your brother committed suicide. All these three people testified at the inquest. You can read the transcript. They all said Hank was worried; he wasn't happy about things. There was no sign of violence on Hank, or the pier."

"How could there be?" said Channing. "Hard asphalt paving doesn't show much. And Hank's body wouldn't show much, either."

"Shut up. I'm telling you. There's no evidence of murder, no reason to think it's murder. Hank was like you, Channing. He couldn't take punishment. He got chicken walking a dark beat down here, and he jumped, and that's all."

Channing said slowly, "Only two kinds of people come to Surf-side—the ones that are starting at the bottom, going up, and the ones that are finished, coming down. It's either a beginning or an end, and I guess we all know where we stand on that scale."

He got up, tossing the packet of letters into Budge Hanna's lap. "Those are photostats. The originals are already with police headquarters in L.A. I don't think you have to worry much, Max. There's nothing definite in them. Just a green young harness cop griping at the system, making a few personal remarks. He hasn't even accused you of being dishonest, Max. Only dumb—and the powers-that-be already know that. That's why you're here in Surf-side, waiting for the age of retirement."

Gandara struck him in the mouth. Channing took three steps backward, caught himself, swayed, and was steady again. Blood ran from the corner of his mouth down his chin. Marge Krist was on her feet, her eyes blazing, but something about Channing kept her from speaking. He seemed not to care about the blood, about Gandara, or about anything but what he was saying.

"You used to be a good reporter, Budge, before you drank your-self onto the scrapheap. I thought maybe you'd like to be in at the beginning on this story. Because there's going to be a story, if it's only the story of my death.

"I knew Hank. There was no yellow in him. Whether there's yellow in me or not, doesn't matter. Hank didn't jump off that pier. Somebody threw him off, and I'm going to find out who, and why. I used to be a pretty good dick once. I've got a reason now for remembering all I learned."

Max Gandara said, "Oh, God," in a disgusted voice. "Take that somewhere else, Chan. It smells." He pushed him roughly toward the door, and Rudy Krist laughed.

"Yellow," he said. "Yellower than four Japs. Both of 'em, all talk and no guts. Get him out, Max. He stinks up the room."

Flavin said, "Shut up, Rudy." He grinned at Marge. "You're getting your sister sore."

"You bet I'm sore!" she flared. "I think Mr. Channing is right. I knew Hank pretty well, and I think you ought to be ashamed to push him around like this."

Flavin said, "Who? Hank or Mr. Channing?"

Marge snapped, "Oh, go to hell." She turned and went out. Gandara shoved Channing into the hall after her. "You know where the door is, Chan. Stay away from me, and if I was you I'd stay away from Surfside." He turned around, reached down and got a handful of Budge Hanna's coat collar and slung him out bodily. "You, too, rumdum. *And* you." He made a grab for the blonde, but she was already out. He followed the four of them down the hall and closed the door hard behind them.

■　　■　　■

Paul Channing said, "Miss Krist—and you too, Budge." The wind felt ice cold on his skin. His shirt stuck to his back. It turned clammy and he began to shiver. "I want to talk to you."

The blonde said, "Is this private?"

"I don't think so. Maybe you can help." Channing walked slowly toward the beach front and the boardwalk. "Miss Krist, if you didn't think Hank committed suicide, why did you testify as you did at the inquest?"

"Because I didn't know." She sounded rather angry, with him and possibly herself. "They asked me how he acted, and I had to say he'd been worried and depressed, because he had been. I told them I didn't think he was the type for suicide, but they didn't care."

"Did Hank ever hint that he knew something—anything that might have been dangerous to him?" Channing's eyes were alert, watchful in the darkness.

"No. Hank pounded a beat. He wasn't a detective."

"He was pretty friendly with your brother, wasn't he?"

"I thought for a while it might bring Rudy back to his senses. He took a liking to Hank, they weren't so far apart in years, and Hank was doing him good. Now, of course—"

"What's wrong with Rudy? What's he doing?"

"That's just it, I don't know. He's 4-F in the draft, and that hurts him, and he's always been restless, never could hold a job. Then he met Jack Flavin, and since then he's been working steady, but he—he's changed. I can't put my finger on it, I don't know of anything wrong he's done, but he's hardened and drawn into himself, as though he had secrets and didn't trust anybody. You saw how he acted. He's turned mean. I've done my best to bring him up right."

Channing said, "Kids go that way sometimes. Know anything about him, Budge?"

The reporter said, "Nuh-uh. He's never been picked up for anything, and as far as anybody knows even Flavin is straight. He owns a haberdashery and pays his taxes."

"Well," said Channing, "I guess that's all for now."

"No." Marge Krist stopped and faced him. He could see her eyes in the pale reflection of the water, dark and intense. The wind blew her hair, pressed her light coat against the long lifting planes of her body. "I want to warn you. Maybe you're a brilliant, nervy man and you know what you're doing, and if you do it's all right. But if you really are what you acted like in there, you'd better go home and forget about it. Surfside is a bad town. You can't insult people and get away with it." She paused. "For Hank's sake, I hope you know what you're doing. I'm in the phone book if you want me. Good night."

"Good night." Channing watched her go. She had a lovely way of moving. Absently, he began to wipe the blood off his face. His lip had begun to swell.

Budge Hanna said, "Chan."

"Yeah."

"I want to say thanks, and I'm with you. I'll give you the biggest break I can in the paper."

"We used to work pretty well together, before I got mine and you found yours, in a bottle."

"Yeah. And now I'm in Surfside with the rest of the scrap. If this turns out a big enough story, I might—oh, well." He paused, rubbing a pudgy cheek with his forefinger.

Channing said, "Go ahead, Budge. Say it."

"All right. Every crook in the Western states knows that the Padway mob took you to the wall. They know what was done to you, with fire. They know you broke. The minute they find out you're back, even unofficially, you know what'll happen. You sent up a lot of guys in your time. You sent a lot of 'em down, too—down to the morgue. You were a tough dick, Chan, and a square one, and you know how they love you."

"I guess I know all that, Budge."

"Chan—" he looked up, squinting earnestly through the gloom, his spectacles shining—"how is it? I mean, can you—"

Channing put a hand on his shoulder, pushing him around slightly. "You watch your step, kid, and try to stay sober. I don't know what I may be getting into. If you want out—"

"Hell, no. Just—well, good luck, Chan."

"Thanks."

The blonde said, "Ain't you going to ask me something?"

"Sure," said Channing. "What do you know?"

"I know who killed your brother."

2
Badge of Carnage

The blood swelled and thickened in Channing's veins. It made a hard pain over his eyes and pressed against the stiff scar tissue on his neck. No one spoke. No one moved.

The wind blew sand in riffles across the empty beach. The waves rushed and broke their backs in thunder and slipped out again, sighing. Up ahead Sunset Pier thrust its black bulk against the night. Beyond it was the huge amusement pier. Here and there a single light was burning, swaying with the wind, and the reaching skeletons of the roller coaster and the giant slide were desolate in the pre-season quiet. Vacant lots and a single un-lighted house were as deserted as the moon.

Paul Channing looked at the woman with eyes as dark and lonely as the night. "We're not playing a game," he said. "This is murder."

The blonde's teeth glittered white between moist lips.

Budge Hanna whispered, "She's crazy. She couldn't know."

"Oh, couldn't I!" The blonde's whisper was throatily venomous. "Young Channing was thrown off the pier about midnight, wasn't he? Okay. Well, you stood me up on a date that evening, remember, Budgie dear? And my room is on the same floor as yours, remember? And I can hear every pair of hoofs clumping up and down those damn stairs right outside, remember?"

"Listen," Budge said, "I told you I got stewed and—"

"And got in a fight. I know. Sure, you told me. But how can you prove it? I heard your fairy footsteps. They didn't sound very stewed to me. So I looked out, and you were hitting it for your room like your pants were on fire. Your shirt was torn, and so was your coat, and you didn't look so good other ways. I could hear you heaving clear out in the hall. And it was just nineteen minutes after twelve."

Budge Hanna's voice had risen to a squeak. "Damn you, Millie, I—Chan, she's crazy! She's just trying—"

"Sure," said Millie. She thrust her face close to his. "I been shoved around enough. I been called enough funny names. I been stood up enough times. I loaned you enough money I'll never get back. And I ain't so dumb I don't know you got dirt on your hands from somewhere. Me, I'm quitting you right now and—"

"Shut up. Shut up!"

"And I got a few things to say that'll interest some people!" Millie was screeching now. "You killed that Channing kid, or you know who did!"

Budge Hanna slapped her hard across the mouth.

Millie reeled back. Then she screamed like a cat. Her hands flashed up, curved and wicked, long red nails gleaming. She went for Budge Hanna.

Channing stepped between them. He was instantly involved in a whirlwind of angry flailing hands. While he was trying to quiet them the men came up behind him.

There were four of them. They had come quietly from the shadows beside the vacant house. They worked quickly, with deadly efficiency. Channing got his hand inside his coat, and after that he didn't know anything for a long time.

· · ·

Things came back to Channing in disconnected pieces. His head hurt. He was in something that moved. He was hot. He was covered with something, lying flat on his back, and he could hardly breathe. There was another person jammed against him. There were somebody's feet on his chest, and somebody else's feet on his thighs. Presently he found that his mouth was covered with adhesive, that his eyes were taped shut, and that his hands and feet were bound, probably also with tape. The moving thing was an automobile, taking its time.

The stale, stifling air under the blanket covering him was heavy with the scent of powder and cheap perfume. He guessed that the woman was Millie. From time to time she stirred and whimpered.

A man's voice said, "Here is okay."

The car stopped. Doors were opened. The blanket was pulled away. Cold salt air rushed over Channing, mixed with the heavy sulphurous reek of sewage. He knew they were somewhere on the road above Hyperion, where there was nothing but miles of empty dunes.

Hands grabbed him, hauled him bodily out of the car. Somebody said, "Got the Thompson ready?"

"Yeah." The speaker laughed gleefully, like a child with a bass voice. "Just like old times, ain't it? Good ole Dolly. She ain't had a chansta sing in a long time. Come on, honey. Loosen up the pipes."

A rattling staccato burst out, and was silent.

"For cripesake, Joe! That stuff ain't so plentiful. Doncha know there's a war on? We gotta conserve. C'mon, help me with this guy." He kicked Channing. "On your feet, you."

He was hauled erect and leaned against a post. Joe said, "What about the dame?"

The other man laughed. "Her turn comes later. Much later."

A fourth voice, one that had not spoken before, said, "Okay, boys. Get away from him now." It was a slow, inflectionless and yet strangely forceful voice, with a hint of a lisp. The lisp was not in the least effeminate or funny. It had the effect of a knife blade whetted on oilstone. The man who owned it put his hands on Channing's shoulders.

"You know me," he said.

Channing nodded. The uncovered parts of his face were greasy with sweat. It had soaked loose the corners of the adhesive. The man said, "You knew I'd catch up with you some day."

The man struck him, deliberately and with force, twice across the face with his open palms.

"I'm sorry you lost your guts, Channing. This makes me feel like I'm shooting a kitten. Why didn't you do the Dutch years ago, like your brother?"

Channing brought his bound fists up, slammed them into the man's face, striking at the sound of his voice. The man grunted and fell, making a heavy soft thump in the sand. Somebody yelled, "Hey!" and the man with the quiet lisping voice said, "Shut up. Let him alone."

Channing heard him scramble up and the voice came near again. "Do that again."

Channing did.

The man avoided his blow this time. He laughed softly. "So you still have insides, Chan. That makes it better. Much better."

Joe said, "Look, somebody may come along—"

"Shut up." The man brought something from his pocket, held

his hand close to Channing's ear, and shook it. "You know what that is?"

Channing stiffened. He nodded.

There was a light thin rattling sound, and then a scratching of emery and the quick spitting of a match-head rubbed to flame.

The man said softly, "How are your guts now?"

The little sharp tongue of heat touched Channing's chin. He drew his head back. His mouth worked under the adhesive. Cords stood out in his throat. The flame followed. Channing began to shake. His knees gave. He braced them, braced his body against the post. Sweat ran down his face and the scar on his neck turned dark and livid.

The man laughed. He threw the match down and stepped away. He said, "Okay, Joe."

Somebody said, sharply, "There's a car coming. Two cars."

The man swore. "Bunch of sailors up from Long Beach. Okay, we'll get out of here. Back in the car, Joe. Can't use the chopper, they'd hear it." Joe cursed unhappily. Feet scruffed hurriedly in the sand. Leather squeaked, the small familiar sound of metal clearing a shoulder clip. The safety snicked open.

The man said, "So long, Channing."

Channing was already falling sideways when the shot came. There was a second one close behind it. Channing dropped into the ditch and lay perfectly still, hidden from the road. The car roared off. Presently the two other cars shot by, loaded with sailors. They were singing and shouting and not worrying about what somebody might have left at the side of the road.

■　■　■

Sometime later Channing began to move, at first in uncoordinated jerks and then with reasonable steadiness. He was conscious that he had been hit in two places. The right side of his head was stiff and numb clear down to his neck. Somebody had shoved a red-hot spike through the flesh over his heart-ribs and forgotten to take it out. He could feel blood oozing, sticky with sand.

He rolled over slowly and started to peel the adhesive from his face, fumbling awkwardly with his bound hands. When that was done he used his teeth on his wrist bonds. It took a long time. After that the ankles were easy.

It was no use trying to see how much damage had been done. He decided it couldn't be as bad as it felt. He smiled, a crooked and humorless grimace, and swore and laughed shortly. He wadded the clean handkerchief from his hip pocket into the gash under his arm and tightened the holster strap to hold it there. The display handkerchief in his breast pocket went around his head. He found that after he got started he could walk quite well. His gun had not been removed. Channing laughed again, quietly. He did not touch nor in any way notice the burn on his chin.

It took him nearly three hours to get back to Surfside, crouching in the ditch twice to let cars go by.

He passed Gandara's street, and the one beyond where Marge and Rudy Krist lived. He came to the ocean front and the dark loom of the pier and the vacant house from behind which the men had come. He found Budge Hanna doubled up under a clump of Monterey cypress. The cold spring wind blew sand into Hanna's wide-open eyes, but he didn't seem to mind it. He had bled from the nose and ears—not much.

Channing went through Hanna's pockets, examining things swiftly by the light of a tiny pocket flash shielded in his hand. There was just the usual clutter of articles. Channing took the key ring. Then, tucked into the watch pocket, he found a receipt from Flavin's Men's Shop for three pairs of socks. The date was April 22. Channing frowned. April 21 was the day on which Hank Channing's death had been declared a suicide. April 21 was a Saturday.

Channing rose slowly and walked on down the front to Surfside Avenue. It was hours past midnight. The bars were closed. The only lights on the street were those of the police station and the lobby of the Surfside Hotel, which was locked and deserted. Channing let himself in with Budge Hanna's key and walked up dirty marble steps to the second floor and found Budge Hanna's number. He leaned against the jamb, his knees sagging, managed to force the key around and get inside. He switched on the lights, locked the door again, and braced his back against it. The first thing he saw was a bottle on the bedside table.

He drank straight from the neck. It was scotch, good scotch. In a few minutes he felt much better. He stared at the label, turning the bottle around in his hands, frowning at it. Then, very quietly, he began to search the room.

He found nothing until, in the bottom drawer of the dresser, he discovered a brand new shirt wrapped in cheap green paper.

The receipt was from Flavin's Men's Shop. Channing looked at the date. It was for the day which had just begun, Monday.

Channing studied the shirt, poking his fingers into the folds. Between the tail and the cardboard he found an envelope. It was unaddressed, unsealed, and contained six one hundred dollar bills.

Channing's mouth twisted. He replaced the money and the shirt and sat down on the bed. He scowled at the wall, not seeing it, and drank some more of Budge Hanna's scotch. He thought Budge wouldn't mind. It would take more even than good scotch to warm him now.

A picture on the wall impressed itself gradually upon Channing's mind.

He looked at it more closely. It was a professional photograph of a beautiful woman in a white evening gown. She had a magnificent figure and a strong, provocative, heart-shaped face. Her gown and hairdress were of the late twenties. The picture was autographed in faded ink, "Lots of Luck, Skinny, from your pal Dorothy Balf."

"Skinny" had been crossed out and "Budge" written above.

Channing took the frame down and slid the picture out. It had been wiped off, but both frame and picture showed the ravages of time, dust and stains and faded places, as though they had hung a long time with only each other for company. On the back of the picture was stamped:

SKINNY CRAIL'S
Surfside at Culver
"Between the Devil and the Deep"

Memories came back to Channing. Skinny Crail, that bad-luck boy of Hollywood, plunging his last dime on a night club that flurried into success and then faded gradually to a pathetically mediocre doom, a white elephant rotting hugely in the empty flats between Culver City and the beach. Dorothy Balf had been the leading feminine star of that day, and Budge Hanna's idol. Channing glanced again at the scrawled "Budge." He sighed and replaced the picture carefully. Then he turned out the lights and sat a long while in the dark, thinking.

Presently he sighed again and ran his hand over his face, wincing. He rose and went out, locking the door carefully behind him. He moved slowly, his limp accentuated by weakness and a slight unsteadiness from the scotch. His expression was that of a man who hopes for nothing and is therefore immune to blows.

There was a phone booth in the lobby. Channing called Max Gandara. He talked for a long time. When he came out his face was chalk-colored and damp, utterly without expression. He left the hotel and walked slowly down the beach.

■　■　■

The shapeless, colorless little house was dark and silent, with two empty lots to seaward and a cheap brick apartment house on its right. No lights showed anywhere. Channing set his finger on the rusted bell.

He could hear it buzzing somewhere inside. After a long time lights went on behind heavy crash draperies, drawn close. Channing turned suddenly sick. Sweat came out on his wrists and his ears rang. Through the ringing he heard Marge Krist's clear voice asking who was there.

He told her. "I'm hurt," he said. "Let me in."

The door opened. Channing walked through it. He seemed to be walking through dark water that swirled around him, very cold, very heavy. He decided not to fight it.

When he opened his eyes again he was stretched out on a studio couch. Apparently he had been out only a moment or two. Marge and Rudy Krist were arguing fiercely.

"I tell you he's got to have a doctor!"

"All right, tell him to go get one. You don't want to get in trouble."

"Trouble? Why would I get in trouble?"

"The guy's been shot. That means cops. They'll be trampling all over, asking you why he should have come here. How do you know what the little rat's been doing? If he's square, why didn't he go to the cops himself? Maybe it's a frame, or maybe he shot himself."

"Maybe," said Marge slowly, "you're afraid to be questioned."

Rudy swore. He looked almost as white and hollow as Channing felt. Channing laughed. It was not a pleasant sound.

He said, "Sure he's scared. Start an investigation now and that messes up everything for tonight."

Marge and Rudy both started at the sound of his voice. Rudy's face went hard and blank as a pine slab. He walked over toward the couch.

"What does that crack mean?"

"It means you better call Flavin quick and tell him to get his new shirt out of Budge Hanna's room. Budge Hanna won't be needing it now, and the cops are going to be very interested in the accessories."

Rudy's lips had a curious stiffness. "What's wrong with Hanna?"

"Nothing much. Only one of Dave's boys hit him a little too hard. He's dead."

"Dead?" Rudy shaped the word carefully and studied it as though he had never heard it before. Then he said, "Who's Dave? What are you talking about?"

Channing studied him. "Flavin's still keeping you in the nursery, is he?"

"That kind of talk don't go with me, Channing."

"That's tough, because it'll go with the cops. You'll sound kind of silly, won't you, bleating how you didn't know what was going on because papa never told you."

Rudy moved toward Channing. Marge yelled and caught him. Channing grinned and drew his gun. His head was propped fairly high on pillows, so he could see what he was doing without making any disastrous attempt to sit up.

"Fine hood you are, Rudy. Didn't even frisk me. Listen, punk. Budge Hanna's dead, murdered. His Millie is dead, too, by now. I'm supposed to be dead, in a ditch above Hyperion, but Dave Padway always was a lousy shot. Where do you think you come in on this?"

Rudy's skin had a sickly greenish tinge, but his jaw was hard. "You're a liar, Channing. I never heard of Dave Padway. I don't know anything about Budge Hanna or that dame. I don't know anything about you. Now get the hell out."

"You make a good Charlie McCarthy, Rudy. Maybe Flavin will hold you on his knee in the death-chair at San Quentin."

Marge stopped Rudy again. She said quietly, "What happened, Mr. Channing?"

Channing told her, keeping his eyes on Rudy. "Flavin's heading a racket," he said finally. "His store is just a front, useful for background and a way to make pay-offs and pass on information. He doesn't keep the store open on Sunday, does he, Rudy?"

Rudy didn't answer. Marge said, "No."

"Okay. Budge Hanna worked for Flavin. I'll make a guess. I'll say Flavin is engineering liquor robberies, hijacking, and so forth. Budge Hanna was a well-known lush. He could go into any bar and make a deal for bootleg whiskey, and nobody would suspect him. Trouble with Budge was, he couldn't handle his women. Millie got sore, and suspicious and began to yell out loud. I guess Dave Padway's boys overheard her. Dave never did trust women and drunks."

Channing stared narrow-eyed at Rudy. His blood-caked face was twisted into a cruel grin. "Dave never liked punks, either. There's going to be trouble between Dave and your pal Flavin, and I don't see where you're going to come in, except maybe on a morgue slab, like the others. Like Hank."

"Oh, cripes," said Rudy, "we're back to Hank again."

"Yeah. Always back to Hank. You know what happened, Rudy. You kind of liked Hank. You're a smart kid, Rudy. You've probably got a better brain than Flavin, and if you're going to be a successful crook these days you need brains. So Flavin pushed Hank off the pier and called it suicide, so you'd think he was yellow."

Rudy laughed. "That's good. That's very good. Marge was out with Jack Flavin that night." His green eyes were dangerous.

Marge nodded, dropping her gaze. "I was."

Channing shrugged. "So what? He hired it done. Just like he hired this tonight. Only Dave Padway isn't a boy you can hire for long. He used to be big time, and ten years in clink won't slow him up too much. You better call Flavin, Rudy. They're liable to find Budge Hanna any time and start searching his room." He laughed. "Flavin wasn't so smart to pay off on Saturday, too late for the banks."

■　■　■

Marge said, "Why haven't you called the police?"

"With what I have to tell them I'd only scare off the birds. Let 'em find out for themselves."

She looked at him with level, calculating eyes. "Then you're planning to do it all by yourself?"

"I've got the whip hand right now. Only you two know I'm alive. But I know about Budge Hanna's shirt, and the cops will too, pretty soon. Somebody's got to get busy, and the minute he does I'll know for sure who's who in this little tinpot crime combine."

Marge rose. "That's ridiculous. You're in no condition to handle anyone. And even if you were—" She left that hanging and crossed to the telephone.

Channing said, "Even if I were, I'm still yellow, is that it? Sure. Stand still, Rudy. I'm not too yellow or too weak to shoot your ankle off." His face was grey, gaunt, infinitely tired. He touched the burn on his chin. His cheek muscles tightened.

He lay still and listened to Marge Krist talking to Max Gandara.

When she was through she went out into the kitchen. Rudy sat down, glowering sullenly at Channing. He began to tremble, a shallow nervous vibration. Channing laughed.

"How do you like crime now, kiddie? Fun, isn't it?"

Rudy gave him a lurid and prophetic direction.

Marge came back with hot water and a clean cloth. She wiped Channing's face, not touching the handkerchief. The wound had stopped bleeding, but the gash in his side was still oozing. The pad had slipped. Marge took his coat off, waiting while he changed hands with the gun, and then his shoulder clip and shirt. When she saw his body she let the shirt drop and put her hand to her mouth. Channing, sitting up now on the couch, glanced from her to Rudy's slack pale face, and said quietly,

"You see why I don't like fire."

Marge was working gently on his side when the bell rang. "That's the police," she said, and went to the front door. Channing held Rudy with the gun. He heard nothing behind him, but quite suddenly there was a cold object pressing the back of his neck and a voice said quietly,

"Drop it, bud."

It was Joe's voice. He had come in through the kitchen. Channing dropped his gun. The men coming in the front door were not policemen. They were Dave Padway and Jack Flavin.

Flavin closed the door and locked it. Channing nodded, smiling faintly. Dave Padway nodded back. He was a tall, shambling man with white eyes and a long face, like a pinto horse.

"I see I'm still a bum shot," he said.

"Ten years in the can doesn't help your eye, Dave." Channing seemed relaxed and unemotional. "Well, now we're all here we can talk. We can talk about murder."

Marge and Rudy were both staring at Padway. Flavin grinned. "My new business partner, Dave Padway. Dave, meet Marge Krist and Rudy."

Padway glanced at them briefly. His pale eyes were empty of expression. He said, in his soft way, "It's Channing that interests me right now. How much has he told, and who has he told it to?"

Channing laughed, with insolent mockery.

"Fine time to worry about that," Flavin grunted. "Who was it messed up the kill in the first place?"

Padway's eyelids drooped. "Everyone makes mistakes, Jack," he said mildly. Flavin struck a match. The flame trembled slightly.

Rudy said, "Jack. Listen, Jack, this guy says Budge Hanna and his girl were killed. Did you—"

"No. That was Dave's idea."

Padway said, "Any objections to it?"

"Hanna was a good man. He was my contact with all the bars."

"He was a bum. Him and that floozie between them were laying the whole thing in Channing's lap. I heard 'em."

"Okay, okay! I'm just sorry, that's all."

Rudy said, "Jack, honest to God, I don't want to be messed up in killing. I don't mind slugging a watchman, that's okay, and if you had to shoot it out with the cops, well, that's okay too, I guess. But murder, Jack!" He glanced at Channing's scarred body. "Murder, and things like that—" He shook.

Padway muttered, "My God, he's still in diapers."

"Take it easy, kid," Flavin said. "You're in big time now. It's worth getting sick at your stomach a couple times." He looked at Channing, grinning his hard white grin. "You were right when you said Surfside was either an end or a beginning. Dave and I both needed a place to begin again. Start small and grow, like any other business."

Channing nodded. He looked at Rudy. "Hank told you it would be like this, didn't he? You believe him now?"

Rudy repeated his suggestion. His skin was greenish. He sat down and lighted a cigarette. Marge leaned against the wall, watching with bright, narrow-lidded eyes. She was pale. She had said nothing.

Channing said, "Flavin, you were out with Marge the night Hank was killed."

"So what?"

"Did you leave her at all?"

"A couple of times. Not long enough to get out on the pier to kill your brother."

Marge said quietly, "He's right, Mr. Channing."

Channing said, "Where did you go?"

"Ship Cafe, a bunch of bars, dancing. So what?" Flavin gestured impatiently.

Channing said, "How about you, Dave? Did you kill Hank to pay for your brother, and then wait for me to come?"

"If I had," Padway said, "I'd have told you. I'd have made sure you'd come." He stepped closer, looking down. "You don't seem very surprised to see us."

"I'm not surprised at anything anymore."

"Yeah." Padway's gun came smoothly into his hand. "At this range I ought to be able to hit you, Chan." Marge Krist caught her breath sharply. Padway said, "No, not here, unless he makes me. Go ahead, Joe."

Joe got busy with the adhesive tape again. This time he did a better job. They wrapped his trussed body in a blanket. Joe picked up the feet. Flavin motioned Rudy to take hold. Rudy hesitated. Padway flicked the muzzle of his gun. Rudy picked up Channing's shoulders. They turned out the lights and carried Channing out to a waiting car. Marge and Rudy Krist walked ahead of Padway, who had forgotten to put away his gun.

3
"I Feel Bad Killin' You . . ."

The room was enormous in the flashlight beams. There were still recognizable signs of its former occupation—dust-blackened, tawdry bunting dangling ragged from the ceiling, a floor worn by the scraping of many feet, a few forgotten tables and chairs, the curling fly-specked photographs of bygone celebrities autographed to "Dear Skinny," an empty, dusty band platform.

One of Padway's men lighted a coal-oil lamp. The boarded windows were carefully reinforced with tarpaper. In one end of the ballroom were stacks of liquor cases built into a huge square mountain. Doors opened into other rooms, black and disused. The place was utterly silent, odorous with the dust and rot of years.

Padway said, "Put him over there." He indicated a camp cot beside a table and a group of chairs. The men carrying Channing dropped him there. The rest straggled in and sat down, lighting cigarettes. Padway said, "Joe, take the Thompson and go upstairs. Yell if anybody looks this way."

Jack Flavin swore briefly. "I told you we weren't tailed, Dave. Cripes, we've driven all over this goddam town to make sure. Can't you relax?"

"Sure, when I'm ready to. You may have hair on your chest, Jack, but it's no bulletproof vest." He went over to the cot and pulled the blanket off Channing. Channing looked up at him, his eyes sunk deep under hooded lids. He was naked to the waist. Padway inspected the two gashes.

"I didn't miss you by much, Chan," he said slowly.

"Enough."

"Yeah." Padway pulled a cigarette slowly out of the pack. "Who did you talk to, Chan, besides Marge Krist? What did you say?"

Channing bared his teeth. It might have been meant for a smile. It was undoubtedly malicious.

Padway put the cigarette in his mouth and got a match out. It was a large kitchen match with a blue head. "You got me puzzled, Chan. You sure have. And it worries me. I can smell copper, but I can't see any. I don't like that, Channing."

"That's tough," Channing said.

"Yeah. It may be." Padway struck the match.

Rudy Krist rose abruptly and went off into the shadows. No one else moved. Marge Krist was hunched up on a blanket near Flavin. Her eyes were brilliant green under her tumbled red hair.

Dave Padway held the match low over Channing's eyes. There was no draft, no tremor in his hand. The flame was a perfect triangle, gold and blue. Padway said somberly, "I don't trust you,

Chan. You were a good cop. You were good enough to take me once, and you were good enough to take my brother, and he was a better man than me. I don't trust this setup, Chan. I don't trust you."

Flavin said impatiently, "Why didn't you for godsake kill him the first time? You're to blame for this mess, Dave. If you hadn't loused it up—okay, okay! The guy's crazy afraid of fire. Look at him now. Put it to him, Dave. He'll talk."

"Will he?" said Padway. "Will he?" He lowered the match. Channing screamed. Padway lighted his cigarette and blew out the match. "Will you talk, Chan?"

Channing said hoarsely, "Offer me the right coin, Dave. Give me the man who killed my brother, and I'll tell you where you stand."

Padway stared at him with blank light eyes, and then he began to laugh, quietly, with a terrible humor.

"Tie him down, Mack," he said, "and bring the matches over here."

■ ■ ■

The room was quiet, except for Channing's breathing. Rudy Krist sat apart from the others, smoking steadily, his hands never still. The three gunsels bent with scowling concentration over a game of blackjack. Marge Krist had not moved since she sat down. Perhaps twenty minutes had passed. Channing's corded body was spotted with small vicious marks.

Dave Padway dropped the empty matchbox. He sighed and leaned over, slapping Channing lightly on the cheek. Channing opened his eyes.

"You going to talk, Chan?"

Channing's head moved, not much, from right to left.

Jack Flavin swore. "Dave, the guy's crazy afraid of fire. If he'd had anything to tell he'd have told it." His shirt was open, the space around his feet littered with cigarette ends. His harsh terrier face had no laughter in it now. He watched Padway obliquely, his lids hooded.

"Maybe," said Padway. "Maybe not. We got a big deal on tonight, Jack. It's our first step toward the top. Channing read your receipt, remember. He knows about that. He knows a lot of people out here. Maybe he has a deal on, and maybe it isn't with the cops. Maybe it isn't supposed to break until tonight. Maybe it'll break us when it does."

Channing laughed, a dry husky mockery.

Flavin got up, scraping his chair angrily. "Listen, Dave, you getting chicken or something? Looks to me like you've got a fixation on this bird."

"Looks to me, Jack, like nobody ever taught you manners."

The room became perfectly still. The men at the table put their cards down slowly, like men playing cards in a dream. Marge Krist rose silently and moved towards the cot.

Channing whispered, "Take it easy, boys. There's no percentage in a shroud." He watched them, his eyes holding a deep, cruel glint. It was something new, something born within the last quarter of an hour. It changed, subtly, his whole face, the lines of it, the shape of it. "You've got a business here, a going concern. Or maybe you haven't. Maybe you're bait for the meat wagon. I talked, boys, oh yes, I talked. Give me Hank's killer, and I'll tell you who."

Flavin said, "Can't you forget that? The guy jumped."

Channing shook his head.

Padway said softly, "Suppose you're right, Chan. Suppose you get the killer. What good does that do you?"

"I'm not a cop anymore. I don't care how much booze you run. All I want is the guy that killed Hank."

Jack Flavin laughed. It was not a nice sound.

"Dave knows I keep a promise. Besides, you can always shoot me in the back."

Flavin said, "This is crazy. You haven't really hurt the guy, Dave. Put it to him. He'll talk."

"His heart would quit first." Padway smiled almost fondly at Channing. "He's got his guts back in. That's good to know, huh, Chan?"

"Yeah."

"But bad, too. For both of us."

"Go ahead and kill me, Dave, if you think it would help any."

Flavin said, with elaborate patience, "Dave, the man is crazy. Maybe he wants publicity. Maybe he's trying to chisel himself back on the force. Maybe he's a masochist. But he's nuts. I don't believe he talked to anybody. Either make him talk, or shoot him. Or I will."

"Will you, now?" Padway asked.

Channing said, "What are you so scared of, Flavin?"

Flavin snarled and swung his hand. Padway caught it, pulling Flavin around. He said, "Seems to me whoever killed Hank has made us all a lot of trouble. He's maybe busted us wide open. I'd kind of like to know who did it, and why. We were working together then, Jack, remember? And nobody told me about any cop named Channing."

Flavin shook him off. "The kid committed suicide. And don't try manhandling me, Dave. It was my racket, remember. I let you in."

"Why," said Padway mildly, "that's so, ain't it?" He hit Flavin in the mouth so quickly that his fist made a blur in the air. Flavin fell, clawing automatically at his armpit. Padway's men rose from the table and covered him. Flavin dropped his hand. He lay still, his eyes slitted and deadly.

Marge Krist slid down silently beside Channing's cot. She might have been fainting, leaning forward against it, her hands out of sight. She was not fainting. Channing felt her working at his wrists.

Flavin said, "Rudy. Come here."

Rudy Krist came into the circle of lamplight. He looked like a small boy dreaming a nightmare and knowing he can't wake up.

Flavin said, "All right, Dave. You're boss. Go ahead and give Channing his killer." He looked at Rudy, and everybody else looked, too, except the men covering Flavin.

Rudy Krist's eyes widened, until white showed all around the green. He stopped, staring at the hard, impassive faces turned toward him.

Flavin said contemptuously, "He turned you soft, Rudy. You spilled over and then you didn't have the nerve to go through with it. You knew what would happen to you. So you shoved Hank off the pier to save your own hide."

Rudy made a stifled, catlike noise. He leaped suddenly down onto Flavin. Padway motioned to his boys to hold it. Channing cried out desperately, "Don't do anything. Wait! Dave, drag him off."

Rudy had Flavin by the throat. He was frothing slightly. Flavin writhed, jerking his heels against the floor. Suddenly there was a sharp slamming noise from underneath Rudy's body. Rudy bent his back, as though he were trying to double over backwards. He let go of Flavin. He relaxed, his head falling sleepily against Flavin's shoulder.

Channing rolled off the cot, scrambling toward Flavin.

Flavin fired again, twice, so rapidly the shots sounded like one. One of Padway's boys knelt down and bowed forward over his knees like a praying Jap. Another of Padway's men fell. The second shot clipped Padway, tearing the shoulder pad of his suit.

Channing grabbed Flavin's wrist from behind.

"Okay," said Padway grimly. "Hold it, everybody."

Before he got the words out a small sharp crack came from behind the cot. Flavin relaxed. He lay looking up into Channing's face with an expression of great surprise, as though the third eye just opened in his forehead gave him a completely new perspective.

Marge Krist stood green-eyed and deadly with a little pearl-handled revolver smoking in her hand.

Padway turned toward her slowly. Channing's mouth twitched dourly. He hardly glanced at the girl, but rolled the boy's body over carefully.

Channing said, "Did you kill Hank?"

Rudy whispered, "Honest to God, no."

"Did Flavin kill him?"

"I don't know . . ." Tears came in Rudy's eyes. "Hank," he whispered, "I wish . . ." The tears kept running out of his eyes for several seconds after he was dead.

By that time the police had come into the room, from the dark disused doorways, from behind the stacked liquor. Max Gandara said,

"Everybody hold still."

. . .

Dave Padway put his hands up slowly, his eyes at first wide with surprise and then narrow and ice-hard. His gunboy did the same, first dropping his rod with a heavy clatter on the bare floor.

Padway said, "They've been here all the time."

Channing sat up stiffly. "I hoped they were. I didn't know whether Max would play with me or not."

"You dirty double-crossing louse."

"I feel bad, crossing up an ape like you, Dave. You treated me so square, up there by Hyperion." Channing raised his voice. "Max, look out for the boy with the chopper."

Gandara said, "I had three men up there. They took him when he went up, real quiet."

Marge Krist had come like a sleepwalker around the cot. She was close to Padway. Quite suddenly she fainted. Padway caught her, so that she shielded his body, and his gun snapped into his hand.

Max Gandara said, "Don't shoot. Don't anybody shoot."

"That's sensible," said Padway softly.

Channing's hand, on the floor, slid over the gun Flavin wasn't using anymore. Then, very quickly, he threw himself forward into the table with the lamp on it.

A bullet slammed into the wood, through it, and past his ear, and then Channing fired twice, deliberately, through the flames.

Channing rose and walked past the fire. He moved stiffly, limping, but there was a difference in him. Padway was down on one knee, eyes shut and teeth clenched against the pain of a shattered wrist. Marge Krist was still standing. She was staring with stricken eyes at the hole in her white forearm and the pattern of brilliant red threads spreading from it.

Max Gandara caught Channing. "You crazy—"

Channing hit him, hard and square. His face didn't change expression. "I owe you that one, Max. And before you start preaching the sanctity of womanhood, you better pry out a couple of those slugs that just missed me. You'll find they came from Miss Krist's pretty little popgun—the same one that killed her boy friend, Jack Flavin." He went over and tilted Marge Krist's face to his, quite gently. "You came out of your faint in a hurry, didn't you, sweetheart?"

She brought up her good hand and tried to claw his eye out.

Channing laughed. He pushed her into the arms of a policeman. "It'll all come out in the wash. Meantime, there are the bullets from Marge's gun. The fact that she had a gun at all proves she was in on the gang. They'd have searched her, if all that pious stuff about poor Rudy's evil ways had been on the level. She was a little surprised about Padway and sore because Flavin had kept it from her. But she knew which was the better man, all right. She was going along with Padway, and she shot

Flavin to keep his mouth shut about Hank, and to make sure he didn't get Padway by accident. Flavin was a gutty little guy, and he came close to doing just that. Marge untied me because she hoped I'd get shot in the confusion, or start trouble on my own account. If you hadn't come in, Max, she'd probably have shot me herself. She didn't want anymore fussing about Hank Channing, and with me and Flavin dead she was in the clear."

Gandara said with ugly stubbornness, "Sounded to me like Flavin made a pretty good case against Rudy."

"Sure, sure. He was down on the ground with half his teeth out and three guys holding guns on him."

Marge Krist was sitting now on the cot, while somebody worked over her with a first aid kit. Channing stood in front of her.

"You've done a good night's work, Marge. You killed Rudy just as much as you did Flavin, or Hank. Rudy had decent stuff in him. You forced him into the game, but Hank was turning him soft. You killed Hank."

Channing moved closer to her. She looked up at him, her green eyes meeting his dark ones, both of them passionate and cruel.

"You're a smart girl, Marge. You and your mealy-mouthed hypocrisy. I know now what you meant when you accused Rudy of being afraid to be questioned. Flavin couldn't kill Hank by himself. He wasn't big enough, and Hank wasn't that dumb. He didn't trust Flavin. But you, Marge, sure, he trusted you. He'd stand on a dark pier at midnight and talk to you, and never notice who was sneaking up behind with a blackjack." He bent over her. "A smart girl, Marge, and a pretty one. I don't think I'll want to stand outside the window while you die."

"I wish I'd killed you, too," she whispered. "By God, I wish I'd killed you too!"

Channing nodded. He went over and sat down wearily. He looked exhausted and weak, but his eyes were alive.

"Somebody give me a cigarette," he said. He struck the match himself. The smoke tasted good.

It was his first smoke in ten years.

Helen Nielsen

DECISION

From *Manhunt*, June 1957

Long before it was fashionable for female crime writers to write "dark," Helen Nielsen was turning out novels such as After Midnight *and* A Killer In The Street*—books that even the most hard-boiled of readers took to. Her novels have been out of print far too long, and deserve to entertain and inspire a new generation. For a good example of Neilsen at her dire best, read on.*

E. G.

RUTH HAD NEVER BEEN IN A COURTROOM BEFORE. IT WAS EXciting—like something from a movie or the television. She paused just inside the doorway, the matron at her side, and as she did so the flashbulbs began to explode, and all the people in the room turned to stare at her. For just a moment she was startled and embarrassed. One hand automatically tugged at the front of her blue wool suit jacket—it had a way of riding up since she'd put on weight. Not that Ruth was plump. Her figure was good—too good for comfort, because Ruth, although she'd trained herself to conceal it, was excessively shy. But she was also feminine. She tugged at the jacket, and then she brushed a wisp of blonde hair from her forehead—and all of this with such a well-practised concealment of emotion that the caption writers would be dusting off such phrases as "stony-faced tigress" and "iceberg killer" to fit under those pictures in the afternoon editions. By this time the flashbulbs had stopped exploding, and a policeman was clearing the way.

Ruth walked forward to the table where Mr. Jennings was waiting for her. He pulled out her chair and smiled.

"Good morning, Miss Kramer. You're looking well this morning."

Ruth didn't answer. She sat down, and then Mr. Jennings sat down beside her and began to fuss with some papers in his briefcase. Mr. Jennings was rather shy himself—and nervous. Ruth had heard it remarked that this was his first capital case, which accounted for the nervousness. Public Defender. She ran the words over in her mind. They had a good sound. This man was going to defend her from the public. No, that wasn't what the words really meant. Ruth knew. She'd learned a great many in her thirty-odd years, and she knew what just about all the words meant; but that's the way they sounded to her when she ran them over in her mind. She liked Mr. Jennings. He reminded her of Allan. Younger and more serious, but just as neat. That was the important thing. His white shirt was freshly laundered, his narrow tie was clipped in place, and his suit must have just come from the pressers. He was clean shaven and smelled of one of those lotions the ad writers call brisk and masculine.

But staring at Mr. Jennings would only make him more nervous. Ruth looked about the courtroom. The jury was in the box, their assorted faces wearing different degrees of strain. Ruth's bland face concealed an inner smile. The jury seemed even more nervous than Mr. Jennings. It might have been on trial instead of her. Then she turned and looked at the spectators. No trial since the Romans fed live dinners to the lions had been complete without them. The public—society. That was a word that amused her even more than the faces of the jury—society. There it was in its assembled might, neither frightening nor particularly offended. Curious was a better word. Curious society awaiting its cue to acquit or condemn, because society never knew until it was told what to do. It was like a huge mirror in which one saw not one reflection, but that of a crowd.

If I smiled, Ruth thought, *they would smile back. If I waved my hand, they would wave their hands. They never do anything of themselves. They never act; they only re-act.*

That was society, and she was outside of it now because she'd broken the first rule. She'd made a decision . . .

Everybody in the neighborhood could tell you how devoted Ruth Kramer was to her parents. Such a good girl. Such a hard

worker. Such a good provider since poor old Mr. Kramer had to
stop working. There wasn't a mother on the block who didn't
envy Mrs. Kramer's relationship with her daughter. Not many
young people were so thoughtful. Not many cared so much.
Everybody in the neighborhood could tell you everything they
knew about Ruth Kramer—which was nothing.

Ruth couldn't remember when she'd started hating her father.
It might have been the time when she was five and caught him
killing the puppies. They were new-born and hardly aware of life,
and maybe it was the only thing to do with times so hard and
food so short; but it was horrible to watch him toss their bodies,
still warm and wriggling, into the post-holes he'd been digging
for the back fence. It was even more horrible to hear him boast
about it later.

"Six-post-holes, six puppies at the bottom. I saved myself all
that work of digging graves."

"Otto, don't talk about it. Not in front of the child," Anna
Kramer would say.

"Why not talk about it? She has to learn to save—work,
money. Nobody can waste anything in life."

Otto Kramer had a simple philosophy. He never questioned
life; he never argued with it. "A bed to sleep on, a table to eat
on, a stove to cook on—what more do you need?" A very simple
philosophy. Worry and fear belonged in a woman's world, and he
had no sympathy for either. If Ruth had tears she could shed
them in her mother's thin, tight arms. There was no other
warmth in the world.

And there was no money to be wasted on the foolishness of
pain.

"A woman is supposed to have babies. That's what she's made
for. I ain't got money to throw away on hospital bills. It's all
foolishness anyway. It's all in a woman's mind."

Otto Kramer spoke and that was law. Anna never argued with
her husband. She just grew thin and pale and cried a great deal
when he was away, and when her time came it wasn't all in her
mind after all. Hidden behind the pantry door, a child heard
everything.

"You thick-skulled old-country men ought to be horse-
whipped!" the doctor said. "You lost a son for your stinginess,

and you damned near lost a wife! Leave her alone now until she gets her strength back—understand? Leave her alone or I'll take care of you myself!"

Crouched in the darkness behind the pantry door, Ruth didn't understand—except that in some way her mother was in danger from this man she was growing to hate and needed protection. She never forgot.

There were a great many things the neighbors didn't know about Ruth Kramer. They didn't know, for instance, that when she was fourteen she slept with a knife hidden under her pillow. Nobody knew that. Not even her mother. But Ruth had watched and guarded for a long time, and by that time the quarreling and night noises beyond the paper-thin walls had taken on a strange and ominous significance. The knife was for her fear—a nameless fear that was doomed to silence.

Anna Kramer didn't like to talk about such things.

"Forget the silly things you hear, child. It's not for you to worry about."

But Ruth wasn't a child. She was fourteen. At fourteen it seems there should be an end to misery.

"Why don't you get a divorce?" she asked.

Divorce! A shocking word. Where had she gotten such an idea? Divorce was a sin! It seemed to Ruth that perpetual unhappiness was an even greater sin; but she didn't have a chance to argue the point. The tight, thin arms were about her again, closing out the world. She mustn't think of such things. She had her school-work to think about, and that scholarship—

Ruth didn't win the scholarship. She suffered a breakdown and couldn't even finish the semester; but in a way, her sickness was a good thing. It gave her time to think things out. There had to be a reason for all this unhappiness, and there had to be a way out. If only they weren't so poor. If only there was a little extra money to fix up the house and have friends and live the way other people lived. Ruth thought it all out and then put the knife back in the knife drawer because it was foolishness, even if it was a sign of rebellion. She knew a better way.

There was no trouble about going back to school. School was an extravagance and a waste on a female. Work was good. Work kept young people out of trouble.

"I went to work when I was twelve years old," Otto Kramer

said. "Fifteen hours a day and a straw pallet in the back of the shop. I had no time for racing around in old cars and playing jazz records all night like young people do nowadays. Hoodlums! Nothing but hoodlums!"

Ruth didn't argue. The old cars and the jazz records weren't to be a part of her life anyway. There was no time. Work was for days and study was for evenings, because her father was wrong about education. He was wrong about a lot of things, but she didn't argue about any of them. Arguments and quarreling were a waste of time. She learned to withdraw from them—to tune out the voices behind the wall at night, just as she tuned up the music on her bedside radio. But she always listened with half an ear, and she never forgot to watch. And she never forgot her plan. Every problem had to have a solution, and she was going to find the solution for happiness. Otto Kramer's house remained a fortress from without; but within, it began to change. The floors were carpeted, the windows curtained, a plumber installed a new sink, and the ice-man didn't have to stop by after the refrigerator was delivered. The plan began to work. Anna Kramer's face learned how to smile; but Otto's remained grim.

"Foolishness! Damn foolishness! Throw money around like that and you'll be sorry!"

And just to prove his point, he lost his job and never did get around to finding another one.

It might have been then that Ruth Kramer began to hate her father; but for the next few years she was too busy to think about it. Every problem had to have a solution. She did her positive thinking and took another course at night school. After that, she got a better job with longer hours. The problem was still there, but there wasn't so much time to think about it. What was happiness anyway? How many people ever knew? When the quarrelling was especially bad, and the tears too heavy—Ruth could never bear to hear her mother cry—she could set a balance again with flowers sent as a surprise, or some new piece for the shelf of china miniatures Anna Kramer so loved. And there was always the music to be turned up louder so the neighbors wouldn't hear. From the outside, everything was lovely. Nobody ever went into the house but the three people who lived inside, enduring one another while the years piled up behind them like a stack of unpaid bills. And everything in life had to be paid for sooner or later. Far back in her mind, crowded now with more knowledge than she could ever use, Ruth knew that.

The bills began coming due when she met Allan.

She'd never thought about men. They were in her world; but they were only names on the doors of offices, or voices answering the telephone. They sat behind desks that always held a photograph of the wife and children, and they sometimes paid compliments and gave raises.

"I wish we had more employees like you, Miss Kramer. I never have to worry about how you're going to do your work."

That kind of compliment—never anything about her hair-do, which was severe and neat, or her suits, which were tailored to conceal her thinness and build up her bustline. Men were hands on desktops, voices on the telephone, and signatures on the paycheck. They were the office wolf to be ignored, the out of town customer to be kidded, and the serious young man who missed his mother to be gently brushed aside. And a dour old man who now sat at home in his chair in the corner like a pile of dirty rags.

But Allan Roberts wasn't any of these things. Allan was that old bill coming due. If she'd known, she wouldn't have been so pleased when he called her into his office that first day.

"I like the way you work, Miss Kramer. You must have been with the company a long time."

A new engineer with top rating, and he'd noticed her out of the whole office staff. Ruth was flattered.

"Twelve years," she admitted, wishing, for some reason, that it didn't sound so long.

"Good. You know more about procedure than I do. You're just the assistant I need on this hotel job."

That's how it started—strictly business. But it was a big job—an important job. It meant long hours with late dinners in some hole-in-the-wall restaurant, with a juke box wailing and a lot of talk and laughter to ease the strain of a hard, tense job. It meant work on Sunday, with Allan's convertible honking at the curb, and Ruth hurrying out before he had time to come to the door. And, eventually, it meant talk at home.

"You're with this man an awful lot," Anna Kramer said.

"He's nice," Ruth admitted. "And smart. I'm learning a lot on this job."

"He looks nice. He dresses nice."

"He's got a responsible job. He has to dress nice."

"Your father used to dress nice. I'll never forget when I met him—silk shirts, derby hat, walking stick."

"My father?"

"Handsome, too. I remember thinking that I'd never seen such a handsome man—and such big ideas for the future."

They'd never talked like this before. Anna Kramer's eyes were far away; then they met Ruth's and changed the subject.

"I suppose you'll be working Sunday."

"I suppose I will," Ruth said.

"We'll miss church again."

"I keep telling you, you should make friends with the neighbors and go with them."

Anna sighed. Her eyes found the miniatures on the shelf.

"You know how your father feels about neighbors. I don't like to start a fuss and get you upset when we have such a nice home now."

Ruth worked Sunday. She worked many Sundays, and then, as much as she dreaded it, the job ended.

"But we're invited to the opening," Allan said. "When shall I pick you up?"

She hadn't counted on that. Working with Allan was fun. Dinner in those small cafes was fun. But a hotel opening wasn't like a concert, or a lecture, or a class at evening school.

"I suppose it's formal," she hedged.

"I hope so. You'll be a knockout in an evening gown."

He was kidding her, of course. Allan was a great kidder. Still, she didn't like to refuse. It might even jeopardize her job. She took a lunch hour for shopping, because she'd never owned an evening dress. That was when she became the last person to be aware of what had been going on under those tailored suits all the years. Allan wasn't kidding.

Cinderella went to the ball. Poor Cinderella, who was always losing things. A dance floor wasn't much good to a collector of Bach, but Allan was gallant.

"I might as well be honest," he said. "It doesn't show because I have my shoes made to order, but I've got two left feet. Let's see how the terrace looks in the moonlight."

The terrace looked the way all terraces look in the moonlight. Ruth was trembling when she pulled away from him. They hadn't taught her anything like that in night school. But she was embarrassed, too. He must have known. He could go back to the office and tell stories in the washroom about how he'd frightened that straight-laced Miss Kramer who was so efficient in so many other things.

"You live with your parents, don't you?"

She expected that. She didn't have to answer. She already felt alone.

"I mean, you don't have any other ties to hold you here?"

She didn't expect that.

"To hold me?"

"There's a new contract coming up in Mexico City. A big one—six months, maybe a year. I'm getting the assignment, and I'd like to have you come along. I think we work well together."

She didn't expect that at all. Mexico City. A Latin beat from the dance floor came up behind them, a deep, throbbing rhythm, and Ruth began to hear it for the first time. To hear it, and feel it, with a stirring and churning starting inside her as if something were being born.

And she could feel Allan's eyes smiling in the darkness.

"I think you'd like Mexico," he said. "I think the change will do you good. Anyway, you've got a couple of weeks to decide."

It was much after midnight when Cinderella came home from the ball. She stopped humming at the doorway and let herself in quietly; but she needn't have been so cautious. As soon as she switched on the lights, she saw her mother huddled in the wing-chair.

"You didn't have to wait up—" she began, and then she saw her mother's face. "What is it? What's wrong?"

The face of a martyr taking up the cross.

"Nothing," Anna answered. "Nothing for you to worry about."

"Nothing? Then why aren't you in bed?"

Haunted eyes looked at her. A thin hand tugged at the throat of a worn robe, and the sleeve fell back to show an ugly bruise.

"Mother—!"

"Go to bed," Anna said. "You had a nice time, didn't you? Go to bed and don't worry about me."

"But you've been hurt!"

"It doesn't matter. It's happened before."

"*He* did it!"

An anger flared up as old as a knife tucked away under a pillow.
"Don't—don't talk so loud! He's asleep now."

"But you don't have to put up with this! You don't have to live with him!"

Anna's eyes swept the room. A beautiful room—perfect, like the miniatures on the shelf. The home she'd always wanted. Some plans did work.

"Maybe he's sick," Ruth said. "Maybe if he saw a doctor—"

"You know what your father thinks of doctors."

"But if he's violent—"

Anna wore a sad smile.

"I told you—it's nothing. It's happened before. You would have noticed if you weren't always so busy. He's an old man, that's all. An old man gets angry when—when he can't do what he used to do."

Anna fell silent. There was shame in her eyes for having almost spoken of the forbidden subject. She got up out of the chair and started toward the hall.

"You're not going back there?"

The sad smile came back.

"I told you—it's nothing. I shouldn't have said anything and ruined your good time. Go to bed now. It's all right. As long as I have you, everything is all right."

The arms closed about Ruth's shoulders in a goodnight embrace. Nothing . . . nothing . . . Ruth turned out the lamp when she was gone and sat alone in the darkness. Nothing . . . She began to tremble.

Ruth didn't go to Mexico City. At the office, her breakdown was written off to overwork on the hotel job. When she returned, Allan was gone. He never came back. For a time there was an empty place where he had been, a kind of misty pitfall with a mental sign in front of it: "Keep Away—Danger," and then the emptiness began to fill up with odds and ends of more work, more books, a course in clay modelling, and a season's ticket to the symphony. At home she played the music louder to drown out the endless quarrelling, and learned not to mention separation, or a doctor, or doing anything at all.

On her thirtieth birthday, Ruth bought her first bottle of whiskey. She kept it in a closet where her mother wouldn't find it. Good people, who didn't do sinful things—such as not facing problems—didn't drink. The bottle helped on the long nights when sleep wouldn't come. A little later, she dropped the modelling class because she'd lost interest in it, and the homework was cluttering up her room, and she had to stop going to the concerts because they made her nervous. But she couldn't sit around the house watching the slow death come. She drove out nights, and in time found a hole-in-the-wall bar where a three piece combo wandered deep into the wild nowhere, and a sad singer sobbed out the woes of the shadow people, who feel no pain and dream old dreams that never come true because they live in the land of no decision.

There were objections, of course.

"I wish you wouldn't go out so much alone," Anna Kramer said, "especially at nights."

Ruth laughed. She laughed a lot lately.

"Alone? How else could I go?"

The hurt look, and then—

"We used to take such nice rides on Sunday."

"I'll take you for a ride on Sunday."

"But every night—out. Honestly, I don't know what to make of you anymore. You'd think I had enough trouble with your father!"

"Oh, God—!"

Then a door would slam, the music go loud, and she'd dig the bottle out of the closet.

The trouble at the office was a long time coming. It wasn't her fault. Everything cluttered, everything a mess. The youngsters were coming in—fresh and eager and green. No use trying to teach them anything. They knew it all. It got so that Ruth hardly talked to anyone except the clown in the sales department who told ribald jokes and made her laugh without knowing why. The trouble was a long time coming, but it came suddenly when it arrived. With gloves, of course. Working too hard. Too much responsibility. Not a demotion, understand, but the hours will be shorter and, of course, the pay. Ruth understood. The strange thing was how little she cared.

She didn't go home after work. She drove around for a few hours, and then drifted back to that hole in the wall where the shadows moaned, and crouched, and waited. Now it seemed that they were waiting for her—that this was the destiny she'd been bound for all these years. This was what came of hiding behind pantry doors and trembling in the darkness with a knife under her pillow. She knew what was wrong. She couldn't bury it in the books or try to hide it in the bottom of an empty bottle anymore. It crawled inside her like a worm of dread, and there was only one way to get rid of it. She ordered a double whiskey to steel her nerve.

The shadow people moved about her with hungry faces. At first she'd come only to watch them; now she belonged. She had only to give the sign. They were waiting. One, in particular, a dark, dirty, unshaven man.

They went out together. They drove to a dark street—dead end. It seemed appropriate.

No preliminaries. This wasn't a high school prom. He knew what she wanted. His mouth closed over hers, and his hands began tearing at her blouse. Ruth shuddered. The stirring that had started with Allan's kiss was churning up like an angry sea. A wall was crumbling. A high wall, a high tower—

But her hands were pushing him away.

He clawed at her, swearing softly. She pushed him back against the door.

"You crazy bitch!"

He came at her again, ugly and cruel. She saw his face dimly—unshaven, leering, smelling of liquor and filth. All of her strength went into her lunge. He fell backward against the door handle. It opened, spilling him out in the street. She had the motor started by the time he'd scrambled to his feet. The headlights caught him for one wild moment as she backed away—an angry and bewildered man, muttering curses and fumbling at his trousers.

She drove blindly, half sobbing. When it was far enough behind, she parked and sat alone in the darkness. The wall had started to crumble, and when a thing started it had to go on until it was done. She smashed the "Danger" sign in her mind and stared deep into the emptiness that was Allan's. Allan was gone. Allan would never come back. She'd never hear his laughter, or see the way his eyes crinkled, or feel that second kiss that had made all the difference. But the world wasn't over. There was other laughter and other eyes, and there *was* a difference! There *had* to be!

But before she could find it, there was one thing she must do. One thing for certain.

She drove home, noticing for the first time how the hedges had become shaggy and how the lawn had turned brown. There were so many things to do, and never enough time. She went into the house. Her father sat in his chair in the corner like a heap of dirty rags. Her mother looked up with anxious eyes. She hurried past them to her room. One thing she *must* do . . .

"Ruth! What are you doing? Where are you going?"

One suitcase was enough. The furniture, the lamps, the books didn't matter. Let the dead bury the dead. One suitcase and tomorrow was enough.

"Why are you packing? What's happened? What's wrong?"

No answers. No explanations. No trouble. Ruth closed the suitcase and started toward the door. They were there, both of them. The woman and the old man. Bewildered, frightened. She tried to get through the door without speaking, but they blocked the way.

"I'm leaving," she said.

"Leaving? For a trip? On business?"

"Forever," Ruth said.

"But why? What have I done?"

Tears were welling up in the woman's eyes. Ruth couldn't bear tears: She tried to push past. Her father was in the way.

"Who do you think you are?" he demanded. "You answer your mother!"

"There is no answer."

"You be careful now! You ain't so damn smart as you think. You ain't no better than us! You'll end up in the gutter like I always said!"

He shouldn't have said it—not ever, but especially not then. An ugly, dirty, unshaven old man. She looked at him and trembled, and then it started again—the shuddering, the churning inside.

"Let me go!" she gasped.

He tried to push her back into the room. He slapped her across the face, and the wall was crumbling again. She had the suitcase in her hand. She swung with all her might. She heard him go down, and then the ugly, evil face was gone . . .

"Ruth—what have you done?"

He was on the floor—quiet and bleeding.

"Your own father! You've struck down your own father!"

Anna knelt beside him, cradling his bleeding head in her arms. "Otto! Otto, are you alive? *Liebchen—*"

Ruth stared at them. The woman sobbing, her head bowed and her tight, thin arms, cradling him closer and closer to her breast. Her child. Her broken child caught up in the great-mother-lust, that subtle rape from which there is no escape save one . . .

And the wall was crumbling so that Ruth's breath came in great, silent sobs. When a thing started it had to be finished, one way or another. She moved slowly toward her mother.

■   ■   ■

The murmur of voices in the courtroom silenced and everybody rose as the judge came to the bench. A handsome, dignified man graying at the temples. Stern and fatherly. He sat down, and everybody sat down. It was about to begin. Exciting. Just like in the movies.

And then a man came across the room and bent down to whisper in Mr. Jennings' ear. Mr. Jennings looked happy. He turned to Ruth.

"Good news!" he said. "Your father has regained consciousness. He's ready to testify that he struck you first—that you retaliated in self-defense."

Of course, Ruth thought. *Somebody has to look after him.*

"That gives you a good chance of getting off completely. We should have little trouble proving that your mother's death was accidental. Everybody knows how devoted you were."

For just a moment Ruth felt the quick stab of panic; and then her poise returned and she sat back quietly. The jury—only faces in a mirror. She'd never let them acquit her. Nobody was going to send her back to that house now that she'd made her decision.

Clark Howard

HORN MAN

From *Ellery Queen's Mystery Magazine,* June 1980

Besides having written a number of bestselling blockbuster novels, Clark Howard has written several smaller and more personal books, at least one of which, The Arm, became a more-than-decent movie. For all his skills as a novelist, however, one might argue that it is his short stories that future generations will remember him for. In his shorter work, Howard tries a variety of voices, techniques, and themes, frequently producing work which even literary writers would envy. The story here is an example of Howard at his very best.

E. G.

WHEN DIX STEPPED OFF THE GREYHOUND BUS IN NEW ORleans, old Rainey was waiting for him near the terminal entrance. He looked just the same as Dix remembered him. Old Rainey had always looked old, since Dix had known him, ever since Dix had been a little boy. He had skin like black saddle leather and patches of cotton-white hair, and his shoulders were round and stooped. When he was contemplating something, he chewed on the inside of his cheeks, pushing his pursed lips in and out as if he were revving up for speech. He was doing that when Dix walked up to him.

"Hey, Rainey."

Rainey blinked surprise and then his face split into a wide smile of perfect, gleaming teeth. "Well, now. Well, well, well, now." He looked Dix up and down. "They give you that there suit of clothes?"

Dix nodded. "Everyone gets a suit of clothes if they done more than a year." Dix's eyes, the lightest blue possible without being gray, hardened just enough for Rainey to notice. "And I sure done more than a year," he added.

"That's the truth," Rainey said. He kept the smile on his face and changed the subject as quickly as possible. "I got you a room in the Quarter. Figured that's where you'd want to stay."

Dix shrugged. "It don't matter no more."

"It will," Rainey said with the confidence of years. "It will when you hear the music again."

Dix did not argue the point. He was confident that none of it mattered. Not the music, not the French Quarter, none of it. Only one thing mattered to Dix.

"Where is she, Rainey?" he asked. "Where's Madge?"

"I don't rightly know," Rainey said.

Dix studied him for a moment. He was sure Rainey was lying. But it didn't matter. There were others who would tell him.

They walked out of the terminal, the stooped old black man and the tall, prison-hard white man with a set to his mouth and a canvas zip-bag containing all his worldly possessions. It was late afternoon: the sun was almost gone and the evening coolness was coming in. They walked toward the Quarter, Dix keeping his long-legged pace slow to accommodate old Rainey.

Rainey glanced at Dix several times as they walked, chewing inside his mouth and working up to something. Finally he said, "You been playing at all while you was in?"

Dix shook his head. "Not for a long time. I did a little the first year. Used to dry play, just with my mouthpiece. After a while, though, I gave it up. They got a different kind of music over there in Texas. Stompin' music. Not my style." Dix forced a grin at old Rainey. "I ever kill a man again, I'll be sure I'm on *this* side of the Louisiana line."

Rainey scowled. "You know you ain't never killed nobody, boy," he said harshly. "You know it wudn't you that done it. It was *her*."

Dix stopped walking and locked eyes with old Rainey. "How long have you knowed me?" he asked.

"Since you was eight months old," Rainey said. "You know that. Me and my sistuh, we worked for your grandmamma, Miz Jessie Du-Chatelier. She had the finest gentlemen's house in the Quarter. Me and my sistuh, we cleaned and cooked for Miz Jessie. And took care of you after your own poor mamma took sick with the consumption and died—"

"Anyway, you've knowed me since I was less than one, and now I'm *forty*-one."

Rainey's eyes widened. "Naw," he said, grinning again, "you ain't that old. Naw."

"Forty-one, Rainey. I been gone sixteen years. I got twenty-five, remember? And I done sixteen."

Sudden worry erased Rainey's grin. "Well, if you forty-one how old that make *me*?"

"About two hundred. I don't know. You must be seventy or eighty. Anyway, listen to me now. In all the time you've knowed me, have I ever let anybody make a fool out of me?"

Rainey shook his head. "Never. No way."

"That's right. And I'm not about to start now. But if word got around that I done sixteen years for a killing that was somebody else's, I'd look like the biggest fool that ever walked the levee, wouldn't I?"

"I reckon so," Rainey allowed.

"Then don't ever say again that I didn't do it. Only one person alive knows for certain positive that I didn't do it. And I'll attend to her myself. Understand?"

Rainey chewed the inside of his cheeks for a moment, then asked, "What you fixin' to do about her?"

Dix's light-blue eyes hardened again. "Whatever I have to do, Rainey," he replied.

Rainey shook his head in slow motion. "Lord, Lord, Lord," he whispered.

■ ■ ■

Old Rainey went to see Gaston that evening at Tradition Hall, the jazz emporium and restaurant that Gaston owned in the Quarter. Gaston was slick and dapper. For him, time had stopped in 1938. He still wore spats.

"How does he look?" Gaston asked old Rainey.

"He *look* good," Rainey said. "He *talk* bad." Rainey leaned close to the white club-owner. "He fixin' to kill that woman. Sure as God made sundowns."

Gaston stuck a sterling-silver toothpick in his mouth. "He know where she is?"

"I don't think so," said Rainey. "Not yet."

"*You* know where she is?"

"Lastest I heard, she was living over on Burgundy Street with some doper."

Gaston nodded his immaculately shaved and lotioned chin.

"Correct. The doper's name is LeBeau. He's young. I think he keeps her around to take care of him when he's sick." Gaston examined his beautifully manicured nails. "Does Dix have a lip?"

Rainey shook his head. "He said he ain't played in a while. But a natural like him, he can get his lip back in no time a'tall."

"Maybe," said Gaston.

"He can," Rainey insisted.

"Has he got a horn?"

"Naw. I watched him unpack his bag and I didn't see no horn. So I axed him about it. He said after a few years of not playing, he just give it away. To some cowboy he was in the Texas pen with."

Gaston sighed. "He should have killed that fellow on this side of the state line. If he'd done the killing in Louisiana, he would have went to the pen at Angola. They play good jazz at Angola. Eddie Lumm is up there. You remember Eddie Lumm? Clarinetist. Learned to play from Frank Teschemacher and Jimmie Noone. Eddie killed his old lady. So now he blows at Angola. They play good jazz at Angola."

Rainey didn't say anything. He wasn't sure if Gaston thought Dix had really done the killing or not. Sometimes Gaston *played* like he didn't know a thing, just to see if somebody *else* knew it. Gaston was smart. Smart enough to help keep Dix out of trouble if he was a mind. Which was what old Rainey was hoping for.

Gaston drummed his fingertips silently on the table where they sat. "So. You think Dix can get his lip back with no problem, is that right?"

"Tha's right. He can."

"He planning to come around and see me?"

"I don't know. He probably set on finding that woman first. Then he might not be *able* to come see you."

"Well, see if you can get him to come see me first. Tell him I've got something for him. Something I've been saving for him. Will you do that?"

"You bet." Rainey got up from the table. "I'll go do it right now."

George Tennell was big and beefy and mean. Rumor had it that he had once killed two men by smashing their heads together with such force that he literally knocked their brains out. He had been a policeman for thirty years, first in the colored section, which was the only place he could work in the old days, and now in the *Vieux Carré*, the Quarter, where he was detailed to keep the peace to whatever extent it was possible. He had no family, claimed no friends. The Quarter was his home as well as his job. The only thing in the world he admitted to loving was jazz.

That was why, every night at seven, he sat at a small corner table in Tradition Hall and ate dinner while he listened to the band tune their instruments and warm up. Most nights, Gaston joined him later for a liqueur. Tonight he joined him before dinner.

"Dix got back today," he told the policeman. "Remember Dix?"

Tennell nodded. "Horn man. Killed a fellow in a motel room just across the Texas line. Over a woman named Madge Noble."

"That's the one. Only there's some around don't think he did it. There's some around think *she* did it."

"Too bad he couldn't have found twelve of those people for his jury."

"He didn't have no jury, George. Quit laying back on me. You remember it as well as I do. One thing you'd *never* forget is a good horn man."

Tennell's jaw shifted to the right a quarter of an inch, making his mouth go crooked. The band members were coming out of the back now and moving around on the bandstand, unsnapping instrument cases, inserting mouthpieces, straightening chairs. They were a mixed lot—black, white, and combinations; clean-shaven and goateed; balding and not; clear-eyed and strung out. None of them was under fifty—the oldest was the trumpet player, Luther Dodd, who was eight-six. Like Louis Armstrong, he had learned to blow at the elbow of Joe "King" Oliver, the great cornetist. His Creole-style trumpet playing was unmatched in New Orleans. Watching him near the age when he would surely die was agony for the jazz purists who frequented Tradition Hall.

Gaston studied George Tennell as the policeman watched Luther Dodd blow out the spit plug of his gleaming Balfour trumpet and loosen up his stick-brittle fingers on the valves. Gaston saw in Tennell's eyes that odd look of a man who truly worshipped traditional jazz music, who felt it down in the pit of himself just like the old men who played it, but who had never learned to play himself. It was a look that had the mix of love and sadness and years gone by. It was the only look that ever turned Tennell's eyes soft.

"You know how long I been looking for a horn man to take Luther's place?" Gaston asked. "A straight year. I've listened to a couple dozen guys from all over. Not a one of them could play traditional. Not a one." He bobbed his chin at Luther Dodd. "His fingers are like old wood, and so's his heart. He could go on me any night. And if he does, I'll have to shut down. Without a horn man, there's no Creole sound, no tradition at all. Without a horn, this place of mine, which is the last of the great jazz emporiums, will just give way to"—Gaston shrugged helplessly, "—whatever. Disco music, I suppose."

A shudder circuited George Tennell's spine, but he gave no outward sign of it. His body was absolutely still, his hands resting motionlessly on the snow-white tablecloth, eyes steadily fixed on Luther Dodd. Momentarily the band went into its first number, *Lafayette*, played Kansas City style after the way of Bennie Moten. The music pulsed out like spurts of water, each burst overlapping the one before it to create an even wave of sound that flooded the big room. Because Kansas City style was so rhythmic and highly danceable, some of the early diners immediately moved onto the dance floor and fell in with the music.

Ordinarily, Tennell liked to watch people dance while he ate; the moving bodies lent emphasis to the music he loved so much, music he had first heard from the window of the St. Pierre Colored Orphanage on Decatur Street when he had been a boy; music he had grown up with and would have made his life a part of if he had not been so completely talentless, so inept that he could not even read sharps and flats. But tonight he paid no attention to the couples out in front of the bandstand. He concentrated only on Luther Dodd and the old horn man's breath intake as he played. It was clear to Tennell that Luther was struggling for breath, fighting for every note he blew, utilizing every cubic inch of lung power that his old body could marshal.

After watching Luther all the way through *Lafayette*, and halfway through *Davenport Blues*, Tennell looked across the table at Gaston and nodded.

"All right," he said simply. "All right."

For the first time ever Tennell left the club without eating dinner.

■ ■ ■

As Dix walked along with old Rainey toward Gaston's club, Rainey kept pointing out places to him that he had not exactly forgotten, but had not remembered in a long time.

"That house there," Rainey said, "was where Paul Mares was born back in nineteen-and-oh-one. He's the one formed the original New Orleans Rhythm Kings. He only lived to be forty-eight but he was one of the best horn men of all time."

Dix would remember, not necessarily the person himself but the house and the story of the person and how good he was. He had grown up on those stories, gone to sleep by them as a boy, lived the lives of the men in them many times over as he himself was being taught to blow trumpet by Rozell "The Lip" Page when Page was already past sixty and he, Dix was only eight. Later, when Page died, Dix's education was taken over by Shepherd Norden and Blue Johnny Meadows, the two alternating as his teacher between their respective road tours. With Page, Norden, and Meadows in his background, it was no wonder that Dix could blow traditional.

"Right up the street there," Rainey said as they walked, "is where Wingy Manone was born in nineteen-and-oh-four. His given name was Joseph, but after his accident ever'body taken to calling him 'Wingy.' The accident was, he fell under a street car and lost his right arm. But that boy didn't let a little thing like that worry him none, no sir. He learned to play trumpet *left-handed*, and *one-handed*. And he was *good*. Lord he was good."

They walked along Dauphin and Chartes and Royal. All around them were the French architecture and grillework and statuary and vines and moss that made the *Vieux Carré* a world unto itself, a place of subtle sights, sounds, and smells—black and white and fish and age—that no New Orleans tourist, no Superdome visitor, no casual observer, could ever experience, because to experience was to understand, and understanding of the Quarter could not be acquired, it had to be lived.

"Tommy Ladnier, he used to live right over there," Rainey said, "right up on the second floor. He lived there when he came here from his hometown of Mandeville, Loozey-ana. Poor Tommy, he had a short life too, only thirty-nine years. But it was a good life. He played with King Oliver and Fletcher Henderson and Sidney Bechet. Yessir, he got in some good licks."

When they got close enough to Tradition Hall to hear the music, at first faintly, then louder, clearer, Rainey stopped talking. He wanted Dix to hear the music, to *feel* the sound of it as it wafted out over Pirate's Alley and the Café du Monde and Congo Square (they called it Beauregard Square now, but Rainey refused to recognize the new name). Instinctively, Rainey knew that it was important for the music to get back into Dix, to saturate his mind and catch in his chest and tickle his stomach. There were some things in Dix that needed to be washed out, some bad things, and Rainey was certain that the music would help. A good purge was always healthy.

Rainey was grateful, as they got near enough to define melody, that *Sweet Georgia Brown* was being played. It was a good melody to come home to.

They walked on, listening, and after a while Dix asked, "Who's on horn?"

"Luther Dodd."

"Don't sound like Luther. What's the matter with him?"

Rainey waved one hand resignedly. "Old. Dying, I 'spect."

They arrived at the Hall and went inside. Gaston met them with a smile. "Dix," he said, genuinely pleased, "it's good to see you." His eyes flickered over Dix. "The years have been good to you. Trim. Lean. No gray hair. How's your lip?"

"I don't have a lip no more, Mr. Gaston," said Dix. "Haven't had for years."

"But he can get it back quick enough," Rainey put in. "He gots a natural lip."

"I don't play no more, Mr. Gaston," Dix told the club owner.

"That's too bad," Gaston said. He bobbed his head toward the stairs. "Come with me. I want to show you something."

Dix and Rainey followed Gaston upstairs to his private office. The office was furnished the way Gaston dressed—old-style, Roaring Twenties. There was even a wind-up Victrola in the corner.

Gaston worked the combination of a large, ornate floor vault and pulled its big-tiered door open. From somewhere in its dark recess he withdrew a battered trumpet case, one of the very old kind with heavy brass fittings on the corners and, one knew, real velvet, not felt, for lining. Placing it gently in the center of his desk, Gaston carefully opened the snaplocks and lifted the top. Inside, indeed on real velvet, deep-purple real velvet, was a gleaming, silver, hand-etched trumpet. Dix and Rainey stared at it in unabashed awe.

"Know who it once belonged to?" Gaston asked.

Neither Dix nor Rainey replied. They were mesmerized by the instrument. Rainey had not seen one like it in fifty years. Dix had *never* seen one like it; he had only heard stories about the magnificent silver horns that the quadroons made of contraband silver carefully hidden away after the War Between the States. Because the silver cache had not, as it was supposed to, been given over to the Federal army as part of the reparations levied against the city, the quadroons, during the Union occupation, had to be very careful what they did with it. Selling it for value was out of the question. Using it for silver service, candlesticks, walking canes, or any other of the more obvious uses would have attracted the notice of a Union informer. But letting it lie dormant, even though it was safer as such, was intolerable to the quads, who refused to let a day go by without circumventing one law or another.

So they used the silver to plate trumpets and cornets and slide trombones that belonged to the tabernacle musicians who were just then beginning to experiment with the old *Sammsamounn* tribal music that would eventually mate with work songs and prison songs and gospels, and evolve into traditional blues, which would evolve into traditional, or Dixie-style, jazz.

"Look at the initials," Gaston said, pointing to the top of the bell. Dix and Rainey peered down at three initials etched in the silver: BRB.

"Lord have mercy," Rainey whispered. Dix's lips parted as if he too intended to speak, but no words sounded.

"That's right," Gaston said. "Blind Ray Blount. The first, the best, the *only*. Nobody has ever touched the sounds he created. That man hit notes nobody ever heard before—or since. He was the master."

"Amen," Rainey said. He nodded his head toward Dix. "Can he touch it?"

"Go ahead," Gaston said to Dix.

Like a pilgrim to Mecca touching the holy shroud, Dix ever so lightly placed the tips of three fingers on the silver horn. As he did, he imagined he could feel the touch left there by the hands of the amazing blind horn man who had started the great blues evolution in a patch of town that later became Storyville. He imagined that—

"It's yours if you want it," Gaston said. "All you have to do is pick it up and go downstairs and start blowing."

Dix wet his suddenly dry lips. "Tomorrow I—"

"Not tomorrow," Gaston said. "Tonight. Now."

"Take it, boy," Rainey said urgently.

Dix frowned deeply, his eyes narrowing as if he felt physical pain. He swallowed, trying to push an image out of his mind; an image he had clung to for sixteen years. "I can't tonight—"

"Tonight or never," Gaston said firmly.

"For God's sake, boy, take it!" said old Rainey.

But Dix could not. The image of Madge would not let him.

Dix shook his head violently, as if to rid himself of devils, and hurried from the room.

■   ■   ■

Rainey ran after him and caught up with him a block from the Hall. "Don't do it," he pleaded. "Hear me now. I'm an old man and I know I ain't worth nothin' to nobody, but I'm begging you, boy, please, please, please don't do it. I ain't never axed you for nothing in my whole life, but I'm axing you for this: *please* don't do it."

"I got to," Dix said quietly. "It ain't that I want to; I *got* to."

"But why, boy? *Why?*"

"Because we made a promise to each other," Dix said. "That night in that Texas motel room, the man Madge was with had told her he was going to marry her. He'd been telling her that for a long time. But he was already married and kept putting off leaving his wife. Finally Madge had enough of it. She asked me to come to her room between sets. I knew she was doing it to make him jealous, but it didn't matter none to me. I'd been crazy about her for so long that I'd do anything she asked me to, and she knew it.

"So between sets I slipped across the highway to where she had her room. But he was already there. I could hear through the transom that he was roughing her up some, but the door was locked and I couldn't get in. Then I heard a shot and everything got quiet. A minute later Madge opened the door and let me in.

The man was laying across the bed dying. Madge started bawling and saying how they would put her in the pen and how she wouldn't be able to stand it, she'd go crazy and kill herself.

"It was then I asked her if she'd wait for me if I took the blame for her. She promised me she would. And I promised her I'd come back to her." Dix sighed quietly. "That's what I'm doing, Rainey—keeping my promise."

"And what going to happen if she ain't kept *hers*?" Rainey asked.

"Mamma Rulat asked me that same thing this afternoon when I asked her where Madge was at." Mamma Rulat was an octaroon fortuneteller who always knew where everyone in the Quarter lived.

"What did you tell her?"

"I told her I'd do what I had to do. That's all a man *can* do, Rainey."

Dix walked away, up a dark side street. Rainey, watching him go, shook his head in the anguish of the aged and helpless.

"Lord, Lord, Lord—"

■   ■   ■

The house on Burgundy Street had once been a grand mansion with thirty rooms and a tiled French courtyard with a marble fountain in its center. It had seen nobility and aristocracy and great generals come and go with elegant, genteel ladies on their arms. Now the thirty rooms were rented individually with hot-plate burners for light cooking, and the only ladies who crossed the courtyard were those of the New Orleans night.

A red light was flashing atop a police car when Dix got there, and uniformed policemen were blocking the gate into the courtyard. There was a small curious crowd talking about what happened.

"A doper named LeBeau," someone said. "He's been shot."

"I heared it," an old man announced. "I heared the shot."

"That's where it happened, that window right up there—"

Dix looked up, but as he did another voice said, "They're bringing him out now!"

Two morgue attendants wheeled a sheet-covered gurney across the courtyard and lifted it into the back of a black panel truck. Several policemen, led by big beefy George Tennell, brought a woman out and escorted her to the car with the flashing red light. Dix squinted, focusing on her in the inadequate courtyard light. He frowned. Madge's mother, he thought, his mind going back two decades. What's Madge's mother got to do with this?

Then he remembered. Madge's mother was dead. She had died five years after he had gone to the pen.

Then who—?

Madge?

Yes, it *was* her. It was Madge. Older, as he was. Not a girl anymore, as he was not a boy anymore. For a moment he found it difficult to equate the woman in the courtyard with the memory in his mind. But it was Madge, all right.

Dix tried to push forward, to get past the gate into the courtyard, but two policemen held him back. George Tennell saw the altercation and came over.

"She's under arrest, mister," Tennell told Dix. "Can't nobody talk to her but a lawyer right now."

"What's she done anyhow?" Dix asked.

"Killed her boyfriend," said Tennell. "Shot him with this."

He showed Dix a pearl-handled over-and-under Derringer two-shot.

"Her boyfriend?"

Tennell nodded. "Young feller. 'Bout twenty-five. Neighbors say she was partial to young fellers. Some women are like that."

"Who says she shot him?"

"I do. I was in the building at the time, on another matter. I heard the shot. Matter of fact, I was the first one to reach the body. Few minutes later she come waltzing in. Oh, she put on a good act, all right, like she didn't even know what happened. But I found the gun in her purse myself."

By now the other officers had Madge Noble in the police car and were waiting for Tennell. He slipped the Derringer into his coat pocket and hitched up his trousers. Jutting his big jaw out an inch, he fixed Dix in a steady gaze.

"If she's a friend of yours, don't count on her being around for a spell. She'll do a long time for this."

Tennell walked away, leaving Dix still outside the gate. Dix waited there, watching, as the police car came through to the street. He tried to catch a glimpse of Madge as it passed, but there was not enough light in the back seat where they had her. As soon as the car left, the people who had gathered around began to leave too.

Soon Dix was the only one standing there.

■　■　■

At midnight George Tennell was back at his usual table in Tradition Hall for the dinner he had missed earlier. Gaston came over and joined him. For a few minutes they sat in silence, watching Dix up on the bandstand. He was blowing the silver trumpet that had once belonged to Blind Ray Blount; sitting next to the aging Luther Dodd; jumping in whenever he could as they played *Tailspin Blues*, then *Tank Town Bump*, then *Everybody Loves My Baby*.

"Sounds like he'll be able to get his lip back pretty quick," Tennell observed.

"Sure," said Gaston. "He's a natural. Rozell Page was his first teacher, you know."

"No, I didn't know that."

"Sure." Gaston adjusted the celluloid collar he wore, and turned the diamond stickpin in his tie. "What about the woman?" he asked.

Tennell shrugged. "She'll get twenty years. Probably do ten or eleven."

Gaston thought for a moment, then said, "That should be time enough. After ten or eleven years nothing will matter to him except the music. Don't you think?"

"It won't even take that long," Tennell guessed. "Not for him."

Up on the bandstand the men who played traditional went into *Just a Closer Walk with Thee*.

And sitting on the sawdust floor behind the bandstand, old Rainey listened with happy tears in his eyes.

Richard Matheson

THE FRIGID FLAME

From *Justice*, 1953

Stephen King and Dean Koontz have both freely acknowledged their debt to suspense master Richard Matheson. Author of such celebrated TV movies as "Duel" and "The Night Stalker," and writer of such classic horror novels as The Shrinking Man *and* I Am Legend *and* Hell House, *Matheson is also a brilliant writer of short stories. Here he is at novelette length—a shorter version of his James M. Cainian masterpiece,* Someone Is Bleeding. *It is difficult to convey the respect and envy Matheson elicits from his fellow scribes. He is one of the best writers of this century.*

E. G.

IT WAS A PRETTY BRISK DAY, AS I RECALL. SKY A LITTLE OVER-hung, the palisades greyish behind the mist. I suppose that's why the beach wasn't too crowded. Then again, it was a weekday and school hadn't let out yet. June. Put them together and what have you got?

A long stretch of beach with just her and me.

I'd been reading. But it got tiresome so I put the book down and sat there, arms around my knees, looking around.

She had on a one-piece bathing suit. Her figure was slight but well placed. I guessed she was about five-five. She was gazing intently at the waves. Her short-cropped blonde hair was stirring slightly in the breeze.

"Pardon me but could . . ." I said.

She wasn't turning. She kept looking at the shifting blue ocean, I looked over her figure again. Very well placed. A model's figure. The kind you see in *Mademoiselle*.

"Have you the time?" I asked.

She turned then.

Eyes. That was my first impression. The biggest and the brownest eyes I'd ever seen, great big eyes seeming to search for something. A frank look, a bold one, meaning a bold curiosity. But no smile. Deadpan. Did you ever have a child watch you from the seat in front of you in a bus?

That's what it was like.

Then she lifted her arm and looked at her watch. "One thirty," she said.

"Thank you," I answered.

She turned away. Her eyes moved to the sea again. I felt the uneasiness of the unconsolidated beachhead.

I rested on my elbows and looked at her profile. Delicately upturned nose. Lovely mouth. And those eyes.

After watching a while to catch her eyes again, I gave up. I was no professional at pickups. I got up slowly and walked down to the water. I felt her eyes following me.

I didn't leap in like athletes do. I stalled, I edged, I shivered. I evolved quick arguments for forgetting the whole thing.

Then I slid forward with a shudder and swam out a little way. Body heat took up the chills, my blood started moving.

On my back, looking up at the sky I wondered if I should speak to her. Whether it was worth it.

Then, when I came dripping back, she asked me if the water were cold.

I jumped at the opening.

"Pretty cold," I said. "I'll give you ten dollars if you go in."

She shook her head with a smile.

"Not me," she said.

I dried myself.

"Does the weather get cold out here?" I asked her. Weather talk, I thought. Always an ample wedge.

"It gets cold at night," she said.

The eyes intent on me again. I almost felt restive. They *were* searching.

I edged a little closer to her blanket.

"Well, I've just come from New York," I said, "and I came to get warm."

"Oh," she said, "is it cold there?"

Weather talk. Enough to start on. We eased into other things. California. New York. People. Cars. Dogs. Children.

"Do you like good music?" she asked me.

"What's good music?" I asked.

"Classical music."

"Sure," I said, "I love it."

The eyes looking harder. Was that the basis of the search?

"Gee," she said.

She sat hugging her knees. The filtering sunlight touched her white shoulders. She couldn't have been more than seventeen, I thought.

I was smiling. "Why gee?" I asked her.

"Because men never like good music," she said. "My . . ."

She stopped. Her eyes lowered.

"What's the Hollywood Bowl like?" I asked her, not wanting to let conversation run down.

She was looking again, shaking her head.

"I don't know," she said, "I sure wish I could go, though."

Too easy, I thought. Where is the hedging, the sly evasions, the mental sparring of a he and she? The moxie?

No moxie in Peggy.

That was her name.

"What's yours?" she asked.

"David," I said, "David Newton."

And so we talked. I'm trying to remember the significant things she said. They came out once in a while in between straight data about her mother, dead, her father, a retired navy man, her profession none and her spirit, obviously stepped on somewhere.

She saw my book and asked what it was. I told her, and we got started on the subject of historical novels.

"They're dirt," she said, "nothing but sex."

Something in her eyes. A hardness. I said why read them if they offend her.

"I'm looking for a decent one," she said.

"I'll write one," I said.

Obvious move. Impress the little girl. I am a writer, what do you think about that, my young lady?

She didn't catch it.

We kept skating around with words. Talking about home and background, school and other things. I told her I'd graduated from the University of Missouri Journalism School three years before. She told me about traveling around with her mother, father and brother until her mother died, then she and Phillip, her brother, not being able to follow the old man from one base to another anymore. So they stayed in San Francisco with a friend of her mother's.

"She was a swell woman," Peggy said. "But her husband—"

"What about him?"

"He was a pig," she said.

A significant remark. Not to me at the time. But later I understood.

Now, though, I just listened halfway, devoting the other half of my attention to looking at her almost child-like face. At the way her hair was parted on the right, the boyish wave of blonde hair over the left part of her forehead. The full lips, delicately red. And those eyes.

How could a face like that give you premonitions? It just didn't. And that was too bad.

We were in the middle of a discussion on jazz when she stood up.

"I have to go," she said.

I felt myself start. I'd almost forgotten we'd just met.

She began to put on her jeans and blouse.

"Well, I have to get back to my novel too," I said standing up. Trying again.

"Oh, that," she said, frowning.

"No, one I'm writing, not reading," I said, giving up subtleties.

We scuffed across the warm sands.

"Gee," she said, "you like good music and you write."

She shook her head. I got the impression she was confused.

"Is it so strange?" I asked.

"Men aren't sensitive enough to do things like that."

We reached a corner on Arizona and she started to turn off. I fiddled around, asking for her phone number, and she fiddled back, finally giving it to me with a brooding reluctance. I memorized the number.

We said goodbye and I watched her walking down toward Santa Monica Boulevard. She moved with a relaxed, effortless grace.

I turned away. I went home and worked on the book with a renewed vigor.

That afternoon I sent a card to a friend in New York. *Met me a cute gal*, it read. *Glad you aren't here.*

That evening I remembered something. I remembered that I'd forgotten to write down her telephone number and now it was gone from my mind.

■ ■ ■

I went to the beach every day for a week but I saw no Peggy Ann.

I gave up three days and wrote heavily. Then, on the fourth day, I got up late, couldn't get up the fortitude to sit in front of my typewriter, ended up by putting on my bathing suit and leaving for the beach.

And while down there, happened to glance up and saw her walking across the sands. My heart beat harder. I realized I'd been waiting for her. Again.

She didn't see me. She was sitting on her blanket rubbing cocoa butter over her legs when I came up with my blanket and clothes.

"Hello," I said.

"Hello, Davie," she said.

It made me feel strange. No one, since my mother, had called me that. Davie. There was something about it.

"I was going to call you," I said, "but I forgot your number and your name wasn't in the directory."

"Oh," she said. "No, I live with another couple and the phone is under their name."

She seemed a little evasive that day. She avoided my eyes, kept looking down at the sand. Then, when she tried, without success, to put the cocoa butter on her back, I offered my services.

She sat stiffly as I rubbed my hand over her sun-warmed back. I noticed how she kept biting her lower lip. Worriedly.

"I . . ." she started to say once and then stopped. She sat quietly. Finally she drew in a deep breath.

"I have something to tell you," she said.

I felt myself tremble slightly.

She sounded so serious.

"Go ahead," I told her.

"I'm divorced," she said.

I waited.

"Yes?" I said.

Her throat moved. "That's all," she said, "I—I just thought you might not want to go out with me when you knew—I—"

"Why not?"

She started to say something, then shrugged her shoulders helplessly.

"I don't know," she said, "I just thought."

She looked so young, so timorous.

"Don't be silly, Peggy," I said, quietly.

She turned in surprise.

"What did you call me?" she asked.

"Peggy," I said. "That's your name isn't it?"

"Yes, but—" She smiled at me. "I didn't think you'd remember."

She shook her head in wonder. "I'm so surprised."

It was one of those things about Peggy. The littlest thing could delight her. Like when I brought her an ice cream cone later that morning.

It might have been a diamond ring.

Peggy lived on Twenty-sixth Street off Wilshire.

It was Sunday night and I was walking up the quiet tree-lined block looking for her house. It was to be our first date.

There were two things in front of the house. An old Dodge. A man watering the lawn. The car was a 1940 model. The man about a 1910 model, pudgy and pasty faced, wearing most unfetching shorts.

"Peggy Lister live here?" I asked him.

He looked at me with watery blue eyes. His expression was dead. He held the hose loosely in his hands. His head jerked a little.

"She lives here," he said.

I felt his eyes on me as I stood on the porch. Then Peggy opened the door.

With heels on she was tall, about five ten, I guess. She wore a sweater and skirt, a brown sport jacket. Her shoes were brown and white, carefully polished. Her hair had been set and combed out painstakingly. She looked wonderful.

"Hello, Davie," she said. "Won't you come in?"

I came in. Those big brown eyes surveyed me.

"You look nice, Davie," she said.

"*You* look terrific."

Again. Surprise. A half-quizzical smile which seemed to say—oh, you're just fooling me.

Just then an older woman came out of an adjoining room.

"Mrs. Grady, this is David Newton," Peggy said.

I smiled politely, said hello. Noticed that Mrs. Grady was one of those unfortunate women suffering from progressive ugliness.

"Going out?" asked Mrs. Grady.

"We're going to get acquainted," Peggy said.

Mrs. Grady gave us a nod. Then she leaned over and called out the window.

"Supper's on, Albert."

We went to the front door and passed Albert. He gave me a sullen look. And her a look. A look that made me start. Because there was almost a possessiveness in it. It gave me an odd feeling.

"Who is that guy anyway?" I asked as we started down the street.

"Mr. Grady," she said.

"That look he gave you," I said.

"I know."

That expression was on her face again. Not quite identifiable. Mostly disgust. But there was something else in it too. I wasn't sure but it might have been fear, I thought. The fear of a child who has come upon something it does not quite understand yet instinctively shrinks from.

I decided to change the subject.

"Where would you like to go?" I asked.

"I don't care," she said, brightening. "Where would you?"

"A movie?" I suggested, without really thinking.

"Well—"

"What am I talking about?" I said. "I don't want to go to a movie. I want to talk to you."

She smiled at me.

"I'd like to talk, Davie," she said.

We went down to Wilshire to the Red Coach Inn for a few drinks. A cute little place; intimate, booths, a man playing casual organ music.

She ordered a vodka Collins and I ordered a Tom. Then she turned to me and, casually, said:

"I think I should tell you I'm madly in love with you."

I took it for a gag, of course.

"Splendid," I said. "That's grand."

But her face wasn't smiling. It made me feel a little restless. Sometimes you couldn't tell what Peggy meant.

We drank a little. It was quiet.

"Would you like to come to a party with me?" she said. On the spur of the moment it seemed.

"Why—sure," I said.

"Good," she said.

"Where is it?"

"At my lawyer's house," she said.

"You have a lawyer?"

"He handled my divorce," she said.

I nodded. I asked her where the house was. She said, "Malibu."

"How will we get there? I plan to get a car but I haven't yet."

"We can get a ride," she said confidently.

Then the confidence seemed to slip. She fingered her glass nervously.

"Davie," she said.

"What?"

"Will you—will you promise me something?" I hesitated. Then I asked what.

"Well, I—"

She looked irritated at her own fluster. "These parties are so—"

Again she halted; then: "You're a gentleman."

"I am?"

"I mean," she went on, "you know how these parties are. Actors and actresses and—well, usually they get all drunk and the men start to. . . ."

"You want me to promise not to touch you?"

"Yes."

I didn't like to say it. She looked delicious then, in that soft light. But I nodded. "All right," I said.

She smiled gratefully.

After a few drinks we started down Wilshire again, headed for the ocean.

"I wish I did have a car," I said.

"It's all right," Peggy said.

We walked and talked. Peggy told me about her mother. Her mother had died when Peggy was twelve.

"Tell me about your marriage," I asked once.

"There's nothing to tell," she said and that was all I could get out of her.

■ ■ ■

When we walked past my room I asked her if she'd like to come in and read some of my published stories. Strange, it didn't seem wrong with Peggy. With any other girl I would have felt obvious, but with Peggy I couldn't even conceive of anything under the table. She had too much—what's the word? Class, I guess you'd have to call it.

Peggy sat on my bed and looked at my stories. I sat across the room by my typing table. I watched her draw up her shapely legs and rest one of them under her, then draw the slip and skirt down. Watched her as she took off her jacket, as she leaned against the wall reading, watched her large brown eyes reading my words. Living in them. She was right there.

She looked up after reading the first one.

"My goodness," she said, awed. "I had no idea."

"Of what?" I asked.

"Of how—deep you are."

I chuckled self-consciously. "I've done better," I said.

She shook her head wonderingly. "You're so sensitive," she said. "Men aren't sensitive but you are."

"Some men are, Peggy," I said.

"No," she said. And she really believed it. "They're pigs. They don't care anything about beauty."

Was that her marriage talking? I wondered. What had it really been like to put that look of bitter conviction on that sweet face?

All I could do was shrug. Feeling a little helpless before her complete and dismaying assurance.

"I don't know, Peggy." I shouldn't have said it.

"I do," she answered.

And there was hurt there too. She couldn't hide it. I didn't want to spoil the evening. I tried to let it go.

But Peggy wasn't finished.

"I've seen it time and again," she said. "My uncle left my aunt with three children to support. The husband of the woman my brother and I stayed with was a drunkard. Phillip and I used to lie in bed on Saturday and Sunday nights and listen to the man beat his wife with his fists."

"Peggy, those are only two examples. In my own family I can give you four examples of happy marriages."

She shook her head. She read some more. And her jaws were held tightly. I sat there looking at her sadly. Wondering if there were anything I could do to ease that terrible tension in her.

The night seemed to disappear, Houdini-like. The first thing I knew we were walking back on the block off Wilshire. It was a nice, starry night. The street was dark and quiet. Peggy took my arm as we walked.

"I *do* like you," she said. "You talk my language."

We talked of different things. Nothing important.

"I should work," she said, a little ashamed. "It's not very honorable to live on—my alimony. But—" She looked at me as if almost pleading. "I don't know how to do anything, and I dread the idea of working in a ten-cent store or something. I did that when I was married. It's—awful."

I patted her hand.

A little later. "Where does your husband live, Peggy?"

"Do we—have to talk about it, Davie? Please."

"I'm sorry," I said.

It was when we were walking past the little park between 24th and 25th Streets:

"Would you like to sit in the park a while?" she asked me.

"Sure," I answered.

So we sat on the grass looking over the mirror-like pond. Watching the moon saucer that floated on the water surface. Listening to a basso frog giving out his roundelay for nothing.

We didn't talk. I listened to her breathing. I glanced at her and saw her looking intently at the pond. Felt her hand on the ground and covered it with mine. And, naturally, without forcing it, found my head resting against hers. Her cheek was firm, soft. The cologne she wore was a delicious, delicate fragrance.

And, then, in a moment, casually, I kissed the back of her neck. Long.

She didn't move. She shivered. Didn't struggle. But her hands tightened on the grass and pulled some out. I wondered what her lowered face was like.

I withdrew my lips. Her breath stopped, then caught again. In time with mine? I wondered.

Her throat moved. "Wow," she said.

I guess I laughed aloud. Of all the words in the world, it was the last I expected.

Peggy looked hurt, then offended. I quickly apologized.

"The word seemed so odd right then," I explained.

"Oh," she smiled, a little awkwardly. "No one ever kissed me like that," she said.

I looked at her in amazement. "What? No one?"

She shook her head.

"But—your husband?"

Her lips tightened. "No," she said. She shuddered and her hands tightened into hard fists. "No," she said again.

"I'm sorry," I said.

She shook her head. "It's not your fault. You just don't—realize. What it was like."

I put my arm around her.

"Peggy," I said, softly.

When we reached the front of her house I took her in my arms and kissed her. Her warm mouth responded to me.

I left her three times. Then, each time, turned to look back. And saw her standing by the picket fence that glowed whitely in the moonlight. And she was looking after me. The way a frightened and lonely child looks after its departing parent.

I kept going back. Holding her. Feeling her press her face against my shoulder. Whisper. "Davie. Davie."

It was while I was walking away the third time that the big car passed me. I didn't notice it. At least not any more than I'd notice any car that passed me on a dark street in the early morning. We'd sat talking till way after midnight.

But at Wilshire I stopped to go back again.

And found the car parked in front of her house. Right behind Albert's old Dodge. I saw a man at the wheel wearing a chauffeur's cap. He was slumped down, staring at the windshield.

Another man was at the door. He had on a topcoat, a Homburg.

At first I thought, Oh my God, it's her husband and he's a millionaire. I felt like creeping away.

Then I saw her framed in the doorway and I suddenly knew I

couldn't leave and I had to know who this man was. I walked past the Cadillac, a sleek, black job. I glanced at her room which faced the street. But the shades were drawn. I turned into the alley and walked up to the side window of her room. I stood there in the darkness, holding my breath. The window was open. I could hear her voice.

"You shouldn't come here like this," she was saying, "at this time of night. What will the land-lady say?"

"Never mind that," said the man. "I was talking about something else."

"I said no and I mean it."

Silence a moment. The man's voice again.

"And who's the new one?"

She didn't answer. I felt my brow knitting. Because the man's voice was familiar.

"Some poor fool who—" he started.

"Oh leave me alone, will you?" she burst out.

"*Peggy.*"

The voice was low and it warned. "Don't keep trying my patience. Even I have a limit. Even I, Peggy."

I heard her skirt rustle, then a long silence. I tried to hear. I tried to look under the shade. Nothing to see or hear. I imagined. I'm good at that.

"Jim," she said, "Jim—no."

Another connection. Not quite secure. The voice. The name.

Then I heard the back screen door shutting and I walked down the alley. As I turned onto the sidewalk I saw a dark figure coming up the alley. Albert. I recognized the form. I didn't know whether he was just out for the air or whether he was going to listen at the window too.

It didn't matter to me.

I'd had enough. I stalked past the black Cadillac and walked quickly toward Wilshire. In my mind I kept seeing her in the man's arms, being kissed, minutes after I had kissed her. Kissing him the way she kissed me. Peggy, the new, the bright; Peggy, the deceiving one.

Goodbye Peggy Ann.

■　■　■

There was someone scratching on my screen.

I raised up on one elbow and looked at the window. She was

looking in. She knocked at the door then. I hesitated. Then I relaxed.

"Come in," I said.

She was carrying her bathing suit and a towel in one hand. A grease-spotted paper bag in the other.

I looked at her clinically.

"I brought doughnuts for breakfast," she said.

Still no answer from me. She caught the look. Peggy was always quick at that. She knew the moment your feelings toward her chilled. Her face fell.

"What's the matter?" she asked.

I didn't answer. Her face was disconcerted. The face I was beginning to love. I tried to fight that but it was just about impossible.

She turned away sadly. "I'll go," she said.

I didn't feel anything until her hand touched the doorknob. Then it seemed as if someone were wrenching at my insides.

"Peggy."

She turned to look at me. Her face blank.

I patted the bed. "Come here," I said.

She stood there, looking hurt. She tried to flint her features, failed, tried again. I patted the bed a second time.

"Sit down, Peggy," I said.

She sat down gingerly.

"I haven't done anything," she said.

"I came back last night," I said.

At first she didn't understand. Then her face tightened.

"You saw Jim," she said.

"Is he your husband?"

"He's my lawyer," she said.

Last connection. The voice, the name, the profession.

"What's his last name?" I asked.

"Vaughan," she said.

"My God."

She looked at me in surprise.

"What is it?"

"I know him," I said.

"You *do*?"

"We went to college together."

"Oh." Her voice was faint.

I shook my head. "My God," I repeated. "Jim Vaughan. Of all the crazy coincidences."

I turned to her.

"Is Jim in love with you?" I asked.

"I—" She looked helpless.

"Is he?"

"I don't know."

"Isn't he married anymore?" I asked.

"They're going to be divorced," she said.

Audrey divorced. I saw her face at college, in my mind. Adoring Jim Vaughan. Divorced.

"Is Jim's brother here too?" I asked.

"Yes."

"My God, it's so fantastic."

I saw that look again and let it go for the moment though there were still many questions I wanted to ask. Jim and I had known each other very well at the University of Missouri.

"It's his party we're—supposed to go to?" I asked.

She looked at the floor. "I suppose you're not going now," she said.

"I don't know," I said. "I'd like to see him again. But if he's in love with you it would be a—little strained."

"If you don't want to," she said.

"Don't you think he'd mind?"

She didn't answer.

"Peggy, come on."

"I had no idea you knew him. But—what difference does it make? I asked you to go with me."

I remembered something.

"Poor little fool," I said. "Why that snotty son. He's as smug as ever. Sure, I'll go. I just want to see his face when he sees me walk in with you."

∎ ∎ ∎

I was putting the polishing touches to my bow tie when the car horn honked outside.

I found the black Cadillac waiting.

Peggy was inside, the door open.

"Hi," she said. "Come on in."

I got in. The door shut and the car pulled away from the curb. Good God, I was thinking, this ices the cake.

Peggy smiled at me.

"What's the scoop?" I asked, quietly so the driver couldn't hear.

"What do you mean?"

"You didn't say we were going in Jim's own car."

"What's the difference?"

I started to answer. Then I chuckled. "Jim will do nip-ups."

"Why?"

She actually didn't know. Not my Peggy Ann Lister, divorced and very wonderful.

I patted her hand.

"Here is the picture, my dear," I said. "You taking Jim's rival to Jim's party in Jim's car. You get it?"

She looked blank. "You're no rival," she said.

It was my turn to look blank. Maybe she was naive, I thought.

I took a closer look at the driver. Affluence, I was thinking. Jim has done well for himself. A Caddy, a chauffeur, a house at Malibu.

But the chauffeur didn't fit. Not quite. Rich men's chauffeur's have non-committal features. They match the upholstery.

Not Walter Steig. That was his name. Steig stood out like a keg of beer among wine glasses. Big and stolid. His face and neck were reddish. He looked like a left-over from the Third Reich. Big and brutish with closely cropped hair of greyish-steel color. Rimless glasses and a stiff, unrevealing expression.

He turned the car onto Pacific Coast Highway and speeded up the ocean. Malibu, I thought, Jim *has* done well. A beach house probably. Fireplaces and french windows and opulence. Jim Vaughan.

I looked at Peggy.

"I'm sorry," I said. "I didn't mean to be rude. It's just that I can't help being surprised that you know Jim. That he's so well off. When I knew him he was—as poor as I am now."

That was poor.

She smiled back. My love was wearing a dark-blue dress that clung fittingly to her figure. Her blonde hair was brushed out again, haloing her head with light curls. Her skin was flawless. No makeup other than lipstick.

Everything seemed fine.

The Malibu house was a lush two-story affair that rambled all over a hillside and ended up like a luxurious animal crouched on a cliff, peering down at the pounding surf way down below across the highway.

It was quite a place. Thick broadloom, everything smart and rich. Jim's taste, all right. I could see that.

"Well—"

And heard him. I turned and saw him standing, one foot below the other on the step that led to the raised living room.

Staring at me.

Prophetic, I thought, that the last time I had seen him and this first time again, the expression I saw was devoid of all concealment. With not enough time to combat shock, it was Jim Vaughan in the raw looking at me. The look had surprise in it. Surprise, and, no hiding it, although he did his best thereafter, distinct and obvious displeasure.

"David!"

The pose was back. His hand holding mine was firm. The smile, the look was one of pleasure.

"If this isn't a coincidence," he was saying.

"How are you, Jim?" I said.

No need to ask. He was in fine shape. From his well-trimmed head of red hair, down through his well-shaven, well-fed face, through his maroon dinner jacket, and down to his shiny, dark maroon shoes. Jim was all right. I almost felt like a tramp in my old jacket, one he'd seen at college no less. And that feeling was a new one for me. When I was with Jim especially.

I'd always felt at least equal, if not superior.

"What are you doing out here?" he was asking me.

His arm around Peggy's waist. Obviously. She looked a little pained but she didn't move away. The move made me feel strange. As if with one calm, assured gesture, Jim was removing her from my sphere.

"Writing," I said.

"Oh, yes, of course," he said as if he didn't know it. "You wrote."

His tendency towards smugness that I'd taken delight in puncturing at school had now blossomed into a full-fledged snobbishness. This, I suspected, was progress to Jim.

Then came a move which sort of put down the groundwork for the coming months.

"Peggy, I've got someone you must meet," Jim said.

■ ■ ■

That was the opener. There were other words, quickly spotted.
But the kicker was me standing alone in the hallway. A few seconds after I'd met a guy who'd been a friend years before, I'd
been dismissed that easily. Jim Vaughan discarding the past like
a scab. He'd said, "We'll have to have a long talk," but I knew
it was only words.

I saw him wedge Peggy into a mass of people standing up near
a large fireplace which was crackling with orange flames. Peggy
looked toward me once, apologetically. But it didn't much ease
my irritation.

I went up the small staircase and into the huge living room.
Just as expected. Lush. High-beamed ceiling, thick, wall to wall
carpeting, huge, solid color furniture, copper lamps. Jim had it.

I looked around. At first I thought there would surely be someone I had known from college. He couldn't have discarded them
all, he knew so many. If nothing else, there would be Audrey. She
and I had been minor buddies at college.

No Audrey. I kept walking around adding unto myself a drink
and a plate of well-catered canapes, a high-class antipasto. I stood,
back to a wall-high picture window and surveyed the room full
of affluent strangers. I got philosophic. I always do when I'm
around people who all have more money than I do.

It was about that time that I saw Dennis.

He was sitting on a couch with a pretty young thing. He was
glowering alternately into his drink and at the mass of people
wherein stood Jim and Peggy.

I went over, sat down. I hadn't known Dennis at college except
by sight. Flitting about the campus like a scholastic phantom,
carrying books and a woman. Always a woman.

"Hi," I said.

The young thing showed her teeth.

Dennis looked at me with his dark eyes. He didn't answer.

"You don't remember me," I said.

"No, I don't," he agreed.

"I'm Dave Newton," I said. "I was a friend of Jim's at Missouri."

Recognition. But no pleasure.

"Oh yeah," he said.

I can't get on very well with people who won't talk.

"You've got quite a home here," I said.

"*Jim* has quite a home."

There it was. Plain as the nose on his sullen face. The resentment. I'd heard Dennis talk once at college. That was one day when I'd come up to him and Jim on the campus. Dennis had walked away saying, "Sure, *have* it your way. You always do anyway."

And Jim had said to me, faintly amused, "*That* is brother Dennis. The brat of the family."

Now, in the present, I saw that Dennis was still the brat of the family.

"Yeah," I said, for want of anything better.

Young thing coughed. Dennis didn't stir.

"I'm Jean Smith," came a gushing introduction. "Dennis is just *awful* about introductions."

I smiled and nodded. I forgot about her.

"Where's Audrey?" I asked Dennis.

He looked at me coldly a moment. I guess he didn't see what he was looking for. He turned away.

"She's sick," he said.

"That's too bad."

"Yeah, isn't it?" he said and was up and moving for the bar. Jean Smith followed him.

I moved for the big group. It was obvious that Jim had no intention of sharing Peggy. She was private property. I stood behind Peggy Lister.

"Peggy, let's dance," I said.

Jim's smile was antiseptic. Toothpaste ad smile.

"Not right now, Dave," he said. "We're rather busy."

Then I was left to stand there unintroduced, the ghost of Hamlet's father at Malibu. I felt a heat churning up in my stomach. I've got a temper. I'll be the last to deny that.

Peggy kept looking at me when she could, trying to smile. But Jim kept closing up the group by edging around so that his back was to me. I looked at the back of his neck. Jim Vaughan, I thought, my old buddy. You dirty, smug louse.

Why didn't she come to me, excuse herself? I figured that she was afraid to. She was a timid girl, really. She could be taken advantage of.

I listened to the talk awhile. Then when my arm muscles felt like rigid glass I just moved around and grabbed Peggy's hand.

"Come here, Peggy," I said aloud. "There's someone you must meet."

I could feel their stares on me as I pulled her away.

"That wasn't very polite," she said.

I took her over to the small open portion of the floor where a few couples were dancing to record music.

"It wasn't polite to bring me here and ditch me, either," I said.

"*I* didn't do anything," she said. "He took me over."

"No, you never do anything," I said. "Peggy Lister, victim of fate."

■   ■   ■

She tried to draw away. I tightened my hold. "You're going to dance with me," I said.

She was quiet then. Her mouth was a resigned line. She held herself stiffly.

"My old friend Jim Vaughan," I said.

No answer.

"Peggy."

"What?"

"Do you want to meet the person I was going to introduce you to?"

No answer.

"Do you?"

"Who *is* it?" she asked, with false patience.

"Me," I said. "I'm all alone."

Her eyes on me. And softness coming back. I felt her hand on my shoulder tighten.

"Davie," she said, softly.

"How do you do," I answered.

Later. A bout. Jim taking her. Then me dancing with her. And both of us standing by, around eleven, while Dennis danced with her. Both of us trying to put on an air of Auld Lang Syne.

"I suppose Peggy has told you about our marriage plans," Jim said. Casually. Jim loved to flick off bombshells.

"No," I said, keeping it casual even though it killed me. "She didn't say anything."

"Well, it's understood," he said. The dampener. And was that a little threatening in his voice?

"Does Audrey understand?" I asked.

The twitching that presages a well reserved smile.

"She understands," said Jim Vaughan.

"The way Linda understood," I said.

Another twitch, without a smile this time. I knew he remembered as I did the time at college when I'd started to date Linda. Linda, who everybody but myself considered Jim's unringed fiancée. And Jim had given me the low-down. Told me that he and Linda were going to be married. Although Linda didn't know it. Although Linda later on left him cold.

"That was a childish thing," Jim was saying now. "I'm past childish things."

I nodded. "I see." Then I said, "I hate to say it, Jim, but I'm in love with Peggy."

No sign. No hint. He gazed at me like an exterminator, sighting on his prey.

I smiled thinly. "I know it isn't very guest-like for me to tell you," I said, "especially after what happened with Linda but— well, there it is."

He looked at me as if making some sort of decision. His greyish-blue eyes examined me carefully through the lenses of his glasses. His thickish lips pursed slightly as he deliberated.

He decided.

"Come in here, David," he said. Father about to tell his son that the birds do more than fly and the bees buzz.

He led the way to the library. He ushered me in. The door closed off the sound of the party. He locked the door. We stood together in the quietude, surrounded by the literature of the ages, all dusty.

"Sit down, David," he said.

I sat. I didn't know what to say. I decided to let him play the scene his own way.

"What has Peggy told you about herself?" he asked.

I sat quietly a moment, trying to figure out what his angle was. Jim was always trying for an angle. It might be hidden at first but it was always there. I knew that from school. He'd lead up, lead up, then sock you over the head with his *coup de grace*.

"Her family," I said. "Her life." I paused for effect. "Her divorce," I said, as casually as possible, figuring that it was the angle he was working on.

James Vaughan, late of Missouri farmtown, now of California society, raised his eyebrows. Most effectively. All right, let's have it, Jim, I wanted to say, you can spare the histrionics. I know you.

"That's what she told you," he said. "That she was divorced?"

"That's right."

A sinking sensation in my stomach. What in hell *was* he driving at?

He looked at me, still deliberately. Until the thoughts of what he might be hiding started to make my skin crawl.

"What *is* it, for Christ's sake?" I asked.

He put one hand into his coat pocket.

"I don't know whether you'll believe what I tell you," he said.

"*What?*"

"Peggy isn't divorced," he said.

"She's still married?"

"No," he said, "not now."

"What about her husband?" I asked, perfect straight man for horror.

He hesitated. Then he said, "Murdered."

I felt the cold sickness explode in me because I knew his *coup de grace* before he said it.

"Peggy murdered him."

2

I sat there and I felt as if the walls were tottering, ready to fall in on me.

"You're lying," I said, weakly, very weakly.

"Am I?"

And I couldn't convince myself that he was.

"I'll have Steig take you home," he said.

I looked up at him. His face was without expression. Certainly there was no sympathy there.

"I should see her," I said.

But without conviction. I didn't want to see her. I was afraid to see her.

"I think it would be foolish to see her," Jim said. And I let him tell me.

I found myself in the black Cadillac, and Steig pulled around the pear-shaped drive and onto the road that led precipitously down to the highway.

I sat in the car staring at the floor. And listening to the wind whistle by the car as it roared along the ocean at eighty miles an hour. Under a cold moon.

     ■   ■   ■

I wrote sporadically. I went to the beach, way up the beach, far from the spot where we'd met. I went to the movies. I read. And, from all activities, absorbed nothing. I was still half anesthetized. I hadn't known her long, a few weeks. But she'd gotten to me.

I thought about her after the first few days of deliberately avoiding any thoughts at all about her.

Murder?

I went to the library and looked through old papers. I didn't find anything. And when I thought some more I remembered about Linda and the lie Jim had told.

I went back to my love. Days after. In sorrow and repentance. And found her on the back lawn, trying to read. But just staring at the same page.

And she was cold at first because she'd been hurt. I didn't let it stop me. I was apologetic. I smiled at her and said again and again and again:

"I'm sorry, Peggy. I'm sorry."

"Murdered!" she said to me. "Is that what he told you?"

I nodded, grimly.

She shook her head. "How could he?" And I felt some slight relish in seeing indications of the chinks in Jim Vaughan's self-forged armor.

"Why, though?" she said. "I didn't murder him."

"Where is your husband?"

"He's dead," she told me. "He died in San Francisco. A year ago."

We sat in the back yard talking. And she kept shaking her head and saying she couldn't understand how Jim could say such a thing about her.

"It is strange," I said. "I never saw Jim involve himself in such an obvious lie before."

"I don't know," she said.

She looked away. "I didn't murder him," she said, softly.

"I know," I said.

"You didn't know it before," she said. "You believed what he said."

"It came as such a shock," I said. "Think of how you'd feel if, out of a clear blue sky, someone told you I'd murdered my mother or my wife."

"I'd check before I believed."

"What would you think if I told you I was divorced, made you think my wife was still alive?"

She didn't answer.

"Let's forget about it," I said, leaning over to kiss her cheek. "I have missed you," I said.

"But you stayed away."

I couldn't answer. I just felt rage at Jim for lying so blatantly to me. At myself for believing him.

It was around that time that I noticed Albert.

He was looking out of his window at Peggy. I forgot to mention it but Peggy only had on shorts and a tight halter.

I called it to Peggy's attention. Her mouth grew hard again.

"Oh." She bit her lip. "I have to get out of here," she said. "Do you think I could find an apartment—or something?"

"Has he—tried anything?"

"No. Not with his wife around. But I'm afraid."

"We'd better get you out of here."

"And he pretends to be so pious," she said angrily, "just like all men. Pretending to be moral when all the time they're just pigs."

I didn't want to get started on that again. Besides, I thought, she was probably right in Albert's case.

Albert turned away from the window when I made it obvious from my look that I felt a severe desire to plant my foot in his pudgy face.

"You sure he hasn't tried anything?" I said.

"No," she answered, "but I know he'd—like to. The other day Mrs. Grady called me to the phone. I had on my shortie night-gown. I was too sleepy to think about putting on my robe. And Albert came out in the hall and saw me."

She shuddered.

"The way he looked at me made me sick," she said. "Like—like an *animal*."

"I'd like to break his neck."

"I don't want any more trouble," Peggy said. "I'll just leave."

"Trouble?" I asked. And, sometimes, wished I'd cultivated a deceiving voice like Jim's. Too often, practically always, my voice is a mirror of my feelings.

She looked at me dispassionately.

"You're still thinking about it, aren't you?" she said.

"About what?" I pretended.

"You're thinking about what Jim told you."

I must have looked flustered.

"I'll tell you what I mean," she said. "Maybe you'll be sorry I told you."

Her sensitive face was cold, hurt.

"When I was eight years old," she told me, "I was attacked by a boy. He was seventeen. He dragged me in a closet."

She swallowed and avoided my eyes.

"When my father found out," she said, "he tried to kill the boy."

I reached for her hand instinctively but she drew back.

Peggy, Peggy.

"I can't help the way I feel," she said, "about men. It's in my flesh. If you weren't—if you hadn't been so different, I'd have run from you too."

"And Jim—?"

"Jim took care of me," she said. "He was always good to me. And he never asked anything in return."

We sat there in silence awhile. Finally our eyes met. We looked at each other. I smiled. She tried to smile but it didn't work.

"Be nice to me, Davie," she said. "Don't be suspicious."

"I won't," I promised. "Peggy, I won't."

Then I said, as cheerfully as possible, "Come on, let's find you an apartment."

■　■　■

I found a car that same day at a used-car lot, and afterwards we found a place for Peggy.

It was a small place. Two rooms, bath and kitchenette for $55.

It wasn't going to be empty for about two days so we went back to her old place. I invited her out to dinner, then to a show or maybe down to the amusement pier at Venice. She accepted happily.

"Let's start all over," she said impulsively during the afternoon. "Let's forget the past. It doesn't matter now, does it?"

I hugged her. "No, baby," I said, "of course it doesn't."

When we went in the house Albert and his wife were sitting there in the front room. That they'd been arguing was obvious from the forced way they broke off conversation. There were splashes of red up Albert's white cheeks.

They looked up at us. The old, sullen resentment in Albert's expression. The prissy, forced amiability in Mrs. Grady's atrocious face.

"Mrs. Grady," Peggy said, "I expect to be moving out in two days."

"Oh?" said Mrs. Grady. With that tone that can only be attained by landladies about to lose a tenant.

Albert looked at her. I felt myself tighten in anger. The look on his face made me want to drive my fist against it.

"Is there something wrong here?" Mrs. Grady asked, a trifle peevishly. "Perhaps—"

"No, no," Peggy said, "it's fine. I just want an apartment, that's all."

"Well," said Mrs. Grady. "Well."

"I just happened to stumble across it today," Peggy said, "or else I would have given you more notice."

"I'm sure," Albert said, his fat lips pursed irritably.

More tightening in me. Peggy moved for her room.

"Excuse me," she said.

I followed without thinking.

"Gratitude," Albert said. And when I was going into her room he said something else. Something about little trash.

I felt myself lurching to a halt. I threw a glance over my shoulder. Then I felt Peggy's restraining hand on my arm.

In her room she looked at me.

"I guess you should have waited outside," she said.

"What's the difference?" I said loud for all to hear. "Change your clothes and let's get out of here."

She put up a screen and went behind it. I saw her halter and shorts flutter over the top and I tried to avoid thinking of Peggy standing there. I tried to concentrate on my rage at Albert. But

your mind is hardly your own when it's distracted by such mer-·
ciless visions.

She came out in a little while. During which time I sat listening
to the angry voices of Mr. and Mrs. Grady, lovable duo. And I
heard the word "trash" used again. Albert wasn't hiding it.

"We'd better go," I said, "or I swear I'm liable to punch that
slob in the nose."

Silence outside. I hoped they heard.

"I wish you could leave tonight," I said.

"So do I," she said. And in her voice I heard the mixture of
revulsion and contempt and, yes, fear.

They were talking when we went out into the front room again.
But they shut up. They looked up at Peggy who wore a light blue
cotton dress and had a blue ribbon in her hair.

"I'm afraid I won't be able to refund your money," said Mrs.
Grady, revealing the depth of her soul.

"I—" Peggy started.

"She's got no claim to it," Albert snapped bitterly, "no claim
'soever."

"I don't expect it back," Peggy said.

"I'm *sure* you don't." That was Albert.

"Shut your mouth, Albert," I said. Surprised at myself how
easily it came.

"*Uh!*" In unison. Mr. and Mrs. Grady were both outraged at
my impertinence.

"Come on," I said and Peggy and I left. Hearing a muffled,
"She'll be sorry for this," from Albert as we closed the front door
behind us.

"You shouldn't have said that," Peggy said as we got into the
car. Then she laughed, and it was nice to hear her laugh again.

"Did you see the look on his face," she said. "It was priceless."

We laughed for three blocks. . . .

I parked the car on one of the streets that lead down to the
Venice pier. And we walked down together, hand in hand.

We tried to hit a swinging gong at a shooting gallery. We
nibbled on buttered popcorn and threw baseballs at stacked
wooden bottles. We went down in the diving bell and watched
tiger sharks circle the silent shell holding us, watched rays and
heard the man say over and over, "They *fly*, ladies and gentlemen—they *fly!*" We rode the little skooter cars and bumped

each other and Peggy laughed and her cheeks were bright with color.

I don't remember everything. I just remember the walking hand in hand, the warm happiness of knowing she was with me.

I remember *Funland*.

It's a strange concession. Nothing really but a big black maze. You wander through it, down inclines, turning corners, searching for an exit—all in a blackness that's complete and abysmal. This sounds pointless, I guess. Until you take a girl. A lot of loafers hang around there. They wait for unescorted girls to go in.

I don't know what it was that made me nervous from the start. Maybe it was Peggy. She seemed to be driving herself, daring herself not to be afraid. Her laughter was forced and her hand in mine shook and was wet with perspiration. She kept tugging.

"Come on, Davie, let's find our way out."

"What did we come in for?"

"To find our way out."

"Progress," I said.

The place was like a coal mine. I couldn't see a thing. It had a dank, rotting odor too, that place. The smell of uncleaned spaces and water-logged wood and the vague, left-over smell of thousands of phantom bodies who had come in to get out.

And there were sounds. Giggles. Little shrieks of deliberate fright. Or were they deliberate? Peggy's breath was fast, erratic. Her laughter was too breathless.

"Babe, what did we come in here for?" I said.

"Come on, it's fun, it's fun."

"Some fun."

She kept pulling me, and I held on tight moving through the blackness that was filled with clumping and shuffling of feet. And more shrieks and giggles. And the sound of our breathing. Unnaturally loud.

"This is scary," Peggy said, "isn't it?"

We touched walls, bumped down inclines, pressed together in the dark.

"Excuse me," I said. It sounded inane.

"All right," came the phantom reply. In a voice that had more fright than elation in it now.

"How do you get out of here?" I said, trying to get rid of the rising uneasiness in me.

"You just wander and finally you come out," she said.

Silence. Except for feet shuffling and her breathing and my breathing. Shuffling along in the dark. With the rising sense that we weren't alone. I don't mean the other people in the black maze. I mean somebody *with* us.

The next thing I remember, the last thing for a while, was a sudden blinding beam of light behind us. A rushing sound behind me. And me whirling around into the eye-closing light. Then feeling two big hands grab my throat, strong arms spinning me now in blackness again. A heavy knee driving into my back, and something hard crashing down on my skull.

And though it was dark, for me it got darker. I felt myself hit the floor and start falling into night.

But not before, on my knees and almost gone, I heard Peggy scream out in mortal terror.

■   ■   ■

Somebody was slapping my face.

I twisted my head away and groaned. Sounds trickled back into my brain. I opened my eyes.

I was still on the pier, half stretched out on the walk, propped up against a wooden fence. A crowd was watching me with that alien and heartless curiosity that crowds have for stretched-out victims of any kind. I heard a voice saying, "It's nothing folks, he just fainted. Don't congregate, please. Don't get the police on me, thank you kindly, I appreciate it. Nothing at all folks, just fainted that's all, he just fainted."

"Peggy!"

I struggled up. The pain in my skull almost put me out again. I fell back on one elbow.

"Take it easy, boy," said the man with the cigar in his mouth, the loud sport shirt, "just fainted, folks. Don't congregate, please don't congregate."

He looked at me. "How's the head?" he asked.

"Where *is* she?" I asked. I grabbed his arm, fighting off the dizziness. "She's not still *in* there, *is* she?"

"No, no, no, no, nobody's in there now. It's cleared out. Stop yelling please. You want the police to come down?"

"Did you see her leave?" I asked.

"I didn't," said the man, still looking around. "Somebody said they did."

"Alone, was she alone?" I slumped against the fence, dizzily.

"I don't know, I'm not sure. *Please*, folks, don't congregate like this. Be a good egg, folks. Give me a break and don't congregate like this."

I pushed up then and started through the crowd, holding myself tight to keep the pain from knocking me on my face again.

I kept seeing her in there. In pitch blackness. With her fear of men. And someone attacking her in blackness. It would drive her out of her mind.

Then another thought.

Jim.

Steig trailing us. Jumping me. Taking Peggy away. It seemed terribly logical to me then.

I started running up the pier for the car and planning to drive to Jim's place to find her. Strange there seemed no doubt in me that she actually was there. Only in a white rage could I be so certain.

I rushed past endless gaudy concessions, the barker voices shrouding me with blatancy. Then, suddenly, I thought, I'll phone him.

In the airless booth my head started throbbing. I gritted my teeth, panting. I looked up Jim's number, sweat rolling down my face. I called the operator and had the call put through.

His voice, assured, dripping with aplomb: "James Vaughan speaking."

"This is David," I said. "Is—"

"David who?"

"Newton!" I said angrily. "Is Peggy there?"

"Peggy? Why do you ask?"

"*Is she there?*"

"You sound hysterical," he said.

"Did you have me attacked tonight?" I asked furiously, not thinking at all. "Did you have Steig take Peggy?"

"What *are* you talking about?"

I suddenly felt my insides falling. If it weren't Steig, then who was it?

"Speak up, David. What are you talking about? What's happened to Peggy?"

I hung up. I pushed out of the booth. I walked a few feet. Then I broke into a weaving run again. I felt a wild fear in me.

I moved off the pier and wove up the dark street past bars with tinkling pianos and a mission with a tinkling piano and tone-deaf converts singing for their supper.

"Peggy," I gasped.

And found her in my car.

She was sitting slumped over on the right hand side. The first impression I got was one of stark shock. She was shaking violently. Just staring blankly at the windshield and shaking. She had her right arm pressed over her breasts. The fingers of her left hand in her lap were bent and rigid.

"Peggy!"

I slid in beside her and she snapped her head over. Her stare at me was wild with fear. I put my arm around her shaking shoulders.

"What happened, Peggy?"

No answer. She shook. She looked at me, then at the windshield again. Her pupils were black planets swimming in a milky universe. I'd never seen eyes so big. Or so terror-stricken.

"Baby, it's *me*. Davie."

She started to bite her lower lip. I could almost feel the rising emotion in her. She literally shook it out of herself.

It suddenly tore from her lips. She threw her hands over her face. Then she drew them away just as suddenly and held them before her eyes in tight claws of blood-drained flesh. She clicked her teeth, clenched them together and tried to hold back the moaning.

But her breath caught. And a body-wracking sob burst from her throat. She dragged her hands across her breasts. And I saw that the front of her dress had been ripped open and one of her brassiere straps had been snapped.

"I'm dirty," she said, "dirty!"

I had to grab her hands to keep her from ripping open her own flesh. I was amazed at the strength in her arms and wrists. Impelled by savage shock she was almost as strong as a man, it seemed.

"Stop it! Peggy, stop it!"

Some people stopped and watched with callous curiosity while Peggy shook and groaned, and tried to claw herself.

"Peggy, please, please . . ."

I wanted to start the car and get away from those staring people. But I couldn't let her tear at her own flesh.

A long shuddering breath filled her. And she started to cry. Heartbroken crying, without strength or hope. I held her against me and stroked her hair.

"All right, baby," I said, "cry, cry."

"Dirty," she moaned, "I'm dirty."

"No," I said. "No, you're not."

"I'm dirty," she said, "dirty."

■   ■   ■

As soon as I could I started the car and drove away from the curious people. I drove along the ocean for a while and then stopped at a drive-in. By that time she'd stopped crying and was sitting quietly, way on the other end of the seat, staring at her hands.

I'd put my jacket over her to cover the torn dress and slip. I ordered coffee and made her drink it. She coughed on it but she drank it.

It seemed to calm her a little. I stayed away from her. She wanted it that way, I knew. She almost pushed against the other door, crouching as if prepared to leap out should I make the remotest suggestion of an advance.

"Tell me what happened, Peggy?"

She shook her head.

"It'll help you if you can tell me."

Finally she did. And the visualization of what she said made me shiver.

"Someone grabbed me," she said. "I screamed for you but— but you didn't answer."

"I was unconscious, Peggy."

For the first time she looked at me with something besides fear.

"You were hit?" she asked.

I bent over and told her to touch the dried blood on my head.

"Oh," she said in momentary concern, "Davie—"

Then she drew back.

"Go on," I said.

"Some . . . some *man* put his hands on me. He tore at my dress. I scratched him. I think I must have scratched his eyes out. Oh, God, I hope I did. I hope he's *blind!*"

"Peggy, stop."

I saw the look of revulsion on her face. Because she had suddenly picked up her hands to look at them.

She made a gagging sound. Then she started rubbing her fingers over her skirt. I saw what it was.

Skin under her nails. The skin of the man in the black maze.

I got a pen knife from the glove compartment and cleaned her nails while she kept her head turned away, her eyes tightly shut. Her hands trembled in mine.

"I think I'm—going to be sick," she said.

I felt sick myself, flicking those particles of someone's skin on the floor. Someone who had terrorized the girl I loved. It was almost as if he were present with us. I thought vaguely of taking those particles to the police but then I just let them fall. I couldn't stand putting them in an envelope.

"Peggy," I said, "do you think it was Steig?"

She couldn't speak for a moment. Then she said she didn't know.

"If I'd had a gun," she said, "a knife, a razor, *anything*. I'd have—"

I felt the muscles of my stomach tighten. Until I told myself that she'd been driven half mad with fear. And I pushed away the thought I was trying so hard to avoid. And came up with another one that had preyed on me since I was conscious again.

"Peggy."

"What?"

"Did he—?"

She closed her eyes.

"If he had," she said, "you wouldn't have found me here. I'd be in the ocean."

My stomach kept throbbing as I drove up Wilshire. The thought of her being alone after this experience distressed me terribly. Worse than alone, alone with Albert. What if he made an advance this night?

And then I thought, what if it were Albert who had attacked her in the first place?"

I didn't know how to put the thought to her. I didn't want to alarm her needlessly. She seemed set on going back to her room. If I made the idea horrible, and she went anyway. . . .

Thoughts. No end to them. And no resolution.

As I turned up 26th I saw Albert's Dodge in front of the house. And another car too. Jim's Cadillac.

I pulled up to the curb. Jim got out of his car and came quickly over to mine. He opened the door on Peggy's side.

"What is it, Peggy?" he asked.

She shook her head.

"Come here," he said.

By the time I got out of the car, he'd led her to his Cadillac and tried to make her get in it.

"I don't want to go!" I heard her say, her voice edging on hysteria again.

"Stop it, Peggy," Jim said. "I just want to talk to you."

Then she was in. And I came up to the car. I looked in and saw their dark forms. I heard Jim's muffled voice.

Steig got out of the car and walked around to where I stood.

"This is private," he said. Guttural. Thick German accent.

"Miss Lister is—" I started to say and found that one of his beefy hands had clamped on my arm. The strength of his grip pressed pain into the flesh.

"Let go of me," I said, gasping.

"You go," he said.

He firmly led me to my car. I couldn't do a thing. He was too big, too strong.

"*Get out,*" Steig said.

My fingers shook as I slid the ignition key in. They shook on the gear shift. My legs trembled on the clutch and the accelerator. My heart pounded violently as I pulled up the street, afraid to look back.

I got out.

■   ■   ■

I jolted up on the bed with a gasp. There was a dark figure standing over the bed.

I threw up one arm to ward off the expected blow.

"Davie, what is it?"

I said, "You startled me, I guess."

"Oh. I'm . . . sorry. It's Albert," she said quietly.

"*What . . . ?*"

Then the light was on. She was over at the sink. She pressed a wet cloth on my skull. To my surprise I saw her wearing a different outfit. She had a dark pair of slacks on and a tight black turtleneck sweater. She'd taken a shower too. I could tell from the fresh smell of her, from the dampness on the lower part of her hair where it had come out of the shower cap. Her only makeup was a little lipstick.

She looked very calm.

"What *about* him?" I said.

"When I went in the house tonight," she said.

"Yes?"

"I—I went to brush my teeth and I met Albert in the hall." She paused.

"*Well . . . ?*" I asked.

"*His face was all scraped off,*" she said.

"Albert," I said.

She turned the cloth over with her gentle, unshaking fingers.

"What did you do?" I asked.

She stroked my hair gently. "I left," she said.

"You took a shower first?"

"No," she said, "I took that before. It was after the shower that I met Albert in the hall."

"You came right here?"

"I stopped to call Jim."

"He didn't stay with you?" I asked, inanely.

She looked slightly surprised. "Of course he didn't," she said, "he just wanted to find out what had happened tonight. He said you called him."

"Yes."

"Why?"

"I thought maybe you were at his house."

We drove back to her place in the morning. I'd told her about Steig roughing me.

"Well, I'll just *tell* Jim," she was saying. "He'll get rid of Steig if I tell him."

"Are you sure?"

"Of course, Davie," she said, "you're his friend, aren't you?"

"I doubt it."

Then I said, "I still think you should move out today. Stay with me one more night. But, my God, don't spend another night there with Albert."

"I won't," she said.

She shook her head then. And her throat moved nervously.

"We'll just pick up your things," I said. "You don't even have to go in the house."

As we drove up to the house and I parked behind the Dodge Peggy's face got suddenly pale.

"Baby, it's all right," I said.

I got out. She got out too.

"Baby, stay here," I said. "You don't have to go in."

"No," she said, "I'll come in."

"Well—all right."

We went up the walk together. I felt in myself that if Albert were there and he said a word to me, I'd knock him down and step on his face.

The front door was open. We went into the living room.

"Is Mrs. Grady home?" I whispered.

"I guess so," she said.

We went into the hall. She went into her room and I followed. Then as she turned to close the door I heard her voice sink to a whisper.

"*Davie. . . .*"

I looked in the direction she was looking. Down at where Albert's room was. My heart jumped.

There was a body sprawled on the floor.

I broke into a run and pushed open the half-open door. I heard Peggy behind me.

Mrs. Grady was crumpled on the floor. Her white face was pointed at the ceiling. In her right hand she clutched something. I couldn't see what it was but the tip was red . . .

Then my eyes moved suddenly to the bed.

Albert was there. He was staring at us, his eyes were wide open.

Albert was no more. And that was when I recognized the instrument in Mrs. Grady's hand.

An icepick.

It had been driven into Albert's brain.

3

Lieutenant Jones, Homicide, was a broad man with horn-rimmed glasses. His mood was surly.

Mrs. Grady was giving her version of what had happened.

"I went in to call him for breakfast," she said. "I found him in there with that—that *thing* in his . . . *oh!*"

"Why did you take it out?"

She shook her head. Then suddenly she twisted her head and pointed a shaky finger at Peggy.

"*She* did it!" she said wildly. "I know it, I *know* she did it!"

I sat beside Peggy on the big flowered couch, afraid to look at her.

"That will do," Jones said.

"*Do!* My husband is dead. He's killed! Do you understand that? Are you going to let her get away with it?"

"I know he was killed, Mrs. Grady," Jones said. "We're trying to find out who did it as soon as possible. If you'll just help us and not throw around accusations."

I sat there numbly staring at him. Listening to the murmur of voices in Albert's room, the muffled pop of flash bulbs, the shuffling of feet.

I kept visualizing Albert lying in there, the icepick hole in his head—and the other. It was almost unbearable to think about the other. Whoever had driven the icepick into Albert's brain had also taken Albert's straight razor and made an enormous bloody slit around Albert's neck. It was long, nearly the whole circumference of the neck. And it was deep. *It was almost as if. . . .*

As if—and I wanted to be sick.

"Miss Lister?" Jones said.

"Y-yes?"

"You were out last night?"

"Yes."

"What's that you said about having trouble with him?"

The way he spoke made me start. As if he were trying to rip away all incidentals and get to the core of everything.

"He was—" Peggy started. She lowered her eyes. "He—"

"Albert tried to attack her last night," I said.

"Lies, lies!" cried Mrs. Grady. "He was a dear, clean man, a dear, clean man."

"You'll have to stop this," Jones said to her, "or I'll have to ask you to leave this room."

She slumped back in silence again, blubbering helplessly, her toothpick shoulders twitching with violent sobs.

I was sitting there suddenly wishing I'd kept my mouth shut.

Because all I could think was that I'd given Peggy a perfect motive.

Jones looked at Peggy.

"Is this true?" he said.

She tried to answer but couldn't. She nodded her head once, jerkily.

Jones looked back at me. "Well," he said, "what about it?"

I told him about the scrapes on Albert's face. I told him about *Funland* and the attack on me and Peggy. My words were punctuated by moans and muffled denials from Mrs. Grady. I didn't know whether she really doubted me or not. After all, I kept thinking, the icepick had been in her hand. And she certainly had a motive.

"Did you see him?" Jones asked.

"You mean last night?"

"I mean last night."

"No, I—"

"Why not?"

"It was pitch black."

"I see," Jones said. But he really said, in effect, thirty days, next case. It occurred to me that he might even think I did it. The jealous lover. I lowered my eyes.

Jones worked on Peggy again. "You two were together then?" he said.

She swallowed. "Yes."

"And you went to—" Jones consulted the pad in his hand, "to Newton's apartment later."

Peggy looked flustered. "I—"

"What time did you go there?"

"She came to my room about—" I started.

"Will you kindly let Miss—" He consulted the pad again. "Miss Lister answer her own questions?"

"About two," Peggy said.

"Why did you go there?" Jones asked.

"Because I saw the scrapes on Albert's face. I didn't want to—"

"Lies . . . lies!" Mrs. Grady again. *"Murderess!"*

Her voice broke off with a choking gasp as two men carried a stretcher into the room, a blanketed body on it.

"Couldn't you go the back way?" Jones asked sharply.

"Alley's too narrow," said a bored cop.

Mrs. Grady was up. Her face was strained and wild. "I'm going with him," she said, "I'm going with my darling."

"That won't do any good," Jones said quietly.

"I'm *going*, I tell you." Her voice was cracked, her eyes almost glittered.

Jones let her go. He said a few words to one of the cops. While he was talking, I turned to Peggy. "Don't tell him how you feel about men," I whispered.

"What?"

I glanced at Jones. "I *said*," I whispered out of the side of my mouth, "don't tell this man how you feel about men. It would only—"

She was looking at me curiously.

"What were you saying to her?" Jones asked me.

"Nothing," I said instinctively.

Jones looked at me coldly. "No talking," he said. Then he sat down as the door shut behind Mrs. Grady and her dead husband.

"How sure are you that the dead man is the one who tried to attack you?" Jones asked Peggy.

"I know how I scratched the face of the man who— And Albert had scratches all over his face too. You saw him."

"I know," Jones said, "did you see anyone else last night?"

"My—lawyer," Peggy said.

"When?"

"When—when we came home from Venice."

"You told him about the attack?"

"Yes."

"Did you suspect the dead man of being the one who had attacked you at the time you were speaking to your lawyer?"

"Not then. I told him later that it was Mr. Grady who had done it."

"You saw him later?"

"I called him before I went to—to Mr. Newton's room." Her eyes were lowered in embarrassment.

Mr. Newton, I thought. Murder, the strange impersonalizer.

Then the doorbell rang. Jones got up and opened it.

Jim. He came in and talked to Jones for a few minutes, and then Peggy went to the station with Jones and Jim. I wasn't invited. As they got into the police car Jim told Steig to follow them.

I tried to catch Peggy's eye as the police car moved away from the curb. But she avoided my look. I guessed because I'd as much as told her I suspected her.

I watched the two cars go down the street. And I felt sick and empty. . . .

That afternoon, back at my room, I was trying to nap when I heard footsteps on the porch and, looking out the window, saw that it was Jim.

"Come in," I said when he knocked. He came in and the first thing I asked him was how Peggy was.

"As well as can be expected," he said, always cryptic.

"What the hell does that mean?"

He took his hat off and looked at me dispassionately.

"If you're going to tell me that Peggy killed Albert, save your breath. I know she didn't," I said.

"And how do you know?"

"I—I know."

"Hardly a legal defense, David," he said. "You always did think with your voice."

"And you," I said, "always did destroy what stood in your way."

A flicker. Gone then. He sighed.

"What's the use?" he said. He reached into his inside jacket pocket and drew out a rich leather bill-fold.

He was holding something out to me.

"Well, take it," he said. He paused for effect. "Are you afraid?"

I reached out a visibly shaking hand and took it.

"Read it."

The clipping was five years old. San Francisco dateline. Picture of a man I'd never seen. And next to him a picture of Peggy.

The headline:

G.I. Student Stabbed
Pregnant Wife Confesses

■   ■   ■

When Jim made his exultant exit, I rushed to my car and drove at near violation speed up Wilshire. And going in the front door without knocking. Pretending to ignore the shudder I got going back into that house.

She was packing, her face very sad.

"Peggy."

She kept packing after she looked at me. She moved around

the room, her motions crisp and tight. I watched her for a moment. And I just couldn't for the life of me, visualize murder in those hands.

I went in and sat on the bed by the suitcase. "Peggy."

No answer.

"I want to tell you why I didn't come back this afternoon."

"It doesn't matter."

"Doesn't it?"

"No."

"I saw Jim this afternoon."

"I see." Coldly. As if she were a woman who didn't care for anything in the world. Instead of a shy, timorous girl afraid of the world and its multiple terrors.

I reached out and grabbed her wrist. She didn't honor me with a struggle. She just stared straight ahead.

"He showed me a newspaper clipping, Peggy," I told her.

Her eyes moved down at me.

"It was the story of how you killed your husband," I said.

She shuddered and her wrist went limp.

"Jim also told me you were living on his money and not on alimony," I said.

I wanted desperately for her to snap out angry words at me and make me know they were all lies. But she couldn't. She didn't speak. Then she said, softly:

"Let me go."

"When you tell me why you lied to me. About so many things."

"I didn't want to tell you," she said.

"Why?"

She bit her lower lip and kept her face averted.

"Peggy, I want some truth! Do you hear me?"

She cut off a sob.

"What sort of a girl are you," I said, "who can speak of love and yet lie incessantly to the person you say you love? What kind of selfish girl are—"

"*Selfish!*"

She jerked away her hand violently.

"Selfish!" she said, "yes, I'm selfish! Very selfish! I was brought up by a father who hated me. Who did everything he could to make my life miserable. I was shuttled around from city to city, never having a home. Only hotels and motels and dingy little apartment houses near naval bases. I had boys try to attack me. I had older men try to proposition me. And to top it all off I married an animal who dragged me through poverty and gave me nothing but filth in return. Filth, do *you* hear! A man who made me pregnant, then tried to force me to get an abortion! A man who had no regard for me. I was a piece of flesh to him. And I killed him and I'd kill him again for the things he did to me! I—I lost my baby in a miscarriage." Peggy gulped, then said, "And now—when I find something good for the first time—when I try to hold on to the only beautiful thing I ever had in my whole life . . . you call me *selfish!* Yes! I'm s-s-selfish!"

Her back was turned from me. She shook violently, crying and trying not to cry. But unable to keep all the pent misery of years from flooding out.

I got up quietly. I stood behind her. I put my hands up to hold her shoulders. Then I drew them back. I didn't know. I felt terribly contrite. Everything seemed to fall into a pattern. Jim had colored an already ugly picture with even uglier hues. For his own purpose.

She cried for a long time. We sat on the bed and I kept drying her eyes with my handkerchief. Later, I asked:

"And the money?"

"Money?"

"Jim's."

She looked at me unhappily. "Why—what's wrong with that? If he wants to give it to me?"

"Baby, you're being kept!"

"He never *touched* me, Davie."

"It's the idea, Peggy."

She looked at me, a little frightened.

"Peg?"

"Yes, darling?"

"Did you—?"

"What?"

I didn't speak. Finally, I said. "If you did it, Peg, I'll understand, and I'll stick by you. I'll—"

"Love my memory?" she said.

"No, I—"

"I didn't kill Albert," she said.

I grabbed at it. I clung to it and it was like a tonic, the first moment of limp ease after a raging fever has abated.

"I believe you," I said.

We moved her into the new place that afternoon, and I tried to get her to tell the police about Jim. But she refused with her little girl logic. Then I suggested that at least we ought to confront Jim himself with his lies, and she refused to do that, too. It wasn't loyal, she said.

So I went alone to see Jim. I didn't find him, but I did find somebody else.

Audrey.

Audrey flung her arms around my neck. She had a silk pair of lounging pajamas on. Black and sheer and nothing else. I could feel the softness of her mold against me.

"Give us a kiss, Dave."

Her soft lips pressed against mine. And I got a sense of tension in her. The way she clung to me. It wasn't right.

Suspicion vindicated by the distinct odor of whiskey on her breath.

That was a shock. Audrey had never drunk at college. She'd just follow Jim around, a disciple to his calloused presence. Treasuring the few scraps of affection he gave her.

"Gee, Dave, it's good to see you," she said.

"It's good to see you too, Audrey."

She drew back, her small hands still gripping my shoulders.

"Let me see," she said. "Oh, yes. You're heavier. Affluence? Or beer?"

I chuckled and leaned over to kiss her cheek.

"Audrey, Audrey," I said, "what transmutation is this? I remember saddle shoes and bright-eyed naiveté. Now I find a new hairdo, sexy pajamas and—well—"

"And liquor?" she said.

I tried to slough it off.

"Come on in," she said, "come on in and talk to me. I'm lonely."

"Is Jim home?" I asked as she led me into the living room, big and empty now.

"He's on business," she said.

I got that too. Too chipper, too much a toss-off. She had found the phrase too easy. And from it I knew there'd been a lot of nights when Audrey had stayed home while Jim went out on "business." The old American synonym for cheating. Yes, it all added up. College had been the preamble.

I sat down, and Audrey got a couple of drinks. Big ones, and straight. She drained hers swiftly and filled her glass again.

We talked for a long while. It wasn't too pleasant.

"Sometimes I could scream," she said later on.

I thought of Peggy. "Sometimes I could, too," I said.

Then I stood up, "I'd better go," I said. Before I forget myself, I didn't add. I went over to her.

"Goodbye, Aud—"

I stopped when she looked me in the eye. Her breath was tortured. It shook her body. Something seemed to be bubbling up in her.

"*I could scream,*" she said.

"Scream," I said.

Suddenly she grabbed my arms and pressed her open mouth against my chest. I heard the muffled sound of her screaming at the top of her lungs into my flesh. It lasted until her breath went. Then she raised her darkly flushed face and looked at me, gasping.

"There," she said, hardly able to speak. "Mostly it's a pillow. Thanks for the nice cushion."

She turned away. I followed her from the room. We stood together by the front door.

"Will you give me a goodbye kiss?" she asked.

She raised on her toes and slid her arms around my neck. She brushed her warm lips over mine. Then she smiled and stroked my cheek.

"You're sweet," she said. "I wish—" She shrugged. "Oh, what's the difference, anyway?"

"Goodbye, Audrey."

"Goodbye, dear."

I went out the door and down to my car. I got in and sat there a long time staring at the windshield, wishing I'd stayed with Peggy.

Then, as I stepped on the starter, light streamed across the porch and leaped on the car.

"Dave!"

I looked over and saw Audrey come running across the porch and down the steps. She had on a long black raincoat with a hood over her head. I saw a maid at the door watching her go. Then the maid shrugged, and shut the door.

Audrey ran around the car, opened the door and slid in.

"How about giving a gal a ride into town?"

"All right," I said, caught off guard.

Back on Pacific Coast Highway I asked her where she was going.

"Santa Monica," she said.

"You're not quite dressed for evening activity," I said.

"Nobody will notice," she said, "where I'm going."

"Where's that?"

"Just drop me off downtown," she parried. "I'm not going any place in particular. I'll probably go to a movie."

"Oh."

I drove in silence a while. Audrey sat staring out at the ribbon of road unraveling under my headlights. Her face was expressionless.

"You can let me off here," Audrey said at Wilshire and 3rd.

"I'll take you downtown," I said.

"You don't have to."

I slowed down at Santa Monica Boulevard and 3rd.

"This is fine," Audrey said.

I kept moving. Down to Broadway. I stopped the car and she turned to look at me.

"I'm not clever, am I?" she said.

Broadway is where all the bars are.

"Come with me," I said. "Meet my girl."

"Oh, you have a girl?"

"Come on. Shut the door."

"No."

"You'll like Peggy," I said.

And from the look on her face I suddenly realized that it was Audrey's husband who wanted to marry Peggy. And I knew that, contrary to Jim, Audrey didn't "understand" it.

Audrey shuddered and pushed out of the car.

"Bye," she said hurriedly and slammed the door.

"Audrey—"

■   ■   ■

She was already turning the corner. I started the car and pulled around. I saw her going into The Bamboo Grill.

I drove to Peggy's and found the note on the door.

Davie: Jim came. He said we had to discuss my legal case. I told him I was waiting for you but he said it's very important. After all, Davie, I have to have a lawyer and I don't know anyone else and he doesn't charge me. I'm sorry but I think I should go. Please call me in the morning. Peg.

Legal case. Fat chance that's what they were discussing. He was pouring more lies into her. I was burned up. I'd told her I was coming right back. She might have waited. After all the tension we'd had between each other—and now this.

I stood beside my car, glowering, wanting to hit back. I was sick of it all. I wanted to write a note telling her it was all over. Something that would hurt. But I knew I had no right to do that.

I didn't want to go home, though.

Audrey. Downtown, alone, my old pal Audrey.

I got into my car and drove back to The Bamboo Grill. She wasn't there, and she wasn't in the next four bars I tried, either. But I had a drink in each of them.

In the fifth bar, I decided to hell with it. I grabbed a booth and ordered another bourbon and water. I drank half of it. And then she appeared. From the cosmos. From the universe. From the ladies' room.

And, even slightly potted and disarrayed, Audrey was out of place there.

She almost passed my table.

"Buy you a drink, girlie?" I said.

She turned to cut me off, then smiled as she saw me.

"Davie!"

She slid in across from me. She still had on the raincoat.

"Where did you come from?" she asked.

"From the cosmos, from the universe," I said.

"I came from the john."

"Won't you allow me to purchase you a magnum of Chantilly?"

"That's lace, isn't it?"

"Who knows? Let us be gay. If it's lace we'll drink it anyway."

We drank a lot. The time seemed to pass. And I found myself sitting beside her instead of across from her. The strong sensation of drunkenness on me. The loss of balance. The sense that you're hyperbrilliant, that your brain, though cased in numbing wool, is glittering like a jewel.

And, around midnight, I remember putting my mouth on hers. And feeling all the animal heat in me dredging up. And not caring. She made no attempt to stop my touching her.

Somehow we were in the car, driving up Broadway. Then over to Wilshire on Lincoln. I remember that. We parked. We were out of the car and into my room. In the darkness, weaving as in a dream. I took off her raincoat, letting all the things I believed in be washed away by the tides of the coarse desire flooding through me.

It was dark. She was in the cool darkness, waiting for me.

And then a car came past the house in the alley, slowly moving out. And the light played on Audrey's face.

In the light I saw her face. It was blank. That headlight was like a spotlight of revelation on those expressionless features.

Her cheeks were shimmering with tears.

"Audrey."

My voice was broken. Something cold billowed up in my body, freezing everything as violently as it had come. I stood there, trembling.

Then I went over, reached down and pulled the blankets over her. Without a word, I bent over and kissed her forehead.

I was afraid to say anything. I was about to straighten up when she put her arms around my neck.

"I'm sorry," she whispered, "I tried to believe it was right. But. . . ."

■　■　■

I almost fell out of the chair in shock when the knocking came on the door. A loud knocking, hard.

I leaped up, wincing at the stiffness in my back and neck. My heart was pounding. My head ached a little.

Suddenly I remembered Audrey with a gasp. My eyes ran over to the dark outline of her.

I didn't know what to do. I just stood there shivering, staring stupidly at the bed, then at the door. I felt myself jump as Audrey stirred restlessly. She moaned a little and turned on her side. I think I was paralyzed. All I could do was visualize Peggy standing out there. My claims of innocence would mean nothing to her.

I started for the door.

"What is it?" Audrey asked in sleepy fright. She was propped up on one elbow.

"Shhh!" I said anxiously.

Then I leaped back as the door was shoved open violently and I saw a figure in the doorway, lit by the hall light. A tall figure, square, powerful.

Steig.

He came in and flicked on the light switch.

I don't know what I felt in those first moments. Shame, fear, anger. But I exploded in his face.

"Get out of here!" I yelled.

My words were hacked off as Steig drove a violent right into my stomach which doubled me over.

All the night seemed to flood in on me. I was bent over, gasping for air. The floor ran like water to my eyes.

Another blow on the side of my head. Like a cast iron mallet it felt. It drove me into the table and sent me and the whole business crashing over onto the floor.

"Stop it!" Audrey screamed, "stop it, Steig!"

I was dragged up. Then a rock exploded in my face and I felt hot blood spurting out of my nose and sharp pain in my head.

"You stay off!" Steig snarled. "*Stay* off!"

I think he might have beaten me to death if Audrey hadn't jumped up and grabbed his arm. She was Vaughan's wife, *Mr.* Vaughan's wife. He couldn't afford to harm her.

He had to let me go. His way of letting go was shoving me across the room. I crashed into the partition that separated the room from the kitchenette. Then I slid down and crumpled into a heap on the rug.

"Let me go!" I heard Audrey screaming.

I couldn't help. I was gone. Falling through a black pit that hurt. And hurt. And hurt.

4

I felt lousy for a couple of days after that.

I drove to Peggy's. She was inside. So was Dennis. And another miserable afternoon began. Dennis was in a nasty mood and he made it plain that he was after Peggy and that he didn't want me seeing her anymore. That led to one thing and another and, finally, a brawl. I took out on Dennis all the anger Steig had built up inside me, and when the fight was over, Dennis was battered and bloody.

While he was picking himself up off the floor, Peggy announced that she thought it would be "nice" if I drove Dennis home.

Very nice.

I drove Dennis home.

The next day, Peggy came and told me that Jim wanted to take us to dinner and to a concert at the Bowl.

Us?

Sure, she said. Us. Peggy and me.

"I'm sure the three of us will love it," I said. . . .

One of the first things Jim said at dinner was, "David, I want to apologize quite sincerely for the terrible mistake Steig made the other night. I guess he jumped to conclusions that were unwarranted."

He shrugged like the genial apologizer he wasn't.

"Steig has been disciplined," Jim said like a stern schoolmaster.

"What did you do," I asked, "take away his pet spiders?"

He smiled. Perfect combination smile. Clever admixture of amusement and aloofness. A look that said to Peggy—there, you see, my dear, I told you that this lout was beyond all appeal to decent behavior.

I drank heavily at dinner. I don't know what was the matter with me. I guess I'm spoiled. I just wouldn't take that evening straight. I couldn't beat Jim in his own territory at a game he made the rules for. I felt clamped and a hapless jerk from the start.

As a result I just drank and sniped like a kid all night.

At the Bowl, I further distinguished myself by falling over a seat.

Afterwards we went to the Mocambo. All I remember is people laughing and cigarette smoke and dancing once with Peggy and her not looking me in the eye.

I drank. The room spun around me. I didn't taste the drinks

anymore. They were just containers of liquid. And Peggy drank some and so did Jim.

Then we were up again. Large denomination bills fluttering out of Jim's wallet like flocks from a sanctuary. And me, God help me, staggering, almost falling. Jim's hand at my elbow, guiding.

"Let's go!" Me, rambunctious. The tough guy. Sing me an old refrain. *"Oh what an ass was Davie!"*

Out in the street. The reaction at last. Sudden quietude in me. A desire to be rid of everyone and everything for good.

"Good night," I said, casually, and walked away from them as Jim was helping her into the car.

"Davie."

Her voice was more irritated than concerned. I paid no attention. I walked quickly up Sunset. The wrong way, I later discovered.

They didn't follow. I suppose Jim talked her out of it. She was just angry enough to let him.

I don't know how long I wandered. The night went on and on and so did I. Everything whirled around, it was just dumb luck I wasn't flattened by a car. I bumped into a couple of people who looked mildly revolted. I tried to get into somebody else's 1940 Ford which I thought was mine.

I don't remember everything. But I remember sitting in a diner and drinking coffee and discussing religion with the cook. I remember sitting on a curb and petting a very patient collie dog who must have been repelled by my breath and my soporific mumbling. I remember lying on my back on somebody's lawn and looking up at the stars and singing a soft version of *Nagasaki* to myself with lyric variations pertaining to the atom bomb.

Then, finally, in some erratic fashion I found my way down to Wilshire Boulevard and got myself on a red bus. I rode down to Western and picked up my car where I'd left it. I drove back to the room.

Key in door lock. Opening of door. Drunken weaving to lamp, turning on of lamp.

Breath sucked out. An icy hand crushing my heart.

On my bed, Dennis.

In his brain, an icepick.

5

I don't know how long I stood there looking at him. Then I stared at my shaking hands, and I was as sober as a judge.

Dennis dead.

Who? The thought finally managed to emanate after the initial shock had faded a little. Who had done this? Another icepick.

Peggy was out with Jim. But how long had Peggy been home? I jumped up and ran out of the room. I got into my car and started the motor.

Then I stopped it and ran back in again. I tried not to look at those glassy, staring eyes and that great patch of blood on my pillow. I drew the light blue bedspread over his body, his face. Then I turned out the light and went into the hall and back to my car.

A mistake. But who ever makes the right move when he's all twisted inside?

I turned off at 15th, and drove down to Peggy's. I saw a light in her living room as I ran across the lawn.

She was alone, sitting in her bathrobe reading a book. I forgot about the night that had gone before. All I could think of was Dennis.

I knocked.

"Baby, how long have you been here?" I asked hurriedly as she opened the door.

"What do you—?"

"Peggy, how long?" I asked, grabbing her shoulders.

She jerked back and her right hand slapped against my cheek. "Get your hands off me!" she said angrily.

She stood there trembling, her chest rising and falling with sharp breaths.

"Dennis is in my room," I said.

"What has that got to do—"

"He's dead," I said.

She stared at me. "What did you say?"

"He has an icepick in his head," I said slowly and watched the look come over her face. A lost look. Her mouth fell open. She stepped back and bumped against the couch. She sank down on it and looked at the far wall.

"He's—?"

I didn't say anything.

"*Dennis?*"

"Yes, Dennis," I said, "how long have you been home?"

"I—I don't know. A few hours, I guess."

"Think!"

"It was—I remember looking at my watch. We were—just turning the corner at Wilshire, I think. Yes, we—"

"What time?"

"Twelve thirty-five. No, twelve forty-five."

I looked at my watch. It was past four.

"Did Jim stay here?" I asked.

"For a while," she said.

"How long?"

"Oh—twenty minutes."

Then she was in my arms crying. Her fingers held tightly to me.

"Davie, Davie, what's the matter with everything?"

"All right," I said, "I know you didn't do it."

She drew back as if she'd been struck.

"Me!" she said. "You thought I'd killed him!"

She pulled away from me.

"Get out of here," she said. "Oh, get out of here!"

"Peggy, listen to me."

"No, I won't listen to you," she said. "I've had enough of you. All you've done is act suspicious and hateful!"

She looked at me angrily, hands clenched.

"Listen, Peggy," I said, "your pride is rather unimportant now. In the past week two men have been murdered. That's a little more important than vanity, isn't it?"

She turned away. "I don't know," she said. "I know I'm tired of everything. I'm tired of it. I'll never find any happiness."

"I'll leave you alone then," I said. "You can go to sleep. But I advise you to call Jim. You'd better find out if he's arranged an alibi for you."

She looked at me but I left. I got in my car and drove back to the room. I was going to walk up to the gas station and call Jones.

I didn't notice the big car as I parked and got out. I didn't notice anything, I was so upset.

But there were two plainclothesmen waiting. And Jones said, "I'm glad you had the sense to come back."

■　■　■

The body was gone. Jones and I were sitting in the room.

"And that's your story," he said.

"Easily checked," I said. "Ask Peggy Lister. Ask Jim Vaughan. I was with them."

"There's a long time you weren't with them."

"I saw other people then."

"We'll find out about Vaughan first," he said.

"Do you really think I'm lying?"

He shrugged. "The pick is from your drawer," he said.

"Are you—do you actually think I did it?"

He shrugged again. "You'll do for now," he said.

"Are you serious?" I said. "For God's sake, why should I come back here if I did it!"

"Come on."

"I told you I was going to call you!"

"Are you coming?"

"Listen—"

"Let it go, boy," he said. "Get some toilet articles and let's get out of here."

That's how I spent my first night in jail. Lying on a cot in a cell. Staring at the walls. Listening to a drunk singing college songs.

In the morning I was taken to Jones' office.

He sat there working on some papers while I waited nervously. I watched his lean, blue-veined hands shuffling through papers. I looked at his thin face, the dark eyes.

Finally the eyes were on me.

"So you were with Vaughan," he said.

"That's what I said. Have you spoken to him?"

"Yes," he said, "we have."

"Well—?"

He kept looking at me and not answering and all of a sudden the bottom started dropping out.

"Oh, *no!*" I said.

He looked at me without speaking. He nodded.

"This is crazy!" I said. "You mean that he actually said he *wasn't* with me last night?"

"He actually said that."

"Well, he's lying! Damn it! Isn't that obvious?"

He shook his head.

My hands started to shake. "Have you asked Peggy?" I said.

"Yes."

It hit me right in the stomach. I felt as if I were going out of my mind.

"Let me get this," I said. "Peggy said I wasn't with them last night?"

"How long are you going to insist on that?" Jones asked.

"Have you heard of people lying?"

"Yes, I've heard of it," he said, looking at me.

"Peggy," I said, "*Peggy*. To lie about me. I just don't get it. I just—don't."

"Tell me what happened last night," he said.

"I told you."

"Tell me again."

I told him. When I finished, he looked at me studiedly.

"That's it, huh?"

"Yes, that's it. I have no reason to lie."

"Except to save your life," he said.

"Listen, Jones," I said, "you're falling right in with that red-headed louse who's trying to shove me around the way he's been shoving people around all his life."

He looked at me a long time until it made me nervous.

"I don't know," he finally said, "whether you're telling the truth or not. I'm inclined to believe you. I don't think you could make up as many verifiable lies on the spur of the moment and then duplicate yourself. *But*—unless either one of those two will change their story, there's not much I can do. Your story *could* be a lie."

I was taken back to my cell.

I spent the morning reading the paper. The story was on the front page. There was no picture of me, just one of the house, a front view. I knew the landlady wouldn't exactly love me after this. Her house would have a reputation now. . . .

About noon a cop opened my cell door and gestured with his head.

"Get your stuff," he said.

I found Steig out in front. I was going to get irate at first and refuse the bail. I decided otherwise.

As we started down the steps, Steig said, "Mr. Vaughan wants to see you."

"I don't want to see him," I said.

"You go with me," he said, assured.

"Listen, tough man," I said, too burned up to be afraid, "I'm not going with you. If you want to try and make me, go ahead. I'll kick you where it will do the most good."

Then I turned on my heel and walked away.

Steig was too amazed at my violence to move. He just stood there, staring after me. . . .

■   ■   ■

I found Peggy in her living room. I went in without knocking. She jumped a little as I entered.

"All right," I said, "let's have it."

She stood up, and I grabbed her wrist.

"*Well?*"

"You're hurting me!"

"You're hurting *me*, too!" I snapped back. "Does it mean anything to you that I might be executed for murder?"

I've seen confused faces in my time. But the look on Peggy's face had them all beaten.

"But he told me—" she started.

"Who told you? Vaughan? Told you what? That they couldn't pin anything on me?"

"I—yes."

"Well, I'm the only suspect," I said. "Who the hell do you think they're going to suspect—Dracula?"

"I don't understand, Davie—"

"Obviously," I said. "Listen, Peggy, maybe you don't realize what's been going on. There have been two murders, *two* of them!"

"But you didn't—"

"I know it and you know and Jim knows. But if neither of you tells the truth about it, who's going to take *my* word?"

"I—" She ran a hand over her cheek.

"What did he tell you?" I asked. "Come on, let's have it. Did he actually tell you I wouldn't be involved?"

"Yes. He told me they—couldn't prove a thing against you. So he said we shouldn't get involved. I mean, *I* shouldn't get involved."

"A dead man in my room with an icepick from my kitchen drawer," I said, "and I wouldn't be suspected! Come on Peggy, what's the matter with you? You're so naive, it's near criminal."

"I know. But he—" She shook her head. "He said we shouldn't!"

"And you just—*took* his word."

"Well—"

"Peggy, when are you going to start using your head?"

She looked up defiantly a moment. Then her shoulders slumped. She lowered her eyes.

"What did he really tell you?" I asked.

Her voice was defeated. "He said he'd re-open my old case. He said I'd be executed for it."

"You can't be tried twice for the same crime!"

"He said—"

"He said, he said! What is he—a Svengali? Haven't you got a brain in your head?"

"He has my life in his hands," she said.

The thought was sickening.

"He has *not*," I said. "He has no control over you. Are you going to set his welfare above mine?"

"Davie—"

"What kind of love do you have for me, anyway?"

"Please, Davie."

"Listen," I said incredulously, "this is serious business."

"I was *afraid*—"

"Afraid," I said. "I'm afraid too, Peggy. Jim said he'd get me one way or the other."

"He wouldn't kill his own *brother*."

"Jim would kill his own *mother* if it served his purpose."

"No."

"It serves his purpose to get me out of the way. And he'll do it too, if you keep lying about me."

She looked at me blankly, then nodded once.

"All right," she said quietly. "This afternoon I'll go to Lieutenant Jones and tell him you were with us."

I took an easy breath. They were short and far between those days. I knew I should start worrying about what Jones would do when she changed her story in midstream. A girl who was proven to have murdered once and suspected of having done it again.

"Thank you," I said. "I'll go now."

I was beginning to sense the end of our relationship. I couldn't see how it could last through all this. Even if I loved her. Let's face it. It *isn't* enough when everything else is lacking.

6

I was wrong. Several days after Dennis' funeral, Peggy and I reached an understanding. She agreed to marry me. We were returning to her place after a day hiking in the woods. I had soothed all of her revulsion toward men; even the miserable, horrible fact that years ago her own father had—I brushed the horror from my mind. Now, my love was going to marry me. I had room for nothing else in my mind.

As Peggy and I entered her place, Jim looked up from the couch. He was dressed informally in a brown suede jacket with a lightly patterned sport shirt under it.

"I've been looking for you all day, Peg," he said firmly. He didn't even glance at me.

"Jim," I said.

"Will you get dressed as quickly as possible," he said to Peggy. "We're to go to a barbecue at Lamar Brandeis' beach house. We're late already. It's not polite to be late at a producer's party."

I held my temper. The axe would fall on him soon enough. I glanced at Peggy.

"Jim, I—" she started.

"Peggy, I wish you'd hurry."

She took a deep breath.

"I can't, Jim," she said.

His eyebrows drew together and I felt inclined to utter a mocking "Bravo" at this splendid bit of facial business.

Jim was looking at her gravely.

"And why, may I ask?" he said, still ignoring me.

"Jim—I—"

She couldn't finish. She seemed halted by those eyes. Those grey-blue eyes on her, probing, demanding, almost hypnotizing.

"Peggy is staying here," I said.

"No one is speaking to you!"

Anger at last! And anger in Peggy's sight. I almost reveled in it. Something ugly that had been veiled too long from her eyes. Now at last, revealing itself.

"Listen, you pompous ass," I started.

"Davie," she pleaded. I stopped and her eyes moved over to Jim. Her throat moved. She bit her lip.

"Jim—"

"Well, *what* is it, Peggy?"

"Jim. Davie and I are going to be married." She spoke quietly, half in defiance, half with the still remaining timidity.

Jim Vaughan's body twitched. Something almost gave. Like a great wall about to topple. He stared at her, speechless for the first time I could remember since I'd met him, so many years ago. Someone had finally hit Jim Vaughan where it hurt.

And, suddenly, it came to me that Jim was in the same boat as Peggy and Audrey. And all of us to some degree. He was starving for real love and he'd never received it. And now it was tearing him apart at last because the shell he'd made to hide himself was cracking.

"It's not true," he said.

She nodded once. "Yes. It is."

Something seemed to drain from his body. He pumped it back with will power. He managed a thin smile.

"Oh?" he said. "And have you told him how you murdered Albert? Is he willing to—"

"Your lies won't work anymore," I told him.

"Lies?"

"I know who murdered Albert. And Dennis. I know about your argument with Dennis. I know that he was wild for Peggy and wouldn't listen to your warnings to keep his hands off her. You killed him!"

He turned and walked to the door. There he turned again. He looked at us, his face a stone mask. His eyes settled on me like the benediction of a cobra.

"Then maybe you also know," he said, "how you'll live long enough to marry Peggy."

Peggy gasped.

"*Jim!* You wouldn't—"

For a moment, Jim's face was stripped of everything. The animal, the hating, frustrated animal showed for that moment. And it was ugly.

"I'll do anything for you," he said. "I've lied, I've cheated for you. Yes, I've *murdered* for you! And now. . . ."

His words went on. But they were lost in the sudden explosion of joy in me.

He had confessed! Peggy was free. Sick in mind and afraid— but free.

I put my arm around Peggy.

"Don't argue with him," I said. "You don't have to argue. Look at him, Peggy. He's beaten."

Those were my words but my stomach was throbbing because I knew that from that moment on my life was in danger. All possible friendship between us was kicked away for good.

His face was cold and murderous.

"I've despised you for a long time," he said, "and now, I'll see to it you bother me no longer."

I tensed myself instinctively, almost expecting him to reach into his pocket and take out a gun. Or an icepick, my imagination said.

I should have known better. That was not his way. Once I'd seen Jim refuse to sweep a floor in his fraternity house room. And he would always have someone else do his dirty work. And murder was dirty work.

He just opened the door.

"Good night," he said as casually as his shaken system would allow.

Then he closed the door quietly and we heard him walking down the path, unhurried, carrying through to the last his pretense that the illusion of his casualness might even deceive himself. We stood there motionless and silent until the sound of his footsteps had disappeared.

Peggy's hands were shaking.

"I never knew he was like that," she said, frightened. "I never even suspected he was like that."

"I know you didn't, Peggy."

"What are we going to do?"

In answer, I went to the phone and dialed.

"Lieutenant Jones," I said when they answered.

I felt her hand grow limp in mine.

"Yes?"

It was Jones. I told him what Jim had said.

"I'll have him picked up," Jones said, "and you'd better come by in the morning. With Miss Lister. Her alibi clears you—but there are still some formalities."

"I will," I said.

"All right. You say he just left 15th Street?"

"Yes."

"All right. Goodbye."

I hung up and looked at Peggy.

"All over, baby," I said.

How wrong can a guy get?

7

At my home, I opened the door—and there was Jim. He was sitting there in the shadows.

I started for him, then stopped as he leveled a gun at me.

"Don't come any closer, David," he said, "or I'll take the pleasure of putting a slug in your belly." Jim had had some fast, stiff drinks on the way over. He wasn't used to liquor, and what he had downed was showing. That smile, the slightly, almost imperceptibly disheveled appearance. The tie knot slightly off center, the hair slightly uncombed, the hat at the minutest wrong angle. All added up. I remembered how Jim had been at college the few times he'd been drunk. He'd been quite unpredictable. And this time he had a gun in his hand. And hate for me.

I moved for my chair.

"I should shoot you," he said, "now, while the opportunity is here."

A car motor. Headlights coming to the curb. I saw them, out of the corner of my eye. My heart thudding. Was it Jones? And, if it was, would he come thudding up on the porch?

It was fortunate that Jim was drunk. Otherwise he surely would have heard the car door slamming, the footsteps on the porch, the shadowy figure that quietly stopped outside of the screen window.

"Now that you're going to kill me," I said, "you can tell me about your murdering Albert and Dennis."

He looked at me with that thin, supercilious smile on his lips. The light reflected off his polished, rimless glasses.

"You killed them, didn't you?" I said, hoping that there was no sign of eagerness in my voice.

His face sobered. "Of course I did. They both stood in my way."

"Albert?" I said.

"He attacked her," he said.

"And Dennis?"

It seemed too good to be true. A confession in the hearing of a police lieutenant.

"Why go on?" he said. He raised his gun.

"And now a third victim?" I said.

Jim didn't point the gun at me. He just let it hang loosely in his hand.

"Who knows?" he said.

"You can put down that gun now," Jones said from the window.

Vaughan twitched a little. But he didn't turn. He seemed to listen a moment as if waiting for Jones to say something else. Then that smile came to his lips again. He seemed too drunk, too emotionally exhausted to feel fright.

"Trapped," he said.

Then Jones took Jim Vaughan away. . . .

I rushed over to Peggy and told her and we decided to drive down to Tijuana the next day.

We packed her clothes and then I went back to my room and packed some things for myself.

I slept that night. I turned out the light without dread. The end of it, I figured, closing my eyes.

No. . . .

Because the next day after I'd gone to a doctor, after I'd picked up a wedding ring, after I'd bought a bottle of champagne to open that night, I found a note slipped under my door.

I opened it.

At first I couldn't believe it. It seemed too cruel a joke.

The letterhead was *Santa Monica Police* and the message said that . . .

I drove as fast as I could up Wilshire. I wheeled around the corner of 15th and jerked to a stop in front of Peggy's house.

I ran in the open door.

She whirled in fright as I entered. Her fingers clenched on the dress she was holding.

"Davie! What is it?"

"Are you finished packing?" I asked quickly. "We have to get out of here right away."

"Why?"

I handed her the note. She looked at it. Then looked up at me, her eyes frightened.

"*Jim?*" she said.

The note said that Jones hadn't shown up yet at Headquarters.

My car raced down Lincoln. Every time I hit a red light I thought it was a plot. My eyes stayed fastened to the road ahead. I wasn't going to the police. I didn't want to stay in town. I wanted to get out fast.

I remember looking out the rear-view mirror.

But I didn't notice anything. Because, without thinking, I was only looking for a black Cadillac.

■ ■ ■

Tijuana. A five-hour drive. Dirty and almost wordless, with me looking at the rear view mirror. With Peggy sitting close by me and glancing at me in fear every once in a while.

We stood side by side in the little place and I slipped the ring on Peggy's finger. It felt wrong though. As if I were being forced into it. As if we really weren't sure but had to go through with it. Inevitable. There was nothing casual, nothing leisurely or pleasant. The nerve-wracking aspect of a man following to kill me. And if I felt uneasiness at the haste of the wedding, Peggy felt it twice as much.

"What is it?" I asked.

For the last ten miles she'd been staring ahead glumly at the highway. She shook her head.

"What *is* it?" I asked again.

She tried to smile and press my hand reassuringly.

"Nothing," she said.

"Tell me."

She shrugged.

"Oh—"

"I guess I know," I said. "The wedding. The way we're rushing. It isn't what we'd hoped for. It doesn't seem like a wedding at all."

"I—" she started. "I guess it's because it reminds me of my first wedding. The same rushing and—I was even more scared then."

"Scared?"

"Of him. Of—my—of George."

"What are you afraid of now?"

"Not of you," she said, but it didn't sound convincing. "Jim, I guess."

That didn't sound convincing either. I tried to get her mind on something else. I thought I knew what she was afraid of.

"As soon as we hear one way or the other about Jim," I said, "we'll have a real church wedding. We'll go back to New York and have all my family at it."

She turned, a smile flickering on her tired face. We'd been driving all morning and afternoon.

"Honest?" she asked.

"Honest."

She leaned against me wearily and was at peace for a moment. She held my arm.

Night was falling over the highway and I was sleepy and tired. And starving too. We hadn't eaten much all day and my stomach was about empty.

I signed the motel registry with as pleasant a smile at Peggy as I could manage.

Mr. and Mrs. David Newton, Los Angeles.

We walked along the gravel path under the sky that was hidden by dust clouds. And we tried to pretend we were happy.

But every sound made us start nervously.

Cabin K. All wrong. A slanty little structure, painted green and white and the paint was probably an inch thick. The shutters hung lopsided and the window curtains hung drearily.

I stood before the door and looked at her. She shook her head once and I didn't go near her. It would have been a tragic mockery to carry her over that dismal threshold. I just opened the door and stepped aside.

She stood inside looking around the room as I put the bags on the bed. The room was terrible. No touch of sweet romance. No fireplace, nor balcony overlooking a lake, nor latticed windows with boughs stirring outside. A dusty floor, a touch of stale whiskey in the air.

I looked at her. And the expression on her face made me forget my own irritation and worries. I took her hand.

"Peg," I said, "I'm sorry. I wish it was a castle. But it's all we can get now. We *have* to sleep."

"I know," she said. Without enthusiasm.

While she was in the bathroom I went down to the manager's office.

"Hey, can I get some food?" I asked.

"Afraid not," he said. "All I got's candy. And that popcorn machine over there."

"How about some ice?"

"Only got a little, mister," he said. "Ice's hard to get around here."

"Look," I said, "we've just been married. And I have a bottle of champagne in my bag. Can't you let us have a little ice? Maybe a pailful or something?"

He looked at me studiedly. Then he got compassion. He got a pail and put a chunk of ice in it.

"Fifty cents," he said.

I paid him and held back the temper.

"What about glasses?" I said irritably.

"Glasses in the cabin."

"I can't get this chunk of ice in the glasses," I said.

He reached under the counter. . . .

"*Violà!*" I cried to her as she came out of the bathroom. I'd chopped the ice into small pieces and decided to chill the bottle instead of putting the ice chips in the glasses. I'd stuck the bottle into the pail. But the ice only covered about two inches on the bottom of the pail. The champagne would never chill.

"Oh!" Peggy said. "Champagne!"

She tried to smile and keep smiling.

She sat on the bed as I opened the bottle. I noticed her glance at the pail, at the object beside it. Then she turned her eyes away and smiled at me again.

She was wearing a long dressing robe. She sat on the bed and watched me. But she wasn't relaxed. Her poise was strained, her lips forced into a smile.

I put down the unopened bottle and sat beside her and put my arms around her.

"Honey, be happy," I said. "It's not paradise, I know. But we're away at last. And we're free of the past."

Her arms clung to me.

"Oh, Davie," she said, "don't let anything happen to me. Don't let anything spoil it."

"I won't," I said, cheerfully.

Then I stood up and opened the bottle.

"Ooops!"

The white foaming champagne spurted out of the bottle mouth and ran onto the floor. I leveled the bottle quickly and poured it into the glasses. Then I put down the bottle next to the pail. I put some pieces of ice into the glasses.

"I shouldn't dilute it," I said, "but if I don't, the champagne will be too warm."

"It's all right," she said.

I handed her a glass. I held my own out to her.

"My love," I toasted.

■　■　■

She smiled. We sat side by side and drank. I was thirsty. The cool tingling of the champagne tasted good. I polished off the glass in two swallows.

"Popcorn, m'lady?" I asked.

She took a few pieces. I tried some. It was stale.

"I wish we could get a steak dinner," I said, "but there's nothing around here. I promise as soon as we get back to Santa Monica or—wherever we're going," I added as her face grew concerned, "I'll buy you a nice, juicy sirloin."

"You'll make my mouth water," she said.

I felt a little lightheaded. I blinked at her and grinned.

"Mrs. Newton," I said.

She smiled dutifully and I poured two more glasses. One and a half really. Peggy had only drunk about half a glass.

I felt the warmth coursing my body and I had a little more popcorn. It made me thirsty. I put the bag aside because it spoiled the taste of the champagne.

The stuff worked fast. I felt as if I were floating. I put my head down on her lap. I reached out casually and stroked her.

She tried to smile but she couldn't.

"Baby," I said.

I kissed her on the mouth. I felt something rising in me. A familiar sensation. Everything had been building it up through the months. And now hunger and lightheadedness were added to it. A cabin isolated. And my brain saying speciously—she's your wife now.

I poured some more to drink.

"Peggy?"

"No, thanks," she said. "Maybe we should—find someplace to eat."

"There isn't any place around here," I said.

"Maybe up the road," she said.

"Honey, not now. I'm tired. I don't want to drive again."

Her chest rose and fell with a shudder.

"Do you think Jim is—?"

I had my mouth over hers to stop her talking about it.

"Now, never mind him," I said. "This is our wedding night."

"Davie."

I started to unbutton her robe.

Her hands held mine. "No, Davie." Gently pleading.

"Peggy, stop it," I said. "What are you afraid of? Have I ever hurt you?"

"I'm sorry. I just—"

I opened another button. She was staring at me, her face white and tense. She looked like some maiden about to be sacrificed to a horrible god.

"*Peggy!*" I said angrily.

She had her dress on under the robe.

"Davie, please don't be angry. Don't you see I'm—"

"See! See *what?*"

"Davie—"

"What do you think marriage is, a *business* relationship?"

"*Davie.*"

I didn't look at her. I had another drink. She drank another glass. We sat there in silence and we both drank. She seemed to be trying to get drunk. Relentlessly trying to lose herself so she could please me. But it seemed she couldn't do it, as if this fear in her were imbedded in her very flesh.

I don't remember every moment. But I do remember that she took off her robe after I acted sullen. She took her dress off and sat beside me in her slip. Her motions were nervous and shaky. She kept drinking. Her lips shook.

She tried to smile. "You won't—"

I didn't answer. My breath was heavier. I could see the lines of her body through the silk now. A beautiful body. My lips pressed against the warm flesh of her shoulder. I thought of all the times I'd wanted her. I thought of Audrey screaming into my chest. I wanted to scream too. Hunger seemed to have been converted into an ugly drive in me. My mind kept trying to stop me, but I kept kicking it aside.

I caressed her. She shuddered.

"Davie." A frightened little voice.

"Stop that," I said.

I heard her throat move. I kissed her throat. She drew away. I pulled her close in what I thought was a gentle way.

She drew away again and stood up.

"I think I'll take a bath," she said.

It sounded so obvious to me. It irritated me. I stood up quickly and slid my arms around her.

"No," I said.

Her eyes like a frightened bird's. Trapped, helpless.

"Peggy, I'm your husband." Thick voice, uncomprehending voice.

"I know, I know but—"

I was lost in a fog. She kept backing away. I followed. I was out of my mind. I grabbed her. She swiftly squirmed out of my embrace.

"No," she said. More firmly now. A little fire in her eyes.

I grabbed her.

She tore away from me. "You're not going to touch me!"

"No?"

I moved toward her and she backed away. I thought about her husband. I threw the thought aside. Almost. Her fright drove me on harder. I could almost understand her husband.

She backed into the bedside table.

"Davie—no!"

I clutched her shoulders.

Suddenly her eyes expanded, her lips drew back as she sucked in a terrified breath. I could almost hear the scream tearing up through her throat.

That was when something managed to lance its way through the thick coating of mindless desire in me. I saw myself. I saw her. And I was doing to her what they'd all done. I was no better than any of them. And the shame of it made me turn away with tears in my eyes and a shaking hand over my eyes.

"I'm—I'm—sorry," I muttered brokenly.

A sudden rushing sound. A biting pain in my right shoulder. I jumped around with a sharp gasp.

She was holding the icepick in her hand and staring at me, her eyes like white dotted marbles in her head, her lips pressed together into a hideous white gash.

■ ■ ■

My mouth fell open. I stared at her dumbly.

I don't know how long we stood there without a sound. She was like a tensed animal, the icepick raised in her hand, her dark pupils boring insanely into my eyes.

I moved back a step then. The words seemed to come from my mouth by themselves.

"You're *crazy*," I said.

She still looked at me, something tight holding her together.

Then she noticed the big drops of blood running over my hand and dripping on the floor. She leaned forward a little, the berserk look fading from her face. The features relaxed. Her arm dropped.

"Davie?" she said.

"Get away from me."

"Davie, I didn't stab you."

I backed away some more.

"Davie, it wasn't you."

"Get *away*."

"I didn't stab at *you*. Davie, not at *you!*"

"I said get away!"

I backed off in horror. And then the idea came and the breath was sucked out of me.

"You killed Albert, didn't you?" I said.

She stopped. She looked at me blankly.

"You *killed* him, didn't you?" I said hoarsely.

"Davie, I—"

"You did, didn't you!"

"What difference does it make?"

"Oh my God!" I cried. "You kill a man and you ask what difference it makes!"

"You said you could forget everything," she said as if that wiped the slate clean.

"Forget that you murdered a man!"

"He wasn't a man, he was an animal!"

"He was a man, a *man!* And you killed him!"

Her throat moved. She started to tremble. She raised her hand. She saw the icepick and then threw it away with revulsion, and it rolled over the floor.

"I didn't," she said weakly.

"You did!"

"Yes, I—I killed—h-h-him. But—"

I felt myself drained in an instant, as if some invisible vampire had bitten me. I staggered back, hardly feeling the stabbing pain in my shoulder at all.

"You lied to me," I said dizzily. "All this time you lied to me."

"No, Davie, no," she said miserably.

She was trying to wipe away the past. It was what she always meant. That we should forget everything, even that she had killed.

"You said what happened before didn't matter. You said it didn't," she said.

"What are you?" I said. "An animal yourself? You kill a man and then you say forget it."

"I was out of my mind. I couldn't help it. I—didn't mean to."

"Why did you lie? Why did you lie to me?"

"Davie, don't." Tears were flooding down her cheeks. "I was upset. I couldn't lose you. You're all I have now. Don't desert me. I need you. I *need* you."

"And you let me think that Jim killed them," I said.

"He killed Dennis," she said, "I didn't do that. What's the difference if Jim dies for one crime or two? Didn't he *say* he killed Albert?"

He'd lied for her. I knew it suddenly. I hadn't gotten any confession from him. He'd heard Jones out there and he'd lied once more to save Peggy.

I just couldn't understand it. All I could think was one thing.

"And we're married," I said. "We're *married.*"

Something hard gripped her features.

"Oh, that's awful, isn't it?" she said, her voice breaking. "That's just horrible, isn't it?"

"I don't think you feel guilty at all," I said, "I think you feel *justified* for everything you did. You think you had a *right* to kill Albert, don't you?"

"I *did* have a right! He was a pig! He tore at my clothes. I *had* to kill him! I had to, can't you see that!"

"No, I can't! I can't see it!"

Something seemed to start in her. Way down. Like a flood of hot lava surging up to the mouth of a volcano. It shook her body as it came up. It made her arms tremble at her sides, made the fingers of both clamp into bony fists.

It exploded in my face.

"You're like *all* of them!" she yelled. "Like every damn one of them! *Defending* each other! *Plotting* with each other against us! Driving us into a pit! A *pit*! *Hurting* us, *brutalizing* us, *destroying* us. Twisting our hopes into knots! And tearing our hearts out! You don't care, oh, *you* don't care! You're all the same, *all* of you! You don't care about us! You don't care if we have minds, you don't care if we're sensitive, you don't care if we're afraid. You just rip the beauty out of our lives and give us ugliness instead! And then you tell everybody what wonderful men you are, how *happy* you've made us! All of you—*pigs*! Get away from me you filthy pig, *you pig*, YOU PIG!"

Her blood-drained fists were crushed against her white cheeks and saliva ran from her twitching mouth. I stood there, paralyzed, looking in blank horror at a girl I'd never seen.

I didn't even hear the door open. The first thing I knew was Peggy turning. And then I looked toward the door.

Jim.

■　■　■

He came across the room quickly. I couldn't move. I watched him take off his top coat and put it over her shoulders. She tried to throw it off but, without a moment's hesitation, he slapped her across the face. Hard. The red flared up on her cheek and she gasped and slowly backed away from him.

"You're coming with me," he said, "don't argue with me. You'd better, if you don't want to be turned in. You don't want to be jailed and executed for murder, do you?"

Her eyes on him were wide and staring. Glassy eyes like an insane cat.

"I'm all you have now," he said. "Your dear *David* wouldn't lift his little finger to save you now!"

His words seemed to whip her into submission. The wildness was gone. The deepest Peggy came into control. The weak Peggy, the Peggy who always needed guidance and discipline. Who could never think for herself. She looked at him like a frightened child would look at its parent.

"Jim, you—" she started, "you won't—let them do—"

"Come on, Peggy," he said. "How long do you think I can protect you from the world?"

She didn't answer. She just stood by him and let him lead her to the door. I stood there bleeding and not feeling it. Staring after them helplessly. Detached from reality.

"You won't let them, will you Jim?" she begged.

He looked at her pathetic face. He heard the lost fright in her voice. And, for the first time in his life, he showed in my sight that there was more than machinery in him.

He drew her against him and pressed his lips gently to her hair. "Peggy," he said, "oh, *Peggy*."

Only an instant. Then he raised his head and his face was hard. "They won't get you," he said. "Not while I live."

I might have been invisible standing there. The blood dripping from my finger tips onto the floor. Me watching a world slip away from me. A rootless detached feeling. As if something I'd called my heart had been torn away leaving me hollow, a shell.

I noticed that there was somebody outside the door. A heavy knock sounded.

"Is there anything wrong in here?" the voice asked. "I heard shouting."

Jim Vaughan spoke calmly, distinctly.

"This is my wife," he said. "I'm taking her away from that man in there."

Muttering. "I knew it, I *knew* it."

Then, at the door, Jim turned. He had his arm protectingly around Peggy's shoulders. And for some reason, all the smugness and the meanness and the cynical detachment seemed to have gone from him.

He looked at me. And it seemed as if he felt as helpless as I did. He had tried to save her again and again. Doing everything he could, even to confessing for her crime. Now, if they were fugitives, it would be Jim they sought for murder. He had thoroughly and completely wrecked his life.

And, despite all that, she had not changed.

And I knew later—not then because I could do nothing but stand there mutely—that Jim loved her. In a way that I and my sort of person cannot understand, much less appreciate. In the old way. The unquestioning way. Defying the traditions of society rather than losing it. Loving in a way that even allowed a man to kill for his love. Right out of the middle ages. Yet, something strangely and perversely noble there.

At least there seemed a sort of quiet unassuming nobility to Jim as he stood there by the silent Peggy. The frightened and weak Peggy who would never in her life be able to face the world without help even if she feared that help above all else. My Peggy Ann Lister.

Jim turned to her then. His eyes were on her only and his whole mind and whole heart held her alone.

"Come away, my dear," he said.

And led her out of my life forever.

■ ■ ■

The police came soon. I hadn't left. They picked me up on a morals charge. Later they called Santa Monica and fortunately Jones was still alive. He gave them the facts and they released me and started after Peggy and Jim. But they didn't catch up with them.

And one day I saw Jones and he told me they'd caught the man who'd attacked Peggy at *Funland.*

"I don't understand," I said, "Albert—"

"Grady didn't do it," Jones said.

"But—the scratches," I said, in a last confusion about my Peggy Ann, "she said she'd scratched the man who'd tried to attack her. And Albert's face was covered with scratches."

"That's right," he said, "they both were scratched. She did both jobs."

I looked at him a moment and then I lowered my head. And I whispered, "God help her."

That's about all. I finished my novel and sold it and made $1700 on it. I talked Audrey into going back to her family in

Pennsylvania. I met some people and laughed again and pretended that everything was status quo again.

I read the papers.

Maybe you read the story, too. It was about a month ago. When they found Jim and Peggy in a Kansas City hotel room. And when they took away the thing that Peggy was fondling in her hands she said they mustn't.

She said they had to let her keep his head because she loved the man.